THE

AWAKENED

A WANDERING STARS NOVEL

JASON TESAR

fourshadow
publishing

THE

AWAKENED

A WANDERING STARS NOVEL

JASON TESAR

This is a work of fiction. All the characters, organizations, and events portrayed in this book are either products of the author's imagination, or are used fictitiously.

This book or parts thereof may not be reproduced in any form, stored in a retrieval system, or transmitted in any form by any means—electronic, mechanical, photocopy, recording, or otherwise—without prior written permission of the publisher, except as provided by United States of America copyright law.

Cover design, interior design, and page layout by JASON TESAR
www.jasontesar.com

Published by
4shadow, LLC

ISBN-13: 978-0-615-38282-1

Scripture quotations taken from the *Authorized King James Version*
Public Domain, 1611

Quotations taken from the *Book of Enoch*
Not in Copyright, Translation by R H Charles, 1917

Printed in the United States of America

Carly, my love
You are my light and laughter
Without you this book wouldn't exist

THE HISTORY AND PROPHECY

ᵃ...the angels which kept not their first estate, but left their own habitation...**wandering stars**, to whom is reserved the blackness of darkness for ever.

ᵇAnd it came to pass when the children of men had multiplied that in those days were born unto them beautiful and comely daughters. And the angels, the children of the heaven, saw and lusted after them...

ᶜAnd they were in all two hundred; who descended.

ᵈAnd all the others together with them took unto themselves wives, and each chose for himself one, and they began to go in unto them and to defile themselves with them...

ᵉ...taught men to make swords, and knives, and shields, and breastplates, and made known to them the metals of the earth and the art of working them...

ᶠThere were giants in the earth in those days; and also after that, when the sons of God came in unto the daughters of men, and they bare children to them, the same became mighty men which were of old, men of renown.

ᵍ...whose height was three thousand ells, who consumed all the acquisitions of men. And when men could no longer sustain them, the giants turned against them and devoured mankind. And they began to sin against birds, and beasts, and reptiles, and fish, and to devour one another's flesh, and drink the blood...

ʰ...and as men perished, they cried, and their cry went up to heaven...

ⁱTHEREFORE, I WILL RAISE UP ONE FROM AMONG THOSE YOU DESPISE. AND I WILL **AWAKEN** HIS EYES TO THE MYSTERIES WHICH I HAVE HIDDEN FROM MEN SINCE THE FOUNDATIONS OF THE WORLD. HIS FEET WILL I MAKE TO TREAD UPON THE PATHS OF DESTRUCTION AND HIS HANDS TO MAKE WAR. HE WILL UPROOT THE SEEDS OF CORRUPTION WHICH YOU HAVE SOWN THROUGHOUT THE EARTH. AND THEN YOU WILL KNOW THAT I AM THE LORD AND MY JUSTICE IS EVERLASTING.

The Book of Enoch 6:1-2ᵇ, 6:6-8ᶜ, 7:1ᵈ, 7:2-6ᵍ, 8:1ᵉ, 8:3ʰ
The Epistle of Jude 1:6, 1:13ᵃ
Genesis 6:4ᶠ
From the writings of Ebnishaⁱ

FORWARD
BY THE AUTHOR

I began writing THE AWAKENED in the winter of 1998. The company I worked for at the time closed down every year between Christmas and New Year's and I suddenly found myself without responsibility for a period of time. For years I'd been toying with a storyline in my mind—inventing characters and visualizing scenes—but had yet to venture beyond the confines of my imagination. As my body moved through the motions of a physically laborious job, my mind wandered, unengaged and unchallenged by my work. The characters became real to me as I spent countless hours experiencing their lives, living their passions and struggles. In the back of mind, I always thought that someday I'd write it all down.

And then *someday* happened. As the snow fell outside, I sat in front of a computer with a cup of steaming coffee and began typing the first scene that I had already witnessed a thousand times in my head. Every last movement and word of the characters, every detail of their environment I could see as if they were right in front of me. But I struggled, coming quickly to the realization that writing is much more difficult than imagining. There is no explanation in imagining. The scenes just play out and make sense because you are both the author and audience. But writing is altogether different. Writing means commitment. Writing means exposing yourself through words that someone else may read. And for an introvert like me, that was a scary concept. Still, I pushed through and after several days I had a very short stack of papers to show for my effort. It was more than I had ever written for a school assignment and it gave me a measure of satisfaction at getting something out of my head and down onto paper.

New Year's Day came and went and the pace of life sped up once more. Until one night, maybe a year and a half later, my wife asked,

"What ever happened with that story you started writing?" We began talking and our conversation didn't stop for several hours. I told her about my characters, where they had come from and what they were going to face. I explained the geography of the Empire, the main plot and subplots. I even told her about the prequel to my story and that one day I wanted to write that as well. When I finished, she was almost speechless. I say *almost* because she did say something very important, something that changed the trajectory of my thoughts and actions.

"You have to write your story—like right now! You can't just keep it in your head! When you're eighty years old and sitting in a rocking chair on our front porch, do you want to be the person who always thought about writing a book? Or do you want to be the person who did it?"

Hearing those words and seeing her excitement was like pouring gasoline on a fire. That was it. I was going to do it; I was going to write my story. From that night on, I committed to myself that I would write at least one night a week. Though a seemingly insignificant amount of effort, it was a major turning point for me. Writing was slow-going at first, but over time I saw improvement. I was gradually becoming able to express my thoughts without struggle. I no longer spent hours agonizing over a few sentences, but could write a couple pages in an evening.

This continued for years until, by an interesting coincidence, I finished my story roughly a week before my first child was born. As the sleepless nights began, I put my writing on the shelf and didn't return to it until a year later. That's when I realized that my story was far from complete. Though I had a few hundred pages, I realized it needed some resolution, and the characters and scenes I'd planned as sequels would need to be pulled in to accomplish it. This was daunting at first, as I realized that I wouldn't be satisfied until I got the whole storyline down on paper. But as I started on part two, I quickly settled back into the routine of writing and found myself looking forward to it. It was like reading a good book, only much better because it was the book that I'd wanted to read but couldn't find at any bookstore. All week I would plan out the scenes and work through the dialogue in my head, so that when I sat down to write I was able to write five pages on a good night.

Two years and a few hundred pages later, I reached a stopping point once again as my second child was being born. And like before, I took a break for about a year. But when the time came for me to start on part three, my passion and commitment were already growing at an exponential rate. Now I reserved two nights a week for writing. And when that wasn't enough, I started getting up early on weekends to squeeze in a few hours before anyone in my house was awake. It didn't take long before this behavior began to spill over into the weekdays also, as I looked for every available moment to continue my story. It was addicting. To make up something out of thin air and then watch it come to life. I finished writing part three of THE AWAKENED in the fall of 2007. What had previously taken me years to complete with the first two parts, I accomplished in six short months. It was a major accomplishment for me and I found I could breathe a little easier having released the story and characters from the prison of my imagination.

But even as I took pleasure in the realization that I'd just accomplished what might otherwise have been a life-long unrealized dream, my imagination refused to be satisfied. Already I was thinking of a prequel. Like a monster that grows when you feed it, this was not just a book I'd written, but the start of an epic saga requiring several series of books to fully bring it to life.

So that is how THE AWAKENED came to be. I hope you enjoy reading it as much as I enjoyed writing it. And if you find that the story finishes sooner than you want it to, don't worry, there's more to come—much more!

— Jason Tesar

HIGH TEMPLE OF THE KALIEL
PLAN VIEW

NORTH ENTRANCE

MOUNTAIN

SOUTH-EAST GATE

OUTER WALL

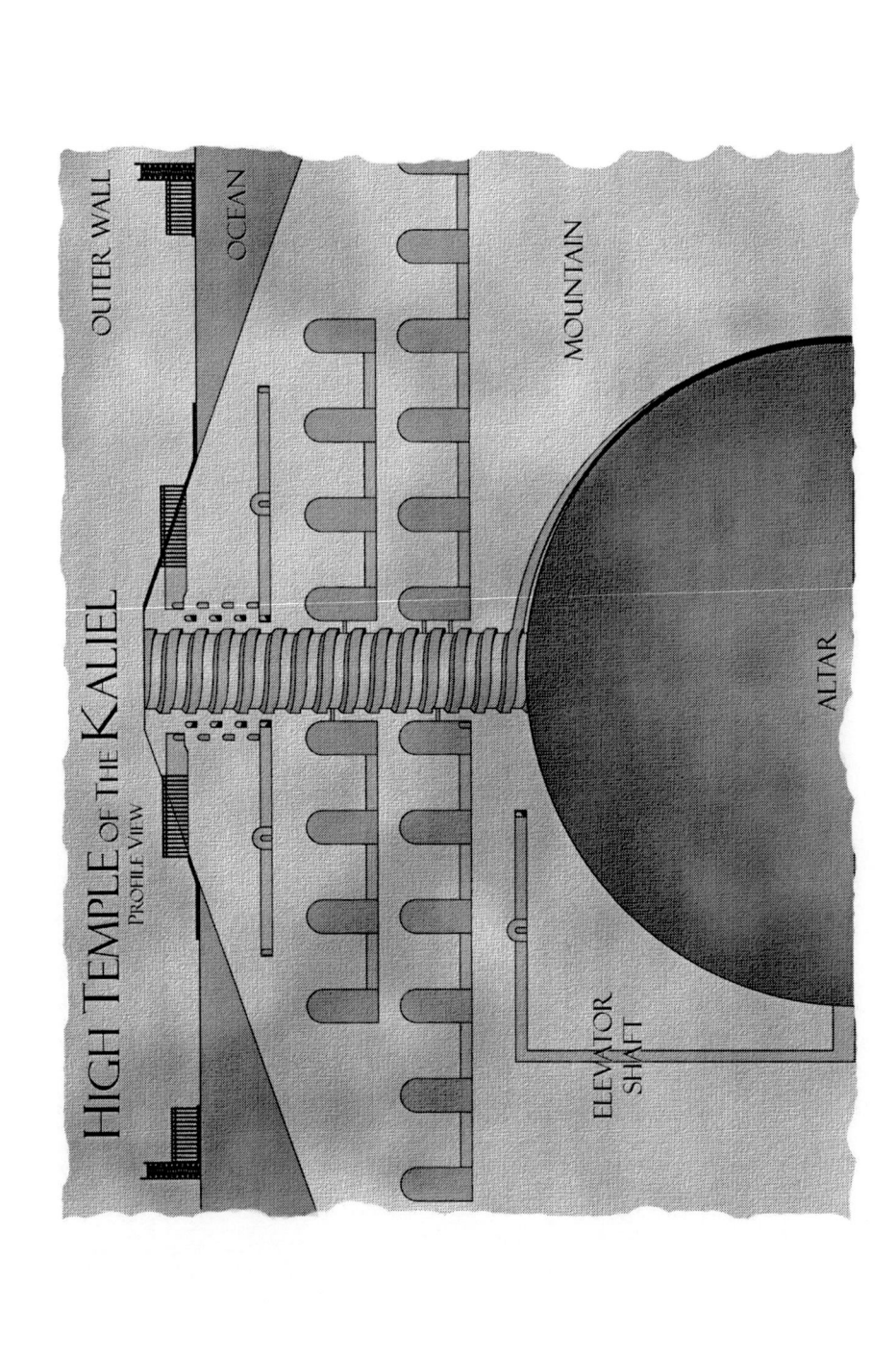

HIGH TEMPLE OF THE KALIEL
PROFILE VIEW

OUTER WALL

OCEAN

MOUNTAIN

ALTAR

ELEVATOR SHAFT

PART I

1

The young analyst glanced quickly around the room, his eyes darting between the flickering computer screens and scores of other technical personnel. His knee bounced with nervous energy, resonating with the frantic mood pulsing through the communications center. As he waited impatiently, he reached forward and grabbed his coffee mug and took a quick swig. It had gone cold. From a television on the wall to his right came the sound of yet another news reporter trying to present a different perspective on the same story that had dominated the media for more than a week.

"...as ocean levels continue to rise across the globe. This only adding fuel to the already heated environmental debate that is drawing new lines of separation between members on both sides of the aisle. But while some argue over the potential cause of this global catastrophe, others believe that the issues of greatest concern are the ghastly death toll and the millions of displaced people in nearly every country, seeking refuge by moving inland. Already, the burden of supporting these refugees is being seen..."

"What did you want?" sounded a coarse voice from behind.

The analyst jumped, spilling his coffee. He quickly wiped at his wrinkled slacks but the coffee had already soaked in. Giving up, he turned to address his superior. "Have you been watching any of this?"

"I'm well aware of what's happening," the older man said, his eyebrows wrinkling into a scowl. "It's on every news station on the planet. But we still have jobs to do. And yours is to gather data on your target."

"But that's why I called you over here. They're the ones that caused it!"

The older man's once impatient body language softened. "Show me."

"Ok–so, I was going over the surface contour data from the satellites when I noticed that the ocean levels were rising faster in the southern hemisphere. And that gave me the idea to run a simulation, comparing the current mapping data to the..."

"Skip to the point, Matthews!"

Setting down his mug, the analyst leaned forward and grabbed hold of the mouse. Frozen on one of the four screens at his workstation was a distorted satellite image. "This is their South American facility," he mumbled to his superior without making eye contact. He pecked a key and un-paused the video footage, the distortion disappearing immediately.

"This is last week," he said. "Watch the atrium roof."

The older man stood with his arms folded, watching the screen.

In the midst of a lush jungle was a compound with high fences topped with razor wire. The interior of the compound had been cleared of all vegetation. At the north end sat an enormous rectangular building with a circular glass roof at its center. A six digit time display showed at the bottom right corner of the screen with the seconds ticking by.

At 10:06:54, the glass roof exploded upward, scattering shards of debris in every direction. A dark object materialized in the void where the roof had been. When it sprouted wings and began to rise in elevation, it became obvious that it was some sort of bird.

The analyst paused the footage and increased the magnification. "You see this rectangular box on the roof?" he said, pointing to the screen. "It's an air-handler manufactured in Germany. I tracked down the schematics and got dimensions. It measures sixteen feet on its longest side, which..."

"...puts the wingspan at about thirty feet," the older man interrupted. "What the hell are they doing down there?"

"...synthetic biology? Who knows?" replied the analyst, un-pausing the footage. "But watch this."

When the time display read 10:07:22, a geyser of water came bursting through the hole in the roof. The analyst zoomed outward, showing the compound engulfed in water in a matter of seconds.

"The amount of water is just unreal. Check this out," he said, typing in a new time signature. The footage jumped forward a few hours, showing the entire valley flooded.

"Where is all that water coming from?" the older man mumbled.

"I don't know. It's way too much to be an underground river or something. But it stopped," the young man said simply. "Here, look at this."

He punched in a new date and the image switched to the present, showing a live feed. He clicked a few times with his mouse and zoomed in again.

"See? The water used to be surging all over this area like it was still coming up from underneath the building. But now the water's calm..." The analyst trailed off as he noticed something new. "Hmm...," he said, clicking the mouse to zoom in even further.

"That's a dive team," the older man said, leaning closer to the screen. "...five of them, and a boat."

"...four," the young man corrected.

"What?"

"There are only four divers. The fifth isn't in a wet suit. See how he's swimming away? It looks like they're chasing him."

"Go back!" the older man said. "Show me how he got in the water."

The analyst quickly scrolled the footage backward until everyone disappeared, then played it again. "There's the dive team arriving. They're getting in the water," he mumbled as he carefully moved through the footage. "And there. The other guy just comes up out of the water a half hour later. And there's the dive team coming after him."

The older man squinted, then stood up straight and grabbed the analyst's phone from his desktop. He punched a button and waited for the call to be routed.

The analyst grinned. "Are we going to take him in?"

The older man nodded. "We have six teams in the area on standby. This could be a major breakthrough for us."

The chopper skimmed low over the treetops, flying parallel to the undulations in the terrain. The large-leafed vegetation bent low from the downdraft. A hundred yards ahead was a gap in the otherwise thick jungle treeline. Seconds later, the helicopter passed over the clearing and a two-lane blacktop road that ran east and west. The chopper swung around to the east and descended into a nearby meadow. When it was still several feet from the ground, five men jumped out and landed in the knee-high grass, moving quickly toward the road. Their camouflaged clothing blended perfectly with the surroundings, as did the camouflaged tape wrapped around the automatic weapons slung across their backs.

The team leader took point and ran for the treeline on the opposite side of the road, while the others followed. Once inside the cover of the vegetation, the team changed direction and began to move west, keeping the road a few yards to their right.

They moved quickly and silently through the dense jungle for a hundred yards before the team leader held up his hand and brought them to a halt.

He put a finger to the spiraled cord coming from his ear and listened, then motioned for the others to move toward the road. Two of his men continued another twenty feet up the road and laid out a spike strip before returning.

As soon as they were in position, the team leader could hear the distant roar of an engine. It grew slowly in volume until an uncovered green jeep came into view around a bend in the road. He summed up the situation with only a glance.

Two men in military fatigues. One driving, the other in the back pointing an automatic weapon at the third man...the prisoner.

The jeep was moving at roughly forty miles an hour when it hit the spike strip. A loud pop cut through the roar of the motor as the tires shredded instantly. The jeep skidded on the wet asphalt as the driver struggled to maintain control, coming to a stop directly in front of the men waiting in the trees.

The timing was perfect, exactly as planned. The team leader brought the stock of his silenced weapon to his cheek and peered through the scope. When the crosshairs were centered on the side of the driver's head he squeezed the trigger. The gun coughed a three-round burst and the driver's head pitched violently to the side, throwing him over the driver-side door.

The other soldier in the rear of the vehicle reacted quickly, jumping to a stance and spinning toward the trees, firing wildly into the jungle.

The group fired in unison, and the soldier in the jeep fell backward with several hits to his midsection. It was over just as suddenly as it had begun. The team moved out of the trees and fanned out, surrounding the vehicle.

"Come on out," the team leader said in the friendliest voice he could muster. But there was no reply. "Come on...you're safe now," he repeated. Slowly, he approached the back of the jeep and peered over the tailgate.

A man cowered in the back, keeping his head down.

"Can you understand me?" the leader asked, but the blank look in the other man's eyes told him the answer. Instead, he waved for the captive to get out of the jeep.

Cautiously, the man rose up on his knees and looked around. He seemed to be assessing the situation. Finally, he got to his feet and moved to the back of the jeep.

The team leader moved back, allowing the man to crawl out of the vehicle, inspecting him as he waited. He appeared to be in his late thirties, with a muscular build and Mediterranean features. He was dressed like he had just walked off a movie set, wearing a black toga, short cropped pants, and leather sandals that laced up his calves. His chest was protected by some sort of primitive armor that looked like leather. *This guy's definitely not a local.* "We're going to the helicopter now," he said, pointing over the man's shoulder.

The man turned to watch the rest of the team make their way back along the road. He appeared reluctant, but finally started moving with the team leader following close behind. When they rounded a bend in the road, the captive turned around with a look of intense fear in his eyes.

"Afraid of flying?" he asked. "You'll be fine." The group leader pointed again, indicating that the man should follow the other soldiers who were already climbing into the chopper.

The captive appeared frightened of the machine, but eventually moved forward, limping on a badly injured foot. One of the crew members leaned out and offered him a hand, which he cautiously accepted.

When everyone was aboard and seated, the chopper lifted off the ground and began to move back in the direction from which they had come. The team leader looked over at the man and saw that his eyes were closed and his head was back against the seat. His skin looked pale and it was obvious that he was getting motion sick. He reached over and touched the man's leg to get his attention.

When the man opened his eyes, the team leader pointed two fingers at his own eyes, then pointed out the window. "Keep your eyes open and watch the trees."

The other man seemed to understand.

As everyone watched the passing jungle, the team leader inspected the strange man whose rescue was the objective for this mission. Whoever he was, he was definitely a long way from home.

2

The sound of lapping waves was faint and peaceful, at first. But eventually it caused something in Bahari's mind to take notice. He awoke with a jerk. He was sitting at the stern of his cargo ship and the rudder handle was an arm's reach away, swaying back and forth in unison with the ocean swells. He grabbed the handle and steadied it, cursing himself for his carelessness.

He looked out across the deck of the ship, laden with cargo, and could not see much farther than the bow. A thick fog had rolled in while he slept, reducing visibility to almost nothing. The mainsail was full with a breeze coming from the northwest. Bahari took a deep breath and exhaled, trying to calm himself; sound was his only navigational tool now. Then he heard it again, the sound of waves breaking off the port bow. Leaning to the side, he pulled on the rudder until the boat slowly began to turn starboard and away from the shoreline. He had obviously drifted off course while he slept and immediately felt guilty for endangering the lives of his crew who were asleep below deck.

That would be my luck! He envisioned the boat smashed into thousands of pieces, washing up onto the shoreline for miles. It sickened him to think of how hard he had worked to get where he was. One careless act could have ruined it all. But the feeling of guilt was quickly replaced by a sense of relief at waking up before anything went wrong.

Bahari kept his south-westerly course for almost an hour, listening intently for the sound of waves. When they had faded to almost nothing, he felt confident that he had reached a safe distance from shore and turned the boat back to the south, resuming his course for Bastul. He could feel the pull of sleep dragging him down and knew that if he stayed in his seat he would only fall asleep again. After securing the rudder handle with a loop of rope and taking a drink from the waterskin stowed beneath his seat, he rose to his feet and walked across the deck, stretching his legs. His tunic was uncomfortably twisted and stuck to his body as if he had just come back from a swim in the ocean. He tried to peel it away from his skin and reposition it, but gave up after a while. He wished he could take it off altogether, but there were laws against that. Citizens of the Orudan Empire were not allowed to be seen wearing only a loincloth. Such dress was only appropriate for slaves, who must not feel a sense of camaraderie with their masters, even in something as seemingly insignificant as clothing.

...although, it would be much more comfortable, especially in this warm, humid air.

He meandered across the deck, walking around crates of fruit and olives, until he found himself standing at the bow of the ship. The fog was starting to thin.

Bahari sat down on a wooden crate and watched the water as it passed by in small ripples. Immediately, his thoughts drifted toward his financial troubles. The growing season had been rough this year, and it meant that he wouldn't be able to pay his debts unless he traveled to Nucotu, where he could get more money for his cargo, and bring back some valuable items on the return trip. But the return trip had been grueling so far—two straight days without sleep.

That's the problem with this line of work—too much time to think and worry. Maybe I'll just have someone take over for me in the morning so I can get some sleep.

Over the next hour, the fog lifted completely and the moon began to carve out the texture of the ocean with its dull light. Bahari rose from his position at the bow and walked back toward the stern, trying to keep from staying in one place too long; the threat of sleep was still heavy on his mind. Suddenly, he stopped in his tracks. On the eastern horizon, a bank of low clouds was rolling away to the south, revealing nothing but ocean as far as the eye could see. There was no land in sight. He scanned the horizon, which was now clear for miles in every direction, but saw nothing. He started to panic as he retraced the night's events in his mind.

And then it hit him. "I missed the turn!" he said out loud. As soon as the thought came to him, everything made sense. Just after midnight he should have reached a section of the coastline that jogged sharply to the east. But he missed it and must have kept heading south, all the while moving farther away from the coast. When he awoke in the fog and heard the crashing waves, it was the western side of the reef which paralleled the coastline.

Bahari glanced over the port side of the boat and searched the water for some sign of confirmation that he was right. It only took a few minutes before he could make out a sandbar reflecting the moonlight from shallow water, only fifty yards away on the port side. He slumped down into his chair and buried his face in his hands. He was going to have to turn around and sail back to the northern tip of the reef.

I've just lost a whole day of travel. I'm not going to make my deadline! How can I explain this to Quartus? He's going to think...

Bahari's thoughts trailed off as his eyes settled on something in the water to the south. A few hundred yards away, just off the starboard side of the bow was a void in the water that didn't reflect the moonlight. At first he thought it might be a sandbar or a small island of rock, but after a few seconds it became clear that the void was moving toward him.

He stooped and pulled out a small wooden box from underneath his bench seat. It contained a looking glass that he had purchased a few years ago. Lifting it to his eye, he scanned the water and found that the object was a ship, roughly the same size as his own. It was shaped strangely with a high bow and low, wide sails. Though it was difficult to tell at this distance, Bahari's ocean-going experience told him that is was moving much quicker than his own vessel.

But that doesn't make sense. It's heading almost straight into the wind.

It was obviously not an Orudan patrol, which Bahari could expect to encounter at regular intervals while sailing along the coast. This ship was bearing no flag or standard of any kind and—thanks to Bahari's carelessness—they were nowhere near the coast. He stomped his foot on the deck.

"Wake up," he yelled to the crew underneath.

There was no response.

He stomped again and repeated himself several times before he heard grumblings from his crew.

One of the men shouted a question in his native tongue.

"I'm turning the boat around. Get ready to row."

He set down the looking glass and untied the rudder handle. Grabbing it with both hands, he set his feet in a wide stance and pulled with all his weight. The ship pitched slightly as it swung sluggishly to the starboard side. The sails began to droop and eventually went slack altogether as the ship came about to the north.

Bahari stomped on the deck once again. "Row as hard as you can...we've got pirates behind us!"

Sixteen long oars slid out of the boat from oval slots along each side of the hull, their blades landing with a splash in the water. The boat began to lurch forward like a wounded animal struggling to regain its footing. Bahari ran across the deck and began to take in the sails and secure them to the mast. He shot a quick glance behind and was startled by how much distance the other boat had already covered. He couldn't understand how it could be moving so quickly into the wind. He hadn't seen any oars, but even if they were rowing, it was impossible to move that fast.

He secured the last of the sails and took his place back at the rudder. He doubted that the other boat was actually a pirate ship. The Orud patrol had cleared these waters of pirates years ago, but he couldn't think of anything better to say. And there was something menacing about the other ship that told him they were in danger.

All of a sudden, a scraping noise sounded from below and the boat began to lose speed. Bahari could hear the murmur of confusion from his crew as their rowing efforts were being hindered. He leaned on the rudder to move the ship away from the reef and instantly the scraping stopped. For a few minutes, the only sounds above the silence were the voices of his crew rowing in unison, bringing the ship back up to top speed. Bahari looked back and watched in amazement as the pursuing ship turned back toward their starboard side, cutting through the water with full sails.

Abruptly, a crunch reverberated through the hull and the ship ground to a halt on the reef, pitching slightly to the port side. Bahari was thrown forward, landing awkwardly on the deck. He quickly grabbed the nearest crate and pulled himself back to his feet. The confused crew came up from below, cursing in their native language, wondering what was happening. But Bahari wasn't paying them any attention; he was staring with dismay at the silent form of their pursuer, which had already closed the distance and was heading straight for their stranded boat. Within a few seconds it became clear that the menacing ship wasn't going to stop.

"Grab on to something," he yelled, but before they were able to, the boat shuddered and rolled sharply to the starboard side, throwing everyone to the deck. The impact came sooner than Bahari expected and his confusion only worsened when he regained his footing and got his first good look at the other ship. He stared at a serpent's head carved into the high prow only a few feet away from the port side of Bahari's ship. The boat was a strange sight to behold; its mast and mainsail sat at a backward angle to the deck. The ship was completely black, including the sails and ropes. There was movement on deck, but the crew of the enemy boat was dressed in black as well, appearing as shifting shadows. The moonlight was insufficient for Bahari to see what the men were doing, but it took only a few seconds before grappling hooks came whistling over the railing to bite into the wooden deck. Bahari fought back the fear in his chest to voice his outrage at this attack.

"What is the meaning of this?" he shouted into the night, but his question went unanswered. "How dare you attack a citizen of the Empire!"

"Stay where you are or you will be shot." The clear, low voice was commanding, leaving the impression that its owner was used to being obeyed. The sound of running footsteps was followed shortly by a line of archers assembling along the starboard side of the enemy ship. Two men slid a plank across the short distance between the two boats, and the man who gave the order stepped from the shadows into the moonlight.

He was almost a full head taller than Bahari and emitted intimidation that was even visible in the body language of the men around him. Just like the other soldiers, the Commander was dressed completely in black. His long-sleeved tunic fell just above his thighs and was gathered at the waist by a leather belt which held a short sword at his left side. He wore black trousers that fell to his calves and boots that laced up his legs, just above the ankle. His chest was covered by a cuirass of boiled leather, with a cloak fastened at his shoulders and falling to the back of his legs. His manner of dress was strange to Bahari, whose only point of military reference was the Orudan soldiers in Bastul. These men were definitely not Orudan soldiers.

Bahari looked over his shoulder and noticed that his crew had assembled in a huddled mass behind him, possibly expecting some measure of protection. He knew he was inadequate to protect them, but turned to give them the only thing he could—a word of encouragement. Before he was able to open his mouth, one of his men bolted across the ship, heading for the railing. He only made it a few steps before he pitched forward and fell to the deck with multiple arrows sprouting from his back.

"I will not tell you again," the Commander shouted.

Bahari turned back and watched as the Commander strode arrogantly across the plank, dropping onto the deck with a short hop. Six other soldiers followed him, dressed similarly, but wearing leather helmets and lacking cloaks. Their swords gleamed with reflected moonlight.

"Who is in charge here?" the Commander asked.

"I am," Bahari answered timidly. He made no effort to conceal himself, realizing that he was the only one on the ship that wasn't a dark-skinned slave.

The Commander walked over to Bahari. "Wrong," he stated and grabbed him by the throat, pulling him close so that their faces were almost touching. "I am in charge." He glanced over Bahari's shoulder at the frightened crew. "Guard them," he shouted.

Immediately, the soldiers surrounded the slaves.

The Commander pulled Bahari a few steps away from the commotion. "What are you doing in these waters?" he asked in a suddenly calm voice.

"I...uh," Bahari stammered for a few seconds, trying to remember what he was doing out here. "I am a merchant. I am delivering a shipment to Bastul from Nucotu."

The Commander eyed him suspiciously for a while before deciding that his story was true. Then a smile slowly crept across his face. "Well, isn't that unfortunate. You took a wrong turn and now it has cost all of you your lives." Still holding Bahari by the throat, he turned to the men guarding Bahari's crew. "Kill them," he commanded.

Bahari began to struggle, but the Commander's grip only tightened until it threatened to crush his windpipe. He could only watch helplessly as the soldiers began to hack their swords into the huddled group of slaves. One by one they began to drop to the deck, slipping on their own blood. One managed to break free of the soldiers and started to run, only to receive a slashing sword across his back. His feet immediately lost strength and he crumpled forward onto the deck.

Rage flooded Bahari's mind, overpowering his fear. He lashed out at the Commander, punching his clenched fist toward the man's face. The Commander reflexively flinched and Bahari's knuckles glanced off the bottom of his chin and struck his throat with a hollow crunch.

Instantly, the grip on Bahari's neck loosened and he was free from his captor.

The Commander stumbled back, grabbing his throat and fighting for breath.

Bahari saw his opportunity and took it. He lunged at the Commander, dropping his shoulder, and slammed into the tall man's chest, driving him to the deck.

A panic seized Bahari's mind and he started running, without a purpose other than to get away from this madness. He saw the opening in the deck near the bow that led down to crew's quarters and altered his course slightly, heading for the door. As he ran, he felt a quick puff of air from a passing arrow brush across the bridge of his nose. Somewhere to his left, he heard the dull thud of another bolt as it struck the deck. The doorway was now only a few steps away and Bahari jumped, headfirst, toward the concealing darkness. Suddenly, his left leg exploded with pain. He pulled his hands toward his face and tightened his body into a ball to prepare for the impact. His jump was a little short and he landed painfully on his left shoulder at the top step, tumbling down the short flight of stairs.

Fighting the pain, Bahari rose out of the shallow water that had filled the lower level of the boat. Surging through the knee-deep flood, he hurried toward the stern of the ship where his quarters were located. Making his way around several crates that had worked loose of their ropes, he passed a section of the port hull where water gushed into the ship through a puncture wound left by a serpent-headed battering ram. Bahari stumbled on without slowing, realizing in an instant why the enemy ship was able to stop short of crashing into his freighter.

The sound of pursuing footsteps could be heard above him, moving in the direction of the stairs at the bow. Bahari reached the stern and stepped into his room, bolting the door shut for the first time that he could remember. Now that he was momentarily safe, Bahari reached down to the back of his left thigh and felt the shaft of an arrow protruding from his leg. He pulled gently, but stopped as waves of pain raced up his leg, making him feel suddenly nauseous.

All of a sudden, something crashed into the door and it bowed slightly inward. Outside the door, he could hear the voices of his pursuers who had found his hiding place. He quickly looked around for a weapon to defend himself, but instead noticed the porthole above his bed. It was just large enough to squeeze through, but he knew the arrow sticking out from his leg would cause a problem.

Again, a crash sounded at the door and the thick wood flexed, threatening to break but for the strength of the iron hinges bolted across its planks.

They'll break it eventually!

Bahari grabbed the shaft of the arrow as close to his leg as he dared touch, and broke it with a quick snap of the wrist. The feathered part of the arrow came off in his hand, leaving the rest of the shaft and the arrowhead in his leg. The sharp pain made his stomach turn.

Now there was shouting outside the door, followed by another loud crash.

Bahari tried to ignore the pain in his leg as he climbed onto his bed and leaned on the wall for balance. The porthole was now at eye-level and he pushed it open, catching a brief glimpse of the moonlight reflected on the ocean.

He gripped the sill of the porthole with both hands and jumped, relying mostly on the strength of his right leg, while pulling with his arms. Squeezing his upper body through the hole proved more difficult than he thought it would be. With the water in sight, he no longer thought about the men behind him. He simply leaned forward and let gravity pull the rest of his body out of the porthole.

It was a short fall into the water below, the world becoming suddenly silent. For a moment Bahari felt a small measure of peace. But it didn't last long as his need for air drove him back to the surface. Once more, his ears were assaulted by the sound of yelling and more running footsteps, which he hoped would conceal his escape.

Quietly, he moved to the hull of his ship to keep from being seen from above. His leg was throbbing now.

I have to think quickly. I have to hide...but where?

Treading water was getting difficult with his leg wound and he knew he couldn't keep it up for long.

Where can I hide that they won't look for me?

Then it came to him. *On their boat!* He knew it wasn't possible to board their ship without getting caught, but maybe he could hide along the hull.

He tried to calm his breathing, then sucked in a big gulp of air, diving beneath the surface. He kicked his one good leg and clawed with his hands along the underside of his boat. The sounds of the soldiers above were muffled and echoing as if he were listening from far away. He felt safer down here, detached from the horrible things that took place above him. When he reached the keel, he pushed off and swam with all of his might for the other boat. It took longer than he expected and he was out of breath by the time he reached it.

He knew that he couldn't surface between the boats without getting caught, so he dove deeper, trying to fight the panic of drowning as he struggled to get underneath the enemy boat. To his surprise, the hull of the ship was shallow and he soon found himself on the other side, heading for the surface. His lungs were burning now and he had to fight the urge to open his mouth and breathe in the water around him. Just as quickly as the thought came to him, his head broke free of the water on the port side of the enemy ship and he gasped for air as silently as he could.

Though still vulnerable, he was farther away from the commotion now and used the opportunity to search along the ship for somewhere to hide. The hull was completely smooth, just as he expected it to be, and he was unable to find a handhold. He made his way cautiously to the stern and found, to his relief, an alcove where the anchor was suspended from a chain that exited the hull of the ship. Bahari swam underneath the anchor, into the shadows of the alcove and gripped the anchor with both hands.

The passing seconds seemed like hours to him as he hung in the water, holding the rusting metal. Occasionally, scraps of coherent sentences floated to him from above deck

"...leave him there. He'll go down with the ship!"

Bahari hoped that the men outside the door to his room had given up on their chase. As long as they were unable to get into the room, they would think that he remained there for the safety that it offered. If they got into the room they would see the open window and know that he was outside the ship. Within a few minutes, he could hear the sound of marching footsteps getting louder as the soldiers left his boat and boarded their own.

The sky was beginning to lighten in the east, which was the only direction that Bahari could see past the anchor and the confines of the alcove. With miles of ocean surrounding him on every side, he started to wonder what he was going to do if the enemy stopped looking for him. Without warning, the ship lurched backwards, putting an end to his wondering as he struggled to hold on to the anchor. Then he heard the voices of men yelling in unison and the ship lurched again. He counted five such motions, accompanied by a shuddering vibration that moved through the hull of the ship each time. On the last attempt, they pulled the battering ram free of Bahari's ship, allowing the weight of the water inside the hull to drag it down the side of the reef. As the enemy ship turned back to the south, Bahari watched from his hiding spot as his cargo ship rolled to the port side and slipped beneath the surface. Everything he had worked for, everything that made his way of life possible came to an end in that moment. Within minutes, the boat was gone, with only an area of bubbles and floating debris to show where it had been.

Despair threatened to overtake him, but he fought it off, realizing the urgency of his situation. *What am I going to do now? I can't hang on to this anchor forever*. Even now, the jagged, rusted metal was biting into his hands. Even if he could hold on, he would be in greater danger once the ship reached its port. *No, I've got to get free of this boat without them seeing me!* Suddenly, the ship began to turn around and as they came back to the sight of the attack, Bahari realized that they were looking for survivors.

Isn't it enough that you attacked us and sank my ship? Is it really necessary to make sure that we're all dead? Pirates would be satisfied with looting and sinking the ship. As soon as the thought came to his mind, Bahari was faced with the obvious conclusion. These were not pirates.

Who are these people? What are they doing out here? Are they looking for something, protecting something, hiding from something? It is an outrage that a citizen of the Empire would be attacked like this!

As they passed the attack area once more, Bahari hoped to come in contact with some debris that he could hide behind, but the ship stayed just barely out of the wreck area. Then as they moved further to the south, he noticed a barrel floating a few yards away. The sky was still mostly dark, offering a small measure of concealment and he knew that the opportunity would not present itself again. So, taking a deep breath, Bahari ducked under the water and pushed off of the boat. The saltwater stung his eyes and it was too dark to make out the barrel. He continued to kick his good leg and paddle with one arm while the other was outstretched, feeling for the barrel. At first, he thought that he had passed it and started to panic, knowing that he couldn't go to the surface to look. But then his hand touched something firm. Swimming underneath it, he surfaced, taking caution to keep the floating barrel between him and the enemy ship. He waited, for what seemed like an eternity, before risking a peek from behind the barrel. When he did, he saw that the ship was only a dark silhouette on the brightening horizon. For the first time since the attack began, Bahari breathed a sigh of relief.

He floated in the water for a moment, clinging to the barrel, trying to come to grips with what had just happened. His most immediate threat was now sailing to the south, but in many ways, his current situation was worse. *Now what do I do? I'm floating in the middle of the ocean and I don't even know where I am or how to get to land!* He shook his head to clear his mind.

He had been heading south along the coast from Nucotu when he missed the turn and ended up on the west side of the reef. As close as he could figure, he was still well north of the halfway point between the two cities and many miles west of the shore. *With a dangerous reef in between!* He would have several days' journey before he could reach the shore. *That's if the tides don't carry me past the southern tip!* For that amount of time, he would need food and water.

Then, as the sky continued to lighten in the east, a smile formed on Bahari's face. All around him, scattered in the dawn light, were crates of fruit drifting away from the sight of the attack. *If the gods are merciful, I should reach land within a few days. And then the Governor will know about this!*

3

The rectangular peephole slid open, showing the eyes of an elderly woman, then shut suddenly. A few seconds later, the large door opened inward and the nurse of the temple of Adussk, the god of healing, bowed in reverence before the Governor of Bastul.

Adair Lorus walked through the door and motioned for the woman to rise. Although it still made him uncomfortable, he had come to expect this reverent behavior from his subjects. Each of the royal guards at his flanks carried spears in their right hands and torches in their left, casting a flickering orange glow around the trio, barely fighting back the darkness of the night.

"I was told you have a man in your custody...a sick man."

"Yes, my lord," the old woman responded. "He has been here since yesterday morning, unconscious and silent until a few hours ago. But then he started moaning your name, so I sent for you. I hope I have not disturbed you," she stated quickly.

"Not at all. Thank you for notifying me. May I see him?" he asked, unnecessarily.

"...at once, my lord." The woman turned to Adair's right and began walking down a long hall. The dark green fabric of her veil and floor-length tunic billowed as she hurried through the dark passage, restricted only by the leather apron tied at her waist. The sound of their footsteps echoed off the stone floor as they passed numerous doorways and candles burning in sconces along the stone walls. The hall turned to the left and continued for another hundred feet before it ended at a door. The woman pulled a set of keys from her apron.

With a nod of confirmation, she unlocked the door and pushed it open. Adair walked slowly into the room, unsure of what he might find. The guards followed closely, their torches adding to the light from a small lamp hanging on the wall. The soft illumination showed a man lying on top of the sheets, covered in bandages, and throwing his head back and forth. If he had been moaning before, he showed no signs of it now.

"Where did you find this man?"

"A soldier brought him to me. He said they found him on the western shore."

Adair wrinkled his eyebrows as he walked over to the bed. "Is he awake?"

"No, my lord. It only appears that way because he moves so much."

Adair stood over the bed with his hands clasped behind his back. It was plain to see that the man was badly injured. He had a large bandage around his left thigh and the skin on his face and arms was burned and peeling. His hair was gray, flecked with brown, and matted on his head. Adair looked at his face but didn't recognize him.

"No..." the man mumbled and then flinched as if dodging something.

Suddenly, a memory sprang into Adair's mind. He had dealt with this man before on the matter of neglecting to pay a shipping tax. Usually, any crime against the Empire, no matter how small, was punishable by death under Orudan law. Adair had shown mercy on the man and let him live. After that, the man tried to repay Adair's kindness by sending word of any criminal happenings around the city, as he became aware of them. Adair had to admit that this man had proven to be a useful informant on several occasions, but he hadn't heard anything from him in almost a year.

As the man's name came back to his memory, Adair said it aloud. "Bahari."

"Do you know him, my lord?" the old woman asked.

"Yes," Adair answered, wondering why Bahari would be moaning his name. "You said he was found on the western shore?"

"Yes, my lord. That's what the soldier told me. I've..." she started, but then trailed off.

Adair turned to her. "What is it, woman? If you know something, tell me at once!"

"I've seen this type of thing before," she answered, her body language more timid than before. "A man gets in a drunken fight and finds himself washed up on the beach. I thought this was another such occurrence," she said, her voice lowering to a whisper. "But when I cleaned the wound on his leg I pulled this out."

Reaching into the pocket of her apron, she produced what appeared to be the dangerous half of an arrow. She handed it to Adair and he took it carefully.

The craftsmanship was better than what the Orud military used, but he couldn't place it.

"How was it positioned in his leg?"

"May I...?" the woman asked, motioning for the arrow.

"Please," Adair said, handing it back to her.

"It entered from the back," she said, holding it up to Bahari's leg. "But it wouldn't come out so I had to take it out from the front. It wasn't easy, but he didn't even seem to notice."

Adair looked back at Bahari and shook his head. *What did you get yourself into this time?* "I am leaving for a while, but I will be back," he said to the woman. "While I am gone, keep his door locked and let no one else see him."

"Yes, my lord," she said with a nod.

Adair strode out of the room with the guards following closely. When he reached the front door, he called over his shoulder to the old woman who was struggling to keep up. "If he wakes up, try to find out what happened."

The sun had just peeked over the mountains to the east and the Bay of Bastul glittered with the first rays of the morning sunlight. Maeryn stood on the balcony of her bedroom with her hands on the stone railing. Her night clothes and long blonde tresses swayed in the light breeze as she took a deep breath of the salty air and exhaled. Adair wasn't in bed when she woke and the sheets were cold. He had obviously left sometime during the night and it was bothering her. It wasn't as if this was the first time. Actually, it was a regular occurrence for someone of Adair's position. But Maeryn was finding it harder and harder to deal with his absences. *When you're the governor of Bastul, everyone needs something from you.* She rubbed the sleep from her eyes and yawned, walking back into the bedroom.

The house was already alive with activity. The slaves had been awake for a couple hours and were scurrying around the house, busy with their duties. Maeryn pulled a fresh white tunic from her closet and slipped it over her head. The purple thread sewn into the hem dragged on the floor until she gathered the tunic at her waist and fastened it with a matching purple silk belt. She walked barefoot to her mirror set against the wall and sat down in the chair which faced it. Voices drifted to her from different parts of the house as she combed her hair, but she hardly heard them. She was unable to stop thinking about Adair and her thoughts turned from irritation at his increasing responsibilities to worry about his safety.

After combing out a night's worth of tangles, she wove her hair into a simple braid that hung down to the middle of her back, tying the ends of the thick locks with a narrow ribbon. On the table next to her comb were two elaborately decorated glass bottles of rose oil, a rare treat in her culture. Adair had purchased each of them on separate occasions from a merchant friend of his that passed through Bastul only a few times a year. She pulled the glass stopper from the older of the two bottles and applied a drop to each wrist and one on either side of her neck.

Now ready for the day, Maeryn left her bedroom and descended the stairs leading toward the center of the house, remembering Kael's excitement about a new project that he and Saba were going to start in the morning. As she reached the first floor, the garden courtyard came into view between white stone columns which supported the overhanging roof. She headed through the center two columns and down a circular set of stairs that led to the gravel floor. The bright morning sun reflected off the top of the house to her left, leaving the rest of the open area in morning shadows. By noon, the sun would be shining straight down into the garden and the many trees and flowers would bask in the warmth.

Just as she suspected, Kael and Saba were at the other end of the garden. As she approached, Saba stood from a kneeling position at the base of a small tree.

"Good morning, Maeryn," he said in a soft voice.

"Mother," exclaimed Kael, running toward her and throwing his arms around her waist.

Maeryn reached down and stroked Kael's shoulder-length blonde hair. His blue eyes were bright, especially when he was excited about something. Most boys his age would be embarrassed to hug their mothers. But not Kael; he was different—special. "Good morning, you two. And what are you working on now?" she asked.

Kael answered excitedly before Saba had a chance. "Saba is going to show me how to graft a branch onto this tree. They are different species, but he says they will grow together if we are very careful."

Maeryn smiled at his excitement, then looked to Saba. "Thank you," she whispered.

"My pleasure," he whispered back.

Saba was an old man, old and wise. He was tall, with silver hair that fell past his broad shoulders and a beard that was just as long. Between the beard and his thick eyebrows, most of his features were covered, except his straight, sharp nose and bright blue eyes.

Adair first met him seven years ago when he needed some information. Adair didn't tell her much, except that he was impressed with the man's wealth of knowledge. It seemed that they had just discussed what to do about Kael's education only weeks before and couldn't come to a decision. They both agreed that the usual Orud upbringing did not interest them. Most of the education revolved around the history of the Empire and the lineage of Emperors from the first to the most recent. Beyond that, the education was simply a preparation for becoming a soldier.

And then Saba came into their lives. He was knowledgeable about many different cultures, history, religions, economics, nature, and weather. Actually, Maeryn couldn't think of a single thing that Saba didn't know about. Not once had he ever responded to a question with "I don't know" as his answer. Yet, he wasn't arrogant in any way. In fact, he was one of the most humble people that either of them had ever met. That, combined with his patient and kind personality made him the perfect tutor for their son. Adair wasted no time approaching him on the matter, taking great care to emphasize the fact that the pay for tutoring the governor's son would be quite handsome. They made sure there was no way he would refuse. And he didn't.

That was seven years ago, when Kael was only three years old, and Saba had since become part of their family. Maeryn watched as he knelt down and talked to Kael. He was so patient and gentle, and Kael's eyes lit up with excitement every time Saba was near. The agreement had always been that he would tutor Kael in a variety of subjects for several hours each morning. The hours would get longer as Kael got older, but at the beginning, the tutoring was to end by midday so Kael would also have the time to play like every child should. The tutoring eventually evolved into something much less formal. The two became friends and did everything together. Whether play or work, every situation became a teaching experience and Kael thoroughly enjoyed every minute of it.

"Have you seen Adair this morning?"

Saba looked up and shook his head. "He was gone before I woke."

Maeryn smiled nervously.

"Have fun, you two," she replied, turning to leave.

As she reached the steps to the house she turned around to watch them from a distance. They were both kneeling by the tree, as Saba pointed at the peeling bark and explained some incredibly detailed information that would have bored her. But Kael was enthralled. As she watched, her thoughts returned to her husband and she wondered how long it would be until she would see him again.

4

The carriage bounced and creaked in response to the stone road underneath, as Adair watched the scenery pass by the window. To the east, rolling meadows stretched from the road to the mountains, the land rising sharply as it drew close to the foothills. Occasionally, a tall row of trees would divide the land, designating a property boundary. To the west, the cobblestone road gave way to patches of grass, clinging stubbornly to the shoulder, which ended abruptly at a steep cliff. The ocean, which was hundreds of feet below only minutes ago, was getting closer now as the carriage descended into a valley. After a few minutes, the road ended at a sandy beach and the carriage came to a halt. Adair quickly opened the door and stepped out, happy to be rid of his method of transportation. He preferred to ride a horse, but because of his position, was expected to do otherwise for safety reasons.

A hundred yards away, at the opposite side of the beach was a wooden guard tower clinging to the side of the cliff like a vine in one of the surrounding vineyards. It reached from the beach floor, all the way to a lookout perched fifty feet above the top of the cliff. Two of the four soldiers that had been accompanying Adair rode up and began to dismount, intending to follow him inside.

"I'll return shortly," he said to them.

They each glanced at the other and then back to Adair, conceding with a nod. Adair turned away and walked toward the guard tower, leaving the men to keep charge of the carriage.

It took him several minutes to reach the lower entry. Two guards on either side of the door tipped their spears in salute. They were otherwise motionless, staring straight ahead without making eye contact. Adair never ceased to be impressed at the discipline of his soldiers, especially those who were stationed at posts far away from the scrutiny of the Governor. It was a small sign, but it confirmed his success at ruling the city. He smiled as he walked past the soldiers and through the stone archway. This room was one of many rooms making up the lower level, serving only as an entrance to the enormous staircase carved into the rock.   Around the other side of the building, facing the ocean, were other rooms of supplies and stables for the mounted patrolmen who rode up and down the coast at scheduled intervals, but this one was completely empty.   Adair waited for a few seconds, looking around at the construction of the room.   He had been here many times, but had never paid much attention to the place beyond its practical uses.   He glanced up to the ceiling and observed thick wooden beams that extended twenty feet over his head from their anchor point in the rock cliff, to where they were supported by slightly larger vertical beams buried in the sand.   The room itself was nearly forty feet wide, but only half as deep.

To his left, a door opened and another soldier walked through.   As soon as he noticed Adair, his casual demeanor disappeared.   "Colonel, it is a pleasure to have your company."   The man bowed his head in respect.   "How may I be of assistance?"

"I am here to see your Lieutenant."

The soldier motioned to the stairs.   "He is up above in the observatory; I will go fetch him for you."

"No; that won't be necessary.   I don't wish to keep him from his work; just take me to him."

"Certainly," the man bowed.   "Please follow me."

He led Adair up the stairs, which switched back and forth across the cliff face.   The soldier climbed slowly out of courtesy for his superior.   After five floors they reached the observatory, which stood even with the top of the cliff.   The stairs ended at a spacious room with a balcony overlooking the ocean.   From here, a ladder extended through the ceiling, leading to the upper lookout.   The Lieutenant was standing at the railing of the balcony, looking north along the beach.   He was dressed much the same as Adair, with a hammered metal cuirass and a short red cloak gathered at one shoulder by a silver torc.   Though he was younger than Adair, he looked ten years older. His sand colored hair was starting to thin on the top and his weathered skin had seen too many years of sun.   Adair walked up behind him, but the Lieutenant was deep in thought and didn't notice.

"Lieutenant," Adair said softly.

The man turned his head, startled.   It took him only a second to realize who was standing before him and he quickly bowed.   "My lord...what brings you from the city?" he asked, unable to hide his nervousness.

"I came to inquire about the man that you found on the beach yesterday."

"Yes, my lord," he replied.

"Tell me everything you know."

"Well," the man started, "I don't know who he is, but I can show you where we found him.

"Please," Adair said, his curiosity peaked.

The Lieutenant motioned for Adair to come farther out onto the balcony and pointed to a sandy finger of land to the north that jutted out from the rocks into the ocean. Adair judged it to be just over five miles away.

"He was found lying face-down in the sand on the other side of that point. It was yesterday morning," he quickly added, getting ahead of himself. "When we came upon him, he was already unconscious. His tunic was torn in many places and he was badly burned by the sun." The Captain looked out at the ocean as he remembered. "His hands and feet were cut and bruised all over. It happens when fishermen get tangled up with the reef. He also had a large wound, high up on his left leg. When he was first brought to me, I thought he was dead, but his breath could be felt under his nose. I had one of my men wash him and temporarily dress his wounds. But we were unable to get him to wake up for food or water, so I sent him to the city to be cared for." The soldier stopped with a puzzled look on his face. "I'm sorry. I didn't know he was important or I would have contacted you immediately."

Adair dismissed the man's comments, not wanting to get sidetracked by instructing the Lieutenant about how everyone was important in one way or another. "Did he speak at all when you had him in your custody?" Adair asked instead.

"No, my lord, he didn't even move," the Lieutenant answered.

Adair only nodded in reply.

The silence was clearly uncomfortable for the Lieutenant. "With all of the activity around here lately, my men have been volunteering to make patrols rather than waiting for me to order them," he said, trying to make conversation.

"What do you mean?" Adair said in a stern voice, his gaze now leveled at the man.

"Oh, I beg your pardon, my lord. I didn't mean to make light of his unfortunate circumstances," the Captain quickly replied.

"No," Adair clarified, waving his hand to the side. "What do you mean by *all of the activity?*"

"Oh!" the Lieutenant exclaimed, a look of relief washing over his face. "I just meant that you are the second person to come asking about the man today."

Adair's pulse quickened. "Who else have you talked to?" he asked, not bothering to hide his look of worry.

The Lieutenant, who was looking more nervous by the second, put his hand on his forehead as he tried to recall the details. "Some of my patrolmen came across a young man...maybe thirty years old, walking along the beach early this morning. He said he was looking for his brother...and that their boat had gone down. I told him where we sent the man and offered to have one of my men escort him, but he refused and ran away."

"I need a horse," Adair blurted out.

"I'm sorry..." the Lieutenant replied, not understanding what was happening.

"Quickly, I need a horse," Adair repeated, much louder this time.

"You can take mine; he's outside that door," said the Lieutenant, pointing to a door by the stairs.

"Have someone notify my men down on the beach that I've gone back to the city." Adair barely got the words out of his mouth before he reached the door. He threw all his weight at it and it flung open, revealing the rolling hills at the top of the cliff. Squinting at the bright sunlight, he found the horse only a few steps away and ran to it, leaping into the saddle in one swift movement. He pulled hard on the reins, turning the horse around and kicked his heels, causing the beast to leap into motion.

"I'm sorry, my lord," the Lieutenant shouted, leaning out of the doorway. "I should have taken him myself."

Adair's heart was pounding as he raced southward along a narrow path which followed the top of the cliff. One specific part of the Lieutenant's story worried him the most. Adair made it a point to know everything about his informants. He knew that Bahari had a wife, but was positive that he didn't have any other relatives.

Adair's horse was running at a steady pace, despite the winding path. It was obviously used to the terrain from being part of a patrol unit. The path eventually curved to the west and descended steeply, connecting with the western road on which Adair had just traveled by carriage only half an hour ago. It was wider and paved with flat stones, being the main thoroughfare along the west coast. The pavestones which kept the sand from eroding into the ocean made travel by carriage easier, but slowed the progress of a horse. Adair steered the animal to the inside shoulder of the road, where its hooves would find traction in the bare sand. The horse was able to gain speed on the unobstructed road and within minutes he reached the outskirts of the city. Whereas the trip by carriage took him all morning, already he was riding past the vineyards and farmland that surrounded Bastul. Slowly, the rural environment gave way to the urban, as houses and structures of various kinds became more frequent. Just before reaching the Market District, the road forked and Adair veered to the right, taking the road that paralleled the water and ran out to the peninsula, encircling the city.

The organization of the Market District, with its large buildings and regulated structure ended abruptly at the Housing District, which had fewer regulations and resulted in a haphazard look of odd sized and shaped dwellings, housing the bulk of the population of Bastul. Adair counted streets as he passed them, turning left at the sixth one, heading across the peninsula toward the bay.

The temple of Adussk was located at the other end of the district, just before the docks. It sat on a man-made island in the center of the Nescus

River, with arched bridges connecting it to either shore. Adair received stares of wonder from the citizens of Bastul as he steered the horse through the western gate and over the bridge. The horse skidded to a halt in the graveled courtyard in front of the building and Adair leaped off, running as soon as his feet touched the ground. His knees were stiff from the ride and he stumbled at first, but ignored the pain and headed up the front steps for the door. He was in too much of a hurry to knock, so he pushed the door open as soon as it was within reach. There was no one to greet him at the entry and he turned right, retracing his steps from the previous night. As he rounded the corner, he almost collided with the old nurse.

"My lord!" she screamed in shock.

"Give me the key to his room," he demanded, his voice sounding louder than he intended in the close quarters.

The lady struggled in her apron for the right key.

"Here's the one," she said as he snatched it from her hand and ran down the hallway.

Coming to the door of Bahari's room, Adair jammed the key into the lock and twisted it, expecting to hear a click. When nothing happened, he pushed on the door, but it didn't move. Without waiting for the woman, he jumped back a few steps and kicked at the door with all of his weight. The lock broke and the door swung on its hinges, crashing into the wall with a loud thud. There, on top of the bed, lay Bahari, unflinching.

Adair rushed over to him, but it was obvious that he was too late. Bahari's skin was a pale blue beneath his sunburn. Adair bent down and put his ear to the man's mouth, listening for breath.

"What is the ma..." the old lady began as she entered the room, but trailed off as she caught sight of Bahari's dead body. "Oh my!" she exclaimed. "I just checked on him not more than twenty minutes ago."

Adair stood up and looked at the woman. "Has anyone been in here?"

"No, my lord...only me!"

"Did you give your keys to anyone after you checked on him?" he asked, trying to calm himself down.

"No, my lord. I always keep the keys right here," she replied with a pat to the front pocket of her apron.

Adair looked back to the body. As his mind raced to find a solution, something caught his eye. Other than being devoid of life, Bahari's body looked strange and Adair stepped back, trying to figure out what was wrong. He realized, after a few seconds of inspection, that there was something wrong about the way his head looked in relation to his body.

"His neck is broken," he said, more to himself than to the old woman. "That rules out death by natural causes." *One thing is sure—the people who caused Bahari to end up in this infirmary were dedicated enough to make sure that he didn't come out alive.* He looked back at the woman. "Someone was in here, and I want to know who."

"I swear, my lord. I checked on him just a short time ago and he was breathing. His fever had broken, and I went to prepare some broth for him to drink."

Adair tried to think his way through the problem, starting with the way in. He had to kick down the door, *so she didn't forget to lock it.* He looked around the room and his gaze settled on the window, which was the only other way into the room. It was small, but the shutters were open. He walked over to it and looked out, seeing that the ground was only a short jump away. *Someone would still be able to climb through if they were determined.*

He briefly considered jumping out of the window and searching for the person, but they would be impossible to track once outside of the temple grounds. The city was too big and the population too large. If someone wanted to hide in this city, there were plenty of places to do it.

"I'll need a moment alone with him," he told the woman, who now had tears in her eyes.

"Certainly, my lord," she replied with a sniffle and started to walk out.

"Oh, wait. I need to see the arrow that you pulled from his leg," he added. It was the only clue that he had to go on.

"Yes, my lord. I will get it for you," she said and left Adair alone with Bahari's body.

He sat down on the bed and grasped Bahari's cold hand. "The gods have not smiled on you today Bahari," he said aloud. Pausing to find the words, he continued. "I will find the one who did this and I will make it right. You needn't worry about your wife; she will be taken care of. I will see to that. May you find the peace in death that escaped you in life."

After a few minutes the old woman returned and handed the arrow to Adair. He fingered the tip of the arrowhead as a matter of habit, before turning the weapon over in his hands. The construction of it showed skill, but nothing unusual caught his attention.

"Thank you," he said to the woman, tucking the arrow in his belt.

"Shall I notify his family, my lord?"

"No, that won't be necessary. I'll take care of it," replied Adair. He rose to his feet and excused himself, a feeling of defeat replacing his prior sense of urgency.

5

The sun was touching the western horizon, turning the dark blue of the ocean a fiery orange as Adair entered the courtyard of his mansion situated in the hills overlooking Bastul. All was quiet except for the voices of his son Kael and Ajani, the youngest of the slaves. Ajani was only slightly older than Kael, but much taller. The two were throwing makeshift spears at a nearby tree, and from the look of determination on their faces, it was a competition.

"Hello, boys," Adair said as he walked up behind them.

"Hello, father," Kael answered without looking. The boy was holding a spear above his shoulder, readying himself for his next throw.

"I don't wish to disturb such a fierce competition, but I was hoping that you might know where I could find Saba?"

"He's gone until tomorrow," Kael answered.

Adair paused with his hand on his chin. "Well, please continue," he told the boys with a wave of his hand and walked toward the main entrance of the house. To the right of the stairs, he found Maeryn sitting on a rock ledge which surrounded a broad-leafed tree. She was pruning a flowering bush with her back turned to him. Adair suddenly found a mischievous grin spreading across his face as he decided to sneak up behind her.

"Those flowers just don't stand a chance at looking beautiful when you are next to them," he whispered in her ear.

Maeryn jumped at the unexpected sound, spinning around.

Adair couldn't help the huge smile of amusement that spread across his face.

Maeryn's startled expression quickly melted. She sprang to her feet and threw her arms around him. "Where have you been? Is something the matter? You left so early!"

Adair rubbed his forehead. "There is always something the matter; never a moment's rest for me."

For an instant, a flicker of some emotion crossed Maeryn's face. Adair had a talent for reading people. It was one of the skills that allowed him to rise so quickly through the ranks to his current position of authority. But sometimes his wife was a complete mystery to him. And now was one of those times. He knew he should ask her what was wrong, but it had been a long day and he wasn't in the mood for an emotional conversation. "Kael said Saba will be gone until tomorrow?" he asked instead.

"Yes. He left just after dinner. I think he was going to visit a friend. Anyway, he said he should be back before sundown. Are you hungry? I could fix you something to eat."

Adair smiled. "I'm starving. That would be great!" He knew Maeryn suspected that something was wrong but dinner would be a good distraction. Besides, he couldn't tell Maeryn what had happened. Especially when he wasn't sure exactly what had happened himself, or how dangerous the situation might be. Whoever attacked Bahari out at sea was thorough enough to search the beach for survivors, and it wasn't safe to involve Maeryn at this point.

It was midnight, and there was a slight chill in the breeze coming off the ocean. Adair had been unable to fall asleep and had wasted away the last few hours watching the curtains at the balcony dance in the breeze. Only minutes ago, he decided that the arrowhead wasn't going to lead him anywhere. Saba was the only one who would be able to make some sense of it and turn it into a usable clue. Unable to bear the boredom any longer, Adair rose from his bed, dressed, and grabbed a cloak before heading toward the guest quarters in the east wing of the mansion. In Saba's room he found a scrap of parchment in one of the desk drawers and laid it on the desk next to a burning candle. Pulling a quill from its ink pot he began to write.

> *Saba,*
> *Something terrible has happened to an acquaintance of mine. I am looking into the matter, but have been unsuccessful in finding any useful information to this point. The only clue that I have thus far is this arrowhead. I leave it in your possession to find out what you can about the people who made it. I have been unable to find any meaning in it and would, therefore, be grateful for any information that would aid me in my searching.*
> *Gratefully,*
> *Adair*

After blowing on the ink to speed its drying, Adair rolled the parchment and tied it with a thread. He slid the arrowhead inside the tube of parchment and left the message on Saba's writing desk before blowing out the candle and leaving the room.

Even in the early morning hours, the streets of Bastul were busy, though to a lesser degree than during the day. The majority of the traffic belonged to merchants, wheeling their carts down to the docks to be ready for business as soon as the sun came up. Groups of men clustered in the shadows nursing bottles of wine, occasionally shouting at the passersby, offering some meaningless challenge before collapsing from the exertion of raising their voices.

Through it all, no one noticed the silent, cloaked figure that walked briskly through the alleys, keeping to the shadows so as not to attract attention. Adair was heading for the Shipping District, just as the merchants, but for an entirely different reason. He would have preferred to take a direct route, but thought it best to stay out of sight. It is not often that someone of his position goes skulking around in the early hours of the morning. *...or, rather it is not often noticed!*

Three blocks from the ocean, he came upon a series of small stone buildings that made up the majority of inns and pubs in the city. Adair peered around the corner and could see a few people hanging around in the street. They were either waiting to be the first customers of the day, or else, they were the last ones of the night. Adair glanced behind to make sure that nobody had followed him and when he was assured, ducked down the back alley. All of the business owner's living quarters faced away from the main street and toward the alley, so Adair walked softly until he found the building he was looking for.

He walked to the appropriate door and knocked softly. When no one answered, he tried again, a little louder this time. The thick wooden door finally opened just a crack, orange candle light spilling from the opening. Adair pulled back his hood just enough to reveal his face to the person inside and the door opened all the way. A short, fat man filled the doorway, waving his hand rapidly for Adair to come inside the house.

After closing the door, the man put a finger to his lips and turned to walk through a low doorway at the back of the house. Once inside the back room he shut this door behind them as well and offered Adair a seat at a small wooden table. The table wasn't the only thing that was small; in fact, it fit the rest of the room perfectly.

"What's the occasion?" the man asked, rubbing sleep from his eyes.

"Why don't you offer me something to drink, Gursha?" Adair said as he took off his cloak and draped it over the chair before sitting down.

"Sorry," the large man muttered, and walked out of the room.

While he waited, Adair studied his surroundings as a matter of habit. The table was obviously where Gursha ate his meals, but the walls were lined with shelves stuffed with an assortment of knick-knacks that didn't appear to be kitchen related. Before he was able to come to any conclusions, Gursha returned, carrying a bottle of wine and two dirty glasses. He set them down on the table and slumped into his chair with a look of exhaustion. Adair waited for Gursha to pour him some wine, but the man was clearly flustered with this meeting and overlooked it completely. Adair wasn't used to meeting his informants in their own homes, so he felt a little out of place, but obviously not as much as Gursha.

"Thanks," Adair said, pouring himself a glass instead. "I can see that you don't prefer to meet in your home, but I can assure you, it will be worth your time."

A greedy smile spread itself across Gursha's wide face and then quickly retreated, replaced by a forced look of seriousness. Usually, Adair didn't have to pay any of his informants. There were other methods of extracting information from people. Some were happy to tell all just to escape the punishment that they justly deserved. Others found themselves in trouble so often that they would do just about anything to have friends in high places. Adair had found that Gursha was a unique case. He ran the pub next door and was a legitimate businessman. But there was a way to get to anyone, and Adair had a special way of knowing people better than they knew themselves. The truth was that the *Dockside* couldn't survive on its own. Adair timed his meetings perfectly to coincide with Gursha's financial troubles and was now in a position of providing the pub owner with a necessary second income, to which Gursha had become accustomed.

"Tell me what you know about a man named Bahari," Adair said as he took a sip of wine, ignoring the stains on the side of his glass.

Gursha grunted and scratched his chin before his eyes lit up.

"A merchant. Hasn't been doing well lately...specially this year with the bad growing season and all. He's in pretty deep with Quartus. Last I heard...took a shipment to Nucotu. Hopin' to get paid better up there."

Adair liked what he was hearing so far. "When is he due to return?"

"Should've been back a few days ago. Missed his deadline from what I hear."

"And why do you think that is?" questioned Adair.

"Don't know. Haven't heard nothin'." Gursha's eyebrows wrinkled as he tried to think of where these questions were leading. "Didn't have nothin' to do with it," he said defensively.

"With what?"

"Well," he paused. "You say he's missin', maybe you think I did sumthin'."

"I didn't say he was missing," Adair corrected. "You did."

Gursha opened his mouth to defend himself, but promptly closed it when he realized that he had nothing to say. Adair was amused at how easy it was to get this man where he wanted him.

"Look," Adair offered. "I know you wouldn't be involved in anything like that. But I want to know, in your professional opinion, why would a man like Bahari not meet his deadline? And think carefully about your answer."

Gursha looked down at the table while he considered the question. Adair knew that this man had all kinds of information in his head. Most of the time, he didn't even realize it. You don't run a local pub without coming in contact with all sorts of people who like to tell stories. But the best way to get information from Gursha was to make him feel as though he is constantly on the verge of losing his precious second income. Fear tended to make this confused man think clearly.

Gursha finally started to speak. "He was doin' better 'till this year. Was close to having his debts paid off. Things turned bad. Maybe he ran away." He smiled as the words came out, pleased with his conclusion.

"However," Adair countered. "He's got a wife. And you just said he was close to paying off his debts. He wouldn't just leave with the prospect of getting paid more in Nucotu." This line of questioning was really irrelevant. What Adair needed to find out was where Bahari was when he was attacked, without revealing any information of his own.

Gursha returned to his thoughts with a look of determination on his face. Adair thought he looked like he needed a push in the right direction. "What are some other reasons that a man might disappear?"

"Two things," Gursha responded. "If he got in trouble..." His speech trailed off as the thought got away from him and then returned in another form. "He coulda been drunk, crashed his boat. Course, he wasn't a big drinker." He paused in mid-thought, still staring at the table. "If he was tryin' to get back on time...probably wouldn't stop to sleep. Coulda fell asleep and wrecked on the reef, people do that all the time."

Adair's attention perked up at this news. "Why is that?"

"Well, if he was comin' from Nucotu, he should've stopped early before passin' by the reef. But if he was in a hurry, he coulda tried to go right ahead through the night."

Adair smiled as Gursha said these words and pulled a bag of coins out of his cloak, setting it on the table. Gursha was visibly relieved to hear the sound of coins clinking together. Obviously, he was worried that his information wasn't valuable to Adair.

"Do you have a map that I can look at?" asked Adair.

Gursha's chair creaked as he leaned back and grabbed a piece of parchment from the shelf, disturbing a layer of dust that seemed to have been accumulating for years. Everything was at arm's length in the tiny room. "Here you go," he said and laid the old map in front of Adair.

Adair unrolled it and set his glass in one corner to keep it from rolling back. After inspecting the portion of the map that showed the western shoreline of Bastul, he stood up and lifted his glass, emptying it in one last gulp. He set the glass down and slid the map back across the table.

"Thank you Gursha. It's always a pleasure." Adair took the bag of coins off the table and tossed them to the fat man who was still sitting. Gursha snatched the bag from the air with an unexpected quickness.

Adair looked at the tavern owner and waited until he had full eye contact. "As always, I was never here, and we never talked about any of this."

"Talked about what?" said Gursha, his sense of humor the only thing about him that was finely tuned.

"Precisely," Adair said and couldn't help smiling.

Gursha grunted as he rose from his chair and showed Adair to the door. When Adair stepped outside, Gursha glanced nervously up and down the street before shutting and locking the door.

The early morning air was cool on Adair's face. The lurching of the ocean was mesmerizing and he realized how easy it would have been for Bahari to fall asleep trying to make it back to Bastul to meet his deadline. But the normal shipping routes between the coast and the reef were used regularly and situations like Bahari's didn't occur often. Bahari was attacked by someone, but it probably didn't happen on the eastern side of the reef. Remembering Gursha's map, Adair wondered if Bahari might have fallen asleep, like Gursha suggested, and missed an important turn just before the northern tip of the reef began, causing him to sail down its western side. There were many strange stories about that part of the sea, folklore mostly, told by drunken fishermen who didn't have much credibility to begin with. However entertaining the stories of sea serpents might be, it was common knowledge to stay away from that side of the reef. It was also dangerous to sail in that water for no other reason than the sharp coral that could sink a boat in a matter of minutes.

The more he thought about it, the more it made sense. And that was where he was headed. He knew it was hopeless, but he had to follow through with checking out the area. After all, it was all he had to go on. Who knew how long it would take Saba to find out anything useful with the arrowhead, or if he ever would? By then the trail might be cold.

As soon as he left Gursha's house, Adair went straight to the docks and boarded a small but fast patrol boat, taking a few soldiers with him. If he did manage to run across the people that attacked Bahari, he would need to be able to maneuver quickly and it would help to have experienced soldiers with him. *I should be at home, in bed next to Maeryn!* But he knew that on nights like these, his mind would race and he would lie awake for hours only to watch the sun rise. This way, at least he was doing something about the situation.

After a few hours of heading north along the shore, the sun began to rise. It peeked over the mountains to the east, only a bright orange sliver at first. The ripples on the water picked up the color and suddenly the whole ocean seemed to glow around them. Within a few minutes, the sun had risen enough to be seen in its entirety above the mountains. The light quickly changed to a pale yellow which illuminated the whole sky and the orange glow disappeared.

As the morning drew on, Adair wondered about the consequences of leaving so suddenly. He had left a message for Thaddius to watch over things for a few days until he could return. But Thaddius wasn't a soldier, just an official elected to deal with the social issues that the governor didn't want to deal with, or else, wasn't able to because of a military absence. Adair held the position of Colonel in Orudan Military, but, as with all colonels, he also ruled over a city and was charged with its protection. Adair found the dual responsibilities taxing and leaned heavily on Thaddius to handle most of the decisions that were not specifically military in nature. He knew that the city would be in great hands for the duration of his short trip, but he was now starting to consider how dangerous this excursion might really be. *What if something happens out here and I'm unable to return to Maeryn and Kael?* It was too much to think about and he shook his head to make the thoughts go away.

"Colonel," one of the soldiers called to him from the main deck, breaking the silence. He walked quickly across the deck and climbed the short ladder to the navigational deck where Adair sat under a canopy. "Sir, if you don't mind me asking, what are we doing out here?"

The soldier was close to Adair's own average height with dark brown hair. He had a fierce look in his eyes and it was obvious that he was asking not out of a sense of fear for himself, only curiosity, but didn't want to offend his superior by questioning his reasons.

"I am investigating the death of an acquaintance. He was attacked out near the reef where we are headed."

After a moment of silence, one of the other soldiers spoke up. "What do you hope to find? If it was pirates, there won't be any sign of them by the time we get there."

Adair smiled. "This acquaintance had an arrow embedded in his leg. Our patrols haven't seen any signs of pirates in years, but more importantly, pirates don't use arrows. They are not trained in the military arts. Usually, they are commoners who rely on surprise to overtake their victims. These men were soldiers. And if they were not our own men, I would like to know what rogue soldiers are sailing through the waters of the Empire."

The sun was directly overhead, beating down on the small crew when they reached the northern end of the reef. They were making excellent time and, as the swift boat made its way around the tip and began heading southwest, Adair's senses began to tingle with anticipation. He wasn't sure what he would find out here on the ocean, if anything. Part of him expected to sail around for hours, not seeing anything that would give him a clue as to what might have happened. Another part of him, the part that got excited in dangerous situations, expected to meet confrontation. He was prepared if that was to be the case.

Much to his disappointment, the minutes turned into hours, and still there was no sign of what he was looking for, whatever that might be. He watched clouds roll in from the north, covering the sky in a thin veil of gray. The sun slowly crept west and eventually slipped behind the horizon, turning the sky from pale gray to a brilliant purple. Adair had just come to the decision that this trip was a failure and was about to give the order to turn the boat around when he noticed something out of the corner of his eye. He scanned the southern horizon, trying to find what had grabbed his attention, but now there was nothing except for a smooth ocean surface.

"Keep your eyes open for anything unusual," he called to the men at the bow.

A few seconds later, he saw it again, but it was only visible when he didn't look straight at it. It was a disturbance on the surface of the water; an area where the reflected light from the sunset danced a little differently than it did in the surrounding water. Being a reef area, there were shallow spots everywhere around them, but something was different about this. It wasn't just a sandbar or a coral shelf.

"What is that?" one of the soldiers asked.

"I'm not sure, but head straight for it," Adair answered, hoping that he'd gotten lucky.

Are my eyes deceiving me? It seemed as if something was there on the water, but he couldn't make out any distinct shape. The men on his boat busied themselves with adjusting the sails to make the change in direction, trying to take full advantage of the wind coming from the west. As their sails bulged once again with air, something inside Adair told him that this was what he was looking for and with every second, he was getting closer.

He was just starting to detect a shape in the shimmering water when it began to change. A dark area began to grow on the eastern side of the shimmer. The darkness seemed to emerge from nowhere and finally detached itself, moving to the left.

A ship! Then another appeared on the right side of the shimmer. Suddenly, his eyes found their focus and it all made sense to him. The ships were emerging from behind a structure on the surface of the water. The pale light in the western sky was growing darker with every second, but now that Adair was able to make sense of what he was seeing, more and more details were becoming visible. It was a circular structure with polished metal walls that reflected the surrounding water, giving the illusion that nothing was there. The camouflaging effect was stunning and it wasn't until the second ship emerged from behind the wall that Adair was able to understand what he was seeing.

The two black ships which had been moving in opposite directions away from the structure, turned north simultaneously, heading straight for Adair's small vessel. It only took a few seconds for everyone to realize that they were not equipped to handle this fight.

"Colonel?" one of his men asked, sensing danger.

"Head for the reef. They won't follow us in there." *We're small enough to maneuver around obstacles and this boat doesn't run deep. If they try to follow us, they won't make it out alive.*

One of the men pushed on the rudder and the small boat carved a sharp turn to the port side and headed for the reef. The others jumped into action, trimming the mainsail to keep the westerly wind. The larger boats moved from their intended flanking positions to a direct chase and they were closing in fast, but Adair already saw what he had come to find. These people were doing something out here that they wished to keep a secret. Judging by what they did to Bahari, they were willing to kill for it. But now Adair knew of their presence. He couldn't hide the smile on his face and soon, the other men were grinning as well, with admiration for their superior.

As soon as I get back to Bastul, I'll bring the fleet back and find out what they're hiding.

As their small vessel entered the shallow water of the reef area, they slowed just enough to maneuver through the sharp coral, while still maintaining their lead. The pursuing boats, which dwarfed Adair's boat, came to a stop as they neared the reef. Adair exhaled a deep breath, relieved to be a safe distance away and protected by the coral. Turning his attention back to the difficult task of navigation, he heard a sharp cracking noise from behind.

All the men turned to look back at the large black boats that had positioned themselves with their starboard sides facing the reef. Their silhouettes were barely visible against the sky in the east. Halfway between them and their pursuers, something landed on the surface of the water. Adair squinted just as it skimmed past the prow, leaving a wake on the mottled ocean surface that quickly faded from view.

An unsettled feeling began to grow in his stomach and his heart began to race as he realized his pursuers had projectile capability. The sunset was almost gone now and within a few minutes, there would not be enough light to navigate the dangerous reef. Just as the thought came to him, he noticed the water in front of the boat getting lighter.

"Hard starboard!" he yelled to the men as he pushed on the rudder.

The boat pitched and swerved to the right. Adair almost lost his footing, grabbing the railing for balance.

Another sharp crack sounded as the crew struggled to adjust the sails, hoping to maintain their momentum. Adair turned to see a splash on the rippled surface of the water as another projectile came skipping toward them. Judging by the angle, it was aimed more accurately than the first.

"Brace yourselves!" As the words left his mouth, the middle of their tiny boat erupted in a shower of saltwater and splinters. The jolt knocked Adair off his feet and he rolled across the deck as the boat pitched to the port side and began to fill with water. He clawed at the wood decking to get a handhold, when his eyes settled on the body of one of his crew only a few yards away. The man's midsection was almost completely missing. It looked as though the projectile went straight through him as well as their boat.

Adair pulled himself to his feet and scanned the boat, trying to get a sense of the damage. Water poured across the deck and the weight was rolling the ship back to its starboard side. The remaining soldiers jumped overboard, abandoning the ship which was nearly ripped in half and sinking fast.

Adair ran to the nearest port railing and dove over the side. The other men were already a short distance away and splashing so loud that Adair could follow them by sound alone. He began to swim east with a steady pace that he could maintain for a long time. *At this point, the most important thing is to keep moving.* It took only minutes to catch up to the others. They had slowed considerably after using up their energy with panicked strokes. As Adair closed in on the men, he risked a look behind, but the light was gone from the western sky and nothing could be seen. Even their sinking boat was only a slightly darker blot on the water.

Shouting voices came across the water from the direction of the enemy ships and Adair's heart dropped. He had hoped they would be satisfied with sinking his ship, but it sounded as though he and his men were being pursued.

"Ahh!" one of his men grunted.

We've reached the coral. "Try to stay on the surface as much as possible. The water is shallow, but we should still be able to get over it if we're careful." Adair tried his best to sound confident for the men, but he was out of his realm of experience. He really wasn't sure how close the coral grew to the surface, but it sounded good, and at this moment, keeping the men from despair was important.

Adair flipped over on his back and began to swim with a backstroke, keeping his body on the surface. Then he noticed an orange light hovering over the water behind them. *A lantern!* The flickering glow illuminated what appeared to be six men rowing and several others standing. Whatever hope Adair had of escaping these men, it had just ended. The rowboat was much too fast for panicked swimmers. *We're not going to make it.*

"We've got to split up," he called to the others. No one acknowledged him. He repeated his words a little louder, but all they could hear was their own splashing. Adair decided not to risk yelling any louder to the men and veered to the left, taking his own advice instead. He quickly lost sight and sound of the other men, but the orange light continued to move forward. Adair adjusted his own course even more to stay out of the light, turning directly to the north.

"Stop where you are!" The words came across the water to him and for a brief second, he thought he had been sighted. Then he heard shouts, followed by complete silence.

I've just lost my crew!

He quickened his pace and continued to swim north. The minutes passed slowly and Adair began to grow tired. After fighting fatigue for as long as he could, he slowed to an easier pace. The glow of the lantern had disappeared. He wasn't sure how long he had been swimming, but he knew that he couldn't keep this up forever. Gradually, the sky lightened and he turned to see the moon rising over the eastern horizon. As it climbed higher in the sky, the concealing darkness vanished.

The orange light of the lantern reappeared a moment later. It was only fifty yards away and it looked like they had already spotted him. The rowboat moved swiftly, coming alongside of Adair as he floated in the water. The men standing in the center of the boat were holding bows, stretched taut with arrows ready.

"Climb aboard," came a raspy voice.

Adair knew it was pointless to resist, though his mind still raced to find a way to escape. Against his instincts and years of training, he swam over to the boat and grabbed the extended hand of one of the rowers.

"That's it, nice and easy," the man with the lantern spoke again.

The rower pulled and Adair slid into the boat, rolling over the side and slumping onto his back with exhaustion. The bottom of the boat had a musty smell like it hadn't touched fresh air in a long time.

The man with the lantern stepped forward and held the lamp over Adair's limp body. "I already know from your late friends that you are the Captain."

Captain? Adair was relieved that his men hadn't told the whole truth. Although the position of Captain evidently gave him some measure of safety, being a Colonel and the Governor of Bastul was something that should stay hidden.

"Yes, that is true," he replied, sitting up and wiping the saltwater from his eyes. "What do you..."

Out of the corner of his eye, Adair caught a sudden movement. He didn't even have time to flinch before something hard slammed into the back of his skull and everything went black.

6

Adair was vaguely aware of being dragged across a smooth floor. He felt the sensation of his legs, from the knees down, sliding on a hard surface. He could hear the footsteps of the men that were on either side of him, half carrying him by the shoulders of his tunic. The fabric was cutting into his skin. There was an elapsed period of time between this realization and when he regained his vision. As soon as he opened his eyes, the sight of his own reflection in the marble, four inches away from his nose, caused a shooting pain in his head. He quickly shut his eyes, but his temples pounded, making it difficult to concentrate on anything but the pain. He tried not to make any sound or movement as he winced. The pain gradually lessened into a dull ache, emanating from the base of his skull, spreading down his neck and into his shoulders. He decided to risk opening his eyes again and found his vision to be blurry. Even through the blur, the sight of the intricate black marble veined with silver streaks passing beneath him was too much. His head began to spin. He shut his eyes and darkness returned, a welcome retreat for his overwhelmed vision.

"Is this the one?" The voice seemed loud in the surrounding silence. The two men had stopped dragging him and were talking with a third man. There was a pause before the reply, probably for some gesture that Adair couldn't see.

"He made it close to the outer wall. We almost didn't know he was there until it was too late." Adair was listening intently for any information he could glean from this. He could feel a slight tug on his right shoulder and his captor continued. "He started to run through the reef, but we got him." There was another pause and Adair wished he could watch this conversation from somewhere other than where he was now. There was much to learn, even from people's body language.

"Take him to the end, last cell on the left," said the third man.

Good, only one guard so far. He took note of this as a matter of habit, knowing that any information of his surroundings would be useful at some point.

Without another word, the two soldiers continued to drag Adair down the hall. He knew that they were going to put him in a cell, probably to be questioned. There was no other reason to keep him alive. *But then my chance to escape is gone.* The thought of trying to get away from these two soldiers and the guard they just passed made Adair feel queasy. He knew under normal circumstances that these two men would be no match for him, but the third man, coupled with the probability of blacking out from the exertion, made the situation very dangerous. But he had no other options. As these thoughts were sluggishly making their way through his head, he felt the soldiers drag him around a sharp corner, turning to the left. Once out of site from the guard behind them, Adair seized the opportunity.

The men were carrying swords at their right sides; the scabbard of the man on the left had been knocking into his arm the whole time. He listened to their steps to get the timing and suddenly reached both arms around the back of the soldiers' legs.

The two men tripped over their own feet, sprawling onto the floor in front of them and losing their grip on their prisoner.

Adair pulled his feet underneath him and pounced on the back of the soldier to his right, pinning him to the ground. He reached down to the man's waist and grabbed the hilt of his sword, attempting to rip it from the scabbard. It stuck at first, the awkward angle not allowing it to come free.

The soldier on the left was quicker than Adair had anticipated, already gaining his footing and pulling his own sword free.

Adair somersaulted forward over the soldier beneath him while keeping his grip on the sword. It came free and Adair rolled to his feet on the other side with the sword in his hand.

The other soldier wasted no time and attacked immediately. Lunging forward, he swung his sword at gut level with a backhanded slash.

Adair back-stepped the passing blade and thrust his sword into the man's chest.

The soldier dropped immediately to his knees.

Adair wrenched the sword out, spinning around to find the other man on his hands and knees. Before he could get to his feet, Adair drove his sword between the man's shoulder blades and the soldier collapsed on the floor.

Adair's head was spinning, but he gritted his teeth and tried to ignore the growing nausea. Darting back to the corner of the hallway, he laid in wait for the guard who was sure to have heard all the commotion.

Mere seconds elapsed before the guard came running around the corner.

Adair swung his sword in a level arc and caught the soldier in the face, stopping his upper body momentum while his legs continued forward and swung out from underneath him.

Adair dragged the bodies into one of the nearby cells and piled two of them in the corner. He stripped off the clothes of the third man and changed into them, using his own to wipe up the mess in the hallway. His head was still spinning a little, but he was feeling better with every breath. The guard had been armed with a spear, but Adair decided to keep his newly acquired sword instead, to complete his disguise. The attire of these soldiers was much different from his own military dress, with leather sandals that crisscrossed up his lower leg, coming almost to his knee. The guard's tunic had long sleeves and only reached to Adair's waist, where a pair of calf-long trousers completed the uniform. The sword was similar to standard Orudan issue, only a few inches longer and slightly narrower.

Who are these people? Everything about them seemed relatively normal; nothing was foreign or outlandish except their secretive presence on the ocean. They weren't part of any group that he knew of, but their skin and features suggested they were from this part of the world. *Does the Emperor know about them?* Just as the thought came to him, he dismissed it. The Empire was the most advanced military in the world and they owed that to two reasons—organization and communication. If the Emperor had any operations so near to Bastul, or even knew of something, Adair would be the first one to know. For the meantime, Adair brushed the thoughts aside and concentrated on finding a way out of this place.

Disguised as one of the enemy, Adair strode confidently down the hallway, turning to the right and heading in the direction from which he had been dragged. As he walked, he tried to take note of any details that might later prove useful. Flames burned in sconces at eye-level along both walls, dimly lighting the hallway. The floor was made of a smooth black marble, highly polished, and it reflected what light the torches cast. The walls were made of a more ordinary stone, duller than the floor, but still black. Adair couldn't find any seams where the stones were joined together. It was as if the whole hallway had been carved out of one giant rock.

He found the place where the guard had stood only a moment ago, a low archway at the end of the hall that opened into a wider and taller area with doorways on the left and right. Another low archway was set into the wall on the opposite side, making this chamber a four-way junction. Adair tried to remember from which direction he had been dragged, but couldn't recall turning around any corners. Then again, he had only just regained consciousness at this point. He decided to go with his instinct and chose the archway across the chamber. It was a hallway, exactly like the one he just left. As he walked, it occurred to him that he must be somewhere inside the walled structure he saw on the ocean.

At the end of the hall was a set of stairs leading up. He climbed carefully with one hand on the hilt of his sword, ready for someone to appear at any moment. The stairs spiraled in a tight radius and after a few minutes, he began to wonder how far the steps would go. With each passing second, his sense of direction was more and more confounded. He thought this place to be a building inside the wall, but it was far too large. With all of the stairs he had climbed, this building would have reached high into the air, clearly visible above the wall that surrounded this place. When he was out on the ocean, just before turning into the reef, he was able to get a good look at the outer wall. Despite its camouflaging properties, he estimated it to be only forty or fifty feet tall, and he was positive that he had already climbed much higher than that.

He trudged on for several more minutes before hearing a change in the sound of the stairwell. His footsteps were starting to echo and he could tell that there was a larger area up above. He moved cautiously up the spiraled stairs as the passage widened, ending at a doorway. It was a low arch without a door just like all the others he had seen, but beyond the doorway was what interested him.

Though his view was limited, he could see what appeared to be a cavern, a hundred feet long with a low ceiling. He could also make out row upon row of barrels and crates lining the left side. A sharp clanking noise drew his attention to the right, but he had to move a few steps forward to get a better view. There, in the soft orange glow of a furnace, were a handful of blacksmiths pounding red hot metal with hammers. One of the men plunged the metal into a bucket and a hiss of steam rose above his head. He tossed the metal into a box set on wheels and another man pushed the cart away. Adair moved closer to the archway and scanned the cavern. There were dozens of groups like the first one, all making what appeared to be weapons.

They're building an arsenal!

Before he had a chance to dwell on the shocking discovery, his attention was drawn to something glittering on the far side of the cavern. It took him a little while to realize that it was reflected moonlight on the ocean, seen through an enormous doorway on the other side of the cavern. Just outside of the opening were several ships moored to a dock, but it was too dark to make out anything else.

Suddenly, the sound of voices came to him, much closer than the metalworkers. They were just outside of the doorway to the right, and they were approaching. Adair turned and fled down the stairs, struggling to keep from tripping as he skipped over several steps with each stride. He reached the bottom of the long, winding staircase in just a few minutes and stopped, trying to calm his heartbeat and listen for signs of pursuit. A moment later, the sound of unhurried footsteps drifted to him and it was apparent that the men were coming down the staircase. He had only an instant to think of what to do before they would reach the bottom. He glanced at the other doorways around him. The one straight ahead would lead him back to the jail cells. He wasn't sure about the other two passages, but either one might be an escape route.

If I run, the men coming down the stairs will be alarmed by the disappearance of the guard. If I stay and pose as the guard, they might pass by and not notice. But in order to maintain secrecy in a place such as this, all of the soldiers would probably know each other well enough to recognize a stranger. They would never buy his impersonation. The footsteps in the stairwell were getting louder and time was running out. Adair chose the doorway across from him, running down the hall and turning the corner.

Along the left side of the hall were the barred cells where he hid the bodies of the soldiers. He ducked into the first one and hid in the corner where the shadows would conceal him. He hoped that the men wouldn't even come down this passage. Perhaps they would take one of the other doors. But to his disappointment, he heard them coming. Now all he could do was wait for the men to pass by and sneak out of this passage when they were gone. *By the sound of the footsteps, there are four or five of them. Much smarter to run and hide than fight.*

A moment later Adair watched as four men passed by his cell without even a glance in his direction. He waited until they got farther down the hallway and then he slipped quietly out of the cell, turning back toward the staircase.

"Get back to your post!" one of the men yelled to him from behind.

Adair raised a hand in acknowledgment without turning and continued around the corner. He heard one of the men laugh and hoped that he wasn't really alarmed. As Adair neared the guard post, two more soldiers appeared from the bottom of the stairwell in the opposite hallway, apparently following the same route as the first four. Adair immediately stopped in his tracks and stood at attention against the wall. If the soldiers were suspicious, they didn't let on. Adair's heart was racing as he prepared himself for conflict, which seemed only an arm's reach away.

Then it happened.

A yell came from down the hallway where the first four soldiers had gone.

They found the bodies!

The second group of soldiers stopped walking and pulled their swords from their scabbards, looking at Adair with suspicion.

The first group came back around the corner.

Adair now had enemy soldiers in front and behind him, and two doorways for escape.

"Get him!" they yelled, pointing at Adair.

Adair sprang from his position and ran for the nearest door, entering a dark hallway with six men in pursuit. The hallway went on in a straight line for a short time before any other passages became visible. At the first sight of a doorway Adair risked a glance behind him to find that he had gained a considerable distance on his pursuers. He passed by the first door and dodged through the second one on the left and kept running. To his surprise, it was another hallway with a large doorway at the other end. As he ran he noticed that there were more passages on either side of this hallway as well. He quickly opted for one of the smaller doorways on the right, thinking that it would not be his first choice if he were chasing someone. Each doorway led to another passage with more choices. He kept running, trying to pick a random route to avoid being caught. After a few minutes, he stopped and tried to listen over his own heartbeat.

Silence. Have I lost them?

With at least a few calm minutes ahead of him, Adair considered his situation. He knew there was no hope of escaping this place by way of the cavern at the top of the stairs; there were too many people. He had to find another way. *In a place like this, there has to be more than one!*

Without the sounds of pursuit, he cautiously pressed on to locate another exit. He moved from the dark room that had been his hiding place and began walking tentatively down the hall. It was eerily silent and Adair drew his sword to be ready for any more surprises.

As time passed he found himself in a hall that appeared to be a main artery inside this maze of tunnels. It was at least thirty feet wide and the ceiling sixty-five feet high. Adair glanced down the length of the hall in both directions and noticed that it curved until it disappeared from sight. This was just the sort of thing he was looking for. If it was a main thoroughfare, it would likely lead to an exit. The only problem was the increased probability of meeting more soldiers along the way. But Adair decided to take his chances. He turned to the right and kept to the outside of the curve, which allowed him the best view of what was ahead.

The minutes passed without any change in the scenery. Adair had just begun to wonder if this hall would go on forever, when he noted a change in the air. The passage seemed cooler and the torches on the wall flickered more than before.

Fresh air. He scanned the walls and ceiling for proof of what he hoped for. Directly above him on the wall, only a few feet from the ceiling, was an opening. It was hard to make out at first with all the shadows cast by the torches. Adair's heart sank when he became sure that this was where the air was coming from. It was more than forty feet above him and there was no way to climb to it on these slick walls. He would just have to find another way out.

He continued down the hall hearing nothing but his own footsteps. A minute later he noticed another hole in the wall to his left. It too was out of reach, but a little lower than the first. It was still too far above the ground to climb to, but there was a pattern developing, and Adair liked the look of it. He sheathed his sword, jogging down the passage a little quicker than before and found another opening in the wall just where he expected it to be. This one was only thirty feet off the ground.

Anticipation propelled him forward at a run, down the curving passage, watching one after another of these holes in the wall spiral closer and closer to his reach. Suddenly his excitement came to a halt. The hallway ended at an arched doorway like so many others he had seen in this labyrinth. He walked a short way into the smaller passage but there was no hole where he expected it to be. He backed up to the last opening he passed and found that it was about ten feet off the ground, maybe more. Adair couldn't remember any time in his life when he needed to be able to jump this high and seriously doubted that he could.

He backed away from the opening and tried to get a better look at it. It appeared to be just a ventilation hole drilled into the side of the wall and seemed large enough for a man to fit through, but there was no telling where it led. As Adair tried to figure out how he was going to get up to the hole, a faint sound came to his ears. He turned his head to listen and could barely make out footsteps. He glanced left and right, but he couldn't see anything in the hall. The way sound bounced off the walls in this passage made it difficult to tell from which direction the footsteps were coming.

He tried not to panic.

He looked to the opening and took a few steps back, trying to find the best position for the difficult jump. When it felt right, he lunged into motion, jumping as high as he could. When he reached the wall, his fingers slapped against the stone several inches below the hole. The rest of his body crashed into the wall before he slid down to the floor.

The hilt of the sword around his waist clanged loudly on the stone floor and he winced at the sharp noise.

The approaching footsteps were getting louder and now he could hear voices as well.

He didn't have much time and needed to make a decision. He could either keep the sword—his only means of protection—and fight his way out, or he would have to get rid of it in order to reach the opening, which might not even be an escape. If he decided to fight, he might do well for a while, but he knew there was no way one man could survive against many trained soldiers.

His fingers quickly went to his belt and began to unfasten it. He took off the sword and scabbard and threw them to his right, as far down the hallway as he could. The belt landed on the stone floor with a clang and skidded to a stop. The sound of approaching footsteps quickened to a running pace and Adair judged the group to be five or more people. Hopefully the belt would lead them away, unless they were coming from that direction, in which case it would only serve to give away the fact that he was in the general vicinity.

Again Adair took a running start and jumped. This time his fingertips grasped the ledge of the opening and hung for a second, but he lost his grip and slid down the wall.

He backed up again and could see the lengthened shadows of running men along the wall, cast by the torches they were carrying. *This is my last chance!* He only had enough time for one more jump and then the soldiers would have him. He sprinted forward stepping into a crouch and sprang off of his left leg, extending it as far as possible while reaching up the wall with his right hand. The ledge came into reach and he grabbed as hard as he could. His fingertips tried to dig into the stone but his grip was fragile. Adair quickly swung his left hand up to the ledge and was able to get a solid grip with both hands and pulled his upper body over the ledge and into the opening. The round hole was just wide enough for his shoulders to pass through. He could see that it continued straight for about twenty feet where a soft light spilled in. Adair didn't know what was on the other side, but at this point, he didn't care. The cramped space wouldn't allow for him to swing a leg up so he reached further into the hole to find another grip. There was nothing but smooth stone. Adair tried desperately to pull his lower body into the passage but his sweating palms couldn't find traction.

"There he is," yelled someone from the hallway below.

Adair couldn't hold back the panic. He was defenseless with his lower body completely exposed. He wriggled from side to side while boosting his upper body on his elbows and slowly began to gain the leverage he needed. But it was all happening too slowly. With one more pull he managed to get his legs into the passage. At the same moment he felt something slam into his right foot followed quickly by the sound of metal glancing off the stone. By reflex he jerked his foot further into the tunnel, but it was too late. A searing pain spread through his foot and leg. He knew he was injured, but he kept crawling, trying to get free of his pursuers.

He reached out with one hand against the stone beneath him and pulled, while simultaneously pushing forward with his knees. He felt like a worm trapped inside a piece of fruit that was about to be consumed. As he approached the end of the tunnel, his surroundings became brighter and the air clearer. His head exited the passage into open air. Craning his neck to look above him, he could see stars shining brightly in the night sky overhead.

Turning to look down, he saw what looked like an enormous well. It was at least seventy-five feet across and had a spiraling staircase carved into the stone along the inside. He looked across and saw other ventilation shafts just like his own, drilled into the stone at regular intervals, eight feet above the stairs. Looking down to the stairs below, he knew that it would be a painful jump from this height, but an instant death if he overshot the stairs and slipped into the darkness below. The staircase had no railing, only steps that dropped off the edge into nothingness. His options were limited and he was in danger of death regardless of whether he went forward or backwards.

It was difficult and painful to turn himself around in the tight passage, but once he changed his direction, he was able to slide backwards out of the tunnel, letting his legs dangle while holding onto the ledge. As gravity began to pull his body out of the tunnel, he realized that his grip was compromised by the slick coating of blood coming from his foot. A feeling of panic surged within him as he realized the peril of his situation.

In a last second attempt to keep himself from falling over the side of the stairs, Adair pushed his feet out a few inches away from the wall and let go, leaning in toward the face of the stone as he fell. His feet hit the ground, sending a wave of pain from his right foot up into his leg. His position caused him to fall forward into the sheer face of the stone and roll down a few stairs before coming to a halt. His foot was throbbing intensely, but he tried to put it out of his mind until he was safe.

Even though the moon was not visible, its light illuminated the opposite side of the well. Adair stood in the shadowed half and looked up to the rim that was almost two hundred feet above. Knowing that the soldiers would inform everyone else of his whereabouts, it was only a matter of time before they closed in on him. He needed to get to the top of this chasm and out of sight as quickly as possible. He began to painfully limp up the spiraling stairs, hurrying almost to a run when he came to the illuminated side of the well.

It seemed like an eternity before he reached the top. Fortunately, the stairs ended in the shadows. Adair crouched down to keep his head from being visible above the rim, while crawling up the last few steps. He waited for a brief moment to listen for any movement nearby. When he was satisfied that it was safe, he peeked over the rim. What he saw amazed him.

He was perched atop a small island of stone that gently sloped fifty feet down to the ocean surface. Docks sprouted from the island like spokes from a wheel. Several hundred feet away from the shore of the island was the inside of the circular wall that surrounded this secluded place. The inside of the wall was made up of hundreds of covered ports. Some were empty and some contained ships. It was too dark to tell for sure, but Adair knew that if even half of the ports were filled, this place contained a fleet that would rival the Empire itself.

One area of the waterway between the wall and the island was teeming with ferries, offloading crates of goods from one of the ships and transporting them to the island. Adair looked back down the stairs and realized that all this time spent running down hallways and hiding from his captors, he had been beneath the ocean. Even as the realization came to him, he denied the possibility of it. *Who could make such a place?*

"Stop right there."

Adair spun around to see two men standing on the opposite rim of the chasm. They both held torches and immediately separated, running around opposite sides of the well. Adair stood and ran up the last few steps, not wanting to get trapped inside the chasm. The stairs ended at a pathway which circled the rim. Other narrow footpaths radiated out from the main path to end at stairways heading down the outside of the hill. He took only a few steps before seeing another pair of men coming up the nearest set of stairs at a full run. Adair paused for a brief moment, unsure of whether he should fight past these men to escape, or run back down the stairs where immediate safety was available. He instinctively chose the latter and rushed back down the stairs into the well.

What have I done? Even through the unbearable pain shooting into his leg, Adair knew that he made the wrong decision. There was nowhere for him to go now but down. He might be able to keep ahead of them, but what would that gain him? They had him trapped now and he was finally starting to feel afraid of not making it out alive.

He ran down the winding staircase as fast as his injured foot would allow him, keeping to the inside of the treacherous steps. Suddenly, a torch landed on the stairs in front of him, sending a shower of sparks into the air before falling over the edge and disappearing into the darkness. Adair didn't even pause to see how close they were or who had thrown the torch; his instinct for survival drove him downward.

Gradually the light of the moon disappeared altogether and Adair ran in complete darkness, dragging his hand along the rock face to maintain a sense of proximity to the edge. After what seemed like an hour, Adair noticed a dull orange glow coming from the center of the darkness below. It was just enough light to illuminate his surroundings. His breath was ragged and his right leg was nearly useless. He slowed his pace and looked up behind him. Far away he could see the bouncing torches of his pursuers. They must have slowed long ago, realizing that his capture was inevitable.

Adair pressed on and within minutes he reached the bottom of the staircase. It ended at a tunnel which led away into the side of the rock face. The tunnel was completely dark and Adair had to move by feel once again. After a slow hundred yards, the passage began to slope downward and veer to the right. The slope gradually steepened until Adair almost tripped down another set of stairs. It was a strange sensation to be underneath the ocean and he marveled at how much work must have gone into building this place, aside from the fact that it seemed physically impossible.

Slowly, the tunnel began to lighten with the same orange glow. His pace quickened in the soft light, as he no longer needed to feel his way through the passage. After several more minutes of descending the curving steps, the tunnel opened up into an enormous cavern, hundreds of yards wide and equally as tall.   Torches burned along the wall, casting an eerie light throughout what looked like a gigantic temple to some unknown god.

Or gods, Adair thought as he noticed great stone statues, at least a hundred feet tall, lining the perimeter of the cavern. Each one was shaped almost like a man, but their features were stretched vertically, with great wings that extended to either side of the statue. The tips of the wings touched the tips of the next statue, so that the whole cavern was encircled by them. Adair continued out of the mouth of the tunnel and ran down the remaining steps, which were carved into the wall of the cavern like the chasm above him. When he reached the floor of the cavern, his feet crunched into pure sand, like the shores of Bastul.

He looked down to take in this unexpected sight and noticed the bloody mess of his right foot. The severed sole of his sandal dragged uselessly across the sand, held to his leg by a thin strip of twisted leather. His foot had gone numb. Across the cavern was a lake whose water was still and smooth as glass. At the center of the lake was a stone dais, thirty feet across and only inches above the level of the water. Narrow footbridges of stone extended from the dais on opposite sides, arching over the water and ending at the sandy perimeter of the lake.

On the other side of the cavern was a large arched doorway. It appeared to be the only other way out of this place. A quick look around told Adair that it would be quicker to head straight over the dais via the footbridge than it would be to skirt the lake. Once his goal was set, he quickened his pace to a run.

The sand slowed his progress and sapped his already depleted energy. By the time he made it to the start of the footbridge, his pursuers spilled out of the tunnel behind him and onto the staircase. Adair ran with all his might up the narrow bridge, trying to keep his footing on the polished stone. His lead on the soldiers had lessened considerably and he feared that he would lose this race. His only hope now was to make it through the archway at the other side of the cavern and hopefully find a narrow corridor where he could defend himself against one man at a time. Even then, they would eventually wear him down.

Slowing little by little with every painful step, he looked across the cavern at the archway and tried to fix his will on getting through that doorway. Just as he took his first step on the dais, the dark hole of the archway began to change. There was movement inside it and Adair suspected that he had failed. When row upon row of soldiers filed out of the archway, Adair felt all hope drain from his body, like the wind being taken from the sails of a boat.

He stopped running and unexpectedly lost his footing on the slick surface. His left foot shot out from underneath him and he landed painfully on his elbow before sliding to a stop. Knowing that the chase was over, he lay back on the stone and stared up at the ceiling.

It only made the situation worse when he saw stars overhead. The ceiling above him had a huge hole right through the middle of it. It took a second before he saw the spiraling stairs and recognized it as the chasm with which he was already acquainted. He could see freedom right above him, but there was no way to reach it. He lifted his head to get a view of his odds at the last moments of his life. Altogether, there were about fifty archers and foot soldiers surrounding the lake. It was over.

Adair looked around and realized he was sitting roughly in the center of the stone dais. Its surface was polished like marble, and seemed to glow with a silver light. Just beneath the surface, as if encased in ice, was a strange pattern of concentric circles like the rings of a tree that had been frozen, then shattered. He ran his hand over the smooth surface and marveled at its translucency. Even more strange was that it was perfectly clean. Adair ran his finger over the surface and rubbed it with his thumb. *Not even a speck of dust!*

It's beautiful. It looked like an altar. *I guess it's a fitting place to die.*

He struggled to his feet as the soldiers advanced up the bridges on either side of him. They were within shooting range now and it was only a matter of seconds before he would see death. His thoughts turned to his family. *Maeryn, with her beautiful blonde hair and gorgeous smile. Kael, with that inquisitive look in his eyes.* Tears began to stream down his face as he realized that he would never see them again in this life.

He looked back to the soldiers marching toward him and noticed that they looked wavy and distorted as if he was seeing them through poorly crafted glass. He rubbed the tears from his eyes and looked again, but his vision didn't change. Adair looked down at his feet and saw his own reflection on the dais spiraling inward. He suddenly felt very heavy as if he had consumed too much wine. He looked up again at the soldiers and saw that they were retreating with looks of astonishment on their faces. Their images continued to distort and pull inward toward Adair as he felt the weight of the world pressing in on him. Suddenly, a burst of blue light flashed in his eyes, sending a jolt of pain through his head. It was the last thing he saw before he lost consciousness.

7

The panel of men staring at Maeryn would have been intimidating, if she were the type of woman to be easily intimidated. But she wasn't. Though she was doing her best to appear that way and the men were buying it.

"Tell us the story again, from the beginning," muttered one of the interrogators.

"I already told you," she began, using the same emotionally stretched voice that she had used from the onset of this interrogation. "I woke up in the early morning and he was gone..." She trailed off as tears began to well-up in her eyes. She covered her face with her hands to show that this was all too much for her. The emotion she felt was real enough, but if Adair wanted the council to know what he was doing, he would have told them. He was definitely in some kind of trouble and she wasn't going to be punished for it. After all, she was ignorant really. Adair hadn't told her anything, probably to protect her. But he did seem different before he disappeared—distant, thinking to himself more than usual. Of course she didn't include any of this information in her story. These men weren't trying to help Adair; they were hoping to catch a deserter. The Empire had no tolerance for anyone who was not wholly devoted to it.

"I'm sorry," she continued after pulling herself together. "It's just...he is always being called out in the middle of the night for one reason or another. His position is very demanding. It's as though the city couldn't function without him."

"On the contrary," stated the man seated at the center of the table. "The city will function without him. In fact, it is the judgment of this council that all possessions and responsibilities of your husband will be given over to an appointed steward for a period of one week."

The statement hit Maeryn like a wave, forcing the breath from her lungs. Under Orudan law a man's possessions included his wife and children. The interrogator was trying to scare her into giving them information. It was working. She started to cry for real this time.

The interrogator's voice rose so as to be heard clearly above her sobbing. He wasn't about to repeat himself. "If your husband does not return in a week, then the appointed steward will gain ownership of those possessions and responsibilities."

In the silence that followed, the words began to sink in. Maeryn continued to cry outwardly to show the interrogator that he had made his point, while inwardly she wept at the thought of Adair being replaced so quickly. *How could they treat us like this, after all he sacrificed for them?*

"Please find him," she pleaded.

"That is all," stated the interrogator and the whole panel of men rose to leave the room.

As they filed out the door, Thaddius separated from the group and came over to Maeryn. He waited until they were alone before speaking. "Adair left a message with one of my servants that he would be gone for more than a day. He wouldn't have done that if he was deserting. I tried to tell them, but they wouldn't listen. I'm sorry."

Maeryn simply nodded in response, wiping the tears from her face.

Thaddius slowly backed up, then turned and followed after the other members of the council.

Maeryn counted to ten before she stopped crying. *I think they were convinced,* she assured herself with a smile of satisfaction. *Men like that have no idea what to do with an emotional woman. They only know how to fight wars and give orders.*

The following day, Maeryn stood on the balcony outside of her bedroom. The sun was well above the horizon and the city glittered with the yellow light reflecting off the surface of the water. She watched a procession of wagons and marching soldiers wind through the streets of the city. Red banners at the front and rear of the procession waved in the breeze, the gold eagle emblem of the Orudan Empire sparkling as it caught the sunlight.

"You're not in charge yet," she said to the man inside the covered carriage half a mile away. "You're only a steward!"

The citizens of Bastul lined the streets, waving their hands at his carriage as it passed them. She was disgusted by him already. *You would think the Emperor himself had come to visit us.* Adair never flaunted his power; he didn't need to. People tended to respect him because of his character first, and his power second. *Unlike this man, who is obviously trying to make up for something he lacks!*

The procession continued along the cobblestone road leading up to the mansion that Maeryn had called home for many years. The pace was slowed considerably when the road became a series of switchbacks as it climbed the hill. When the procession finally reached the top and entered the courtyard,

Maeryn decided to go downstairs and meet this prideful man who thought he could take over for Adair.

Exiting the house, Maeryn walked through the garden situated between the guest wing and slaves' quarters of the mansion. Adair had the garden built as a gift to Maeryn, following the customs of her ancestors. Trimmed trees and shrubs dotted the landscape, separated by rings of brightly colored flowers. The north end of this secluded paradise was open to the hilltop courtyard, containing stables, soldiers' housing, and various other structures, all surrounded by a pale stone wall.

She stopped at the entrance to the garden and waited at the top of a short flight of steps that descended to the gravel courtyard. The last of the rearguard were just entering through the north gate when, farther to her left, a guard reached up and opened the door to the most expensive looking carriage of the whole procession. Maeryn was glad that she had sent Kael away at first light to spend the week with Saba. Until she knew what kind of man this steward was, it was better to keep her son away from him.

The man who climbed out of the carriage blinked at the harsh morning light as if he had just awoken. He was a tall man, taller than Adair, but much thinner. His jawline was narrow and coupled with his protruding nose, made him look like a rodent. He was dressed as every other Orud male of importance; he wore a pure white tunic underneath a metal cuirass. The sculpted abdomen and chest muscles of the cuirass looked out of place on his narrow frame. Over his clothing he wore a red cloak fastened at the left shoulder with a golden torc. He appeared uncomfortable in this elaborate style of dress. *So you have no prior experience!*

He smiled when he looked in Maeryn's direction and spoke loud enough for everyone in the courtyard to hear him. "Hello. You must be Maeryn." He spread his arms wide and lifted them up to the sky, keeping his gaze fixed on her. "Now this is a mansion fit for an emperor."

After his brilliant observation, he strode confidently over to the garden's entrance and climbed the stairs, stopping when he reached Maeryn. His height was imposing and he knew it. He stood uncomfortably close, by social standards, looking down on her. "I am Lemus," he stated with a smile that was too big. "You may show me around my new home."

"You're to be a steward only," Maeryn corrected, "until my husband returns."

The tall man glanced quickly around the courtyard to see if anyone had overheard. Suddenly, he bent down until his mouth was close to Maeryn's ear and she flinched in response. When he spoke his voice was a whisper. "If you ever speak to me in that tone again I'll have that disrespectful tongue of yours cut out of your mouth. If the coward ever does turn up, he won't be allowed to return to his former position." When he straightened up to his full height, he still had a smile on his face. He gestured past Maeryn toward the garden. "You lead the way."

The days dragged on and Maeryn's anxiety increased. Her once optimistic attitude about Adair's absence was being steadily worn down with every passing moment. It wasn't unusual for Adair to be gone for long periods of time, but this was starting to scare her. It only complicated her emotions to be sharing a house with Lemus. The more time she spent with him, the surer she became of his mental instability. He had the look of a starved and unpredictable animal. After showing him around the mansion and answering hundreds of his questions, Maeryn tried her best to avoid him, spending most of her time on the balcony staring at the city below. On days when Lemus stayed close to the house, she would go with one of the slaves into the city and help shop for food and other supplies.

As the morning sun rose over the bay, Maeryn watched from her balcony as she always did. Clouds had rolled in during the night and the sun was struggling to warm the air through the gray blanket. The skies over Bastul only lightened to a hazy purple. It made everything look drab which seemed fitting to Maeryn. It had been weeks now, but Adair had not returned. She feared the worst, that he was dead. Nothing except death would have kept him away for so long. Tears began to well up in her eyes and blurred her view of the city below. There was bitterness growing inside her. To be honest, it had been there for some time. It was the Empire and its stranglehold on their lives that angered her.

When she first met Adair, he had taken refuge in her parent's barn, having been wounded in a battle that took place a short distance from her home in the north. She nursed him back to health with her mother's help and in time, got to know Adair. The two of them fell in love and when it was time for Adair to leave, Maeryn's father begged him to take Maeryn. It wasn't a difficult decision for either of them; Maeryn was the most beautiful woman Adair had ever seen, Adair was a kind and respectable man who offered a life apart from the harsh conditions in which Maeryn had been raised.

But Adair was a soldier, and she knew what kind of life came with marrying a soldier, though Adair's love blinded her from that reality for a long time. He was a man of genuine character. The confusing part was how he could be so kind and still function as a soldier. Didn't soldiers need to be rough and crude by nature in order to do what was required of them? When they were first married she used to worry about his safety for that same reason. However, it wasn't long before Adair's reputation on the battlefield made its way to her ears. Everyone said he had a way with people. He was a born leader. People listened to him out of respect, without having to be ordered. He inspired others by being ferocious in the face of enemies and he instinctively knew where and how to move on the battlefield. Slowly, his reputation earned him higher and higher positions of authority. Eventually he was granted the position of Colonel and with it, governorship of Bastul. But somehow, the enormous responsibility became a weight around his neck. And it wasn't just Adair; Maeryn felt it as well. They started to feel trapped. Now Adair was gone. The probability of his death caused a loneliness in Maeryn's heart that went deeper than anything she had experienced before. She was bitter that their lives always had to be in accordance with the goals of the Empire. *The good of the nation always outweighs the good of individuals.* She was tired of living a life dictated by others.

"It's beautiful, isn't it?"

The voice behind her was startling.

"The Southern Jewel is what they call it in Orud." Lemus was staring past her and looking at the city which surrounded the bay and sprawled into the foothills of the mountain-range to the east. If he realized he had startled her, he wasn't showing it. He seemed to be reveling in his newfound power.

Maeryn wasn't sure how to respond and only managed to nod and smile.

"Now what do you have to cry about?" he asked in an almost believably caring tone, noticing the tears on her face.

She just looked at him and couldn't manage to find any words. If he was dense enough not to realize, then he could go on wondering for all she cared.

He walked over to the railing and stood next to her. "I think I've been pretty generous so far," he stated calmly. "You've had several days to yourself. I don't know of many men who would wait that long for a new wife."

Maeryn's heart began to race at the sound of his lusting voice. She knew what it meant to have another man assume all of Adair's responsibilities. She knew that her body would soon belong to Lemus as well, but the transfer of authority hadn't been made official yet. It was clear that Lemus didn't care.

"I need more time, please," she whispered as she turned and walked into the bedroom.

Lemus' footsteps came quickly behind her and she ran for the bedroom door in a panic. She only made it a few steps before Lemus caught hold of her braided hair, snapping her head backward with searing pain.

"I wasn't asking," he said with gritted teeth in her ear.

She scrambled to get away but he was too strong, using his full weight on her back to force her to the ground. She wanted to scream, but she knew that there wasn't anyone to come to her aid. The only souls in the house were slaves who wouldn't think of interfering. She was helpless and the only thing she could do was lie still.

She wasn't sure how long she lay on the floor after it was over. Her hot face was pressed against the cool stone floor. Her eyes traced a crack in the stone as it meandered from underneath her nose to a point in the middle of the room where it fragmented into a dozen other cracks. She never noticed little things like that before. Probably because she was always distracted by how good her life used to be.

Maeryn struggled to her feet, moving slowly at first. Her body ached and her scalp was tender from Lemus pulling on her hair. As she stood in her bedroom she noticed the wet area on the stone floor where her face had been only a moment ago. It was proof that she had been crying, but right now, she couldn't feel any emotion.

She watched her feet move in small steps toward the door of her bedroom and figured they must know better than she where to go. She felt detached, as if the whole thing were a story told by a friend that was now beginning to fade from memory. Maeryn's feet continued to move and when they stopped, she found herself in the garden. A slight wind had picked up and the air was a little cooler than normal. The clouds were gone, but the sky was still hazy as if some invisible force was trying to dampen the sunshine.

She sat down on a low stone wall that ringed a flower bed, and winced at the pain it caused. She watched as the leaves danced in the breeze and wondered what it would be like to be a flower; no one to please, no one to bother you. All you would have to do is stand in the sun with your friends and be beautiful. People would admire you for what you were and they would feed you and take care of you. Without warning, a wave of sorrow overwhelmed her and the tears began to fall.

The following day, while watching the city from her balcony, Maeryn saw Kael and Saba walking up the cobblestone road. She couldn't contain her excitement, turning to run back inside the house. After two steps, she stopped and doubled over in pain. Her excitement had gotten the better of her and she cursed her own stupidity. Her body hadn't healed enough for her to run and she waited until the pain in her abdomen faded, leaving only a dull ache between her legs. By the time she got to the garden, the two were just entering the courtyard through the north gate. Maeryn walked down the steps and crossed the bare expanse between them, the gravel crunching softly underneath her sandaled feet.

Saba stepped to the side and watched as Maeryn bent down to embrace her son, moving carefully.

"Oh I've missed you," she said, kissing Kael on the forehead.

He showed no signs of embarrassment, as others of his age might have. He just smiled and hugged her back.

Maeryn stood up, rubbing tears from her eyes, trying to regain her composure.

Saba made eye contact and gave her a questioning look.

Maeryn returned his gaze and placed her hand on Saba's arm. "Well," she managed. "I guess it's time for you to meet him," she said, giving Saba a wrinkled eyebrow as an answer. Taking Kael by the hand, she led them across the courtyard, toward the house.

Before they reached the garden steps, Lemus stepped out from behind the slave quarters and leaned against the building, exuding the arrogance that Maeryn had come to expect from him. "Come introduce yourselves," he ordered.

Saba slowed his pace as if he knew, just by looking, what type of man this was.

Lemus straightened himself and came out onto the steps, stopping just before the bottom. His face was beaming with forced happiness and he appeared to wait patiently while the three crossed the courtyard and stopped at the bottom of the steps.

Lemus towered above Maeryn and Kael with the added height of the steps upon which he was standing, but was still only level with Saba. It was obvious that he was uncomfortable with this arrangement; it defeated the whole purpose of standing where he was.

"I am Saba," stated the old man, looking directly into Lemus' eyes. After a few seconds of silence, it was apparent that Kael didn't feel like introducing himself. "And this is Kael," he added.

Lemus looked down at the child and waited for him to say something. When nothing happened, he bent down and waved a hand in front of Kael's face.

Kael did nothing but blink.

"Is your child deaf?"

Maeryn decided not to acknowledge the question.

"Or just a half-wit perhaps," Lemus continued with a sneer.

Saba decided to comment on the observation. "It is difficult for a child to know what to say when confronted with a man of such power and majesty as yourself." The statement was obviously sarcastic to those who knew Saba, but the serious way he delivered it confused Lemus, who took a moment to decide whether or not he agreed.

"Very well then," he replied. "Come inside; you must tell me what you've been up to." The four walked through the garden and into the house together but Lemus led the way and missed the smiles shared between the others.

8

The next day, Maeryn pulled a chair out onto the balcony that had become her refuge. There was something soothing about watching the ocean glitter in the sunlight. Lemus left for the city just after sunrise and she hadn't seen him since. She felt safer when he was gone. He was so unpredictable. She tried to shake the thoughts out of her head and think about more positive things, but it was difficult. She kept thinking about Adair and why he had abandoned his family.

He didn't abandon you, or anybody else for that matter! That's not the kind of person he is.

She was worn out by the emotional drain of wavering between bitterness about her situation and worrying about the safety of Adair. She closed her eyes to picture Adair's face. It came instantly. His deep brown eyes, strong jaw, his dark hair...

Abruptly, the sound of screaming jolted her from her thoughts and the vision of Adair vanished. She listened for a second and realized that it was coming from the courtyard on the other side of the house. Maeryn jumped to her feet, and hurried through her bedroom and down the stairs, following the screams. She knew somehow it was related to Lemus.

When he heard the screaming, Kael was watching a grasshopper cling to a blade of grass on the side of the cobblestone road, just outside of the wall which surrounded the hilltop estate. He knew it was Ajani as soon as he heard it. Though the slave boy hadn't ever screamed about anything as far as Kael could remember, he knew his voice well. Kael immediately rose to his feet and ran between two guards who were standing at attention on either side of the entrance into the courtyard. Once inside, Kael darted across the gravel landscape and headed for the garden. He took the short flight of stairs at the entrance in two leaps and skidded to a halt. What he saw on the other side of the garden made his body go weak with fear.

Lemus was crouched over the crumpled body of Ajani who was lying on his side, trying to shield his face. The screaming had stopped but the dull thud of Lemus' fists pounding the body of the child underneath him was even worse.

"I'll teach you to talk back to me," grunted Lemus between excited breaths.

"Stop it," screamed Kael, but Lemus didn't listen. He just kept hitting Ajani who had stopped moving. "Stop it," he yelled again in the loudest voice he could manage, but Lemus didn't even seem to know he was there.

The paralyzing effects of fear quickly gave way to empowering feelings of anger. *I have to stop him!* He ran back down the steps and turned right, reaching the supply shed in seconds. He threw open the doors and stepped inside, looking for anything that could be used as a weapon. Seeing a pitchfork leaning against the wall, he grabbed it and ran back toward Ajani as quickly as his little feet would carry him.

When Kael reached Ajani, there was an eerie silence. Lemus was standing with his head pointed toward the sky, facing away from Kael. His arms hung limp at his sides, blood dripping from his knuckles. Ajani was covered in blood and lay on the ground unmoving.

Rage welled up inside Kael and he ran at Lemus, holding the pitchfork in front of him.

Lemus continued to stare at the sky until the last second when he turned and jumped to the side.

One tine of the pitchfork punctured his right thigh and he yelped as Kael kept charging, driving it into his leg. When it hit something hard, Kael let go and took a few steps back, realizing what he had just done.

Lemus yelled at the top of his lungs as he grabbed the gardening tool and angrily ripped it from his leg. Without pausing, he gripped the shaft with both hands and lurched forward, swinging the handle at Kael.

Kael wasn't fast enough to dodge it but put his hands up to guard himself. The thick wooden handle crashed into his forearm and then his face, breaking through the useless defense. Kael felt his head thrown to one side and his feet lifted off the ground before his whole body hit the dirt.

Maeryn screamed as she saw Kael's tiny body thrown to the ground. "What are you doing?"

Lemus turned toward her and then looked to the guards just coming in through the gate. He ignored her as if she hadn't said anything at all. "Put that brat in restraints," he ordered the guards.

The two soldiers ran to Kael's limp body and each grabbed an arm.

Maeryn came down the steps from the house. "Don't you dare touch him," she shouted.

"Stay back or you'll be put to death as well."

Maeryn stopped dead in her tracks and turned to Lemus, who was now standing with a bloody pitchfork in his hand, looking as though he was waiting for an opportunity to use it. It took her a second to realize what he had said. "...as well?"

"Any attack on an Orudan soldier is punishable by death." He threw the pitchfork across the garden and it clanged off the stone building.

It was only then that she realized what had happened. She saw the body of Ajani lying in the dirt, the blood running down Lemus' leg, the pitchfork, and her son being dragged away.

"But he's just a child," she pleaded, tears now running down her face.

Lemus repeated himself. "ANY attack is punishable by death." It was a law well known throughout the Orudan Empire, but no one had ever heard of it being applied to a child. Of course, no child had ever attacked an Orudan soldier.

"But..." she began, not really knowing how to argue the matter.

Lemus pointed his finger at her and spoke loudly over the sound of her voice. "You are both under my custody and therefore my property. If you wish to join your son in death, by all means, keep talking."

"NO!" Maeryn screamed with everything that was in her. She felt panic take over her mind and body, telling her to run after Kael. He needed her protection, but she knew that Lemus would kill her. She began to shake with frustration, overwhelmed with emotions that she couldn't act on. The internal conflict was too much and she felt her knees start to wobble.

Another pair of guards entered the courtyard. "Go fetch me a doctor," Lemus said to one of the men. "And you, give me a hand." The other soldier quickly ran to his aid, throwing his arm around his superior and helping him limp his way out of the garden.

Maeryn's knees gave out and she collapsed in the dirt. Her sobbing drowned out everything around her.

She lay in the garden for some time, in a trance, vaguely aware of what was going on around her. Someone must have taken Ajani away because he was gone by the time she gained enough strength to lift her head. She remembered one of the slaves offering to help her and she shooed him away, but she didn't remember how long ago that had been.

Maeryn feebly climbed to her feet. The drag marks from Kael's feet ran next to her and she traced the path with her eyes. They led toward the courtyard and disappeared around the slave quarters.

She started moving. Her eyes were still crying, but she was disconnected from them. When she came to her senses, she found herself in the kitchen. At some point she must have decided to kill him. She was holding a butcher knife and wasn't sure exactly how it came to be in her hand. It felt comforting there, resting heavily in her clenched fist. She felt powerful, unlike the past couple of weeks. She looked at the long blade and the idea to kill him made sense. *Adair is dead. Kael will be executed. I've lost everything now! If Lemus ever intends to get rid of me, I should at least take him with me. I won't be able to do it during the day. He's too strong for that. No, I'll wait until he sleeps.* Of course, she would be executed as soon as they found out who did it, but it seemed a fitting end to everything that had occurred in the last few weeks.

"There are better ways to get back at him, Miss."

Maeryn turned around to find Zula standing in the corner of the kitchen. This slave woman was in charge of the whole house and had been with their family for several years. Maeryn hadn't heard ten words from her in the entire time she worked for them and it was strange to hear her speak now.

"What?"

"I know what you feel, Miss. If you kill this man, you will be put to death. That would not be enough punishment for what he has done."

"You don't understand," Maeryn countered, trying to sound as authoritative as possible. As soon as she said it, she regretted her words. Although she wasn't his mother, Zula had raised Ajani from a baby.

"I understand better than you, Miss," the dark skinned woman shot back. "I have seen more trials in my life than you will ever see, even if you were to live ten lifetimes." As Zula spoke, her intense dark eyes fought back the tears that had every right to spill down her face. There was an incredible strength in her that Maeryn had never noticed before, but when she spoke again, her words were softer. "You are a strong woman who has lived an easy life. But that has changed. You will see how the rest of the world lives now." She paused. "There are better ways to get back at a man, especially one of such power." Zula turned around and started to walk out of the kitchen.

"He's going to kill him," Maeryn cried after the slave woman. Tears began to run down her face again and she suddenly felt embarrassed for crying in front of a woman who had seen so much heartache. "Did you see what he did to Ajani?"

"Yes, ma'am, I did," the dark-skinned woman said flatly, turning back to Maeryn.

Maeryn wiped the tears from her eyes. "How can you just stand there as if nothing happened?"

"...because it is useless to do anything about it, and I have had much practice pretending nothing has happened."

A moment of silence followed as Maeryn considered Zula's words.

"Before your husband, I had another master. He was a cruel man." She paused, unable to speak what she was thinking. Tears rolled down her cheeks, but her eyes never faltered. "There were many things he did to me, and the others. There was nothing we could do. That was my whole life until I met your husband. After a while, you learn to hold it in."

"But why should I hold it in?"

When Zula continued, her voice was almost a whisper. "Because it's a gift. It'll make you stronger than you ever thought possible. It'll make you smarter. It'll build inside you until the moment comes when you find a way to make him suffer in such a way that it repays all of the things he's done to you."

It was clear that she was speaking directly out of her past. Maeryn was at once intrigued and scared.

"You are a strong woman, Miss," Zula said, her voice now sounding normal. "Don't let him break you." Zula turned and walked away, the conversation ending just as abruptly as it had begun.

Maeryn was speechless. Not only had Zula spoken as eloquently as any educated woman, but it was unheard of for a slave to speak so boldly to her master. She risked her own safety in order to share the honest truth. It was a much-needed message. *And she's right. It's not enough to kill him while he sleeps, especially when I would forfeit my own life in the process. No! There is more that can be done. I won't give Lemus the power to destroy my life.*

9

Saba walked quickly down the dark hallway toward Lemus' study. The guard standing at attention outside the door straightened up as Saba neared. It seemed strange that the usual faces were not seen anymore in the mansion, having been replaced immediately as Lemus took control. But that was the least of Saba's worries on this night.

"I need to speak with him," he told the guard.

The man nodded and opened the door behind him, disappearing momentarily. His muffled voice could be heard through the door. There was a pause before he came back and tilted his head toward the room. Saba pushed the door open and strode into the room, his temper already rising.

Lemus sat at his desk, the glow of candlelight illuminating piles of parchment in front of him. Some were stacked in neat piles while others were spread out haphazardly, like a strong wind had blown through the room. He lazily lifted his head as Saba entered and motioned for Saba to come closer. "Come in. I've been meaning to have a few words with you."

Saba walked to the front of the desk, ignoring the few empty chairs along the wall. "I want to talk with you about Kael."

"Yes. I'm sure you do. My guards at the jail tell me that you have been over there, bothering them constantly to let the boy go." Lemus sat back in his chair.

"Yes. Of course I have. How could I do anything different?"

Lemus smiled at this. "Well, I have a few ideas. To start with, you will stay away from the jail. The boy attacked me and his actions were punishable by death. He has already been executed, so you are wasting your time. I understand that you were his tutor?"

"Am his tutor," Saba corrected.

Lemus laughed. "If you are indeed smart enough to call yourself anyone's tutor, then you should know that when someone is dead, it is no longer appropriate to speak of them in the present."

Saba gave no reaction to the man's reply.

"Well, isn't that interesting, a teacher with nothing to say? That's good. Finally you are starting to get the hang of this." Lemus paused while he scooted his chair back and stood up to look Saba in the eyes. "I do have something to say to you, however. Your room has been emptied and its contents packed in boxes. I have provided a cart and a mule to carry your belongings. You will find everything waiting for you in the courtyard. I suggest that you take advantage of my generosity and leave the city tonight. I understand that you have many connections in the surrounding territory; I'm sure that you will find a place to stay."

"You have no right," Saba began, his voice suddenly rising above the normal conversational tone. "This has been my home and these people my family before anyone had ever heard of you..."

"I have every right," Lemus shot back, interrupting. "This is my home now and I do not wish to take care of old men who have the ability to take care of themselves. But more importantly, I no longer require the services of a tutor."

Saba opened his mouth to say more, but Lemus kept talking.

"If you have heard nothing of what I have said this night, hear this. My soldiers have orders to kill you on sight, if you are ever found in this city again. Take your belongings and leave. This is your last chance."

Saba stood motionless for a moment, looking into the eyes of Lemus. He had so many things to say, but none of them would accomplish anything except to risk his own life. After a few seconds, he spun on his heels and stormed out of the room. As he walked down the hallway, he overheard Lemus' voice.

"No more visitors."

"Yes, my lord," the guard replied.

Kael found himself lying face-down on the floor of a small, dimly lit room. It was a stone floor with layers of dust covering everything except a few scuffled footprints and a small area in front of his face, cleared by his breath. Out of the corner of his eyes he could see that the walls and the ceiling were the same color as the floor and he assumed that they too were stone. At the other end of the room, he could barely make out dark vertical stripes that had the look of iron bars.

He lifted his head to get a better look at the room, but his vision began to swim and he suddenly felt nauseous. Putting his head back down on the dirty floor, he took deep breaths and waited for the nausea to pass. The floor felt cold against his hot face, which seemed to pulse with its own heart beat. After his stomach settled, Kael managed to lift a hand to the side of his head where Lemus struck him. It felt swollen. The tips of his fingers passed over crusted areas of dried blood. The skin was bruised and sensitive to the touch.

Kael closed his eyes and rested his weary body, letting his ears explore the surroundings that his eyes were not yet able to. After a while he could make out the sound of water dripping. Someone coughed and it sounded far away. Suddenly, he heard a loud creak and a metal clang like a door closing.

Footsteps could be heard, faintly at first, but growing louder with every step. Eventually they stopped in front of the metal bars of his cell. Kael opened his eyes and squinted to see who it was, but his vision was blurry; he couldn't focus on anything beyond the metal bars. He blinked a few times, but it didn't seem to help much. He dared not lift his head again, so he waited to see what would happen.

The squeal of metal upon metal sounded harsh against the silence. Whoever it was had opened the door and stepped into his cell, leaving the door open behind him. The blurry shape moved slowly forward and Kael looked up without lifting his head. The person began to take shape and definition as it got closer, revealing the man's features and the bandage around his leg.

"Are you surprised to see me?" asked the man.

Kael didn't answer.

"Oh, it wasn't quite as bad as it looked. You, on the other hand, don't seem to be doing so well."

The sounds of Lemus' voice hurt Kael's ears, which felt hot and tender. He tried to ignore both the man's loud voice and the intended message of his words. Suddenly, there was a flicker of blurred movement and Kael felt Lemus' foot crash into his stomach, throwing him against the back wall. All of the air shot out of his lungs and he started to panic, fighting for a breath. Just when he thought he couldn't go any longer without air, his lungs started to work again, accepting only small breaths at a time.

Lemus stood in the middle of the room, unmoving.

Kael pushed himself up into a sitting position to be ready for another attack. He still felt a little nauseous, but the fear was causing it to wear off quickly.

Lemus didn't advance, but stayed in the middle of the room and crossed his arms.

"That's better," he said, as if Kael had been wrong to be lying down before. "You know, your father wasn't perfect either." He trailed off, trying to choose the right words.

"Did you know...did he ever tell you what he did with criminals? I'll bet he didn't. It's actually quite admirable." Lemus took a few steps forward and crouched down in front of Kael.

"Your father knew that everyone had a use to the Empire, even criminals. Usually they could be bribed in some way, or turned into informants, but sometimes that wouldn't work. So your father would put them in jail, keep them without food or water for days, until it was time. Then a jailer would come in, put a black bag over their head and lead them into the execution room. There they were given the opportunity to confess all their wrongdoings or be tortured and if they withheld nothing, they would be released. But they weren't released. After the torturing, the executioner would come out and..." Lemus dragged a thumb across his neck. The stubble under his chin made a loud scratching noise in the small room.

Kael showed no expression toward Lemus' story and it angered the tall man.

"It is a practice I intend to continue and I am pleased that you have chosen to participate." A large smile spread across his face. He was trying to scare Kael, but it wasn't working. Lemus rose to his feet, wincing slightly in the process and turned around. Kael noticed his limp just as his features began to blur into a vaguely man-shaped blotch in his vision. The loud metal clang of the door signaled the end of the one-sided conversation.

The next few days were much the same as the first—at least it seemed like days, though it was impossible to tell without seeing the sunlight. Everything looked just the same to him. The same stone walls, the same flickering torchlight from down the hallway. Hunger gnawed at him like an insect buzzing in his ear. He was uncomfortable no matter what he did. Sitting, standing, pacing the floor; nothing seemed to help.

Mother's probably worried. I wonder if she even knows I'm here. Poor Ajani. He wasn't moving and I can't remember anything after Lemus hit me. Kael still remembered the first time he saw a dead rat. It was just lying there on its side, its mouth open, like it died in pain. He remembered the nightmares he used to have and how he would cry when he thought about how it used to be a live animal, and now it was just a lump of dead flesh. *I hope Ajani's not dead! And Father too. I hope he's alive, out there somewhere on a secret mission that he has to do by himself.* It was lonely in this cell. *I wish Saba was here with me. He always makes things fun and interesting.*

The creaking sound of a metal door interrupted his thoughts.

It must be morning. There was always more movement and sounds right after Kael woke up, only this time, he hadn't slept.

He heard footsteps coming down the hallway and the sound made his heart quicken. He wasn't sure why he was scared, maybe they were finally bringing some food. Lemus was probably just trying to scare him for a few days, letting him think about what he had done.

The footsteps were getting louder and Kael instinctively backed away from the bars. A large man appeared in front of his cell. He was a jailer and it looked to Kael as if this man hadn't seen the light of day in several years.

He was fat, with pale skin and uneven stubble that made him look like he was dead. Kael had never seen a dead person before, but he imagined that they would look like this. The man pulled a ring of keys from his belt and began to unlock the cell door. Kael watched for several seconds before he noticed the piece of black fabric hanging from the jailer's belt. *A hood!*

All at once, Lemus' story came back to him. He was coming to take Kael to the torture chamber. Kael backed away, but there was nowhere to go.

The jailer hooked the key ring back on his belt and pushed open the door, stepping into the cell. With one hand held out to the side of his overweight body to prevent the prisoner from escaping, he pulled out the black hood.

Kael saw an opening and ran toward the man, ducking under his legs.

The jailer was quicker than he looked. He pulled his legs together just in time to catch Kael by the waist. Kael tried to kick and wiggle his way out from the man's legs, but the jailer dropped to the ground, pinning him in place. It felt like a horse had fallen on top of him. There was nothing he could do but wait and try to keep breathing. The man slipped the hood over Kael's head, then pulled his arms behind him and tied them with rope.

Then the man stood up and lifted Kael to his feet, shoving him down the hallway. Kael stumbled along, not knowing which direction to go. The sour smell of the hood made his head spin and combined with the inability to see, Kael lost all sense of direction. The jailer's heavy hand grabbed hold of his shoulder and pushed him along.

They walked in this manner for a short while before the jailer pulled Kael to a stop. The jingling of keys could be heard as the man searched for the one to open the door that must be in front of them.

Kael could barely make out the orange glow of torches through the thick hood. He waited until the man let go of his shoulder, then jumped away and ran down what he thought was the hallway. He followed the line of the torches, keeping in between where he thought they were. The laugh of the jailer was loud and unexpected. Suddenly he hit a wall with full speed where one should not have been and slumped to the floor. His head was ringing and he fought to stay conscious as the smell of the hood over his head made him want to vomit.

The jailer caught up with Kael and pulled him to his feet again.

It's useless. There's no way to escape.

The jailer shoved him through the door that was now unlocked and immediately Kael felt a difference in the air. They were outside. The crunch of gravel under his feet was the only sound as the jailer pushed Kael's shoulder, keeping him moving forward. After a short distance, they stopped again.

"Put him in the back," someone said.

Then, Kael was lifted off the ground and into the back of a covered wagon. A harsh clank sounded as the iron gate was shut and locked. *Is this the executioner? Is he taking me away?*

Outside the wagon, someone mumbled something.

"He'll have a witness," the jailer replied. His voice was hushed, but Kael could still make out his words.

"I don't like this," the other man said.

"Just stick to the plan and keep your mouth shut."

The carriage began to move. Kael waited nervously, completely confused. He expected to be taken to the executioner's chamber to have his head cut off, but something else was happening.

After a few minutes, the wagon stopped again and Kael was taken out and walked across a wooden dock. He could hear the lapping of the water underneath him and the creak of the timbers that supported their weight. They changed direction a few times, then walked across a plank and onto the deck of a ship. His footsteps sounded more hollow than before, and the ship moved with the gentle motion of the water.

Kael was taken below deck and stopped in front of an open door. Suddenly, the hood was pulled from his head and he was shoved from behind. With his hands still tied behind him, he fell to the floor in the middle of a small room. The door slammed behind him. Kael lifted his head and saw that his room was completely bare. No furniture and no windows except for a small peep hole in the middle of the door. It was another jail cell.

The ship began to move and Kael crawled to the corner of the room, leaning against the wall for support.

Where are they taking me?

The sound of retching echoed down the hallway and Zula quickened her pace toward the noise. Patches of sunlight dappled the steps leading up to the master's chambers and Zula rushed past, wondering what horrible thing was happening now. At the top of the stairs, she pushed open the bedroom doors and turned toward the bathing room, relieved that Lemus had left the house early in the morning. There, hunched over in the corner, was Maeryn, unaware that anyone else was in the room.

It took Zula only a second to realize what was happening. "Whose child is it in your womb?"

Maeryn lifted her head, startled, but didn't turn to face the slave woman. "What are you talking about?" she mumbled, still facing the wall.

"Don't bother trying to hide it from me," countered Zula. "It is going to be obvious in a few months anyway."

Maeryn turned around. Her eyes were red with tears and her skin was a few shades paler than usual. "It's Adair's."

"Are you sure?" the slave woman asked, not wholly believing her answer.

"Yes I'm sure." Maeryn stared at the ground and began to cry again.

Zula resisted the urge to hug the other woman. Maeryn would need to toughen up quickly if she hoped to survive now, although, it was becoming obvious that she didn't care either way.

"You're worried about the safety of this child because of what happened to Kael."

Maeryn replied only with a nod.

"How will my new master know that it is not his child?"

Zula's question hung in the air as Maeryn considered the words. After a long silence, she lifted her head. "You're right. He would have no idea that it's not his child." The tears had stopped, replaced by a gleam of hope in her eyes.

Zula pushed on, hoping to further encourage the lady. "It would be the safest way to bring this child into the world. Men like him think nothing of hurting other people, but are protective of their own children."

Maeryn's face turned from one of anguish to one of restrained happiness in a matter of seconds. "Thank you."

"M'lady, might I make a suggestion?" the dark-skinned woman asked, fully intending to give her opinion anyway. When Maeryn didn't object, she continued. "Your life may have changed for the worse, but you have many opportunities around you. You must choose to see them."

Maeryn nodded her head, considering the words.

Even Zula had to admit the oddity of giving advice to her master, but something told her that this woman was different. This woman would listen and not be offended.

"Zula, would you please fetch me some water to clean this up?"

"I'll clean it, Miss."

"No. I couldn't let you do that," Maeryn objected, repulsed by the thought.

"I don't mind. You need to get some rest." Zula turned around and walked away, not leaving any more room for discussion.

10

The passage aboard the prison ship had taken days. *How many? It must be five or six.* Kael was never allowed out of his cell, so he couldn't be sure. But now it was evening. The stars were out as they led him from the docks into a stone fortress in the side of a mountain. There was no hood over his head this time as the Orud soldiers prodded him down a hallway. On both sides were cells. Some were empty, but most contained at least one person, huddled in the corner. They quickly left the cells behind and continued down a corridor that seemed to stretch on forever. Kael shuddered at the thought of going so deep into the mountain.

Finally, at the end of the hall were two torches flanking an iron gate. One guard lowered his spear toward Kael's chest, while the other pulled out a knife and grabbed hold of his tunic.

"What are you doing?"

"Shut up," the guard said.

He began to cut Kael's tunic from his body, while Kael held as still as he could, helpless with his hands tied behind his back. When the tunic was gone, the guard grabbed Kael's loincloth and cut one side, nicking the skin.

Kael flinched, then felt a trickle of blood move down his thigh.

"Hold still," the guard snapped.

Tears of shame began to roll down his face and he shut his eyes to make them stop. He was completely naked now.

"Go," the soldier ordered.

Kael slowly walked through the unlocked gate, fearing what he would find inside. As his eyes adjusted to the dark, the harsh sound of the slamming gate rang out among the stone walls and floor, making him jump. In the darkness he could see movement. There were other people in the cell, lots of them. And the cell was big. But it was too dark to see clearly.

Moving to his right, Kael felt for the wall, then slid down and huddled on the floor. He pulled his knees up to his chin and waited. For what, he didn't know. He wasn't about to sleep, so he just stared into the darkness and waited.

Hours later, a guard lit torches along a hallway outside the chamber opposite from Kael. With the illumination, Kael could begin to make out the features of his surroundings. It was a circular chamber, a hundred feet across. The only way in or out was the gate that Kael came through, behind and to his left. On the opposite wall were three barred windows showing a view of the hallway outside their cell. It was like a pen used to corral animals. Only there were no animals. There were children, dozens of them, all boys like himself. None of them had clothing.

Kael shifted his weight and a fist-sized chunk of rock fell from the wall behind his shoulder. He reached out and grabbed the jagged shard and placed it back in the void it left. Then he paused. *I wonder if there's a way out of this place.* Scanning the walls, his eyes settled on the barred windows. He wondered how far apart each bar was and if he might be able to squeeze through.

And Kael wasn't the only one. Just as the thought occurred to him, a boy climbed up into one of the windows and reached his arm through the bars. A small group quickly formed around the boy, cheering him on. He was small, smaller than Kael, but it was obvious that he wouldn't fit through. His shoulder and chest could fit, but the bars were too close together to allow his head to get through.

Kael stood up and started to walk over, then stopped abruptly as he saw something dark sprout from between the boy's shoulder blades. Some in the group let out screams of shock, and scattered like rats. The boy fell backward off the window ledge and landed hard on the stone floor. His lifeless body lay perfectly still with a spear thrust through his chest.

"Stay back from the windows," a guard yelled from somewhere in the hallway.

Kael instantly lost his breath and slumped to the ground. His heart raced with fear, but he couldn't take his eyes off the boy. His motionless body lay on the ground, his mouth open in a grimace of pain. Where a living being used to be, there was now only dead flesh. *Just like a rat!* He started to cry and covered his face with his hands so that the others wouldn't see him.

The day dragged on, if it was in fact daytime. Kael kept to himself, as did most of the other children. The dead boy's body still lay under the window; no one had come to take it away. Kael overheard some of the boys talking about food. Usually they were given something to eat in the middle of the day, but that didn't happen this day. When nightfall came, signaled by the guard extinguishing the torches in the hallway, the air grew cold and Kael found himself shivering. *It's never this cold in Bastul. Where have they taken me? And what kind of jail is this?* As the temperature continued to drop, he huddled against the wall and wrapped his arms around his legs in an attempt to keep warm. It worked for a while, but then the shivering returned. He tried sleeping, but was too uncomfortable. His stomach began to growl. The minutes crept by slowly and Kael couldn't help himself as he started to cry again.

Shortly after the guard came to light the torches, the air grew warmer. Kael stayed huddled against the wall and slept for a few minutes, enjoying the relief from the cold. When he awoke, he could see that most of the other boys were clustered in groups now, except for a few others scattered around the chamber that were still asleep. But after a few minutes, he noticed that they weren't sleeping. Their skin looked pale and they weren't moving. *They froze to death!* Kael suddenly felt nauseous and his stomach heaved, but there was nothing to vomit.

By midday, the hunger pains in Kael's stomach returned, and with them, a growing anger. *We're all starving to death. How can they treat children like this?* A sudden squeal and the sound of the opening gate brought Kael out of his thoughts and turned everyone's attention to the one side of the room.

Running through the opening came a wild boar, grunting in agitation. It ran forward about ten feet and stopped, looking around at its new surroundings.

Kael immediately backed away, knowing that boars were extremely dangerous.

The other boys did the same, all except one. He had dark hair and scars on his back like he had endured many beatings. He walked forward cautiously, with his hands held out to either side.

The boar turned its head to look, then shifted its weight nervously. As the boy approached, it grew more agitated, grunting and turning toward the threat.

The boy continued to come forward, slowly making his way to the animal.

The boar charged forward, squealing as it ran.

The boy turned to run just as the wild beast made contact with his legs. He tripped and fell to the ground.

The boar was on him in an instant, biting mercilessly amid screams of pain and desperation.

Another boy ran forward and kicked the boar in the side of the abdomen, but the animal easily absorbed the blow and turned to attack him as well.

The rest of the boys, including Kael, backed away from the savage struggle. After a few minutes, it was over. The screaming had stopped and the air was still. The boar was breathing heavily, blood dripping from its sharp tusks. The two bodies of the boys lay on the floor, their skin lacerated beyond recognition.

Kael clenched his fists in rage. They were without food. They were naked and left to freeze in the night. And now, they were trapped in a cage with a dangerous animal. It was all too much!

A few of the boys broke away from the group and started moving slowly toward the boar. That's when it dawned on Kael. *We can eat it! If we can kill it.*

"We have to do this together," one of the boys said, "or we'll just end up like the others."

Kael searched the crowd and found the one who had spoken the first intelligible words since their captivity. He was short, with sandy colored hair. He looked to be about twelve, just a couple years older than Kael.

"We need to surround it and attack at the same time," he told the small group that was now forming around him. Roughly half of the remaining boys were joining in, while the other half backed away, scared by the prospect of death.

Kael walked over. If there was going to be a meal, he was going to make sure that he was included. As he approached, the other boys began to spread out and move in the general direction of the boar. There were thirteen including Kael. They started slowly, getting into position so that they formed a circle around the animal. Then, they began to close in and make the circle tighter.

"Tighten up over there," the boy instructed. "He's going to run as soon as he gets nervous. Don't let him out of the circle."

When they were within ten feet, the boar bolted and tried to run between two boys who dropped on the animal's back. The circle closed in quickly and fell on the animal, but not before it turned on the first two boys. After a few seconds of struggle, one of them fell to the ground, bleeding from the stomach and screaming.

The rest of the group pounced on the animal and beat it furiously with their fists, but it didn't seem to make a difference. Someone else tripped and the boar was on him in an instant.

Kael reached in and grabbed hold of the animal's neck, attempting to pull it off the boy. But the boar turned quickly and punctured his left forearm with its tusk. Kael stumbled back a few steps, squeezing his arm as the blood flowed down to his hand. Anger boiled inside him. *I have to kill it. I have to eat. I can't die here.* Then a thought came to him.

He ran over to the section of wall where he had spent the first night. Feeling along the stone blocks, his hand settled on the loose chunk that had fallen out. He pulled the jagged rock out of the wall and turned it over in his hands so that the sharpest point faced outward. Then he ran back and jumped over the crowd, landing on the animal's back. Grabbing a fistful of coarse hair to keep from being thrown off, Kael brought the rock down as hard as he could on the animal's head. It flinched and let out a squeal—its first sign of weakness.

Kael held on with all his might and continued to beat on the animal's skull while the other boys punched with their fists and kicked with their feet. After a few seconds, the animal fell over on its side. Kael fell to the ground with it, but kept hammering with the rock until his arms and face were covered in its blood. The group slowly backed away when they realized that the animal was dead.

When he knew that he was finally out of danger, Kael slumped to the floor in exhaustion. His left arm was numb from the puncture wound. He let go of the bloody rock and as it fell to the ground, he saw that two of the fingers on his right hand were broken and sticking out at odd angles.

There was no wood to make a fire, so the boys tore at the flesh of the boar like ravenous wolves. They had all gone without food for so long that taste meant nothing. They were going to die if they didn't eat the raw meat. By the time the guard came to light the torches, two others died from their injuries. But despite the growing numbers of human bodies now littering the chamber, Kael slept a little better, without the gnawing hunger pains. His small group also huddled close together for warmth. It was strange at first, being naked. But they all knew that survival was more important than their pride.

For the next few days, Kael's group continued to eat off the animal carcass, while the others began to die off from starvation and exposure to the cold night air. Every morning they woke to find a few more bodies on the floor. Kael thought that they should give some food to the others, but he didn't say anything. They had risked their lives to kill the boar while the others stood back in fear. The consensus among his group was that they had earned it.

Kael's face exploded with pain. He flinched and rolled to the side, stopping in a crouching position. It was dark. *Is it night? Was I sleeping? What's happening?* In the darkness, he could just barely see that the others were attacking as a group. The carcass of the boar was being dragged away. And the boy who had punched him lunged forward again.

Kael thrashed from side to side as the boy, who was much bigger, grabbed hold of his wrists and wrestled him to the ground. He pinned Kael on his back and began to drive a knee into his side. With each blow, Kael felt a shooting pain through his ribs and the air pounded from his lungs. In a moment of panic, he lifted his head and lashed out with his teeth, catching the larger boy in the neck. When Kael realized where his mouth was, he bit hard with his teeth and immediately felt blood fill his mouth. The boy screamed and thrashed violently, but Kael just bit harder until the flesh came off in his mouth.

The boy released his grip on Kael's wrists and slumped over, convulsing for a few seconds before going still. Kael pushed him off and struggled to his feet. The fight was over, and most of his group had survived. The others were all dead. It had been a fight for survival. But that fact didn't make Kael feel any better. He knew he had just killed someone and the thought made him feel more horrible than he'd ever felt. He leaned over and tried to spit the blood out of his mouth, but the taste wouldn't go away. His stomach heaved and he vomited on the cold stone floor. When he finished, he walked away from everyone and slumped down against the wall. He started to cry again and didn't stop until he fell asleep.

"How many?"

"All of them."

Kael woke at the sound of the voices which echoed through the chamber.

"I'll pay you a fair price," someone said.

The voices were coming from outside the gate where the boar had been let in. But then the conversation was over and the only thing that could be heard was the sound of retreating footsteps.

Kael wondered what the exchange of words meant. The only interaction with whoever was on the other side of the wall had been negative. *The boy they killed. The boar. What's it going to be this time?*

After what seemed like half an hour, the iron gate opened. Growing up in the port city of Bastul, Kael had seen many foreigners from different parts of the surrounding territories, but never anyone who looked like the man walking through the gate.

His skin was pale, but with a yellowish tint. His black hair was pulled back into a single braid that ran all the way down to his waist. His oversized clothing consisted of what looked like a skirt that reached down to sandaled feet, with a jacket that covered his arms. The deep blue fabric shimmered in the torchlight, like the most expensive kind that his mother used to buy in Bastul. In his hands, the man carried several small loaves of bread. And behind him, five other men followed who looked just like him, but dressed in long robes of a dull brown color. Each of these men also carried bread and folded clothing as well.

The strange man walked over to Kael's group.

The boys shrank against the wall.

"My sons," he spoke softly. "Do not be afraid. They cannot hurt you any longer. You are mine now and I will protect you." As he spoke, the man leaned down and began to hand out the loaves of bread, one by one, to each of the boys.

When Kael accepted his loaf, he looked into the dark, slanted eyes and saw compassion.

"After you've eaten, please clothe yourselves. We will make a journey to my home where you will be my guests."

Kael accepted the folded brown clothes and sandals from one of the other men, and dressed quickly. He was relieved to be able to cover himself. And for the first time in many days, he felt some measure of relief.

11

Saba had been lying low for a while, staying with a friend who lived just outside of the city limits. He had been trying to keep busy with other things, but it wasn't working well. How could he leave Maeryn alone with that murderer? She wasn't safe and he felt it was his duty to keep an eye on her, which was why he found himself walking along the busy streets of Bastul. He was trying to keep close to the most crowded areas, working his way up the hill toward his former home, hoping to blend in and thereby escape the eyes of the soldiers patrolling the city.

The market district was teeming with merchants hawking their goods. Saba had to run off a particular child who wouldn't take "no" for an answer. He was trying to sell a few small fish that he said he had just caught in the bay. It was obvious that the child was working for someone else, probably only receiving a small percentage, if anything, for the sale of the fish. Eventually the child returned, following at a distance. Saba moved out of the main flow of people and over to a cart of figs. The fig merchant scurried quickly around the cart to meet this new customer.

"Fine day, isn't it?" he said, in a shrill voice, easily piercing the cacophony of noises from the surrounding crowds.

"Yes, it is. I'll have one please."

"...only one? Why, a man of your size could not be filled by such a small..."

"I'll have one," he stated firmly, not wishing to barter.

"Fine...fine. Here you go. It just seems a shame for a man like you..."

Saba dropped a coin on the cart and took the fig, leaving before the man finished his sentence. He walked back into the crowd and continued along the street, waiting for the boy to approach him again. He wasn't about to buy the fish when the money would be taken from the boy anyway, but the child could eat a fig and his master wouldn't even know. After a few minutes, Saba felt a tug on the back of his sleeve. He spun around quickly, already knowing what he would say to the child.

But instead of the boy, Saba found a group of soldiers with their spears lowered, spreading out to prepare for a confrontation. The one who had tugged on his tunic stood close, his spear raised in confidence that the situation would be resolved verbally.

"Sergeant," Saba said, not at all surprised by the situation.

"Come with me," the soldier commanded.

Saba was escorted to an alley between two rows of merchant shops. There were eleven soldiers in all, including the sergeant. Five guarded the front of the alley and five guarded the back. The leader stayed close to Saba and spoke in a hushed voice.

"I have orders to kill you on sight." He looked up and down the alley to make sure that no one was listening. "Since you are a friend of Adair's, I will only ignore my orders once and I do so at my own peril. Leave this city or I will be forced to kill you."

Saba nodded. "Thank you, Sir, for your kindness. I will do as you say."

"You'd better," the soldier warned. As he walked out to the street the others fell in behind him.

Saba waited awhile in the alley to catch his breath. There was just no way to keep in contact with Maeryn and the guard was very clear about what would happen if he tried. He had no choice but to leave. Someday, perhaps, he would return.

Maeryn will have to fend for herself. As the thought came to him, it was accompanied by doubt. He knew it would not be easy for her.

Kael's body recoiled, anticipating danger. His breaths were shallow and rapid, his eyes darting back and forth, searching for the threat. Suddenly, he remembered where he was and a wave of relief washed over him. *I was just dreaming. Safe now.*

The boys had traveled with the kind stranger and his men for a few days by ocean and land. Upon arriving at his mountain-top estate, they were fed, bathed, and their wounds dressed. Kael looked down to the bandage on his left forearm and the splint that kept his broken fingers from moving. With the other hand, he rubbed the stubble on his head where his hair used to be. The wound from Lemus had also been cleaned and dressed.

It had been late in the evening when they arrived, so he didn't get a good look at his surroundings. But it was light outside now. His room was larger even than the one he had in Bastul. Gray stone walls surrounded a polished wood floor. Across the room to his right, was a giant wooden door standing eight feet tall. It was constructed of thick wooden planks, held together by ornate black hinges which spanned the width of the door and bolted to the frame. The only other objects in the room were a small table of rough hewn timber in the corner, and a chest at the foot of the bed. Along the left wall was a window large enough for him to fit the table through. It was covered by thick wooden shutters that blocked almost all of the light, except for a tiny amount that seeped through the sides next to the wall.

A whistling sounded as a breeze was trying to force itself through the edges of the shutters. Leaving his bed, he walked to the window and opened the shutters. He was at least twenty feet off the ground, staring down at a gently rolling meadow with a high stone wall a hundred yards away. Beyond the wall, tufts of long pale grass protruded from clumps of snow that clung to the side of rocks and shadowy areas created by the setting sun. Kael had never seen snow before, though Saba had explained it to him. To the right, the meadow slowly rose until it blocked the horizon, leaving only a clear blue sky above. To his left, over the rooftops of several square buildings and one large circular structure, a wall of enormous mountains capped with white snow covered the horizon. *Where am I?* The mountains that he knew of, the ones north of Bastul, were not this big and never had snow on them.

When he walked back to the bed, he noticed a neatly folded pile of clothing on the chest. On top was a tunic, which he quickly picked up, expecting to slip it over his head. But when he unfolded it, he was confused about how it was supposed to be worn. There were long sleeves, which were unusual for Kael, but at least he knew where to put his arms. The material was a dull brown color, but soft and slick, like it had been polished. He slid his arms into the appropriate places and paused, trying to decide what to do next. The front of the tunic was open, like a coat, with two flaps of fabric hanging in front of him. He wasn't sure how to proceed, but it was obvious that he needed more clothing; the tunic only hung down to his waist. He grabbed the other item of clothing and unfolded it.

"Pants," he said out loud.

The only reason he knew what they were was because his father had recently explained them to him. The soldiers in the Northern Territory wore these as the weather got colder. He slipped them on and fastened them at the waist, using the ties sewn into the front. He was not accustomed to wearing anything on his legs, but was grateful in light of the crisp chill in the air.

A knock sounded at his door. His heart quickened a little as he walked over and pulled on the handle. It didn't budge and the metallic sound of a lock being opened made him jump. Kael stepped back and the door opened to reveal a short man that looked like one of the servants. His skin had a yellow tint and his eyes were wide-set. Kael assumed that his hair was black, but could only look at his eyebrows for proof; his head was also shaved. Kael wondered if his own head was shaved for some purpose other than to treat his head wound.

When the man spoke, it was in a language foreign to Kael, but the inflection told him that it was a question. Kael shook his head to show that he didn't understand. The man looked at the floor for a moment before speaking again.

"Awake?" he asked in a strange accent.

Kael thought the answer was obvious, but nodded his head anyway.

"You dress...come with me," he continued, pointing at the flaps of fabric hanging from Kael's tunic.

Kael looked down at himself and then back to the man. "I don't know how...it's different than..."

Before he could finish his statement, the man stepped into the room and grabbed Kael's tunic. He wrapped the flap on Kael's right side across his body and secured it with ties on the inside of the left flap. He repeated the process with the other side, securing it to ties on the outside of his tunic. Kael watched, confused until the man was finished.

With that completed, the stranger walked over to the foot of Kael's bed and picked up the footwear off the floor. He placed them in Kael's hands and lifted his robe, showing Kael his own feet. These sandals were not really sandals at all. They completely covered the feet, but didn't extend to the lower part of the leg. They had laces, but instead of wrapping around the legs, they slid through holes and criss-crossed on top of the feet. It took a moment, but Kael eventually got the hang of it. The man waited patiently until Kael was finished.

Suddenly, he bent down and patted Kael's foot. "Shoe," the man said. He stood back up and nodded his head. "Shoe," he said again and pointed at Kael's feet.

"Shoe" Kael repeated, receiving a smile from the man.

"Come," he said, motioning for Kael to follow him as he left the room.

The tall doorframe opened into a long hallway that reminded him of the one in his home. The man turned to the left and walked down the hallway and Kael quickly fell into step behind him. Their footsteps plodded softly on the wooden plank floor, with the slight hollow sound of being above the ground. As they walked, Kael noticed that everything about this place was foreign. Not only were the ceilings constructed differently, but the stone walls were a dark gray color and seemed to be fitted together without mortar. Everything in Bastul was built from a white stone and covered with plaster on the inside.

"Where am I?"

The man slowed his pace and looked back over his shoulder, then shook his head.

Doesn't he know? Or maybe he can't say.

"Far away," the man replied and continued walking as if the answer was sufficient.

"Where are we going?"

"They tell me—wake child, bring him here."

The hallway ended at a landing overlooking a cylindrical room with stairs curving down to the next floor in both directions. The man chose the right-hand stairs and quickened his pace down to the lower level. Kael had to jog to keep up with him. The pair moved so quickly that Kael scarcely had time to notice the large iron sconces along the wall, illuminating the room as well as a discolored area of the stone wall where something had hung for a long period of time. There were no decorations.

It looks abandoned.

When they reached the bottom, the man slowed his pace to a walk and turned to the left, entering another hallway that led underneath the one outside Kael's room, heading in the opposite direction. The hall terminated at a large rectangular doorway, similar to what Kael was used to seeing at his home. It led to a spacious circular room lit with many torches. A crackling noise drew Kael's attention to the right where he saw a stone fireplace that jutted out from the wall. He could feel the heat on his face, even though it was twenty feet away. The walls of the room were stone, like the rest of the building. He looked up at the ceiling and saw that it was vaulted toward the center of the room. Thick beams radiated from the highest point, angling down to where they were embedded in holes at the top of the wall. Doors were placed at regular intervals around the circular wall, mirroring the hub and spoke construction of the ceiling.

At the center of the room was a long, wooden table set with an assortment of foods. There were plates of steaming meats arranged in groups of colors from dark to pale brown. In addition, there were plates of cheeses, fruits, vegetables, and an assortment of breads. Two large pitchers sat at one end of the table, and though Kael couldn't see inside of them, the cups arranged around the pitchers told him that they contained the beverages. The whole room was filled with a mixture of aromas from the feast before his eyes. It was so much to take in all at once, that it took Kael a few seconds to notice that most of the other boys were already seated at the table.

Kael counted eleven chairs, eight of which were filled. Each boy's head was shaved, just like Kael's. Filling the ninth chair at the head of the table was the kind stranger who rescued them. That left two open chairs and Kael assumed that one was for him.

"Please have a seat," spoke the man at the head of the table who had now risen from his chair.

As Kael took his seat, he saw another robed man entering the room from the same place he had entered, followed by the boy who had been their leader during the attack on the boar. He seemed even more stunned than Kael by the surroundings. He was ushered to the table as well and when they had both taken their seats, the man at the head of the table pushed in his chair and remained standing.

"Now that you are all here, let us begin."

Suddenly, a door on the other side of the room opened and several men in robes came out. They surrounded the table and began to serve the food onto plates and pass them out, as if they had been waiting for a signal. As they worked, the man at the head of the table continued to speak.

"My name is Ukiru and I have a few things to say before we share our first meal together. The ten of you have been rescued from certain death. When I found you, you were naked, starving, and killing each other just to stay alive. This is no way for a person to live. But just as you were rescued, you were also redeemed for a purpose. You see, the world has cast you out like refuse. But I believe that you have a great deal of worth. Each one of you had a different beginning, but that is no longer relevant. Your former life was a breath away from ending. And that is how you should think of it. Dead! What is important now is that your lives are not your own. You have been rescued and given a wondrous gift, a new beginning."

His speech halted momentarily as he began to walk around the table. He was shorter than most men Kael had met and had a steady, careful gait, like the acrobats who used to perform in Bastul during the festivals.

"I worship a god who is powerful beyond any human comprehension. He used to rule this world until its inhabitants stopped worshiping him and became distracted with other, less-important things. So, he left this world and its people to their own devices for a time. This was many, many years ago. But the time is coming soon when he will return and claim this world once again. He will drive out all those who oppose him and those that worship other gods, bringing justice to this unjust world."

Kael looked around the table and could sense that the other boys were just as confused as he was. In Bastul, talk of such things usually involved many gods. Most families had several gods in particular that they worshiped and prayed to throughout the day. One time, Saba told him of a group of people far to the east who believed in one god who created everything. But he was still confused. *What does this have to do with us?*

After making several passes around the room, the man had reached the head of the table again and paused behind his chair. "I know that this sounds strange. And right now you are probably wondering why you are here and what all of this has to do with you."

A few of the boys nodded their heads in confirmation, but Kael didn't move. It seemed like the man had just read his mind.

"I will try to be as plain as possible. A short while ago, the god whom we worship spoke to our High Priest."

Several murmurs could be heard around the room from the robed attendants.

"The High Priest told me that the time of our god's return is short at hand. He appointed me to a task. From the farthest reaches of the Orud Empire, choose ten children, boys. Choose from among those who have been cast out by the world, and bring them to this place to be raised in the order of an ancient and forgotten priesthood, the priesthood of the All Powerful. Once you reach the age of adulthood, you will present yourselves as gifts to our god, warrior-priests. He will then return and you will become his instruments of justice to reclaim his kingdom. And so I searched, and that is when I found you, caged like animals. There were only ten of you left and I believe the All Powerful himself preserved you for this task."

At this, the boys shifted in their seats.

Ukiru raised a hand in protest. "Now I know what you are thinking. This all sounds so strange and is too great a responsibility for mere children. I will not lie to you. It is perhaps the greatest responsibility that has ever been entrusted to mankind. But I will be honest with you. I am jealous of you all. It is a responsibility that I would have for myself. But I will have to be content with being your instructor. I assure you this will not be as difficult as it seems to you now. You will all be given the finest education. Your training as priests will be balanced with your training as warriors. You will make a steady transition from the boys you are now to the men you will become—the most powerful men this world has ever seen."

"What if we don't want to?" came a voice from across the table. It was the child who had led the attack on the boar.

"There is always one who must question," replied the man, with a smile. "But it is a good question. Why would you not want to do this? You will be fed and clothed. You will do more, see more, and learn more than any other child in this world. It will also be a lot of fun. And when it comes time for you to present yourself to the All Powerful, you will know that you are the most fortunate person in all the world."

"They can't keep me here," the boy said to himself, his voice almost a whisper.

"My dear son, there is nowhere for you to go. Even if you did try to leave, you are weeks away from the nearest city and you would starve before you reached it, that is, if you didn't freeze to death first. But of course, I could not let that happen. And I hope that you will come to love your new home."

Kael wished the boy would stay silent. He didn't see any reason to argue with the man. Although he missed his home and family, Kael figured that this was much better than the fate that awaited them in prison. He, for one, felt fortunate already.

"Now that I have told you why you are here, I welcome you and consider it an honor to be entrusted with your safety. Let us eat, and afterward I will show you around your new home. There will be no further introductions tonight; we will get to that tomorrow morning. For now, enjoy the feast."

The food was delicious, but Kael found it difficult to eat very much. Several of the other boys didn't have as much trouble, however, and refilled their plates more than once. For the duration of the meal, the robed attendants stood around the perimeter of the room with their hands behind their backs. When one of the children cleared their plate or finished the last sip of water or tea, the attendants quickly came forward to offer more.

When everyone had eaten as much as they could, Ukiru rose to his feet and announced that it was time to show them around their new home. Some of the other boys stood up as well and Kael followed their leading. As soon as the chairs were empty, the men around the room began to clear the table. Ukiru beckoned for everyone to gather around him so that he could begin the tour. When the group was assembled, Ukiru pointed at the door through which Kael had entered the room.

"I assume that you are already familiar with your living quarters? All of you boys have separate rooms on the upper level of this hall." Turning to the right, he walked to the next door along the wall, which was bigger than any other in the room. He slid back a large bolt and pushed open the door. "This is the main entrance."

Kael tried to see out the door, but most of the view was blocked by the other boys standing in the way. He moved around to get a better look and saw tapered stone columns along a stone path which began at the door and extended through a courtyard area before reaching an open gate. Beyond that, the path continued for a short distance before curving out of sight.

Ukiru shepherded the boys back inside and shut the door, sliding the bolt into place once again. "This next door," he continued, "leads to the other living quarters; it is where the rest of us sleep. The hall itself looks identical to yours."

The next item along the wall was a huge square pillar which mirrored the one on the opposite side of the room, only this one didn't have a fireplace built into it. The next door led to what Ukiru called *the lawn*, but said that he would show it to them later on. The next door led to the kitchen, but that was made obvious by the robed men entering and exiting with piles of plates and eating utensils.

Ukiru walked to the final door around this circular room, positioned to the left of the fireplace. He indicated that the group should follow him before opening the door and walking through it. Kael followed the line of boys and found himself outside, under a covered walkway. Large round beams were set into the ground on either side of the walkway, supporting an elaborate roof much like the one in the dining room. Each support beam had a torch mounted to it. Ukiru led the group down the path where it turned left in front of a square building with one door. On either side of the door, running the entire length of the building were windows shaped like the door turned on its side. Ukiru walked over to the door, unlatched it, and pushed it open. He waited until all of the boys were inside of the first room before explaining.

"This is our classroom, where our studies will take place. Each morning you will assemble here for instruction in a number of subjects."

The room was shallow but wide, with a number of chairs and desks arranged in a semicircle, all facing toward the back wall. As he spoke, Ukiru wove through the line of desks and made his way to the back of the room, opening one of two doors along the back wall. The boys followed him into a room filled with books. Some were arranged in piles on tables, others were set on end inside of shelves.

"This is our library. We have assembled together all of the writings that will be needed for our instruction, as well as many others that you may find informative."

Ukiru walked back through the classroom and out the front door, waiting under the covered walkway for the children to file out of the building. When they were ready, he continued along the path to where it ended at a huge circular building with a conical roof, raised at the center and gently sloping to the perimeter. The path stopped at two wide doors which Ukiru slid to each side.

"We call this place *the arena*. It is where most of your weapons and combat training will take place."

Kael was stunned at the size of the building. It was hundreds of feet across and he couldn't imagine why all of this space would be necessary. It looked like a barn. At the center of the room was a bundle of support columns stretching up to the ceiling. The room was divided into pie shaped sections that radiated from this point. The section where they were standing was completely bare with a soft, sand-covered floor. Some of the other sections had raised floors, while others had wooden structures either hanging from the ceiling or sprouting from the ground. It all seemed confusing to Kael, but he was sure that it would be properly explained at some point.

The boys followed Ukiru to the left as he walked around the perimeter of the building and through another set of wide doors. The smell of livestock reached Kael's nose and it was obvious where they were headed, even before Ukiru began to explain the stables.

"Some of your training will occur on horseback and as you can see, we have plenty for everyone."

As they moved down the center aisle, horses shifted uneasily in their stalls on either side. The aisle eventually became an intersection, with one path leading straight ahead and another leading between two stalls on the left side of the room. Ukiru chose the left path and slid open another set of wide doors. A robed man waited on the other side of the door.

Turning around to address the group, Ukiru spread his hands wide. "This is *the lawn*, where our outdoor training will take place."

It was an enormous grass-covered field, hundreds of yards across. The large field was lined with iron torches at the perimeter, huge structures that were set into the ground like trees.

As they made their way across the field, Kael was amazed at the softness of the grass. He even stopped and bent down, running his palms across the lush blades. The way that it was carefully maintained reminded him of his mother's garden in the courtyard back home. When he looked up again, the group was already across the lawn and heading for a path on the other side. Kael had to run to catch up.

At the edge of the lawn was a gravel path that wound its way through low walls of sculpted shrubs. Ukiru was in the process of explaining something to the group when Kael reached them.

"...they take care of all of this. In fact, there are many places throughout the monastery where the monks have created tranquil surroundings for meditation."

It sounded to Kael like Ukiru was answering someone's question. After glancing around, he saw what must have prompted it. On one side of the path, the shrubbery opened to form a circle, twenty feet across. Boulders were placed randomly throughout the meditation spot, with rings drawn into the sand around each one, as if the sand were actually water. In the center of the circle was a short platform of polished wood.

Ukiru led the group farther along the path until they reached another small circular building with vaguely square structures sprouting from its sides. As they entered the building Kael realized that it was the dining hall where the tour had started.

"This concludes the tour and our time together today. While you were away, your rooms were prepared for you. Your servant will help you get acquainted with your new home. He will be your escort for the remainder of the week and answer any questions that you may have. I will see you all tomorrow morning in the arena where your training as warrior-priests begins. Rest well; you will need your energy." With that, Ukiru walked across the room and through the doorway to his living quarters, his blue robes fluttering as he walked.

12

Kael awoke before the sun and dressed himself with the clothing he found in the chest at the end of his bed. Just as he finished lacing his shoes, a knock came at his door and he opened it to find his servant standing in the hall.

"It is time," he said, in his strange accent.

Kael left his room and followed the man down the hallway. "What's your name?" Kael asked when they reached the stairs.

"No name. Only, one who serves All Powerful."

"Why don't you have a name?"

"Cannot talk of this," he said, shaking his head and quickening his pace down the stairs.

Kael wrinkled his eyebrows, then watched his feet as they took the stairs at a rapid pace to keep up with the servant. "Well, my name is Kael."

They retraced their steps from the night before, taking them down to the dining hall and out a door on the right side of the room. The sky was growing brighter in the east as the pair moved down the covered walkway toward the arena. The air was incredibly cold and Kael crossed his arms in front of his chest in an attempt to keep in his body heat. As soon as they entered the arena, the air was warm and Kael got the shivers as his body readjusted to the new temperature. He was only the third boy there. The other two were looking out the windows lining the far wall. In the few minutes it had taken to walk to this building, the sun had just started to peek above the horizon. The view was majestic, overlooking a valley of rolling hills, turned a pale yellow from the cold air. The sky was awash with orange and pink light reflecting off the thin wisps of high clouds hanging in the air.

Kael expected to see Ukiru, but he was not in the building. The servant led Kael over to the far side of the room where the others were standing. The floor of this pie shaped section of the arena was a raised platform covered in canvas. Ten square mats were arranged on the floor in a double line and Kael could only assume that they would be part of the morning's event.

"He will be here soon," the monk announced. "I will go now."

The other boys turned around from the windows and Kael suddenly felt awkward being in this strange place without an escort. Even though he was supposed to think of it as his new home, he still felt like a visitor. One of the boys walked toward Kael with a smile on his face.

"My name is Coen," he said with an outstretched hand.

Kael was so surprised by his joyful manner that he almost forgot to respond. "I'm Kael," was all he said, shaking the boy's hand. Then the thought occurred to him that in all their time together in that prison, no one had introduced themselves. They hardly talked at all. It was like they had turned into animals while trying to survive.

Things are different now.

Coen was short, like Kael, though a few years older. His shaved head was just starting to grow thin black hair. He had a large nose and full lips that almost looked like a girl.

"That's Berit over there," he said, pointing at the other boy who was still standing at the window. Berit waved and turned back to looking at the sunrise.

"He's a little shy. So where are you from?"

Kael was just about to answer when he was interrupted by some of the other boys entering the building, their attendants turning and leaving just as promptly as Kael's had done.

"Do you like it here?" Coen continued.

"Uh...I...I don't know yet," Kael stumbled. *This kid sure likes to talk. At least he's nice though. I'd hate it if he were mean and talkative.*

The rest of the boys came in seconds later, some in groups, some alone. None were as talkative as Coen. Berit continued to stare out at the valley, which was now a series of rolling shadows carved out by a blinding orange rising sun. Two of the other boys talked quietly with each other, but mostly, the room was silent.

Suddenly, Kael noticed that Ukiru was standing by the wall, only a few feet away. Somehow he had slipped in without anyone noticing. "I trust that you all slept well last night. This morning we will start with introductions. Everyone pick a mat and stand in the center of it. I want you to state your first name only, loud enough for everyone to hear. We'll start with you," he said, pointing to the boy who occupied the leftmost mat at the front of the room.

The boy shifted his stance, uneasy at the unwanted attention. "Donagh," he mumbled. His accent was thick and guttural sounding. He was tall and appeared muscular, even beneath the thick clothing that each boy was wearing. Kael couldn't tell if his hair was brown or black.

Ukiru nodded in response and shifted his gaze to the second boy in the front row. Berit seemed even more nervous than Donagh, but it showed in a different way. His scalp and face turned a bright red beneath his sand-colored eyebrows. "Berit," he stated in a pinched voice.

"Horace," the next boy offered, merrily. He was of average height, but a little thick through the midsection. He also had sand-colored stubble just starting to grow on his odd shaped head and skin that turned red easily, though the redness seemed to be concentrated on his bulb-shaped nose.

Coen was next in line and announced his name without any signs of nervousness. He was clearly comfortable in front of people. Kael on the other hand was dreading his turn. Not for any reason, particularly. It just made him uncomfortable that it would soon be his turn.

"Narian," came the deep voice from the last boy in the row. He was just as tall as Donagh, though his features weren't as dark and his smiling face made him look friendly.

Instead of choosing Kael, who was standing behind Narian, Ukiru pointed back across the room to the boy at the other end of the row.

"Arden," the boy said, in a loud and clear voice. He, too, had an accent and Kael wondered how they had all ended up in the same jail together. Arden was only a little taller than Kael, with a protruding nose that was even larger than Coen's.

The next boy waited until Ukiru pointed at him before speaking his name. "Soren." This was the boy who had become their group leader while in the prison. Kael could tell he didn't like following rules.

"Rainer," said the next boy. The only thing that Kael noticed about him was that he looked younger than all the rest of the children in the room.

"Jorn," stated the boy standing next to Kael. He was the shortest one in the room and also the pudgiest. The tiny hairs on his scalp were thick and black, and it reminded Kael of his father's beard.

Finally it was Kael's turn. He felt his face turn red and his voice tightened a little as he spoke his name. Suddenly, his turn was over and he felt a sense of relief.

Ukiru nodded and began to pace across the floor. "Thank you all. Now, I only asked for your first name because I do not care to which family you belong. I do not care what country you were born in. All those things are dead now, just as your former life is dead. We will only know each other by the names that were spoken here today. That is all that matters."

Kael could see that a few of the boys were finding it hard to concentrate on Ukiru's words. The view of the rising sun behind him was distracting.

Ukiru noticed and immediately walked back to the front of the room to regain his audience. "Every morning we will meet here at sunrise and begin the day with some exercises. I will instruct you until you memorize each step and position. These exercises will help you gain balance, coordination, and flexibility at first. Eventually, when they are committed to memory, you will find that these movements also help to clear your mind of distractions. A clear mind is essential to hear the voice of the All Powerful. In time, these exercises will become a meditation." He now had the attention of everyone in the room.

"Place your feet together and stand straight," he said, demonstrating the stance. "Pull your shoulders back and look straight ahead. Put your hands together in front of your chest and close your eyes. I want you all to remain quiet, so quiet that you can hear yourself breathe, so quiet that you are able to hear your own heart beating."

Kael had his eyes closed, but could hear a few of the boys snickering. It felt a little strange to be standing in a room full of strangers with his eyes closed. But even though it was awkward, he must have been more comfortable than some of the other boys, who were whispering to each other.

Oh well. Just try to ignore them.

"Breathe in deeply and hold your breath for a moment," said Ukiru, sounding a little irritated with the uncooperative children. "Now let it out and continue to breathe deeply, concentrating on the sound of your heart.

Kael kept his eyes closed and tried to follow the instructions. He could hear his heart beat and felt a sense of peace and comfort at the sound of Ukiru's voice.

"Now open your eyes. Move your left foot out to the side and stand like this," he demonstrated. "Extend both of your arms out from your body and hold this position."

Kael followed Ukiru's mesmerizing voice, as he led them through many different poses and stretches. Most of the time was peaceful, barring the occasional suppressed laugh from one of the other boys. Kael's limbs were a little shaky with fatigue, though none of the exercises were difficult for him. He used to spend many hours at a time climbing trees and balancing on the branches. Such feats of daring bravery were part of his ongoing competition with Ajani. *I wonder if Ajani is still alive.* He had stopped screaming long before Kael was able to stop Lemus from beating him. He couldn't remember anything after Lemus hit him with the handle of the pitchfork. He felt tears begin to form in his eyes and shook his head to stop them. *I can't cry here.*

"Now place your feet together again and stand up straight. Put your hands together in front of your chest and close your eyes."

They ended up in the same position in which they started. Kael found himself breathing heavily, despite the ease with which he moved through the exercises. When he opened his eyes on Ukiru's command, he felt invigorated. Horace and Donagh were trying not to laugh at some private joke they shared.

"Very good. Perhaps tomorrow we will not be as distracted." Ukiru's gaze landed on Horace and Donagh who quickly became serious. "Before we have the morning meal, your servants will show you to the washroom. We will assemble in the dining hall in fifteen minutes." After Ukiru left the room, Donagh and Horace finished laughing at their joke. All of the boys filed out of the arena, following their servants down the covered walkway.

The washroom was located on the first level, off the hallway between the dining hall and the sleeping quarters. There were several stalls of toilets off to the right side of the room, as well as a circular fountain in the center for washing face and hands. Kael didn't need to relieve himself, so he walked over to the fountain. Water gurgled from a short pedestal in the middle, spilling over the side where it filled the basin. He leaned over and noticed holes on the inside of the basin, a few inches from the rim. The water level was slightly above the bottom of these holes, causing the water to drain out just as fresh water from the pedestal replaced it. He dipped his hands in the water and was surprised to find it warm. It felt soothing and he immediately splashed some on his face and rubbed the sleep from his eyes. Jorn was the next one to come to the fountain and was surprised at the temperature of the water as well. Just as the boys began to talk about it, a voice came from the hallway.

"You're curious about the water?" Ukiru stepped from the hallway into the washroom.

"Yes," both boys answered at the same time.

"This monastery was built hundreds of years ago in this location for just that reason. All around us, the land is alive with heat. In some places, steam comes from holes in the earth. Our predecessors channeled that heated air and brought it to these buildings. There are vents throughout these rooms and even in your bedrooms where the heated air comes through to fight back the chill of the winter months. One area, which you will see later this evening, has steaming water coming from the ground, which was made into a bath."

The rest of the boys were finished and had started to gather around the fountain to hear Ukiru. "Finish washing; the meal is ready," he said and left just as suddenly as he arrived.

Kael was already finished and followed Ukiru back to the dining hall. When they arrived the table was already set with food. Each place at the table was set with a cup of tea and a steaming bowl of a thick grayish substance. Kael sat down at the same place he sat the previous night. One by one, the rest of the boys came into the room and followed his example. Horace and Donagh sat together and started to grab for their food before everyone was seated.

"Wait," said Ukiru. "We will have a moment of silence to thank the All Powerful for providing this meal and all the things that surround us. Ukiru closed his eyes and most of the other children did as well. Kael looked around at each face until he stopped at Soren, who winked at him and smiled, refusing to close his eyes. Eventually Ukiru opened his eyes and cleared his throat. "Let us eat," he announced and proceeded to lift the steaming bowl to his lips.

The gray substance in the bowl appeared to be mashed oats and grains. Kael thought it tasted bland, but was thankful to have something in his stomach. He hadn't yet gained all his strength back from his time in prison.

After breakfast, Ukiru rose from the table and led the boys out of the room. They walked as a group down the covered walkway and entered the square building that Ukiru said would serve as their classroom. The desks and chairs were still arranged just as they had been the previous day. Ukiru motioned for everyone to take a seat before he addressed them.

"This is the study," he began. "Every morning after breakfast, we will meet in this room. Here you will learn everything from history and astronomy to arithmetic and the arts of war. Some subjects, of course, will require you to have obtained a certain amount of knowledge beforehand. So we will start with reading, writing and speaking. These three skills form the basis of all knowledge. How can we learn or communicate what we have learned if we cannot read, write, or speak?"

"But we already know how to speak," answered Horace.

"Ah yes! But to speak and to communicate are altogether different, aren't they?"

Horace squinted.

Ukiru quickly spoke a sentence in a foreign language.

All of the boys looked at each other in confusion.

"You see...I have spoken, but I have not communicated to you what I wished to communicate. What I said was—cry in the classroom so that you may laugh on the battlefield," he repeated. "It is a saying where I come from. It means that if you train hard in the arts of war, so hard that all your tears are shed in the classroom, then when it comes time to go into battle, you will be fearless in the face of your enemy. You will laugh at how easy it is compared to your training."

Ukiru turned toward Horace. "You see, speaking is not the same as communicating. Once you have mastered these three skills, you will have the foundation that will be needed in the future. Some of you have already had a great deal of instruction, while others have had none. Nevertheless, we will all start at the same place and we will learn together."

As the sun peaked in the sky, the boys' stomachs began to growl. Everyone filed out of the study room and returned to the dining hall where another meal had been prepared. Breads, cheeses, and meats adorned the table, accompanied by a large pitcher of water. The boys ate greedily as they all seemed to be adjusting to their new surroundings with ease.

After the midday meal, the boys were dismissed for a period of one hour. Ukiru told them that they were free to do anything while their food settled in their stomachs, but they must assemble in the arena afterwards. Donagh and Horace went back to their rooms to sleep, while Berit left in the direction of the library. Kael left the dining hall in search of the meditation area by the lawn. When he got there, Coen was already seated in the middle of the rock garden.

"You can sit next to me," he offered with a smile.

"No thank you," Kael replied. "He said there were other spots around here; I think I will go look for another one."

Kael turned around and started walking back to the dining hall when he noticed a narrow path to his right. Part of his free time was gone already, so he decided to tour the place by himself and get a better feel for his surroundings. He took the path and found that it curved around the main building through a thick stand of trees and stopped in the front courtyard. A wider stone path ran from the front of the building through the courtyard and out the front gate. Kael followed it and found himself outside of the stone wall which surrounded all of the buildings.

A dirt path broke off from the main thoroughfare and ran to the south. It wasn't a constructed path like the others around the monastery; it was simply an area where repeated foot traffic had worn away the ground cover. Kael took the path and followed it as it swung to the east for a while, running parallel to a ridge that obscured his view of the horizon. Eventually, the path turned south again and began to climb the steep ridge. Kael thought that his time was probably getting short, but now he was curious to see what was beyond the ridge. It took him a few minutes to reach the top of the path and he was breathing heavily by the time he made it.

To the south, as far as the eye could see, the ocean glittered in the midday sun. Kael was surprised by the sight, expecting to see only land and perhaps a few mountains. The path descended from the top of the ridge to a rocky area which marked the edge of a cliff. Kael stood on the rocks and looked down at the water, hundreds of feet below. Until this moment, he wasn't aware of how much he missed the ocean. He would have to come back to this place when he would have more time to enjoy it. Reluctantly, he turned around and followed the path back to the monastery. He tried to walk quickly, even running in places, until he came to the arena. He was almost sure that he had been gone more than an hour, but when he entered the building, there were only a few monks waiting. Within minutes, Ukiru walked into the building, talking with Narian and Rainer. A few minutes later, Coen walked in and came straight over to Kael.

"Did you find your meditation spot?" he asked as soon as he was within earshot.

"Yes," Kael answered with a smile.

One by one, the others came into the building. When all were present, Ukiru directed the group over to a section of the arena with a polished wooden floor. "Each day after the midday meal and your time of rest, you will all come to this building. Here you will be trained in the practices of war. As priests of the All Powerful, you will be persecuted and attacked for your positions of authority. You must all learn to protect yourselves against those that would wish to harm you and rebel against our god. These practices are an ancient art, recorded thousands of years ago and handed down from generation to generation among his faithful servants. As the classroom learning will shape your mind, these practices will shape your body so that your whole being will be a perfectly tuned instrument for the All Powerful."

Kael drew in a deep breath and shifted his weight in anticipation. After a morning of sitting in chairs and listening to Ukiru speak, he was ready to stretch his muscles and use his body instead of his mind.

"Everyone gather around me in a circle."

The boys drew near and Kael could tell by their expressions that they were also excited about the opportunity to train as warriors. When all of the children had gathered around, Ukiru continued speaking.

"All of the stances and positions that you learn during the morning's meditation will be applied to the afternoon lessons. Each position is either an attack or defense posture that will be the basis of your training as a warrior."

As the afternoon advanced into evening, Ukiru explained each stance and its use in warfare. All of the positions, whether attack or defense, were modeled after some animal which demonstrated an ability in nature to defend itself against or advance upon an enemy. All of the boys seemed to prefer the afternoon to the morning, except for Berit, who kept quiet the whole day and didn't show a preference for anything in particular.

When the sun began to slip below the mountains to the west, Ukiru ended their activities and led them back to the dining hall where, once again, the table was set with a meal. The boys ate quickly to replenish the strength expended during the afternoon. Already, some of them were making friends, joking and laughing during the meal. Kael didn't talk to anyone, but sat back and watched the way people interacted with each other. His thoughts drifted back to Bastul where his mother and Saba lived. He hoped that they were well and worried for their safety, having to live with such an evil man as Lemus. Most of all, he wondered where his father was and if he had returned while Kael was away.

When the evening meal concluded, each one of the boys was escorted to his room for the remainder of the night. When Kael got to his room, he immediately crawled into bed and pulled the covers up to his chin. Voices drifted to him from down the hall and Kael realized that not everybody was exhausted. *Oh well. I'll be well rested in the morning and they won't be able to keep their eyes open.*

13

Kael arrived at the *arena* after Coen and Berit, but only had time to say a quick "hello" before the other boys arrived. Ukiru wasted no time and immediately began the morning's exercises. Just as Kael suspected, Donagh, Horace, and Rainer looked as though they hadn't slept at all. During one of the seated positions, Horace actually fell asleep, much to the amusement of the entire group. Ukiru, however, took exception and considered the lack of attention a lack of respect.

"I understand that all of you will need time to adjust to your new life, but I will not tolerate this behavior," he directed to the whole group. "All of you arrived at your rooms in plenty of time to get a sufficient amount of sleep. It would be wise for you to use that time for its intended purpose."

Kael's heart beat loudly in his chest and he felt his face get hot. *It's not fair that the rest of us are scolded for their mistake!* He kept his mouth shut, wanting Ukiru's anger to pass as quickly as possible.

When they resumed their exercises, Rainer kept his face toward the ground, trying to hide his snickering mouth.

Each day of the week continued in the same fashion, with Ukiru familiarizing the children with the daily routines. He explained that their real training wouldn't begin until the start of the following week. In the meantime, the boys had fun acquainting themselves with their surroundings. For six days, they repeated the pattern until the morning meal of the seventh day.

Ukiru sat at the head of the dining table and spoke to the group. "The seventh day of the week is free time for you to do whatever you wish. We will have meditation and the morning meal after which you may retire to your room or spend your time with all manner of activities. There are games that can be played indoors or out. We have a library of books from which you may read. They day is yours to spend as you wish. We will all assemble here in the dining hall at sundown for the evening meal and the rest of the evening will be unscheduled as well. The seventh day is a day of worship unto the All

Powerful and will not be a day for learning anything except to hear his voice speaking quietly to us. I hope that you will spend some of the time in meditation."

The other boys hardly paid any attention to his last words. Everyone was so excited to have a free day that they immediately began to chatter amongst themselves.

Kael, however, was intrigued. *His voice speaking quietly to us? Do gods speak at all?* Ukiru kept talking of this All Powerful as if he were a person, but the gods that Kael learned about in Bastul were just statues. Sometimes people talked to them, but they never talked back. Or sometimes people left food offerings or lit candles for them, but they never gave anything back.

These thoughts quickly gave way to relief at having a break from the routine. When he lived in Bastul, he would study in the morning and have every afternoon as play time. He and Ajani would explore, hunt, fish and occasionally wander into the city where they were not supposed to go. Kael was told that his father's position made it dangerous for him to travel into the city without a guard. Of course, guards only inhibited the boys from doing many of the things they would normally do to occupy their time.

Ukiru's loud but calm voice brought them all back to attention. "Settle down everyone." When the children were quiet he continued. "Your servant will show you what games we have for you to play. Now that the meal is finished, you are free to go."

The table exploded into a frenzy of activity. Most of the boys jumped out of their chairs and rushed out of the room as quickly as possible. Berit rose slowly from his seat, pushed his chair in to the table, and left in the direction of the library. Kael remained seated at the table with Ukiru.

"Do you not wish to join the others?" he asked the child.

"I stayed behind to ask you a question," Kael replied.

"Please," Ukiru said with nod.

"Where..." he began, then paused. *Where are we?* Something told him to keep the question inside. "Do you hunt?" he asked instead.

"Well," Ukiru breathed as he sat back in his chair. "There aren't many things to hunt at this elevation. It would take a whole day to descend into the jungle where the monks do their hunting, but I've heard that there are ground squirrels that live in the rocks a few miles from here. The monks here occasionally hunt the little creatures for the meat. I'm told it is quite a delicacy. Would that suit you?"

"Yes, it would," Kael replied with a smile. "We hunt a lot where I come from."

"Yes, I know. So you are a hunter?"

Kael nodded.

"I am as well. I've not been able to hunt for quite some time. Although, squirrels are not exactly a formidable foe. May I join you?"

"Yes, Sir," Kael replied, unable to contain the excitement in his voice.

"Then we shall make a day of it." Ukiru rose from his chair. "Let's pack a few provisions and I will have one of the monks accompany us on the short journey."

They left the dining hall and within half an hour, Kael, Ukiru, and one of the robed servants were walking across the valley northeast of the monastery, choosing to go on foot rather than take the horses. Pale grass crunched beneath their feet as they walked. The cool morning air felt strange in Kael's lungs but it smelled sweeter and was more refreshing than the salty ocean air of Bastul. They quickly descended into the valley below and came upon a small river, flowing back to the south. Ukiru pointed out that this fresh water continued south until it fell off a cliff and into the ocean. They turned to the north and headed upstream into a forest of short pine trees. Crossing the river at a low, rocky shelf, they continued their ascent up the other side of the valley where the river narrowed to just a stream. As the sun crept higher into the sky, they left the water's edge and climbed east until they reached a bank of rocks, exposed by the eroding soil.

The silent monk simply pointed at the bank.

Ukiru nodded. "This is the place."

They stopped and laid their provisions next to a tree. The monk laid out weapons for the hunt and beckoned for Ukiru and Kael to come over and choose what they wished to use. Ukiru put his hand out, indicating that Kael should go first. Then he stood back and watched.

Kael looked at the assortment of weapons on the ground—a crossbow with a bundle of bolts, a spear, a sling with a leather bag of shot, and a bow accompanied by a quiver of arrows.

"What are you going to use?" he asked Ukiru.

"Well, they are small, fast creatures. I think I will use the crossbow for speed and accuracy."

"Me too."

"I'm sorry but we only brought one of each. Had you chosen first, the crossbow would have been available to you. Now you must choose between the other three."

Kael thought for a moment and then bent down, grabbing hold of the spear.

"Are you sure that is the best choice?"

Kael stopped, reconsidering the positives and negatives of each weapon. Then he shrugged his shoulders. "This will work. I'm good with a spear."

Ukiru smiled as if he wanted to say something, but didn't.

When they had chosen their weapons, Ukiru and Kael set off in search of their prey with the monk following at a close distance, carrying a quiver and a few other provisions. Kael wasn't sure of how to approach these animals, so he stayed close to Ukiru and followed his lead. Ukiru led the hunting party up a collapsed section of the rocks and then began to traverse the shelf above.   He explained quietly that the ground squirrels could be seen scurrying from the shelter of the rocks to forage for food. They would be quick and their dusty brown fur was a perfect camouflage for this rocky terrain. They walked for almost an hour before any sign of movement.

All of a sudden, Kael noticed a small brown shape dart out from the rocks.   He raised his spear and waited for the rodent to turn around and come back before throwing his spear. The squirrel, startled by the sound above, sprang to the right as the spear struck the ground only inches away. It paused for a second before heading for the safety of the rocks.

Ukiru took aim and loosed his bolt, pinning the animal to the ground.

The three hunters scrambled down the rocks and gathered up their prey. The monk placed the squirrel in a cloth bag and slung it over his back.

Ukiru patted Kael on the back. "That was excellent. You have very quick reflexes."

"Thanks," Kael replied, even more determined to catch his prey.

They continued to hunt along the rocky slopes until the sun had passed its zenith.   When they turned around and began to make their way back to the starting point, Kael chose to walk along the bottom of the rock wall, several yards behind Ukiru who stayed on top. Along the way Kael remained silent, scanning the rocks for another chance.

"You were about to ask me something this morning," Ukiru called down.

Kael wrinkled his eyebrows.

"At breakfast," he continued. "You were about to ask me a question, but you mentioned hunting instead."

Kael was surprised that he had noticed. "Where am I?" he finally asked.

Ukiru smiled. "You will know in time. For now, I will say that you are a long way from Bastul."

"Why is it a secret?" Kael asked.

"Because you need to forget about your old life. You must come to see this place as your home and all of us as your new family. The more you think about Bastul, the harder it will be for you to adjust to this place."

Suddenly, movement at the corner of Kael's vision interrupted the conversation.   Ukiru raised his crossbow, but Kael had already sighted the rodent and thrown his spear. The animal rolled to its side, pierced by the spear, and slid to a stop in the dirt.

Kael looked to Ukiru whose eyebrows were raised.

The hunting party gathered the remainder of the provisions next to the tree and headed back to the monastery with two squirrels to show for their efforts. Kael was finally starting to feel comfortable in his new surroundings, although he hadn't really made friends with anyone yet, like some of the other children. Coen seemed friendly, but then again, he was friendly with everyone. It was comforting for him to hunt; it reminded him of his normal life in Bastul.

The return trip took less time, and was considerably easier than climbing the valley earlier in the morning. No one spoke the entire way back and Kael was perfectly content to follow the other two men, listening only to the sounds of nature and a few quiet footsteps. The monastery was also silent when they returned and Kael couldn't help wondering where all of the other children were. The monk took the squirrels and promised Kael that the meat would be part of the evening meal.

"You should wash up, it will be evening soon." With that, Ukiru excused himself.

After washing his face and hands in the bathing room, Kael went to his room to change his clothes. He felt himself rushing in order to get back outside and find out where the other children were. He quickly found a fresh tunic and rushed downstairs, pulling it on as he went. He wandered for several minutes before entering the library where he found Berit sitting by a window. The large, dust-covered book on his lap suggested that he had been there for quite some time.

"Have you been in here all day?"

Berit looked up from his reading with a startled look on his face. It was apparent that he had grown accustomed to the privacy and silence. "Yeah," was all he said in return.

Kael waited a few minutes, hoping that the other boy might elaborate on what he was reading. When nothing happened, Kael realized that Berit might not be the best person for striking up a conversation.

"Do you know where the others are?"

Berit looked at Kael without lifting his head. "I think some are out back," he said with a nod. "I heard them earlier."

"Thanks." Kael tried not to look hurried when he left the library. Even though he had been gone all day with Ukiru, he was beginning to feel like he had been left out of something. He exited the building and circled around to the back, but was disappointed to find that the back of the building butted up to the wall which surrounded the whole monastery. Kael turned around and made his way to the front courtyard, exiting through the front gate, but there was still no sign of the other children. Then he remembered the cliffs overlooking the ocean that he found on the second day after his arrival. He hadn't been back since that day and decided to wander in that direction. As he neared the ridge to the south, he heard laughter. He stopped walking and waited a few minutes before he heard it again and realized that the sound was coming from the other side of the ridge.

By the time he reached the top he was winded, but the ocean view made the climb worth the effort. The sound of laughter drew his attention to the right and he could see Donagh, Horace, Arden, and Coen gathered around a pile of small stones. As he walked toward them, Horace threw a rock toward a stick planted in the ground. His stone flew wide of the target and landed in the sand. Horace stepped back and Coen, who had already chosen his stone from the pile, stepped forward.

"What are you guys doing?"

"We're trying to see who can hit the stick first," Horace replied, as he walked to the pile and chose another rock. "Do you want to try?"

"Sure," Kael said with a smile.

"Grab a rock and you can go after me," said Donagh.

Coen's attempt fell short and Donagh stepped forward. He took a few hops to gain momentum and heaved a rock the size of his fist toward the target. It landed with a dull thud at the base of the stick and moved it slightly.

"That's the closest one so far," Arden said. "Now it's your turn, Kael."

Kael had been watching the others and had forgotten to choose a rock. He quickly picked the first one his hand closed around and stepped up to the line dug in the dirt.

"Your foot can't cross the line," Donagh said, his competitive nature showing through.

"Okay," Kael replied, inching back more than necessary from the line. The rock he had chosen was shaped strangely and didn't fit well in his hand. He threw it anyway and it flew over the stick and bounced in the dirt.

The minutes passed and the pile of stones shrank with every attempt. The other boys were starting to grow bored of the game. When it came time for Horace to try again, he ran across the line with his arm cocked. Coen began to laugh as Horace stopped only a few strides short of the stick and threw the rock as hard as he could only to miss it completely. Exhausted with his wasted effort, he collapsed on the ground in a fit of laughter. Soon everyone joined in and all of the boys rolled on the ground clutching their stomachs. When the laughter subsided, they all stayed lying on the ground looking up at the few wispy clouds high overhead.

"Where were you today?" asked Arden.

"Who, me?" Kael replied.

"Yeah, we haven't seen you since this morning."

Kael hesitated. "Uh...I went hunting squirrels with Ukiru."

The other boys rolled over and looked at him. "Where did you go?" asked Coen.

"Up the other side of the valley." Kael could see the jealousy in their eyes. "One of the monks took us. We should all go next week," he quickly added.

"Yeah. That would be..." Coen began, but Donagh interrupted.

"We should be getting back. It's almost time for the evening meal."

At his words the other boys got to their feet. As they started to walk back toward the top of the hill, Kael decided to try one more time to hit the target. He knelt at the pile and moved the rocks aside, searching for just the right one.

"Come on, we need to get back," Coen yelled.

"I'll be there in just a second," Kael yelled back. "Just one more try." As he looked down at the pile, his hand closed around a smooth rock. It was elliptical in shape and narrow, growing sharp at the edges. He held it up for a second to inspect the shape and could almost feel how it would fly. He stood up and faced the target, imagining the way it would arc through air and curve slightly in the wind. He stepped forward and threw it, feeling it spin off his pointer finger and cut through the wind just as he imagined.

CRACK!

The stone hit the stick and cut it in half.

Kael stared in disbelief.

"Whoa! How did you do that?" Coen yelled, running back down the hill toward the severed stick.

Kael ran toward the target and arrived just after Coen, who was holding the top part of the stick for inspection. The cut was smooth halfway through the stick where the rock had impacted, while the back of the stick was splintered.

"Good throw," Coen said, patting Kael on the back.

Kael looked up the hill to see if the others had witnessed it, but they had already crested the hill and started down the other side.

"Wait till they see this," Coen said, running off in the direction of the others.

The midmorning sunlight streamed through the window of the study where Lemus sat at a desk strewn with papers. The quill stood upright in the ink pot, untouched. This room, as well as all of the others in the house, overlooked the bay of Bastul. It was difficult to get any work done with such a majestic view just outside of the window. Lemus sat back in his chair and placed his hands behind his head. Closing his eyes, he let the sounds of the ocean occupy his attention. The position of Governor had, so far, proven to be more difficult than he had originally expected. Not only did he have the rotation of soldiers to plan out, always keeping a state of readiness for the defense of the city, but it also seemed as though someone always needed his attention. Whether it was a ruling on some minor matter, or his presence at some occasion, he always had a list of things to do. After only a few short weeks it was all becoming a big headache to him.

As he allowed the slight breeze coming through the window to wash his thoughts away, a knock came at the door. The soldier who stood guard next to the door turned and unlatched the bolt. The motion startled Lemus who had forgotten that anyone else was in the room. The door swung open to reveal two men escorted by another soldier. The guard looked back to Lemus who waved his hand for the men to be let in.

As the two men came into the room, Lemus sized them up in a matter of seconds, deciding that they were not a threat. Even if they did something unexpected, it would be three trained soldiers against these two, who looked like priests. They were dressed in long dark robes that covered everything except for their faces.

"Sir. These men asked to speak with you. They are unarmed." The soldier stepped to the side, his escort duty complete, and watched the men cautiously.

"What do you gentlemen want?"

One of the robed men stepped forward, bowing his head. "Are you the Governor?"

Lemus was silent for a second, not expecting to have to answer questions. "Of course I'm the Governor! What do you want?" he repeated louder.

"I apologize, Sir. I just want to be sure that I'm dealing with the highest authority in the city."

Lemus nodded his head for the man to continue.

"We are looking for a man that we are told lives here. He goes by the name Saba."

Lemus laughed. "He did live here, but he was escorted off the premises a few weeks ago. What do you want with him?"

"Our employer wishes to speak with him."

Lemus smiled. "Sounds like trouble. Well, I'd be happy to pass on trouble to that meddling old man. He has many friends in the area, but the Captain of the Guard could probably steer you in the right direction." Lemus turned to the men's escort. "Take these men to the Captain; make sure they have everything they require."

"Yes, Sir," the soldier replied.

The two robed men bowed their heads to Lemus. "Thank you for your hospitality."

Lemus nodded his head and watched as the escort led the men out of the room. When they entered the hallway, Lemus noticed Maeryn standing to the side holding a tray. "Bring her in here," he said to his guard.

"Yes, Sir," came the reply.

As Maeryn came into the room, she moved through a shaft of light next to the doorway. For a split second, Lemus could see the outline of her bare skin through the fabric of her tunic. Just as quickly as it appeared, the vision vanished, leaving Lemus in a state of shock. Had it not been for her, he might not have asked to take Adair's position.

"I thought you might like something to eat. You've been working all morning without a break." Maeryn set a tray of sweet bread on his desk, on top of the papers he should have been working on.

Lemus stared at the bread and then eyed Maeryn suspiciously. "Thank you. I was starting to get hungry." He continued to stare at her, but was more than a little distracted by her bright blue eyes and fair skin. She was so different from any other woman he had seen. "What's wrong now," he said, when he came to his senses.

"What do you mean?" she asked.

"Why the sudden change of heart—bringing me something to eat? I suppose it's poisoned and you're trying to kill me."

"No," she protested.

He interrupted what she was about to say. "I have spies everywhere and if I even hear a whisper of a rumor about you trying to harm me, I won't even wait for the jailers to carry out your execution. I'll kill you myself."

"No...of course I wouldn't try anything. It's just..." she trailed off. "I've been thinking a lot lately."

"About what," he asked, interrupting her again.

"I've really...it has been difficult for me to adjust to being without Adair. But all that has changed and I want to start over with you. By law, you are my husband now and I will respect that. My former husband abandoned me for some reason and left his responsibilities behind. Those are not the actions of a respectable man of Orud. I know that now. Anyway, I thought you might be hungry."

Lemus continued to stare at her for a moment, looking for signs of deceit. He considered himself to be a good judge of things like that. But instead of lies, he saw only beauty. "It's good that you have finally accepted the truth. Adair was a coward and did not serve the Empire well. I have much work to do, so if you will excuse me," he said, motioning for the guard to open the door. "Thank you for the bread."

The soldier closed the door after Maeryn left and returned to his guard position. It was silent in the room for a moment as Lemus inspected the slices of sweet bread arranged on the tray. "Come here," he commanded the soldier.

"Yes, Sir," replied the man who quickly came to Lemus' side.

"Eat this," Lemus said, handing him a slice of bread.

The soldier hesitated, unsure of whether or not this would violate any rules of conduct.

"Go on," Lemus insisted.

The guard took the piece of bread from Lemus' hand and stuffed the whole slice in his mouth and chewed quickly.

After the guard swallowed the bread, pretending not to enjoy it, Lemus rose from his chair and stepped back. "How do you feel?"

"Good, Sir."

"How is the bread?" Lemus questioned further. "It's alright, you can tell me."

The guard was visibly uncomfortable with the whole situation. He finally answered. "It's good, Sir. ...very sweet."

Lemus stared at him for a moment, expecting the soldier to drop dead at any time. When nothing happened, he sat down at his desk and greedily ate the whole plate of bread.

Maeryn had been nervous all day, hoping that her words had done the job. She was certain they had the moment she left Lemus sitting at his desk, but as the day wore on, she began to lose her certainty. As night fell, she prepared herself for bed in one of the spare rooms at the end of the hall. Lemus had long ago confiscated her bedroom and claimed it for his own. She combed her hair and braided it loosely. A small part of her really wondered if Adair had left on purpose. But just as quick as the thought came, it vanished in the face of logic. *That's impossible. He loved us very much. It was the Empire that took him away.* Maybe they didn't know where he was, but they were definitely responsible for his disappearance.

Suddenly, Maeryn was aware that the door to her room was open. She turned to see Lemus standing in the doorway. He looked startled, as if he had been watching for a while and had just been spotted. If that was the case, he tried not to show it.

"You shouldn't sleep in here anymore," he said, walking forward a few steps.

"But I thought you said..."

"Never mind that. Wouldn't it be nice to sleep in your own bed again?"

She doubted that he cared about her quality of sleep. She had prepared herself for this moment and knew exactly what to do. "Yes. I miss sleeping in my own bed." She rose to her feet and followed Lemus to the master bedroom. When she entered the room he closed and locked the door.

I'm not going anywhere. If anyone is setting a trap here, it's me.

When Lemus turned around Maeryn was standing close. She reached up and placed her hands gently on his face. He instinctively bent down and kissed her. Maeryn felt like she would throw-up and took a deep breath to clear her mind. *I planned for this to happen.*

Lemus walked her over to the bed and sat her down. When he began to take off his tunic she started to panic. *Can I really do this?* The question hung in her mind, waiting for an answer. She took another deep breath. *Of course I can; I have to. I have no other choice!* It wasn't any comfort, but it worked. She watched Lemus pull off his tunic and untie his loincloth. He was skinny and looked even more repulsive without his clothes. Somehow the whole scene was funny and she was able to think more clearly when she concentrated on the humor and nothing else.

This is just the first step. Win him over tonight and you'll have him. You've got a baby to think about now, a baby that needs a safe place to live. Eventually he'll grow comfortable with you and that's when you'll make your move.

14

Saba turned from the western road and headed northeast into the hills, making his way on foot as the sun began to set. The outskirts of Bastul were populated by farmers who were attending to various tasks outside, trying to make the most of the daylight. Most of these hardworking people waved to Saba as he passed along the road and he couldn't help but think of the contrast in lifestyles between the city and country folk. These farmers worked from sunrise to sunset, sometimes even longer. But within the city, the workday had already ended hours ago so that the citizens of Bastul could enjoy baths and leisure time before their evening meals.

The small dirt path wound through the foothills for a short distance before cutting into a deep canyon dividing the mountain range. The setting sun cast strong shadows that separated the canyon into areas of intense orange light and patches of complete darkness. By the time the path climbed out of the canyon and leveled out into an area of rolling meadows, the sun had dropped behind the ocean. Saba turned off the road and followed a walking path between fields of mature lettuce and cabbage, ready to be harvested.

Just as expected, Trenus was still outside, washing the soil from his hands at the well. It was difficult to see in the fading light, but he was a short, sturdy man, with light brown hair. His clothing, like all country folk, was similar to what a slave might wear. His tunic, now stained with dirt from a hard day's work, was not made of white linen, but a coarser, thicker material that would stand up against the harsh lifestyle. His sandals were not really sandals at all, but boots that covered his feet completely and laced on the top of the foot. Trenus waved as soon as he caught sight of Saba. It took a few minutes before they were within earshot of each other and by that time, he had finished washing his hands.

"Are you hungry?" he asked.

"Starving. I've been walking most of the day."

Trenus smiled. "I've got a stew going. Come inside."

The main house was a humble wood building with tiled roof and walls plastered on the inside. The layout was a departure from most houses in this region. There were only a few doors off the main living area and it contained a limited amount of practical furniture. Obviously, Trenus had built this place for function only.

"Have a seat." Trenus pointed to a table on the opposite side of the room. It was situated only a few feet from the stove, upon which a pot of stew simmered.

"Thank you," Saba replied, slumping into the chair, grateful to be off of his feet. Once he caught his breath, he looked around the room. He had only been here for an hour a few days ago to drop off his belongings before he went back to the city to check on Maeryn. He felt bad now at barging in on Trenus, though it didn't look as if it hindered his life one bit.

"What does that look mean?" Trenus asked, looking back at Saba while stirring the stew.

Saba decided to give him an honest answer. "This place needs a woman's touch."

"Yeah, I know. Maybe some day it will have that. But for now, I kind of like it."

Saba nodded his head. "I must say, it is...efficient."

Trenus laughed. "That's one way to say it." He brought two bowls of steaming food over to the table and set them down. Pulling back his chair, Trenus was about to sit down when he realized that he had forgotten the spoons. "Oops," he said, turning around to grab those as well. "I'm not used to entertaining company." He handed one to Saba.

"That's quite all right. Thank you, by the way, for letting me stay here."

Trenus waived his hand in dismissal. "Never mind that. Tell me how it went, though it seems obvious by your quick return."

"I only made it as far as the Market District before I was spotted."

"Soldiers?" Trenus asked. "And they let you go?"

"Yes. I think I've worn out my welcome."

The room was silent for a few minutes as the men began to eat their food.

Eventually, Saba looked up, wiping stew from his beard. "It looks like I will have to find something else to do."

"Well...you know you're welcome to stay here as long as you need?"

"Thank you. I guess I'll unpack my things tonight."

Trenus pointed at a door to the right of the stove. "That's my only empty room and it's used mostly for storage, so you'll have to forgive the mess."

"I'm sure it will be just fine. Thank you."

Several minutes passed before Trenus got up to refill his bowl. He offered to do the same for Saba, but the old man politely refused. "I've got so much on my mind that it has ruined my appetite."

"Are you sure it's not the stew?" Trenus asked, his face wrinkling into a smile.

Saba couldn't help but laugh. "No, it's not the food. Actually, you could probably make quite a living in the city selling your meals." Saba suddenly felt relieved. Trenus had a way of lightening the mood that made for easy conversation.

"So," Trenus began. "Even though we've been acquainted for years, I still don't really know much about you."

"What would you like to know?" Saba asked.

"I've never asked you how old you are."

"No, you haven't," Saba replied with a smile, trying to match the man's sense of humor.

Trenus laughed before rephrasing his statement into a question. "Okay. How old are you?"

Saba looked down at the table. "Actually, I'm not sure."

"What do you mean? It's a simple question."

Saba looked up and smiled. "Yes...for most people, it is a simple question. But I'm one of the exceptions."

Trenus took his seat and began to eat from his second bowl of food, still carrying a puzzled look on his face.

Saba decided to make the attempt to enlighten him, though he was hesitant about sharing this information. "I've actually never told anyone this before."

"Well, I'm honored," Trenus replied. "But please, continue."

Saba leaned back in his chair and crossed his right leg over his left, settling into a comfortable position that seemed to imply a long story would follow. "My first memory is of waking up inside a small, tent-like structure. I found myself lying on a bed of animal skins, clothed in a soft leather robe. There were no other people in the tent, so I just lay there, taking in my surroundings. Hours must have passed before I tried to sit up. It seemed like something I should be able to do, but when I tried, my body wouldn't respond." Saba looked up at the ceiling, trying to recall the details. "A few minutes later, a young woman came into the tent. She had long black hair and dark skin and was dressed the same as myself. I immediately wondered if I was an elder of this woman's tribe. I only thought of being an elder because I could see my own hair, which was already white at that point, reaching down to my waist. Indeed, she moved about the tent as if I was supposed to be there. I don't know why, but I felt compelled to get her attention. Without the use of my body, I felt frustrated. For some reason, it took a long time before I realized that I could try speaking. I called out to her, but my words only came out as a grunt. When she heard me, she spun around, startled. She looked at me as if I was a ghost and her skin became pale. Once she got the courage, she ran out of the tent, screaming at the top of her lungs. What shocked me more than my encounter with this woman was the fact that I knew she was screaming a foreign language, but I understood every word. She kept saying, over and over, 'He is awake. The old one is awake.'"

Trenus set his spoon carefully into his bowl and leaned back in his chair. He had completely forgotten about eating and was now staring at Saba with his full attention. "How long ago was this?"

"Twenty years."

Trenus' eyebrows shot up. "You were already an old man back then..." he trailed off, trying to make sense of the story.

"I can see that if I tell you the whole story, you might end up more confused than me. So I'll try to skip to the point. Apparently I had been living with these people for some time. They were a nomadic tribe, following herds of wild animals and living off of what they hunted. I tried to ask them how long I had been with them, but they didn't seem to understand. I asked them if they understood the passage of seasons and if they did, to make a mark in the dirt for every full cycle that I had been with them. The younger people all looked to an old man who was the elder of the tribe. He began to draw lines in the dirt."

"How many?" Trenus blurted out.

"Nearly one hundred."

The room was silent for a while, before Saba spoke again. "Of course, his answer would be impossible. I don't think he understood my question. Although they understood seasons, they had almost no knowledge of past generations of their own people. They concerned themselves only with the present. So...as you can see, I'm not sure."

"And you have no memory of anything before?"

"Nothing," Saba replied.

After minutes of silence, Trenus shook his head. "I've never heard of something so strange."

Saba lifted his hands and shrugged his shoulders. "I agree with you. But that's all I know."

"What brought you to Bastul? I assume that all of this took place somewhere else?"

"Yes it did, in another country," Saba replied, answering Trenus' last question first. "I began having dreams about a place that I had never seen. The dreams compelled me to search. I kept moving, staying with different people until the terrain around me matched what I saw in my dreams."

"And that place was here?"

"Yes, in Bastul."

After the meal, Trenus helped Saba move his belongings from the barn into the spare room. Trenus insisted on doing most of the work, handing a candle to Saba and telling him that lighting the way was all that was necessary. The work was completed in under an hour and when the last crate had been moved, Trenus bid Saba goodnight and headed to his bedroom.

Though he had walked for almost an entire day, Saba's mind was still racing with worry about Maeryn and he knew that sleep would not come easily. So, he decided to unpack his essentials and spent several minutes just trying to make heads or tails of how the soldiers packed his things. He finally located his clothing and laid it out in piles on the floor as there was no chest to put it in. In fact, there was no furniture in the room at all and Saba laughed to himself about what he would do for a bed. His belongings were either packed hastily in wooden crates, or thrown into linen bags and he knew that unpacking everything was too ambitious a project for one evening. Instead, he grabbed the nearest bag and began to untie the top. It rustled as if it was filled with paper and after opening the top and removing a few handfuls of its contents, that guess was confirmed. There were papers and writing utensils and even a book. Saba realized that this bag contained everything that used to reside on his desktop in his bedroom. Several of the papers were smudged with half-dried ink from the tips of the writing quills. Luckily, Saba was in the habit of corking the ink pot after every use, or this whole bag would likely be a dripping mess.

Reaching down into the bag, his hand settled on a rolled up piece of parchment. He pulled it out and questions immediately came to his mind as he couldn't remember putting anything like this on his desk. Turning it over in his hands, he saw that it was tied with a thread to keep its rolled shape. With his curiosity peaked, he quickly slid the thread off the tube of parchment and unrolled it, wondering how he could have missed this sitting on his desk.

> Saba,
>
> Something terrible has happened to an acquaintance of mine. I am looking into the matter, but have been unsuccessful in finding any useful information to this point. The only clue that I have thus far is this arrowhead. I leave it in your possession to find out what you can about the people who made it. I have been unable to find any meaning in it and would, therefore, be grateful for any information that would aid me in my searching.
>
> Gratefully,
> Adair

Saba put the parchment down and grabbed the bag, turning it upside down and shaking it to empty the contents. A few more papers fell out, but no arrowhead. He quickly rifled through the other bags that were present, shaking them to determine their contents until he found one that made a knocking noise when he set it on the floor. He untied the bag and dumped the contents onto the floor. Amid a shower of dried leaves and feathers, something heavy fell out of the bag and landed with a thump on the floor. He pushed aside the growing pile of debris until he found the arrowhead. Moving it closer to the candle, he turned it over in his hands, inspecting every feature. The construction was similar to what the Orud military used, a metal head sharpened to a double-edged point, set into the shaft and held in place with a metal pin that extended through the whole arrangement. The pin and shaft were both wrapped tightly with silk thread that wound around the base of the head. The silk was frayed in a few places and was starting to unravel. Saba sat down on the floor and picked at the thread, until it was completely unwrapped. As he started to pull the head from the shaft, he noticed a circular engraving in the wood that was covered by the thread. At first glance, it looked like a wreath. But upon closer inspection, Saba could see what looked like winged creatures gathered around in a circle with their wing tips touching.

Saba put the arrowhead down and sat back. For the first time in his life, he felt a twinge of memory, a link to his forgotten past. It was a faint feeling and didn't provoke anything specific, but he had the sense that he had seen this symbol before.

Three weeks had passed since Kael arrived at the monastery. So far, he was enjoying himself, though he missed his family. He wondered if his father had ever returned. His thoughts often drifted to his mother, who was probably very sad to be missing her husband and her son. Sometimes at night, when everyone else was asleep, Kael would lie awake and picture his mother and father standing in front of him. He would tell them that he was okay and that he was being taken care of. He would try to explain all of the things he was learning and how Ukiru said that they would be the best-educated children in all of the Empire, maybe even the whole world. He knew they couldn't hear him, but maybe his thoughts would somehow find their way back to Bastul and they would be comforted. He always hoped.

Except for missing his family, Kael couldn't have imagined a better place to live. The morning exercises were becoming a way of meditation, just as Ukiru said. In the silence of the sunrise, Kael found that it was easy to lose himself in the peacefulness of feeling his body move in harmony with his surroundings. Most of the other boys still joked with each other the whole time, but he just tried to ignore them. The midmorning studies were fun, but they weren't as fun as learning from Saba. Still, Ukiru was a very good teacher. But Kael's favorite part of the day was the physical activity in the afternoon.

The sun was bright through the open doors and the air was warmer than usual. Just as every other weekday, Kael stood with the other boys in the arena, facing Ukiru.

"For several weeks now, you have learned how to move your body and breathe steadily to create a strong center of balance. Some of you have grown bored with these exercises. But I assure you that they are necessary. Now that you have a basic understanding of balance, we will progress to defense."

Kael's attention was peaked at the man's words. It was obvious that the other children were excited as well.

"Everyone spread out. Each of you will be paired with an attacker." Ukiru walked among the boys, directing their steps until each child had plenty of room around him. A group of monks, who had been standing off to the side, now joined in, each facing one of the children. "The man in front of you is your partner. In a few minutes, he will try to attack you, and if you have paid attention to what you were supposed to be learning to this point, you will avoid his attack."

Kael's heart quickened slightly at the thought of confrontation. He wasn't sure what to expect.

"Your defensive position for this exercise will be the one you learned during our morning meditation called Tiger. Assume this position now." At Ukiru's command all of the boys leaned back and brought their hands up in front of their bodies. "Rainer, what does a tiger do?"

The boy looked around, unsure of the correct answer.

"It crouches," whispered Coen.

"Thank you, Coen," Ukiru said with a stern face. "A tiger crouches to be ready at any moment to spring into action."

"Oh," Rainer said aloud as he realized he was standing straight-legged. He quickly bent his knees and looked at the others to make sure he was in proper position.

"Very good," said Ukiru. "Now, your attacker will rush at you and try to grab you. From this position," Ukiru demonstrated, "you will lift your back foot and lunge one giant step backwards." One of the monks, at Ukiru's signal, rushed forward, trying to grab his clothing. Ukiru jumped backwards just as he instructed and evaded the attacker's hands. His quick and graceful movements made it look easy. "Now it's your turn."

Kael loosened his stance and made sure that his knees were not locked. He waited for Ukiru's signal and the attacker lunged as soon as it was given. Kael was expecting more of a delay, but was still able to easily avoid his attacker. Arden was not so lucky. His attacker grabbed him before he could move and he ended up tripping over his own feet. Sounds of muffled laughter could be heard as he got back to his feet.

"Once more," Ukiru said. "Back into position. Everyone ready? Go."

Once again the monk grabbed at Kael, but this time he was better prepared and was able to get much more distance between himself and the attacker.

"Very good," Ukiru commented, when he saw that everyone completed the exercise successfully. "Now if you will notice, jumping backwards only gives you a little more time before your attacker reaches you. Even though you have evaded him, he can simply keep advancing toward you. And I have never met anyone who could run backward fast enough to outrun someone who is moving forward. So, this time we will jump to the right using the same technique." Ukiru motioned for his attacker to advance and easily jumped to the side, returning to his crouching defensive position. "Now you do it. Ready? Go."

This time Kael's attacker got close to catching him and when he was finished, a quick look around the room showed that he was not the only one. Horace was straightening his clothing after being grabbed by his partner.

"Do it again, but notice that you are moving to the side and not backward. You will not have as much time to get out of the way. Instead of reacting, try to anticipate your attacker's move. Bend your knees and be ready. Wait for the slightest sign of movement, then spring out of the way. Get in position."

Kael watched the attacker's feet, waiting for Ukiru's signal. Suddenly, the monk sprang forward and Kael jumped out of the way, barely missing the grasping hands. "Very good. Some of you were ready. Do it again. This time don't wait for my signal, watch your attacker."

The second time Jorn failed to evade his attacker, but the third time, everyone was successful. As the afternoon progressed they learned to evade their advancing attacker by jumping in combinations of different directions.

At the end of their time each child was breathing heavily and Ukiru had them line up once more. "You all did well today. Some of you may have noticed that when evading to the side, your attacker left himself exposed and vulnerable on that side. What you learned today is the basis for a counter attack. But that will have to wait until tomorrow. Go and get washed up for the evening meal. You are dismissed."

As each of the boys walked unhurriedly toward the main building, the monks stepped back and lined up near the door. Kael's heart was beating rapidly when he walked out into the open air. The sun was beginning to set and the air had grown cold, but it felt good to his overheated skin. The evening meal tasted better than anything Kael had ever eaten and when it came time to retire to his bedroom, he was unable to keep himself awake to think about how much he missed his family. He didn't have much time to think of anything at all before his eyes closed and he fell into the deepest sleep he could remember.

Maeryn lay awake in the early morning hours, watching the moon-shadows dance along the wall. The nauseous feeling in her stomach woke her and it was just the moment she had been waiting for. She spent many nights lying next to this evil man trying to decide how to tell him that she was pregnant; to convince him that the child was his. There was no way to tell how he would react. Eventually, she realized that the best way to break the news was to let him find out by himself, to make it appear as if the two of them were discovering it together. Shortly after arriving at this decision, the sickness went away and Maeryn began to lose hope that things would go her way. That was one week ago. But tonight, the nausea returned, and the feeling was strangely welcome.

She climbed out of the bed, being careful not to wake Lemus. She had planned the whole event and if he woke now, it would ruin everything. She tiptoed her way to the bathing room and found the toilet. Breathing heavily, Maeryn flexed her stomach to make it irritated. It took a while and she began to wonder if anything would happen at all, but finally her stomach obeyed and she began to gag. After a few seconds passed, she could hear Lemus stirring in the bed. *He's probably annoyed at the disturbance of his sleep.* She decided to make it louder so that there was no chance of him falling back to sleep. Her stomach heaved again and she did her best to make it as loud as possible. After several minutes, Lemus was standing in the doorway.

"What's wrong?" he asked in a muffled voice.

"I'm sick," Maeryn mumbled between gags, trying to look as pathetic as possible. It wasn't difficult under the circumstances.

"Well that's obvious isn't it," he shot back, his irritation never too far below the surface of his personality. "Why are you sick...is it something you ate?"

"I don't think so." She hesitated, wanting him to draw it out of her.

"Well, what's the problem then?"

"I think I'm with child."

Lemus stared at her with a blank look on his face. "How long has this been going on?"

Maeryn lifted her head from its drooped position and looked him in the eye. "A few days," she lied. "I thought it would go away, but it hasn't."

"That's ridiculous. There is no..."

"It usually happens in the morning," she interrupted, trying to distract him from his train of thought. "...but sometimes at night."

Lemus stood speechless for a moment and Maeryn secretly rejoiced at the way everything was turning out. "I have work to do in the morning," he finally blurted out, but with less conviction than she was used to hearing in his voice. "I'm going back to bed."

As Maeryn listened to his retreating footsteps, she knew that it had worked. Not one word was mentioned of Adair. In fact, it seemed that Lemus had all but forgotten about him. If he acted as she expected he would, it would be days before he would revisit the subject. *He won't like the idea of having a child at first. But when he accepts the fact that it will happen regardless of how he feels, he'll change his opinion. In a few days, he'll come bursting into the room, talking about the legacy he will leave to his children, as if the whole thing was his idea in the first place.* Maeryn had never been the type of person to manipulate others, but now it was a matter of survival. Her old life was gone, forever changed. This was her life now and it was horrible for the most part. But like Zula said, she would have to change the way she looked at the world, to find little things to make her happy. And, she had to admit despite her new position in life, she felt more powerful than she ever did before...and that made her happy.

15

In the grandest library in all the Empire the smell of old parchment hung in the air, unable to clear out from the lack of ventilation. But that is exactly what one would want out of a suitable library. The old documents needed to be kept away from the elements, protected from sunlight and air. Saba sat alone at a stone table amid rows of shelving that reached to the thirty foot arched ceilings. The journey to Orud had been exhausting, taking months, but Saba was no stranger to travel. It seemed that most of his life, what he could manage to remember, had been spent moving from one place to another. His arrival in Bastul marked the longest stretch of stillness, but that had now passed. Though tiring, Saba had grown accustomed to the peacefulness of traveling through the land. So accustomed, in fact, that if he spent too much time indoors he began to grow restless.

Well, you'd better get used to being restless, old man! You're going to be here for a while. He pulled a thick book off the top of the stack to his right and set it down in front of himself. It contained paintings of the numerous crests of the most important families in the Orudan Empire. Saba thought that it would be a good place to start looking for a match to the symbol on the arrowhead. As he leafed through the pages, his mind began to wander. There was something about that symbol that seemed familiar, but he had been unable to figure it out during his travels.

One painting made him pause in mid thought, but it was only a likeness of an eagle and he began to turn the pages again. He picked up the trail of his last thought and retraced the steps that brought him here. Unable to remember anything about the symbol, he decided instead to research the arrowhead itself. The construction was typical of what the Orud military used, so he had the idea of searching through the family crests for a lead. But so far, it had proven useless. He reached the end of the book and closed it, frustrated with the lack of progress. He had been here for two days already and without results.

I need to try a different approach. Saba rose to his feet and began to walk down the aisles of books, hoping that something would jump out at him.

After a few minutes, he found himself lingering near a section that documented the various religions of the regions that the Empire had conquered. *It wouldn't be a religious symbol would it?* He picked up one of the books and quickly turned a few pages, immediately seeing an improvement. Most of the content was text, but the few drawings were much more similar in style than what he had been looking at before. He set the book back on the shelf. *Something older, more elaborate perhaps.* He walked further down the aisle and slowly, the documents turned from books to scrolls. They were not labeled like the books, so he grabbed an armful and headed back to his table.

It was tedious work going through the scrolls, untying and unraveling them, only to find that they were also a dead end. After several hours of searching, Saba decided to go back to his room at a nearby Inn and get some rest. Perhaps tomorrow would bring better results. After placing all of the scrolls and books back in the places that he found them, Saba climbed the stairs leading up to the first level of the library. There was no light coming in from the windows and the custodian waved to him from behind his candle lit desk.

"Will I see you tomorrow?" he called out.

"First thing in the morning," Saba replied, waving as he headed for the entrance.

The vestibule of the library was a long and wide corridor with columns lining the sides. Between each fifth column was a statue of the gods of Orud, their bodies partially clothed and posed in some dramatic gesture. At the end of the hall, two great wooden doors stood ajar, allowing the cool air to make its way inside. Saba stepped through the doorway and walked into the night air of Orud. Apparently he had been down in the basement longer than he thought, as he looked to the darkened sky. The view from this vantage point always took his breath away. The library was perched atop a small knoll within the academy district, surrounded by various temples and schools. From the terrace, Saba could see a great deal of the city and the flickering light from torches spread out for miles. The beauty of this city was unrivaled and Saba realized that one needn't look far to see it. The flat stone streets curved throughout the city lined with alternating iron torch posts and planted trees. The vegetation within the city was maintained by an enormous force of gardeners enlisted by the Emperor himself.

Saba took a deep breath and descended the library steps to the street below. Crossing the road, he walked south for a few blocks before turning east along the street that would eventually lead him to the Inn. It had taken a few days to find a place to stay, but luckily, he still had plenty of money from his days of tutoring Kael.

Kael! As soon as the name came to him, his heart dropped. He was such a special boy. Inquisitive. It broke Saba's heart to think of how his life had come to an end. He was yet another innocent casualty of this brutal life.

Suddenly, Saba's senses became alert. Perhaps it was a noise or a smell. He couldn't be sure but it felt like someone was following him. The sensation wasn't foreign to him, as he had noticed it during his travels to Orud as well. The last few days before his arrival were spent with the occasional glance over his shoulder, but the feeling went away when he entered the city limits. Now it was back again and it was unsettling. He quickened his pace toward the Inn and kept his eyes moving, checking each alley as he neared it.

"Sir," called a voice.

Saba stopped in his tracks and looked around.

"Sir, may I have a word with you?" came the voice again. It echoed slightly off the stone buildings on either side of the street.

Saba turned around and saw a dark-robed man walking briskly in his direction. If he was trying to be stealthy, he was not very good at it. "My good man, it's late and an old man needs his rest," he replied. Turning back around, Saba began to walk faster than before.

"Please Sir, I must speak with you," the man pleaded.

Saba tried to ignore him, only glancing behind to make sure that he was showing no signs of aggression. To his surprise, the man had stopped walking. *Good. If you mean me no harm, then whatever you have to say can wait for the light of day.* When Saba looked ahead, he saw another man dressed like the first, standing under a torch post half a block away. "What do you want," he called out, trying not to sound scared.

"We wish to speak with you about a very important matter," the second man called back.

"It is late. Perhaps we can talk over breakfast."

"No," the man behind him said, from much closer than before. "We have been waiting for you for too many years. We are done waiting."

Saba turned back around, looking to the nearest alley for an escape route, but the shadows in the alley began to move. He turned to run across the street, but all of the alleys around him began to empty with men, their cloaks billowing in the slight breeze. In a matter of seconds, he was surrounded by more than twenty strangers.

"What do you want to talk about?" he called out, turning in circles to keep an eye on the nearest man.

One of the figures stepped forward. "We are looking for someone and we need your help."

"Who are you looking for?" he asked the man. Suddenly, he heard a step behind him and whirled around to confront the man, but it was too late. Something brushed passed his shoulders and immediately cinched his arms to his side.

"We're looking for you," the man replied with a calm, methodical voice.

Saba looked down at the rope which now restricted his movement and felt panic. He tried to scream for help but one of the men stuffed a rag into his mouth, muffling the sound. Saba was helpless in that instant, and his only emotion was fear. Suddenly the vision of the streets of Orud disappeared as someone slipped a cloth over his head. Saba dropped to his knees, not knowing what was happening and powerless to do anything but comply.

Then the struggle stopped, just as suddenly as it had begun. Saba knelt on the ground, wondering why they were not dragging him off or beating him. He received only silence for an answer, which was no answer at all. Then, faintly, he heard the sharp clipping sound of hooves on stone. It was a horse. *No, several horses.* And they were moving in his direction. Saba waited a few seconds, listening intently, also making out a wagon, presumably pulled by the same horses. Saba struggled to his feet, yelling for help as loud as the rag in his mouth would let him. He took a few steps in the direction of the horses before he felt a sharp tug on the rope around his arms. He lost his balance and fell back to the street.

"Settle down old man," an amused voice commanded. "That's your transportation, not your rescue."

The man's words were confirmed when the wagon, pulled by a team of horses, stopped next to Saba. He was lifted to his feet and escorted to the rear of the wagon where he was, to his surprise, gently placed inside. As he lay on the floor of the wagon which jostled with the movement of the horses, Saba's fear slowly gave way to reason and he tried to make some sense of the situation. *Is this an arrest?* These men were not soldiers, so that was not a likely answer. *Whoever these people are, they have not harmed me other than scaring an old man half to death. They must want me alive!* That, at least, was an encouraging thought as the horses took him away.

Kael was awakened by a tapping sound at his door. At first he thought it was a dream, but it happened again. The night air was cold on his skin as he threw back the covers and went to the door. It made a creaking sound when he opened it, loud as a trumpet in the stillness of the night. Donagh and Narian were standing just outside of the door.

"Are you hungry?" Donagh whispered.

"Why?"

"Cause we're all going down to the kitchen to get some food."

Kael peered out into the hallway and saw several of the others standing in the shadows, waiting.

"Were not supposed to. We'll get caught."

Narian leaned closer. "That's why we'll have to be quiet." Kael could see Narian's teeth as he grinned.

"Alright," Kael said. "Let me get dressed."

"Hurry up," said Donagh as Kael ran back to his bed and pulled a tunic from the clothes chest. When he rejoined them in the hallway, the group stopped at Berit's door. He was the only one left. Donagh tapped at the door and it opened almost immediately.

"What are you guys doing?" he asked before anyone could explain.

Soren made his way to the door. "We're goin' down to the kitchen to sneak some food."

"Whose idea was that?" Berit asked, suspiciously.

"Mine," Soren answered. "Now get some clothes on; you're coming with us."

"Alright. Hold on." Berit closed the door.

After several minutes Donagh knocked again. "What's taking so long," he whispered, as loud as he could.

The door opened and Berit came out into the hallway, fully clothed.

Horace laughed out loud. "Were not going on a journey, were just going to the kitchen."

"Be quiet," Soren said in a harsh whisper. "You're going to get us caught. Let's go."

The boys followed Soren to the end of the hall where he signaled for them to stop. "I'll go down and make sure that it's safe." He crept down the spiraled stairs, keeping close to the wall so they wouldn't squeak. It was several minutes until he came back up, waving the group forward.

They went single file down the stairs, running quietly from shadow to shadow until they made their way through the dining hall and into the kitchen. "Everyone grab something and we'll take it back to my room." Soren was the oldest and no one had any problems following his lead, especially when he seemed to know what he was doing. They all looked around for anything edible; fruit, bread, anything that could easily be carried back upstairs. Kael was eyeing a cheese block when Horace came out of the ice room struggling to lift a piece of salted meat twice the size of his own head.

"Find something smaller and hurry up," Donagh told him.

Arden tried to stifle his laughter as Horace slipped going back in. He was promptly silenced by Soren, but couldn't keep from giggling under his breath. When Horace came back out empty handed, Arden started to laugh all over again.

"Let's get out of here," Soren said, and they all followed him back upstairs. Creeping down the hallway, they stopped at Soren's bedroom. "In here," he waved to the group. One after another, the group piled into his room until he locked the door and opened the window to let in some moonlight. Kael and Berit sat on Soren's bed and Soren joined the others on the floor. Everyone placed what they had taken from the kitchen in the middle. Soren and Narian began to divide the spoils and deal out everyone's portion.

"Soren. Where are you from?" asked Coen, stuffing a chunk of bread into his mouth.

"Nortuk," he answered simply.

"Did you ever go on kitchen raids there?" Coen asked, his smile reflecting the chuckles around the room.

"Yeah, all the time. In fact, that's the only way to get food where I come from."

Coen was confused and the other boys were intrigued. "Didn't your parents feed you?"

Soren glanced around the room at the curious faces. "No. My father died when I was a baby; I don't even remember him. And my mother died a few years ago, so I had to learn to fend for myself."

Coen was so shocked that he was speechless for a few seconds, which was a long time for him. "So, where did you live?"

"Well, everywhere I guess. I just wandered around the city, mostly looking for places to sleep and get food. It took a while, but I found this tavern in a rich part of the city. They used to throw away the food that their guests didn't eat. They had these barrels in a back alley where they put the old food until there was enough for someone to take it away."

As Soren spoke, all the boys listened with full attention. Kael thought that they had probably never heard of such a thing before. Or, at least, that's how it looked. He, on the other hand, would often run across such boys in Bastul, when he and Ajani would sneak into the city. Some of them were very nice, but others were mean to everyone they met.

"I remember one time," Soren continued, "I showed some of my friends to this place. They weren't too careful. I told them to wait until nighttime when everyone was sleeping, but they were hungry and they didn't want to wait. It was only barely past sundown when they ran over to the barrels and started tipping them over, looking for food."

Some of the boys had looks of disgust on their faces. Soren stopped his story. "Have you forgotten already what it's like to be truly hungry?"

Kael immediately thought of their time in jail, and cringed. He just wanted to forget.

When everyone went back to chewing on their food, Soren continued. "Anyway, the owner came out. I guess he must have heard my friends. I was waiting across the alley and I saw the whole thing. The owner saw the barrels tipped over and grabbed one of my friends. The rest of us started to run, and we didn't even see, at first. Well, he started hitting on this kid."

"What did you do?" asked Coen.

"What do you think I'm trying to tell you?"

Coen laughed. "Sorry. Go ahead."

"So we all turned around and went back. By the time we got there, the kid was beaten up pretty bad. The rest of us weren't even sure what we could do about it. But we had to do something. When we gathered around the man, he must have panicked, because he took my friend and threw him against the wall. The kid hit his head pretty hard on the stone. The owner tried to run back inside, but I chased him and hit him in the back of the head with a stick that I was holding. He fell down, just inside the door like he was sleeping. The others helped me drag him out into the alley and we just started kicking him until our legs were too tired to kick anymore."

"What happened to your friend?" Donagh asked.

"Oh. He didn't make it."

Everyone was silent, except for Coen. "He died?" Coen asked.

"Yeah. It was that last throw against the wall that did it."

"What about the owner?" Coen asked with a look of disgust on his face.

"Oh, I'm not sure. But I hope he died too. We never went back there after that."

Kael had a nauseous feeling in his stomach. After the horrible experience of their imprisonment, he was disgusted by the thought that someone might live like that their whole life. And the callous way that Soren spoke of the whole event gave him the shivers. "I hope it wasn't like that all the time," Kael said.

"No, not all the time, but I have a lot of those kinds of stories. The rest of the time we just wandered around, bored and hungry."

"Well, I'm starting to get tired. I'm going to bed," Arden said, standing up and stretching. His thoughts were echoed by most of the other boys who left the room as well. Kael stayed, as did Berit and Narian. Through the night, they traded stories of their homes and parents. Kael didn't say much, but asked lots of questions. Their lives were fascinating, but Soren definitely had the hardest time.

When morning came, Kael found himself on Soren's bed, facing the wrong direction. Narian was gone and Berit was asleep on the floor, huddled in a ball. Soren was putting on his shoes.

"You guys had better get ready or you're going to be late." Soren's words awakened Berit who promptly ran out of the room with a look of panic on his face.

"Sorry I took your bed," Kael said as he was leaving.

"Don't worry about it. I can fall asleep anywhere."

"Thanks," Kael said, and went to his room to get ready for morning meditation time.

The morning's exercises were a struggle because of the lack of sleep, but Kael made it through. The late morning studies were the most difficult, however, as Kael couldn't seem to keep his eyes open. As Ukiru spoke of the history of the Orudan Empire, his voice sounded like the steady beat of the ocean waves, lulling him to sleep. By the time the afternoon rolled around, the sleepiness had faded, replaced by excitement for the coming lessons.

As always, Ukiru stood facing the boys in the arena. "We are fast approaching the year's end. You have all learned many things that will be of great use to you in the future. However, your studies thus far have only been concerned with how to control yourself in various situations. The next logical step in the training of a warrior is the control of his horse."

The boys bristled with excitement. For most of them, a horse represented the life of the wealthy and not something that everyone was privileged to have.

Ukiru waved a hand, and at his signal, ten horses walked into the arena, each one led by a monk. "A horse is a valuable tool in the arsenal of a warrior. With knowledge of how to use it well, it can be a great advantage in any war. Use it without proper knowledge and it can be a great distraction. I have seen many men go down in battle because they did not have command of their horses. These beasts are powerful. It is best to have this power working for you and not against you. Today we will begin learning how to ride a horse. The best way to learn is to do, so everyone choose a horse and we will help you up." Ukiru walked to the nearest horse where he waited to help Rainer.

The boy's father was wealthy and Rainer knew horses well. He grabbed as high up on the saddle as he could while placing his foot in the stirrup. With one fluid motion, he pulled himself onto the horse.

"Very good, Rainer. I can see this is familiar to you."

"Yes, Sir. My father owns many horses."

"I'm sure he does," Ukiru replied. "But the 'All Powerful' is your father now, and he owns many horses as well. In fact, all of the horses that have ever lived are his. You must put your old life behind you and press on."

His last words were spoken loud for the whole group to hear. "Is everyone ready?"

"No, Sir," came a muffled reply.

"Who said that?"

"Me, Sir," said Jorn, stumbling out from behind his horse. Jorn was a stocky child and was having difficulty pulling himself onto the horse.

Ukiru walked over to help the boy. "Jorn, you are heavier than the other boys, but you are also stronger. Use your weight to your advantage. Lean into the horse and pull hard with your arms."

The boy tried again, following the advice of Ukiru. He was able to stand on the stirrup, but was unable to swing his leg over the animal. Ukiru grabbed his foot from the other side of the horse and pulled his leg over the saddle. "This takes much practice. It will come in time."

After each child was mounted on his horse, Ukiru motioned for one of his own. When the monk brought it the children gasped at its beauty. It was black and shiny and walked with gracefulness. All of the other horses were brown in color and didn't look quite as strong as Ukiru's steed. He took the reins from the monk and ran his hand down the nose of the animal. "First we will start with a few basic commands. These horses are already trained, so for now, you will simply learn to command them. At some point you will learn to train one of your own, but that will come later."

After a few simple lessons on how to control the horse, Ukiru sprang up into position with ease, not bothering to place his foot in the stirrup. Apparently he didn't need the help. They rode out of the arena and into the bright sunshine. There was a chill in the air and several patches of snow clung to the shadows, leftover from a storm that had passed through a few days ago.

Kael was excited to ride. His father used to take him on rides before it became dangerous to travel around for pleasure. There were many things that his father wasn't able to do because of his position within the Empire. *But I guess that's why they found Saba.* A thought suddenly came to him. "Did you know that far to the east is a tribe of people who train their horses to obey their voice?" The thought of Saba sparked a memory of one of his lessons.

"Yes, Kael. That's right." Ukiru slowed, letting Soren take the lead. "But in battle, there are many voices. Whose voice will the horse listen to? No, it is best to lead these animals by hand. A rider must always have one hand on the reins, which is why it can be a disadvantage in battle. But if trained properly, a rider can never lose to a man on the ground."

Kael was about to say that these people also train their horses to be lead by hand or by the pressure of the rider's legs to accommodate any situation. But he suddenly didn't feel like finishing his story. He only sulked for a few minutes before the enjoyment of riding overcame him once more. The sun felt good on his back and the lurching motion of the walking horse was mesmerizing, like being in a boat.

The group rode for a few hours before circling back to the stable, arriving just as the sun went down. Ukiru leapt off his horse and helped the children down as well. When Kael's feet touched the ground, he found it difficult to walk. His knees were cramped and his feet hurt, despite the fact that he had not walked on them for hours.

"Everyone is dismissed. Wash up and we will have our meal." Ukiru handed the reins of his horse to a stable hand as other monks came out to take the rest of the horses.

Later that night, as Kael lay in bed, he thought back over the months that had passed since he arrived at the monastery. It was fun to learn everything that they were being taught. These boys had all become friends to him. And Soren was a closer friend than any. He saw things and went places that most people three times his age would never get to. But even with last night's raid of the kitchen, Kael couldn't help feeling like he didn't belong here. No matter how much he enjoyed his time here, he felt even stronger a growing sense of isolation. *What's wrong with me? I have friends...food. I'm training as a warrior. Most kids would love to have this life.*

The question kept crossing his mind. He rolled over and pulled his pillow over his head to block out the sound of his thoughts, but it didn't help.

16

The screams echoed down the hallway and Lemus felt his nerves cringe. He didn't have the patience to sit and wait for the birth of his son. It was driving him mad to do nothing but stare at the floor. He decided, instead, to get some work done. Walking down the hall, he stopped at the door to his study. He wasn't eager to deal with his new responsibilities either, but under the circumstances, he had no choice.

He entered the room and sat down at his desk which was covered in an assortment of parchment scraps. Charts, lists, and maps of various sizes filled his vision. He slowly began to organize the mess that had been building for a week. He tried to clear his mind of everything but the problem at hand. A shipment of armor and weapons would be arriving in three days from a neighboring city and he had to make sure that it arrived safely. He had come across several bits of information that led him to believe the shipment would be attacked.

He had already rescheduled the ships to arrive at midnight, which was unusual. Hopefully, the would-be attackers would be thrown off a bit. Although the city of Bastul never seemed to sleep, the population on the streets would be considerably less at that time of evening, making it easier to spot anything out of the ordinary. Still, there was the problem of extra reinforcements. There was no good place from which to pull guards. Lemus buried his face in his hands and massaged his temples. He was having trouble concentrating. Suddenly a knock sounded at the door.

"Yes?" Lemus responded, waiting for an answer.

The door opened slowly and the face of a female servant peeked through.

"Yes, what is it?"

"Sir, the baby is coming."

Lemus raised an eyebrow. "Is it here yet?"

"No," she answered timidly.

"Come back when my son is born."

The woman nodded and pulled her head back from the room.

"Make sure he is cleaned up before you come again," he yelled at the retreating sound.

Now...back to business. Where was I? Oh yes, reinforcements. He scanned a map of the city, letting his vision pause at the major defense points. Each had only the minimum number of soldiers necessary. Finally he stopped at the armory. *Thirty guards.* He thought it seemed a bit excessive. *I'll leave two guards there and move the rest to the docks for just a few hours.* He looked back to the docks lining the bay. *Twenty-eight extra men should be plenty.* He would have them dress in plain clothes, not their uniforms, and hide them in the dark alleys near the docks. They would be quick to join the fight if the attack came from the bay. If it came from the streets he would be able to cut them off before they could reach the ships. Another knock interrupted his thoughts.

"Yes?" he said, annoyed.

"It is time for you to see the baby," came the voice from the other side of the door.

Lemus jumped to his feet and walked briskly to the door. As he opened it, the servant girl flinched. He ignored her and strode quickly down the hall. His heart was racing and he couldn't think of a time when he had been more excited. The thought of having a son who would follow in his footsteps gave him such a joy that he finally realized what all the fuss was about. He never thought of himself as the type to be married and have a family, but over the course of the last few months, the idea had grown on him. Finally, there would be someone whom he could train, instruct and guide through life, steering him past difficulties while teaching him how to lead people. It was an opportunity that Lemus' own father had neglected completely. The excitement was almost too much to bear.

Halfway down the hall he found the spare room where he had chosen for the baby to be born. Maeryn had wanted to be in the bedroom, but Lemus insisted that the mess be kept to a room that was rarely used. Three of the servant women were gathered around the bed and Maeryn was sitting up, propped by pillows. She was holding what looked to Lemus like a bundle of cloths. As he got closer he could see the pink face of the baby protruding from the bundle.

"Give him to me." Lemus grabbed the baby from Maeryn. "He's lighter than I thought he would be." Pulling the baby close, he moved some of the blankets out of the way of the baby's face, then noticed that the women were staring at him. "What?"

Maeryn looked at Zula.

What's that expression she's wearing?

"It is a woman child." Zula answered instead, with the cautious look of a mouse about to be struck by a snake.

"What?" he asked, partially because of the strange wording from the slave woman, partially from unbelief. "What did you say?"

"It is a girl, not a boy...Sir," she corrected.

Maeryn watched as the blood drained from Lemus' face. His arms went slack and Zula caught the baby girl before he had the chance to drop her. Then the blood returned and his features burned with anger. His eyebrows wrinkled as he backed away from them and turned, storming out of the room.

The women looked at each other in disbelief. Maeryn had expected something bad to happen, but everyone seemed shocked at Lemus' silence. The girl who announced the arrival of the baby to Lemus was still standing out in the hall, unsure of what to do next.

Zula gave the baby back to Maeryn who had tears running down her smiling face, despite the awkward event with Lemus. "She looks like her father." It was a statement that didn't ask for confirmation.

Zula agreed anyway. "Yes, she does. I am proud of you, my lady."

Maeryn was unsure what the woman meant, but was too exhausted to ask.

"Your strength has been tested and you have proven to yourself that you are strong. I know that you will raise your daughter to be the same way."

Maeryn cried tears of joy as she looked from Zula to her new daughter. "Aelia will be strong indeed as long as she is in the presence of women like you."

The soft light of the morning filtered in through the window of the birthing room. Maeryn lay awake watching Aelia's body expand and contract with each breath. She seemed so peaceful as she slept, unaware of the world she had been born into. Maeryn felt more at peace than she had in a long time.

"When is it coming?" came a faint voice from outside her window. A scrap of someone else's conversation drifted into the room from the courtyard. Maeryn listened for a recognizable voice. It didn't take long before she heard Lemus' hissing.

"Two days from now...at midnight."

Maeryn's interest was peaked at the hushed voices. She leaned closer to the window to catch more of the conversation.

"What should I do?" asked the other man.

"Leave two men behind at the armory. The rest of you will be reassigned to the protection of the shipment."

"Is that really necessary?" The other man seemed to be confused about his orders.

"I have received information that the rebels will attack the ship as it docks in the harbor. You and your men will trade your uniforms for less obvious attire." Lemus paused, apparently enjoying his own brilliance.

Maeryn imagined that the other man was probably smiling with a devious grin that would only serve to make Lemus think more highly of himself than he usually did.

"What do you expect to happen?"

"The docks will already be guarded with the usual amount of security. Perhaps the rebels will attack from the sea; however, I find that unlikely. Instead, I think they will be waiting a short distance away from the docks in the city. Your men will be disguised in various places near the docks as drunks, fishermen, and whatever other rabble can be found at that time of night wandering the city. We will stop the rebels before they can even reach the boats."

A quiet laugh echoed slightly off the stone buildings and made its way to Maeryn. It was obvious that Lemus' underling was trying to flatter him.

"Make sure that your men are ready. If you sense that any of them are not up to the task, you must tell me at once. I will deal with them. We cannot have any mistakes."

"Yes, Sir," the other man answered.

The retreating footsteps signaled to Maeryn that the conversation had come to an end. Ever since she realized that she was pregnant, she hadn't given much thought to the idea of getting back at Lemus. She had been focused on how to keep her baby safe from the monster who was now her husband. She remembered how Zula had once told her that there were better ways to get back at Lemus than to kill him while he slept. Until this morning, she hadn't understood.

Zula was right. This is much better!

Maeryn lived with the man responsible for governing the city of Bastul and she had access to information that other men would kill to have. She remembered that while Adair was Governor, he had kept informed on the Resistance movement. They were a subversive group of people living within the Empire and among its citizens. Adair never spoke of what these people stood for, but she remembered that he had even communicated with them on several occasions through a local fisherman who relayed messages. Throughout his time as Governor, he had managed to avoid any major confrontations. The fact that they were now planning to attack a shipment in the harbor meant that they didn't think too highly of the new Governor.

"Zula," Maeryn called as carefully as she could without waking the baby.

"Yes, ma'am," the slave woman replied, coming in from the hallway.

"Is Lemus gone?" she whispered, tilting her head toward the window.

The woman walked to the window and peered out. "Yes, ma'am," she answered after a few seconds. "Shall I fetch him for you?"

"No," Maeryn answered quickly, wondering if the slave woman was being facetious. "I was thinking that I would like to have fish this evening for dinner. I would like you to go into the city and buy some from a certain fisherman."

"But, ma'am, we have plenty of fish here." Zula was obviously confused.

"Yes, I know, but he is a friend of the family and it has been a long time since he has heard from us. I am also going to send a letter for you to deliver to this man." Maeryn motioned for the writing utensils on a nearby desk and Zula quickly brought a quill along with a sheet of parchment and an ink pot.

"Thank you," she said as the woman handed her the items. "Give me a few minutes to write the letter and then you can go into the city."

"Yes, ma'am," Zula said and left the room to finish what she was working on before she was called.

Maeryn dipped the quill in the ink and paused to look at the baby. *One day, I'll be able to tell you who your real father is. And we won't be forced to live a lie.* She looked back to the parchment and began to write.

I have recently become aware of information that may be of some use to you. There is a shipment coming to Bastul at midnight, two days from now. There are rumors that the Resistance has made plans to attack the shipment as it reaches its destination. I can assure you that measures are being taken to solve this problem and the attack will likely be unsuccessful. Your lives will be at great risk should you choose to continue with this course of action. I have heard from a reliable source that the armory will be emptied of all but two men on the night of the shipment to deal with this rumored threat. Perhaps the cargo of the ship is not as important as the contents of the armory to a movement such as yours.

Maeryn blew on the ink and folded the parchment into thirds. When she was finished, she noticed Zula standing in the doorway. "Would you please seal this with Adair's symbol?" she asked as she handed the letter to the woman.

Zula nodded. "I will be back in a few hours. Do you need anything else while I am in the city?"

"No thank you, just the fish."

As Zula turned to leave, Maeryn felt a pang of guilt. "Zula..."

"I know, ma'am. He won't ever know. I'll be careful." She gave a knowing smile and left the room.

The jostling of the wagon stopped, waking Saba from his uneasy sleep. For a moment, he forgot where he was, but the aching in his joints quickly reminded him. *Why have we stopped?* He couldn't see anything with the covering over his head, so he sat still, waiting to see what his captors would do. He had been in the back of this wagon for close to a week now, or so he guessed. Several times a day they would stop and allow him to get out and walk around. It was during these times that Saba was able to relieve himself. *But it's too soon since the last break!* Saba began to grow nervous.

To his left, Saba heard the sound of metal grating on metal.

"Get out," one of his captors said.

Saba tried his best to comply with the command, but his body was stiff. Once out of the wagon, the man placed a hand on Saba's shoulder and pushed him forward. Saba's heart began to beat louder as he anticipated something terrible.

"Where are we going?" he mumbled through the gag in his mouth.

"Huh? Did you say something? It sounds like you have something in your mouth." Laughter broke out from the other two men who were following at a safe distance, probably waiting for Saba to try and run.

He didn't bother. He didn't repeat his question either.

The ground under his feet suddenly became smoother and the stranger pulled on Saba's shoulder to stop him. He briefly heard the creaking sound of wood and then they were moving again. After a few minutes he stopped Saba, reaching up to the back of his neck to untie the bag.

"Welcome to your new home," he said, as he lifted the covering off of Saba's head.

After seeing nothing but darkness for a week, the light was intense. Saba could only open his eyes for seconds at a time. What he did manage to see was a fenced area of well-trodden soil, containing a few buildings, one of which was directly ahead of them. Saba spat his gag onto the dirt, then took a deep breath. The air was cold, but smelled clean and damp and the soil under his feet showed signs of recent rain. He quickly noticed that his captors were not dressed the same as the cloaked men who had attacked him in the city of Orud. These men wore black as well, but were garbed like soldiers with long-sleeved leather tunics and trousers that reached down to their calves.

"In you go," he said and pushed Saba toward the nearest building.

One of the soldiers ran ahead and opened a wooden door in the stone structure. Once inside, Saba's eyes could relax, though there wasn't much to look at once his eyesight returned. Along the right side of the building was a long narrow room with a fire pit in the floor on the far end. A few crudely built chairs surrounded the pit with others arranged near a table in the corner. Along the left side were thick wooden doors with narrow viewing slots carved into them at eye level. The three men walked Saba down to the far end of the building and opened the last door, pushing him inside.

"Make yourself comfortable," said one of the soldiers as the others laughed. The door was shut and locked, and once again, Saba was alone. A quick look around the room was all that was needed to take inventory of his surroundings. There were no windows, only a small cot and a hole in the floor that smelled of urine. Saba walked over to the cot and inspected it with a probing hand. *I think I'll stand.*

The next few days were as uneventful as his trip in the back of the wagon. They fed him regularly and kept the fire going outside of his room, so that the chill night air never made it to his cell. It was the inconsistency of the situation that confused him most. *What do they want from me? Why keep me locked up, and yet tend to all my basic needs?* It didn't make any sense. Saba set his pondering aside at the sound of voices. Footsteps preceded the sound of jingling keys and suddenly, the door was open.

"Come on, old man, it's your turn," said a soldier whom he hadn't seen before.

"My turn for what?"

The guard smiled. "You have a big day tomorrow, don't you want to look your best? You don't have a choice in the matter anyway. Come on, get out of your cell," he said before Saba had the chance to answer.

Saba was escorted back the way he entered the building. On his right, he heard sounds coming out of the other cells. He tried to remember if there were people in the cells when he came in, but before he could recall, the door opened and the guard pushed him outside.

The chill in the air made him feel instantly awakened. For the first time, Saba got a good look at the place where he was being held prisoner. It was a compound with several stone buildings that appeared to be randomly placed within a high stone wall surrounding a dirt courtyard. *Although the term 'courtyard' is usually reserved for more hospitable surroundings.*

A thin fog obscured most of what was beyond the wall, but a few trees which stood close to the wall could be seen. Saba noted that they were some variety of pine, which meant that they must have traveled north from Orud and had climbed a considerable amount in elevation.

"Keep moving," the guard said in a bored tone.

Saba got the impression that these men were either being paid to do what they were doing or else they were just following orders. They didn't express any malice toward him, in fact, he felt almost ignored, but for the attention needed to prevent his escape. *Like watching animals.*

They walked across the courtyard toward a building that looked much like the one Saba had been sleeping in for the past few days, except for a small wing that extended off the main structure at an angle. As they approached the extension, the door opened and a guard led another old man from the room and the two began walking in the opposite direction. When they passed, Saba could see that the man's head had been shaved as well as his face. Neither guard said anything as they passed each other, as if they had done this a hundred times already.

Saba was pushed through the doorway and into a small room with a wooden floor that sloped downward toward a center drain. One man was sweeping gray hair off of the floor while another was setting down a bucket of soapy water with a rag draped over the side. Saba's escort pushed him toward a chair that sat in the center of the room.

"Take off your clothes and sit," he commanded.

Saba looked at the man with raised eyebrows.

"Hurry up, I don't have all day."

Saba unfastened his belt and pulled his tunic over his head, tossing both to the side of the room. He had just settled into his chair when he noticed the silence. He looked around at the three men and received suspicious looks in return. *Why are they acting so strange?* The man who had been sweeping left the room and came back with two more guards. There were now five men in the room and four of them stood guard around the perimeter while the first guard stepped closer to Saba with a short blade in his hand.

"Now don't move. I don't want to hurt you, but this thing will take your ear clean off if you're not careful."

Saba nodded that he understood and sat still while the guard rubbed soap suds into his hair and proceeded to shave his head. He watched the hair that used to fall down to his shoulders drift toward his feet and onto the floor. It only took a few minutes before the man was done and moved around in front of Saba.

"Put your head back," the man said carefully.

Saba obeyed, tilting his head back while another man started on his beard.

"You know, I could do that myself?" Saba offered.

"And let you get your hands on this razor? That doesn't sound like a good idea to me. Now shut your mouth so I don't accidentally cut your throat."

Saba closed his mouth and tried to keep as still as he could. Shaving his beard took longer than shaving his head, but before long, the man was finished.

"Take that bucket and wash yourself. And hurry up, we're running late."

Saba got to his feet and walked over to the bucket, rinsing his head and face first. After scrubbing himself with the rag, he tipped the bucket over his head and let the cold water wash over his skin. Despite the shocking temperature, it felt refreshing to bathe for the first time in weeks. "Do I get something to dry off with?" he asked, setting down the bucket. When he looked up at the men, they were all staring at him again. "What do you keep looking at?" he growled, not able to tolerate the awkwardness.

"How old are you?" one of the men asked.

"Old. Why?"

A different man answered this time. "You sure don't look that old." He looked back to the man who had performed the shaving. "We might have made a mistake with this one."

"Never mind," the guard said, putting down the razor and handing Saba a towel. "Dry off and put your clothes back on."

17

Two nights after writing the note, Maeryn stared at the ceiling of her bedroom and waited impatiently. She was not sure of the time but it had to be close to midnight. After feeding Aelia and putting her back to sleep, Maeryn's mind began racing. Soon, the events that she had possibly affected in a tremendous way would unfold, if the letter reached its intended destination. Zula had delivered it with no problems and made it back to the house without seeing Lemus. But since then, there had been growing in her mind a sense of doom. At first, she was pleased with herself and the idea that she could slowly destroy the man who tried to replace her husband. The Empire to which Adair had devoted himself had so quickly abandoned him, even though he had gotten into trouble by serving that very same Empire. It was exciting to think of the privileged information to which she had access on a daily basis. If she was careful, she might be able to do great damage to the Empire that had stolen her true love away. But now she was scared of the consequences of her actions. Maybe the letter was not the smartest thing to send. If Lemus found it, he might suspect her, and he had proven that he had no reservations about sending family members to their death. But she had already sent the letter and there was nothing to be done about it now but to wait. As she watched the moon reflections cast by the ocean dance along the ceiling of her bedroom, she eventually drifted off to sleep.

The sound of a baby crying jolted her awake. She glanced around the room, now awash with the orange hues of early morning, looking for the crib and found it at the foot of the bed. Aelia was sleeping soundly and Maeryn wondered if the sound that had awakened her had been just a dream. She pulled the covers back and got out of bed to stretch her legs. Suddenly, the sound of approaching footsteps echoed loudly in the hallway. She could tell that it was Lemus; he had a certain attitude that permeated everything he did, including the way he walked. The footsteps passed the door to her room and entered the master bedroom at the end of the hall. From the agitated sound of the footsteps, his plans must not have gone well. Maeryn waited for a few moments, then left the room while Aelia was still sleeping.

She found him out on the balcony that used to be her favorite place to think. Since Aelia had been born, Lemus had not let her return to the master bedroom because of the child's crying. He told her that a man of importance with his amount of responsibility could not afford to be disturbed at night with crying children. It was just as well though; she enjoyed not having to share a bed with him. Lemus was standing at the railing, overlooking the city as it began to sparkle in the increasing light of the sun.

"Are you alright?" she asked quietly and carefully.

He didn't respond, but continued to stare out into the bay. After several seconds, Maeryn started to wonder if he hadn't heard her at all. She tried once more to bring him out of his thoughts.

"Things are not well. You seem troubled."

"I don't wish to talk about it," he stated flatly.

She didn't want to give up so easily. "Well, if you decide that you want to talk, I'll be in my room; sometimes it feels better just to get the words out." As she turned to leave, Lemus let out a sound as if he started to say something, but decided not to. Maeryn stopped and waited for him to say what was on his mind.

"There was trouble last night," he said at last.

Maeryn waited for the rest of his story and when it didn't come, she coaxed him out of his silence with more questions. "What kind of trouble?"

Lemus turned around from the railing and walked back into the bedroom. He slumped down on the bed and crossed his arms. "Last night..." he began and then drifted off.

Maeryn figured he was either too worked up to think straight or else he was uncomfortable discussing the details of his business with her.

He took a deep breath and started again. "Last night there was a shipment of armor coming in."

"And?" Maeryn questioned. "What was the trouble?"

"It was supposed to be attacked by a group of rebels...or so the rumor said. So I pulled most of the men from the armory to help guard the shipment." The despair in his voice slowly gave way to anger at being outsmarted. "Apparently the rumor was just a diversion because they attacked the armory while we waited for them at the harbor."

"Oh no!" Maeryn did her best to sound surprised. "What happened?"

"The two guards were killed and the rebels stole everything. Every last weapon and piece of armor is gone."

"That's horrible," Maeryn said with as much disgust as she could muster. "Who do they think they are that they should try to rise up against the Empire?"

Lemus picked his head up and looked at her with piercing eyes. Maeryn thought that she might have sounded a little too eager. When he smiled she felt a great deal of relief.

"Your patriotism is admirable, but there's more. While we waited at the harbor we heard the sounds of fighting. I sent a man to check on the matter and he came back a short while later to inform me that the armory was under attack. So I pulled the guards from their positions at the harbor and we went to confront the rebels at the armory. By the time we got there most of them had disappeared. We defeated the ones we could find, but the bulk of them got away."

"I'm sorry," Maeryn offered.

Lemus continued without acknowledging her words. "When we got back to the harbor..." He trailed off and his skin grew red. He clenched a fist and finished his statement. "The rebels attacked the ships when we were at the armory. They looted the entire shipment and set the ships on fire."

Maeryn really was speechless this time. She had to admit that the rebels were more devious than she had previously thought.

"Apparently there were two groups and they knew exactly how we were going to respond." Lemus put his head in his hands and massaged his temples.

"What will you do now? Do the soldiers have no weapons?"

"No, no," he assured her as if he were speaking to a child. "All the soldiers here have weapons and armor, but I have an additional three hundred soldiers arriving in six weeks and now I won't be able to arm them."

"Oh!" Maeryn tucked that bit of information away in her mind as well.

"What's worse is that I must dispatch a report of the state of my army to Orud at the end of the month."

"Perhaps the Empire will ship more armor when they hear of this attack. Maybe they will even send more than armor to aid you." Maeryn offered whatever suggestions came to mind. It was actually easier to make conversation when the words were not planned out beforehand.

"I don't know what is worse, the Empire knowing of this failure or the fact that the dispatch rider could be attacked on the way and the report stolen." Lemus got to his feet and walked back out on the balcony. "Before last night, I wouldn't have considered that the rebels were this well organized. But it is clear now that I have underestimated them and I mustn't let it happen again. This report will contain every detail of the state of my army and it cannot fall into their hands. If they are able to plan such a successful attack, then surely they are a force to be considered and it would not go well to have my enemies privy to all of my military capabilities."

"Is there no other way to send a report to Orud? Maybe you could disguise the rider." Maeryn couldn't feel the least bit of pity for this man; the man who had raped her, had her only son executed, the man who almost killed little Ajani, sent Saba away and tried to take the place of Adair. She had to fight the urge to celebrate his failures right in front of his face.

"I can think of no other way that would be sure to escape the rebels...not after tonight."

"I don't pretend to understand how one would govern an entire city, but perhaps there is a solution. I have heard of a man in the city who raises birds and trains them to do all sorts of amazing things."

Lemus darted a quick, angry glance at Maeryn. "What does this have to do with anything?"

"I'm sorry. I just meant that perhaps this man could help you. Zula told me that he has trained birds to fly all the way to Cerrar and back. The rebels would not be able to catch a bird if you sent the report that way."

Lemus laughed out loud and turned around to face Maeryn. "You were right...you can't even pretend to understand all that I must deal with. But it does feel better to talk about it. Leave me alone now, I must figure out what to do."

Maeryn smiled and left the man to his thoughts. By the time she got back to her room she was overflowing with excitement. She had no idea that the information she gave to the rebels would have such a potent effect. It was a scary thing to write that letter, even scarier to have it delivered into the hands of the enemies of the Empire. She had partially expected to be caught and executed, but fortune had smiled on her this day. And the way Lemus opened up and told her such useful information, it was better than she had hoped for. For the first time since losing Adair, she felt that her future held promise. Aelia was still sleeping soundly and Maeryn stood over the child and watched as her tummy rose and fell with each breath.

The evening proceeded slowly as Saba worried about the so-called *big day*. He didn't sleep well and found his mind racing with anxiety the whole night. Finally, morning came much the same as all the rest. The guard brought him a bowl of porridge shortly after his waking and Saba sat in the corner, half chewing, half drinking his breakfast. He tried to pass the time by thinking about the garden back in Bastul. He had helped Maeryn with much of the planting and looked back on those times with fondness.

A few hours after breakfast, voices began to stir outside of his cell. He could also hear muffled shouting coming from outside of the building. He rose to his feet and walked over to the door, trying to peer out of the observation slit in the thick wood. When his door suddenly opened he was as shocked as the guard, who quickly jumped back and grabbed for his sword. Saba held up his hands in protest. "No. No. I was just trying to listen."

When the guard regained his composure, he waved for Saba to come out of his cell. He pointed to the open door at the end of the room. "Get moving."

Saba complied and headed for the door with the guard close behind. As he exited the building, the scene in the courtyard made his heart race. Dozens of old men were being ushered into groups and lined up side by side. All wore looks of fear and confusion on their faces and Saba couldn't help but wonder what was going to happen to everyone, himself included. The guard shoved him toward the nearest group where several others were arranging the old men into orderly ranks at the points of their swords. Saba did his best to comply with their commands and not appear to be a threat, all the while thinking as fast as he could how to escape. When the last of the prisoners were brought into formation, the guards stepped back and joined the others at the perimeter of the courtyard. Saba looked around and made a mental note of the number of prisoners. *Ten in each group. Probably ten or twelve groups. At least a hundred in all.*

Suddenly, a dead silence fell over the crowd. Saba stopped in mid thought and instantly knew the reason. An overwhelming sense of dread poured over him. Not the kind that would make one want to run and scream, but the kind that is so powerful, it makes one paralyzed.

At the far right corner of the courtyard, a small group of soldiers appeared through a narrow gate. They strode confidently toward the groups of old men and stopped a short distance away. Pausing only for a moment, the small band of dark clad men separated to reveal a mysterious figure waiting at their center. He was covered head to foot in a black cloak which hid his face and even his hands. The soldiers escorted the figure to the first group of old men, where he proceeded to grab hold of the frightened prisoners by their necks, lifting their heads. Saba watched as their leader, or so he assumed, carefully inspected each prisoner as one might do when buying livestock. Slowly, one by one, the cloaked man dismissed the prisoners, who were then taken away to a large building on the opposite side of the courtyard.

The time went by at an agonizingly slow pace as the cloaked man made his way through more than half of the prisoners before coming to Saba. Although the man stood almost a foot shorter than Saba, like all the other guards and prisoners, he was still intimidating. Even at such close proximity, Saba was unable to see his face through the shadow cast by the thick hooded cloak.

Suddenly, the man's hand snaked out and grabbed him by the chin. Twisting Saba's face from side to side with incredible strength, he stepped closer. After a full minute of silence, he let go. Saba exhaled his breath and lowered his gaze to the ground, apparently passing the inspection. He began to feel dizzy and took a few deep breaths, but his vision was beginning to blur. The ground started to spin around his feet and Saba quickly shut his eyes to make it stop.

AHH...SARIEL!

A voice forced itself into Saba's mind, pushing his own thoughts aside.

I'VE FOUND YOU AT LAST

Saba opened his eyes and looked at the cloaked figure who was still standing in front of him.

YES,
THAT'S RIGHT.
YOU DIDN'T THINK I WOULD FORGET ABOUT YOU, DID YOU?

Though Saba couldn't see his face, somehow he knew that the words were not coming from his mouth. Saba looked around at the guards who were now taking the remainder of the prisoners away. None of them were speaking. Saba looked back to the shadow beneath the hood. "How are you doing that? Who is Sariel?"

YOU DON'T ASK THE QUESTIONS HERE.
NOT THIS TIME!

The voice in Saba's head exploded with fury.

YOU HAD YOUR CHANCE AND NOW IT'S MY TIME!

Saba was confused. He heard the man's voice in his head, without hearing him speak. It was as if he was hearing the man's thoughts.

"Take him to the chamber and get rid of the rest of these," the robed man said audibly and in a completely different voice, waving a hand dismissively at the other old men.

Suddenly, Saba was being pushed across the courtyard toward one of the smaller buildings, in the opposite direction from the rest of the prisoners. A guard ran ahead and produced a set of keys, unlocking the door into the small structure. Just as Saba reached the doorway, he heard screams. He only had time to glance over his shoulder before being shoved through the door, catching a glimpse of smoke pouring from the windows of the large stone building where the other prisoners had been taken.

Saba stumbled to the ground just inside the doorway. When he lifted his head, he saw a square room, twenty feet across, with stone walls and floor. There were no windows or features of any kind, aside from a small hole in the floor at one corner. The thick wooden beams that made up the ceiling were the only break in the visual monotony of the room. Saba scrambled on his hands and knees to the other side of the room before turning around and sitting against the wall.

The cloaked man entered the room and held up his hand. "Leave us," he said to the guards, who promptly did as they were told, locking the door behind them. "Now," he turned his attention toward Saba, "I have someone who wants to speak with you."

Saba quickly looked around the room, wondering if they were alone. The room was completely empty. He looked back to the mysterious figure whose head was bowed and arms crossed. His body seemed to shudder before he lifted his head and resumed a more normal body language. Once again, Saba felt an overwhelming sense of dread that made him feel dizzy with nausea.

When the man spoke it was not with the inaudible thoughts as before, but his voice was also not his own. "Sariel, you were a hard one to find, though I didn't expect you to make it easy for me. Nevertheless, I succeeded."

"You must have me confused with someone else," Saba replied, at once confused and terrified.

"Ha!" barked the man. "Do you not recognize your old friend? Surely the depth of your treachery cannot be so easily forgotten? I admit the physical manifestation is a bit of a change," he conceded, waving a hand in front of himself, "but you must be joking?"

"I'm afraid I don't know what you are talking about," Saba pleaded.

The man took a few steps closer and knelt down, pulling the hood of his cloak back away from his head. Saba's confusion fled, replaced with a feeling of disgust. The man's eyes were rolled back in their sockets and his facial features were contorted, as if struggling to resemble something they were never meant to. When the man spoke again, Saba realized that he was not conversing with the man before him, but whatever had taken control of his body and mind.

"You honestly don't know me anymore." The statement seemed to come as a complete shock to the man.

Suddenly, Saba's vision blackened and he fell on the floor, unable to control himself. Images flashed in his mind. Maeryn, Kael, Adair, scenes from their time in Bastul flashed through his mind in a random succession. Saba felt as if his head would explode from the pressure. Places and people whirled by from a time when Saba was looking for Bastul. Then, the images stopped. For a few moments, there was only darkness. The pain was the most excruciating thing Saba had ever experienced. *He's looking for something...in my mind.*

A sharp pain exploded in the front of Saba's head, and more images flashed through his mind, things that he had never seen before. *Are they memories of the past? Visions of the future?* As soon as the question formed in his mind, Saba realized that these were old memories from a time before he lost his memory. Then, the images stopped. Saba could see again. He was lying on the floor of the small building with his face on the stone floor. He tried to move, to sit up, but his body was limp with exhaustion. Then the voice in his head spoke once more. Calmly this time.

I KNEW IT WAS YOU.

The words or thoughts disappeared from Saba's mind and the man began to speak audibly once more.

"How fortunate that you should lose your memory after what you did to me. I often wondered how you were able to live with yourself. In your mind, you are a different person. But that doesn't change what happened. For thousands of years I have been alone with my thoughts, trapped in a prison of your making. I have been waiting for an opportunity to return and take my revenge, and it has presented itself. It is so close now that I can taste it. For now, you will stay confined to this jail until I can come and deal with you myself. My only regret is that your sentence won't last as long as mine. You will die much too soon."

Saba watched from the floor, still unable to move, as the hem of a black robe passed in front of his face and floated across the room. The door opened and the man's cloaked silhouette stood in the doorway.

"Enjoy your new home," the man spoke, with his own voice this time. Then the door was shut and locked and Saba heard only silence.

18

The bright sunlight did little to warm Kael as he sat on a rock outcropping overlooking the ocean. The air was cold and still, except for the occasional gust of wind. There were hardly any clouds to be seen in the whole sky, though it would not have mattered to Kael anyway. He sat, legs crossed, with his eyes closed. He had found this spot shortly after arriving at the monastery; though, at that time, it wasn't the hiding place that it had now become. Seven years had passed, and with each year, Kael felt more and more distant from the people around him. His heart had grown heavy and he couldn't figure out why. But it was always therapeutic to hear the ocean and feel the breeze on his face. Some days, when he had free time, he would sit in this place for hours with his eyes closed and try to feel everything that was happening around him. Today was no different.

Darkness filled his vision, but his memory, in combination with his imagination completed the picture. Years of watching the waves below, the wind as it passed through the pale grasses in the field behind him, told his mind what should be happening when his eyes were closed. The sound of his heart beating was loud in his head, even though he was not doing anything strenuous. He had lost track of how long he had been in this position, but it didn't matter. It was soothing to his soul.

He tried to think back over the time he had spent in this place and the friends he had made. Even though he knew almost everything there was to know about each of his brothers, as they called each other, he was sure that they all knew far less about him. With the passing of time he found it harder to relate to those around him. Even the things he was learning in class made less sense lately. Sometimes Ukiru would be teaching a subject and it would remind Kael of a long time ago, when he and Saba would talk for hours. It seemed like he was doing more listening than talking lately.

Kael tried to push the thoughts out of his head. He had been dwelling on this matter for too long now and was tired of it consuming his mind. He took a deep breath and replaced the negative imagery in his head with the soothing feeling of nature. He could feel the air stir to his left and blow gently across his face. He imagined all of his negative thoughts floating away on the breeze. He imagined them tumbling and dancing like leaves off the cliff and out over the water. Occasionally one of the leaves would fall from the group and swirl downward until it was too small to see. The rest kept tumbling into each other as they moved farther away until they too were lost to sight. Somewhere off to the right, just above the cliff face, he imagined the air stirring, driven by a lone seagull. It flew in from the ocean and hovered for a second above the rocks before spreading its wings for the slow descent of its landing. When it reached the ground, it let out a screech as it tucked its wings close to its body.

Kael suddenly felt silly to be imagining such things, even though it was fun to let his mind wander for a time. He opened his eyes to the bright sun and blinked at its harshness, unable to stop himself from yawning.

A second screech sounded and Kael glanced to his right. It took him a second to realize that the seagull perched on the rocks, only thirty feet away, was real. He shook his head and looked back, but the bird was still there. He slowly got to his feet and watched as the bird, previously unaware of his presence, leaped off the cliff and spread its wings to catch the air. It glided for a while before it began to beat its wings, slowly descending to the beach below.

Did I watch the seagull come to a landing, or were my eyes really closed when it happened? Kael continued to watch the bird as it retreated. *No. I'm sure I had my eyes closed the whole time.* But just as he came to that conclusion, he dismissed the idea as impossible. *If I had my eyes closed, then I saw it in my mind before it even made a sound. I'm definitely not feeling well.* Turning around, Kael headed back to the monastery to get some sleep.

Kael slept from before sundown until the next morning. He awoke feeling refreshed and realized that it had been quite some time since he had slept so well. The morning's activities passed in a blur, as they usually did, and Kael found himself in the arena, standing next to the other young men, awaiting the opportunity to act upon the instruction of Ukiru. The instructor, who was now only taller than a few of his pupils, paced back and forth in front of the group.

"In combat, a warrior may easily find himself in a situation beyond his control. Facing a number of adversaries at once may be such a situation. Regardless of how much you train and practice the skills of fighting, there are times when you cannot control what is happening around you. The only way to prepare for such a time is to be able to recognize a bad situation and avoid it before you become trapped. Today we will split up and each of you will have a group of adversaries from whom you will have to retreat and defend yourself. Offensive tactics are not allowed in today's training. The way to succeed today is to avoid being trapped by the enemies who outnumber you and to hold out for as long as possible."

As Ukiru ended his introduction, the group split up and each person found his own space at the edge of the arena. The sand crunched beneath Kael's feet as he walked away, his footsteps producing an intriguing rhythm. He tapped the soil with the wooden staff he held in his right hand between each step and watched as it left a dimple in the soft earth. When he reached the edge of the arena, he turned to find his adversaries following at a short distance. There were eight monks in all, dressed in their usual attire and carrying staffs of their own. He looked around and noticed that most of the others had only five enemies, except for Soren, who had eight as well. When starting a new training session for a particular fighting concept, they always used wooden instruments, eventually moving on to bladed weapons when a level of proficiency was attained.

Kael gripped the staff firmly in both hands. *So we're supposed to carry a weapon, but we can't use it.* He always liked how weapons felt in his hands, like they were alive and just wanted to move. He had the urge to twirl the staff around his body. He had done so a long time ago and was chastised severely for it. Ukiru used him as an example that day to explain that a weapon was not a toy and should never be treated as such.

The enemies stopped twenty feet away and gathered in a bundle. Everyone looked to the center of the arena where Ukiru stood with his hand raised in the air.

"Begin," he shouted and his hand dropped.

Immediately the group in front of Kael spread out into a line and started to advance. Kael quickly moved to the left. The men on the left side ran wider to flank him and he quickly doubled back to the right, slipping past the men who waited to trap him there by the wall of the arena. Slowly at first, but with increasing frequency, he could hear the crack of wooden sticks hit each other as the other students tried to defend themselves. The sounds of combat meant that the others were not faring as well, as the purpose of this lesson was evasion.

Kael now had his entire group of enemies lined up behind him and closing in fast. He slowed his pace and turned out toward the middle of the arena so they couldn't use the wall to their advantage. Again they fanned out, hoping to encircle him and he backed away from them, dodging to the side of the group and closing the distance before they could use the advantage of their numbers against him. It became a dance after a while and his body moved through the evasion methods he had learned so thoroughly, allowing his mind to wander as his enemies chased him to no avail. After several minutes the sounds of struggle and wooden staffs beating against each other dwindled to nothing and Kael realized that he was the only one left who had not been defeated. Somehow, he didn't take any pleasure in the thought. He was beginning to get frustrated with the concept of evading the enemy. He knew what Ukiru was trying to teach by this exercise, but he didn't find it very efficient. He was also starting to get fatigued from the monotony.

Suddenly one of his enemies lunged forward and Kael realized that he had let the man get too close. He dodged to the side as the man swung his staff in an overhead motion, trying to bring it down on Kael's head. Kael raised his staff and deflected the blow to the side, sending his enemy tumbling past him into the sand. His knuckles ached as he realized the blow glanced off his hand. Kael quickly swiveled around and jabbed the man in the back with his staff.

"You're out," said Ukiru to the monk from a short distance away. The monk stayed on the ground and pretended to be a slain enemy.

Kael turned back to the group only to find that two others were advancing at a run. It was too late to run away from them. He instantly made the decision to run at them and try to break through, which would place him, once again, beyond the reach of the other five enemies. It was only an instant before the two were upon him. The man on the left swung his staff at waist level and the other man jabbed for the chest. Kael spun to the left and blocked the jab, throwing the enemy's staff in the way of the second adversary. The two blows met each other as Kael used his spinning momentum to dodge to the right of both men.

"What are you doing?" Ukiru yelled from across the arena.

Kael decided that there wasn't enough time to stop and defeat the two men. Instead, he ran for the safety of the open area behind the other five men. Ukiru was shouting something in the distance, but he wasn't paying attention any more. The pain in his hand fueled his frustration with this exercise. *I guess I'm just supposed to run around until one of them wounds me enough to slow me down. That's no way to fight.*

As he ran to the edge of the arena it occurred to him that he just didn't trust any of the things he was being taught. *Is that what's bothering me?* As the thought came, it triggered a memory from two years ago when he pointed out a flaw in one of the attack stances that Ukiru was teaching. The awkward position left the attacker unable to step backwards quickly and, therefore, the attacker would not have enough time to react if the defender decided to rush him. He had never seen Ukiru lose his temper the way he did that day. After being scolded and belittled in front of the rest of the young men, Kael was sent to his room without dinner and was not allowed out until the next morning. Ever since that day, Kael began to find problems with many other things about their training. It eventually bothered him so much that he devoted much of his personal time to developing his own methods of combat, though he would never have the chance to use them anywhere other than in the privacy of his own bedroom.

The seven remaining enemies stopped in the middle of the arena at Ukiru's command. Kael could see the instructor's face, flushed red with anger. "You men," he shouted at a group of other monks who were standing nearby. "Join in with the others." At his command, twenty other monks joined the ranks and Kael's enemies almost tripled. "If you insist on disobeying me, this will indeed become a painful lesson."

The rest of the students were watching intently.

Maybe I will get the chance to put my private studies to good use. Kael closed his eyes and breathed deeply. He tried to put everything out of his mind but the awareness of his own body. Ukiru's yelling voice slipped into silence. The vision of twenty-seven monks with wooden staffs blinked out of sight and quickly gave way to silence and darkness.

Kael could feel his heart beating heavily in his chest.

He could feel his lungs expanding and contracting as air rushed in and out of his body.

The sand moved beneath his feet as he shifted his weight from left to right.

There was another sensation as well, just at the edge of his perception, but still out of reach. It nagged at him until the sound of approaching footsteps caused him to open his eyes.

Suddenly, in that instant, he saw and felt the position of every man in the approaching group. Not only could he see and hear the enemies approaching, but he could actually feel them as if they were an extension of his own body. It took only a fraction of a second for him to know where the weakest point of the mob was. And that was where he ran. The faces of the monks dropped as the young man charged willfully into the insurmountable odds.

Kael closed the gap on the group before they had the chance to shift their order around to meet him. Even if they had the time, there was hardly any reason for twenty-seven men to think about the perfect way to approach one young man. And that was the weakness that Kael planned to exploit. As he came within striking distance, Kael twirled his staff above his head in open rebellion against the instructions of Ukiru, and brought it down at the limit of his reach on the head of the closest man. The blow caught the monk by surprise and shoved his head downward toward the sand, causing him to topple forward.

Kael kept his forward momentum and stepped onto the monk's back, springing off of his defeated enemy in a spinning motion. His staff flicked outward as he spun through the air, smacking into hard surfaces in rapid succession. Kael didn't have time to notice what he had struck until he landed in a somersault and came to his feet again. Turning around, he saw the group now trying to deal with the changing direction of their prey. Four men were lying on the ground, holding various parts of their bodies in an attempt to soothe their pain.

He had just broken through the thinnest part of the mob and would not get the same opportunity again. The remaining men split into two groups and began to circle back on Kael, trying to flank him on either side. Before they could get into position, he sprinted to the left and watched as their ranks broke formation. The men in front ran as fast as they could to keep Kael from getting around the left side of the group. As the closest man approached he swung his staff in a level arc aiming for Kael's head. Kael ducked under the attack and rolled onto his back, sweeping at the man's leg with his staff. The counterattack caught the monk on the knee and brought the man to the ground as well as two others behind him who tripped over their fallen comrade.

Kael tried to keep his momentum, but was too slow in getting to his feet. By the time he regained his footing and spun to meet his attackers, they were too close to run from. He crouched into a defense position of his own making and waited for the men to advance. The rear group spread out to encircle him as the group in front attacked to keep him from running.

Three monks advanced and the one in the middle jabbed his staff out at Kael. Parrying the jab with a two-handed block he struck the monk in the face with the same motion. Before the attacker on the right had time to bring his staff up to protect himself, Kael spun around and jabbed his own staff into the man's stomach. The third monk swung for Kael's head and Kael dropped to his knee, spinning his staff once above his head and smashed it into the man's chest, driving him backwards into his group.

Kael could feel a blow coming for the back of his head and spun to block the attack, but he was too late. The staff knocked him on the side of his head and dazed him for a moment. Then he was jolted by another blow to his back. Several more strikes crashed into his body before he fell over to the ground.

"That's enough." Ukiru's voice stopped the attackers and they slowly backed away. Ukiru stood over Kael and stared at the defiant young man. After several seconds of silence, Ukiru spoke. "Take him to his room."

Kael felt his arms lifted as two monks dragged him from the arena. He could see all of his fellow students watching in stunned silence as the men removed him from the training area. Even though he had taken several hard blows, Kael didn't feel very much pain. He decided that it would be best, however, to let the monks continue dragging him as if he couldn't walk. When they reached his room, the two men laid him down on his bed and left without saying a word. Kael rolled onto his back and stared at the ceiling. He couldn't remember now why he had done what he did. He only knew that it was important at the time. An appropriate emotion might have been regret, or even anger, but he just felt numb. One day, those buried emotions would come boiling to the surface, but for now he took a deep breath and closed his eyes.

When he awoke it was to the sound of the others returning from their meditation the following morning. Loud footsteps pounded down the hallway as each of his fellow students came back to their rooms for a change of clothes before breakfast. Kael looked down at his own body, still dressed in the dirty clothing from the previous afternoon. A soft knock at the door came as a surprise to Kael who rarely had anyone else in his room. *Not lately anyway.* Usually, the others would gather in Soren's room if they wished to socialize.

"Come in," he called.

The door opened and Ukiru stepped inside, carefully closing the door behind him. Kael's heart, which was so willing to defy this man yesterday, now trembled at the coming confrontation. Ukiru walked over to the bed and sat down slowly next to Kael with a calm look on his face.

"Are you hungry?"

The question seemed out of place to Kael. "Yes," he answered, not noticing his hunger until Ukiru mentioned it.

"You may come down to breakfast after we are finished talking."

"Okay," Kael responded, still unsure of how to read the man's body language.

"Are you hurt in any way?"

"No. They're just bruises; they'll heal."

Ukiru breathed deeply and exhaled. "What were you doing yesterday? I was trying to teach you all how to stay out of danger and you ran straight into it. I don't understand why you disobeyed me."

Kael wanted to explain everything to him, but how could he? How was he supposed to tell his mentor of seven years that the methods he is teaching are wrong? What words could he possibly use to explain what was impossible to prove; that he just knew something was missing? "I don't know," he mumbled instead. "I don't know."

Ukiru was obviously hoping for more of an answer and waited for Kael to elaborate. When nothing more was said, he stood up and walked over to the window. "You want to know what I think? I think that you still look back to your old life and wonder what would have happened if you had never come here."

Kael shrugged his shoulders, not really agreeing, but not necessarily disagreeing.

Ukiru continued. "This world rejected you and you were nearly dead when I found you. By the authority of the All Powerful and the direction of our High Priest, I saved you from that life and gave you the opportunity of another. This life," he motioned with his arms, "is a blessing. It's a chance to see what the All Powerful may accomplish through us. But I don't believe that you have given yourself wholly to it, or to him."

Ukiru spoke truthfully. Kael realized in that instant that he hadn't. Hadn't fully given himself to the training. Hadn't given himself fully to the god that Ukiru so often spoke of. As soon as Ukiru mentioned the All Powerful, Kael felt a twinge of uneasiness. He had never been able to reconcile his religious instruction with the concept of a single god that he had learned from Saba all those years ago. *Maybe my former life is really holding me back.* "Sometimes I feel like I'm just going through the motions, like this whole place is just one big exercise."

"Exactly," Ukiru spoke, suddenly looking encouraged. "Isn't that what life is, a preparation for what is to come when we die? But that doesn't mean that we should walk through life as though our actions don't matter. They do matter a great deal. This life is where our character is shaped and we become who we are supposed to be. I think that you are holding back in many ways, that you are keeping a small part of yourself reserved. You must trust that the All Powerful can do great things through you if you surrender yourself completely to him." Ukiru paused to look more directly at Kael.

He's trying to make sure that I understand.

"The humorous part about all of this is that, even though you are holding yourself back, you are still the most talented of all the boys here."

Kael wrinkled his eyebrows. "That's not true."

"Why do you disagree?"

Kael looked to the window and let his mind wander through all of his years of memories at the monastery. In every subject, whether in the classroom or the arena, Kael knew that he excelled. He wasn't always the best, but he was always near the top of his class. "Soren beats me every time in war strategy."

"Yes, but that is only one area. In the years that I have known you, I have seen glimpses of absolute perfection in individual combat that the others cannot even touch. Just think of what you could become if you would only trust my instruction."

Kael looked down at the bed and fumbled with the edge of his blanket.

"Please trust me; it is the only thing holding you back."

Ukiru stretched out his hand and waited.

Finally, Kael grasped it firmly. "You're right, I'm sorry."

Ukiru smiled. "No words, only actions." It was a saying that he was fond of and Kael thought that it was appropriate for the situation. "Now, it is time for breakfast," Ukiru said, walking to the door.

"I'll be there as soon as I change my clothes."

"Very well," Ukiru said and quietly left the room.

Kael lay back on his bed and stared at the ceiling. Ukiru was right. He had been holding a part of himself back, following all of the rules, but never really giving himself to his studies. Especially during meditation, when they were all supposed to focus their thoughts on the All Powerful, he always felt like it was make-believe. *Maybe I'm the one who is fake!*

He knew that there was only one more year until their pilgrimage and he decided to forget about everything that had just happened. He knew that he had to push aside his feelings of mistrust and forget about the combat methods that he was developing on his own time. He could see how all of these things were clouding his perception. *One more year. I need to see what I'm capable of.*

Another knock at the door interrupted his thoughts. "Come in."

Soren's faced peeked around the door. "How are you doing?"

"Fine," Kael replied.

"Are you coming to breakfast?"

"Yeah, as soon as I get changed."

Soren walked into the room and smiled. "You're still wearing your training clothes. You didn't have time to change since yesterday?"

"No," Kael replied with a laugh. "I fell asleep as soon as I got back to my room."

"Oh," Soren said, searching for the right words. "What happened yesterday?"

Kael exhaled loudly. "I'm not sure. I guess I just got frustrated with constantly retreating and running. I didn't think that running was the best way to deal with eight enemies, but I guess I was wrong, huh?"

"Yeah. But it sure was a good show," Soren said with a mischievous smile. "You were amazing. I've never seen someone move that fast before. You must have defeated a dozen of them before they got you."

"...nine actually."

"They looked like they hit you pretty hard," Soren stated, but it was more of a question.

Kael pulled his shirt off and showed him the bruises that were still forming on his back.

"Oh yeah," Soren said, "those'll be good ones in a couple of days."

"Oh well," Kael offered, "you always say the best lessons are the ones you learn, not the ones that you're taught, right?"

"That's right," Soren replied, walking over to the door. "I bet you'll never forget this one. Any way, you'd better hurry before the food is all gone."

"Okay, I'll be there in a second," Kael called to the retreating footsteps.

The air smelled clean and fresh following the recent storms that had passed over the city, washing everything with three days of rain. The bright sun was out now, drying the soil and a fresh humidity hung in the air.

Maeryn sat on the steps of the garden and watched Aelia play in the flowers with one of the servant girls. Nearly seven years old now, she was looking more and more like Adair every day. Lemus had no suspicions about the child's origins. Once he believed something, he never again questioned it. His stubbornness was a large part of his detestable personality, but it had a positive side.

The sound of rushed footsteps brought her out of her thoughts as Lemus entered the garden from the courtyard on the opposite side. He strode across the groomed soil in a hurry. Maeryn hoped that he would ignore her and keep walking by, but to her disappointment, he stopped briefly in front of her.

"Come with me," he commanded.

Maeryn looked to Aelia who was oblivious to anything but the clump of newly picked flowers in her dirty hand.

"She'll be fine," he added, hurrying up the steps and into the house.

Maeryn rose to her feet and tried to keep up with Lemus' pace.

Lemus stopped at the nearest room and motioned for Maeryn to follow. Once the two were inside he shut the door. The dusty room was strewn with books and papers. Several pieces of furniture were piled on top of each other in one corner. Adair had used this room to store things that he didn't want elsewhere in the house and it looked as if it had not been entered since then.

Lemus was visibly angered. "Many years ago, you mentioned a man who trained birds to fly between cities. Where can I find him?"

"Oh," Maeryn said. "That was such a long time ago. I'm not sure if he still lives in this region."

"Well, where did he used to live?"

Maeryn had to resist the desire to ask why he needed this information. When he was in a mood like this, he needed to feel important. She decided that it was best to just answer as soon as possible. "His name was Cornelius. He used to perform tricks with his birds in the City Square to earn money. That was the only time I saw him." It was the most direct answer she could think of.

Lemus nodded his head and his anger seemed to be pacified slightly.

After a moment of silence, Maeryn thought it was safe to ask questions. "What's wrong?"

Lemus looked up from staring at the ground.

Maeryn thought he might be waiting for her to ask.

"I sent out the census report last night. I used one rider as a decoy and a second rider to carry the report. The decoy left the city at midnight and rode to a checkpoint beyond the city limits where he was to wait for the second rider. The report left shortly after that, but the rider never made it to the checkpoint."

"Oh my!" exclaimed Maeryn, truly surprised, but exaggerating for effect.

Lemus' countenance changed as he enjoyed laying his burdens on Maeryn. She had worked hard to get to this point and now that she had gained his confidence, he spoke to her about everything. It made him feel important to impress her with the difficulty of governing the city, especially all of the problems he had to deal with on a daily basis. "We haven't even found his horse yet."

"Do you think it could be the rebels?" Maeryn asked, playing ignorant.

Lemus barked out a laugh. "Of course it's the rebels. Who else would have the nerve to do something like this? I can tell you one thing though, this won't carry on for long. They have grown from an annoyance to a menace and I will put a stop to them."

That's what you have said all along. Since the attack on Lemus' ships in the harbor, Maeryn had kept the rebels well informed of his plans for counterattack. It was because of her intervention that there hadn't been any major confrontations since that night. "What will you do?" she asked instead.

"I will see this bird-man of yours and find out if it is possible to send my report that way. Now that the rebels know the state of my forces, I will have some reorganizing to do. It will take much thought and patience, but I will dedicate my time to finding every last one of these vermin and exterminating them. They have sought to undermine the Empire and they will receive a just punishment." Lemus opened the door and walked confidently down the hall, not bothering to say goodbye or even to thank Maeryn for her time.

Maeryn, pleased to be rid of Lemus, walked back to the garden and resumed her position on the front steps. Aelia was leaning over the low wall surrounding the fountain and was running her hand through the water. The servant girl was trying to convince Aelia to come away from the fountain, but the gurgling water proved to be much more interesting than anything else at that moment.

Maeryn watched her daughter play and felt a sudden pang of guilt. Aelia had no idea about the circumstances surrounding her birth. As far as she knew, life was normal. She had a father and a mother who loved each other and her life was happy. That was how Maeryn intended to keep it. It would do more harm than good to tell her the truth—that Lemus was not really her father. All of the other horrible things that Lemus had done would go unmentioned as well. But what bothered Maeryn more than anything was the knowledge that Aelia had become a tool of her deception. If it had not been for her birth, Maeryn was sure that none of this would have worked. She had used Lemus' love for Aelia as a way to secure her own safety and was now using that safety as an inroad to do whatever she could to strike back at the Empire she had come to hate. That was the bottom line and it hurt to think about. Maeryn tried to shrug off the painful thoughts. *It won't do any good to think about that now. This is your life, and you must live it. One day, when Lemus has been brought to his lowest point, you will destroy him and then you will be free.*

19

Saba sat in the corner of the cell that had become his unwilling home for many years now. His hair and beard that had been shaven before his encounter with the cloaked man, now hung well past his shoulders. His body was thin and weak from inactivity and lack of proper nourishment. The guards only brought one meal a day, no longer concerned with keeping him unharmed. He tried his best to move around the cell and stretch his limbs every day to keep his body from becoming completely useless, but there was only so much he could do.

For all the years he had spent in this cell, there were only two things that occupied his time—the coming of his meal brought by a guard at dawn every morning, and the thoughts in his own head. The latter proved to be the more exciting of the two lately. When the cloaked man, or the being that was contained in his body, searched Saba's memory, he brought images and sounds out of a place where they had been forgotten. Most of them were forgotten once again, as Saba was unable to hold on to memories that had no connection to his present life. But a few lingered with him still and had actually grown more vivid with the passing years.

One such memory was an image—the symbol on the shaft of the arrowhead that Adair had given to him so many years ago; the symbol that took him to Orud where he was captured. All he had to do now was close his eyes and the memory came instantly to him.

Saba stared at his own hands, the skin smooth and healthy. In his hands he held a scroll. The edges of the discolored parchment were ragged and worn, as if they had seen many years of use. On the page in front of him was a sketch, drawn in the same ink as the surrounding text. Ten winged creatures, vaguely human, with their arms and wings outstretched, formed a circle. His hands reached down and placed the scroll into a small stone sarcophagus and slid the heavy lid over the top.

Saba walked through a cave with a rough dirt floor and arched stone ceiling covered with stalactites. The tunnel of the cave widened as it turned around a bend and stopped at a wall of water. It was the backside of a waterfall. Saba ran toward it and jumped. For a second, there was a muffled cacophony of sounds, until Saba's falling body emerged from the waterfall into the sunlight. He continued to fall a short distance until he splashed into a pool of water. Swimming back to the surface, his head broke free and he drew in a few quick breaths. All around the pool was dense vegetation and a forest of a bright green color, suggesting regular, heavy rainfall. On the bank of the pool stood three men of a primitive culture. Each brown-skinned native wore only a loincloth and carried a short spear. They were barefoot and had no adornments aside from the white bones that pierced their noses. Saba swam in their direction as one of the men waved his hand, beckoning him to come closer. Just as Saba reached a shallow area where his feet dug into the soft sand, he stood up and looked behind at the waterfall.

Saba opened his eyes and was confronted by the drab jail cell once again. No matter how long he dwelled on the memory, he couldn't make it tell him any more. It started with seeing his hands, and ended with the waterfall, no matter how many times he revisited it.

Kael stood in calf-deep grass, which was now green from the spring rain. The breeze made the grass sway and ripple like ocean water. Sweat began to bead on his forehead as the sun beat down on his body. He stood firm on the ground with his arms extended, holding a bow stretched taut and ready to fire. On his left, a few paces away was Soren, and on his right, Jorn. All of the students were standing in a line and each held a bow, waiting for the command to loose their arrows. Kael closed his eyes and imagined his surroundings, trying to recreate the strange event that happened on the bluffs and again during his encounter with the monks. Since that day, he attempted to bring back the sensation at the start of each exercise, but it proved to be elusive. It was like trying to train a muscle that he wasn't even sure existed. He steadied his thoughts and concentrated on his breathing. In his mind's eye, he could begin to feel the grass waving in the breeze as if each blade were a hair on his arm. He could feel the targets made of hay and canvas lined up out in the field in front of them. Each student had his own set at varying distances based on the limit of each student's skill level. Kael's own target was set at almost twice the distance of the others, next to Soren's.

Ukiru's voice spoke softly. "Fire when ready."

Almost immediately, Kael felt seven bolts fly at their targets, all striking their mark, some more accurately than others. The eighth arrow was loosed only a second later by Rainer who missed his target. The other students scrambled to restring the second in a series of three arrows. Soren and Kael still held back waiting for a break in the wind.

"You first," Soren whispered, when the breeze died down.

Kael opened his eyes and saw his target. Even at its great distance, Kael could feel it as if he were asked to reach up and touch his own nose. He aimed for the fist-sized red circle painted in the middle and loosed his arrow. It flew quickly to its target followed by Soren's. Both arrows struck inside of the circle. Immediately, Kael plucked another arrow from the quiver at his right leg and set it to the bow-string. In one motion he raised the bow and pulled the arrow back, resting his hand just below his cheekbone. The rest of the students and their attempts had disappeared now and the only thing in Kael's mind was his own target. He aimed and released his second arrow just as a gust of wind blew. The arrow struck the target only inches to the left of the red circle, blown off course by the wind. He grabbed his third and final arrow and aimed while the wind continued to blow. Closing his eyes, he could immediately feel the path that the arrow should take. He didn't stop to question it, but aimed almost a foot to the right of the target and several inches higher than the last shot. He released his last arrow and quickly opened his eyes, watching the bolt arc through the air, fighting the wind. It struck the target with a loud crack.

"What was that?" Horace yelled.

Kael couldn't see his third arrow and began to question whether or not he missed completely.

"Let's go see," Ukiru suggested and everyone ran out to the targets to see the results.

As Kael got closer, it became clear what had happened. His third arrow struck the center of the red target and split his first arrow in two pieces. The split pieces of the first arrow were still lodged in the target so that they looked like one arrow. Kael looked to the left and Soren was staring at him.

"You know...you're making us all look bad," he said with a smile.

Kael smiled in return just before noticing that Soren's target had all three arrows inside the red circle. "Not with a pattern like that..." he countered.

Kael felt a hand on his shoulder and turned to see Ukiru behind him. "Good shooting, you two," he said in a quiet voice so as not to make a scene. "Kael, what happened is very interesting, but you must work on your consistency."

Kael nodded, his joyous feelings immediately deflated.

"Soren, excellent job," he congratulated the young man. He searched for something more to say, but there was nothing for him to critique. Instead he patted his student on the back and turned to address the rest of the students.

"Are you pleased with your results?" he shouted to be heard over the sound of the waving grass. A few mumbled words were the only replies he received. He waved for everyone to follow him back to their starting positions and addressed them on the way. "It is easy to reach a high level of proficiency with bow and arrow when shooting once. It is quite another matter to be consistently accurate when shooting multiple times in a row. In a war setting, archers must shoot one arrow after another and it is not enough to simply let one fly. Each arrow must count as if it were your last."

When each student reached his starting position, Ukiru pointed at the targets in the field. "The target in front of you is your enemy. He is charging at you and you have no other weapons but your bow. Visualize the small red target on his chest and fire three more arrows. Don't try to hurry. Don't panic. Simply pull an arrow from your quiver, set it to the string, pull back, aim, and release. Do this three times until your enemy is defeated." Ukiru raised his hand and each student readied himself.

Kael was already visualizing the target in his own way. When Ukiru's hand dropped, he pulled an arrow from his quiver and began the fluid process of firing once, twice, and three times. When he released his last arrow to join the other two inside of the red circle, he looked around and noticed that he had finished before all of the others, except for Soren, who was enjoying the competition.

The next day, Kael found himself waiting on a bench in a hallway. He was staring at the floor when the door opened. He rose to his feet and walked into a room where Ukiru and three other monks were standing around a table. As he walked closer, he could see a large map spread out on the table covered with small wooden statues. It was an elaborate game that Ukiru had devised to teach his students the principles of warfare strategy.

"One day has elapsed. Your scout has just returned to inform you that the enemy has breached the northern wall of the city." Ukiru leaned over the table and pointed to a black statue on the map to indicate the new information.

Kael looked over the pale statues representing his own forces, most of which were still far to the east. The objective of this game was to take the abandoned city in the center of the map and use the advantage it offered to defeat the opposing forces. It looked like he was going to have to take the role of the attacking army in this game. Somehow Soren, who was waiting outside another door, had managed to move his army to the northern wall fast enough to take the city while most of Kael's forces were waiting for the foot-soldiers to catch up. He had already put himself at a disadvantage by his lack of aggression.

"Pull the army back from the wall and set up a camp until the other soldiers arrive." *I'm already committed to a siege. I might as well wait until the full force of my army is ready.*

"Very well," Ukiru nodded his head. "Please wait in the hall."

Kael walked out to the hallway and resumed his position on the bench. After a few minutes, he was summoned back into the room. The map looked very different from when he had seen it last.

"Half of the enemy's army has taken up residence in the city and is guarding the walls with archers. The other half has come out of the eastern gate and is attacking your unguarded camp." Ukiru's face was unreadable, but Kael knew that he must be disappointed.

Kael looked to his foot soldiers in the east and saw that they were now close enough to attack. "The archers will retreat from the camp and the foot soldiers will attack." Once again, Ukiru nodded his head and Kael left the room to give Soren his turn at the map.

Long moments passed before Kael was let into the room. When he came back and looked at the map, he saw that Soren's forces were now all inside of the city. "What is the status of my army?" he asked immediately.

Ukiru pointed to the map. "Your foot soldiers pushed the enemy back into the city, destroying a quarter of his forces. But most of your archers were destroyed in the process."

Kael shook his head and tried to think of some way to take a defended city with only a few archers and the rest of his army. This game required an active imagination to understand how each stage might progress. Kael thought that the northern gate must have suffered some damage when Soren's forces broke through. "All of my forces will move to the northern gate. The archers will provide cover for the foot soldiers to attack the gate." Kael turned and left the room before he had the chance to see Ukiru's expression. It didn't matter anyway; Ukiru hadn't shown one bit of emotion since this game had started. He was obviously doing his best not to show favoritism.

As Kael waited in the hallway, he became aware that Soren was taking longer and longer on each turn. He must be choosing his actions very carefully. He had always been the best at this sort of competition. He had a way with people and knowing what they were capable of. Kael, on the other hand, had long since lost the patience for this sort of game. There was so much speculation involved that it became difficult to make decisions. Kael preferred to confront an enemy face to face, study his actions, and react. That is why he enjoyed the physical combat training the best. The principles and actions were all real and substantial.

"Come in, please," one of the monks said, peering around the door.

Kael rose to his feet and entered the room where Ukiru and Soren stood by the table. "This exercise has reached a point where the smallest of decisions will affect the outcome. Now that your two forces are within close range, you will be able to see everything that your enemy is doing; therefore, you are both allowed in the room at the same time." Ukiru waved Kael over to the table to update him. "The rest of your archers were killed in the attack. They could not compete with the range of the archers on the wall. However, they provided enough cover for your foot soldiers to breach the gate. You lost one quarter of your foot soldiers taking the gate, but you still have half of your original forces."

Kael surveyed the map and noted the location of Soren's forces. "How has my enemy reacted?"

Soren looked up from the map and winked at Kael, who smiled in return.

Ukiru answered. "After breaking down the gate, your soldiers have found themselves in a narrow corridor leading into the courtyard of the city. Your enemy has massed his foot soldiers in the courtyard to meet your attack and has placed his archers on top of the corridor to fire arrows down on your soldiers. You have already lost several men in the initial surprise."

Kael looked up at Soren who was now expressionless. "The soldiers in the rear will lift their shields over their heads to defend against the volley of arrows." Kael tried to imagine actually being in that situation. "The entire unit will drive the enemy back into the courtyard and get out of the narrow corridor."

Ukiru looked to Soren for his instructions. Soren looked straight at Kael. "My foot soldiers will push back to keep his forces inside the corridor. And my archers will continue to shoot." Ukiru looked back to Kael for his response.

"What is the status of both armies?" Kael asked.

"Both forces are dwindling, but the archers have given your enemy the advantage," Ukiru responded, still waiting for Kael's decision.

Kael knew that it was just a matter of time before he was defeated. It was strictly a numbers game now. His soldiers were evenly matched against Soren's, but the archers were bound to take out a few of his men, even with their shields above their heads. "My forces will retreat out of the northern gate."

Ukiru looked to Soren for a nod of confirmation before picking up the pale statue from the courtyard and placing it back in the corridor. He then reached for a black statue and placed it outside of the gate. "The other half of your enemy's force exited the western gate and has come behind you. Your men are now trapped in the corridor by a force in the courtyard, another outside of the gate, and archers above you. Your men are defeated."

Kael immediately looked up from the map and extended a hand to Soren. "Well done."

Soren grasped Kael's hand and shook it. "Thank you," he said with a smile on his face.

Ukiru turned to Soren and clasped a hand on his shoulder. "You are the winner of this competition. Congratulations."

Soren only smiled in response.

"Now, you must finish packing. Tomorrow we begin our pilgrimage. We must be ready to leave at first light."

The two young men walked out of the room together and Soren put his arm around Kael. "You put up a good fight."

"No, I didn't," Kael argued. "You're just saying that to make me feel better."

"Yeah. You're right. You didn't stand a chance," Soren said, patting Kael on the back. "Come on. I've got to hurry. I haven't even started packing yet," Soren said, running ahead.

"We were supposed to start a week ago," Kael yelled, but Soren had already rounded the corner and was out of earshot.

The light from the quickly sinking sun filtered through the trees, leaving the ground in the garden dappled with alternating yellow light and purple shadows. Maeryn sat on a rock ledge surrounding an island of flowers, carefully pruning them by snapping off the dead parts of each plant. The soft humming of a melody drifted to her ears from across the garden and it brought a smile to her face. Aelia liked to sing and it warmed Maeryn's heart to have the child in her presence.

Life is difficult to understand sometimes. It seemed like such a long time ago that she was surrounded by very different circumstances. She used to watch while Kael and Ajani would play in the courtyard. Saba would always be nearby, ready to give an explanation to the boys about how something worked. Eventually, when the sun went down, Adair would come home and everyone would sit down to a meal together.

Life was different then. Maeryn knew that even in her current circumstances she was more fortunate than most, but somehow, that didn't make her feel any better. It was peaceful in the garden, among the trees and flowers. Somehow, regardless of the things going on around them, the plants and trees kept growing, kept going through their seasons. They would shed leaves or change colors depending on the species, but eventually, all would bloom again. *What will my life look like when it blooms again?*

"Ma'am?" came a voice behind her. Maeryn was so deep in thought that she had not heard the footsteps in the coarse sand.

"Yes," she replied, turning to see Zula standing patiently behind her. The woman held a piece of parchment in her hand, which she extended to Maeryn. "Thank you, Zula."

"Yes, ma'am," she replied with a nod and quickly turned and walked away.

She is a strange woman to figure out. One moment she would speak with such passion, disregarding every manner expected of a slave. Then the next moment she would be polite and follow all of the rules to perfection. Maeryn thought that it must be difficult for such a passionate woman to keep quiet. And it seemed to be getting more difficult for her. Indeed, Maeryn herself was finding it more difficult lately to be in the presence of Lemus and not say all of the things she wished to. She only hoped that Zula would not make a mistake in front of that man, for her own sake.

Maeryn turned the letter over in her hands and the sight of the wax seal on the other side sent her heart racing. She immediately lifted her head and glanced around the garden to make sure that no one was watching her. The slight movement of Aelia at the other end of the garden was the only presence she could see.

She broke the seal on the letter and unfolded the parchment.

I know not the final destination of this letter. Nor do I know to whom it is sent. What I do know is that the one who reads it has proven himself time and again to be a true ally. For that I must extend my appreciation as well as the offer of my aid in any circumstance where I may be of assistance to you. As I do not know your identity, I will trust that if you ever need anything that is in my power to give, simply communicate it to me and it will be done. As a gesture of my trust in you, I wish to give you information as well. Please forgive the generalities as I do not wish to endanger anyone with specifics. Indeed this letter is already incriminating and I hope you will follow my advice and burn it as soon as you are able. In the past, Bastul has not been a major focus of our efforts throughout the Empire. Therefore, it has gone overlooked for some time. Lately, certain events have brought Bastul to the forefront of our attention, due in large part to your own contributions. However, we do not have enough allies in your city to make any difference. Therefore, I must ask a favor of you, if you wish to continue this relationship, but it will require much patience.

The Empire has been built upon the backs of slaves who reap none of the benefits of its citizens, but who must labor every day for its welfare. The city of Bastul has one of the largest slave populations in the Empire and I believe that these people are the key to developing a large base of sympathizers to our cause within your city. My request is that you take note of every slave within Bastul and find out if there are any who would not want the chance to change their way of life. From the information we have received from you in the past, I feel confident that you are the man for this task. My hope is that you are willing to take this next step and become an active part of our cause. However, if you do not wish this relationship to continue, simply burn this message and I will not contact you again.

I await your reply.

Maeryn quickly folded the parchment into its original form and looked around the garden to make sure that no one was watching. Her heart was still beating loudly in her chest in stark contrast to the silence in the garden. Aelia had only moved a few feet from her last position and was now staring in awe at the butterfly flexing its wings on her arm.

Maeryn looked back at the letter, afraid to open it again. Somehow it seemed more dangerous if she were to reread it, as if the first time had been an accident. Many thoughts raced around her head, crashing into one another and making it difficult to think clearly. She raised her hand to her eyes and massaged them until her mind cleared. The words of the letter shocked her in many ways. She had no idea that the Resistance was so elaborate and involved so many cities. It made perfect sense that a movement such as this would not be limited to Bastul, but for some reason, she hadn't considered the vastness of it and the consequences of involving herself in such a cause. When she first wrote a letter and gave it to Zula, it was a result of her own personal struggle with Lemus and a desire to see him fail. She didn't realize what she was getting herself into. But the more she thought about it, the more sense it made. *Who else is capable of doing this task? Who else has my position and is not fiercely loyal to the Empire? What about the attack on the shipment in the harbor? If Bastul really has been 'overlooked', what kind of power do they have in other cities?* It all became too much to think about. Maeryn knew that she would need to think more on this matter before deciding, but something inside her already knew the answer.

"Aelia?" she called out.

"Yes, Mother," came the reply from behind a flowering bush, followed by a sweet little face.

"Let's go inside, the sun is almost down."

20

Tears flowed down Saba's face. He had no images to recall, only the feeling of a deep and immense sense of loss. Someone had died in his past; someone he loved deeply. In the recent months since this memory—if it could be called such—came back, there were several occasions when the feeling would overwhelm him and he would cry until his body fell asleep from sheer exhaustion. He would wake, only to find that the feeling had not gone away, but had only lessened in intensity. Eventually, he would heal and begin to feel normal for a while until it happened again, unexpectedly. As far back as his time in Bastul, Saba had wished that he could remember what was in his past. But on these occasions, he knew that the pain was too great for him to experience and that it was a blessing to have no memory of it. He wondered now if there were other painful things in his past; things from which he was being protected by his own forgetfulness.

Kael sat at the prow of the ship, watching as waves broke into white foam around the hull. From somewhere behind him he heard the laughter of Horace and Donagh as they shared a joke. They had all been at sea for weeks now. Initially, the trip had been an exciting break from their normal routine. But when the first day of the week arrived, they began with the usual morning meditation, followed by all of their normal instructions in various subjects. The afternoon's physical training consisted mainly of hand-to-hand combat while trying to keep one's balance during the rocking, swaying motion of the boat at sea. It was difficult at first, but Kael found that the rhythm of the ocean was like everything else in nature; it felt alive and seemed to have a predictable pattern once you got to know it.

But Kael wasn't thinking of any of that right now. He was preoccupied at the present with trying to catch a glimpse of their destination. He had been told, along with all of the others, that they would reach the temple before sundown, and he had grown tired of being at sea. Finally deciding not to torture himself any longer, he got to his feet and moved past the others, taking a seat at the stern. The view was much of the same. Stormy skies and ocean as far as the eye could see. The only difference was the wake left behind the large boat.

It was strange to think how much time had passed since he had left Bastul. He had stopped counting long ago, but it must have been close to eight years. Things had changed drastically in the past year for him. Ever since that talk with Ukiru, Kael realized that he had been living in the past.

The past is past, but the future is yet to come, Ukiru would say.

Kael laughed to himself. It was funny how well you got to know people when you spent enough time with them. Although in his case, he didn't have any choice. It wasn't as if he could go anywhere. Still, he was starting to enjoy his life again. He was living in the present now, and looking toward the future. Ukiru told all of them that by the end of the trip, they would get to see the temple, meet the High Priest, and receive a commission straight from the All Powerful. Kael knew that it was just another step in his training, but it would give him a taste of what his purpose in life was to be, and that had recently become very important. He was no longer a child, he realized, but a young man being prepared to go out into the world as a messenger for the All Powerful.

"What is that?" yelled an excited voice from the front of the ship. Kael turned around and looked to the southwest, off the starboard side of the ship. About half of a mile away, the low-lying clouds had parted, allowing a bright shaft of daylight to stream down to the ocean in a column of brilliant pale yellow.

"Wow," remarked Kael as he walked back to the prow. "That's beautiful."

Soren turned around and noticed what Kael was looking at. "No. I think he was talking about that."

Kael turned from the spectacle and followed Soren's pointing finger toward the southeast where the boat was facing. At first he didn't see anything. "What am I supposed to be looking at?" he asked for clarification.

Arden turned around. "Don't you see it?"

Soren waved a hand at Arden and turned back to Kael. "Look closer at the water."

Kael looked back to the ocean and after several seconds he noticed something different. It was still more than a mile away, but the shimmer on the water was slightly different, duller somehow.

"Is that where we are headed?" asked Jorn.

Kael wasn't sure to whom he was speaking until he realized that Ukiru was standing behind him. "Yes, Jorn. That is where we are headed."

Ukiru always had a fatherly tone in his voice and Kael realized that it was getting more noticeable as time went on.

"What is it?" Jorn asked, still confused.

Ukiru couldn't help but smile. "I'll explain it when we get closer," he answered, adding to the mystery of the situation.

During the next few minutes, all of the boys stared in wonder at what they couldn't understand. The clouds began to break apart and more light streamed down from overhead. The glittering light reflected off the water making it more difficult to see the object of their fascination. Suddenly, as they moved closer, its silhouette broke apart from the horizon and became a substantial object.

Ukiru's timing was perfect. "What you are looking at is a circular wall surrounding the location of the High Temple of the All Powerful. The surface of the wall is covered in sheets of polished metal to reflect the image of the water around it. It is not too much different from a mirror; only, instead of reflecting one's face, it reflects the water around itself, thereby concealing what is behind the wall."

"Is it floating?" asked Coen.

"That is a good question," Ukiru replied. "It is not floating, but underneath the water, the wall is anchored to the ground. The water is very shallow by the wall and we must circle around the wall and enter from the south where there is a deeper channel through which boats may travel."

As soon as Kael realized what he was looking at, a question formed in his mind. "Why is it necessary to hide the High Temple?"

Ukiru turned to Kael, somewhat shocked by the question. His agitated features slowly gave way to his usual calm demeanor as he gave Kael an answer. "This world is no longer loyal to the All Powerful. Therefore, it is not safe to leave the temple exposed to anyone not specifically looking for it. For that matter, followers of the All Powerful are not safe to roam about freely in this world, which is why your training has included combat."

"I thought the temple would be bigger," Donagh pointed out.

"Actually, it is very large; you just can't see it," answered Ukiru.

"What do you mean?"

Ukiru smiled. "It's under the surface of the water."

"How can you build a Temple under the water?" Donagh asked in a deep voice.

Ukiru turned to face Donagh, apparently liking his line of questioning better than Kael's. "I don't know how one might build a temple under the water, but this one was originally above the water. You see, thousands of years ago, the gods built this temple. Everything that you see now was once dry land and the waters were not this deep. The temple was carved out of a mountain and the people would come here to worship. There was a great war between the gods, and the one that we call the All Powerful emerged victorious. He chased the other gods away, never to return again. But eventually, this world stopped worshipping him and he left until such a time as he would return to claim the world that is rightfully his own. After he left, the oceans rose and buried the temple beneath the water. It has remained this way for thousands of years until now."

"Why would he leave?" Kael asked, interrupting.

Ukiru tried not to show his frustration. "The All Powerful left this world to give everyone the opportunity to see how detestable life would be without him. We have had many years to make our decision and still the people of this world choose to live without his guidance, or most of them anyway. But now the High Priest has heard the voice of the All Powerful and has restored the temple. We are, at this very moment, preparing for his return."

As Ukiru answered the questions of the young men, the boat made its way around to the south side of the wall and was now within a hundred yards of the structure. As they approached, its camouflaging quality began to lose its effectiveness as the individual sheets of polished metal could be made out from one another by their riveted seams.

"The wall conceals the top portion of the mountain which is the only part above the waterline," Ukiru continued explaining. He was about to say something else when he realized the boys were not paying attention. Everyone was watching as a section of the wall slid sideways to reveal a glimpse of the interior through a narrow channel, just wide enough for their boat.

Kael looked over the side of the boat and could see a distinction between the shallow water and the darker, deeper channel through which they were sailing. As the ship left the open ocean and entered the confines of the channel, the water abruptly changed to glassy smooth. The air was more still as well, the wind being blocked by the surrounding wall. As if waiting for a signal, dozens of oars sprouted from the hull of their ship and began to propel the boat through the channel and into a courtyard of sorts.

It was even more impressive on the inside. All around the interior of the wall were covered ports filled with various sizes of ships. Some were tiny and others were larger than any ships Kael had ever seen. Rising from the center of the harbor was an island without trees or vegetation of any kind. What did cover the land, however, were numerous buildings and structures as well as a multitude of different piers jutting out a short distance into the channel like spokes on a wheel. Most of these docks had small rowboats moored to their sides. But the strangest sight of all was the enormous cave burrowed into the island.

Narian, who had been silent for most of the trip, finally spoke. "Is that how we get into the mountain?"

"Yes, it is one of four entrances. There are three more facing the north, east, and west." Ukiru seemed pleased to hand out information that pointed to the glory of the High Temple.

As their boat approached the island, six men walked out from the shadows of the cave entrance and quickly made their way down to the pier. These men were dressed all in black, much different than the monks who staffed the ship on which Kael stood. Their long-sleeved tunics fell only to their waists and they wore loose-fitting pants that ended several inches above their calf-high sandals.

The boat came to rest next to the pier and the six men secured the ship to the dock with ropes. Ukiru extended a walking plank from the ship to the dock and motioned for the young men to exit the boat. As they did so, the six men on the pier formed a single file line, shoulder to shoulder, parallel with the pier. Kael wondered whether these men were monks or soldiers as he walked down the plank and finally stepped on to the pier.

Luckily, Coen had the same thought. "Are these men monks as well?" he said in a hushed voice to Ukiru, not wanting to offend the men by speaking about them in such close proximity.

"No," Ukiru answered, matching Coen's hushed tone. "These men are guards of the High Temple, soldiers in a way."

After everyone was assembled on the dock, Ukiru led the group up to the island. They walked in single-file following a raised deck that passed between buildings and led to the southern entrance in a straight line. Kael glanced behind him to see the six men no longer standing at attention, but hurriedly unloading their supplies from the ship.

As they made their way into the cave, the gray light of the overcast skies gave way to the flicker of torchlight. The cavern was enormous in size. The ceiling was at least thirty feet overhead and it stretched a hundred feet deep before disappearing into the shadows.

"First, I will show you around the temple and you will see how close it is to being fully restored. Then we will have our evening meal." Ukiru directed his words to no one in particular, although Jorn's stomach was growling audibly. "This is the supply storage area and as you can see, the temple can sustain many people for over a year without the need of outside assistance."

Kael tried to estimate the number of wooden boxes lining the walls of the cavern but quickly gave up. The boxes were stacked four high and four wide in columns that lead all the way to the back of the cave. They were not labeled and so their contents were a mystery, but Kael thought that they must contain food in order for the temple to be independently sufficient.

This time it was Soren who questioned what he was looking at. "Why is it necessary to have this many supplies?" His voice echoed slightly.

Ukiru didn't stop and only turned his head as he kept the group moving. "Oftentimes, a temple will become a place of refuge for its worshippers. We already know that the world is not friendly to the All Powerful and his followers, so every precaution must be taken to ensure that they always have a refuge."

The group moved through the cavern and made its way to the back where the torches on the wall did little to illuminate their surroundings. The silence was broken only by the sound of their own footsteps on the stone beneath them. It took a few seconds for Kael's eyes to adjust, but eventually he could make out a wide doorway at the top of a short flight of stairs toward the back of the cavern.

Ukiru walked up the steps and paused for a moment when he reached the doorway, waiting for the others to catch up. "Stay close to me and don't wander; it is easy to get lost here."

Everyone proceeded through the door and down the spiraling staircase on the other side. The steps were wide enough for two people to comfortably walk side by side. Kael found himself at the end of the line and decided that he would prefer to walk alone so that he could get a good look at this place without having to carry on a conversation. Something about this place unsettled him. Maybe it was the black stone walls, or the way he felt all alone when he lagged behind, as if the world had passed him by. He ran his fingers along the wall and was surprised at the smoothness of the stone. Suddenly he realized that the others had gotten ahead of him and he quickened his pace.

The staircase ended at a hallway that branched into three directions. At the intersection stood a guard, dressed like the others from the dock, but holding a spear at his side. He didn't even move to acknowledge their presence. Ukiru passed by the man and nodded, taking the path on the right. This hallway seemed to stretch forever with doorways lining both sides. As they walked, Ukiru explained what most of the rooms were used for and even offered a little history as to their original design. After what seemed like an hour of walking, which didn't make sense to Kael who thought that they should have reached the other side of the island already, Ukiru turned to the left and followed a narrow passage. Everyone had to duck to keep from bumping their heads except Jorn who walked all the more tall under the circumstances.

The narrow passage opened into what seemed like a gigantic cavern. "This is one of the major passages in the mountain through which large groups of people would pass in order to make their way to the temple," Ukiru explained.

"I thought we were already in the temple," questioned Horace.

Ukiru's smile wasn't visible, but Kael could hear it in his voice.

"Not yet. And you will not get to see it right away. It is still being prepared for the ceremony. But I will take you to the entrance."

Ukiru again turned to the right and began to walk at a brisk pace. Kael finally understood the reason that they had never reached the other side of the island. This enormous hallway, like the previous one, curved slightly to the left making a large circle. They were closer to the center of the island now and the curve of this passage was more noticeable than the last. The torches flickered much more in this passage and the air seemed fresher.

As the rest of the young men tried to keep pace with Ukiru, Kael couldn't help but wonder how this temple was constructed. He looked to the ceiling, which was more than fifty feet above him and marveled at what it must have taken to carve such a large amount of stone out of this place. His gaze drifted to the walls and quickly fixed itself on a hole to his left. It was far above the ground, almost at the ceiling and he could almost smell the fresh air coming in through it.

"Stay close," echoed Ukiru's voice from farther ahead than Kael realized.

As he jogged to catch up he noticed another hole in the wall ahead. By the time he reached the group he could see it more clearly. This one was slightly lower than the previous one, but still too far away to see if it led to open air. As the minutes went by, Kael watched as the holes continued to appear at the same frequency, with each one being slightly lower than the one before. Finally, the passage ended at a large doorway, blocked by a wooden door that seemed as solid as the mountain itself. Kael looked up and saw the last of the windows only nine or ten feet above the ground. It was completely dark, but fresh air was definitely coming in through it. The window was circular and looked large enough to fit a grown man through.

A loud clank startled Kael and brought his attention back to the group. Ukiru was pushing the door open and beckoned for the young men to follow. They all stepped into a well-lit, dome-shaped room with two doors. The one straight in front of them was ridiculously large and covered by a thick curtain. The other door to the right seemed to be the only thing in this whole mountain sized appropriately for normal human beings.

Ukiru walked to the smaller door and knocked. "That curtain covers the entrance into the temple. We will eat our evening meal first and then I will take you inside to meet the High Priest." The door opened and Ukiru walked through.

Immediately, the smell of food came to Kael's nose. The rumble of Jorn's stomach brought a bit of hushed laughter from Donagh and Horace. As they followed Ukiru into the small room, Kael noticed the man holding the door was dressed in robes like the monks at the monastery, only his were all black.

Inside of the small room was a ring of large pillows circled around a pedestal. Ukiru motioned for everyone to take a seat. Being the last in line, Kael was the last to find a pillow. The intimacy of the setting was strange and made him feel uncomfortable.

Ukiru looked at ease sitting on his pillow with his legs crossed. He extended both arms out to his sides and addressed the group. "We have come to the end of our journey and I'm sure that you are all hungry." At these words, the monk who was holding the door approached the group and placed a silver tray of cheeses and bread on top of the pedestal. He walked back to the corner of the room and opened a wooden chest, producing a silver goblet and filled it with wine from a bottle. He walked back to the group and placed the goblet next to the tray of food.

"Is that all there is?" asked Jorn, sounding sincerely worried.

"My dear Jorn, your question is an honest one." Ukiru paused, thinking of the right words to say. "This is only a small meal to take the edge off of your hunger. But in a few minutes, you will meet the High Priest who will lead you in a meditation where you will be met by the All Powerful. Please believe me when I tell you that food will be the last thing on your mind. In fact, I doubt that you would be able to keep anything in your stomach if you were to eat too much." Ukiru took the tray and handed it to Jorn. "Take a few pieces and pass it around."

As each person chewed on the small amount of cheese and bread, Ukiru continued. "Until this point, I have attempted to show you everything that I know about how to protect yourself, lead others, and be a useful tool for the work of the All Powerful. The time has come for all of you to meet him. This is a great privilege, reserved only for a select few. And everyone who has come into his presence has been unable to keep his grip on consciousness, including myself. I do not say this to scare you, but I want you to realize that after this experience you will feel a presence in your life that will guide and protect you. The All Powerful will accomplish great things through you and you will never experience a greater life than this one which has been given to you. I have shown you everything that I know in our time together, but after tonight there will be another who will instruct you."

Ukiru isn't going to instruct us anymore? Kael felt a tinge of sadness. He tried to imagine what the next part of his life would be like.

It seemed that they had only been in the room for a few minutes before Ukiru stood and waited for the others to do the same. "It is time," he stated and walked toward the door. The monk who had fed them opened the door and the group followed Ukiru out into the dome shaped room. Ukiru waited by the large curtain until everyone was present.

Again, Kael was the last in line. There was a tension in the air that made him feel uneasy. *It's probably just the anticipation of an important event.* But it felt more like something terrible was about to happen. He looked around at the others to see if he was the only one who felt worried, but they only seemed excited.

"You are entering the temple of the All Powerful and so I will remind you that I expect the highest level of respect from all of you." With these words,

Ukiru pulled hard on a thick rope to one side of the curtain and it glided slowly sideways to reveal a dark tunnel. The effect was a little anti-climactic and the boys looked back and forth at one another, clearly expecting something different. "Follow me," Ukiru added, and proceeded into the darkness.

For a few seconds, Kael was unable to see anything and had to rely on his sense of sound to guide him, listening to the footsteps ahead of him. But slowly, a soft glow began to reflect off the walls and the silhouettes of the figures ahead could be made out. The glow quickly grew into a flicker of sharper yellow light and the echoing sounds of footsteps diminished. The tunnel ended at a large wooden cage set into a hole in the wall.

Ukiru grabbed hold of the cage and opened the front like a door. "Everyone in," he instructed.

With hesitation, the others walked into the wooden cage and moved to the rear. Kael followed, while Ukiru brought up the rear after closing the door. Then, grabbing hold of a lever on the ceiling of the cage, Ukiru pulled it sharply and the cage began to descend.

As their descent began to quicken, Kael's stomach began to tighten.

"What is this?" asked Rainer.

Ukiru, still holding the lever, turned his head. "It is a lift that is used to transport supplies between the various levels within the mountain. It is also the quickest way to the temple."

After several minutes of watching the stone walls and occasional tunnels pass by, the lift began to slow. Kael watched Ukiru's hand on the lever as he controlled the speed of the descent.

Ukiru began to apply more pressure to the lever until the lift stopped completely. Then he walked to the front and unlocked the door which swung outward over another smooth stone passage.

The group exited the lift in the same order they entered it. Then the young men waited for Ukiru to close and latch the door.

When the instructor was finished, he walked to the front of the group and proceeded down the short passage that ended at another thick black curtain. Without hesitation, Ukiru reached up and pulled the curtain aside. The passage gave way to an enormous cavern that stretched away so far that the other side was lost to the shadows.

"Ouch," Horace whispered as someone bumped into him from behind. The group had unknowingly stopped a couple steps inside, unable to walk and appreciate the majesty of their surroundings at the same time.

The cavern was spherical from the ceiling down to the walls, ending abruptly at a sand floor, smoother than the beaches of Kael's childhood. Around the perimeter of the cavern were enormous statues of creatures with great wings reaching out to either side. They looked almost like men, but their features were stretched lengthwise. There was a bonfire burning a short way out into the cavern, from which heat could be felt even at this distance. The most visible thing in the whole place was a large hole in the roof where moonlight streamed down in a column to illuminate a circular stage at the center of the sand floor. The stage was surrounded by a moat of still water that reflected the moonlight onto the cavern ceiling.

In front of the fire was the silhouette of a man. He was tall, a full head taller than Ukiru who immediately started walking forward. The High Priest, or so Kael assumed, spread his arms wide in welcome, revealing the draping of a heavy cloak covering his entire body, including his face. Ukiru stopped short and knelt before him. The straggling group behind him followed his example and knelt in the sand.

"My lord, High Priest of the All Powerful, I bring you ten young men from the farthest reaches of the Empire. All ten have been raised in accordance with the instructions given to me. All ten I now present to you as gifts to the All Powerful." Ukiru rose to his feet and the young men did the same.

Suddenly, the High Priest, who had been completely silent until now, spoke with a commanding voice. "Young men, present yourselves."

Kael stepped forward with the others and assembled into a single line like they had been instructed to do on several previous occasions.

The High Priest walked to the end of the line and stood in front of Coen. "Coen, do you present yourself as a gift to the All Powerful, to be an instrument for his glory on this earth?"

"I do," Coen answered uneasily.

Kael's heart was thudding in his chest as he waited for his turn. After Berit and Donagh, his turn came and he answered the same as all the others. When the High Priest moved on, Kael felt no sense of relief. His nausea persisted. Jorn was the last to answer, after which, the High Priest moved back to the center of the line and faced the group.

"Come with me," he said and began to walk across the sand to the center of the cavern. As they approached what now looked like a stone dais, Kael could see arched bridges attached to either side, which extended across the moat to disappear into the sand. It was at one of these bridges that the High Priest stopped the group. Once again they gathered in a line as they were accustomed to doing from all of their time at the monastery. The man in front of them walked three steps up the archway and turned to face them.

Kael was startled at the volume of his voice when he began to pray. "Mightiest of all gods, the one we call All Powerful, we beseech you to meet us here in this place."

Kael looked to either side and noticed that some of the young men had their eyes closed. He took this to be the proper conduct and closed his eyes as well.

Suddenly, the High Priest began to speak in a language that Kael had never heard before. Usually he could guess languages, or at least the region they came from, just by the sounds. But this was one that he could not figure out.

Kael could feel his shoulders and neck muscles tightening with each passing minute. With his eyes closed, he couldn't help but concentrate on the mesmerizing words of the High Priest and his own heavy breathing. His heart beat in a loud, steady rhythm that fell in line with the cadence of the High Priest's voice.

Kael was unsure of the passage of time. It could have been minutes or possibly hours since the prayer had begun. Unexpectedly, a soothing sensation washed over him and calmed all of his anxieties. It was a peaceful feeling that changed his mood about the whole situation. Suddenly, the prayer being echoed off the stone walls of the cavern seemed majestic, even if he couldn't understand any of the words. The air was cool and the sand felt soft beneath his feet. An overwhelming sense of belonging welled up in his heart and for the first time in a long while, Kael felt truly happy.

The beat of his heart, the cadence of the prayer, and the rhythm of his own breathing grew louder and louder until they became one symphony of sound. At some point, Kael lost all sense of direction and feeling of his body, but it didn't matter because the feeling of intense joy drowned out everything else.

Kael opened his eyes and saw nothing but darkness. The cavern, the High Priest, and all of his friends had disappeared. It wasn't a scary feeling, but a feeling of intimacy. There was another presence there with him and Kael felt comforted. He seemed to float in nothingness with the company of this other being for minutes before any perceptible change took place. When it happened, it was so subtle that, if he hadn't been paying attention, he could have easily missed it. It was as if he was at the bottom of a large lake staring up at someone who was talking to him from above the surface of the water. But the change wasn't anything as simple as a vision. Neither did it make as much sense as words. Instead, ideas floated into his head from somewhere else. Peaceful feelings that made him imagine that he was waiting on the front porch of his home and an old friend was walking toward the house. The friend waved and Kael waved back. A wild excitement welled up inside him, although he couldn't make out the face of the visitor. After several minutes, the friend stood in front of Kael. His features could not be seen, but his calm presence could be felt. He didn't speak but Kael could feel that he had been traveling a long distance and wished to come inside and rest. Kael turned and opened the door and led the friend inside. Kael realized that the house was nowhere that he had ever been before, but he knew exactly where everything was located. He showed the man to a sitting room with many comfortable chairs and gave him the best one in the room. As the man made himself comfortable Kael took a seat across from him and eagerly sat down, not knowing why he was so excited to visit with this stranger who seemed so familiar. As he watched the figure across from him, a fleeting thought crossed his mind and vanished just as quickly as it came. There was a sense of being in this situation before, but then he lost the thought and the man was talking and Kael forgot all about it. His words carried no sound, but Kael had a vague sense of satisfaction, as if the communication were making sense. It must have been hours that Kael sat and listened to this man speak, when the memory returned in a flash. Suddenly, Saba was sitting across from him, dressed exactly how the stranger had been dressed. Saba spoke in his soft, gentle voice and Kael smiled at the sight of an old friend. All of a sudden, Saba's face vanished in a grimace of pain and the stranger sat before Kael once again. His demeanor was different this time, replacing the calm friend was the body language of one who had been severely offended. Kael reached his hands out and pleaded with the man. He apologized for thinking of someone else and tried to explain that he was only reminded of Saba because of his kindness. The stranger didn't want to hear any explanations and abruptly stood to his feet. Kael ran to the man, but he was too fast. The stranger had already turned and was running toward the staircase leading up to the topmost portion of the house. Suddenly, Kael began to panic, as if there was something up there that he didn't want this stranger to see. The man was fast and could leap several stairs at once. Kael quickly lost sight of the man, but continued to run as fast as he could. By the time he made it to the top, he could see that the door to the top room had been smashed in. Kael ran into the room and skidded to a stop. The stranger's back was turned to him and he was kneeling down, about to open a wooden chest that lay in the middle of the floor. Suddenly, Kael became aware of a pitchfork in his hands and a feeling drifted to him from somewhere in his memory, a frenzied sense of protection for what was lying on the floor. Then he ran at the stranger and drove the pitchfork into his back.

Abruptly the vision vanished and Kael was once again aware of his body. Only this time, he was lying down in the sand. His eyes wouldn't open and he could still feel the presence of the stranger in his mind. His body began to simultaneously itch and convulse as if someone else were trying to get inside of it. Kael drew in a deep breath and tried to block out all other thoughts except for his own heartbeat. He could feel the extremities of his body and began to flex his muscles. First his fingers, then his toes and slowly the rest of his body came under his control. Eventually his vision returned and he opened his eyes. Briefly, he caught sight of an orange glow like a dying fire and then the attack returned.

This time, it was in his mind. Hundreds of images flashed in front of him, some were from his childhood and it seemed that some were from his future. He watched himself crawl on the floor as a baby and then the vision changed to himself as an old man crippled on the floor. Images of dying people and feelings of suffering shot through him like lightening. The most intense feeling of hatred that he had ever felt washed over him like an ocean of sewage. He felt hopeless and alone and all of a hundred other negative emotions at the same time. He reached out for help and suddenly the images stopped and the stranger stood over him with an extended hand. Kael felt exhausted and dirtier than the lowest human being on the face of the earth. But something inside him, something that was truly his own, would not let him take that hand. Instead, he kicked at the man and spit on him. Just as quickly as the defiant thoughts came to him, the flood returned. He saw his mother being hacked to pieces by a barbarian. When he turned his head he saw his father being stretched by horses until his limbs pulled away from his body. As the images flashed in front of him, he grew cold and numb. It was like being in the presence of a massacre and not being able to blink or even close his eyes. Kael knew that his eyes were deceived, but he still cried at the horrible things that he saw. Hours seemed to pass before the images in his head stopped.

The first pleasant feeling was the cold sand beneath him. His body had sweat so badly that his clothes stuck to his skin as if he had been swimming in the ocean. The cavern ceiling was far overhead and the moonlight that had been streaming down before was gone now. The only light was from the fire, which was now only a small pile of glowing embers. He turned his head and saw several figures lying on the ground but could not make out who they were. Whoever was to his left was still standing and he thought it might be Narian. Suddenly, the figure began to wobble and lean back. Footsteps crunched by Kael's head as one of the monks ran to catch whoever it was who had just lost consciousness and lay them safely on the ground. When the monk walked back to wherever he had been standing, Kael could see who it was that was next to him. Donagh's calm face leaned slightly to the right where Kael could get a good look. He didn't seem to be in any pain, but just laid there in the calm posture of someone in a pleasant dream. The exhaustion of the events caught up with Kael and he found his eyes drooping. He tried to resist sleep, for fear of experiencing any more of what had happened, but sleep overtook him.

21

Bright morning light was shining in Kael's face when he awoke. The soft rocking motion of his bed told him that he was back on the ocean. He opened his eyes and sat up. The other young men were all in their beds sleeping soundly. Kael wondered, but doubted that the others experienced the same thing that he did. The sound of footsteps startled him and he lay back on his bed, pretending to be asleep. For some reason, he felt guilty, like he shouldn't be awake. He could hear Ukiru walking around the room, stopping at each sleeping body. Kael's heart was beating loudly as he waited for Ukiru to pass by. Unexpectedly, he felt a warm spoon against his mouth and the aroma of soup filled his nostrils. He allowed the nourishment to be poured down his throat. Ukiru lingered over Kael a bit longer than the rest before moving on and eventually going above deck.

When he was gone, Kael sat up to see if any of the others had been awakened by the feeding, but he was still the only one. His head ached and his muscles hurt like he had been training for combat all day. He rose to his feet and stretched his weakened body, surprised by the toll that the ceremony had taken on him. After more than an hour of pacing around the room in silence, Kael returned to his bed and tried to sleep again, but couldn't get comfortable. It was like torture, waiting below deck for someone else to wake up, but there was nothing he could do. So Kael passed the time by imagining what had happened in Bastul while he had been away and he was alone with his thoughts until dusk.

The sun had dipped toward the western horizon, off the port bow of the ship, when Kael's thoughts finally resolved into a decision. All day he had been struggling with how to continue at the monastery. He wasn't sure of when they would finally be sent out into the world, but he knew that he had to leave soon. If the being that attacked his mind and body was really the All Powerful, then Kael didn't want any part of him. He still felt like he needed to bathe after the whole experience, though he knew it wouldn't do much to clean the polluted feeling inside of him.

"So, you're awake too?"

Kael spun his head around and saw Berit sitting up on his bed. "Yeah, I just woke up," he lied.

"My head hurts," Berit grumbled, and turned to look out the porthole situated above his head.

"Mine too," Kael lied again. His headache was actually gone, lessening and eventually disappearing over the course of the many hours he had been awake.

One by one, the others began to wake up. The only one who seemed to be in the mood for conversation was Coen who immediately began talking about his amazing experience. As the sluggish mood wore off, everyone began to chime in about this or that incredible feeling or experience. After several minutes, Kael realized that he was alone in his experience. Everyone else had done exactly what they were supposed to do except for him. Suddenly the conversation stopped and Kael realized that someone had asked him a question.

"What?"

"I said," Arden repeated, "how long before you passed out?"

Kael tried to look mystified to share in their excitement. "I lost all sense of time, so it's hard to say."

"I know," Jorn blurted out. "That's exactly what happened to me!"

"So you are all awake now," announced Ukiru who was standing on the stairs, watching his group of students. "Why don't you continue your conversation up here and get some fresh air."

Coen was the first one up the stairs and Kael waited to be the last. The group assembled at the bow of the ship and Kael leaned over the railing to watch the water as it split around the ship in smooth strips of white foam. The chattering continued around him and he was content to just look at the ocean until Ukiru tried to draw him in.

"Kael. What was it like for you?"

Is that skepticism in his voice? Kael wondered if he knew what happened and then dismissed the thought because there was no way that he could. "Uh..." he stammered, searching. "I just don't have the words."

Ukiru nodded, apparently satisfied. "That's a good way to describe it."

Saba sat on the floor against the door, with his ear pressed to the wood, straining to hear anything that might be happening outside. He heard a footstep near the door and pushed himself back, frightened that someone was coming. He waited for a moment, then leaned in again. As soon as his hands touched the door, he felt a strange sensation pass through his body. It lasted only for a second, but in that moment Saba could swear that he *felt* the inner workings of the lock on the door. Reeling back in surprise, Saba listened carefully for movement outside while his mind raced with questions.

Slowly, he leaned forward against the door. But nothing happened. *Did I imagine it?* He placed his hand near the lock and waited, attempting to recapture the feeling. When he closed his eyes, it came again.

The sensation was dulled somehow, muffled at first, but with concentration, Saba regained the clarity of the first occurrence. And then it was obvious, like looking at a picture, only more interactive. Saba could feel the bolt running through the iron lock on the door into the housing on the door jam. And just as one might wiggle their finger, Saba knew without even testing his knowledge that he could move the bolt without having to touch it. But his excitement at the discovery was too great to allow him to be satisfied with that knowledge; he had to test it. And just as he expected, the bolt slid back at his will. It screeched slightly, grating on the inside of the door jam, and Saba paused to make sure that no one heard. When nothing happened, he tried again and the bolt slid free of the door jam. *How is this possible? And who am I that I can do such things?*

He pushed gently on the door and it moved open, allowing him an inch of visibility to the courtyard and the wall beyond it. There were no guards to see along his narrow path of sight, but that didn't mean they weren't out there. There was a change of guard every night at midnight, or so it seemed to his limited senses. And that had occurred more than an hour ago. Pushing harder on the door, he opened it far enough to peek his head out. Just as he suspected, to his left a guard sat outside on a crude chair, slumped back against the building. Saba smiled to himself. *It's nearly impossible for a guard to follow the same routine for years without losing vigilance.* This man had probably become bored with his task long ago, and tonight was just another night to get some sleep while the old man inside the jail couldn't possibly escape anyway. *But this old man has a few tricks.*

Saba pushed the door open a bit wider and walked quietly out of the cell, slipping into the night.

The hours dragged on into days as their ship cut a northeasterly path through the ocean. When they sighted land, Coen spoke up.

"Are we traveling faster than before?"

"No," Ukiru answered. "It is only that you were asleep for several days at the beginning of this return trip, so it seems shorter."

They kept the land on the starboard side of the boat and continued traveling north until there was only ocean again as far as the eye could see. Kael didn't feel much like talking and kept to himself most of the time. Ukiru allowed them to skip the usual morning routine of meditation and instruction, explaining that they would need some time to think about what the All Powerful had shown each one of them. They would resume their studies after they returned to the monastery.

Kael had been doing nothing but thinking for days now and he would have liked to do something else to take his mind off of it. All of the old feelings of mistrust were coming back to him, only stronger this time. His meeting with the All Powerful was not what he had expected it to be. They were always taught that he was a loving and merciful god who was heartbroken when the world turned away from him. But the intense hatred and wretchedness that Kael felt from being in his presence made him think that they had all been lied to. Anyway, he was tired of thinking and just wanted to sleep. When the sun went down, Kael went below deck and lay on his bed. It was quiet with everyone else above deck, talking about the whole experience. Kael shut his eyes and let the gentle rock of the ocean soothe him to sleep.

Sometime during the night, he began hearing voices. When he lifted his head, he realized that most of the others were gone. Berit and Horace were still sleeping. The thump of footsteps moved up above, heading for the stairs. Shortly after, Coen peeked his head down.

"You guys better wake up."

"What's going on?" Kael asked.

"We've reached the island and some of the monks are loading our stuff into the wagons. Ukiru said we could take a few of the horses and ride back to the monastery. If we're quick, we could be back in our own beds before the sun comes up."

"Where are the others?" Berit asked.

"Soren and Narian are waiting for us; the rest already left."

The remainder of the night was a blur for Kael. He felt half-asleep most of the time. Immediately after leaving the small desolate harbor of their island, the horses began to climb. It was slow going at first, but after climbing for the first few hundred feet, the path leveled out and the horses began to pick up speed. The sky was still dark when they got back and Kael went straight to his room and collapsed on his bed.

The next day was unusual compared to their normal routine. They didn't have to get up at a certain time, nor were they required to do any of the activities to which they had become accustomed. Kael woke up just before noon and wandered down to the kitchen where one of the monks was starting to prepare the evening meal. He gave Kael something to eat and shooed him out of the kitchen. For a few hours, Kael wandered around the monastery, letting the silence clear his head. He didn't know where the others were, but he also didn't care. He eventually found Berit in the library where he usually spent his free time, but neither one of them was in the mood for conversation, so Kael moved on. Finally, Kael arrived at the top of the cliffs overlooking the ocean and took a seat on his favorite rock.

The past eight years of his life had been quite strange, he realized. How many children grow up in a bustling port city like Bastul, living the life of a privileged few, only to have that life ripped away in an uncontrollable string of events that leaves you to grow up in a monastery?

He stood up suddenly, trying to shake off the questions. He wanted to do something instead of thinking, so he walked around looking for rocks to throw over the edge and finally found an area where a boulder was falling apart under the relentless forces of nature, slowly eroding into a pile of rubble. Kael picked up a handful of stones and tossed them, one by one, over the edge. He watched the smaller ones zigzag through the air as the wind moved them. The larger ones fell without any perceptible movement other than straight down. The surface of the ocean was too far down for Kael to see them hit, but it was something to keep his mind occupied.

The hours of daylight diminished and the sun began to slip behind the mountains. Kael made it back to the monastery just in time for the evening meal. Everyone seemed to be in good spirits and even Kael was happier after a good meal.

"Before we retire for the night, I just want to say a few things." Ukiru stood up to address the group. "I am proud of you all. We made a difficult and long journey, but it was for a great purpose. The All Powerful has met each of you in a different way and has seen your future. In a short time, I am expecting to hear a message from the High Priest. The message will contain a commission for each one of you. For the next two years, you will continue to train in a more specific manner related directly to your commissioning. Until we receive this message, our days here will look much different. There is cleaning and reorganizing to do and I'm sure it would be a welcome break from all of the recent traveling. So, get your rest tonight. Tomorrow things will begin to change around here in preparation for the coming months. I assure you that the next two years will go quickly and before you know it, you will be back in the world of men once more."

Everyone clapped their hands together and cheered at Ukiru's words; everyone except Kael. The feelings of contentment and gratefulness which used to reside in his heart had vanished, replaced by a sense of uneasiness and doubt. As the others went off to their rooms in high spirits, Kael had to pretend in order to not draw attention to himself. Ukiru had been acting strange toward him ever since their time at the temple and Kael was doing his best to appear as normal as everyone else. When he lay down to go to sleep, his mind was racing. He tossed and turned in his bed for hours until he couldn't take it anymore.

I know what I have to do!

Quietly, so as not to disturb anyone, Kael began to lay out a few articles of clothing on his bed. He got dressed and wrapped the rest in one of the sheets from his bed. Easing open his door, he peered down the hallway until he was certain that all was clear. As he tiptoed out into the hallway, every sound seemed amplified in the silence. Even the sound of his own breath threatened to wake up the whole monastery. He continued moving cautiously until he found himself outside, heading through the outer wall and along the path that would eventually lead down to the harbor. He wasn't sure how he was going to get off of the island, or what he would do once he did. But it didn't matter, he just knew he had to go. The moon was nearly full, illuminating the fields and casting shadows beside trees. Within several minutes the monastery began to disappear into the darkness behind him and Kael was feeling better with each step.

Suddenly, a shadow flitted behind a tree at the corner of his vision and Kael stopped in his tracks. His heart was beating in his ears, making it difficult for him to listen for further signs of movement. He waited for a few seconds, but there were no other noises.

"Who's there?" he called out, more sure with every passing second that it wasn't just an animal.

"Where are you going?" came a voice out of the woods.

Kael immediately recognized Ukiru's voice. Now he was scared. He looked around, but wasn't sure where Ukiru was, and had forgotten exactly where the voice had come from. "I can't stay here," he shouted, the panic rising in his voice.

"And I can't let you leave." A figure, silhouetted by the moonlight, walked from the trees and onto the road, fifty feet away. Ukiru was silent, standing sideways as he watched Kael with the careful but relaxed look of someone in complete control.

Kael's heart was beating powerfully in his throat. But he choked down his fear. "It's all a lie. This whole...place. You. Your so-called god. Everything!"

"You choose to see it that way," Ukiru responded calmly.

Kael didn't know what else to say. He knew the truth, but Ukiru was deceived along with everyone else. Once Kael experienced the true presence of the All Powerful, felt the hatred and filth of being near him, his fragile faith began to unravel. He was lost now, unsure of anything but the powerful need to leave. Any trace of gratefulness at being rescued from the prison, cared for, and trained, was swept away by an overwhelming sense of betrayal. And then a thought occurred to him, a thought that would have seemed ridiculous until this very moment.

"You didn't rescue us from that prison, you miserable liar! You put us there. You locked us up like animals to see who would survive!" Kael was yelling now, his volume in sharp contrast to the silence of the night.

Ukiru turned to face Kael. "Pack animals develop their own hierarchy, especially under threat of extinction. Humans are no different. I had to have a winning team, to see who was capable of survival."

"You bastard!" Kael shouted between gritted teeth. "How could you do such a thing? We were just children."

The figure before him, who now seemed more like a complete stranger than a friend, crouched slightly into an attack posture.

Kael had seen this many times before, but it was never directed at him. He dropped his bundle of clothes on the ground because he knew that it would only be a hindrance. "If I had a sword, I'd cut you down right here!"

In response, the ring of sharpened steel rang clear as Ukiru pulled his sword from its scabbard, a shaft of reflected moonlight moving down the length of the blade. "The All Powerful was displeased with what he saw in you. It was obvious to him that you were never one of us. I told you time after time that you must let go of your past, but you just wouldn't listen."

For a moment, the two stood still.

Then Ukiru burst into motion.

Kael spun on his heals and ran as fast as his feet could carry him. He lengthened his stride and breathed steadily as he had always been instructed to do. A quick look back told him that he was keeping just out of Ukiru's reach, even if he was closer than expected. The monastery came back into view and Kael circled around to the right following the outside of the perimeter wall, not wanting to get trapped inside the grounds of the monastery.

He was gliding now across the meadow between the monastery and the ocean cliffs. The ground started to rise before him and he sprinted up the hill as his legs burned and his lungs gasped for air. Another panicked look behind showed that he had gained a few strides on Ukiru, but not nearly as much as he had hoped for. The older man was still as fit as a man half his age and ten times more deadly when the chase was over.

Cresting the hill, Kael picked up speed and started down a slight decline. He suddenly realized that he had been heading for his favorite spot and knew that now he was trapped between Ukiru and the cliffs. He slowed to a stop.

Ukiru stopped just past the peak of the hill, knowing that he had already won. "You're trapped," he stated, hardly out of breath.

Kael turned and stared into the eyes of his mentor, his mentor who had now become an enemy. Slowly, a calm presence came over him, slowing his heartbeat and breathing. It was a familiar sensation that made him feel safe, and consequently, he felt a confidence stir up inside him. "You can't have me!" Kael yelled, turning toward the cliff.

Ukiru lunged forward, but it was too late.

Without hesitation, Kael ran and jumped off the edge, spreading his hands to the air.

Ukiru only caught a brief glimpse of the swirling fog as it enveloped Kael's body. When he reached the edge of the cliff, he stood for a moment, shocked at the outcome of the situation. Already, the words were forming in his mind of what he would say to the other students. *Kael was a traitor and his true self was revealed to him at the temple. He threw himself over the edge because he couldn't tolerate his own unworthiness.* Ukiru tried to look down at the ocean, but it was obscured by the fog.

I'll have to send some men down to recover the body, or what's left of it. Re-sheathing his sword, Ukiru turned and headed back toward the monastery.

PART II

1

The feeling of falling was gone, replaced by a suffocating presence. Adair was conscious of his limbs moving sluggishly around him. At first, there was only the feeling of pressure against his body. Then his skin began to detect temperature.

I'm cold!

The awareness that he was under water suddenly dawned on him and caused an initial panic. But his years of conditioning as a soldier took over. He stopped struggling in the water and held still, trying to determine which direction was up. A bubble escaped his lips and rolled sideways across his face, telling him the way to the surface.

He opened his eyes and felt the stinging saltwater. At first, his vision was cloudy. Then a flashing light drew his attention to his left. He turned his head and peered through the darkness.

There was another flash of blue light that turned white at the edges, illuminating something next to it. As Adair watched, the object moved.

It was the head of some creature.

Adair suddenly felt vulnerable and kicked his legs hard. He grabbed at the water and pulled himself upward. Without being able to see, he had no idea how fast he was swimming, but it seemed too slow.

Something crashed hard against his head and he winced, letting out a mouthful of air. Instinctively, he lashed out with his hands and felt a smooth surface above his head.

I'm trapped!

Again, panic threatened to overtake him.

He glanced in all directions, then noticed that the darkness was less intense to his right. He moved toward it and as he did, the water began to grow lighter. He swam faster. Then the light was above him. He swam upward again, but this time, nothing was blocking him.

Starved of air, he began to move the air from his mouth down to his lungs and back again. It didn't help, but seemed only to distract his body from the fact that it would soon drown.

Faster and faster he swam and the light above grew more intense. He looked down into the darkness below and could now see a black shape coming up through the murky water beneath him.

He kicked his legs harder, then looked again.

The dark creature was gaining on him. Bubbles were coming from its distorted face, as two long fins propelled it through the water.

Adair looked up and saw the surface. He was only ten feet away, but it felt like a mile.

He broke through the surface into a hazy sunlight that instantly blinded him. He gasped for breath, taking in large quantities of air. Without the benefit of sight, he randomly chose a direction and began to swim as fast as his limbs would carry him, dreading that at any second he would be pulled under by the creature below.

It took only a few seconds for his eyes to adjust. To his surprise, he saw land.

That's not possible! I shouldn't be anywhere near land.

He turned around and saw that he was in the center of a muddy bay, roughly a mile across. There was land on every side, covered by lush, green vegetation.

Then he saw the creature. It was only ten yards away, its head sticking out of the water. Light reflected off one giant eye at the center of its black face. Its breath hissed in and out. All of a sudden, another head popped out of the water...then two more.

There's four!

Adair turned and swam for the shoreline. His heart was racing from both fear and exhaustion. Though he struggled with every ounce of his being, his progress seemed terribly slow.

Something grabbed his ankle from behind.

Without looking, he kicked hard and broke free of the grasp.

A second later, something clamped down hard on his legs.

Ready to fight to the death, he spun around and punched the head of the nearest creature with all his might. The hit landed on the side of its giant eye and it reared back.

Adair's hand exploded with pain and he knew instantly that he had broken bones.

But he was free again.

He backed away quickly, grabbing at the water to get some distance between him and these things, whatever they were.

The one that he punched reached up to its head with two arms and began to pull its face apart.

Adair flinched in horror, then stopped.

It was a man. He was removing something like a shield from his eyes and lifting it over his head. He spit out something from his mouth that was connected to a rope running over his shoulders. His head was covered in a tight black fabric of some sort, with an opening that only revealed his dark-skinned face, now covered in blood from a gash in his forehead.

The man spoke harshly in a foreign tongue.

Though Adair didn't understand the language, he could tell that the man was cursing.

The other man who had grabbed him, turned around and raised one hand into the air, waving it back and forth.

Adair looked over the man's shoulder and could see a dark shape floating on the water a hundred yards away.

Is it a boat?

Then, there was a bark, followed by a faint growling sound that got louder as the boat raced across the water. Adair watched in amazement. *I've never seen a boat move this fast. What's driving it? There's no wind. I don't see any oars. What kind of boat is this?*

The growling ended abruptly as the boat veered to the starboard and came to a stop. The wake moved past Adair, lifting him slightly as he treaded water.

A man aboard the boat stood up. His strange clothes were mostly green, with patches of different colors all over. He wore pants and a tunic that covered his arms all the way to the wrists. He yelled at Adair in the same language that the other men had used. Then he waved his hand and beckoned Adair to come to him.

Adair kept still.

The man aboard the boat reached for something hanging from a strap around his neck. He raised it to his shoulder with both hands, then leaned his head to the side and closed one eye.

He's aiming!

Adair looked at the object in the man's hands. If it was a crossbow, he couldn't see the arrow, or a bow string for that matter. There was nothing intimidating about it. There were no sharpened points, nothing to impale him. He thought briefly that he should be alarmed, but somehow he was not.

A few seconds of silence passed as the man peered at him through one eye.

Then the man moved his weapon a few inches to the left. A flash of fire exploded from the weapon, accompanied by ear piercing claps of thunder in rapid succession.

The water next to Adair burst into numerous fountains, reaching up to the sky. Adair flinched. When the water settled, he looked back to the man in the boat.

He was still aiming his weapon. With one hand, he waved for Adair to come to the boat.

This time, Adair obeyed.

When he neared the boat, another man reached down and grabbed hold of his tunic and pulled him from the water and into the boat. He dropped Adair to the floor, then backed away toward the stern.

Slowly lifting his head, Adair noticed that there were a total of three men. The other two also had similar weapons on straps around their necks, pointing them in his direction.

Adair looked to the empty prow of the ship, then back to the men. *They want me to move.* He obeyed, moving cautiously. When he had gone as far as he could, he stopped, leaning against the soft side of the boat.

What is this? The boat appeared to be made from a pliable skin of some kind, stretched over a rigid structure of bones. He had never seen anything like it.

A low growl startled him and he turned toward the stern.

Two of the men were still pointing weapons at him, while the third was sitting down and holding on to a handle.

That must be the rudder control!

Without warning, the boat lurched into motion and Adair fell to the deck. When he adjusted to the motion and regained his footing, the two men guarding him looked suddenly tense.

It should have worried Adair, but instead, it comforted him. He had seen the same thing, time and time again, with inexperienced soldiers who guarded prisoners. Any sudden movement brought them face to face, in an instant, with the prospect of having to kill a man. Most of them just froze with a look of intensity on their faces.

...just like these men.

Adair couldn't suppress the smile that came to his face.

But this only angered one of the guards, who started cursing at him.

Adair turned away and looked out across the water. It seemed as though they were skimming over the surface of the ocean, faster that any horse could run. The constant growling from the back of the boat told Adair that it was somehow linked to their movement. He had no idea where he was or what he had gotten himself into. These men were not the same as the ones he encountered off the coast of Bastul. As he looked around, everything was foreign. He didn't recognize a single feature of the landscape.

He retraced the events in his mind, running from the enemy soldiers and ending up in that large cavern. He ran across the bridge over the moat and onto the circular stone area. That's when he started to feel a great pressure upon his body. Then he was in water.

What happened? Am I dead?

Then he looked down. His sandal hung uselessly from his right foot. He raised his foot slowly and looked underneath, seeing the deep gash that was still bleeding. His two small toes were numb and unmoving.

Well at least I haven't gone insane!

They reached the shore in only a few minutes. The growling sound lowered to a whisper and the boat coasted in the shallow water, coming to an abrupt stop on the dark sand. One of the men jumped into the water and moved around to cover Adair's flank, aiming with his weapon. The other man, also pointing his weapon, nodded for Adair to get out of the boat.

Adair stepped cautiously over the prow and onto the sand.

One of the guards walked up on to the bank and started toward the forest.

Adair followed, with the second man behind him, aiming at his back.

The third man turned the boat and headed back out to the middle of the bay.

A few yards ahead was another strange sight—an iron chariot with thick, black wheels. It too, was green, just like the guards' clothes. Adair couldn't tell which end was the front; there were no reins and no horses. One end of the chariot had a large flat area that looked like it was made to carry cargo. This was where the men herded him, pushing him forward while keeping a tight grip on their weapons.

Adair climbed into the chariot and sat down on the deck.

One man followed him into the cargo deck and sat against the railing.

The other man climbed into another tight compartment where there was a chair of some sort. Reaching down, he touched something in front of him and the chariot barked like a dog, then proceeded to growl in a similar manner as the boat, though the pitch was lower and sounded more powerful.

Adair stared in fascination. Was there an animal inside of this chariot? Or was it something worse? Perhaps these men were sorcerers and moved about by demons. As it jolted into motion, Adair lost his balance again, but quickly realized that he was at the back of the chariot. After only a few seconds he was amazed. The ground would have been impassable to any other chariot he had ridden in. But somehow, this one rode over the ditches and holes in the road as if they were sitting on a cushion.

As they ascended the shore of the beach, Adair took note of his surroundings. Trees were down all along the shore and the low vegetation was covered in mud. In fact, it looked like this shoreline hadn't been a shoreline for very long. Looking back at the bay, Adair could see that the vegetation ran all the way to the water, and even into the water in some areas.

Flood, he concluded. *This water hasn't been here for very long.*

Moving uphill away from the water, the muddy terrain gave way to a wide, smooth road. Adair looked down and noted the black surface that spread for perhaps twenty feet on either side of them. There were no cobblestones. The chariot picked up speed on the smooth terrain and Adair scooted closer to the deck as he began to feel unsafe.

Shades of green flashed by as they nearly flew through the forest, made up of trees with leaves bigger than a man's torso. Occasionally, they passed an open meadow with grass taller than a man. The air was incredibly humid. He remembered his first such experience when being stationed in Bastul. He and Maeryn had moved to the coast from the mountainous inland terrain in the north and noticed a difference in the air. But this was different. It was as if the air was actually wet. Adair wondered if it rained in this foreign place, for it seemed that the ground would always be full of water. And that explained why the trees and other plants were as big as they were.

They rode for nearly an hour, winding through the forest, all the while climbing. Adair became mesmerized by the rhythm of the chariot and the passing trees. He was exhausted and could have fallen asleep in an instant. But a sharp popping sound brought Adair out of his trance as he instinctively flinched. The popping was immediately proceeded by a horrendous squealing as the chariot skidded to a stop on the road.

Adair grabbed hold of the railing to keep from being thrown to the side. Out of the corner of his sight, he sensed movement. Before he could react, the guard at the head of the chariot seemed to flinch as one side of his head exploded in a shower of blood. His body slumped sideways in the seat.

Adair turned to his right and looked at the thick treeline on the side of the road. There was nothing but a tangle of vines and thick leaves.

The guard next to him pointed his weapon into the trees. It flashed with fire and jolted in the soldier's hands as he waved it back and forth.

Adair covered his ears and lowered himself below the railing.

As he watched the guard, plumes of blood sprouted from the man's back as his body convulsed. The life left his eyes and his body dropped to the deck. Adair could see small wounds on the man's chest and wondered how something so small could kill instantly.

Adair's heart beat quickly in his chest and the fear of being chased returned. He peered carefully over the railing and was shocked by what he saw.

Man-shaped objects were moving slowly out of the trees. But it was as if they were partially invisible. Adair squinted, trying to make sense of what he was seeing. As they spread out, he could see that they were men wearing multi-colored clothing that made them blend in with the forest. He counted five of them and they had now formed a semi-circle only twenty feet from the chariot.

Adair ducked down below the railing and tried to think of how to get out of this situation. After only a few seconds, one of them yelled something. Adair stayed where he was, listening.

Again, the man yelled something.

The language was foreign to Adair, but sounded different than his former guards. There was also no hint of anger in the voice, which was again different than the guards. Nevertheless, Adair stayed where he was.

A few seconds later, a face peered over the rear of the chariot. It was a man, but like none he'd ever seen before. He wore a hat with a brim that was curled upward on one side. His skin was smooth and multicolored, like his clothes, with patches of brown and various shades of green. But his eyes looked normal and despite the strange situation, Adair didn't detect any danger.

The man spoke again, quieter this time, and waved for Adair to come out of the chariot.

Adair rose to a crouching position, looking around the chariot. The other four men were standing at ease. They also had the strange looking weapons hanging from straps around their shoulders and necks. They were pointed at the ground and only being held casually.

Again, the man at the rear of the chariot waved for him to get out.

Adair stood up and made his way to the man, who backed up and waited.

When he reached the ground, the man said something to him, but Adair didn't understand.

Then the man pointed over Adair's shoulder at the other men who had started walking along the road. Adair understood and followed as the group leader walked behind him. After several minutes, a low thrumming sound could be heard. When they rounded a bend in the road, Adair stopped, frozen with fear.

The low thrumming sound was now like a hundred chariots, coming from a giant beast that hovered over the ground in a nearby clearing. It was like an enormous green locust, with buzzing wings that lifted it off the ground.

The group leader pointed at it and said something.

Adair shook his head in protest, but four of the other men were already starting to walk in that direction. Again, the leader pointed.

Against his better judgment, Adair obeyed. Perhaps it was because he knew that he really didn't have a choice. Whoever these men were, they were able to kill quickly and efficiently, and that was something Adair could respect.

The men moved without hesitation, only the leader hung back with Adair. As they neared the beast, still exuding the deep pulsing sound, it became more difficult for Adair. Then, a door opened in the side of the locust, and another man in a helmet reached out his hand from the inside.

Adair realized that like the boat and the chariot, this was another method of transportation. He watched in fascination as the first four men climbed into it.

The fifth man now stood behind him, waiting.

Adair swallowed the lump in his throat and walked forward, taking the man's hand and climbing into the belly of the beast.

The fifth man quickly followed.

Adair followed the example of the others and sat on the padded benches that lined the interior. Suddenly, the locust rose into the air and Adair felt his stomach began to twist. They were already thirty feet in the air before the man in the helmet shut the door.

Adair leaned his head back and closed his eyes, trying to fight the nausea in his gut.

Someone touched his leg.

Adair opened his eyes and the group leader was looking straight at him and shaking his head from side to side. The man pointed two fingers at his own eyes and then pointed out the window of the beast as he spoke in his foreign tongue.

Adair understood, and kept his eyes open, looking out the window. After only a few seconds, he felt better. Then he realized that the feeling was something like sea sickness. It was better to be above deck than below where you couldn't see anything.

Adair watched the trees fly by below them.

We're flying, he realized!

The group leader said something and Adair turned.

The man repeated the phrase and Adair thought he heard something recognizable. One of the four words sounded like a greeting in an ancient tongue, before the establishment of the Orud Empire. It was the word for *welcome.*

Again, the man repeated the phrase.

"Welcome Soth Am…" Adair attempted, mimicking the sounds.

The man smiled, then repeated the phrase.

Adair listened carefully, then imitated the words. "Welcome to South America."

All the soldiers laughed. Adair had no idea where South America was, but he knew that it was nowhere near Bastul. Somehow, he knew he was in a different world altogether.

2

The streets of the market district in Bastul were teeming with merchants and their customers. Hundreds of people clamored to find the best deal or offer the best service, screaming over one another's voices. Maeryn and Aelia stood under a yellow silk shade, searching through piles of rich fabrics. Silk, satin, wool, and linen were all arranged neatly in stacks, organized by color. Aelia, now sixteen years of age, pulled a roll of ocean blue satin from the stack in front of her.

"What about this?" she asked her mother.

Maeryn looked up and examined the fabric, reaching out a hand to feel the quality. "That's perfect," she replied. "Even the pattern would go well with this," she said, lifting her arm which was draped with pure white linen. "Hang on to that, but keep looking."

"Alright," Aelia replied, tucking the roll under her arm.

As Aelia turned around to continue the search for the makings of her coming-of-age dress, Maeryn was struck by how beautiful her daughter was. Her wavy chocolate colored hair fell to the middle of her back. Aelia preferred not to braid it or wear it gathered on the top of her head, as was the current trend. She always kept it loose and the look was even starting to catch on with a few of her friends. She had brown eyes just like her father and some of his other facial features as well. And like Kael, Aelia had inherited her mother's lean frame.

Kael.

As soon as the thought came, a pang of sadness gripped her heart. It seemed like so long ago, but she never failed to remember the pain.

"My lady," someone behind her called. Maeryn ignored the voice, always having a difficult time keeping anonymous when she went into the city.

"My lady," the voice repeated, from closer than before.

Maeryn turned around and searched the crowds. Just inside of the bustling street stood a woman that looked just as ordinary as everyone around her, but Maeryn's heart jumped in her chest. She recognized the lady as a messenger for the Resistance movement, though Maeryn usually dealt with someone else to carry out her correspondence. She immediately spun around and called to Aelia. "I'll be right back."

Aelia waved without taking her eyes off the fabric in front of her.

Maeryn strode quickly over to the woman and nodded for her to follow. After fighting the swarms of people moving up and down the street, the pair made their way to an alley between a meat seller and a masonry building.

"What is the meaning of approaching me in public?" Maeryn barked at the woman, unable to contain the fear in her voice.

"I'm sorry, but it was necessary. Your main contact has been captured."

"My..." Maeryn stopped, unable to formulate a question with all of the thoughts that suddenly collided in her head.

"He was bringing a message to you when he was taken into custody. Your husband has not been to see him yet, but the soldiers sent for him almost an hour ago."

Maeryn swallowed hard, struggling against the panic that threatened her sanity. "What do they know?"

"Nothing yet, but the torture hasn't begun. My lady, he will protect your identity with his very life," she offered as a consolation.

"Yes, I know," Maeryn replied. "But you don't know my husband; he will find a way to make him talk." *Being cruel is one of the only things at which he is proficient.*

The woman only nodded her head. "I must go now. I don't want to put you in any more danger than necessary."

"Thank you," Maeryn said and watched as the woman walked down the alley and melded back into the crowds.

After paying for the fabric, Maeryn took Aelia back to the mansion and left her in Zula's care. She had to call upon her acting skills, which had been honed by years of practice, in order to keep from drawing Aelia's suspicion. But inwardly, fear and panic were building. If Lemus managed to get any information out of her contact, Maeryn's life would come to a swift end. Of that, she was sure.

Just over an hour after the woman had approached her in the market district, Maeryn was seated in a carriage, making her way west along the foothills to the north of Bastul. The stone road separated the farms on her right from the ocean cliffs on her left. It was a slow journey, but it was the only way that the Governess could travel without drawing attention to herself, and privacy meant just as much as speed in this situation. Maeryn would much rather have raced out of the city on horseback, but that wasn't practical.

After what seemed like an eternity, the carriage turned off the road to the north and onto a dirt path that divided two fields. Maeryn's heart quickened with anticipation of the coming meeting. She had suspected long ago the identity of the Resistance leader of Bastul, but had never seen fit to confirm it. Now she had no choice. Her time of secrecy with Lemus was coming to an end and she had to act quickly. If this meeting went as she hoped it would, the Resistance would offer her and Aelia refuge and passage out of the city.

The carriage bumped and bounced its way to the northern end of the enormous estate. Finally, the main house came into view, and Maeryn smiled at the rustic beauty of the place. The main house was a stone structure that seemed to enjoy spreading out in the openness of its rural habitat. It had a tiled roof and branched off in many directions like roots of a tree, searching for water. Behind the house, several smaller buildings contained the stables and slave quarters. In the distance, row upon row of citrus trees marked the beginning of the orchard.

The carriage came to a stop fifty feet from the main house on a graveled path that circled a small stand of trees before heading back out to the main road. Maeryn, eager to be rid of the uncomfortable transportation, immediately opened the door and descended the steps before the driver or guards were able to help her down. She took a few steps to stretch her legs before looking back to the soldiers who were now scrambling to join her.

"It's alright," she waved at the men. "I'm fine."

Almost immediately, a slave came out of the main entrance and walked toward Maeryn. As soon as she was close enough to recognize the Governess, she bowed her head.

"I'm here to speak with the Commissioner," Maeryn called out, not wanting to waste any time.

"Yes, my lady," the woman replied and turned around, walking quickly toward the house.

For a moment, there was complete silence, or as close to it as Maeryn had heard in a long time. Occasionally, a gust of wind would blow through the nearby trees or a bird would chirp, but mostly silence.

"Please stay with the carriage. I won't be long," Maeryn told her guards, before heading toward the house.

Before she reached the entrance, a man came out of the house with his arms stretched wide. He wasn't an old man, though his hair had turned completely white. He was wearing a white linen tunic draped with a white cloak over one shoulder. It was a formal outfit, usually saved for appearances at public meetings. "Governess...why...you must be exhausted. Won't you please come in out of the sun? Can I get you something to drink perhaps?"

"No thank you," she replied. "I'm not thirsty. Besides, I've been sitting for the last hour. I would however welcome a stroll in your orchard."

"Certainly," he said with a smile. "May I join you?"

"Well, I should hope so," Maeryn said, laughing. "I came to speak with you."

"Of course. Please come, it is lovely this time of day."

The two walked in silence until they reached the start of the orchard, a small but elaborate iron gate with vines woven through the decorative bars. The Commissioner led Maeryn through the gate and along the right side of the orchard where the ground was shaded by a row of tall eucalyptus trees. The air smelled sweet and fresh and somewhat eased Maeryn's anxiety. Still, her growing concern caused her to break the silence.

"I'm sorry to disturb you."

"Oh, it's no bother. Your visit could never be a disturbance."

An awkward silence passed as Maeryn tried to compose her thoughts, but to no avail. She couldn't seem to start the conversation.

The Commissioner looked at the ground, recognizing Maeryn's struggle. "Well, I assume you have something important to say, otherwise, your words would not be so carefully chosen?"

"Yes," Maeryn replied. "I just don't know how to say it other than to be completely direct. So I guess that is what I will do."

The Commissioner nodded his head and waited.

"Thaddius, I know who you are."

"Of course you do," he said with a smile.

"No. I mean that I know you are the Resistance leader here in Bastul."

Thaddius stopped walking and turned to look Maeryn straight in the eye. "My lady, I beg your pardon," he said, the jovial nature now gone from his voice.

Maeryn realized that she had called him out without exposing herself. Suddenly, she knew what she had to say, but it felt awkward to speak it out loud. "I'm your contact on the inside. I'm the one who has been helping the cause." There, she said it, and there was no way to take it back.

A silent moment passed as Thaddius stared into Maeryn's eyes. Then, his features softened into a smile. "I'm shocked that it is you...or any woman for that matter. Apparently your instincts are better than mine."

Maeryn felt instant relief. With Thaddius' confirmation she suddenly realized why Adair had so little conflict with the Resistance during his rule. Thaddius had been Adair's social Commissioner, handling the non-military responsibilities of governing Bastul. "How have you been?" she asked. "I haven't seen you since Adair's disappearance."

"Yes, I know. My...responsibilities have been steadily declining since then. It seems that your new husband considers himself an expert in all things. And that includes the social needs of the citizens of Bastul. So, I am no longer needed."

"I'm sorry to hear that," Maeryn replied. "But it makes sense when you consider the increase of Resistance activity since Adair ruled."

"Do you think it's obvious?" he asked suddenly.

"Oh no," Maeryn replied. "Lemus doesn't know your identity...yet!"

Her last word caused a visible change in Thaddius' body language. He suddenly looked tense. "What do you mean *yet*?"

"Well. I guess this brings me to the point of my visit. My main contact was intercepted earlier today. When I left Bastul, they had..."

"Yes, I know," he interrupted. "If that is what you mean about the threat to my identity, you have nothing to worry about."

"Thaddius. Forgive me for my rudeness, but I'm not concerned about your identity. I'm worried about my own. Now, you may think that your messengers are well trained to keep things hidden, but you don't know Lemus. He is the cruelest man I've ever known. And now that the key to all his frustrating dealings with the Resistance resides in his jail cell, he will find a way to get the information that he needs."

"So what do you suggest I do? Have the messenger killed before he can talk?"

Maeryn was immediately repulsed by the idea. Although, she had to admit that it would solve the issue. "Can that really be done?"

"Not at this point. He is too heavily guarded," Thaddius answered, without a trace of hesitation.

Maeryn thought for a second. "Can the Resistance offer safe passage out of Bastul for me and my daughter?"

Thaddius' jaw dropped. "But that would undermine everything that we've worked for. You are the key to the whole plan."

"Yes, but the plan can't succeed if I'm dead, now can it?"

The two stared at each other for a few seconds before Thaddius turned away and continued walking. Maeryn hadn't realized that they stopped until that moment. As she caught up with the Commissioner, he spoke in a sad tone.

"It won't be immediate. I'll need some time to make arrangements."

"Of course," Maeryn offered. "Anything you could do would be appreciated."

"My lady, I'm not going to do this for you. I will do it for the cause. Maybe you can still be of use somewhere else. But understand this," he said, turning to look her in the eye. "The Resistance will not succeed unless its members are just as willing to give their lives as any Orud soldier would for the Empire. Until we reach that point, we are condemned to struggle."

Maeryn tried to look back into those fierce eyes, but the man's conviction made her feel small.

"Go back to your home," he said. "I'll send an escort as soon as I can."

"Thank you," Maeryn replied, not knowing what else to say.

The rain fell softly, but steadily, causing the leaves of the forest to twist and dip with the weight of each droplet. Through the patchy clouds, the rays of the afternoon sun appeared as solid as tree trunks, reaching down to touch the earth. Kael adjusted the hood of his cloak to keep the rain out of his eyes so he could watch the ground, anticipating where his horse would step. This particular terrain, a ridge of crumbling rock that ran down from higher inland areas and ended at the eastern coastline ninety miles north of Bastul, would have been treacherous during normal weather, but the rain complicated matters. It took nearly half an hour to safely descend the path that ended at a smooth shoreline. Once the horse's hooves touched the wet sand, Kael nudged the animal and it sped to a gallop.

No longer concerned with the ground underfoot, Kael let his thoughts drift. The rain stopped and only the cool, damp air remained, blowing across his bearded face. He loosened the hood of his cloak and immediately the air caught the leather and pulled it away from his head. Without the restraint of a covering, Kael's blonde hair—now reaching to the middle of his back—fluttered in the wind. He drew in a deep breath as his mind returned to a time past.

The long blades of grass were dancing in the wind, swaying in unison. The air smelled of a sweet fragrance and Kael wasn't sure whether it was the woman sitting in the grass in front of him, or the purple blossoms on the trees behind her. She had a smile on her face, revealing her perfect white teeth and soft lips. Her skin was smooth and golden colored, in beautiful contrast to her straight black hair, which was also dancing in the wind. Long wisps blew across her face as she tried to tell Kael something funny, but there was no sound. She gracefully reached up and moved her hair out of the way, laughing at the hopelessness of the situation. Kael reached his hand toward her, beckoning her to continue, but she only tilted her head toward his hand.

Kael's eyes snapped open as he tried to shake off the sense of loss and the associated pain. Needing a distraction, he grabbed hold of the reins and kicked his horse into a run.

As the day wore on and the sun dipped behind the trees to the west, Kael sighted something emerging from the forest less than two hundred yards away to the south. He steered his horse just inside of the tree line to his right as a precaution, and continued forward. It took only a moment to see that it was the mainsail and mast of a ship.

As he neared, his heart began to beat more quickly, knowing that what he was witnessing was cause for alarm. The boat, which had now entered the ocean from a river outlet, was long, sitting low in the water, with a high prow that curved like a talon toward the sky. Its hull was polished for speed through the water and its crew was a motley assortment of rough-looking men. It was a Syvak warship, and it wasn't the only one. Kael counted twenty-one gray sails before the trees and rocks upriver obscured his view.

As he watched from the security of the forest, another six vessels came nimbly downriver to join the others in the sea. When all were present, the agile fleet turned to the south and caught the full force of the wind in their sails. Within minutes, the enemy ships were no more than discolorations on the ocean's horizon.

Kael kicked his heels into the flanks of his horse and the animal burst into a run. As he leaned into the beast and prepared himself for a rough ride, his mind raced with explanations. The Syvaku used to live throughout the southern territory of what is now part of the Orudan Empire. After being driven from their land, they settled in the lands far to the southwest of the Empire's boundaries and gained an infamous reputation for their brutal raiding of the coastal cities. But it had been many generations since the Orudan Empire established its dominance in that part of the world. It was from these very people that Kael's mother was descended. In fact, Kael's own name had it's origins with the Syvaku. To his knowledge, no one had even seen them in the last fifty years, let alone in this part of the Empire. Whatever their intentions, they were headed south for Bastul.

3

The night dragged on as Maeryn waited in anticipation for the escort that Thaddius had promised. She hadn't heard from Lemus yet, which meant that he hadn't gotten any information out of the captured messenger. Still, Maeryn's heart had been racing for most of the day and now her exhausted body refused to stay awake any longer. Despite her worry, she fell asleep only seconds after her head touched her pillow.

Maeryn awoke to the sound of knocking. She didn't know how long she had slept, only that her slumber had been fitful. She jumped out of bed and raced to the door, pulling it open.

"I'm sorry to disturb you, m'lady. There is a man at the gate who claims to have a delivery of fabric for you," the guard stated, obviously skeptical.

"Yes. They were to send it as soon as they received their shipment. Let him in immediately," she replied, hoping her explanation quieted his suspicion.

The guard left, returning after a few minutes leading a tall, dark haired man carrying a bundle under his left arm.

The guard nodded and Maeryn returned the gesture, indicating that she was alright to be left alone with the man.

"Please come in," she said to her guest. "When I requested to have it immediately, I didn't intend for you to come at this hour. The morning would have been fine," she said to him, loud enough for the retreating guard to hear.

The tall man smiled and walked into Maeryn's bedroom.

Maeryn shut the door behind him and turned to see the man toss his bundle on the bed. "That was smart."

"I was told you were in the market district this morning, so I thought this would sound believable."

"Well, it seems to have worked," Maeryn said with a smile. "So, what is the plan?"

The man paused for a moment, staring at her before replying. His expression disappeared quickly, but Maeryn saw the disappointment in his face. "It's to look like a kidnapping. I have a few men waiting to cause a disturbance at the north courtyard gate. While the guards are distracted, we will ride through with horses from your stables."

"Aelia will come as well," Maeryn stated.

"Of course."

"Then how will it look like a kidnapping if the three of us ride through the gate?"

"You will have to be tied...both of you," he spoke plainly, not showing any regard to Maeryn's position and the courtesies that she was used to.

Maeryn looked over to the bundle on the bed.

"No," he said, anticipating her question. "I knew the guards would search me." He then lifted his cloak and revealed a thick rope belt around the waist of his tunic.

"Where do we go after we get through the gate?"

"We will travel quickly by the north road into the mountains and then cut back to the west, making our way to Thaddius' land."

"That's it? Has he no other plans than that?" she asked.

"Those are my instructions. Although, I heard that Thaddius was making arrangements to have a boat ready for you in Nucotu, but that's all I know."

Maeryn turned from her kidnapper and walked toward the balcony, trying to hide the tears that were welling up in her eyes. Now that the time had come, she felt herself immobilized with fear. It was one thing to plan and write letters to people, but it was quite another to take the only surviving member of her family and run from the Empire aided by a group of criminals. All of a sudden, it seemed too much for her to bear.

Leaning on the railing, she breathed in the fresh night air and tried to calm herself.

"M'lady?" the escort questioned, using the appropriate address for the first time since their meeting. "We don't have time to waste. This is a dangerous mission and we must leave at once," he argued, following her out to the balcony.

But Maeryn was no longer thinking about the logistics of escaping. Instead, she stared down into the city as her eyes began to glow with the reflected orange light of fire. There were foreign ships in the bay that brought memories from her childhood. She watched as fires began to spread from the bay throughout the water district, lighting up the night sky. The battle was too far away to see individuals, but she could make out the bouncing light of torches being carried through the streets by running men. To her right, a collection of torches gathered together and soon, a building was burning. She stood motionless for a few minutes, trying to digest the vision before her.

"We're under attack," the escort said, and Maeryn nodded in response.

Suddenly, all of her anxieties washed away and a plan began to form in her mind. No longer was she concerned with escaping Lemus' wrath. The battle that raged before her eyes was the perfect distraction that she had been waiting for. And the more she thought about it, the better she felt that it wouldn't be necessary to abandon her years of carefully laid plans.

"I've changed my mind."

"What?" questioned her would-be kidnapper.

"Oh I hope Thaddius is thinking what I'm thinking," she said, more to herself than the man beside her. "This is it. Tonight we will all evacuate the city. Look. The soldiers will have their hands full."

"But...we don't even know what is happening!" the man protested, still looking down into the city.

"What does it matter? It is happening and it's perfect for our needs." The moment the words came out of her mouth, she knew they sounded cold and devious to this man, but she didn't care. In fact, she knew that she lacked the compassion she once had, when she was with Adair. Times had changed, and so had she. When she looked back to the city, the only emotion she could feel was excitement for the enormous trick that was about to be played on the Empire.

"Go now, as fast as you can to Thaddius and tell him that we must move tonight. I will send up the signal as soon as you leave."

"But...m'lady..."

"Go now," she ordered. "Any second now, guards will come and take me to a safe place and I will be unable to escape their protection. You must hurry!"

The man took a few steps backward and paused, a smile spreading across his features. "I had hoped that I would live to see this day. Thank you for not abandoning us!" Then, he turned and ran for the door.

Maeryn turned back to look at the city, trying to gauge how fast the skirmish would reach her hilltop estate. So far, it looked as though the water district was the center of the confrontation. But war was unpredictable. Adair had taught her that. It could be minutes, or it could be hours before her life was in danger.

Maeryn turned and left the balcony, walking through her bedroom and taking a narrow spiraled staircase to the right of her door. The stairs wound through a dark passage and opened into a small enclosure on the roof of the mansion. Just as she hoped, she was alone on the rooftop. She left the enclosure and walked to the middle of the flat, gravel covered roof and stood at the base of a wide flagpole, carrying the Orud standard. With a few quick glances to make sure she was alone, Maeryn untied the rope at the base of the pole and let the flag drop to the ground. Her heart was beating loudly in her chest, but she pushed aside her fear and continued with her mission, acting out the motions that she had practiced a hundred times in her mind.

Untie the knots, starting at the top.
Turn the flag over.
Thread the rope back through the holes.
Tie the knots again, starting at the bottom.

Then, as quickly as her hands would move, she pulled on the other end of the rope that led to the top of the flagpole and watched as the standard of Orud rose into the night, turned upside down. As soon as the dishonored flag reached its limit, Maeryn tied off the rope and ran back for the safety of her house.

Descending the spiral staircase, Maeryn saw a shadow of movement across the wall. Whoever was there was standing outside her bedroom, waiting. Maeryn stopped and moved to her left, against the wall. She held her breath, despite her urge to gasp from the exertion of running. If it was Lemus, then her life was over. She might be able to keep away from him if he chased her up the stairs, but where would she go once atop the roof? Maeryn tried to think of a way to escape, but her panic overwhelmed her ability to think. She stood against the wall, frozen with fear.

"Mother!"

Maeryn drew in a deep breath, wondering if her ears had heard correctly.

"Mother," Aelia called again.

"Aelia," Maeryn cried, running down the last few steps and into the hallway.

"Mother, what's happening," she asked. Her expression of concern resembled Adair.

"We have to leave. We're in danger."

"What's going on?" the young lady questioned.

"The city is under attack and we have to leave."

Aelia looked around and then returned her gaze to her mother. "I'll call the guards."

"NO!" Maeryn shouted, surprising even herself. "The guards won't be able to keep us safe. We must go by ourselves where we're not expected."

"Okay," Aelia replied, trusting her mother completely. "What about father?"

Maeryn paused, the question catching her off guard. "He'll know what to do. It's his responsibility to defend the city." Maeryn knew it wasn't much of an answer, but she didn't want to lie to her daughter. *More than I already have.*

Without waiting for her daughter to reply, Maeryn grabbed Aelia by the arm and ran down the hallway, her mind racing with plans to escape the guards and leave the city.

Six miles south of the guard tower, the northern boundary of Bastul, Maeryn crouched behind a bush along a dirt road. Aelia and dozens of escaped slaves waited a mile to the west, in the forest that covered the foothills. They were being guarded by armed soldiers of the Resistance movement. It was their planned rendezvous point for the evacuation, and with every passing hour, more slaves could be seen running in a crouched position along the side of the road, darting between the foliage for cover.

The sky was lightening to the east, though the sun couldn't be seen through the trees. It had been a while since anyone had come up the road, and Maeryn's body was getting stiff from the awkward posture. *Or maybe it's the lack of sleep.*

Suddenly, the sound of a galloping horse could be heard. Maeryn pulled her head back from the road and lay on her belly at the base of the bush, trying to hide herself as much as possible. Seconds latter, an Orud messenger raced by on horseback, the hooves pounding into the earth in front of Maeryn's face with an intensity that could only be brought about by war. As the rider faded away to the north, the forest returned to silence once again. Maeryn waited for several minutes before getting back to her feet, to continue the waiting.

Two hours later, after directing another fifteen slaves from the road to the rendezvous point, Maeryn decided to head back to the hidden camp. They were supposed to meet at sunrise and she had waited more than an hour longer than agreed. She started up a small dry creek bed created by rain runoff. Finding a footing in the soft sand was difficult, but the jagged narrow path was free of underbrush, making it the only viable passage. After several minutes of slow progress, the sound of a breaking twig brought Maeryn to her hands and knees.

She waited, listening intently for another sound to tell her whether or not she was in danger. Then, the face of a young Resistance guard peered through the trees.

"M'lady," he whispered.

"Yes. I'm coming back."

"He's already at the camp."

"Who? Thaddius?"

"Yes, m'lady."

Maeryn got to her feet once again and struggled up the hill, knowing that questioning this guard any further would not tell her why Thaddius hadn't come by the agreed route. She decided to save her questions for Thaddius himself. Letting the young man take the lead and the task of clearing a path, Maeryn followed, making much better time than she had on her own.

A half hour later, Maeryn and the guard crested a small hill and descended into a sparsely wooded valley. Hundreds of slaves and dozens of Resistance soldiers were gathered in a clearing near a cluster of boulders. Mothers were hugging their children. Fathers were crying tears of joy. And the soldiers stood around the perimeter of the clearing, their emotionless faces a direct contrast to the situation, though Maeryn understood perfectly why these men weren't rejoicing as well. They knew, as she did, that their journey had only begun.

"Where is Thaddius?" she said to the nearest soldier as they neared the camp.

A guard pointed to the right side of the camp where Maeryn could see a waving arm. Apparently Thaddius had already spotted her. Maeryn raised her hand in acknowledgement and pushed past the crowds toward him. When the two met, Maeryn sensed his excitement. His face had a tense, but lively expression.

"Why didn't you come by the road?"

"I had intended to, but I had no choice. The barbarians attacked from the west as well."

Maeryn's eyebrows went up. "Your farm?" she asked.

"They burned it," he said flatly. "We barely escaped. We had to wait in the foothills for hours before it was safe to move. So..." He nodded toward the group of slaves and soldiers that had been his traveling companions. "Here we are."

Maeryn looked around and caught sight of Aelia pushing her way past a group of men with tears in her eyes. Ajani was close behind. She turned back to Thaddius and opened her mouth to speak, but the white-haired man interrupted.

"Maeryn, I must tell you that I am very much relieved by your decision to continue with the plan. As unfortunate as this disaster is for many, it was brilliant of you to recognize the opportunity within the situation."

"Thank you," she mumbled, distracted by the sight of Aelia. "Excuse me for a minute please," she apologized.

Turning away, she came face to face with her crying daughter. "What's the matter?"

Aelia turned to Ajani and the slave stepped forward. "M'lady. Mother has not arrived yet."

Maeryn looked into the eyes of the severely scarred young man and saw the determination that had become as distinguishing a part of his person as his wounds. "Go find her, but be quick. We will be leaving soon."

"Thank you, m'lady," the slave replied, running away as fast as he could.

Actually, Maeryn corrected herself, *he's no longer a slave. He's a free man.* With Aelia comforted at her side, Maeryn turned back to Thaddius who had been waiting patiently. "So, are we still planning to march north?"

4

Dacien Gallus, Captain of the Guard for the city of Bastul, leaned against the side of a stone building in the heart of the Market District, or what was left of it. Only the stone structures still remained; everything made of wood had been reduced to ashes the previous night. Dacien and his standard bearer were all that was left of a contingent of cavalry that had been roaming the streets of Bastul, cutting down any barbarians in their path. But something had gone wrong. The barbarians had organized themselves and set an ambush for the soldiers, trapping them in an alleyway before chopping the legs of their horses from underneath them. Most of the soldiers were slain in the alley as well. Two more were picked off during the retreat. And now, the Captain and his standard bearer, who was bleeding from a fatal wound to his abdomen, found themselves trapped against a building, surrounded by five barbarians. In a matter of minutes, he would be alone.

They were howling like dogs, pounding their weapons on the street to intimidate the soldiers. Dacien had long ago lost the strength to lift and swing his sword, though he was doing his best not to show his weakness. He had been fighting since midnight, and the sun had risen over an hour ago. The sound of their guttural noises had turned from frightening to annoying and Dacien was about to make his last desperate attempt to leave this world fighting.

Unexpectedly, the savage on the Captain's right side fell forward to the cobblestone street, a battle-axe lodged in his back. Dacien risked a quick glance to see who had thrown the axe and the angry barbarians looked as well. Twenty yards away stood a man who could have been mistaken for one of the savages at first glance. His blonde hair fell well past his shoulders and his beard was gathered into a thick braid which reached a handbreadth past his chin. He wore loose fitting trousers and a tunic, both of an indistinct color, giving him a foreign look, but much different than the savages who turned to face this new enemy.

Dacien watched as one of the barbarians ran toward the stranger, raising his double-bladed axe. As the savage approached with a level swing, the man stepped inside of the blade's arc and grabbed the handle of the axe, pivoting on his right foot. The barbarian, bested by his own momentum, lost his grip on the axe and tripped over the stranger's outstretched leg, falling backwards to the street. The man turned quickly and buried the head of the axe into the barbarian's chest.

With two of the five dead, Dacien began to hope that his luck had changed. The Syvaku, however, were enraged by this new threat. Another barbarian, the largest of the group, shouted a few harsh commands and the trio immediately split. Leaving only one man to deal with Dacien and his companion, the other two began to stalk their new enemy, spreading wide to cover each flank.

Dacien tightened his grip on his sword and prepared for his own confrontation, but the barbarian in front of him was clearly more concerned about his fellow raiders. Returning his gaze to the stranger now standing in the middle of the street, Dacien watched in fascination as the man calmly waited for the barbarians to approach.

Suddenly, the man burst into action, springing to his right to pull a spear out of a soldier's dead body.

Within seconds, the barbarian leader closed the distance, but the stranger whirled the spear around his body and struck the butt of the weapon against his enemy's knee. An audible crack sounded as the barbarian's shattered kneecap forced him to his knees. In an instant, the stranger darted past the kneeling enemy, running the blade of his spear across the man's throat before spinning around to confront the next.

The barbarian in front of Dacien, who had been growing more uncomfortable by the minute, turned away from the wounded soldiers and began to run down the street in the opposite direction.

Dacien smiled at his new-found freedom, but was startled when the retreating barbarian was struck in the back with a spear and fell to his face on the cobblestones. Dacien turned back to the skirmish on his right, surprised to see the stranger facing his bloodthirsty enemy unarmed.

The barbarian circled, swinging his crude sword from side to side as he closed in.

The stranger waited patiently, stepping backward with caution. Then he burst into motion and rushed the barbarian, striking quickly with two kicks. The first struck the barbarian's hand, dislodging his weapon. The second collided with his face, knocking the large man back a few steps.

The barbarian quickly shook off the pain and growled like a dog. His fury empowered him as he dropped his shoulder and ran toward the stranger, yelling at the top of his lungs.

But the barbarian's agile enemy sprung from the ground, driving his knee into the man's face.

Dacien's jaw dropped as he watched the large man stumble backwards with blood gushing from his nose. The stranger didn't hesitate for even a second as his foot struck out like a snake, crushing the barbarian's windpipe.

After falling back to the street, it didn't take long before the savage stopped his gasping.

"Are you men alright?" the stranger called to Dacien.

Looking down to his standard-bearer seated against the building, Dacien was disappointed to find the man's head slumped forward. He turned back to the blonde-haired stranger. "I'm afraid it's too late for my friend, but I'm alive thanks to you. Tell me how I can repay you."

"Just answer one question," said the stranger. "Where can I find the Governess?"

"The lady Maeryn?"

"Yes."

Despite the man's actions, Dacien couldn't help but feel distrustful of this stranger as soon as the question was spoken. "If I knew for certain, I wouldn't tell you. But since I don't know, there is no harm in telling you that the lady and her daughter disappeared from their estate sometime last night after the Syvaku attacked us."

"I'm sorry...did you say 'daughter'?"

"Yes. Miss Aelia," Dacien replied, watching the stunned look on the man's face.

"Was it the Syvaku?" the stranger asked.

Dacien hesitated, but could see the concern in the man's face. "We don't think so. The lady had a visitor late in the evening, a man delivering something she purchased earlier in the day at the market. We only allowed him inside at her request. An hour later they were reported missing. We think they may have been taken by the Resistance."

"I have to find them," the man stated simply, turning to look up the hill to the east.

"There are no clues in the mansion, no way to track them. I had several men searching all evening and they found nothing," he offered, hoping to save the man the trouble.

"I must go," the man replied, turning to walk away.

"Wait," called Dacien. "What is your name?"

"Ka... Caleb," the man answered, turning around.

"Well, Caleb, my name is Dacien Gallus. I am Captain of the Guard. I've never seen anyone who can fight like you. If you don't find what you are looking for, I could use your help. The remainder of the Syvaku are retreating to the farmlands north of here and I need every able-bodied man."

The stranger nodded and turned away, heading for the Governor's estate at the top of the hill.

Dacien smiled, while rubbing the muscles in his right arm. He noticed the man's hesitation when he asked for his name. He thought the man almost said *Kael*. Dacien remembered hearing stories many years ago of the Governess' son and his confrontation with Lemus. But the child had been put to death. Dacien's curiosity was peaked, but he would have to save his questions for the next time he crossed paths with the man. And he had a feeling it would be soon. Watching him fight the barbarians had been like watching a choreographed dance. *He won't find anything at the mansion. And when he realizes that his searching is in vain, he'll come looking for a fight.*

The crunch of Ajani's footsteps on the gravel of the courtyard was a lonely sound. His plan was to check all the outlying buildings first and then head to the mansion. However, after checking the storehouse, tool shed, and the soldier's quarters, he was beginning to think the estate was deserted. He made his way to the stables and could immediately hear the buzzing of flies. His stomach cringed at what he might find. Walking through the open doors, he could see blood flowing from the stalls on either side of the room, pooling in the dirt walkway that divided the building in half. He continued on, glancing briefly in each stall, only to find the same sight. The horses' throats had been slashed by the barbarians, the animals left to die in the very cells in which they slept.

He pressed on, making sure to be thorough in his search. Entering the last stall on the left, Ajani fell to his knees, unable and unwilling to stop the tears that poured down his face. A primal scream emanated from his throat and escaped his mouth, shattering the air. The sound was almost completely unfamiliar to him. He could only remember one other time in his life that he had reason to scream the way he did now. But the scars on his face and body, evidence of that incident, seemed insignificant to what lay before his eyes.

The sight of the tunic, the familiar and unmistakable fabric, covering the form lying face-down in the straw, gripped his heart. The clothing was torn, her skin cut and bruised.

BARBARIANS!

Her hunched posture told the story of unspeakable acts, her failed attempt to crawl away from their cruelty. He took in the scene through a flood of tears and approached the body. Kneeling solemnly at her side, he gently lifted and turned the lifeless form. Grief caught in his throat as he mouthed, "Oh Mama..." But no words came, no sound escaped his lips. His roughened fingers traced lightly over the bruises and disfigurement as he lowered his lips to kiss her forehead. With great reverence he slowly laid her back on the straw. He crossed Zula's arms upon her chest and, in a futile attempt at dignity, covered her with the remains of her garment.

It was unclear to Ajani how much time had elapsed as he found himself standing outside of the stables, staring at the blue expanse of the sky. The tears had stopped flowing and now he felt a deep hollow in his soul, a void left by the only person that mattered to him. He was alone in the world now, the last of his family.

The silence was finally intruded upon by the unmistakable form of Lemus stumbling through the northern gate into the courtyard. He was limping badly and his tunic was cut open at the back and soaked with blood. He didn't seem to notice Ajani as he lurched awkwardly toward the entrance to the garden.

Ajani watched with a mild curiosity, as though an ant were crawling by. *How easy it would be to stretch out a foot and crush it!* Then Ajani found himself moving, following the man only a few paces away. They were in the garden now and Ajani's pace was quickening, the gap between them closing.

Lemus heard the footsteps and turned. "Oh it's you," he grunted. "Help me. I must get to my study."

But Ajani ignored him, rushing forward and shoving the Governor to the ground.

Lemus winced as he fell on his back, gritting his teeth. "What do you think you're doing? I'll have the guards hang you by your neck. You're nothing but a treacherous bastard, all of you. Even my own wife betrayed me."

Ajani kicked him in the stomach as hard as he could and the words immediately stopped.

As Lemus struggled to breathe, silence once again returned to the garden. In the distance, Ajani could hear that several people had entered the courtyard. He assumed that they were the guards Lemus had spoken of, but it didn't really matter who it was. He had already made up his mind about how this conversation would end.

He leaned down toward Lemus and whispered into his ear. "The best part of the betrayal..." he paused for effect. "...is that Aelia isn't even your daughter. Maeryn was pregnant by Adair before she met you."

The presence in the courtyard was growing louder; the footsteps were getting closer. But Ajani ignored them. Instead, he widened his stance, bent over Lemus' struggling form and clenched his fists. He could see the panic in his master's eyes, eyes that used to show only cruelty. Ajani hoped that Lemus understood what was about to happen. He hoped that the scars on his own face would communicate what he couldn't say because he didn't feel much like talking anymore.

5

After leaving Dacien, Kael made his way uphill, carefully to the north. His path was erratic, taking him from building to building, staying out of sight to keep from being caught up in any more confrontation. Not that confrontation bothered him. Indeed, it had become a way of life for him. But now that he knew where to start searching for his mother, and surprisingly, his sister, confrontation would only slow his progress.

After the better part of an hour, Kael crested the rise upon which the mansion stood. He stepped cautiously through the gate; the courtyard spread before him. It was eerily silent, but the sound wasn't the strongest assault on his senses. The sight of the mansion and its surrounding buildings, situated within the graveled expanse of the courtyard, was almost too much to bear. Kael felt emotions that had no names. It wasn't sadness. Neither was it joy. It was an odd mixture of too many feelings and Kael shut them down immediately. He didn't have time to waste.

Dacien said that Maeryn received a visitor, so the first place to inspect was the house. The embedded gravel crunched on the dirt as Kael strode across the courtyard. It seemed much smaller than he remembered, though still large by anyone's standards. The garden entrance came into view and more memories began to flood Kael's mind. He heard laughter. He saw his father's mischievous smile. He heard Ajani scream. These things were distractions that he chased away with one conscious thought.

The trees and flowers, the half that were still standing, seemed fuller and more mature. Even in its state of ruin, the garden still held a peaceful ambience. Suddenly, Kael slowed at the sight of a dead man lying in the dirt. A quick glance around told him that there were no longer any threats present, so Kael moved forward again. Recognition came almost immediately, even though the man no longer had any distinguishing features to his face.

"Lemus," Kael said aloud.

The gangly man lay on his back, with one arm on his chest. His tunic was blood-soaked and his face was so swollen as to be unrecognizable as human, had it not been attached to the man's body.

"...looks like the Syvaku hated you as much as I did!"

Kael waited for a moment, staring down at the object of his hatred. This man's presence in Kael's life had changed everything. In his early years at the monastery, when Kael wasn't missing his family, he would lie awake in his bed, imagining the ways in which he would end Lemus' life. And now, many years later, the man was reduced to a cold lump of flesh, *by an enemy of his own making, no doubt.*

Kael wondered what kind of policy would have provoked such a violent reaction from the Syvaku. But he brushed the thought aside and stepped around Lemus' body, heading for the main entrance into the house.

His search began in the master bedroom and when that produced nothing, he initiated a systematic check of every room in the house. After searching in vain for some sort of clue for over an hour, Kael began to believe that the Captain had spoken correctly. There was nothing to see. Everything looked just as it should, deserted and ransacked. Refusing to give up, Kael moved his search to the other buildings around the mansion. Other than the body of an old slave woman that he found in the stables, his searching had turned up nothing.

The sun was now high overhead and Kael sat on the stone steps leading down to the bay of Bastul. The wall that surrounded the estate also included a portion of the harbor which was reserved for sensitive shipments that could be offloaded within the security of the enclosure. From the docks, cargo would be pulled in horse-drawn carts on a paved path that zigzagged up the hillside to where Kael now sat. His vantage point gave him a view of the entire city and as far as he could see, smoke filled the horizon.

The hot sun burned down through the haze clinging to the city and beads of sweat began to form along Kael's forehead. For months he had been traveling with Bastul as his goal. Though he had called many places home over the years, cities and villages that had never even heard of the Orudan Empire, they were all temporary. Bastul was always his home. He wasn't exactly sure why he didn't return immediately after leaving the monastery. Maybe it was just a series of events that kept him away. Or maybe he just wasn't ready. Whatever the reason, it all seemed meaningless now. As he sat on the steps and watched the burning city below, Kael felt more lost than ever. His mother was missing, gone without a trace, along with a sister he had never met. He had separated himself from all the people he called friends in order to come back to Bastul. And now, his journey had proven pointless.

I could use your help.

The words of the Captain came back to him.

Kael sat motionless for a moment, wondering if there was any value in joining the fight. After all, what loyalty did he have for Orud, except that his father was a soldier? He wasn't sure why he had chosen to fight the Syvaku men in the city. Maybe it was because they were taunting the Captain and would certainly have killed him.

After several minutes of silence, Kael rose to his feet and began to move. His decision was simple. He would take the only opportunity presented to him—to help the Captain of the Guard. Perhaps later, Kael's life would move in another direction, but for now, this was enough. It was something he could do.

He left the estate by the northern gate and skirted the city to the north, staying just off the main road. He retraced the route he had taken earlier in the morning and found the clearing where he had tethered his horse. There was no sign of the animal, but that was to be expected. With the city in chaos, Kael left enough slack in the reigns for the horse to pull free if necessary. Within minutes of a sharp whistle, his horse appeared at the edge of the clearing. Kael quickly mounted and headed off to the west in search of the remaining soldiers.

The rest of Kael's day was spent riding along the foothills between the mountains to the north and the farmland to the south. As the sun dropped to the west, Kael found signs of movement, disturbed earth along a riverbed. The same river flowed from the mountains through the center of Bastul before emptying into the bay. Kael followed the tracks upriver, deep into the mountain range, until they diverted into the surrounding forest. Less than an hour before sunset, Kael caught his first glimpse of human life since leaving his parents' estate.

He was aware of the soldier's presence several minutes before the man jumped out from behind a thick hedge of shrubbery. The terrified soldier held his spear in front of him, ready for an attack.

"Identify yourself," he commanded.

Kael raised his hands to show that he wasn't a threat. "I'm looking for Dacien Gallus, Captain of the Guard. He said that he could use my help with the rest of the Syvaku."

"You look like one of them. What is your name?"

"Caleb."

The soldier turned and waved his spear. In response to the signal, another man stepped out from the cover of trees, twenty yards away, and headed off through the forest to the east. The first man turned his suspicious gaze back to Kael and held tight to his spear.

Kael waited patiently while his story was checked out and, after a few minutes, he was surprised to see the Captain himself walking through the trees.

"You're later than I expected," he called out.

Kael smiled. "I don't remember making any agreements, but I'll try to be more punctual in the future." As the Captain neared, Kael dismounted from his horse and shook his hand.

"I'm glad you've decided to join us." Dacien nodded his head back in the direction from which he had come. "Walk with me; I'll explain our dilemma."

"...dilemma?" Kael questioned. "What's happening?"

"Well," Dacien breathed. "As far as we know, there are about thirty barbarians left. We chased them into these mountains a few hours ago, but they suddenly stopped running. I lost two men in their counter attack. Now they're using the cover of the trees to keep the fighting spread out. It's their strong point and our weakness."

Kael didn't have to look around to get his bearings. Though he was never allowed to venture far when he lived in Bastul, he had a firm understanding of the surrounding areas from studying maps with Saba. "They have open fields to their north and the forest thins out to the east. Your horses and archers give you the advantage if they move into open terrain."

"Exactly," Dacien replied. "We think they are waiting until nightfall before they begin to make their way northwest, through the forest. If they split up, they will be impossible to contain in the dark."

"If you put the majority of your men in the trees to the west, is there no way to keep them here and wait them out? Eventually, they'll have to leave."

"Unfortunately, I have less than fifty men and I don't have time to spare. I have to make haste to Nucotu in order to send a dispatch rider to Leoran. They have to be informed of what has happened here."

Kael lifted his head in understanding. "So you need to go into the forest after the Syvaku before sunset?"

Dacien nodded. "We're just trying to work out a plan...and work up the nerve. None of us can stand the thought of letting them go after what they did. But it's not going to be easy to go in after them."

The two men had come upon a small clearing in the midst of their conversation. Soldiers from Bastul stood at attention, grouped by their weaponry. Spearmen, archers, swordsmen, and a handful of cavalry readied themselves for battle, tightening straps, sharpening blades. Each man wore a look of determination with a hint of fear.

"Here we are," Dacien said quietly. "Caleb, I wouldn't normally discuss battle plans with a complete stranger, but these are unusual times and I don't sense any deceit in you. Thank you for your help."

Kael nodded distractedly, taking note of the resources at their disposal.

"Well, your specialty seems to be the spear, so let's head over to the men and get you outfitted."

"Actually, my specialty is the sword, but might I make a suggestion?"

Dacien paused. "After what you did in the city, I would welcome any advice you may have."

Kael looked back to the roughly equal groupings of soldiers now lining themselves up in standard attack arrangements—spearmen in front, followed by swordsmen, then archers. "The standard formations would leave your men vulnerable in this instance. You said that the Syvaku are spread out, hiding behind trees?"

"Yes, that's correct," he replied hesitantly.

"You might consider three-man groups spread ten yards apart. Each group would contain one spearman, one swordsman, and one archer. Have your riders cut sideways in front of these groups to flush out the barbarians on an individual basis. Their strength in this scenario is their ability to attack and hide, which appears undisciplined and chaotic to you. But lining up your men in one large group will only leave them unable to move and react to the barbarians' random attacks. A small group still retains the advantages of long, medium, and short-range attack capabilities, yet allows for flexibility to deal with the enemies' tactics." The words flowed from Kael's mouth with more authority than he intended and when he was finished, he hoped that the Captain was not offended.

"Interesting," Dacien replied. "You have had training in the arts of war."

"Something like that," said Kael, waving his hand in dismissal. "If you would like, I'll ride out in front."

After contemplating the idea for a minute, Dacien replied. "Yes. I think that would be a good idea."

After introducing Kael to the men, who numbered almost fifty, Dacien relayed the plan to the group. The soldiers, without question, began to assemble themselves. Kael mounted his horse and grabbed a shield and spear, opting instead for a weapon with a longer range than the short, Orud-style sword made exclusively for thrusting.

The groups spread out ten yards apart, just as Kael suggested, and began to move slowly forward into the darkening forest. Kael and five other riders rode a short distance ahead and began to cut left and right through the trees, trusting in the speed and agility of the horses to keep them out of danger.

Almost immediately, a barbarian jumped out from his hiding place and swung his axe at one of the riders. The Syvak warrior missed and gave away his position. The nearest group of Orud soldiers quickly closed-in and the archer struck his mark before any combat took place. Seeing the effectiveness of their strategy, the soldiers' confidence began to grow. In a matter of minutes several more confrontations occurred to the same end.

The plan was working.

But the darkness of night was closing in quickly and barbarians were growing more reckless with each attack. Dacien called the riders to himself and changed the strategy.

"We need to speed this up. Ride farther ahead and seek out barbarians for yourself. Kill them on your own if you can. Those of us on the ground will move quicker to give you support."

Kael and the rest of the riders accepted the change immediately, spurring their animals into motion. Suddenly, the soldiers from Bastul were charging through the forest, trying to keep up with the horses. The rider on the left flank went down, but a nearby group came to his aid and dealt with the barbarian. The horse was lost, but the rider escaped uninjured.

In the failing light, sound became the dominant sense. Sharp clangs of warfare sounded from numerous directions. The soldiers, trying to beat back the night, abandoned their fears and charged into the forest, knowing that the remainder of the Syvaku must be dealt with immediately.

Kael closed his eyes and kicked the sides of his horse. As the animal's hooves dug into the soft earth, Kael expanded his senses to take in all of his surroundings. In his mind's eye, he could see every trunk and limb around him. The sound of the running beast beneath him was a warning call to the Syvaku. As he passed between the trees, warriors stepped out from their hiding places, only to be cut down before they could even see their enemy. It became a dance, one that Kael had perfected.

After half an hour, and the complete loss of light, the soldiers from Bastul gathered together in a small clearing. Kael rode near and listened to the hushed sounds of urgent discussion as the soldiers quickly decided the best strategy. Suddenly, the air grew lighter around them as several trees began to go up in flames. Within seconds, the forest all around was burning and Kael realized that the barbarians were about to make their final attack.

"Gather together," shouted Dacien. "Archers in the center, spearmen form a perimeter."

Kael and the remaining cavalry urged their animals into motion and began to move around the group, keeping an eye on the burning trees. For several minutes, the only activity was the fire, its flames climbing the trunks of the surrounding trees. Embers and ash began to fall from above as the leaves were consumed.

Kael could see the tension in the faces of the spearmen as he rode around the circle. It was a common tactic that the Syvaku were using; waiting until the soldiers from Bastul began to mistrust their eyes. Staring at the flames had a way of dulling the senses. Each time Kael circled the group, he could feel a presence at the east side of the clearing. Sometimes the feeling would increase in intensity, presumably as the barbarians moved near. Other times, it would almost completely disappear, only to return from another direction. Kael knew that the enemy was waiting for the right time, as well as the right approach. Of course, he couldn't tell the soldiers from Bastul about his feelings. It wasn't something that they would believe or understand. But

Kael had stopped long ago trying to explain. He had learned through trial and error to trust his instincts.

Suddenly, from the west side of the clearing, an axe spun through the air, catching one of the horsemen on his right arm and knocking him from his horse. The circle of soldiers tensed, wanting to help their fallen friend, but not willing to break the formation. The horseman rose to his feet, blood dripping from a deep gash in his upper arm as well as a minor wound to his abdomen. As he jogged to catch up to his horse, a form appeared at the edge of the clearing, running for the fallen rider.

Kael spun in his saddle and shouted. "Guard yourself," but it was too late. The barbarian approached from the other side of the man's horse, unseen until he darted to the rear of the animal and delivered a fatal blow with his crude sword. Just as the Orudan soldier fell to his knees, the barbarian was thrown backwards by the impact of three arrows.

Kael looked back to the circle and saw the concentration of all the men focused on the west side of the clearing and the events that had just occurred.

"Don't be distracted," he yelled to the men, searching for the presence of the barbarians. And then, to the north, he felt it. It wasn't as strong as he expected. Then he sensed another larger group of men to the south and instantly knew the Syvak's plan.

"Beware the diversion to the north," he shouted, breaking away from the group and riding directly to the south. As the flaming trees neared, he could hear the commotion behind him as several barbarians charged into the clearing to draw the attention of the Orud soldiers. Kael dropped his shield and pulled a sword from the scabbard hanging from his side. Now armed with a spear in his right hand and a sword in his left, he raised himself from the saddle and stood in the stirrups to gain the extra mobility.

Almost immediately, figures began to dart out of the forest, coming from both sides of his horse. Kael stabbed with the spear and swung the sword downward, toppling three men in seconds. After going through the flames, Kael stopped his horse and watched as the majority of the remaining barbarians charged back through the flames toward the Orud soldiers. Kael jabbed his right knee into the saddle and his horse turned left to follow behind the Syvaku.

In their blind fury, the barbarians ran forward, concentrated solely on their goal to kill the soldiers. Kael used this to his advantage and struck down one after another from behind, his enemies only realizing what was happening as they fell to his weapons.

The barbarians spilled out into the clearing and were immediately assaulted by a volley of arrows. In the light of the clearing, Kael noted that Dacien's estimation of thirty Syvaku was far too conservative. They numbered closer to fifty, nearly matching the number of men from Bastul.

As the first rows of barbarians impaled themselves upon the spearmen's weapons, Kael ducked to the right and rode along the rear of the Syvaku. His weapons lashed out, striking many as he spurred his horse to a gallop. Nearing the end of their ranks, he turned around for another pass, just in time to see the circle of Orud soldiers spread out to keep from being surrounded. The rear ranks of the Syvaku pulled back in order to flank the soldiers, and Kael lost his opportunity.

He quickly jumped down from his horse, no longer needing the charging power. Instead, he opted for his own maneuverability and ran to confront the enemy. Axe blades swung by him as he dodged in and out of clusters of untrained raiders. With each step he jabbed and slashed, not even pausing to see the men fall around him.

The final confrontation lasted only a few minutes and when the last Syvak fell to the ground, Kael glanced around to assess the damage. The soldiers from Bastul had lost over half of their numbers, but their Captain was still alive. The remaining men jabbed their weapons into the air and shouted their victory, regaining a small measure of the dignity that had been taken from them by their enormous losses earlier that day.

After searching the surrounding area for additional enemies, the remainder of the group from Bastul marched back through the trees and headed southwest. They arrived at the edge of the forest at midnight and made camp in the foothills northwest of Bastul. Most of the men went directly to sleep, but a handful, including Dacien and Kael sat around a small fire, replaying the day's events in their heads. After a long period of silence, Dacien spoke.

"Once again," he directed to Kael, "I thank you for your help."

Kael only nodded in response, staring at the fire.

"You were probably responsible for a third of them," he continued, murmurs of agreement coming from the other soldiers.

"No," Kael protested.

Dacien shrugged his shoulders. "I know what I saw." He paused for a moment. "What will you do now?"

Kael thought for a second. "I...don't know. I might ask you the same question."

"In the morning, we'll head back to the city for whatever provisions are left. Then we'll leave immediately for Nucotu."

"Are you leaving anyone behind to secure the city?"

Dacien smiled. "There's nothing left to secure. Anyway, we'll come back after I get a message sent to Leoran. They have to know what's happened."

Kael nodded again and looked back to the fire. There were so many thoughts running through his head that they all muddled together. For the first time in his life, he felt without purpose. After several minutes of silence, he stood up.   "Would you mind if I accompany you and your men to Nucotu?"

Dacien laughed. "Of course not. You're one of us now. Besides, you're handy to have around. I just may need my life saved again."

Kael smiled in return. "Thanks. I'll see you in the morning."

"Good evening," the soldiers spoke softly.

6

"Maeryn," spoke Thaddius, softly.

Maeryn turned her head and looked at him. "I know...it's time." She was sitting atop a boulder along the southern rim of the valley containing the refugees from Bastul. Her hair fluttered in the breeze coming off the ocean as she stared out upon the rolling hills. She couldn't see Bastul from her viewpoint, but she knew it was out there. And somewhere within the city limits, Zula and Ajani were trapped, by capture or death, unable to return. The Resistance couldn't wait any longer. They had to begin their long trek to the north. "Still no word?"

"Nothing," said the Resistance leader. "I'm sorry," he added.

"I'm sorry as well, but they knew our timeline. We'll leave whenever you're ready."

"Nightfall is quickly approaching. It will be best to move under the cover of darkness."

"Then I'll tell the people to be ready by sundown," she said, climbing down from the rock and starting down into the valley.

The remainder of the day passed slowly as Maeryn tried to rest in preparation for the coming night. There was a mixture of fear and excitement in the camp and it seemed that Maeryn wasn't the only one who had trouble resting. The Resistance guards, on the other hand, seemed to have no difficulty taking turns napping in the shade of the trees. Maeryn thought that they must be used to conducting their activities at odd hours.

By the time the evening meal was ready, Maeryn couldn't stand being still any longer. She walked down from her napping area to the bottom of the valley where the refugees were beginning to gather. The smell of food immediately made her mouth water. The provisions for this trip had been planned out long in advance, with each person responsible for bringing something of value to the whole group when they left the city. Some brought simple, light cooking utensils, while others brought water containers or sacks of grain. It was accepted that this meal would be the last before the strict rationing would be enforced, and Maeryn tried to concentrate on enjoying what was available.

After assembling into lines to collect their dinner, the crowd dispersed into the surrounding areas to enjoy their meals. Aelia came over to Maeryn and sat down, her food untouched.

"Eat up. This is the best meal that we're going to have for a while."

"I know," Aelia replied. "But I don't have an appetite. Are we really going to leave without Ajani and Zula?"

Maeryn turned to her daughter with tears in her eyes. "We have to."

"Why?"

"Look at all these people," Maeryn replied. "We can't jeopardize their lives for the sake of two people, even though they are our friends. It just wouldn't be right."

Aelia picked at her food. "Is there anything we can do?"

"I'm afraid not," Maeryn answered. After a long pause, she added, "Actually, that's not true. There is something we can do. We can make sure that these people escape to freedom, so that the work of Ajani and Zula is not wasted."

Aelia smiled in response. "Do you think they're alright?"

Maeryn paused, deciding not to shield her daughter from the realities of what they were doing. "No, Aelia. I don't know what has happened to them, but their absence tells me that they are unable to come to us...for whatever reason."

Aelia nodded and then looked to the ground as tears rolled down her face.

Maeryn reached over and put her arms around her daughter, letting her own tears flow as well.

After sunset, the group headed north through the hills, staying well away from the road that lead from Bastul to the northern watchtower. The road continued on a northeasterly course for several miles before ending, the construction of the direct route to Orud having been abandoned long ago in favor of more immediate concerns.

After skirting the guard tower and its area of visibility, the group slowly made their way east to the shore. This first leg of the trip took the entire night and by sunrise they made camp in a ravine along the coastline. Maeryn took the opportunity to rest her aching feet and to talk with the former slaves of Bastul. She was surprised by their optimism, knowing that she and Thaddius had good intentions, but almost no control over the outcome of this situation. But when compared to the lives to which they had become accustomed, the goal of reaching their destination seemed entirely plausible. By the time they began moving again, the weight of this realization began to change in Maeryn's mind, turning into a determination to see this through to the end.

They began to move again a few hours before sunset and continued along the shoreline, heading for a secret location to the north. The first few hours before the setting sun proved to be productive, with the aide of the light and the smooth terrain. But as the sun waned, so did the speed of the group. Thaddius told Maeryn that the need to travel by night would lessen with their increasing distance from Bastul. And just as he suggested, the following day's travels were spent almost entirely in the light.

On the third day of travel, a few hours after sunset, Thaddius stopped the group and instructed his guards to make camp. Maeryn helped prepare a small meal before the people retired for the night.

As soon as the provisions were put away and the cooking supplies packed, Maeryn found Thaddius. He was discussing the plans for the following day with his soldiers.

"Have we arrived?" she asked, as soon as he had passed out the guard's orders.

"Nearly. Our destination is less than an hour from here."

"And the preparations that you spoke of...they are in order?"

"One of my scouts has just returned," Thaddius said, nodding to a man who was just now sitting down against a rock to eat his meal. "Everything is in order."

Although Thaddius wasn't very old, his stark white hair gave him the wise look of a man twice his age. His face appeared calm, reflecting the light of a nearby fire. He seemed to be at peace, even though their actions would earn them all a death sentence if they were discovered. Maeryn thought that it was as good a time as any to have the conversation she had been pondering all day.

"Thaddius. You haven't explained to me what is to happen now that we have left Bastul."

"That's correct," he replied.

Maeryn, seeing his reluctance decided to be more forceful. "I need to be included in the planning of this excursion."

Thaddius' eyebrows raised. "I didn't know you wanted to be."

"Yes, I do."

"Well, what do you wish to know?"

"Everything. I think I have a right to know. Eventually, these people will start wanting some answers and they are going to look to me. In fact, I've already had to dodge a few questions today about our destination."

"Yes, I suppose that is true. However, it's late and we all need rest. I'll tell you tomorrow's plans, but the rest will have to wait until we have a better time."

"When will that be?" she asked, sounding more forceful than intended.

"Tomorrow evening."

"Very well. What is the plan for tomorrow?"

"Shortly after we set out, we will reach a cove. In the cove is a grotto at the water's edge. I've made arrangements to have boats hidden in the cave."

Maeryn looked back to the scattered groups of slaves shifting uncomfortably on the surrounding rocky terrain. "How many boats?"

"Enough," he answered. "It's a large cave," he added. "Each boat will carry a specified number of people and we will travel the rest of the way by sea."

"And what is our final destination?"

"Well now, that would be part of tomorrow's conversation."

"Good enough," Maeryn stated. "But tomorrow I want to know everything."

Thaddius nodded and Maeryn turned away to find Aelia and their sleeping quarters for the evening. As she walked away in the darkness, she realized that Thaddius' conversation was different than any other that had occurred in the past. It took her several minutes to realize that she had never asked him anything specific before. Nothing about his intentions, plans, or his resources. He had always taken care of his responsibilities and left Maeryn to take care of hers. *Perhaps he feels threatened.* Though she knew it didn't make any sense. Ultimately, he had complete control over the situation, even if he needed her as a mediator for the slaves. *What is it then?*

And then it came to her. *He doesn't trust me. He's testing me, buying time to see if I'm going to quit.* Suddenly Maeryn understood. Only hours before the evacuation of Bastul, she had been willing to abandon all of the plans and the entire slave population of Bastul to save her own life. *At least that's the way he sees it.*

In that moment, Maeryn understood that she would have to portray herself as one who was willing to die for the cause. It would be the only way to gain his trust. But more importantly, in order for this to work, she would have to become that person in reality, one who is willing to set aside her individual desires in order to seek a greater good. After everything that she had been through since the disappearance of Adair, she wasn't sure she could do that. She had learned to focus on surviving, looking to her own safety. *How can I now abandon the one perspective that has kept me alive all this time?*

As she walked among the rocks protruding from the hillside, her heart grew heavy and for a moment she doubted that she was capable of what she was doing. *People like Thaddius and Adair are made for this sort of thing. Am I kidding myself?*

And then she saw the figure of a young woman, waving her arms. It was Aelia, beckoning her mother to come and rest in the soft sand. In that instant, her confidence was restored. *How many men could have accomplished this?* She had come up with a plan and had seen it through, at the threat of her own life, to protect and raise her daughter for the last sixteen years. Perhaps even Thaddius was not capable of such steady determination.

Maeryn smiled as she waved back to Aelia. *I will keep going. I will keep going because the consequences of giving up are unthinkable.*

The following morning, the group cleaned up their camp in record time, everyone excited to reach the next leg of their journey. And within an hour of setting out, just as Thaddius said, Maeryn could see the coastline jog sharply to the west, indicating that somewhere, beyond sight, was Thaddius' cove. The terrain rose slightly for several hundred yards, and the bright morning sun had everyone sweating profusely by the time they reached the top of the ridge that surrounded the cove.

Suddenly, one of the Resistance soldiers, who always walked far ahead as a scout, raised his hand and crouched to the ground. All of the slaves looked around in confusion and slowly began to imitate the man, responding to the sense of urgency on his face.

Maeryn's heart began to beat rapidly as she looked over to Thaddius, crouching a few paces away on the right. The scout waved him forward and Thaddius began to move, staying low. Without an invitation, Maeryn followed, intending to be part of every decision made on behalf of this group from this point forward.

As she and Thaddius came within whispering distance of the scout, who was now joined by several other soldiers, Maeryn could see the source of the man's alarm. There, on the northern side of the cove, just visible over the horizon of the ridge, were two Syvak warships. Their sails were slack and they appeared to be anchored. Maeryn looked to Thaddius, who paid her presence no attention. His mind was consumed with the task at hand.

"They have found our cave," he whispered intensely to the scouts.

"What are they doing here?" one of the men asked.

"I thought they all fled after the attack," offered another.

"None of that matters," broke in Thaddius, stopping the unnecessary conversation. "We need only be concerned with how to be rid of them."

Everyone nodded in agreement, but no one offered any constructive ideas. Maeryn looked out to the small bay and was alarmed to see tiny shapes in the water next to the warships.

"What are those?" she asked

Thaddius lifted his head. "Our boats!" he hissed through gritted teeth. "We have to put an end to this, NOW!"

"We outnumber them," Maeryn stated. All the men looked at her as if she was crazy. "I know they're dangerous, but there is strength in numbers.

If all of us," she said, sweeping her hand back to the massive group of crouching slaves, "were to swarm them, our losses would be minimal."

"And who is going to make them do it?" one of the scouts asked her.

Maeryn looked around the small group of soldiers to find Thaddius smiling. "I will," she answered plainly. After a few quick nods of agreement, she turned and made her way back to the slaves.

The former captives of Bastul came close as she approached. Deciding that they were well out of earshot from the Syvaku, she raised her voice enough for all to hear. "Listen to me. Your freedom was not gained by simply escaping Bastul. From this day forward, your freedom will be a prize for which you must fight. And today is the first day of that struggle. Even now as we speak, the same barbarians who attacked Bastul are down in that cove, stealing the very boats that were reserved to carry you to freedom. There is no time to delay, or even to think. We must act now. Though they are warriors, they will not risk their lives for a losing cause. That is why we must act as one, intimidating them with our numbers."

As Maeryn spoke, a sense of calm came over her and the words began to flow. She didn't ask permission. She commanded without hesitation. There would be no second guessing, for there was nothing else to do but act. The freedom of these people before her lay not in her hands, but in their own. "We will head back to the trees and then make our way quickly and quietly to the other side of the cove. I will give you more specific instructions when we get there. Let's go," she said, rising to her feet and striding confidently toward the forest. The slaves followed without hesitation. From the corner of her eye, Maeryn saw Thaddius say something to his men, but she couldn't hear.

Minutes later, Maeryn, the soldiers of the Resistance, and the mass of former slaves poured out of the forest above the cliffs on the north side of the bay. Half of the group split off and followed the gently sloping shore leading to the beach. The other half climbed to the highest point of the cliffs, directly over the entrance to the cave and the Syvak warships. Screaming at the top of their lungs, the slaves began hurling rocks at their enemy.

Three of the barbarians came out of the cave, running along the sandy shore to confront their attackers, but stopped short at the sight of their numbers. As rocks rained down upon them, the warriors turned back and ran for their ships. Along the decks of the warships, a flurry of activity erupted as blonde-haired barbarians readied their ships to sail. When the last of their brethren boarded, the ships lurched into motion, driven by the strength of the oarsmen.

Thaddius turned to a smiling Maeryn with a look of panic on his face. "If they escape, they will return with more men."

Maeryn, unsure of how to respond, watched as Thaddius ran back up the incline, heading toward his soldiers atop the cliffs. Maeryn followed as fast as she could manage, understanding instantly what he meant to do.

As she neared the top, the Resistance soldiers were already in motion, lifting rocks above their heads and heaving them over the cliff, aiming for the warships.

"Large rocks," Maeryn yelled to the slaves. "We must sink the ships."

The first of the Syvak warships was gaining momentum and its slack sails were beginning to fill with wind as it headed away from the cliffs. A great cheer went up from the crowd as one of the slaves, a large and muscular man, hefted a boulder the size of his head, over the cliff. It landed with a crack on the stern of the enemy vessel, splintering wood as it crashed through the hull. Almost immediately, the ship began to take on water and its forward progress halted. It took only minutes before it slipped beneath the surface, leaving its angry crew treading water. Suddenly, another cheer came from the slaves as the second ship, still close to the mouth of the cave, pitched to one side and began to sink.

Maeryn ran to the edge of the cliff and watched in fascination. And then, just as suddenly as the cheering began, it stopped. Only now did the group see the rope attached to the stern of the warship. As it sank beneath the blue-green waters, the small sailing vessels that were meant to transport the slaves were pulled into a straight line. Then, one by one, they were pulled under by the weight of the larger warship.

Thaddius ran down toward the beach, hoping in vain to help the situation. But nothing could be done. And as Maeryn looked out in despair across the waters of the cove, she became aware that their situation had suddenly taken a drastic turn for the worse.

The next few hours were a blur of activity as the exhausted barbarians made their way across the bay to the opposite shore, only to be dispatched by the waiting Resistance soldiers. Thaddius and Maeryn entered the cave to find that two thirds of the transportation boats had gone down with the Syvak ship. The remaining boats, seventeen in all, were still neatly stacked along the back wall of the cave.

"They'll each carry ten," Thaddius spoke softly, his voice echoing inside the earthen chamber.

"We can fit more," Maeryn responded.

"No. We can't risk sinking in the middle of the ocean. They'll only safely carry ten."

"What do you mean for us to do then?" Maeryn shot back.

"I DON'T KNOW!" Thaddius yelled, showing frustration for the first time since Maeryn had met him.

"I'm sorry," Maeryn offered. "I know you didn't mean for this to happen."

Thaddius nodded and glanced around the cave, running through the logistics in his head.

"Maybe now would be a good time for you to tell me the plan. Or what it was originally."

Again Thaddius nodded his head and turned back toward the entrance to the cave. "Walk with me."

Maeryn followed in silence until they exited the cave and started along the sandy beach. The sun was now at its peak, but the heat felt good on Maeryn's skin, chilled from her time in the dark cavern.

"There is an abandoned Orud outpost on the eastern tip of the island Tur'cen. It was used as a staging area for the slave traders. The plan was to take the boats up this coastline, east across the channel, following the southern coast of Tur'cen to the outpost."

"What then?" she asked.

"There," Thaddius continued, "we would make a temporary encampment for the slaves. I figured it would take several months for myself and a few of my men to travel to Orud and make arrangements to bring everyone safely and secretly into the city."

"Do you have any specific ideas about how you will accomplish this?"

"I did. But that doesn't seem to be the most immediate concern."

Maeryn looked out across the waters of the bay while choosing her words carefully. "Somehow, the present difficulty can be overcome. But I want to know how the ultimate goal of this venture will be accomplished. If that isn't figured out, then none of this," she said, pointing back to the cave entrance, "really even matters."

"Alright. The slave trade has slowed considerably in the past ten years, but there are still ships coming in from the east on a regular basis. If we could gain control of one ship, we could smuggle all of the slaves into Orud without any suspicion. The Orudan guard would be expecting a ship of slaves and that's exactly what would arrive. But, in order to make that happen, I would have to travel to the Resistance headquarters in Orud."

"In Orud?" Maeryn questioned, unsure if he spoke correctly.

"Yes, hidden in plain sight. It's right under the nose of the great Orudan Empire, in its capital city."

"And where exactly is it?" Maeryn asked, sensing Thaddius' discomfort at the direction of the conversation. "I understand your hesitation to tell me, but I think I've earned it."

"In the temple of Equitus, the god of equality."

"How poetic," Maeryn said with a smile.

"Yes. And once there, I would have to convince our leader to make the arrangements, for he is the only one with the connections to accomplish such a task."

"That sounds impossible."

"Yes, well, you asked."

"Who is the Resistance leader?"

Thaddius shook his head. "I've never met him. In fact, I don't know anyone who has. He keeps his identity hidden even from his own followers. It's safer that way."

"How..." Maeryn began, but Thaddius interrupted.

"No more questions. We've got to figure out how to get all these people to the island outpost."

Maeryn bit her lip, frustrated at the abrupt end to the stream of useful information. "Well, the quickest way would be for you to take the remaining boats and half of the slaves, and then come back for the rest of us. Meanwhile, we would march north, making your return trip much shorter."

"Does this mean that you are volunteering to stay behind?"

"As long as you leave me a few of your soldiers...yes."

Thaddius smiled. "You do realize that this process could take several weeks and with three trips across the channel, our risk of being spotted by an Orudan patrol increases threefold?"

"Do we have any other choice?"

"I suppose not. Then we'll set out in the morning."

"Agreed," Maeryn replied with confidence, though in reality, she had never been so scared in all her life.

7

Kael awoke before sunrise and left the group of sleeping soldiers. He walked a good distance away, following the edge of the forest until he came to a small hill overlooking the farmlands to the west. Behind him, the dark sky was just beginning to lighten along the horizon. As was his daily ritual, he stood with his hands at his sides and bowed his head. Eyes closed, he began to steady his breathing and concentrate on his heartbeat. Automatically, his body began to move, flowing gracefully through various stances and positions. As his body expended energy, his movements seemed to generate energy of their own, replenishing what was expended, and more. Almost immediately, the familiar but unexplainable sense of his surroundings came to him. Though his eyes were closed, Kael could feel each blade of grass swaying in the breeze; he could sense every contour of the rolling hills.

By the time he was finished, the sun had just cleared the eastern horizon. Kael hurried back to the encampment and found that nearly everyone was awake. A small meal was being prepared over the campfire and the remainder of the men were packing their belongings and readying themselves for the trip back to Bastul. The group ate in silence and within half an hour, they were moving south. The short trip took only a few hours and when they crested the hills to see the city below, the small group of soldiers—all that remained of the Bastul guard—stopped in their tracks.

The once glittering city called the "Southern Jewel" was now only a dark, smoldering blemish upon the face of the earth. The group began to move, slowly. Kael glanced around and saw that many of the men had tears running down their faces, though they made no noise. As they descended out of the foothills, Kael realized that his own feelings of grief couldn't possibly measure up to those of the men around him. Though he had returned, Bastul still remained only a pleasant memory of his past. But for his traveling companions, it was their home.

Upon entering the city, the soldiers were greeted with mixed reactions. Some of Bastul's citizens were excited that help had finally come. Some were angry that the soldiers had come too late. Kael watched Dacien to see how he would respond, but he didn't clarify to the people that his men had been part of the original defense of the city and were, just now, returning from pursuit of the enemy. It wasn't the time or the place, Kael realized. It would accomplish nothing to explain.

The soldiers continued moving through the city, some on horseback, witnessing the aftermath of the attack. The only structures that remained standing were those made of stone. Everything else smoldered, threatening to flare up at a moment's notice. It took several hours to reach the hilltop garrison and by the time the men arrived their energy was nearly spent.

Before the men completely lost their concentration, Dacien called to his second in command. The man immediately responded and came near.

"Have the men gather what provisions are left, if any. I will take a few men and ride to Nucotu. We will depart this evening, or sooner if possible. I am leaving you in charge until I return."

The man nodded sharply, understanding the importance of what was being asked of him.

"I know that this task will not be easy, but you must do what you can to help the people. Some sense of order must be restored. And you may tell them that I have gone to get help from our neighboring cities."

"Yes, Sir," the man replied, leaving to carry out his orders.

Dacien turned to look at Kael, but spoke nothing.

"Just let me know when you are ready," Kael said. Pulling on the reins, he led his horse back to the gate and left the courtyard.

Two hours before sundown, Dacien, Kael, and eight other soldiers started out from the city of Bastul on horseback, by way of the western road along the coast. By sundown they had passed the western guard tower, which marked the northwestern city limit, and turned north into the uneven coastal terrain. Just before midnight, they made camp in a thin stand of trees, each man going directly to sleep without any conversation.

Sunrise came quickly as the small group broke camp and continued their north and west passage, changing direction to follow the smoothest terrain. The sky was clear for the remainder of the day and even after sundown when they gathered around a fire to eat their evening meal.

Sometime during the night a storm blew in from the sea. The rain fell steadily for hours, drenching the ground around them. Without a fire or breakfast, the soldiers broke camp and continued north. Along with the rain came a strong wind that made conversation between the men impossible. The days dragged on in solitude and Kael had only his thoughts to occupy the time.

The weather failed to improve and two weeks after setting out from Bastul, the small group of soldiers, moving swiftly along the beach, rounded a sandy point to see the small town of Nucotu. The trip had taken nearly twice the anticipated time, but the men were relieved just to reach their destination.

The coastal community was originally one of several waypoints setup between the larger cities of the region. Their purpose was to shelter and sustain messengers responsible for maintaining communications throughout the Empire. The town had grown through the years to include a community of farmers and fishermen as well.

But on this cloudy morning, it was immediately obvious that something was wrong. An eerie silence pervaded the area, interrupted only by the soft and steady falling of rain. Dacien rode at the fore and directed the men to move closer to the tree line on the right.

Kael followed in the second position and surveyed the environment. The main dock was partially collapsed into the water and there were no boats to be seen. *Strange for a fishing community.* Immediately, Kael feared the worst—that Nucotu had also been attacked. For the moment, he set the thought aside and cleared his mind to be ready for surprises.

As they entered the city, the column of soldiers spread out to search each building thoroughly before moving on, but they were all deserted. After an hour of searching to no avail, Dacien took two men and rode inland to search the farmlands. Kael and the others continued moving through the town center and ended their search near midday.

In the main meeting hall, Kael found dry wood and cold ashes in the fire ring at the center of the room, and set to work on building a fire. Within minutes he had a small flame and began adding fuel. Once he coaxed the flame into a blaze, he invited the other soldiers to warm themselves, then walked outside, volunteering to keep watch.

It was obvious that the inhabitants of Nucotu had left in a hurry...a disturbing observation. After finding a good sheltered vantage point atop a knoll, Kael settled himself against the trunk of a tree and considered the implications. *If Nucotu was part of the Syvak attack, then this was a coordinated assault or possibly invasion. The attack on Bastul was serious enough to result in a direct retaliation against the Syvaku, but an invasion would mean a large scale war within the Orud Empire.*

Before dusk Kael returned to the meeting hall and switched guard duty with another soldier, finding the evening meal prepared and waiting for the Captain's return. No sooner had he warmed up than Dacien entered the hall with the remaining soldiers. Their faces were solemn.

"What did you find?"

Dacien shook his head and proceeded to speak, his voice barely above a whisper. "One of the larger farms had a barn that was burned down. We searched the ashes and found bones."

"Human?" Kael asked, already knowing the answer.

"Yes."

"How many?"

"I would guess that all or most of the citizens were in the barn when it was set aflame."

A moment of silence followed, not out of respect for the town's inhabitants, though they were deserving, but because it seemed wrong to speak until each person had time to consider what they had just heard.

It was Kael who broke the silence. "Let us sit. I would like to share something that hasn't made sense to me until now."

Slowly, the men made their way to the fire, settling upon the floor with their meals, though most didn't have the stomach to eat. Kael took a few bites of hard bread and swallowed before speaking. "One day before my arrival in Bastul, I was traveling along the eastern coastline. At the mouth of a wide river I witnessed a long formation of Syvak warships entering the ocean. Once the small fleet was assembled into formation, it turned toward Bastul and sailed from my sight. I arrived at the end of the fighting in the city when we met."

"You mean the ships sailed from the river?" Dacien asked with surprise.

"Yes. Their ships have wide, shallow hulls without a keel, making them highly maneuverable in shallow water. And their sailing ability is unmatched." At this, a few of the soldiers grunted with disapproval, not ready to agree with any statement that put Orud behind another nation or people.

"I don't mean any disrespect, but it is a fact. Their entire culture is based upon their sailing and navigational skills. They have weaknesses, but this particular skill is unmatched and unquestioned."

"What are you suggesting?" Dacien asked.

"I believe that the Syvaku descended upon this town quickly and surprised the citizens, dispatching them quietly and thoroughly, taking care to prevent anyone's escape. Then they used a river only a few miles to the north of here to make their way inland. Judging by the disproportionate number of ships to foot soldiers that attacked Bastul, I would guess that they have been transporting their soldiers to a base camp somewhere along the river. They are most likely using the branching river systems to place solders in strategic locations throughout the southern region. And if this is the case, the Syvaku are not just attacking but invading."

"That is a lot of speculation," Dacien said flatly.

"True," Kael conceded.

After a few seconds, Dacien looked back to Kael. "If what you say is true, then our situation has indeed become significantly more complicated. I was expecting to find a dispatch rider in this town to send word to Leoran. But now we will have to deliver the message. And I can't communicate your suspicions to the General without any proof. But to search for the proof means delaying the delivery of this critical message which is my first priority." Dacien looked at the floor, not expecting anyone to answer. He was simply speaking out loud the decisions that were his to make.

In the absence of discussion, one of Dacien's men spoke up. "If they are using this river to the north as an entry point, shouldn't we also hold the river, or at least monitor it?"

Kael responded immediately. "No. At this point it would be a waste of time. The attack on Bastul is an indication that they reached a point of readiness with a sufficient number of soldiers and other resources. You won't see any more ships along this route."

Dacien looked to Kael as soon as he finished speaking. "Take two of my men with you. Ride upriver and follow it until you find confirmation of your theory. Make sure that my men see it as well. I don't mean to offend you, but the General won't accept intelligence from a scout that I met on the day of the attack. We will ride north for Leoran and deliver our message. If you do indeed find confirmation of what you seek, ride north and find our trail if you can. Otherwise, we will wait there for your arrival. You can leave at first light."

Kael nodded. "We'll leave now."

8

The night passed at an agonizingly slow pace as Maeryn found it impossible to sleep with all that was on her mind. She ran the numbers in her head over and over. They had set out from Bastul with nearly five hundred slaves. *With seventeen boats carrying ten people per boat, it will be three trips with or without the Resistance soldiers. Which means there's no other way out of this situation.* She had already told Thaddius that he should take the first group and that she would stay behind, but her mind wouldn't stop trying to come up with a better solution.

Sometime in the early morning, she awoke from a nightmare. She had been dreaming that she was underwater, her ankle tied to the ropes that connected their escape boats. She could see the Syvak warship beneath her, disappearing into the darkness amid a flurry of tiny bubbles. The rope around her ankle pulled her through the water, downward toward the darkness. It didn't take long for the panicked feeling to go away, and when it did, it was replaced by a sense of relief that she had actually fallen asleep.

Morning quickly erupted into a frenzy of activity as Thaddius and sixteen of his men boarded the remaining escape vessels and began to help the slaves of Bastul aboard. The provisions would be split equally between the three trips, in case there were any accidents along the way. Once underway they would fish to supplement their stores of food. Each vessel was fitted with six oars and a small sail to accommodate a variety of situations. The rowing, when necessary, would take place in shifts to spread the work evenly among the passengers. Shortly after sunrise, the first group departed the cove, turning north as they entered the broader expanse of ocean. Maeryn watched, her anxiety growing with each stroke of the oars. At last the boats disappeared from view and Maeryn knew that her most difficult trial had just begun.

"Everyone, clean up! Let's get moving," shouted Garust, the next ranking officer among the Resistance soldiers. Maeryn already suspected a hint of a tyrant, but she hoped it was only the over-eager response to his new responsibilities. She had seen it many times with soldiers in Bastul.

All at once, she felt two opposing emotions, longing for Adair and repulsion for Lemus. It was amazing, but since she had left the city, she hadn't thought about Lemus. It never even occurred to her to fear that he might come after her. But now that she thought of it, the concern seemed valid. Although, it seemed so small in comparison to what she was now facing. And with that, she dismissed it from her mind.

The remaining slaves, now numbering just over three hundred, broke camp in under an hour and quickly assembled double file. Garust sent two men ahead as scouts to find the best path and with the return of the first, the column began to move. Maeryn and Aelia were positioned near the middle of the group; Garust thought it best to have them visible to all the slaves.

It was in this moment that Maeryn realized her role and power in this situation. For some reason, the Resistance soldiers had neither the respect nor authority over the slaves that Maeryn had. *Perhaps it's because I'm a woman, or because the Resistance fighters are soldiers. They earn the automatic disdain of the slaves.* After pondering this thought for the better part of the morning, Maeryn came to the conclusion that her planning of the exodus from Bastul must have given hope to her current traveling companions. *All those years I worked to establish lines of communication throughout the slave class of Bastul, I never considered the effect it would have on the people.* She imagined herself as a slave, chained to a detestable way of life, without hope of change. Then, she imagined what it would feel like to hear rumors of messages being passed from one slave to another. *Finally, you would be approached and asked to report information about your masters and their affairs. Your fear would be great, but equally matched by the anticipation of something undefined. Perhaps change? Your feelings would slowly grow into hope that someone would act, that someone would use the supplied information for some greater purpose, perhaps something that would affect your own life in a positive way.*

As Maeryn considered these thoughts, she looked around at her traveling companions. Her gaze was met with the smiles of men, women, and children alike. It was in this moment that her resolve was hardened and she promised herself that she would never abandon these people as she had been abandoned. She couldn't let them be captured or fall back into a life lived against their will. If anyone understood their pain and suffering, it was she.

After saddling their mounts, Kael and the two soldiers from Bastul rode north to the mouth of the river. The moonlight reflected off the gently flowing water as they turned inland. Already, Kael could feel the discomfort of his companions.

"Is there something you wish to say?"

"Do you plan to travel by night? How will we be able to see what we are searching for in the dark?" The shorter man was bolder in his speech, compared to the tall, fair-haired one.

"This is just for tonight. We will stop tomorrow evening and travel only by day from then on."

With that, the men were silent and remained so for the rest of the evening. The travel was slow without proper light or a defined path, but as the sun began to rise in the east, their progress quickened. By the time the sun was a hand's breadth above the horizon, they spread out to become less visible to any spying eyes.

At midmorning, they stopped to breakfast together and it seemed that the others were not used to the solitude. The conversation started as soon as the first bites of food were swallowed.

"What exactly do you hope to find?"

Kael smiled. "I hope to find nothing. But if we see any sign of a temporary dwelling, cold camp fires, or any sentries, then my fears will be confirmed."

There was silence for a few minutes before Kael spoke again. "When we're finished with our meal, I'd like to spread out even farther. I don't want anyone to ride along the opposite side of the river, it's too exposed. I'll ride along the base of the mountain," Kael said, pointing to the low mountain chain running along the south side of the river. "If you stay in the trees, you won't be visible from above, but we'll have visible contact with each other beneath the foliage. If you see or sense anything, stop riding and signal me."

Kael could see the irritation in their faces. Though he had already proven himself to the men in battle, they couldn't stomach taking orders from a scout.

"Oh yeah...one last thing. You should remove your cloaks and armor; anything bright in color or able to catch the sunlight will give you away." Before the men had time to object, Kael held up his hand. "I know you don't like it, but it is for your own good. Even scouts in the Orud army are not required to wear the royal color," he protested, indicating their red cloaks. "You've been given a new charge by Dacien and for the time being, you are considered scouts."

The men slowly nodded in approval and swallowed the last of their meal. "Let's go," they ordered, attempting to regain their dignity.

For the remainder of the day they followed the river to the east, with Kael traversing the foothills and the others staying between his position and the river. They camped at nightfall without a fire and repeated this rhythm for another three days until the river forked, one branch continued southeast, while the other turned due south.

"Look," the tall soldier said, pointing across the eastern branch to the northern shore. "It looks too large to be animals."

Kael followed his outstretched arm and saw the large area of trampled grass beneath the trees. "It's too far away to tell for sure, but I agree with you. I think we should follow the southeastern branch; it should lead us toward the eastern sea, where I saw the Syvak warships."

Suddenly, the dark-haired soldier shifted his gaze and looked over Kael's shoulder.

Kael turned around slowly and saw it immediately, movement in the rocks to the south of their position. Whoever it was, he was staying just below the horizon to keep his silhouette from being visible, but he moved with too much confidence to be invisible.

"We must keep talking as if we haven't seen him."

The men nodded quickly and casually, adapting to the situation with ease.

"Why don't you two take to the southern branch, along the shore? Make it look as though you seek a place to cross. If he has been watching us for any length of time, then he'll expect me to go back to the foothills. From there, I will try to ascend to him unseen."

The men turned and headed to the river and Kael steered his horse to the foothills. Within minutes, Kael lost sight of the crest of the mountain and immediately began to look for his passage. It didn't take long to find a steep valley that carved its way into the mountainside. Kael dismounted and placed the reins of his horse over a low-hanging branch. Then he sprinted as fast as his legs would carry him up the valley. He knew that time was of the essence. If the enemy scout lost sight of Kael for too long, then he would start to get suspicious. Kael had to reach him before that happened.

Still running, Kael's legs began to burn, but he pushed on until he approached the crest of the hill. Taking in large amounts of air, he slowed himself to a crawl, then veered toward the southern slope of the valley and climbed his way out. He came out into a stand of trees that offered some protection, but limited his visibility. Kael scanned the mountain top while creeping forward, looking for some sign that he wasn't alone. Then, the scuffle of a boot upon a rock sounded to his left. Carefully, he moved forward a few steps and froze.

There in front of him, only twenty paces away, was the Syvak scout, moving sideways along the rocks with his eyes toward the river. Kael was startled at how close he already was to the man. Breathing steadily, he moved silently forward, keeping just behind the scout's peripheral vision.

As he neared, Kael watched in confusion as the man lifted his hands to his face. For a moment, Kael wondered if he was about to sneeze. Instead, he cupped his hands around his mouth and howled like a dog. Suddenly, Kael could hear the faint sounds of commotion coming from the river. It was a signal and his companions were in danger.

Kael burst into action, no longer concerned about silence.

The startled man spun around just in time to see a boot crash into his face. The force of the kick whipped the man's head backward and his body followed obediently, crashing to the ground. Without breaking his stride, Kael reached down to the man's head and gave it a quick twist, feeling the neck snap.

Without hesitating to even verify the man's death, Kael ran down the mountainside, dodging branches and clusters of boulders. The descent seemed to take twice as long as the ascent as every passing second felt like an eternity. The slope flattened in time with the thinning of the trees and suddenly, the shoreline was visible. Kael glanced left and right, but couldn't see around the bend of the river. He had no idea where his companions were. Guessing, he turned right and followed the river to the south. And to his dismay, he found the body of one soldier lying face down in the rocks. The dark hair told him immediately who it was.

A few seconds later, he came across the other, wounded. He was propped up on one elbow, holding his short sword in front of him. Two barbarians lay dead at his feet. Downriver, another Syvak was wading through the water toward him, grinning like a carnivorous predator over its fallen prey.

Kael ran to the wounded soldier and took the sword from his hand. "Can you walk?"

"Is this the best time to ask?" he replied, shocked by Kael's calm demeanor.

"Don't worry about him; he'll be dead in just a few seconds. Can you walk?" he repeated.

"Uh...I think so!"

"Good," Kael said with a grunt, helping the man to his feet. Turning around boldly, he stared at the barbarian who now seemed unnerved that this newcomer didn't wear a look of fear. Kael marched toward the man, entering the ankle-deep water with such confidence that the Syvak took a step backward and stumbled.

Kael lunged at him with the first sign of weakness.

The barbarian stepped back again and stumbled, sending out a flailing arm to regain his balance.

Kael slashed quickly, severing the limb at the elbow. The Syvak's forearm spun through the air and landed with a splash.

Falling backward into the water, the man stared in disbelief at the remains of his arm.

Kael surged forward again and plunged the Orud short sword into the man's chest, forcing his body under the water. He held the sword in place for a few seconds before pulling it free.

The body sluggishly began to drift downriver.

Shaking off the blood and water, Kael wiped the blade clean on the sleeve of his shirt and walked back to the soldier standing on the bank.

The Orud soldier accepted the sword without a word.

"How badly are you injured?"

"I'll live. I'll limp for the rest of my life, but I'll live" he responded, looking down at the deep gash in his leg.

Kael looked around to see the other dead barbarians. "You fought well today."

A few seconds of uncomfortable silence followed as the man struggled to find the words to show his appreciation. Instead, he stepped forward, wincing in pain, and extended his hand. "My name is Caius...and I'm honored to travel with you."

Kael accepted his handshake. "...and I, you!"

The night was cold without a fire and neither man had the stomach to eat anyway. The day's confrontation and the loss of a friend had sapped their energy. Both went to sleep as soon as the sun began to set. The next morning was bright and most of the chill was gone from the air. Kael had to wake Caius, who looked pale and exhausted.

"Can you ride?"

"Always," he replied with a defiant smile. "What's the plan?"

"The men we encountered yesterday were either scouts or sentries. It's good, but not enough of a confirmation. We need to cross the river and follow the southeastern fork."

"I'm ready when you are," Caius replied.

As planned, the two crossed the river and followed the southeastern fork along its southern bank. By midday, the land began to rise around them and they moved away from the river to maintain a vantage over the water. Kael decided to stick close to Caius as his wound wouldn't allow them to travel apart safely. After a gradual rise in elevation, they spurred their horses up a final steep and rocky grade, arriving at the top of a short mountain. The view stretched out for miles.

Following the river bend, Kael's eyes traced the landscape for any sign of confirmation of his theory.

Breathing heavily, Caius squinted into the sun. "If I were a sentry, this would be my choice for a post."

"Indeed," Kael replied. "In fact, I'm surprised that we didn't encounter someone as soon as we crested the hill."

"Maybe there isn't a larger group," Caius offered.

After a long pause, Kael responded. "Or maybe it's because they're on the move and this location has already been scouted."

Caius turned and followed Kael's outstretched arm pointing to the northeast.

"...the cloud of dust, just below the horizon."

"I see it. There must be three of four hundred of them."

"Yes. It looks like they're on foot." Kael turned to look at Caius. "I apologize, my friend. We don't have time for you to rest and heal. We have to ride fast to warn Leoran."

"I understand."

"Is this enough confirmation for you?"

"...plenty. Just give me a minute to change my dressing and we can get going," Caius replied, reaching down to the blood-soaked bandage on his leg.

He dismounted and removed the wet bandages, only to find that the wound had reopened since the morning. The bleeding was considerably less than the previous day, but still more than Kael wanted to see. It was a difficult situation considering the urgency of their information, but Kael couldn't ride ahead and leave this man alone in his current state.

Caius bound the wound with a tight dressing, remounted his horse and nodded to Kael. Kael nodded in return and turned his horse back to the west where he had noted a decent point to cross the river earlier in the morning.

Traveling was slow through the mountainous terrain, but sped considerably as the land began to flatten. A week after setting out from the river fork, Kael and Caius came across the trail of Dacien and his men. They had apparently moved inland from the coast to take advantage of the easier route. After studying the remains of one particular camping spot, Kael estimated that they would be more than a week ahead. He told this to Caius with the conclusion that they would not rejoin their companions before they reached Leoran. He didn't add that it was mainly Caius' wound that would keep this from happening; the man had enough to deal with.

At the midpoint of their six week journey to Leoran, Kael began to notice a drastic decline in Caius' health. The final straw came one afternoon as Kael was following. He put Caius in the lead, hoping that deciding which route to take would keep Caius' mind occupied, away from the pain. As they began a slight decline into a shaded valley, Caius slipped from his horse and landed awkwardly in the dirt. Kael quickly dismounted.

"Are you alright?"

The man only groaned in pain, lying face down on the ground.

Kael lifted his head and saw that his eyes would not focus. "We'll stop here for the evening. Just close your eyes and rest; I'll take care of everything. Just rest," he repeated.

After carrying him to a more secluded location, Kael built a small fire and gave Caius some water. He wouldn't take food, even in small amounts, and eventually, Kael stopped trying to force him. After a few hours, Caius slipped into a deep sleep. Kael took advantage of the dying sunlight and inspected the unconscious man's bindings.

The outer bandage was clean, but as Kael unwound it he could quickly see that the wound was festering. The inner bandage was saturated with a yellowish fluid and when removed, the skin showed itself to be bright red in a large area around the wound. The gash was covered over with a putrid-smelling greenish scab and it was obvious that infection had set in. Kael sat back and slumped to the ground, frustrated by the thought of what this man would have to endure in the next few days.

Sometime during the night, Caius began to moan in pain. Kael checked his forehead and confirmed that he had a fever. Neither of them slept at all the rest of the night, as Kael made regular trips to a small stream nearby for fresh water. Midmorning on the next day, Caius started vomiting and couldn't keep down even water. The minutes stretched into hours and the hours into days. Kael knew that he was losing precious time but he had to see Caius through the worst. And that time eventually came the following morning when Caius shook Kael awake.

"What..." Kael mumbled, disoriented. "How are you feeling," he asked, as soon as he came to his senses.

"Better," Caius replied. "How long have I been out?"

"...a few days. Can you eat?"

"I'll try a little."

Kael rose and immediately set to making a light broth over the fire. When it was prepared, he gave a small cup to Caius and watched the feeble man try to consume the hot liquid.

After seeing him take a few sips, Kael smiled and then spoke. "Listen. You're not fit to travel. And I have to notify Dacien of what we've seen."

"I know," Caius responded with a downcast look, disappointed with himself.

"I can leave you my waterskin and the rest of my rations, which should last you another few weeks. As soon as I reach Leoran, I'll send a rider to come back for you."

As Kael spoke, Caius reached to his shoulder and unfastened his torc, allowing the red cloak of Orud to fall to the ground. At this, the man winced, not for the pain, but the dishonor of allowing the cloak to touch the ground, unattached to his uniform. Without the strength to pick it up, he gestured to it. "Take it. Dacien will never believe you otherwise."

Kael quickly knelt and lifted the cloak from the dirt. "Thank you. Is there anything I can do before I leave?"

"You've done plenty. Now go quickly. You hold the lives of many more than just mine in your hands."

After a few minutes of readying his horse and supplies, Kael mounted and looked down to his friend. "I'll send someone back."

"I know you will. If I don't get the chance later, I want to thank you for saving my life."

"Of course," Kael replied. "But you will have another chance. You owe me an ale the next time we meet."

"Fair enough," Caius laughed.

Kael nodded to his friend, then turned his horse to the north and kicked his steed into motion.

9

The travel on foot had been grueling, but fortunately Maeryn, Aelia, and the freed slaves of Bastul were getting close to their destination. One more day to the north would bring them to a point along the eastern coast where they would meet up with Thaddius. The former Commissioner of Bastul had planned to take the first third of the slaves to their hideout on the island of Tur'cen and return to rendezvous with Maeryn's group.

Lost in thought, a commotion at the front of the group caught Maeryn by surprise.

The lead scout was running back along the column of travelers toward her. "My lady. Thaddius has returned."

Maeryn looked to where the man was pointing. Out in the ocean were several white dots floating in contrast with the deep blue water. "Perhaps he grew impatient with our progress," Maeryn replied.

"Indeed," came the reply with a smile.

Another hour brought the two groups together in a joyous reunion on the shore. Thaddius relayed that the trip was a success and that all was exactly as planned at their island encampment. This instantly gave hope to all who heard. Suddenly, their struggle seemed to have purpose and their efforts were not in vain. After the reunion, they moved a mile to the north where the terrain offered a bit of seclusion from any patrols that might pass by. The sun fell quickly, but the weary travelers were now experts at setting up camp. As the sky darkened, the smell of cooking food filled the air.

"How are you holding up?" Thaddius asked Maeryn as they sat eating their meal.

Aelia seemed more interested in the conversation and only picked at her food.

"Fine. Were you waiting long at the meeting place?"

"No. In fact, I didn't wait at all. Being out on the water makes me nervous. The Orud patrols aren't nearly as heavy as they used to be. But it would be easy to spot us, especially with the repeated crossings to the island.

When I saw that you hadn't arrived, I immediately turned south. I would like to get this over as quickly as possible."

"That reminds me," Maeryn replied. "How will you notify headquarters that we are in place?"

Thaddius shifted his weight and remained silent. It was obvious that speaking of these matters in front of Aelia made him uncomfortable. Ultimately, it didn't matter. There were no secrets now; they were all in this together. But that didn't seem to make it any easier to get Thaddius to talk.

"Aelia dear, I would like just a bit more soup."

"Yes, Mother," she answered, taking Maeryn's cup and walking off in the direction of the nearest fire.

"You were saying..." Maeryn said to Thaddius.

"Actually, I wasn't."

"Thaddius, why do you insist on keeping secrets, even now when we are all risking our lives together?"

"I suppose it's a habit."

"So tell me about the plan as a means of overcoming your habit," Maeryn replied, pushing farther.

"Alright," he said after a few moments of silence. "The need for Orud patrols along the southern islands waned as our enemies became fewer and fewer. Without this purpose, the navy was put to other uses, specifically slave trading. The eastern point of Tur'cen was used as a staging point for slaves. The great ocean faring vessels from the southeastern seas would bring large groups of captured men and women and offload them at the island. From there, they would be loaded onto smaller, more maneuverable ships that could navigate the shallower water among the islands. Once the slave trade declined, the larger ships became obsolete and the smaller vessels would perform both tasks and would eventually make the trip from the southeastern seas to Orud without stopping."

"And what does this have to do with us?" Maeryn interrupted.

"I was getting to that. Once we are in place, the headquarters will be notified and arrangements will be made to route an empty ship to the island. The ship will dock at the abandoned post and we will all board for our trip to Orud. We will ride into the capital city in broad daylight just as any other arriving slave shipment. After arrival, it will appear as if the slaves are given to their new masters, when in fact, each master will take his new subjects to their respective assignments to support the Resistance throughout the Empire."

Maeryn was shocked. "Assignments? I thought they were to be freed!"

Thaddius held a finger to his lips, cautioning Maeryn. "They will be free...they are free," he corrected.

"Yes, free to be subject to someone else's rule!"

"Maeryn, are you so naïve as to think that these people will be released to wander the countryside? Until we can make a permanent change, they will never be free under this Empire. This is a new chapter in all our lives. We are giving them the chance to fight for their own freedom. They will not be subject to new masters, but will have the freedom to act as any of my soldiers do, though their responsibilities will not be as great. What more can we hope for in this day?"

Maeryn sat silent, pondering his words.

"I will tell you this. They will enjoy a great deal more freedom than you did as the wife of Lemus. And under those circumstances, would you have called yourself a slave?"

"I hadn't thought of it like that. What's to become of me and Aelia?"

"I don't know; I was only told of the others. I suspect that you will be given a few choices, but you need to be prepared to keep serving the Resistance as you have through the years. I'm sorry if you expected something more grandiose."

"I'm not sure what I expected. How will you notify the headquarters?"

Thaddius shook his head. "I think I will leave that answer until another time."

Maeryn started to protest but Thaddius was firm. "Such things are only discussed at the highest levels of authority and responsibility. You're just going to have to trust me." Rising to his feet, he brushed the sand from his clothes. "I will leave in the morning with the second group and will return as soon as possible."

Maeryn watched him walk away and tossed the remainder of her soup into the sand. The weight of Thaddius' words made her heart ache. She hadn't really thought about it, but as his words sunk in, she realized that her expectations were inappropriate. She had wanted to go back to a life of true freedom, a life like she had with Adair. But it seemed that she had just traded one type of captivity for another.

Leoran, the capital of Orud's southern region, was spectacular to behold. It was a city built on a lake that was miles across at its widest span. Ivory colored stone walls rose from the lake's glassy surface, separated every hundred yards by towers flying Orud's red flag. Kael's horse raced across acres of open field, heading for one of two roads spanning the water that separated the mainland from the city walls. As with any city, people tended to gather on the outskirts. Leoran was no different, with various sizes of buildings and tents strewn about the landscape with no apparent logic to their locations. Through this maze of civilization, Kael directed his horse until he reached the stone paved road leading across Lake Leoran.

After miles of travel and weeks of hunting for small game to satisfy his appetite, Kael arrived at the gates to the city. Well guarded by a contingent of Leoran soldiers, the gate kept non-citizens and other rabble from even stepping foot on the road across the lake.

"Halt!" cried the soldiers, thrusting the points of their lances forward at an angle.

Kael pulled on the reigns and stopped his horse.

"Identify yourself," demanded the soldiers.

"I am a scout for Dacien Gallus, Captain of the Guard of Bastul."

After a few minutes of careful inspection of his belongings, the guards allowed Kael to pass. The road was over a mile in length and perfectly straight. Kael kicked his steed and sped to a gallop. The air was surprisingly still, and for the first time in weeks, Kael looked around and marveled at the beauty of the landscape. The smooth water reflected the bright sunlight and the golden grasses of the surrounding fields. There was a time when Kael thought more about such things, but the urgency of the situation flooded his mind and he found himself racing for the city walls.

As he closed within a hundred yards of the city walls, a small group of men exited the shadow of the entrance. One man waved his hand and Kael instantly recognized Dacien. Seconds later, Kael dismounted and grasped the hand of his new friend. But the fact that Caius and the other soldier were not present made the situation awkward.

"Where are they?" Dacien asked, turning to lead Kael into the city.

"I found the confirmation that I needed, but we were attacked. Caius was badly injured and the other man didn't make it. Caius and I made it half of the way here before he was overcome with sickness. I saw him through the worst of it, but I had to leave him in order to reach you in time."

Dacien looked skeptical but momentarily set it aside for the more obvious issue. "We'll send someone back for him. In the meantime, come inside and rest and tell me the reason for your urgency; I'll assume you had a good reason to leave one of my men alone and injured."

Dacien's idea of rest wasn't nearly as luxurious as it sounded. Kael was hoping for a pub, but was instead taken to Dacien's temporary quarters and given a plate of cheese and some wine. After a few swallows, Kael could feel his muscles relax.

"Alright," he breathed, exhaustion showing. "We followed the river inland for three days..." Kael said, and continued to recount the happenings of the last few weeks, from the ambush to Caius' sickness.

"Where did you leave him?"

"Three weeks back, along the route you followed here. You will find him in a shaded valley next to a stream." Kael reached into his travel bag and pulled out Caius' cloak. "He also gave me this and said you wouldn't believe me otherwise."

The disappointment of Dacien and the others in the room was tangible. It was as if the air was stolen from their lungs at the same moment. Dacien hung his head and when he raised it again, his eyes were holding back tears.

In that moment, Kael understood the significance of the cloak. "He didn't intend to make it here alive...did he?"

Dacien confirmed Kael's questions with a shake of his head. After a minute of silence, he straightened his shoulders as if to set aside his grief for another time. When he spoke again, his voice was quiet and deep.

"You said there were hundreds of Syvaku moving on foot?"

"Yes. They were headed north, and based on what happened at Bastul, I believe they intend to attack Leoran."

"They'll need more than a few hundred to take this city," argued another soldier. Kael didn't recognize him and assumed he was a Leoran citizen.

Dacien looked back to Kael. "We have a few weeks at most. I will call a council with the General tonight and explain these things."

Kael opened his mouth to speak, but Dacien held up his hand in protest. "I know, but your word won't be trusted. I'll tell him myself. Besides, with your hair and less-than-groomed manner of dress, you might be mistaken for a Syvak yourself!"

Kael scratched his beard. "I was meaning to ask you, where can I wash up?"

Kael was given an escort—or a guard as he saw it—to show him to a bath house. The baths were separated into two sections, one for the regular citizens and one for the military. The soldiers enjoyed many more comforts than the rest of the population, with servants waiting at full attention to tend to every need. After a quick swim, Kael moved to a small, fire-heated pool to relax his tired muscles. Almost instantly, his thoughts turned to Caius.

What courage. To face your death alone, without hesitation. And what was that look on Dacien's face? Horror? Suspicion? I wonder what he thinks of me now! Just stay alive, Caius. You just need to make it until we send someone for you.

"Excuse me, Sir?"

Kael turned to the servant.

"Shave?" asked the man, showing Kael the razor.

Kael was about to send him away, but paused. "Please," he accepted instead.

The night air was cool on Kael's newly shaven face. Perhaps it was the bath, or his new look, which was sure to please Dacien. But for some reason, he felt good about where he was. Even though he had traveled for nearly a year to return to the city of his birth, only to find it demolished and his mother missing, he didn't feel out of place. In fact, he felt like he belonged here.

He stopped walking and leaned over the stone wall. His guard stopped as well, always keeping a few paces of distance between them. Gazing out over the water, Kael smiled at the beauty of Leoran. Night had fallen and all along the banks of the lake, the firelight of numerous homes and businesses reflected off the water. He always felt the need to explore his surroundings and had spent the last few hours wandering the city with his silent companion. He was at once uplifted by the signs of life and saddened that these people were in danger.

There is always someone who seeks destruction!

Feeling a sudden sense of urgency, Kael headed back in the direction of Dacien's living quarters in hopes that the General's council had already met. He returned to an empty room, but didn't have to wait long until Dacien returned.

"Well?"

Dacien slumped into a chair. "You look different."

"So you approve?" Kael asked with a smile.

"Do you care?"

"Not really," Kael admitted. "So what happened?"

"It was...strange."

Kael raised his eyebrows. "Would you care to elaborate?"

"He wasn't the least bit skeptical of your information."

"Well that's good news," Kael replied, wondering what was the matter with his friend.

"He's mustering an attack party to intercept the Syvaku, and he's leading it. It was as if he was bored and wanted something to hunt. I cautioned him that this enemy is unpredictable, but his mind was already made up."

"So when do we leave?" asked Kael.

"We don't. The General wants to handle this matter with his own soldiers. He's leaving at dawn."

Kael felt a little relieved, but mostly offended at being excluded from this fight. "What did he say of Bastul?" he asked to change the topic.

Dacien straightened his posture. "We spoke of that before you arrived. He was sympathetic to the condition of the city. But he was also quick to point out that Bastul is one of the most remote cities in the Empire and not likely to receive much in the way of aid from Orud. It seems that we will have to rebuild slowly, using the resources available."

A few minutes of thoughtful silence passed before Dacien rose from his chair. "I will see you in the morning. I'm sure the General could use some help getting started."

Kael took the hint and headed for the door, only to find that his escort was waiting outside to see him to his own quarters. "Good evening," he said to Dacien and walked out.

Morning came far too quickly for Kael, who awakened to a bright shaft of sunlight streaming in through an open window. He lay still for a few minutes, aware that he hadn't slept this well in months. Suddenly, the realization struck him that he had overslept. Dacien had asked for his help, although not in a very eloquent manner.

Within seconds, Kael had donned his clothing and was headed out the door. Nearly tripping over his escort, Kael let out a laugh. His amusement wasn't matched by the man who quickly straightened his clothing and proceeded to stand at attention. Kael brushed off the man's sour demeanor and headed toward the stables.

The city was alive with activity; people were rushing here and there. For most, it would have been easy to get lost in a new place, especially with the change in appearance from night to day. But Kael possessed an ability to memorize his surroundings and rarely lost his way. Navigating the streets as if he was a citizen, he reached the stables without any hesitation, only to find them empty. "Where are they?" he asked aloud, mostly to himself.

"They've already left."

Kael turned to his escort. "That would have been useful a few minutes ago."

But once again, his companion had grown silent, as if he would only speak to point out Kael's mistakes.

With all the morning's bustle, it took nearly half an hour to reach the city gates. He found Dacien standing outside the walls on the road which spanned the lake. "Sorry. I must have overslept."

Dacien dismissed the apology with a quick shake of his head. "It doesn't matter. The General left before I could be of any help. There," he said, pointing to the southwest. "You can see the rear of the party just before the forest edge."

Kael scanned the horizon and caught sight of the standard bearer, just in front of the supply train. Kael shook his head in disapproval. "Is he expecting a long confrontation?"

"What do you mean?" Dacien replied.

"Why do they have a supply train?"

"So the animals aren't over-burdened with the weight of the weapons and armor."

Kael nodded, anticipating the answer.

"Would you care to elaborate?" asked Dacien with a smile.

Kael smiled in return, enjoying the banter developing between them. "A fully loaded wagon cannot move as fast as if each rider were to carry his own weapons. And given the terrain that they will encounter, they will need to be agile in their travel. Supply trains only make sense when staging long range campaigns against an enemy in flat open territory."

"And where did you learn this philosophy of war?" Dacien asked, half joking and half serious.

Kael avoided the question. "I only mean that those men are vulnerable against the Syvaku and the way they fight."

"Really? So if you were the enemy, how would you do it?"

"Attack the Leoran soldiers?"

"Yes."

"Well," Kael paused. "Since you ask, I would have scouts several miles out front. These men would see the Orud standard in plenty of time to relay their findings. I would then anticipate the path of the Leoran and stage an ambush in terrain that gives me an advantage. I would attack quickly at the supply train first and separate the soldiers from their weapons. Then, they would be nothing more than men on horses, no match for the fierce ground warfare style of the Syvaku."

Dacien looked puzzled and skeptical at Kael's answer.

Kael continued. "Anyway, I just fear for their lives. Who is this General and how much experience does he have?"

"Actually..." Dacien countered, "...he's quite a formidable opponent. I can assure you that if he lacks anything in strategy, he more than makes up for with brawn. Big as an ox and just as strong. I have been told that he cannot be bested in hand-to-hand combat. No, I think he will do just fine against your Syvaku.

"Oh, my Syvaku?" Kael replied. In reality, they were his mother's people and so he was related to the enemy, but he thought it best to keep this to himself.

"Come," said Dacien. "You need breakfast; I can smell your hunger from here."

"Well, I apologize for hurrying to your aid. Next time perhaps I will move at a more leisurely pace." Even though his words spoke sarcasm, Kael felt embarrassed.

10

The days passed by slowly for Maeryn as she watched the ocean from the security of her vantage point. She had many hours to herself to ponder Thaddius' words and to prepare herself for the work that lay ahead. But these thoughts were distracted by the fact that Thaddius hadn't yet returned and it had been seven days. The trip was only supposed to take six days and she was getting nervous. Watching until the sun went down, Maeryn returned to the camp for the evening meal and then retired to her bed. Aelia quickly fell asleep but Maeryn struggled for several hours.

Sometime in the early morning, Maeryn felt a hand on her shoulder. She jumped and then realized that it was the evening watch, a younger male slave that had agreed to keep a lookout for Thaddius' return.

Maeryn rose to her feet and quietly followed him out to the shoreline. Visibility was poor but she was just able to make out the small sailboats. They waited patiently and eventually the boats came to shore in a disorderly clump. The Resistance soldiers stumbled out of the ships with weak knees. Maeryn scanned the crowd for Thaddius, realizing that something was terribly wrong and wanting an answer. But Thaddius didn't appear. Before she could say anything, one soldier approached her.

"My lady..." the man paused to catch his breath.

"Where is Thaddius? And what is wrong with your men?"

"My lady, we have taken ill...all of us. Thaddius was not well enough to make the trip."

"What's wrong?"

"The food, my lady... The supplies at the outpost are spoiled. We didn't know until after... We're dying!"

The soldier's words trailed off as her mind began to spin with questions. *What are we supposed to do? Should we continue to the outpost? Will we catch the sickness? Where are we supposed to go if not to our original destination?*

"How many?"

"Only Thaddius and a handful of others are left."

Maeryn looked to the sky and her emotions welled up, even though she knew that crying wouldn't help the situation. "Thank you for coming back; I know it must have been difficult," she managed to say.

"Of course, my lady. We had to return the boats. You still have a chance, but I don't think we're well enough for the return trip. It's probably better to stay separated until..." The man stopped before stating the obvious.

"Thank you," was all she could think to say.

The rest of the night was sleepless for Maeryn. She hadn't bothered to wake anyone from her group. They would need their rest. After hours of great consternation, she knew that they had to continue on to Tur'cen. There was no going back; there never was! Once this decision was realized, Maeryn began to ponder the realities of reaching their ultimate goal in light of the current grave situation. Getting to the outpost was the easy part. From there, they would have to quarantine the sick from the rest of the group, discard the food and set out to replenish the food stores with fresh supplies. Winter was fast approaching and starting from scratch would make for a tough season. With any luck, Thaddius and the others would pull through.

That's when it hit her. What if Thaddius died before she arrived? He was the only one who knew the protocol for contacting the Resistance leader. Without Thaddius, this whole trip was meaningless!

The sun had just risen when Maeryn awoke. The smell of cooking food told her that the rest of the camp was already stirring. Aelia was gone and probably helping with the breakfast. She felt exhausted and didn't remember coming to her bed, but she had apparently returned at some point during the night. Almost immediately, her fears about Thaddius returned and she realized that for all her worry, she hadn't reached a conclusion during the night.

After a few minutes of walking, she came to the secluded place where the soldiers had retired for the evening. An eerie feeling crept over her as she saw that all of the men were still lying down. She hoped that they were just tired from their trip across the channel, but the smell of vomit confirmed her worst fears.

"They're all dead," she heard herself say. Their lifeless skin looked pale in the morning light, as though bleached by the sun. She was at once overcome with grief for these men, who had suffered an evening of agony, and fear for herself and the others that remained. Thaddius was likely dead and that meant that they were lost, stranded in the middle of nowhere, hiding from an empire that would kill all of them for their rebellion. It was too much. There was no one to impress and no way to be positive about the situation. The tears began to flow and she couldn't stop them. Her cry turned into a wail and she collapsed on the sand.

Why did Adair leave me? Why can't I go back to the only happy time in my life? He was everything. Since he left, all I've managed to do is survive. And now even that prospect has changed.

Long moments of silence passed before Maeryn finally rose to her feet. Her face was dry and she felt relieved somehow. She had tried for so long to be brave and had lived through her fear. And now she had come to the realization that she could die at any moment. There was no way to go back to the life she had with her first husband. That was past and though it saddened her, she also felt a sense of satisfaction at having experienced those happy times. Adair, Kael, and Bastul were gone, as well as Thaddius and all of his soldiers. All she had now was Aelia, her new friends, and a renewed sense of purpose. She couldn't change the past, but she was willing to die to change the future. She would make sure that these free people would survive, and if it was possible, she would be happy again. But first, there was much work to do.

After almost a week in the beautiful city of Leoran, Kael was starting to feel at home. However, the sense of belonging quickly faded with the first signs of bad news. Refugees from the northwest coastal cities began arriving in scattered groups. As these displaced citizens of the Empire brought their necessities with them, they also carried stories of the blonde barbarians who had ransacked their homes and destroyed their towns. With each passing day, Kael's understanding of the scope of this crisis deepened. There were several groups of barbarians moving throughout the southwest region, not just the group from Bastul.

In the absence of the General, Dacien commanded the remaining soldiers of the city and placed them in support of the efforts to house the travelers and to heal the wounded. Eventually, the arrivals slowed and stopped altogether and as soon as the city closed its gates Dacien sought Kael's council.

Kael waited at the southern wall, overlooking Lake Leoran and the reflected light from the evening activity along the shoreline.

"These are strange times, my friend."

Kael nodded silently.

"Never did I think that I would see the day an enemy dared to attack the Empire." Dacien let out an exhausted sigh. "I've seen my share of skirmishes, but they've been minor by comparison. This...this is something else."

Kael didn't respond. It wasn't that he was trying to keep silent; he just didn't know what to say.

Dacien seemed to understand and continued to talk anyway. He had a way of putting people at ease when he wanted to. After a few minutes of one-sided conversation, they were interrupted by one of Dacien's soldiers.

"Excuse me, Sir!"

Dacien nodded for the man to continue.

"Sir, you should come with me and hear for yourself. We have just received urgent news from Ampur."

Dacien followed at a brisk pace with Kael close behind. As they walked, Kael's mind was racing. He had noted a few days prior a pattern to the arrival of refugees. The first groups came from the north, and each successive group from cities and towns farther to the northwest. Ampur was situated almost directly west of Leoran and Kael guessed that the barbarians were moving southwest and sacking every town they crossed, thereby displacing the citizens and sending them to the capital city of the southern region for shelter.

The walk took only minutes before they reached the town hall. A small group of soldiers was gathered around a man who had clearly ridden hard to deliver his message. His face and clothes were speckled with mud and his eyes were red around the edges.

Dacien stepped into the circle and introduced himself as the ranking officer in charge. "I understand you bring news from Ampur?" Before the man could speak, Dacien called for some wine and then turned his attention back to the stranger.

"Ampur was sacked four days ago by an army of barbarians. We think they are Syvak."

"Yes. We've been housing refugees from cities to your north and east. How large was the army?"

The exhausted man took the cup of wine offered by an attendant, but appeared too distraught to drink it. "...perhaps eight hundred."

This response met with whistles and exasperations throughout the crowd, but the man continued talking.

"But they haven't stopped. After Ampur, they turned east. I only managed to survive because I had a mount. They're moving on foot and I believe they are heading for this city."

Dacien was already nodding in confirmation, anticipating the man's message of impending doom. "Thank you for your warning and your courage. We will see to it that you are taken care of. Is there any other information?"

"No, Sir."

"Then we will leave you to get some rest."

"Thank you, Sir," the man replied with relief.

"Guards," Dacien shouted. "Make preparations for additional housing. In the morning, I want you to bring all Leoran citizens inside the city gates and make them as comfortable as possible. Lieutenants, we will meet in the war room in half an hour."

The group immediately dispersed at Dacien's orders and went to their various tasks.

The war room was an essential fixture in every major city within the Orud Empire. It was a gathering place for strategic military planning. Though the surroundings varied, every war room contained, as its focal point, a map of the surrounding terrain on a raised platform in the center of the room. The map was the result of years of tedious observation and documentation of the city, the lake and the nearby forests and mountain ranges. And it was around this map that Dacien, Kael, and the Lieutenants were gathered.

"We were notified that perhaps eight hundred barbarians are approaching afoot from the west. Given that Ampur was attacked only four days ago, I would estimate that they will reach the shores of Leoran in less than a week. We have also confirmed that a smaller army of two to three hundred is approaching from the south. But given their distance, we must first make preparations to address the army from the west without the help of the General. Secondly, we must also be prepared if the army from the south is not stopped. Altogether, we might need to withstand an attack of one thousand or more. If this is a coordinated attack, we may not have the option of dealing with these two groups separate from each other. These are the scenarios that I see. Does anyone have anything else to add?"

Without any arguments or other input, Dacien launched into planning for the first scenario. Immediately, Kael was struck with a sense of familiarity. How many years did he plan and strategize warfare in this manner. And just as when he was young, he held back his opinions as this was not his strength. He marveled at how Dacien commanded authority and moved from one preparation to the next in a logical fashion. He began with an assessment of Leoran's resources from cavalry and foot soldiers, to the possible uses of the small naval fleet that could control the massive expanse of water surrounding the city. There were only a few instances of disagreement between the Lieutenants, which Dacien diffused in seconds, quickly finding a solution that met everyone's needs. After two hours of planning, the soldiers agreed to the strategy and retired for the evening.

Kael went back to his quarters and lay awake for the majority of the night. Even though he knew to leave these large scale matters to others more equipped than himself, his mind continued to work on the problem at hand. It was like chewing a tough piece of meat, lots of work with no progress.

He wasn't sure how long he had been asleep, but when he was awakened to the sound of alarm, he felt as though it couldn't have been more than an hour. An attendant led him back to the war room where he found a smaller group of men than the night before, as well as a few new faces. At first glance it was obvious who these men were. There were six in all, four of them with minor wounds. When Kael came within earshot of the group he picked up on the conversation.

"...no. It happened so fast! We were moving up a mountain pass through a dense forest. They came out of nowhere and attacked at our rear. They stole our supply train and rode the wagons back down the pass. We tried to pursue but they cut the legs of our horses out from under us."

Sounds of disapproval rose from the group at the mention of such treachery. The Empire took great pride in their horses, as they were one of the main distinctions between it and other nations' military forces. Their cavalry gave them a distinct advantage over foot soldiers. However, Kael understood the lack of respect on the part of the Syvaku. Their pride was their navy. Being a seagoing people, they had no use for horses.

"After that, we were trapped. Our only weapons were our spears, which were too long in such a tight space. They picked us off one by one until we left the cover of the forest."

"And what of the General?" Dacien asked.

The man hung his head in shame. "Our archers were at the front of the column when the attack started. The first volley wasn't well organized and someone hit the General by accident; he didn't even have the chance to fight."

Dacien looked shocked. And in that instant, their worst case scenario became a reality. After a few seconds of stunned silence, Dacien turned to make eye contact with Kael. Slowly, his questioning look was replaced by determination.

In that same instant, Kael realized another result of these events. The capital cities didn't have Colonels. And with the General's death, and that of his Captains, Dacien became the highest ranking officer in the southern region by default. It wasn't just that these soldiers were looking to him as an experienced officer, but now they were obligated to follow his command under Orud law. Now, with this quick twist of fate, Dacien inherited the position of General and all the responsibilities and problems associated with it. Despite the weight of the consequences, Dacien seemed unfazed, concerned only with how to handle the current situation.

When the Syvak warlord arrived at the southeastern shores of Leoran with the remnants of his army, he found that his other forces from the west had already arrived. They were eight hundred strong, much larger than the ranks that he had been traveling with. But that was to be expected. He anticipated Bastul to be much more difficult than the other coastal cities. So far, everything was going as planned.

Following the example of the forces already in place along the north shore, the warlord instructed his men to raid and set fire to every wooden structure along the outskirts of the city. Once this was accomplished, the remainder of the day was filled with the felling of trees, erecting temporary shelters and other such activities to support a long-term siege.

While the Syvaku soldiers worked to secure the eastern entrance to the city, the warlord rode north to make contact with his other army already in position for the attack. As he rode his massive steed, he noted that the Leoran army was making no attempts to defend the city. The soldiers simply stood atop the city walls and watched from the safety and separation of miles of water. Perhaps they were confident that their location would protect them. Indeed, the only way to reach the city was via the two roads extending from the north and southwest walls of the city, each stretching more than a mile. But soon, everything would be in place and the city's unique location wouldn't matter.

With the following morning came the unusual sight of three Syvak warships anchored near the northern entrance. This would have given the barbarian warlord more confidence, if not for the fact that the number should have been twenty. Apparently, the Leoran soldiers had anticipated this avenue of invasion and had sunk large, sharpened timbers in various spots along the river that fed into the north end of the lake. And though the Syvak were experts at navigating nature's obstructions, man-made traps were altogether different. This angered the warlord as he hadn't anticipated his enemy's ability to prepare for the same attack that he had used on another city, hundreds of miles to the south.

By midday, the Syvak armies were in motion. They had gained confidence with the arrival of their warships. The foot soldiers marched past the entrances to the north and southeast and proceeded along their respective courses. The larger northern army was escorted by two of their vessels, one on either side of the raised road. The third warship escorted the smaller army. Not surprisingly, the Leoran guard didn't confront them until they neared the city walls. Just as they came within range, the Leoran began volleys of arrows. Because of the elevation difference, the Syvaku had to get closer to the walls before they could return fire. And though they were not protected by city walls, as were the Leorans, they were well protected by animal skin shields supported on wooden frames held over their heads.

In the ensuing hours of conflict, it became apparent that they couldn't match the strength and accuracy of the Leoran archers. After losing one hundred and fifty men to the first attack, the Syvak General pulled his men back from the gates to regroup. A few hours later, he ordered the second attack, this time with makeshift siege ladders, courtesy of the nearby forests.

The warships stayed just out of arrow range and supported the new efforts of the foot soldiers by using small catapults to launch boulders over the tops of the walls. This ingenious use of the war-machines originally intended for land combat soon proved its worth as it began to take its toll on the Leoran guard.

By midday, the larger northern army managed to get their siege ladder raised against the city walls and looked to be on the verge of breaching the gate. But suddenly, one of the warships burst into flames and the foot soldiers lost their confidence. It seemed that the Leoran soldiers also had catapults and were adept at the use of flaming pitch. And as all the attention was diverted to this flaming mass atop the water, the General almost failed to notice another of his warships sinking into the lake.

The flaming ship also served as a diversion to the start of another of the Leoran's defenses. Unused during the earlier skirmish, massive trebuchets mounted atop the city walls began launching iron spears out into the lake. The Syvak General saw the momentum of the battle starting to turn in favor of the Leoran soldiers and quickly ordered his men to retreat. As the sun began to set, the warlord called his Captains to his large tent along the northern shore and planned their next attack. The meeting lasted several hours and after it was concluded, the two Syvak camps grew silent with exhaustion. After a difficult and fruitless day, the invaders slept soundly, vowing to take up their struggle with the light of the next day.

The General was awakened to the sounds of screaming. The massive soldier rose from his bed and stood a full seven feet tall. His blonde hair was braided in a thick knot that ran down to the middle of his muscled back. It took only seconds to don his uniform, consisting mainly of animal skins and a chain-mail shirt. He grabbed his double-bladed battle-axe and ran from his tent.

Immediately, his ears were assaulted by a deafening hum that came and went in waves. He did his best to ignore the sound and tried to get an understanding of the status of his army. As he glanced around, he could see dozens of his men struggling on the ground pierced by arrows. Looking toward the city, he was surprised to see the sails of small ships filling the lake. The Leoran navy had sailed within bow range while his army slept and were raining arrows down upon his forces. At once he cursed himself for this oversight and the Leoran for their creativity.

He barked orders to his men to raise their shields and regroup out of the range of the boats. The sky was growing light to the east before the northern army managed to pull back from their temporary dwellings and rally to their leader. But something didn't seem right. His soldiers continued to fall, pierced with arrows. It was as if the Leoran archers had doubled their range.

And how were their arrows finding their marks now that his men had their shields?

In that instant, the rising sun crested the mountains to the east, throwing morning light across the landscape. Suddenly, the Syvak warlord noticed hundreds of points of light glinting across the lake on the eastern shore—the cavalry of Leoran riding around the lake in his direction. And then it dawned on him! He turned around and gazed into the forest to the north and finally understood what had been troubling him. A second group of Leoran archers were hidden in the woods. His forces were being assaulted from two directions. And just behind the archers, another unit of mounted soldiers!

Kael lowered his spear and yelled. "Charge!"

Suddenly, the entire cavalry jumped into action, as if they were one being. The perfection of it was awe-inspiring. They broke from between the ranks of archers and exited the forest with spears lowered. Within seconds they overtook the barbarians, running them to the ground. Kael left his spear in the first barbarian and continued forward, slashing and stabbing with his sword. Its short and broad construction was designed for stabbing in close quarters combat, but was also highly effective in this situation where the enemy was packed in tight groups. The Syvak didn't have any time to prepare a defense and fell quickly to the cavalry.

Without seeing, Kael sensed movement to his right and instantly dropped his head. The whistle of a passing axe blade sounded in his ear, immediately followed by a jolt, as something rammed into his horse. He struggled to keep his grip and managed a glance behind after regaining his seating. In the midst of the confrontation, the retreating Syvak warlord plowed through the Leoran cavalry. He was almost standing in the saddle of his enormous steed, cutting a path through the soldiers with a long, double-bladed battle axe. He swung the weapon with a two handed stroke from side to side. One after another, the Leoran riders fell before this monster, while his massive horse charged forward without any direction from the reigns. Two of the warlord's Captains followed in the wake of their General and the three burst out of the fray and into the open land, veering northeast to avoid the Leoran archers in the forest.

Kael looked to the east and caught sight of Dacien leading the other unit. He lifted his sword into the air and Dacien returned the gesture. Kael immediately spun his horse around and dug his heels into the steed's flanks. Immediately, he was thrown into motion. Moving low in the saddle, he reached down and pulled a spear from the body of a dead barbarian. Sheathing this in a thong built into the saddle, he steered toward a less dense part of the battle and broke into a full run. After clearing the struggle, he headed toward the northern forest.

"I need a bow," he yelled to a nearby archer. And just as he reached the archer, the man un-slung his quiver and held both up in the air. Kael grabbed the bundle in passing and made a mental note to find the man and thank him later.

The sounds of warfare quickly faded into the distance as Kael entered the forest. Although he raced at top speed in pursuit of the barbarian leader, all was eerily silent. The cool autumn air rushed past his face and the morning sunlight filtered through the trees, throwing a sparkling light into his eyes. Under different circumstances, this would have been an enjoyable ride.

A familiar feeling now took over, a calm but intense awareness that he had become accustomed to over the years. Every tree and every leaf on every tree could be felt, as though they were extensions of Kael's own body. And there, only twenty yards ahead, was something that felt out of place. As he neared in proximity, his sense grew more accurate. And then there was movement.

Instinctively, Kael dove to the left, moving his body out of the path of danger, clinging to the side of his saddle with all his might. From behind a tree, an axe cut through the air where his abdomen used to be and glanced off of his right leg, still exposed atop the saddle. Kael winced as the steel bit into his flesh, but managed to retain his grip. Pulling himself upright with one swift movement, Kael spurred his horse on, knowing that he had to keep up his speed in order to catch the warlord.

A brief glance over his shoulder confirmed that it was one of the barbarian's Captains that stayed behind for the ambush. The man, stunned by his inability to dispatch such an easy target, paused for a second before taking up the chase.

The forest opened into a wide meadow and Kael could see the other two men hundreds of yards ahead. As soon as they noticed their enemy hadn't been stopped by the ambush, the second Captain veered off course and circled around, charging back to face Kael. The leader continued north, disappearing behind a rising knoll.

Kael let go of the reins and set an arrow to the bow string. As his horse continued forward, Kael rose in his saddle and twisted around, drawing his bow on the Captain behind him.

A warrior must always retain his grip on the reins!

The words of an old mentor came to his mind, and with them, a rising anger. Kael loosened his stance to take up the surging of his steed and closed his eyes, feeling the path of the arrow. And when he found a connection between himself and his target, he loosed his arrow.

One... two... three... four, he counted in his head, before the Captain pitched backward with an arrow sprouting from his neck. And just that quick, the anger left him, and only the intensity of the present was left.

Turning back around, he quickly surmised that the second Captain was now too close to draw another arrow. With the bow in his left hand, he pulled the spear from its sheath with his right.

The charging enemy pulled his axe free and leaned forward in his saddle, preparing for the impending clash.

Kael held the spear under his arm, letting the barbarian see the lance and draw his own conclusions. Within seconds they were upon each other.

Just before impact, Kael wrenched the reins to the left and spun the lance over his head, bringing it into a slashing motion. The Syvak, anticipating Kael's attack to be a frontal stabbing motion, had already committed to his movements with his shield across his chest and a desperate swing for Kael's midsection.

Kael, out of the man's reach, extended his arm and spear, swinging over the barbarian's attack to slash the side of his throat. The only flesh that wasn't protected by chain mail yielded easily to the nine inch blade on the end of the spear. Kael didn't even bother to look back, knowing instantly that his enemy was dead. He sheathed his lance once again and set another arrow to the bow, all the while maintaining his speed.

After topping the grassy knoll, Kael could see the warlord a hundred yards ahead. He had gained on the retreating enemy, apparently due to the breed of horse and its enormous rider. The tufts of hair around the animal's hoofs were indicative of a northern breed meant for pulling large loads, not racing across open ground. Kael drew back his bow, but couldn't get the same sense of accuracy that he had only seconds ago. He aimed high and loosed his bolt anyway, and wasn't surprised when it glanced harmlessly off the Syvak's chain mail seconds later. The giant barbarian didn't even flinch as he charged into the nearby forest, disappearing behind the leaves.

Kael caught up quickly and dashed into the forest, his sleeker animal at an advantage in this terrain as well. Minutes later, he came upon a small cliff and followed the edge to the northwest. As the trees cleared, he caught sight of the warlord heading down a landslide of loose gravel and sand, descending quickly into the shallow canyon. Kael only had one second to decide.

Without hesitation, he drew his bow and released. The bolt struck the enemy's horse in the right shoulder and the beast flinched, losing its footing. As it began to fall, the Syvak warlord rose in his saddle and jumped from the animal. Kael rode to the top of the landslide just in time to see the cloud of dust and the commotion of the animal struggling to regain its footing. Kael slowed his pace and descended carefully into the canyon in pursuit.

As the dust settled, Kael could see the warlord face-down in the wet sand. A small stream ran through the bottom of the canyon, only ankle deep in most places. The man's horse had stopped at the bank on the far side of the canyon only fifteen yards away. Kael's shot had been perfect, not enough to lame the animal, but just enough to make it lose its balance. With some care, the animal would be as good as new.

Kael discarded the bow, the last arrow having served its purpose. Pulling the lance from its sheath, he urged his horse forward. The Syvak leader was sprawled on the damp earth, a battle-axe slung across his back. Kael looked for a gap in the chain mail, finding it at the pit of his left arm. Aiming, he thrust his lance forward.

Suddenly, the barbarian spun over and caught the blade of the spear with his hand and pulled it free of Kael's grasp.

The unexpected movement pulled Kael off of his balance and he fell forward out of his saddle. There was no way to recover, and though he tried to hit the ground in a roll, he wasn't quick enough.

The barbarian's foot crashed into his right side and Kael felt his ribs break.

Satisfied with his attack, the Syvak backed away to watch Kael suffer and struggle for air. It was the Syvak way to build fear into their prey before the kill. As Kael moved from the ground to his hands and knees, the giant reached slowly behind his head and pulled on a leather thong, releasing his battle-axe from its sheath. Slowly, methodically, the giant walked to his horse and retrieved his circular shield, knowing that Kael wasn't going anywhere.

In contrast, Kael felt as though everything was happening much too fast. He struggled to catch his breath, only to find that his lung capacity was greatly reduced. Each breath invited a piercing pain through his abdomen, followed by muscle spasms that prevented him from satisfying his lungs' need for air. Pushing through the pain, he managed to crawl over to his spear lying in the stream. Grabbing it, he rose to his feet and turned to confront the barbarian.

The Syvak stood a full head taller than Kael and was now holding his double-bladed axe in one hand and a giant shield in the other. Kael knew that he was disadvantaged against his opponent in almost every way, not to mention that he could hardly move without excruciating pain. He grabbed the spear with both hands and crouched into a defensive posture.

The Syvak rushed in swinging his axe in a flat arc. Kael jumped out of range, but was disappointed to see that the barbarian allowed the axe to continue its motion as it spun back around and over the man's head. He never put his full weight behind the attack, and therefore never let his own momentum work against him.

Smart. This is going to be more difficult than I hoped.

The minutes passed in agony as the Syvak pushed Kael across the valley and up against the northeastern bank. Normally, it would have been Kael's strategy to let the barbarian attack and expend his energy, but in Kael's weakened condition, he was expending much more energy just to stay out of reach.

Suddenly, the Syvak attacked with a full force blow.

Kael moved instinctively, at the sharp protest of his body, and dodged the attack. The axe swung wide and Kael moved in, battering the barbarian's knuckles with the shaft of the spear.

The Syvak dropped the axe, but quickly pulled his shield up to deflect Kael's next jab, while moving inside of Kael's effective weapon range.

The shield dropped just in time for Kael to see a massive fist crash into his face. He fell backward, but quickly rolled to the side, dodging the sound of splashing footsteps. Stumbling away from his enemy, Kael stalled to allow time for his vision to return.

The barbarian was now ten paces away and advancing slowly, more cautious of Kael's abilities, even in his weakened state, though Kael didn't share the man's perception. A quick evaluation of his condition told him that he was in trouble. His nose was certainly broken. The ribs along his right side were crushed, and the leg wound from the forest ambush was bleeding heavily.

The Syvak continued to advance, shield raised, with nothing more than bruised knuckles.

Kael backed away from him, scanning the ground for something to use as a weapon, unsure of where his spear had gone. And there in the water, lay a bundle that had traveled with Kael for many years. He always kept it with him and it must have fallen in the initial struggle as he was pulled from his horse. Kael bent down and grabbed hold of the long, narrow wooden case. He opened it quickly and unwrapped its contents as he kept his eyes on the Syvak.

But the barbarian leader wasn't foolish enough to allow his enemy the chance to produce another weapon. He rushed in immediately. Kael quickly pulled the ancient weapon free of its ceremonial wrappings and held it out in front of himself. The Syvak stopped his approach for a moment, then reconsidered when he saw the condition of Kael's weapon.

Kael felt desperate as he held up the monstrosity of a sword. It was completely foreign looking to this region, with a narrow and curved blade, whose texture was mottled. The guard was elaborate, but looked fragile and the handle was wrapped with a rough thread for grip. In truth, the ceremonial sword was not intended to function as a weapon and was a gift given by an old friend. Kael felt horrible for allowing it to be used as such, but he was indeed desperate.

But the warlord had allowed this fight to last for too long and had grown impatient. At the sight of Kael's ridiculous weapon, he lunged forward and swung his shield at Kael in a back-handed motion. Kael met this attack with a slash of his sword, burying it into the shield.

The barbarian cursed in pain and jerked the shield backward, taking Kael's weapon with it.

Kael backed away in disbelief as the man dropped his shield with the embedded sword, blood pouring from a gash on his forearm. Something about this strange turn of events emboldened Kael and suddenly, his senses were heightened. He circled around to the west of the barbarian and backed away to plan his attack.

The Syvak saw what was happening and smiled, apparently pleased at the opportunity to kill this pest with his bare hands.

Bursting into motion, Kael surged through the shallow water and broke into a full run.

The barbarian grinned and lunged forward to meet Kael, dropping his head for a tackle.

Just before they met, Kael sprang from the ground into a pivoting flip and in one fluid motion, caught hold of the barbarian's head and spun it backwards with a crunch as the skull separated from the spine. The flipping motion carried him over the top of the Syvak's body as both men crashed to the ground with a dull thud.

Kael lay still for several minutes still tangled with the lifeless body of the Syvak warlord. All was silent except for the sound of running water and the rustle of leaves. Kael's heart pounded while his breath came in ragged gasps. Slowly, he released his grip on the man's face and rose to his feet. The pain in his ribs intensified and he knew that he had caused even greater damage to himself with this final attack.

Both Kael's horse and the barbarian's had kept their distance from the fighting, but hadn't run off. Kael left the body and stumbled over to the Syvak's shield. The sword was still embedded in the splintered wood. Kael reached down and wrenched it free, inspecting the damage. The metal of the blade had flaked off in several places, the edges curled back to reveal a dark, glass-like material. It looked like a child's replica, covered in metal to make it look more authentic.

Strange. It was unfortunate that he had resorted to using the gift in such a way, but he would have it repaired at the soonest opportunity. He gathered the original wrappings for the sword and placed it back into its wooden container, securing it with a leather strap.

Surveying his surroundings, he could see evidence of their struggle everywhere—footprints, discarded weapons, and even splatters of blood on the sand. He walked to the Syvak's body and stood over it, marveling at the strength and skill of this foe. Fighting was usually simple for Kael, and rarely did his opponents present a challenge. *But this one...he was a worthy adversary!* The barbarian's body was sprawled on his back, with his head twisted and facing down toward the sand. Kael bent down and grabbed the head by the hair and rotated the face into a more natural position. The flowing water had rinsed the blood and dirt from the skin and left the face pale, but clean.

Kael allowed his gaze to linger for a moment before standing up. Then suddenly, he felt a pang of recognition.

Bending down, he lifted the man's right hand and pulled back the leather shirt sleeve. Scanning the skin of his forearm, he found confirmation of what he feared. There on the skin was a two-inch scar running parallel with the protrusion of muscle. Kael dropped the dead arm and stood, feeling sickened.

Narian!

Images flashed through Kael's mind, memories from his time at the monastery. He could see Narian dueling with Ukiru and losing his temper. The mentor taught the student a quick lesson in the danger of a bladed weapon. The wound healed quickly but left a scar and served as a reminder to all the students that their instructor was not to be confronted in anger. So many of their lessons revolved around controlling one's emotions. But Kael couldn't control the emotions rising in him now. He wished he could confront his old mentor and fight to the death. Even if he didn't prevail, Kael wanted the chance for revenge.

Dacien, though exhausted from the fight, never stopped until the battlefield was rid of the bodies of the enemy. These were thrown on a fire and not given the earthen burial that his soldiers received. By midmorning, the majority of the fields were cleared and Dacien began to worry about his friend. Kael had chased after the barbarian leader hours ago, and hadn't yet returned. He feared the worst and so kept working to rid his mind of the pointless questions plaguing him.

By midday, Dacien had resolved to ride north with a search party the following day to find Kael's body and give him a proper burial. But then, a murmur rose within the crowd of soldiers and Leoran citizens working around the lake shore. The murmur slowly rose to cheering and Dacien stopped to see what was happening.

Relief washed over him when he looked north and saw his friend atop a trotting horse at the edge of the forest. Though he had only just met Kael a few months ago, he felt a strange kinship with him. Dacien had lost a few soldiers this day, but the possibility of losing Kael saddened him greatly.

As these thoughts crossed his mind, he noticed a second horse being led behind Kael's. As Kael reached the shores of Lake Leoran and could be seen clearly, Dacien could see he held a spear upright with something large on the end. It was several minutes before Dacien realized that it was the barbarian's head. The crowd cheered with a riotous noise, but Kael didn't react. He simply rode forward, leading the Syvak's enormous horse, and behind it, a makeshift litter carrying the warlord's body.

Dacien rushed to his friend, calling for the crowd to give him some room.

Blood poured from a gash in Kael's leg. His nose was clearly broken and his face stained with blood, turning purple and beginning to swell.

Dacien instantly felt compassion and pride for his friend. The beheading was hard to stomach though and was not a practice of the Orud Empire, one of the things separating them from other barbaric nations. But it seemed to be effective as Dacien could tell that it earned Kael a mixture of fear and reverence from the Leoran soldiers. The citizens seemed more appalled than anything.

Grabbing the reins of Kael's horse, Dacien looked up and made eye contact with his friend, who only stared blankly in return, as though he were looking through Dacien. Kael didn't seem like the kind of person to be bothered by intense warfare, but it was clear that something was deeply wrong.

"You can rest now. Come back inside the city," was all he could think to say.

11

The weeks passed quickly for Maeryn as she carried out her plans on the island of Tur'cen. Just as anticipated, Thaddius and the other two thirds of the freed slaves were dead when Maeryn arrived. It was a horrific sight, made worse by the fact that the bodies had to be moved away from the encampment and buried. Maeryn did her best to organize the remaining members, now only one hundred and fifty, into groups for providing food, water and shelter. After the many weeks of traveling, the group had become quite efficient in providing for itself. Maeryn was relieved that they had become self-reliant and didn't require much in the way of leadership. But despite this, they still looked at her with great admiration, though she didn't know why. Her only conclusion was that they were counting on her to deliver them, and she was committed to doing just that.

Following three grueling weeks of labor, Maeryn left Aelia and the group and set sail for Orud. She took with her two older men, experienced in sailing and fishing in the bay of Bastul. The air had grown cold and winter was fast approaching. Though it wasn't smart to sail during this time of year, or to travel in general, everyone knew the gravity of their situation. After discarding all the original supplies at the outpost, they were too far behind to store up enough food for the winter. Aelia was in tears when Maeryn left, but it was understood that if Maeryn wasn't successful in her quest, none would survive the winter. She gave them specific instructions to be diligent in their foraging and fishing, and to gather wood to keep the fires burning. This was not a time to relax, but a time to survive.

And after a heartfelt goodbye, Maeryn left for Orud in one of their small sailing vessels to make the arrangements that Thaddius spoke of. She hadn't a clue how to make contact, but remembered what Thaddius had said about the Resistance headquarters being in the temple of Equitus. She knew nothing of the protocols for making contact, but there were no other options.

After enduring two weeks of freezing nights and eating only what could be caught on the way, Maeryn arrived in Orud. At once, she encountered feelings of relief and fear. The presence of a bustling city excited her after living on the run for the past months. At the same time, she was a fugitive hoping to make contact with an underground movement working against the Empire, and for this reason she carried a secret that could cost her her life. In spite of this, Maeryn tried her best to stroll with confidence down the streets of the city with her two slaves following loyally behind her as they were expected to.   She knew that they wouldn't pass careful social examination as they were dirty from their travels and not presentable to the general public. But she hoped to blend in and keep from being noticed.

Without so much as a warm meal, Maeryn asked directions to the temple and walked straight to it. The afternoon sun was warm on her skin and the white stone of the temple walls reflected intensely. There were no people outside the temple which made her feel even more nervous. Her stomach growled, followed by an intense wave of hunger, but she swallowed hard and marched up the steps. Her companions waited outside as they weren't allowed in places of worship.

Once inside, the intense sunlight gave way to a soft glow coming from colored glass in the ceiling. The interior was circular with a giant statue of Equitus in the center. She was reclining on a rock, bare-breasted, holding scales in one hand, the other outstretched with her palm upward, as if to suggest that she would accept the petitions of those seeking justice and equality. The temple was almost empty, except for a man on his knees at the opposite end, and a small group to Maeryn's left.

She looked around the room to see if there were any clues as to how she should proceed, but there was nothing. After circling the building and examining the walls and all sides of the statue, Maeryn found herself back at the entrance. She received only a few curious stares from the worshipers, but otherwise was ignored.

"I have a message to deliver," she announced suddenly. Her voice rang out in the quiet marble interior.

The others in the building glanced at her, shocked by the disturbance of their silence. A soft voice from one of the women replied. "The Lady will hear your petitions."

"No. I want to speak with someone."

"Sister," called the man from across the room. "Didn't I ask you to wait for me?" Rising to his feet, he walked briskly toward Maeryn. "I am sorry, ladies. My sister is not well and doesn't understand."

Three of the women just stared in disgust, but one nodded in acknowledgement of his words.

"Sister," he said, taking Maeryn by the arm and leading her outside. "Please don't disturb these worshipers..." His words trailed off as soon as they were out of temple. "What do you think you are doing?" he asked in a low whisper. He was clearly enraged. "Who are you?"

"I'm sorry," Maeryn replied. "I didn't know what else to do."

"WHO ARE YOU?" he asked, his voice rising as he eyed the slaves suspiciously.

Maeryn wasn't sure if she was speaking to the right person, but decided to risk everything. She didn't know how else to proceed. "Thaddius is dead. All of his men are dead."

The man's expression softened. "Is this some sort of prank? Who do you think I am?"

Maeryn ignored his words and proceeded to explain her situation. "I am Maeryn, the Governess of Bastul. I took five hundred slaves and fled from Bastul with Thaddius and several soldiers..."

The man quickly put a finger to Maeryn's lips and glanced over his shoulder. No one was near the temple and they were obviously alone. "Come with me and don't speak another word until you are instructed."

Turning quickly, he walked around the building and entered a garden of dense vines through an iron gate. Maeryn looked to her two companions, then followed. Trees lined the perimeter of a low stone wall, just tall enough to offer privacy. The layout, like most others in Orud architecture was circular. Vines all but covered the wall, showing only the occasional patch of white stone. At the center of the garden was a fountain with a smaller statue of Equitus rising from the water.

The man held out his hand, indicating that they should stay and wait for him. He angled over to where the garden intersected with the temple building and disappeared from sight behind the trees. After a few minutes he came back.

"Come with me."

Again, Maeryn followed with her two companions. Once past the trees, the wall opened into a short and narrow doorway. Their escort stood to the side and beckoned them to enter. Maeryn could see that the vines had been moved away to reveal this secret place. Stooping to fit through the doorway, she was startled by a presence inside to her right. As her eyes adjusted to the darkness, she could make out a bladed spear and the dull glint of light reflected off armor. Though this should have evoked fear, she was relieved that they were in the right place. The man was obviously a Resistance guard.

After all were inside the crowded space, their escort led them down an unlit passage. Following only the sound of footsteps, Maeryn began to feel trapped. Then slowly the light returned. The footing changed to a descending staircase and the walls opened to reveal a small cavern. Everywhere she looked, Maeryn saw ancient symbols chiseled into the stone, looking menacing in the flickering torchlight. She wondered if they had any significance to the Resistance, or if they had merely adopted this place as their home.

"Please wait here," the man said and disappeared through another doorway.

Maeryn waited patiently, trying to think of what she would say. The minutes passed slowly and she found herself thinking of the two men who had accompanied her on this trip. They were good people; they were all good people. Always willing to work hard without complaining, even when their efforts seemed futile.

They nodded back at her and she realized that she had been staring. "What's taking so long," she wondered aloud as she turned her eyes to the symbols on the wall.

"Come with me."

The voice startled Maeryn. The man didn't seem to notice and simply turned to walk back through the door behind him. Again, Maeryn followed until they arrived at another cavern, this one larger than the first. Tree roots lined one side of the space, indicating that they were either near the surface, or the trees were very large. A small stream flowed through the center of the room only to disappear into a hole in the wall to Maeryn's right. Their escort pointed to the other side of the room where there were small, square boulders arranged in a circle.

"He will be with you shortly."

Maeryn raised her eyebrows and looked at her companions. They only shrugged their shoulders.

By the time their new guest joined them, Maeryn was ready to fall asleep. The sound of trickling water and the cool damp air were relaxing.

"Maeryn," came a soft voice from across the room.

Maeryn stood as the young man walked over. He was of medium height with straight black hair. He had a soft quality about him that, when coupled with his impeccable manner of dress, indicated that he was very conscious of his looks. He wasn't quite what she expected, young enough to be her son. When he was close enough, he extended a hand.

"Maeryn, it is a pleasure to finally meet you."

"And your name?" Maeryn replied.

The man shook his head. "I'm sorry, but you understand the need for secrecy." It was a statement that sounded like a question. "I understand that Thaddius will not be joining us?"

"Yes. The provisions at the outpost were spoiled. He and many others are dead because of it."

"I'm sorry to hear that," the man replied honestly. "So are you all that remains?" he asked, gesturing to the others.

"No," Maeryn corrected. "There are still one hundred and fifty waiting at the outpost."

"Congratulations on your success. We were doubtful that any would survive."

"I would hardly call it a success. We started as five hundred."

"Yes, that is horrible. I'm afraid that was Thaddius' responsibility," he replied, starting to sound defensive.

Maeryn was angered. "And what is your responsibility?" she asked. "You orchestrated this."

"Oh my...no! According to Thaddius, this was your idea. And I had nothing to do with it."

"Who are you?" Maeryn asked. "Aren't you the Resistance leader?"

The man chuckled. "I am flattered that you would think so, but no. I am, however, able to speak on his behalf."

Maeryn paused for a moment, realizing that this man was here to support her and not the other way around. She was pleased that Thaddius had cast her in such a good light. It was her idea after all, but all the details were handled by Thaddius.

"Here is what I need. I have one hundred and fifty freed slaves hiding out on the island of Tur'cen. Their supplies will not allow them to last the winter. Therefore, whatever arrangements were made for transport must happen immediately."

The man raised his eyebrows. "That is not possible. The slave boats will not be traveling again until the spring time. Without this disguise, we are unprepared to grant your request."

"What are we supposed to do? Winter is coming and we will starve on that island. We need to be evacuated immediately."

"I understand, but the arrangement was..."

"I don't care," Maeryn interrupted. "For someone who is working for a cause, you're not trying hard enough. I am offering you hundreds of new supporters and my own services as well. And for such generosity, I expect to be accommodated."

The man was speechless.

"If you cannot provide a larger vessel, then I demand that you provide food and clothing so that we may survive the winter."

The man took a deep breath and replied after a long moment of silence. "Let me see what arrangements I can make."

Maeryn nodded, her heart now beating fiercely in her chest.

"For now," he continued, "come with me and we will get you settled. Are you hungry?"

"We are famished. But we don't have much time, we must get back."

"Of course. But I must send word to our leader for authorization of your requests. Until we hear back, you are our guests." The man turned and beckoned for them to follow.

Maeryn turned around and smiled at her companions who had tears of joy in their eyes.

After a hearty stew, the guests were shown to their quarters. Maeryn was given her own room and was grateful for the accommodations. She didn't bring any belongings and so didn't need any time to settle in. Instead, she asked if there was anywhere to bathe.

"That is one of the best things about this place," replied the man. "Come with me."

They walked along more torch-lit passageways, descending even farther into the earth. Faintly, the sound of water came to Maeryn's ears.

"These passageways extend to various parts of the city. This one leads to the ocean." Just as he finished his explanation, the walls widened to reveal an underground spring which formed a small lake. "There on the far side, you can see daylight."

Maeryn looked and could see a small crack of daylight shining through the wall of the cavern on the other side of the lake.

"The spring runs to the ocean through that passage," he said, pointing to where Maeryn was looking.

It was a beautiful sight to behold and the thought of a bath warmed Maeryn's weary heart.

"I will have fresh clothing put in your room. There are plenty of secluded areas for your privacy. Take all the time you need."

"Thank you," Maeryn replied.

"Of course," the man responded with a smile.

"How long will it take to get authorization?"

"You must know that your request may not be granted, but you should receive a response in just a few days."

"Oh, so he's close?"

"Who say's it's a he? And no...not necessarily. There are many means of quickly sending messages."

Maeryn nodded. "Just let me know as soon as possible."

The man only smiled and retreated, leaving Maeryn alone in the cavern.

Maeryn's time at the Resistance headquarters moved quickly, filled with warm meals and regular baths. It was strange though, not seeing the daylight since she arrived. And though her time was enjoyable, she grew uncomfortable when she thought of Aelia and the others back on the island. She hoped they were doing well and couldn't wait to return.

Just as promised, the dark-haired man came to her quarters after two and a half days. Maeryn's traveling companions were with him.

"I have a message for you."

"And?" Maeryn asked, with anticipation.

"Your request has been granted."

Maeryn couldn't help herself. She hugged the man and then apologized, as he tried not to show his blushing face.

"I also have this," he said, handing her a small rolled piece of paper.

"What is it?" she asked.

"It is a message from our leader. You are very fortunate."

"What do you mean?" she asked, proceeding to read the message containing only two lines of text.

glad to hear that you are safe
look forward to seeing you in the spring

"It is unusual for him to send personal messages."

"So it *is* a he," she replied with a smile.

He ignored the joke. "Have you heard directly from him before?"

Maeryn smiled. "Yes, he sent me a letter many years ago. It took me a moment to realize who it was from."

"Well you are fortunate indeed. The leader doesn't have any contact with those who are not officially part of the Resistance."

"How does one 'officially' become part of the Resistance?" she asked.

"I will let him tell you, since it seems that he wants to meet you next spring. Oh yes, your request has been exceeded."

"What do you mean?" Maeryn asked.

"I have been given instructions to assign you one of my men as well as a larger vessel. It won't transport your refugees, but it will be large enough to carry supplies back to the island. I will need the rest of the afternoon to get your shipping papers prepared and to make other arrangements. But you must defer to my man's authority, especially when in public. It is important that you appear in your proper womanly role so as not to raise any suspicions. He will take the three of you to the shipyards tomorrow and you will set sail for Tur'cen."

Maeryn couldn't believe her ears and she couldn't keep the tears from her eyes. "Thank you," she said simply.

The morning after the battle's end, Kael was up and out of his bed, after being treated for a broken nose and ribs, as well as a deep wound on his right thigh. He didn't remember much of the previous night, only that he somehow made it back to Leoran. What was clear in his mind, perfectly clear, was his encounter with Narian. He replayed the events over and over in his head. And as he did so, several questions came to mind.

Is Narian leading this invasion? Did he escape from the monastery too? Should I feel guilty? No! I will not feel guilty about killing him! He chose his actions and happened to come across my path. If it wasn't me, it would have been someone else.

Actually...it probably wouldn't have been anyone else. With his upbringing and the training he received at the monastery, Kael had always excelled in combat. In fact, he had never met a worthy opponent since his escape. That is, until Narian.

I almost didn't make it out of that one alive!

He tried to shrug off his current train of thought. The city of Leoran was beautiful in the morning as Kael strolled along the city walls overlooking the lake. After a few minutes of concentrating on the present and trying to forget about the previous day's events, Kael became aware of something. As he passed the Leoran citizens, he noticed a hesitation in their demeanor, a mixture of fear and awe. Whispers and hushed voices passed among the people, and when he looked them in the eyes, he received nods of respect. Though not the kind that seems to accompany friendship or trust, but something else. He wondered if it had something to do with not remembering how he got back to the city. It was almost as if he had drunk too much wine the night before and embarrassed himself. *Oh well.* He made a mental note to ask Dacien about it when he got back.

Kael recovered quickly over the next few weeks. His leg wound closed up and he was eventually able to remove the bandages. The swelling and discoloration on his face subsided and the ability to breathe through his nose returned. But the pain in his ribs lingered. Just when he started to forget about his limitations, a jolt of pain would return as he performed some minor activity that would otherwise not have been a problem.

But more important than his physical injuries, Kael felt a wound in his soul. Seeing Narian brought back memories of his past, memories that he'd been trying to forget for a long time. These memories would steal hours of his day before he realized it. Dacien must have thought his friend had gone crazy.

In fact, Kael hadn't shared more than three conversations with him since the battle with the Syvaku. The first conversation was strange, as Dacien relayed the events that Kael had forgotten. Since that time, the two had begun to grow apart, and Kael wasn't sure why. He only knew that he felt uncomfortable around Dacien, like a disapproving parent. Though Dacien never said anything to that effect, Kael felt it nonetheless.

One day, just before the first winter storm, Kael found himself at the city square after one of his many walks to clear his mind, which was increasingly difficult to clear. The market was busy with the normal activity, but Kael's attention was drawn to the unusual sight of a slave trader with his products on display. As Kael neared, he caught a few of the words being shouted to potential customers. Apparently this enterprising man had found a way to profit from the misery of others by rounding up all the homeless slaves of Bastul after the Syvak raid. With the death of their masters, there was no one to contest this man, who simply took them by force. No doubt he had a few thugs nearby for his own safety, but far enough away to stay out of sight so as not to present a negative image that might affect his sales. *Too late. I can see your evil from right where I stand.*

Scanning the faces of the slaves, Kael felt disgusted. For too long, the Empire used slave labor as a way of building and sustaining its gluttonous appetite. The labor of many supported the lifestyle of a few.

All of a sudden, Kael froze. There before him was a man his own age. His dark skin was marred with scars from a long time past. His face was distorted to the point of being grotesque. As Kael looked around, it was clear that the Leoran citizens were also uncomfortable at the sight. Kael looked back to the man's tall and muscular frame and knew in an instant who it was that stood before him.

Stepping forward into the space between the crowd and the slaves, Kael stopped in front of Ajani.

"There he is," yelled the trader. "A man who knows a good deal when he sees one. You won't find a more reasonable price."

The crowd began to back away from Kael as the trader approached.

"I'll take this one," Kael announced.

"Of course, a fine specimen. Hard on the eyes, but strong as an ox," the man nearly shouted, trying to stir the crowd into a buying frenzy.

Kael turned to face the man and stared deep into his eyes.

The trader shifted uneasily and shot glances around to the stunned crowd that had grown eerily quiet.

"On second thought," Kael responded. "I'll take them all."

The man looked stunned, then quickly replied. "...such generosity. I can see that you are a man of great importance..."

Kael interrupted. "You are correct, Sir!" Now it was Kael who was shouting. "And I believe that you have misinterpreted my meaning. I will take all of these men and women. And my payment will be the sparing of your life!"

"But..." the man stammered.

"Leave this city quickly or I will have to reconsider the terms of our arrangement!"

Instantly, Kael was aware of three men hanging back in the crowd to his left and another behind the slaves to his right.

Kael leaned in close to the man, whose face was red with anger. "Call off your men or they will die in front of you today."

The trader's eyes shifted toward the crowd and then back to Kael.

The hesitation in the man's body language was telling, as Kael shot out a hand and gripped the man by the throat. The citizens scattered, revealing the trader's hired thugs standing in the open. They began to approach cautiously until the sound of marching footsteps filled the courtyard.

"What is the problem here?" called a voice from the Leoran soldiers, who were now fanning out to contain the skirmish. "Caleb, sir, these men have a right to be here."

"Of course they do, and we've just made an arrangement. He has agreed to give me all of these slaves and I have agreed not to kill him and his men."

There was no reply from the Leoran guard. Kael slowly released his grip and the man gasped for air. Seconds of tense silence passed and finally, the trader backed away with Kael's piercing stare boring into his skin. Eventually, the man and his hired muscle left the courtyard and headed for the southeastern city gate.

Kael asked the guards to unchain the slaves. And as the shackles fell off of Ajani, Kael stepped forward and embraced his childhood friend, who seemed confused and unsure of how to react.

That evening, a knock brought Kael to the entrance of his quarters. He opened the door to find Dacien with an agitated look on his face.

"Come in; we need to talk," Kael said.

"You're damn right we do!"

In all the time he'd known Dacien, which admittedly wasn't very long, Kael had never known him to swear or lose his temper. Even during times of extreme pressure, which constituted the majority of their friendship, Dacien was calm and even tempered.

Kael poured two glasses of wine and gave one to Dacien. Both men drained their cups quickly, after sitting down to make themselves comfortable.

"First you attack a man in the city square, then you steal his property. And now..."

"Now wait a minute," Kael interrupted. "If I'd attacked the man, he wouldn't still be alive. And those people you refer to as *his property* weren't rightfully his to begin with."

Dacien continued with a quieter tone of voice. "And now I understand that your slaves are presently at the baths, being attended to as if they were Orud royalty...and feasts prepared for them from the winter food stores built up by the citizens of this city."

"I will repay the cost, whatever it is."

"I don't care about the cost, Caleb; this city is indebted to you. What I care about is that a man whom I call a *friend* is losing control of himself."

Kael was immediately struck by the awkward sound of his fake name. He was holding back a part of himself and his secrets were interfering with his friendship. "He was my childhood friend...my first friend. What was I supposed to do?"

"What are you talking about?"

Kael couldn't find the strength to answer. How could he explain the happiness of his childhood, contrasted with the sadness of his time at the monastery, all pivoting upon a single moment of desperation to defend his friend against the beatings of an evil man? How could he explain without having to explain his entire past? He wished it could all just go away.

"Caleb. You're not making any sense these days, ever since the battle. You're angry and it's eating you up inside. Whatever the problem is, learn how to deal with it and stay out of trouble. I grow weary of making excuses for you." Dacien rose to his feet and stormed out of the room with a slamming door to emphasize his exit.

12

Maeryn stood at the prow of the ship and pulled her thick cloak tight against her chin. The driving wind was bringing a large storm cloud from the east that tried to block the rising sun. It was ominous and should have worried her, but the return trip was almost concluded and they would soon arrive at the island. She hoped that her friends had fared well in her absence and was excited to be bringing food and winter supplies.

Gradually, the rocky coast on their port side passed into their wake and Tur'cen came into view. Maeryn was surprised at the amount of elation she felt. But she quickly realized that, though she was cared for while in the Empire's capital city, she dearly missed her daughter and had come to think of the slaves as her family.

Former slaves, she corrected herself.

Swinging around to the southern tip of the island, the man who had taken the role of her husband piloted the ship into a partially hidden cove. With the island now blocking the wind, all became silent. Maeryn scanned the shoreline for signs of movement, but no one could be seen. It seemed an eternity before the boat slid to a stop in the soft shore.

Without waiting for help, Maeryn jumped down to land with a splash into water reaching to her knees. The three men aboard, quickly attended to the sails and dropped anchor. Maeryn waded to the dry sand and walked inland, glancing around.

Maybe they're hiding. But after several minutes, she started to feel a sickness in her stomach. She wouldn't even dare to think or utter the fear in her heart, instead pushing her emotions aside. Her two traveling companions and mock husband now joined her on the beach.

"So where is everyone?" he called, his arms wide.

"Mother!" came a yell from the trees.

Maeryn spun around to see Aelia running out from the protection of the forest. Her swift feet left gentle impressions in the sand as she ran for her mother. Maeryn threw off her cloak and met Aelia, the two embracing with tears in their eyes.

"Are you alright?" she said, pulling back from her daughter and taking the girl's face in her hands.

"I'm fine, Mother; I missed you."

"And the others...are they well?"

"Everyone is fine!"

Maeryn pulled her close again, holding tight.

"Mother!" exclaimed Aelia, pulling away embarrassed as she noticed the handsome stranger only a few paces away.

"Oh," Maeryn mumbled as she noticed the source of her daughter's concern. "Don't worry about him; he's here to help us." She knew that Aelia wasn't concerned about a stranger in their midst, but she wasn't ready to acknowledge her daughter's budding interest in men. She knew it would come eventually, but she wasn't about to encourage it.

Slowly, other familiar faces began to materialize on the beach. And it wasn't long before they all had the boat unloaded, the supplies moved to the camp and the ship stowed out of sight. The hours passed quickly as Maeryn settled back into island life. Everyone was eager to hear of her trip, and it was all she could do to put them off until the evening meal, when she could recount her story for all to hear.

Later that evening, after assessing the food storage, it was decided that they could easily spare enough food for a celebration feast. Maeryn thought it completely appropriate, given the trials they had endured. Immediately, word spread through the camp and was met with smiles and tears of joy. Fires were built and the smell of food enveloped the camp. Roast lamb, fish, and all manner of fruits were prepared so that all could eat their fill. And as the activity of dinner slowed all of the island residents gathered around their respective fires and stared at Maeryn, anxious to hear her story. Maeryn wiped the tears from her eyes and stood before her friends.

She recounted their entire journey, from the time they left the island. And even though she couldn't adequately express it as she wanted, it didn't seem to matter. Her friends listened with rapt attention to every word. They shared in her struggles and envisioned themselves at her side as she traveled to secure their freedom. And though it should have occurred earlier, Maeryn didn't fully realize the weight of her responsibility until halfway through her tale. It dawned on her suddenly and she had to concentrate to keep from trailing off and ruining the moment. She knew, even as she continued, that she would have to ponder that thought at a later time and give it her full attention. But this moment wasn't that time. So she moved on to the climax of her story.

"...and that's when he told me that we would be given a larger ship to carry all the supplies we would need for winter. And in the springtime, he would send a ship large enough to carry us all to Orud."

Cheering went up from the crowd at the mention of their rescue. Maeryn waited until their applause died down.

"He will send a slave ship and we will travel in broad daylight under that disguise. Once we reach Orud, he will stage a pretend market where powerful men of the Resistance will purchase you and take you away to your respective posts throughout the Empire. Now I know that this sounds suspicious, but it's actually quite brilliant. There will be no cause for any citizens to suspect what is happening, because it is a common occurrence. The difference is that you will not be owned by anyone, but will be spreading throughout the Empire to help free your own people from bondage. The Resistance has made great progress recently, but they can use all the help they can get."

Slowly, the looks of concern changed into smiles as they considered the plan. After a few minutes, nods of approval could be seen all around.

"Now, let us all get some rest and we can talk more in the morning."

As the crowd began to disperse, several came to Maeryn and offered their thanks. The women embraced her, while the men simply put a hand on her shoulder. Maeryn felt awkward, knowing that it wasn't her provision that would save these people. That honor would go to the leader of the Resistance. Still, she felt blessed that what she did have to offer was put to good use for their cause.

The thick, humid air made breathing difficult. Coupled with the constant buzzing of insects, it made Saba feel as though everything around him was alive. Indeed, the rich and moisture laden earth beneath his feet seemed capable of growing anything. He was stripped to the waist and following a dark-skinned man through a dense jungle of vines and broad-leafed trees. After nearly three days of walking on a more or less flat grade, they began to descend steeply into a valley. The trees seemed to close in on him and the light grew dimmer as the sun was choked from view. They moved quickly despite the lack of a defined walking path. The man ahead of him was weaving and darting through the foliage, relying upon memory to guide him. And from the increasing noise in the air, Saba suspected that the man's memory was good.

Steadily, the faint sound of water grew to a deafening roar. And just when it seemed as though the sound couldn't get louder, the trees opened to show a magnificent view. They were standing on a precipice with a narrow gap separating the cliff on which they stood from a wall of vegetation only thirty feet away. Craning his neck, Saba estimated that the opposite cliff face reached a hundred feet above them. The most amazing sight, however, was the frothing white water cutting through the vegetation to plummet hundreds of feet below them.

Saba's guide moved along the cliff to the right, not showing any hint of the amazement that Saba felt. It was to be expected, he thought, considering that these sights would be commonplace to the man. Saba followed and after several minutes they came upon a strange sight—a thick rope, tied to the branch of a tree, extending across the gap between the cliffs to disappear into the middle of the waterfall. Though it was woven from vines, it was thick and appeared sturdy. The guide stopped and looked to Saba with a questioning expression.

Saba held out his hands indicating that he didn't understand.

The man responded by shaking the rope and pointing to the waterfall across the chasm.

"Behind the water is what you seek," said the man in his native tongue, a hint of anger in his voice.

"I don't understand. Can you show me?"

"NO! I am not permitted to walk the holy ground. 'Only holy man' say the elders."

Saba looked back to the waterfall and the realization of what he was about to do began to set in. The sacred burial ground for the holy men of this tribe was located in a cave behind the waterfall. He would have to use the rope to swing across the chasm and through the water to get to it. It was all starting to feel familiar.

"How do I get back?" he asked.

The man pondered the question for several seconds before answering. "Keep rope. I will pull you up."

The man's answer lacked confidence, which caused Saba's stomach to sink. But something compelled him to walk forward nonetheless. He grabbed the rope, untied it from the tree branch and stepped to the edge of the cliff. He knew that if he hesitated, it would only give him the chance to consider how dangerous this was. So he didn't hesitate. Instead, he grasped the rope firmly with both hands, took a deep breath, and launched himself away from the cliff.

Saba's heart immediately leaped into his throat as he caught a glimpse of the bottom of the chasm. Before he had time to ponder the pain of falling from this height, his breath was stolen by the sudden temperature change and immense downward force exerted on his body upon entering the water. The shock was short-lived as he passed through the falls. Instinctively, he loosened his grip on the rope and began to drop, longer than expected. When he hit the hard ground on the other side, the impact knocked the wind from his lungs. He stumbled, off balance, and fell to the ground, losing his grip on the rope. In a moment of panic at the thought of being trapped, he lunged for the rope as the downward force of the water whipped it across the dirt floor toward the waterfall. Just before the edge of the cliff, Saba's finger made contact with the rope and he quickly grabbed it with full force. Momentarily relieved, Saba rolled over onto his back and struggled to regain his breath.

It took several minutes, but finally he rose to his feet and stared at the rushing water, keenly aware that he had almost just lost his way out. And yet, something inside him drove out the fear. He knew that he was walking down the path of his hidden memories, and that gave him confidence. Despite his desperate circumstances, there was no place he would rather be.

The deafening water at the mouth of the cave gave a shimmering glow to the surroundings, providing much more light than he would have expected. But as the cave narrowed toward the back, into the mountain, the glittering light was quickly lost. The natives had long ago dealt with this problem by keeping a torch and flint along the wall to the right. After fumbling with the crude instruments for a moment, Saba had a light source that chased away the darkness. Without hesitating, he began to follow the path and his eyes slowly adjusted to the orange glow of the torch. The cave continued to narrow until he found himself on his hands and knees, struggling to squeeze between the rocks and dust. Then, the passage suddenly widened into another cave and Saba could hear its size before he could see it. The sound of his feet on the uneven path was lost to the nothingness of this new space, no longer echoing as it did a few minutes before.

Holding up the torch, Saba let the light stretch across the cavern and was surprised by what he saw—numerous stone sarcophagi covering the floor, arranged in perfect rows. The natives, by what Saba could observe of their culture, didn't appear to be adept at working with stone. However, the piles of stones around him, some carved with intricate designs, argued with his original observation. Walking along the mounds, from row to row, Saba felt drawn by something, although he wasn't sure what he was looking for. It should have been unsettling, walking amongst the remains of the dead, but it was anything but unsettling. There was an overwhelming sense of peace that allowed him to search the entire length of the cavern without once feeling nervous.

Suddenly, Saba stopped. There, in front of him at the back of the cavern was a mound of a different sort. It was small, only a few feet square. He bent down to touch the stones, prepared to search through them, but stopped. *What if this is the resting place of a child, or the ashes of a holy man that didn't require a full size coffin?* Somehow he knew this wasn't the case. And so he proceeded to remove one stone at a time until a weathered wooden box was uncovered. He slowly raised the lid and lifted the torch over the top. Inside, bathed in the flickering glow of the fire above his head, Saba could see an object wrapped in an oiled cloth. Carefully, he lowered the torch and propped it against the sarcophagus behind him. Then, using both hands, he gingerly lifted the cylindrical pouch out of the pile of stones and rested it in his lap. His heart began to beat rapidly, for what reason he didn't know, just that he felt on the verge of discovery.

With a deep breath, he untied the leather thong that bound the pouch and began to peel away the layers of oiled cloth and lay them in a pile on the dirt floor. There were many and it soon became apparent that this object was a prized possession worth protecting. Finally, the last layer came off and Saba held a scroll in his hands. It was plain, without decorations. It was much older than any of the scrolls he found in the libraries of Orud. It was ancient. He inspected it as well as he could in the faint light, holding it close to his eyes. Then he slowly and carefully began to unroll it...

A sudden jolt of fear surged through his body. There, in his shaking hands, was a symbol that caused him to lose his breath. The same symbol, in fact, that was carved into the shaft of an arrow given to him by the Governor of Bastul so many years ago.

He couldn't understand his own emotions at this moment. He should have felt relief, even excitement at the prospect of discovering a clue to the mystery that had eluded him for so long. But instead, he felt a growing sense of dread. Cautiously, he unrolled the scroll and found the first passage of text. The written language was like nothing he had seen before, and for a few minutes he stared at the graceful strokes, carefully scribed on the crude parchment. And then, the ink strokes on the page began to communicate, and Saba began to read and understand.

THE WORDS OF SARIEL, ENTRUSTED TO HIS FAITHFUL SERVANT EBNISHA

At once the tears began to flow from his eyes as Saba read his true name. He understood immediately what he was holding in his hands and why he had reason to fear. He continued reading and with the discovery of each passage, he wept harder as memories came back to him. Faces, cities, experiences that warmed his heart alongside enemies, sufferings and trials that angered him and left him with a profound sense of loss. He kept reading until his eyes began to blur and the words ran together, all the while, he cried for the memories that he now regretted.

His body shook, waking him. Complete darkness surrounded him.
How long have I been here?
It may have been hours, or even days. Searching around the dirt, his hand closed upon the torch. It was cold, giving no indication of the length of time that had passed. Grasped tightly in the other hand and feeling as though it weighed the equivalent of the sarcophagus against which he leaned, was the scroll that had drawn him to this place. With a great deal of effort, Saba—or *Sariel*—rose to his feet and began to feel his way through the dark,

toward the sound of rushing water. With the return of his memory came an impending sense of doom that quickened his steps and gave him a sense of urgency. *Time is running out for everyone! I have to hurry; I have to get back to Orud!*

Kael strode across the courtyard, his footsteps echoing off the surrounding stone buildings. His thick winter cloak was clasped at his neck by a golden torc, a symbol of high ranking in the Orud military. Although he wasn't technically an Orud soldier, he had earned his place among them and their respect. Dacien had sent for Kael, though he didn't say why. But the situation felt quite serious.

Following a wide street north from the courtyard, Kael traced his way to the General's quarters, a magnificent columned structure that Dacien was uncomfortable with. He wasn't used to such extravagance and was having a difficult time adjusting to this part of his responsibilities. Kael smiled to himself as he climbed the steps leading to the front entrance. There a pair of guards pulled their spears away from the door and allowed him to pass. The interior was decorated with sculptures and plants growing from large pots around the room. Kael moved quickly through the foyer and into the center of the house where Dacien waited with several of his other officers.

"You called?"

Dacien nodded. "Please sit."

Kael moved to where Dacien indicated and sat at a large circular marble table.

"I've asked all of you to join me because I've received word back from Orud."

Kael looked around the room and saw eager expressions among the eight other men.

"The Emperor has heard our request for aid and is gravely concerned about the state of the Empire. It seems that the Korgs have broken through the northern border and have taken the city of Orlek. The struggles in the north aren't nearly as widespread as the Syvaku attacks, but the timing of the two is suspicious."

"What will the Emperor do?" asked one of the men.

"Well, he hasn't promised to give aid. In fact, there was no direct answer to our request. Instead, he is calling for all his Generals to assemble in Orud next spring."

"That's not a good idea," voiced Kael.

"I know," replied Dacien. "To have all the Generals in the same place at the same time—especially while the Empire is under attack from numerous enemies—is concerning, indeed. Nevertheless, we have been ordered to the capital."

The other men shook their heads, but didn't look surprised, as if this type of ridiculous mandate was common.

"One other thing...I've also been ordered to bring the one responsible for the death of the Syvak warlord."

Kael's eyebrows rose.

"The Emperor feels that you would be an inspiration at a time such as this," he said to Kael. "So, my friend, it seems that we will journey together once again."

Kael nodded, a little surprised that Dacien had used the word *friend*. They still weren't on good terms as far as Kael knew. And in Dacien's defense, Kael hadn't put much effort into patching things up between them. He still had a great deal of affection for Dacien, and had come to miss the time they used to spend together. But he just wasn't prepared to discuss the details of his past and he knew that conversation—which was sure to occur eventually—was necessary to making things right.

Instead, he had been spending his days with Ajani, trying unsuccessfully to reacquaint himself with his old companion. Sadly, it seemed that even that friendship would never be the same. *Sometimes, there's just no going back.*

The weeks passed, turning into months that were long and dreary. Kael, fully healed from his injuries, began to train again. Rising early every morning, he rode out of the city to the surrounding forest and found a place of solitude where he could stretch and strengthen his muscles. The motions of his exercise came back quickly, along with the familiar, but unexplainable sensation that had become second nature to him. As he moved his body through his exercises, his awareness broadened to encompass the surrounding leafless trees, and the long blades of golden grasses swaying in the breeze.

And then, out of curiosity, he tried something new. He pushed on the limit of his awareness, trying to force it outward. Just as one might scan the edges of a crowd in search of someone, ignoring those people that were in the immediate vicinity. Kael pushed his awareness outward and was surprised by its obedience. Suddenly, he became aware of more, in a wider area surrounding himself, though the clarity lessened.

Just like sight. The details are more difficult with greater distance.

I wonder...

Allowing the feeling to fade, he focused only in one direction, and felt a path extending away from himself to a range of nearly thirty feet. Grass, earth, trees, even wind currents...everything between himself and the extent of his awareness could be felt as though he was connected to it.

Interesting!

And then, he relaxed his body and pushed his awareness farther away, hoping to find the limit of his ability. Sixty, seventy, eighty feet away, he pushed until the clarity began to decline. And when it did, he narrowed his area of concentration and pushed more. His knees began to wobble and he knew that the strain was taking a toll on his body. But now he was determined to know what he was capable of.

Forcing it to go farther, narrowing his focus, his right hand began to tremor. His head began to ache and a trickle of blood ran down his lip. And just before he lost consciousness, he could feel at the other side of the clearing, a tiny beetle clinging to the bark of a tree. It began to scurry away, emitting a sense of panic as it crawled upward. And then darkness rushed in like a flood...

Staring up at the sky, Kael quickly realized what had happened. He sat up and glanced around, confirming that he had passed out where he stood. He tried climbing to his feet, and could feel the shakiness of his limbs, the same feeling that he experienced after intense labor.

He looked across to the edge of the forest at the other end of the meadow, to where he felt the beetle. It was nearly two hundred yards away. A smile crossed his face as he considered the implications of what he had just learned. In the past, he hadn't been able to control his awareness to this extent. But when it came upon him, he was able to guide weapons to their mark with deadly accuracy. It seemed to act as a muscle that tired quickly unless trained regularly. But somehow, in the months that he had neglected its training, this muscle, this ability, had become far stronger.

Two hundred yards...this is going to be quite useful!

13

The morning sunlight shone bright through the surrounding foliage which held the vibrant colors of spring. The soft, but steady sound of the water lapping at the shore reminded Maeryn of Bastul. She used to stand at the railing of her balcony and watch the sun rise over the eastern horizon to reflect brilliantly off the numerous buildings and ships near the bay. She felt a deep sadness at the loss of her beloved city, but those feelings were confounded by her other memories of that time, unpleasant things that she wished to forget. It all seemed so far away, and with any luck, it would stay that way.

She stood now at the sandy shore of a secluded bay and watched as the procession of former slaves made its way down to the slave ship anchored just a few yards from the dry ground. The morning had been filled with tears, both of happiness at the realization of their freedom and sadness at their parting with each other. Unfortunately, Maeryn and Aelia would not be accompanying their friends to Orud. There would be no valid excuse for them to be aboard a slave ship. Instead, the others would make the journey days ahead, while mother and daughter would wait and allow distance and time to separate them from the slaves they had helped to escape.

The fewer suspicions, the better.

It took hours to load everyone aboard the ship. It was awkward seeing so many bodies in so little space, but appearances were important at this stage of their plan. The man that brought Maeryn back from Bastul was apparently in a position of authority as he commanded the crew of the slave ship. Though he wouldn't be traveling with his men, he instructed them nevertheless. And, after instructions to the crew, he turned to address his pretend captives.

"All of you must listen carefully." Immediately, the joyous expressions inspired by the first taste of freedom fled from all the faces. "When we arrive in Orud, it is critical to our success that you appear as anyone would expect. For some of you younger ones, you didn't directly experience the horrors of capture and transport to this Empire. Therefore, you must learn from your elders. I know that living on the run from Bastul hasn't been easy, but it is much different than the experience of a new slave. For the older ones among us, this is the only time when I will recommend that you remember your experiences. Relive them and let your grief show. Use this time before we reach Orud to get back into those feelings. We must put on a show and appear no different than any other slave ship. I don't want to see any smiling or hear any laughing. If you are tempted to feel anything other than downtrodden, think of this. Our mission is not complete. If we are caught, we will all be executed. More importantly, our cause may be compromised. From the time you set sail, until the time you reach your assigned post, there will be no more friendly interactions. You will be treated as slaves and will address the crew as masters. We cannot afford to waste the years of effort and progress that have brought us to this point. The next weeks will be difficult, but you have all endured worse in the past, and I beg you to hold fast to what you know, that your freedom is within your grasp."

When he finished speaking, the crowd was silent. There were no more words to speak as all were deep in thought. Maeryn watched Aelia wipe the tears from her eyes. Maeryn's own eyes were surely red, but without tears. The time for mourning was over, and they needed to look ahead to the task that lay before them.

After much waving and shouted farewells, the anchor was raised and the slave ship was rowed out of the bay. When it reached the open sea, the sails were raised and the wind took hold. From the narrow view of their hideout, Maeryn, Aelia, and the Resistance Captain watched the slave ship disappear from view. Though she had been preparing for this moment for such a long time, Maeryn still felt unprepared for the gravity of the situation. This was a turning point in her life and she would never again be the same. As Aelia held tight to her side, sobbing, Maeryn was keenly aware that something momentous had just occurred and she was now on the other side of it.

Kael cinched down the strap holding his knapsack to the saddle. All of his belongings were now secure and attached to his horse. Stepping back, he surveyed the rest of the General's brigade that would accompany him and Dacien to the capital city of the Empire. Ajani, who was always close-by these days, waited by his own horse as Kael walked down the length of the small column. The spring sunshine warmed his skin and seemed to intensify the smells of the city. Horses stamped, their tails whipping back and forth. Men yelled instructions to each other along with the occasional crude joke. In all, only twenty-two soldiers and eight slaves would be making this journey, including Kael, Dacien and Ajani. However, Kael refused to refer to his dark-skinned friends as slaves.

Whatever questions there were about the purpose of this trip, Dacien knew that the southern region couldn't spare many soldiers, let alone its newly appointed General. He chose only the minimum traveling guard to accompany him as the surrounding cities would need all the hands that could be spared to help rebuild.

After a quick status check, all men signaled a state of readiness. The column moved slowly through the city to the northern gate, the horse's hooves ringing loudly on the stone streets. The citizens of Leoran lined the streets and waved goodbye to the soldiers. After exiting the northern gate, the men rode along the bridge connecting the city to the surrounding shore. It was a beautiful sight to behold as sunlight reflected on the glittering lake surface, throwing tiny flashes of light across spear tips and helmets. For all the times that Kael felt at peace with being alone, this was one of the moments when it was amazing to feel part of something important. There was a sense of power and majesty riding with the General of the Southern Region of Orud. Before they reached the mainland, the quaking leaves of the nearby forest could be heard. The majestic sound combined with the gleaming color of new growth, made for an awe-inspiring moment.

The first day of travel brought them to the eastern edge of the forest where they stopped earlier than normal. It would take more than a day to cross the plains that awaited them and Dacien didn't feel hurried. The evening passed slowly as all the men adjusted to a night outdoors, which hadn't occurred for most of them since the previous autumn.

Kael woke early and helped break camp, while others prepared a quick breakfast, after which they continued on with their easterly trek. Kael had spent the first day at the back of the column with the slaves, but decided now to ride up front with Dacien. He invited Ajani who declined for fear that it wasn't appropriate for a slave to ride in front of soldiers. Kael tried to change his mind, but to no avail. After several minutes of discussion, Kael conceded. In the end, Kael realized that it was for the better, as he had some issues to work out with Dacien.

"How long will it take to reach Orud," he called to Dacien as soon as he was within earshot.

Dacien looked back to acknowledge, but waited until Kael was closer to respond.

"It would only take a few weeks if not for the mountains that we will have to cross. The second half of our trip will be slow."

After minutes of silence riding in parallel with his friend, Kael spoke. "I uh..." Kael stuttered, trying to think of a way to start the conversation that he knew needed to take place.

"We need to talk," Dacien replied, sensing the difficulty.

"Yeah," Kael breathed. "I've...never really...told you anything about myself." The words were forced and Kael knew that it sounded just the same.

Dacien looked over. "I had hoped that you would tell me in time. After all, you know everything about me."

Kael realized that it was true. He had been a good listener to Dacien, but had never offered anything from his own life. In that moment, he realized how difficult it must be to befriend someone who doesn't respond.

"I'm sorry; it's just difficult when..." Kael trailed off.

Dacien waited patiently.

"I guess it's difficult when you have something to hide," Kael blurted out. *Oh well, you're committed now aren't you!*

Dacien's eyebrows raised. "What do you mean?"

"It's kind of a long story," Kael offered, trying to buy some time to figure out how to tell him.

Dacien let out a laugh that caused some birds to take to flight from a nearby tree. "How about a month?" he asked, spreading his arms out to either side. "Will that be enough time?"

Kael smiled, glad to have the mood lightened. "Alright... Perhaps I should just start at the beginning."

Dacien nodded.

Kael was tired of keeping his life a secret. Did it really matter what people would think of him? After all, most of his childhood was a series of accidents, things that happened to him. He had no control. What would Dacien do when Kael told him of his involvement with the man who had led the invasion of the Southern Region?

Oh, who cares! Here goes nothing...

"My real name is Kael Lorus, son of Adair Lorus, the Governor of Bastul. My mother's name was Maeryn."

Dacien didn't even blink.

Kael swallowed, then continued. "When I was young, my father disappeared and no one could figure out what happened. My mother feared the worst, but she never really got any answers. So, after weeks of nothing, the council reassigned the governorship to a wicked man named Lemus."

Dacien smiled, not out of pleasure, but out of understanding.

"Lemus became my father, but I never acknowledged him as such. He was cruel to us and life became very difficult. One day, I heard screaming coming from the garden. I ran toward the sound and found Lemus standing over my friend Ajani." Kael motioned to the back of the column and Dacien nodded, finally understanding.

"Ajani was covered in blood and Lemus just kept pounding on him. So I grabbed a pitchfork from the shed and attacked him."

When Kael paused, Dacien jumped in. "He used to have this bad limp that he would never speak of."

"Yeah...I did that," Kael replied proudly. "I ran it right into his upper leg. That got his attention on me and saved Ajani's life, though you can see that his scars exist even to this day. I'm not sure what kind of life he had after that.   Anyway, Lemus turned his attention on me and knocked me unconscious.   I woke up in the Bastul prison and was held there for days without food or water. I was ten years old. Lemus came by to torment me. I think he was trying to decide what to do with me. I can't even imagine what my mother must have been going through at the time"

As Kael's words began to flow, Dacien's attention peaked.   Kael continued his story throughout the day, telling of his time in the northern prison and the first few days at the monastery.   When the sun neared the western horizon, the General's group stopped and pitched their camp in a slight depression in the plains east of Leoran.   They set up quickly and lit fires to cook the evening meal.   Kael felt a sense of relief in sharing his experience with Dacien, but was now anxious to finish his story.   He knew, however, that their trip would last many days, and so he bid Dacien a good evening and went to eat with Ajani and the others.

In the following days, Kael continued to ride with Dacien and tell him of his unusual upbringing and the other boys that were his friends.   Kael paced himself and tried to be thorough, while Dacien listened intently, never having heard such a story in all his life.   After a week and a half, they began to see the Anodkem mountain range on the horizon.   It was an ominous sight, in spite of the well-maintained and traveled roads leading through the passes, all the way to the city of Orud.   As they reached the foothills, Kael's story reached the end of his time at the monastery.

"So what happened next?" Dacien asked.

Kael ran toward the edge of the cliff and jumped, arms spread out. For a second he felt weightless, but the moment passed in an instant. Suddenly, he plunged through the fog and felt a heavy sickness in his stomach. The wind raced past his ears, blocking out everything with a roar. Sightless, deaf, and unable to scream from the terror that gripped his heart, Kael knifed through the thick air into nothingness.

He wasn't prepared for this moment, even though something inside him had told him to jump. But as he had trained himself to do over the years, he closed his eyes and calmed himself. As the wind rushed past, he struggled to block out the images that threatened to control his mind, images of his splattered body strewn across the rocks below.

A warming sensation came over him now as he began to feel the nothingness of his surroundings. Slowly, the nothingness turned into swirling air currents and jagged protrusions of rocks and they moved past him at incredible speeds. Farther down, and approaching quickly, the surface of the water swayed in its endless motion.

His body...the ocean...the two objects moving closer and closer together.

Kael reached out with his sense, stretched it toward the water...and pushed. He pushed with all his might and felt his speed decrease. It was an action of instinct, born out of desperation. He didn't think he could control himself, he just reacted. He kept pushing until he felt consciousness slipping away from him. And then he hit the water, feet first. It felt thick and solid, like mud, trying to deny his entry. But his speed was too great and he couldn't be refused. The wind was knocked out of him as the water moved to escape the space he now occupied. Plummeting beneath the surface, he struggled to maintain his grip on his awareness, fearing that he would drown otherwise. And still he descended, almost expecting to reach the bottom. But there was no bottom to be reached. The ocean was an endless mass, able to swallow him, remove him from existence in this world.

And then he was motionless. It was a startling realization, an absence of the horror that had just occurred. Now there was a lack of sensation, no deafening roar...again weightlessness. Seizing the opportunity, Kael kicked his feet to propel himself upward to the surface. One of his legs didn't work. It hung, useless, from his hip. But it didn't matter; he was alive. The only thing that mattered now was reaching the surface and breathing air.

He kicked his one good leg and clawed with his hands, moving the water out of the way that separated him from the precious air above. Darkness and silence surrounded him now; only the muted grunts of his own struggles to accompany him. His lungs burned with desire. They began to pump in and out, demanding air, but he wouldn't open his mouth. To do so would only invite death to win this battle.

Suddenly, he burst through the surface and gasped, as though he were taking his first breath. His lungs thanked him and he breathed deep the fresh, life-giving substance.

As he treaded water, Kael became aware of a dull ache in his left leg. It was too soon to tell where the pain was originating from, but it didn't matter. He was alive. He was free. The escalating pain would tell him soon enough what had happened. But that didn't seem important now. It was a wonder that he hadn't broken all the bones in his body.

He looked upward. The air was clear for almost a hundred yards, but the top of the cliff, much higher, was shrouded in fog. Kael was curios about how far he had fallen, and what he had just endured, but is seemed that his curiosity would just have to wait. For now, he had to concentrate on survival. "Now what do I do?" he asked himself.

"I escaped," he replied simply.

"Oh," came Dacien's mumbled response.

Kael wasn't quite ready to reveal his abilities just yet, especially when he didn't even understand them himself. There was just no good way to explain. *Better to leave that for another time.*

"And..." Dacien prodded.   "Actually...never mind" he reconsidered. "We're stopping soon anyway; we'll pick this up tomorrow."

14

Maeryn, Aelia, and their escort arrived in Orud three weeks after the slaves had set out from the isle of Tur'cen. The bay was choked with vessels of all shapes and sizes, attending to the various needs of the city. Fishing boats, merchant ships, and slave traders prowled the waters, slowing their entrance to the docks. It was just after noon and the sun was intense overhead, signaling that the coming summer would be warm, indeed.

After unloading their few possessions—for they were supposed to appear to be traveling for leisure—they climbed into a coach and began their ride through the city. Immediately, Maeryn knew that they were not headed for the underground headquarters that she had visited last fall. She must have appeared concerned, because their escort quickly offered an explanation.

"We have a different route and destination this time."

Maeryn nodded. "I can see that."

"My lord explicitly instructed that your accommodations be more suited to a woman of your stature."

"Oh," Maeryn exclaimed. "I shall have to thank him. That's very kind!"

Aelia was smiling at these words, as she longed to have a comfortable bed and a good meal.

The city passed by at a comfortable pace and Maeryn contented herself with watching through the window. The city was magnificent. All the streets were paved with stones and lined with lamp posts. Everywhere she looked, flowers were beginning to bloom in their designated areas of each intersecting road. Aelia, tired from the journey, leaned her head against her mother and was asleep within minutes. The slight bouncing of the carriage was rhythmic and Maeryn too, began to feel the pull of sleep. Instead, she let her mind drift, recalling her beautiful garden in Bastul; a gift from Adair.

It was now mid afternoon and Maeryn was getting hungry.

Aelia had awakened and was stretching her arms. "How much longer?" she asked, breaking the silence.

"Only a few minutes," replied the man sitting across the cabin.

The seats faced each other, which would have made the silence awkward, but Maeryn had grown accustomed to long periods of quiet. They had been traveling northeast along the coast of the bay, rising in elevation. The terrain had become rockier and their surroundings more rural with groves of trees arranged at regular intervals, extending from the road.

The wagon turned south off the pavestones and started down a dirt road toward the sea. After dropping around a low hill, the carriage turned to a stop in front of a large residence. The driver came around and opened the door, extending his hand to Maeryn. She nudged Aelia to go first, and then followed, stepping down to the ground.

The view was breathtaking. The entire eastern bay of Orud lay before them. To their left, a sprawling mansion extended along the rocky cliff to the northeast, and beyond that, a vineyard. It reminded Maeryn of their home in Bastul, only much more elaborate.

"My lord will be joining us tomorrow. For now, follow me and I will help you get settled in."

"Thank you," Maeryn replied and followed their escort, turning to give a quick smile to Aelia who was beaming from ear to ear.

Once inside, they were taken up a set of marble stairs to the second floor, then down to the end of the hall. On the right, double doors opened into a spacious guest room with large windows to the south and the east, with views of the bay and vineyard respectively.

"I hope this will do?"

"I've been living in the forest on an island," Maeryn laughed. "I think the accommodations will be just fine, thank you."

"Would you ladies care for some tea and a light snack? You must be famished."

"We would, indeed," Maeryn replied.

The escort backed out of the door with a bow and disappeared down the hall.

Maeryn turned to Aelia. "Well," she said, arms outstretched.

"Mother, I love it!" she exclaimed. Running to the south windows she stopped to gaze out at the water. "How long do we get to stay here?"

"I'm not sure. At least until tomorrow, but hopefully longer."

Aelia continued her inspection of the room, stopping by the east windows to stare at the vineyard.

"The plan was to get the slaves to Orud; we didn't discuss anything after that."

Aelia didn't seem to be listening, but Maeryn didn't mind; she was speaking more to herself than anyone.

After tea and some miniature flaky bread loaves, the two rested until evening. Maeryn fell asleep, and when she awoke, Aelia was gone. Startled, she rose quickly and went searching for her daughter. But, as expected, she found her almost immediately, wandering in the vineyard.

"Aelia," she called. "Don't run off like that."

Aelia waited until her mother was close. "Mother...it's safe here. And I'm not a child anymore."

"I know. It's just that I don't think we can completely let our guard down...not yet."

Grabbing her hand, Aelia pulled Maeryn along and the two walked in the cooling air of the afternoon. The setting sun filtered through the leafy vines, covering them in dappled light, and the smell of sweet wet earth surrounded them.

"Mother," Aelia questioned. "Why didn't you tell me sooner about father?"

"You mean Lemus?"

"Right," Aelia replied.

Maeryn knew she would have to have this conversation eventually. Yet there had always been too much to do, too many responsibilities, too many people counting on her. There was never enough time. But now their mission was completed. And here in the vineyard, with the evening breeze, there was finally peace. To her credit, Aelia had been patient. Initially, it was difficult for her to be torn from her life and told that the man she knew as her father was anything but. Eventually, she left the topic alone and contented herself with the tasks at hand. She was an impressive girl, mature for her age. With a deep breath, Maeryn answered.

"I'm sorry if your life hasn't turned out the way you hoped. It hasn't exactly gone as I planned, either. Life has been very difficult since Adair disappeared. I only kept it a secret because I feared that Lemus would harm you if he knew you weren't his child."

"He wouldn't have harmed me."

"Actually," Maeryn corrected, her heart now pounding. "...he would have. I never told you this, but you had a brother."

Aelia stopped and turned toward Maeryn with an intense look in her eyes.

"Yes," Maeryn continued, tears instantly coming to her eyes. "His name was Kael," she managed to say with a choked voice. "Lemus was beating Ajani one day and Kael tried to defend him. He had Kael executed for it."

Maeryn was sobbing now, the emotions just as real as the day it happened. Aelia held her mother until the tears subsided.

"I guess I was scared too...for myself. If I was only the mother of Adair's child, what would he have done to me?"

"It's alright mother, you didn't have a choice."

Maeryn took a deep breath and continued walking. "I do now. We both do. I'm sorry that you've had to make sacrifices, but things are going to be different now...you'll see."

Aelia smiled. "Tell me about my real father."

"Ahh," Maeryn breathed. "...now that's something I like to talk about."

Kael huddled down in the cargo hold of a merchant ship. The light was dim and after pulling a tarp over himself, he was sure that he had a good hiding place. His leg was throbbing again and he was quite sure that he had broken it in the fall.

After days of swimming to the southeast, he had reached the mainland. There, he slept in a seaside cave and after the first light of day he began to slowly make his way south along the coast. Years of studying maps in the library of the monastery had given him a good sense of landmass proportions and their relation to each other. And after their trip to the temple of the High Priest, Kael had been able to pinpoint the location of the monastery after they returned.

It was with this confidence and knowledge that he had moved south into the small port town of Suppard. After rummaging though garbage for something to eat, Kael searched specifically for a fully loaded merchant vessel, one that appeared to be on its way out of port. And now that he felt well hidden, he allowed himself to drift off to sleep.

"Hey," called a deep voice, loud inside of the confined space.

Kael's eyes snapped open, but his body was frozen still. There was no possible way that he could be seen.

"They're looking for you, you know! Yeah...real mean crowd."

Kael wondered whether to stand up, but something told him to stay still. Maybe the man was drunk. Surely he couldn't see.

"Well, normally I'm a nice fellow...normally. But some people are just rude. I don't much care for rude people. So I'm gonna catch some sleep now. We push out in the mornin'. If you have a home, you should go. Otherwise, anything aboard my ship when we set sail is my property." The man paused for a moment. "Hello? Sure are quiet aren't you? Well...good night."

The voice was followed by stumbling footsteps, retreating up the stairs. The pounding in Kael's ears slowly decreased, as he wondered how the drunken man knew that he had a passenger. Maybe he was just bluffing. Either way, Kael stayed awake from then until morning.

The ship lurched and rocked as it left the port and headed for the open sea. With each passing minute, Kael felt more and more relieved. Distance was what he needed, distance between him and the monastery. It didn't matter that he had just spent days swimming and walking on a broken leg, without food and water. It only mattered that he got away, got his freedom. Kael stayed hidden in the cargo area for the rest of the day and the night as well.

"Alright now," called that same deep voice. "You've been down here long enough. Come out where I can see you. I won't bite."

Kael lifted off the tarp and struggled to his feet, figuring that it didn't make sense to keep hiding when the man knew that he was there.

"Come over here son, and let me get a good look at you."

Kael stepped out from the crate he had been hiding behind. His leg shot with pain, resisting the movement so that Kael stumbled slightly.

"What's wrong with ya?"

"...leg's broken," Kael managed through clenched teeth.

"Well for cryin' out loud boy, when were you gonna tell someone?"

Kael paused, not sure of how to react to this man, who didn't seem to pose any immediate threat. "...when I got to safety."

"Well...you're here. Come on, let's take a look at that leg."

Kael didn't move. "You're not going to turn me in?"

The man, who had already turned to go up the stairs, looked back to Kael and smiled. "Son, we all done things we ain't proud of. That don't matter to me or the rest of the crew. What matters is what you do from now on. Now follow me so we can get you fixed up. Won't do me a bit of good with a broken leg."

Kael began to inch forward, his muscles severely cramped by staying still for so long. It took a second for the man's words to make sense. "What do you mean I won't do you a bit of good?"

The man barked a laugh that filled every inch of the hull. "That was the deal. A safe place to hide in exchange for your service. I told you that when we set sail, anything aboard my ship became my property."

Kael doubted if this man's made up rules were considered legal anywhere in the Empire, but he didn't really care. It was a convenient hiding place, a way to disappear.

Limping after the Captain, Kael ascended the rough stairs to the deck of a large merchant vessel. It looked different in the daytime than at night when he stole aboard. Larger crates of some unknown cargo were stacked neatly in rows and secured to the decking, most likely the cargo that wouldn't fit down in the hold. As he followed the man aft, he received shifty glances from the crew as they attended to their duties. They were a rough looking bunch with smirks and scowls on their faces. Kael wondered what they were thinking.

The Captain opened the door to the aft cabin and motioned for Kael to follow. Once inside, Kael sat down and the Captain called for a splint to be brought.

"Hungry?"

Kael nodded, wary of the man's kindness.

"I hope you like fish," he replied, serving up some stew into a bowl and dropping it in front of Kael.

Kael lifted it to his lips and gulped it down, though his tongue protested.

"Good?" the Captain asked.

Kael just smiled and placed the empty bowl back on the table. "Aren't you going to ask why I'm hiding here?"

"Don't care cause it doesn't matter. We all have our stories, but we don't talk much here. No...most these folks'd rather work with their hands and forget about what goes on in their heads. No questions around here."

Kael nodded, liking this man more and more with every second. One of the crew came in and delivered a small strip of wood and some dirty rags, torn into strips. The Captain took the supplies and thanked the man, closing the door after him.

"Well, let's get a look at that leg."

Kael held up his hand. "It's broken just below the knee. And there's some damage to my hip, but there's nothing you can do about that. Here, the splint should go on this side."

The Captain handed the supplies over to Kael. "Sounds like you've had some experience with this."

"Yeah," Kael mumbled.

"What else do know about? Are you a sailor, fisherman?"

"No," Kael replied, revealing nothing.

"Hmm," the Captain sighed. "Looks like Bestio will get promoted. You can take over his cleaning duties. Oh, my name is Gryllus, but folks just call me 'Captain'."

Kael extended his hand. "Caleb," he lied.

15

Maeryn sat atop a rocky ledge that overlooked the eastern bay of Orud. Aelia was napping in their room, which left Maeryn alone and watching the tiny white sails move along the water. The breeze moved through her hair and the sun warmed her skin. And though she had many days like this on the island, this was different. The emotional weight that she had been carrying was now gone. And in its place, a sense of peace—which was strange for Maeryn, because if she really stopped to consider her situation, she should have felt lost. No longer did she have a sense of purpose. The mission for which she had risked her life was complete.

No... the people. I didn't just risk my life for a mission.

And now what? She was in a strange place with strange people, and no idea of what was going to happen next. But somehow, that didn't matter. She was at peace. For all of the long and grueling years past, she felt like a bird that had broken free of its cage and was now able to fly anywhere. Did the bird fear the freedom, the unknown?

No!

It was how the bird was meant to live.

A noise turned her attention from the ocean back to the mansion. To the left of the large structure, one of the servants was pointing toward her, and next to him stood a tall man. She couldn't tell anything about him from this distance, but she knew instantly who it was. He thanked the servant and proceeded to cross the expanse of swaying grass between them.

Maeryn rose to her feet and waited patiently.

"Maeryn," he addressed her in a kind voice.

He was tall, with thick, dark hair, graying at the temples. His piercing blue eyes looked as though they contained great wisdom, but also humility that immediately put Maeryn at ease.

Maeryn bowed. "I don't know your name, but I am honored to meet you."

"It is I who am honored to meet a woman of such courage and strength. What you have done is valuable beyond measure."

Maeryn blushed.

"One day, when we have managed to change this Empire, minstrels will sing ballads of your heroism, and we will feast in your honor."

"I think it will be you that they sing of," she countered. "But thank you. You are very kind. And thank you for your hospitality." She gestured to the mansion.

"I trust you have been well cared for?" he asked.

"Of course...much different than our island home," she added.

"Yes, I'm sorry about that, about all the confusion. I hope it wasn't too awful."

"No, no," Maeryn corrected. "I didn't mean it like that. I only meant, well..." she stammered.

"Shall we go inside?" he interrupted.

"Of course," Maeryn said quickly. She felt mortified. Had she offended him? Their island hideout wasn't his fault; it was part of Thaddius' plan.

Just try to keep your mouth shut. Less talking, more listening!

The Resistance Leader—Maeryn wasn't sure of his title any more than she was of his name—walked slowly back toward the mansion. The grass was soft underfoot and Maeryn walked by his side, listening to him explain where all the slaves had been reassigned. He confirmed that the *sale* had gone smoothly, without complication or suspicion.

After arriving back at the mansion, they continued to discuss what the Resistance was doing throughout the Empire. Maeryn had so many things that she wanted to ask and say, but she managed to follow her own advice and let him do most of the talking. In this way, conversation flowed freely into the evening. Aelia joined them for a short time before leaving to walk in the vineyard, her favorite place since their arrival.

The time passed quickly and, as the sun began to set in the west, their benevolent host called for a more elaborate supper than what had been planned. After a few hours of preparation, a feast of lamb and duck was laid out before them. Wine from his own vineyard flowed freely for his new guests. Maeryn couldn't think of the last time that she had enjoyed herself more. And the smile on Aelia's face made it all the more special.

As the evening activity slowed, the Leader rose from the table. "I'm afraid I will not be able to stay. I have to leave the city for a few days to attend to other matters."

Maeryn was visibly disappointed.

"But I must say that I haven't felt such joy in a long time. Maeryn, Aelia, thank you very much for your pleasant company."

"Will you come back?" Aelia asked.

"Of course... Until then, make yourselves comfortable. Consider this your home. If you wish to go into the city, you need only ask and it will be done. Oh yes! Maeryn, I understand that you had a beautiful garden in Bastul."

Maeryn wiped tears from her eyes. "Yes I did," she replied with a questioning smile.

"I have called for flowers and plants of every imaginable type. You will receive them tomorrow. I would very much like to see your talents, and also learn what makes you happy," he added. "That is...if you still enjoy such things."

"I do indeed," Maeryn breathed, hardly able to find the words.

"Splendid! I will return in a few days and will hopefully get to stay longer next time. Good evening."

And just like that, this gracious stranger exited the house and walked down the front steps to his awaiting carriage. Maeryn stood at the doorway and watched as the team of horses pulled the carriage up the road and out of sight.

Life and work aboard the merchant ship would have been hard for anyone, especially with a broken leg. But Kael found it to be a welcome break from the rigorous training at the monastery. Within the first weeks, the Captain realized that swabbing the decks wasn't the best use of Kael's time. Instead, he set him to the task of fishing, as well as other sailing duties. Kael welcomed the work as a time to do just as the Captain mentioned—to work with his hands and try to forget about all the things that muddled his thinking.

During his second week, Kael began waking early in the morning as he had done at the monastery. Intending to find a secluded spot to perform his morning exercises, he circled the ship, trying to avoid the few crew members that were manning the sails as the others slept below.

After a few minutes, he found himself at the bow of the ship, where the large crates blocked visibility of the prow and the last five feet of deck leading up to it, the perfect spot. But as Kael glanced around to verify his privacy, he noticed a man standing on top of the crates just above him. Kael stepped to the side to get a better view. Suddenly, a bolt of fear shot through his body and he froze where he stood.

Long, dark hair, flowing in the wind

Slanted eyes

His slow, steady movements were following a pattern that Kael knew all too well.

With his heart pounding in his chest, Kael moved aft. In his haste to retreat, he almost tripped over the Captain.

"Whoa there! Where you headin' in such a hurry?"

"Who is that?" Kael demanded, though careful not to raise his voice.

"Why don't you go introduce yourself?"

"No thanks," Kael replied.

"Kinda looks like the men who were lookin' for you."

Kael turned to look the Captain in the eye. "Is he?"

The Captain paused for a moment, studying Kael's face. "No," he finally answered.

"Well what's he doing here; does he work for you?"

"He's on my ship, ain't he?"

Kael didn't reply; he was still waiting for an answer to his first question.

"I keep him around for protection. That little guy's an animal when he wants to be. You wouldn't know it to look at him, but I've seen him take down guys twice his size. He earns his keep. And he's pretty handy to have around when you get in a tight spot."

The next day, Kael rose before dawn and went up to the prow of the ship. As expected, the dark-haired man stood on the crates, facing the bow and performing his exercises. Kael climbed up the last crate, just fore of the mainsail and watched from twenty feet away. It was fascinating. His motions were slightly different than Ukiru had instructed, but eerily similar. The difference was the lack of aggression in his body language, more peaceful. Though it was evident that he was capable of much more.

Kael sat down and rested, feeling a strange connection to this man, drawn to him and yet wary at the same time. He continued to watch for a few minutes longer and then began to feel uncomfortable, like he was listening in on someone else's conversation. The man never acknowledged Kael's presence, but Kael knew that he was intruding.

The following morning, Kael rose before the sun and made his way to the stern of the ship. The roof of the aft cabin was level and sturdy. Here he stood, unsteadily with the rocking of the waves and his splinted leg. He was no longer concerned with keeping his exercises private; the crew was used to the sight of the dark-haired man and all but ignored him.

Still unsure of the man's name, Kael tried to clear his mind and concentrate only on his own movements. Though the soreness was gone, he still had limited movement due to the splint on his leg. Nevertheless, he attempted the exercises that he had developed over the years at the monastery. Of course, he still remembered what Ukiru had taught them, for they all performed those exercises each morning. But alone in his room, he had developed his own in accordance with his own style of fighting. On rare occasions, he had allowed his methods to show during their afternoon training, much to the disappointment of their teacher. After being severely reprimanded, Kael had learned to pretend that such things didn't exist. Only after he had regained Ukiru's trust, did he take up his own methods once again, and only then in secret.

Other than the few rebellious occasions during combat training, Kael had no experience to prove the effectiveness of his methods. But the exercises he developed just seemed more natural. During periods of free time, he used to spend hours in the hot spring pool near the stables, practicing the movements. Submerged in water, he learned to feel how the water reacted, and compared his methods to those of Ukiru.

A yell broke his concentration. It was the dark-haired man who had climbed to the roof without detection. He barked another harsh phrase in his native tongue and took a few steps toward Kael. He was much younger than Kael first thought, close to his own age.

"You're interrupting," Kael replied.

The man looked stunned. "What are you doing?"

"I don't see how that's any of your business."

He took a few more steps toward Kael, growing more irate. "Who taught you to do that?"

"I taught myself," Kael replied simply. He was aware that this man expected fear as a reaction, but Kael wasn't the least bit intimidated.

"Liar," the man replied. "The ways of my people are sacred and forbidden to outsiders."

"These aren't the ways of your people."

"Because you have desecrated them, and made them into an abomination."

"If it bothers you, you should leave and give me the quiet respect that I have showed you these past days."

He rushed toward Kael, clearly displeased with Kael's responses.

Kael crouched in a defensive posture and brought his hands up, causing the man to stop and reconsider.

Then his leg shot up toward Kael's face with a surprising speed. Kael dodged to the side and caught the man's leg, using the momentum to pull him off balance. But Kael's own movements were stiff and limited because of the splint. As a result, they both fell to the roof. Kael rolled to his feet and spun around to face the man who was already on his feet and ready for another attack.

Kael waited, and waited. But nothing happened. The man backed up and stood from his crouching position. "Heal yourself. When you are well we will test our skills again."

"...no need," Kael replied. "I'm well enough to defeat you now!"

The man shook his head. "There is no honor in this. I will give you time." And with this statement, he turned and left.

"How long did it take you to heal?" Dacien asked, thoroughly intrigued with Kael's story.

"Another month or so."

"Then what happened?"

"I defeated him and gained his respect. After that we became the best of friends."

Dacien shook his head. "No, no, no! You can't just skip through it. What happened?" he repeated.

Captain Gryllus was not happy about the situation and the potential of having two injured crew members, but knew the importance of honor and respect among men. He finally gave in to their desire for confrontation one evening when sailing through shallow waters. He anchored the ship at sunset and excused the crew from their duties.

There was a buzz of tension about the boat. The rest of the crew wondered how crazy the new kid must be to face the resident warrior, who commanded everyone's respect. Kael understood what was happening. The pack leader, if they could be compared to animals, was threatened and responded with aggression. At the monastery, it was Soren, and he had never challenged that authority. But this felt different. He wasn't at the monastery any more; he was free. And he had promised himself, while swimming through miles of ocean, that he would never again allow himself to be dominated. His days of submission had passed. It wasn't that he wanted to be the pack leader, nor did he want to be a follower. He just wanted to be left alone. And shrinking from a fight was no way to mark your territory.

As the sun slipped below the horizon, the crew lit torches and gathered at a recently cleared section of the cargo deck, forming a loose circle around Kael and his opponent. The short man had refused to give his name. Now the two warriors stretched themselves, stripped down to just lightweight pants rolled at mid-calf. The Captain joined the crew as well, concerned for the safety of his men.

Kael, ready and willing, made eye contact with his opponent and gave him a nod. The man nodded back and the two turned to face each other.

The crew immediately went silent. The warm summer air was cooled slightly by a breeze. The crackle of torch flames and water lapping at the hull were the only sounds. Kael widened his stance and heard the sound of the deck creak beneath his feet.

His opponent jumped into action, throwing a front roundhouse kick followed immediately by a spinning back kick toward Kael's midsection. Kael retreated, blocking the kicks with his forearms. The man continued to advance with a variety of kicking attacks that covered the distance between them. Kael parried the attacks, keeping his opponent at a safe distance, studying his style and looking for an opportunity. But his technique was flawless. No over-extensions. No loss of balance. This man was truly an artist.

More kicks, followed by more blocks. Then Kael realized the man hadn't yet used his hands. Was it because they hadn't been close enough, or was it that his opponent was weak in this area and was purposely keeping Kael a kicking range? Kael assumed the latter, knowing that it would be painful if he was wrong.

The man spun a back kick and Kael rushed in, slipping inside the range of the kick, which glanced harmlessly off his hip. Driving his fist into the man's kidney, Kael quickly followed with an upward elbow to the face.

The man's head snapped backward with a spray of blood erupting from his nose, the blow knocking him back a few steps. Kael advanced to close the distance and take advantage of the situation. But a low kick to his bad leg cut his balance out from under him, followed by a quick jab that rattled his jaw.

Kael dropped to the deck and rolled to the side. The sound of advancing footsteps told him what his eyes couldn't. As soon as his feet came in contact with the deck, he pushed off and spun around with a kick to the ankles, but there was nothing to impact.

The man leapt over the kick and came down with an incredible force, driving his knuckles into Kael's face. Kael took the hit and pushed himself upward, burying his shoulder into the man's chest. He picked his opponent off the ground and slammed him to the deck, buying himself some time and distance.

The crew was amazed at the demonstration, never having witnessed such equally matched skill in all their lives.

Kael felt his awareness heighten and knew that his opponent's end was near.

The man was back on his feet with a look of determination in his eyes. He advanced quickly with a front kick.

Kael blocked the kick with his foot, then followed with a high snap-kick to the face. Just as his foot fell back to the deck, he followed with the opposite, landing a kick to the stomach. As the man doubled up, Kael followed with an upper cut to the face that sent him sprawling to his back.

"That's enough," yelled the Captain, stepping in between the men.

Kael already knew that it was over, and stood still, heaving in large breaths.

His opponent rose to his feet and stood to face Kael. With a quick bow, he acknowledged his defeat and turned to leave.

"Hey," Kael called, pushing past the Captain. "I'm Caleb," he said, extending his hand.

The man grasped Kael's hand in a firm hold and shook it. "My name is Matsuri, and I am honored to meet you."

16

Maeryn hadn't felt this happy in many years. She wasn't running from anything, or keeping any secrets. But most of all, she was safe. It was a feeling that she thought would never return. Once in her life, with Adair, she knew what is was like to be cared for and protected. And then there was Lemus. Ever since then, she had been trying to survive in one way or another.

Now she found herself sitting in the sunshine, her hands dirty with the rich, dark soil of the Orud foothills. All around her were flowers of every color and shape imaginable. Her new benefactor hadn't lied when he described them. Not just flowers, but trees and shrubs as well.

After inspecting and cataloguing what had been given to her, she asked the head servant where the garden was to be planted.

"My lord has given you free reign. You may choose the location."

Maeryn couldn't contain her smile. She began immediately to plan the arrangement and quickly determined the locations for the trees and shrubs at various points around the mansion. She saved just a few for the garden itself, but only to provide contrast to the flowers that would be the primary focus. After marking their locations in the dirt, the servants set to work digging holes.

By midmorning, she had outlined the structure of her flower garden between the vineyard and the cliffs leading to the ocean. The servants had already begun to unwrap the burlap from the root balls of each tree and had started to plant them in their respective holes.

Aelia had just completed organizing the flowers by type and color, when the head servant brought their morning tea.

"Would you care to take a break?"

"Of course," Maeryn replied.

Aelia ran over and accepted a steaming cup. "Thank you," she offered.

The man simply nodded and turned back toward the house.

As Maeryn sipped her tea, she marveled at how quickly things had changed from constant dread to happy simplicity. If she was tired, she could go to her room and nap. If she felt bored, she could take a walk in the vineyard or ride into the city. She could do whatever she wanted, but right now, she was focused. She put her arm around Aelia and gave her a quick squeeze, then set down her cup, ready to begin planting.

The higher elevations of the Anodkem Mountains were damp with melting snow. This, combined with the rocky terrain, made for slow passage. For several days, Kael and Dacien were forced to separate, the entire column riding single file through dense forests and over wide-spread rock slides where the ground shifted beneath them.

When they began to descend from the heights, their progress quickened and, once again, Kael joined Dacien at the head of the group. Kael's story-telling helped to pass the time and so, almost immediately, Dacien asked him to continue.

"Well," he began. "As I mentioned, Matsuri and I became close friends. We would rise early and perform our morning exercises together, though each in our own way. It was difficult for him at first, but eventually he came to accept it. The Captain was pleased to have two warriors aboard his ship; it gave him a certain confidence that helped immensely in his trading affairs. He had an extensive trading route that stretched across the northern edge of the Empire and west to the islands, then north and east through the various port cities of other countries. Finally, he would end up back in Orlek in the northeastern territory. The whole circle took two years; I stayed with him for almost three cycles.

> *"Caleb," Matsuri confessed. "I will be leaving soon."*
> *Kael wrinkled his eyebrows. "What do you mean?"*
> *"This is not my home. I have seen what I came for."*
> *Kael didn't understand and it must have showed on his face.*
> *His friend took a deep breath before explaining. "For many years, my people never left our fortress city. The young children would grow and take the place of those that had passed on to the next life. But years ago, one of our citizens committed a crime and then disappeared. Many of the youth saw this as proof of what they had been feeling for a long time, that our lives were too confined. After much debate, the elders passed a law that gave any male youth of twenty years, the opportunity to leave for a period of ten years. After living in the outside world, the young man was to return to our city and address the elders, giving his decision to either stay in the city for the remainder of his time, or to leave forever. They were confident that the wickedness and depravity of other peoples would be intolerable."*
> *"So it is time for you to return."*

"Yes," replied Matsuri.

"Were you the first to leave?"

"No. Three others left before me. I will not know their decisions until I return."

"What have you decided?" Kael asked.

"I have spent ten years away from my home. During this time, I have seen many things. I do not agree with the elders that the outside world is completely wicked. There are many bad people, and some good. There are things that my people need to learn and that I can teach them. So I have decided to return to my home and help my people live and carry on future generations. But there are some things that they need to change or they will not survive."

"It took me several days to come to the realization that Matsuri's decision troubled me. I was losing a great friend and I couldn't find a way to accept it. So I confronted him and told him just that."

"How did he respond," Dacien questioned.

"Better than I expected."

"This isn't about you," Matsuri objected. "What am I supposed to do?"

"Take me with you," Kael offered.

Matsuri didn't respond.

Kael couldn't tell if he was actually considering it, or if the idea was so preposterous that it didn't deserve a response. "You said yourself that things need to change. Well, this would be a big change."

"Hmm," Matsuri grumbled. "No outsider has ever set foot within the city walls. It is forbidden."

"Why? We have lived together for six years now. We're practically family."

Matsuri was silent for a moment. "You're absolutely right."

"I am?" Kael replied, stunned at his friend's response.

"Yes, though they will take some convincing." Matsuri paused, thinking through his decision. "Yes. It is a good idea," he concluded.

"We stayed another week, then bid farewell to the Captain and the rest of the crew. In our honor, they provided an elaborate dinner at one of our port cities. We ate and drank as much as we could, retelling stories of our time together. It lasted well into the following morning. Then we purchased two horses and some provisions and set out for Matsuri's fortress city."

"What was the port?"

Kael paused, growing uncomfortable. "I can't say; it was one of the conditions of being able to see Matsuri's home."

"Oh, I see," Dacien replied, somewhat disappointed. "Can you tell me what the fortress city is like?"

"Only that it sits high atop a mountain plateau with a stone wall and turrets around its perimeter. From the towers, one can see for many miles in all directions. Its location has been the source of much confrontation through the years, within its country. Much like Orud, it governs a narrow stretch of land that connects two larger landmasses. All land-based trade routes and military movements are forced to go through the area. There is also a great river that flows through this territory, making passage difficult. The river is what carved the land away to form the plateau. Because of this, the water splits into two paths and surrounds the mountain upon which the city sits. It is here that the water grows shallow and passable."

"Oh," Dacien interjected. "I see where this is going. So they taxed everyone for passage?"

"No," replied Kael. "In fact, Matsuri's people wanted only to live in peace. But this was difficult in that every clan and warlord had to pass through this area under the watchful eye of the city above them. This created many suspicions and rumors, such that the city was thought to be in the service of some clans, selling their intelligence information to certain clan leaders. This brought them into the middle of conflicts that they only wished to avoid. Then, one enterprising warlord, who sought to unite some of the clans and thereby secure his leadership over the entire country, knew that controlling this piece of land was crucial to his success. So he sent hundreds of soldiers to conquer the city, only to meet with defeat. But he was not easily deterred, so he sent thousands more and again, met defeat. This struggle lasted a few years and greatly angered the warlord because he couldn't afford to lose such men at a time of establishing his dominance, but he needed desperately to control the plateau and river passage."

"So he decided to try one last time. Knowing that he couldn't best them in combat, for all of the inhabitants were skilled warriors, he laid siege to the city and tried to starve them out. After a month without evidence of anyone trying to leave, he sent men to spy atop the walls. All but one were killed, and the remaining soldier informed him that they were completely self-sufficient, growing their own food within the city."

Dacien laughed at the situation. "I would like to have seen the warlord's face at that moment."

"As would I," Kael continued. "At this, the warlord knew he had been defeated, though not in the traditional sense. So he flew the white flag of peace and requested conference with the city leader. His request was granted, and the two met at the base of the mountain, each with their own guards ready to fight to the death. The city leader hadn't given his title or name, so the warlord wasn't sure how to properly address him, or if this was in fact the leader at all. Nevertheless, he told the man that the warriors of the fortress city were superior and that he would offer them peace in return for his soldiers to train under these extraordinary men. Thinking that this was a trap, the city leader denied the offer, stating that their ways were sacred and not to be shared with outsiders, and though they desired peace, they were willing to endure the alternative to protect their ways."

"Oh," Dacien interrupted. "So that's why Matsuri was so upset with you."

"Exactly," Kael continued. "Their ways held a high price. Anyway, the warlord then offered to pay heavily for their knowledge of passage through the area. Again, the request was denied. Finally, at his wit's end, the warlord stated that he would pay heavily if only the city leader would appoint men to be the warlord's personal guards. Before the man could answer, the warlord stated that these men would be allowed into areas and be privy to knowledge that few were allowed. Seeing that this warlord was determined and likely to become the king, the city leader liked this arrangement as it would place his people in a position of power without compromising their ways or lifestyle. So he agreed."

"Wow," Dacien exclaimed. "...to be so fortunate that a future king would grovel at your feet. Those warriors must have been extraordinary."

"Indeed," Kael confirmed. "I cannot tell you of the layout or any details of the city or its internal workings, but I can say that it caused quite a commotion when I entered the city with Matsuri."

"Wait," interrupted Dacien. "Before you get to that, I have a question."

"Please," Kael said with an upturned hand.

"If their ways were so sacred, how is it that you came to know them? Was your instructor affiliated with these people? What was his name?"

"Ukiru," Kael replied. "Yes I believe he was, though I never received definite confirmation. You see, I haven't ever told my story to anyone except you. So I didn't discuss the matter during my stay at the fortress city. Instead, I came to suspect the same as you, and looked for hints of confirmation. The look of these people, their features, how they dressed and carried themselves were all very similar to Ukiru. But the most interesting observation was the story of a dissenter, a criminal."

"From the time of his childhood, one man seemed opposed to the traditions of his people. He escaped from the city as a young man. From time to time, they heard rumors of his whereabouts. From what they could glean, the man moved slowly through the country, making money from his ability to fight in staged matches. He was noticed and hired by a particularly brutal warlord and became the Captain of his forces. They were unsure of the details, but apparently something went wrong and they learned that the warlord had been assassinated and the young man was nowhere to be found. There were two possible conclusions to this rumor. One could say that this young man killed his former employer and fled the country. The other possibility is that someone else had assassinated the warlord, and because of the young man's failure to protect his employer, he was executed."

"And you believe the former," Dacien concluded.

"Yes," Kael confirmed.

"Very interesting," Dacien stated, seemingly satisfied. "So what did they do when you showed up with Matsuri?"

Kael looked at the sun declining toward the western horizon. "Perhaps that's a better story for tomorrow."

Dacien looked ahead and realized that he had been completely engrossed in the story. "Yes," he replied. "Let's find a place to make camp."

17

Maeryn was sitting on the covered porch, looking southeasterly at the bay, with her garden filling her peripheral vision on her left. The flowers were a nice addition to this beautiful property and they made her feel more at home. Footsteps to her right startled her. She turned her head and saw the Resistance leader standing at the corner of the house where the porch wrapped around toward the entrance.

"I'm sorry. I didn't mean to startle you. You seemed lost in your thoughts."

"Oh, that's quite all right. I was," she replied, standing and walking over to him. "I come out here to clear my mind. It really is magnificent." Her hand swept through the air, indicating the view of the ocean.

"I prefer the view in that direction," he stated, pointing toward the flower garden.

Maeryn followed his line of sight to see what he meant. "Oh?" she blushed, realizing what he was saying.

"It looks beautiful and complements the surroundings."

"Thank you," Maeryn replied. "It is easy when you have so many choices."

"Nonsense," he dismissed. "Few people have your talents, no matter how much they are given."

Maeryn was quiet, never quite sure what to do with the man's compliments, which were never in short supply. She was about to reply when the man began speaking; they both interrupted each other. "Sorry," Maeryn apologized, deferring to him.

"I was just going to suggest that we take a walk."

Maeryn agreed and as they descended the steps toward the vineyard, he reached for Maeryn's hand. She let him take it, and instantly, she felt her senses tingle. At the back of her mind, a question was begging for an answer, something that needed to be answered before she could completely open herself up. But for now, she pushed it aside and decided to enjoy the moment.

With all the time Kael and Dacien spent together, the rest of the group had fallen into silence, every man to his own thoughts. Always mindful of the critical social dynamics, Dacien took the opportunity at the evening meal to try and bring the group together. After they had pitched their tents and cooked a simple soup, they sat down by the campfire to eat.

"We have made very good progress and should reach Orud in just a few weeks."

This met with murmurs of response, but nothing worthy of a conversation.

"Have you ever been to Orud?" Kael asked, sensing Dacien's intentions and trying to help the situation.

"Yes, once."

"What is it like?" chimed in another soldier.

Dacien smiled, seeing their efforts begin to slowly take effect. "It's magnificent. All of the streets are paved. Lamp posts line the streets so that at night, the whole city glows with life. From spring to fall, flowers bloom everywhere you look."

"Did you have a favorite place within the city," another asked.

"Well, I spent a few days in the eastern bay area on an errand for the city of Bastul. That was back when I was messenger. It was difficult to stay out of trouble," he admitted.

The men around the fire smiled with mischievous grins.

"The night life is quite intoxicating. I ended up spending the majority of my time drinking with sailors and fishermen...a good bunch. I ate well and lived like one of the High Council. But when my errand was accomplished, it was nice to get back home to Bastul. One could get lost in Orud. There is something more satisfying about a quite peaceable life."

The men raised their bowls to Dacien's words and continued eating.

"I imagine you all miss your city as well?"

Nods of affirmation could be seen all around. "None of us have been this far from Leoran before," one man stated.

"Well," Dacien replied. "It is for a good purpose. Be thankful that your home still exits. Mine is destroyed and I don't know if the Emperor will ever support such a costly rebuilding. But you men...your home stands proud. And you travel to the capital city to support the defense of this Empire. Your mission is important and when it is accomplished, you will return to your families and friends."

"Thank you, Sir," one man replied. "If you don't mind, I'm going to try to get some sleep."

"...of course. We all should," Dacien said as he rose to his feet. "Good evening."

"Good evening," came several echoes as the group dispersed.

The next day, travel resumed as usual, with Kael and Dacien in the front. For the first few hours, conversation was difficult as they moved over terrain that alternated between rocky and sandy, with the occasional forest to navigate. Just before midday, they began climbing into yet another mountain pass where the land was more stable.

"So how was your reception at the fortress city?" Dacien asked finally.

"Uncomfortable."

"I can imagine."

"I've never felt so out of place in my life. Matsuri led me right up to the city gates. We were met before we got within a hundred feet. Matsuri began to speak rapidly with the guards. I couldn't tell if it was the just the language, but every word sounded harsh and intense. Finally, after much negotiating, we were allowed in. They eyed me suspiciously the whole time."

Dacien laughed. "I can picture you in that moment."

"Well it wasn't funny at the time. I had the feeling that I could end up defending myself against a hundred angry men at a moment's notice. But that never came to pass. They were cautious, but respectful."

"We traveled through the city to Matsuri's home, as the custom was to first seek out one's father. It was the father who was responsible for delivering the child's message to the elders. I wish I could describe the city to you, but it is forbidden. It is the most beautiful and peaceful place I have ever seen."

"What did Matsuri's father think of you?"

Kael shook his head. "At first, not much. He was angry with Matsuri. They spoke for a long time. In the end, I think Matsuri lied to him. From what I could gather, he convinced his father that it was better for someone like me, who had somehow managed to learn their ways, to be within the city and not out spreading their secrets, or something to that effect. So in the end, they came to accept me. But not easily. Once Matsuri confessed his defeat in our fight, everyone in the city wanted to fight me, as a way of restoring their honor. I wanted nothing to do with it."

"They wouldn't accept that, would they?" Dacien pried.

"No. In fact, I suffered many beatings trying to keep from fighting Matsuri's people. But in the end, I decided that the quickest way to reach an understanding with these people was to fight their best warrior."

"Did you lose?" Dacien asked.

"I wanted to," Kael replied honestly. "I was trying really hard to stay as unnoticed as possible."

"But..." Dacien prodded.

"But I never lose," Kael replied flatly. It wasn't conceit or pride, it was a fact, and Dacien seemed to accept it as such.

"Anyway, things were different after that. They seemed to accept me as one of their own."

"Oh, come on," exclaimed Dacien. "You can't just leave it at that. Tell me what happened."

"No," Kael insisted.   "I am not trying to glorify myself.   We've experienced battle together and that should be enough. I am simply trying to recount my life, so that you will know that I have nothing to hide, that you can trust me."

Dacien slowed his horse. "I do trust you."

"No you don't," Kael contended. "You've always been suspicious of me. That was the issue in Leoran, though you wouldn't ever say it."

Dacien stared into Kael's eyes and finally looked away, as though someone had just spilled his secret. "I'm sorry I interrupted.   Please continue."

The lack of Dacien's denial told Kael that he had guessed right. He always tried hard to read people, but it wasn't one of his strengths. But in this case, he was right. "Altogether, I spent four years there...three of which were the best years of my life."

"Why only three," Dacien asked tentatively.

"Well...it all started when I fell in love with a girl."

Dacien's eyebrows shot up and he whistled a quick and simple melody.

"Yeah," Kael replied. "At the monastery we were constantly told that women were a powerful distraction, capable of beguiling a man that would otherwise have been impervious."

Dacien tilted his head. The look on his face said that he agreed.

"In all my years at the monastery, I never met or talked to a girl. Then, aboard the merchant vessel, we were surrounded by women at every port. But all they wanted was money. They would laugh and pretend to like you, but there was nothing real about it."

"Then I met Suriku and everything changed.   She was completely different. She was innocent and shy at first. But I was patient. Eventually, she too came to be comfortable around me. I tried hard to learn her language so that I could talk to her. Over the next few years, we grew very close and spent much time together."

"But when the elders saw that it was more than a friendship, they confronted us and refused to let use see each other any more. Apparently, the elders had grown more and more interested in pleasing their newly appointed King. If there was such a thing as royalty in the fortress city, Suriku's family was it. Her father was one of the elders and was descended from a long lineage of elders. They had been trying for years to arrange a marriage between the King and their princess, Suriku."

"Wow. You sure have good taste," Dacien interjected.

"Yes I do," Kael confirmed. "So my last year at the fortress city was miserable. I couldn't even see her. The situation angered Matsuri to no end. It was precisely the kind of thing that he hated about his people, the kind of thing he wanted to change. Arranged marriages and vying for the King's good will, these were evils that he believed his people could overcome. Later that fall, the King came to collect on what had been promised to him. The elders were pleased, but Suriku couldn't stop crying. Matsuri was furious and couldn't stand the situation. It burned inside him."

"The King took Suriku with him and prepared to leave the city, but Matsuri chased after him." Kael paused, the emotional pain too deep for words. It had been two years, and still felt as though it happened yesterday.

Dacien saw that this part of his past was difficult. He waited patiently.

When Kael continued, his words were softer and quieter. "He tried valiantly and slew five men, but there were just too many. The King's men ran him through with spears. The King immediately protested to the elders, wanting to know the meaning of Matsuri's actions. It was in this moment that the elders chose the fate of their people. They actually apologized to the King for this outrage!"

"I ran to Matsuri, but he was already dead. Then I heard yelling and realized what I had done. The King was arguing with elders, stating that they pretended to keep their ways sacred. Yet they allowed a white man inside of their city. He then promised to return in the spring to allow his new bride to see her family, and threatened to bring his armies with him if I wasn't exiled. The elders quickly apologized and promised that it would be as he asked."

"I sat in the dirt, with Matsuri's body in my hands, and watched the woman I loved be taken away by the King. After the funeral, the elders wanted me to leave immediately. I wasn't in much of a mood to argue. Matsuri was the reason I had come, and he was dead. Suriku was the reason I wanted to stay, and she had been promised to another man. So I packed my belongings to leave that night."

"As I was leaving, an old man called me over to his front door. He was a master blade smith and former elder that I had become friends with over the years. He invited me into his house for a moment, wishing to say goodbye. He was a man of great wisdom and I had come to enjoy our conversations. He told me that the elders no longer concerned themselves with the old ways and had corrupted themselves with the King. He apologized to me and stated that Matsuri was a true warrior and would have been greatly respected if he had been born in a previous generation. Then he gave me a gift, a ceremonial sword that had been in his family for many generations. It was held in a wooden case, wrapped tightly with silk fabric. I didn't understand, but he just patted me on the shoulder and said that he knew I hadn't tried my hardest when fighting their best warrior. 'You wanted him to feel good about himself,' he said. I protested, but he insisted that he had never seen such a warrior in all his life. 'This sword has great sentimental value and this city is no longer a place of honor,' he said. 'As long as you carry it, I know that my ancestors will be pleased.'"

Dacien pointed to Kael's saddle. "Isn't that the one you used against the Syvak warlord?"

"Yeah," Kael replied hesitantly. "I ruined it in the process. It was clearly not made for combat, but I had no other option."

"Somehow I think the old man would be pleased to know that his old relic had drawn blood."

"Yeah," Kael smiled. "I suppose you're right."

Dacien grinned. "I know a skilled bladesmith in Orud, the best in the Empire. I'm sure he can fix whatever damage was done."

Kael nodded silently.

"So then you left the city?"

"Yes. I wandered for a while, then made my way to a port city. I thought I would try to find another merchant ship. And I eventually did, but it wasn't the same as when I sailed with Matsuri and the Captain. I spent the next two years traveling. It was lonely, but I saw many amazing things, places that have never been put on any map. Eventually, I began to feel like something was terribly wrong. I had no place to call home and no friends. I tried many things to keep from feeling empty, but nothing worked. It was then that I made up my mind to return to Bastul. I don't know why I hadn't thought of returning to see my mother before this point. She had, most likely, agonized over my disappearance. But the thought hadn't occurred to me until then. Lemus was no longer a concern for me. I thought briefly about what the consequences of my return would be, but I knew there was nothing he could do to me that I couldn't prevent. And so I made my way back to my home."

"I set sail from Nijambu in the south. The Captain misjudged his bearings and we didn't sight land until we were well north of Bastul. He didn't think I was paying enough for him to turn around, so I purchased a horse and left the ship with more than two weeks of travel between me and Bastul, while the Captain continued on to Orud."

"Then I made my way south along the eastern coast, where I saw the Syvak ships leaving the river and entering the ocean. And I guess you know the rest of the story from there."

Dacien nodded and was silent for a few moments, searching for words. "You have seen many things my friend. Amazing and unfortunate things."

"Now all I want is to have somewhere to call home. But it seems even that is being taken away."

"That's what we've fought for, Kael. And that's why we go to Orud. It won't be taken away, not while men like us are willing to fight. You have a gift, and now a worthy cause to put it to use."

Kael smiled in return.

18

Kael, Dacien, and their traveling companions, descended from the Anodkem Mountains to see the plains of Orud stretched out before them to the north. It was fertile land with crops as far as the eye could see. It was nice to see signs of civilization as they picked up a paved road and followed it toward Orud. As they traveled, citizens waved to them from the fields as they planted their crops. As with most Orudan cities, the surrounding territories were typically used to sustain the city itself with the base essentials, various grain crops and livestock, and Orud was no different. In fact, it was the model for all other cities to follow.

The city sat on a narrow stretch of land that ran north and south. To the east and west were massive bay areas supporting the fishing industry, as well as a multitude of trade vessels. With one port to the east and one to the west, Orud was naturally positioned to be the trade center of the region.

Circular in shape, the city walls stretched for miles. Dacien led them through the outskirts and up to the city walls, where the guards questioned them about the nature of their travel. Once past the gate, the surroundings immediately took on an urban feel, much like Leoran. And just as that city had a relationship with the water, so to did Orud. A wide channel ran through the middle of the city and connected the east and the west ports. It was an ingenious solution to the logistics of trade, which allowed Orud to heavily tax merchant vessels for a short journey through the city to the opposite bay, when it would have taken months to sail around the northern and southern landmasses that comprised the Orud Empire. The city's position allowed this concept to be applied to land as well, with the main thoroughfare running through the city's northern and southern gates. Kael marveled at how the design of everything within and without the city, only reinforced its dominance and people's reliance on it.

By mid afternoon, the group had checked in with the city officials and been given a place to stay, as they had been expected. Kael settled in quickly to his new temporary residence, enjoying the comforts that the city had to offer. For most of the men, a bath was the first priority. The group met up together again in the evening for a hot meal and discussed their forthcoming responsibilities.

"Tomorrow, at midday, I will go before the Emperor and the High Council, to explain our struggles against the Syvak and share our experiences with the Generals of the other regions. None of you are permitted to attend, and it's just as well; it's going to be an uncomfortable process that will take the remainder of the day."

"What are you going to say to them?" asked one of the soldiers.

Dacien thought for a moment. "I've never done this sort of thing before. I'll start by listening, then I'll tell them of the Syvak's attempt at invasion. I'll ask for support to rebuild the cities and increased aid to scout and protect the southern territory. The Emperor has traditionally focused most of his efforts on the constant struggles on the northeastern border, neglecting the southern territory. But with these recent developments, Orud is at greater risk from an attack based out of our territory. The cities are sparse and there are more areas to hide an invading force."

Another man, who had been looking more and more uncomfortable with himself, finally said what was on his mind. "I mean no disrespect, my lord, but isn't it foolish to gather all the Generals in one place at a time like this."

Dacien nodded gravely. "Indeed, but it is not my decision. I must obey the summons despite my reservations." After a few moments of silence, Dacien rose and announced that he would retire for the evening. "Make sure that you are all reachable tomorrow in case you are called into the council."

And with that, the group dispersed.

Maeryn answered the knock at the door and opened it to find the head servant.

"My lady, your presence is required in the master's chambers."

"Oh?" Maeryn questioned, not liking the sound of his statement.

"Please come with me."

Maeryn followed, nervous about what would take place. She and her benefactor had been spending increasing amounts of time together. And it was clear that there were mutual romantic feelings between them. But they hadn't acted on those feelings, apart from holding each others' hand. She wasn't sure about the depth of her own feelings just yet, but a sickening feeling in her stomach told her that her precious world was about to come to an end.

This is it, Maeryn. Now he wants to collect on all that you are indebted to him for. I should have known better!

The servant opened the door to the master's chambers. And there in the middle of the room, stood the man who had treated her so kindly. His clothing had been removed so that he was bare down to the waist. But something was out of place. Another servant was there, as well; scarlet clothing draped over his arm.

Maeryn walked into the room and jumped slightly as the door was shut behind her.

"Thank you for coming."

Maeryn nodded, still trying to make sense of the situation.

The servant unfurled a scarlet tunic and draped it over his master's shoulders.

As he fastened it at the waist with a braided, gold belt, Maeryn couldn't help but ask. "What is this? What is going on here?"

"I am answering a summons. The Southern General arrived yesterday and the High Council convenes in a few hours," the master replied calmly.

"I don't understand," Maeryn replied.

The tall man waived his servant away and turned to look Maeryn in the eyes. His own were a piercing blue, which contrasted with his dark hair. He was quite handsome, with an authoritative look about him. Then, the corners of his eyes relaxed.

"That is why I asked for you. My name is Magnus Calidon. I am General of the Northern Territory of the Orudan Empire. I am leaving to the city to answer a summons by the Emperor, who has called the High Council and all of the Generals to discuss matters of grave importance to the safety of the Empire."

The General spoke in short, concise statements. Even so, Maeryn was speechless. Her mind raced to understand and comprehend what he had just said. After a moment of silence, she spoke.

"...but...you're the Resistance Leader."

He smiled. "Yes I am."

Maeryn paused again looking at the floor. "But how is that possible?"

"Maeryn, please sit down." He took her by the arm and led her to a chair near an open balcony. Once she was comfortable, he continued. "I hope you appreciate the weight of what I am confessing to you. Only a select few know about the double life that I lead. I could be executed for what I am doing, and yet I am telling you, not out of necessity, but out of choice. And I hope that it conveys the depth of what I feel for you."

"But what are you doing?" she asked, trying to look past the admission of his feelings to his true intentions.

He thought carefully. "I have watched the Empire build itself through detestable means. You are well aware that abolition of the slave trade is the focus of the Resistance efforts. Yet the Empire's crimes go even farther than this. They tax their own citizens to death just to maintain their extravagant lifestyle here at the capital."

Maeryn glanced around the room and started to speak.

"I know that statement seems hypocritical," he interrupted. "But this mansion is the fruit of my own labors, not the taxation of the working class. I am a wealthy land owner, and have done well for myself through my vineyards and other holdings. And because of this, I am keenly aware of the burden that the Empire places on its citizens."

"Oh," Maeryn muttered, her argument disappearing quickly.

"There are many things I could criticize about the Empire, but I have chosen to implement change from within. In the Northern Territory, I have forbidden the purchase of any additional slaves. Those that are within my borders are the property of citizens, and I can't do anything about that. But I have been successful in stopping the continuance of this evil, and it has had a significant impact on the slave trade industry."

"How do you hope to accomplish such an enormous task?"

Magnus smiled. "I know it seems enormous, but it isn't impossible. Look at what you accomplished in Bastul. What you have done, what we have done together, it has made a powerful statement. One that the Emperor can't ignore for much longer."

Maeryn breathed heavily. "Why are you telling me this?"

"Because I need your help. I want you by my side."

Maeryn turned away, feeling uncomfortable about her own indecision in the face of this man's open declaration of his feelings. "I'm flattered," she said finally. "I appreciate all of the kindness that you have shown to us."

"But?" he prodded, waiting for a few seconds. "I have been dangerously honest with you. I would expect the same courtesy."

"Alright," Maeryn exhaled. "Since I was a child, the quality of my life has been dictated by the man who takes care of me. With my first husband, my life was a joy because he was a good man. Then I was forced to marry Lemus and my life became a living hell."

Tears flowed freely now from Maeryn's face as she laid out her feelings.

"He was a cruel man and took everything of value away from me. Then I escaped, and somewhere in the process, I settled into this new life where I was in charge. And now I meet you, and you show me kindness that I haven't seen in many years."

Maeryn stopped to wipe the tears from her eyes.

"I am grateful to you, but I am not going to give up my freedom and have my life dictated by another man just because he is rich and kind."

Magnus turned away and looked at the ground.

Maeryn felt a twinge of regret at her words, but after a moment's consideration, she decided that it was exactly how she felt. "You asked for honesty."

"You're right, I did," he replied. "That's what I like about you. You are a strong woman who gives straight answers. It is something that is becoming rare in my experience. Everyone is interested is saying just the right thing to keep me happy."

After a few seconds of silence, Magnus continued, his voice much quieter.

"Maeryn, I don't want to force anything on you. I just want to have you with me. I will accept whatever terms you offer."

Maeryn nodded blankly, unsure of how to respond.

"Just think about it. I'll be gone until tomorrow, but I don't need an answer right away. Take all the time you need."

19

Kael left word with the servants at the guest quarters of the Emperor's palace. Dacien had given him the whereabouts of the bladesmith that operated in the blacksmith district. Opting to walk instead of taking a carriage, he was better able to experience the feel of the city. The Palace sat at the center of the city with roads extending outward like spokes from a wheel. Each pie-shaped segment of the city contained a different set of related industries, beginning with the more superficial at the center and ending with the more practical at the city walls.

Kael moved at a leisurely pace down one of the main avenues between the blacksmith and masonry districts. There was a great deal of traffic, both pedestrian and horse-drawn carts. Most were of the working class wearing functional clothing stained from their labor. At one point, a contingent of soldiers marched through in formation toward the capital. Kael stepped aside and let them pass, observing the unity of their movements. They were a tightly organized and disciplined group of soldiers, and presented a formidable appearance.

About a mile from the barrier wall that ran around the perimeter of the city, Kael turned right down a narrow alley. Counting eight storefronts, he stopped in front of a stone building with a small wooden door and an engraved metal sign indicating that he had found what he sought. Immediately to his left was a larger set of double doors, large enough to fit two carts sided by side. Kael guessed that this was a shipping and receiving point and briefly wondered if his sword was too small a task for this operation.

He knocked and waited, but no answer came. Then, he lifted the latch and entered the door, which opened to a small waiting room with chairs. At the back wall, a window looked through to the shop where bright flashes of fire cast orange light in all directions, reflecting off numerous metal surfaces. Kael walked to the window and peered into the shop just as a door to his left opened. He leaned back from the window and turned to see a short man covered in black soot and wearing an apron.

"Can I help you?"

Kael gave him the name of the man Dacien had suggested.

"Wait here," he replied.

Kael waited, but grew impatient after a few minutes. He had just turned back to the window when the door opened again.

"Yeah, what can I do for you?"

This man was tall and thin, with several days of stubble on his face. Like the other man, he was wearing a leather apron and was covered in soot.

"My name is Caleb. I was sent by Dacien Gallus of Bastul; he says you are a talented bladesmith."

"Oh, he does, does he?"

Kael started to reply, but the man kept on talking.

"I haven't seen him in years. Last I knew he was hoping to make Captain. So how's he doing?"

Kael waited for a few seconds, until he was sure he wouldn't be interrupted. "He's doing very well. In fact, he's now General of the Southern Territory."

"Oh?" the man questioned. "How'd that happen?"

"Well, we've had some trouble in the south. A good man can move quickly through the ranks in times of war."

"Yeah, I heard about that. I didn't realize that was Dacien."

Kael nodded, wondering how word had spread so quickly when they had just arrived in Orud.

"So that means you must be the one who killed the barbarian leader?"

Kael lifted his eyebrows. "You heard about that, too?"

"I hear lots of things," he said. "But then again, everyone's heard that."

"Everyone, huh?" Kael mumbled.

"Everyone," the man repeated. "So what can I do for you? Any friend of Dacien's is a friend of mine."

Kael took the bundle from under his arm and laid it on a nearby table. Untying the silk threads, he opened the wooden case and pulled out a long object that was wrapped in cloth.

The man stepped forward with a smile on his face.

Kael pulled the cloth away to reveal the ceremonial sword from the fortress city. Holding it gingerly, he handed it to the man who accepted it carefully.

"Dacien knows what a sucker I am for this type of thing. ...started out making swords and spearheads by myself, but then I found that other things were more needed. ...like fasteners for boats, and door hinges. I had to hire a crew to keep up. But this...this is my passion."

The man's words warmed Kael's heart, for he spoke as one who loved what he did. And in Kael's experience, that quality was usually reserved for only the best. He instantly knew that this precious heirloom was in good hands.

"What happened to it?" he asked.

"Well," Kael explained. "It's really only a ceremonial sword, but I found myself in a tight spot and needed to defend myself."

The man looked up from the sword in his careful hands. "This is it, isn't it? This is the sword that killed the barbarian."

"Not exactly," Kael corrected.

The man looked back to the object in his hands, inspecting it. He cocked his head when he inspected the blade, fingering the curled flakes of metal, peeling back from the edge of the blade. "What's this?"

Kael leaned closer. "I think it's glass, covered with metal. It's not a real blade, which is why it shouldn't have left its case."

"That's unusual," the man stated. "It would have been easier to just make the center out of a cheap metal than to use glass. The man that crafted this was a master bladesmith, even if it's useless as a weapon."

"The man that gave it to me was indeed a master bladesmith, but this sword was crafted even before his time. I know it's strange, but I would appreciate it if you could just repair it as best you can. Cover up the glass and make it look as though it wasn't used to chop down a tree."

"I'll do the best I can, but metal doesn't stick to glass. This is going to be difficult."

"That's why I came to you; Dacien said you're the best in the Empire."

"Did he now?" he asked skeptically. "Well you sure know how to get a man to do something," he said with a smile. "I'll do the best I can, but I'm kind of busy and I'm not sure when I will be able to get to it."

"That's no problem," Kael replied. "What do I owe you?"

The man waived his hand. "...depends on how much time it takes. I'll let you know when I'm finished."

"...fair enough."

"Where do I find you when I'm done?"

Kael thumbed toward the north. "I'm staying at the Imperial Palace with Dacien. Just send a message to the guards and they'll find me."

The man turned back toward the door to the shop. "Say hello for me, and tell him to bring his lazy self down here when he gets a chance."

Kael smiled and waved as he left the building.

Dacien fidgeted as he waited to be announced at his entrance to the Court of the High Council. His stomach was tied in knots and he couldn't believe how quickly this had all happened. One day, he was leading troops through exercises in Bastul; the next, he was waiting to go before the most powerful men in the Empire.

"Your majesty," his escort announced. "...Generals...members of the Imperial Council, I present to you Dacien Gallus, General of the Southern Territory of the Orudan Empire." The man followed his loud proclamation with confident strides down the center aisle of nearly empty seats.

Dacien followed, observing that this meeting was not open to other citizens, which would explain the empty seating and eerily silent, echoing feeling of the large stone room. As with most places in this city, pillars and statues adorned the walls, while painted ceilings told the ancient stories that all citizens learned at an early age.

Dacien walked between the semi-circle of council members and turned left, ascending a few stairs to take his seat beside the Commander of the Northern Naval Fleet. Once seated, he took note of his surroundings and the important group that he was now part of. There were six non-military members of the High Council sitting opposite from him, each representing a major industry within the Empire. On his side of the room were the two naval Commanders making up the flanks of the opposite side of the semi-circle. He and the General of the Eastern Territory were positioned just inside of that, followed by the Northern General completing the circle. The Emperor sat behind the Northern General, but his throne was seated higher than the rest, such that he could see all in attendance. Dacien's escort bowed low and left the council, shutting the massive double doors behind him. The booming sound made Dacien swallow the lump of apprehension that had lodged itself in his throat.

"My esteemed guests," the Emperor began. "Thank you all for joining me at this most troubled hour. I have asked you to come so that we may discuss the state of the Empire. I am troubled by the reports that I am receiving from all the territories. It seems that some ancient enemies have renewed strength as of late, and are doubling their efforts against our beloved home. I would now like to open this discussion to hear your thoughts."

"Emperor, council members, and Generals," came the strong voice from the Northern General to Dacien's left. "Thank you for your hospitality in welcoming us here today. I must say, however, that this is a dangerous time to call together the people in this room. Indeed, as the Emperor has stated, our enemies have doubled their efforts. And you have long been familiar with our struggles in the North and East," he stated, inclining his head to the young General from the East.

It was common knowledge that the Northern and Eastern territories shared a common threat in the Korgs, another barbarian people who had recently sacked a city within Empire boundaries.

"The Korgs have breached the border and taken the city of Orlek. And while I'm honored to be here, our soldiers are without their Generals."

Several murmured their agreement. Dacien heartily agreed with him, but decided to hold his tongue until he got better acquainted with his new responsibilities.

"General," the Emperor replied. "I understand your concern, but a unified Empire is the best defense against our enemies. You all know the process. We will be here for the better part of a week, and if the council decides that it is appropriate, you will return to your homes. But you will not leave without hearing the concerns of those in other regions. I'll not have each territory working to its own ends; we must determine a unified solution."

The "process" to which the Emperor referred was his way of leading without making any decisions. Dacien had heard many rumors from his superiors through the years that the Emperor was always greatly concerned with pleasing the council, and didn't seem to have an original idea in his entire being. But his pleasing of the council is what got him to the position he now held. This meeting was to last four days, the first of which was to decide on a clear statement of the problem, the second to discuss possible solutions, and the last two days to turn the solution into a well conceived plan. Dacien had to admit that it was a good process, but the implementation had rarely been wise. Sighing at the thought of being in this room for days, Dacien tried to clear his head and make the best of it.

If they think that the taking of one northern city is cause for concern, they need to hear what I've experienced!

Kael quickly ate his roast lamb, thoroughly enjoying his stay in Orud. The food was extravagant, and the wine was superior to anything he'd ever tasted. He had already cleared his plate before the others were half-through, sitting back in his chair and enjoying the warm feeling that was settling over him.

"It was difficult to say the least," Dacien explained. "The Emperor seemed to be opposed to everything the Northern General had to say. Of course, he disagreed in the most polite way possible."

It was the evening of their third day in Orud, and Dacien, Kael, and the others from Leoran were seated at their evening meal. Dacien was recounting the day's events in detail. And though he probably wasn't supposed to talk with such ease, Kael and the others were having fun.

"And most of the other council members were useless. There is one young man, influential despite his age. I don't know what industry he supports, but he is in alignment with the Northern General. One can observe the lines of separation as if they were drawn on the floor; in one group, the Emperor and the two naval Commanders, along with a handful of the council members; in the other, the Generals from the North and East, along with a majority of the council led by the young man."

"And what side are you on?" Kael asked.

Dacien grinned. "I suppose I agree with the General from the North. His answers make sense, whereas the Emperor..." Dacien trailed off, not wanting to speak poorly of his superior. But he was too honest a man to stifle his intuition.

"I've heard it said that the Empire has grown fat and lazy, that we no longer have the resolution of past generations. That's how I feel when I listen to the Emperor." After a long pause, Dacien spoke again. "Please excuse me; I have a long day tomorrow and I must turn in early."

"These meetings will be the death of you," commented one soldier.

"I believe you are correct," Dacien replied. "Good evening."

In the cool of the evening, Kael walked across the courtyard of the Imperial Palace, heading for his room. Walking at a leisurely pace, he took in his surroundings. The massive trees and fountains of water brought Dacien's words to his mind.

...the Empire has grown fat and lazy...

"Good evening, gentlemen," Kael greeted the guards as he approached the guest quarters.

"My lord, you have a message."

"Is it urgent?"

"No, my lord. It was the blacksmith; he wanted to see you. He was excited, but it wasn't an emergency."

"How long ago?"

Perhaps an hour," the guard replied.

Kael looked up at the dark sky, dotted with stars. The wine had made him sleepy and he considered waiting until morning.

"...excited?" he asked.

"Yes, my lord," the man confirmed.

"Very well," Kael mumbled to himself. "Now I'm curious."

"Do you require an escort, my lord?"

"No thank you," Kael protested, uncomfortable with being called a lord. He really wasn't a landowner, though the guard's assumption wasn't misplaced. Typically, one didn't travel with a general without being a man of considerable status himself. The thought brought a smile to Kael's face.

So you're a man of status now? Very impressive!

It took much longer to reach the blacksmith's shop at night. Most of the shops were locked up, and the alleyway was completely dark, except for a faint orange light coming from a crack in the door.

Kael knocked.

A small window—only big enough for a pair of eyes—opened at the center of the door.

"...you left me a message?" Kael asked quietly.

The door quickly opened and the blacksmith ushered him inside. The man's eyes were red and he looked as if he hadn't slept in a while.

"I suppose it's going to be expensive?" Kael asked.

"No, no," the man protested. "There's no charge."

Kael was surprised, and about to ask for clarification, when the man turned and walked through the door into the shop. Kael followed, feeling the sense of excitement that the guard described.

"Do you want to tell me what's going on?"

The man shook his hand dismissively. "You have to see it."

Kael walked quickly after the man, taking note of the furnaces and waist-high anvils placed around the perimeter of the room. Each furnace had a rack of hanging instruments beside it, hammers and other tools for shaping red-hot metal. The room, which was large enough to be a barn, had the smell of coal and sweat.

"...over here," the man mumbled.

He stopped at one of the work stations, where an object lay on the anvil wrapped in cloth. Kael walked up behind the man and stepped to the side to get a better view. The door to the furnace was open and a white light spilled outward, bringing with it an intense heat.

The blacksmith turned to Kael and lowered his voice. "It looks much different than you remember, but I think..."

Kael, worried about the condition of his ancient gift, ignored the man and leaned forward, pulling the cloth from the anvil.

"...you'll understand when you see it," finished the man, his voice trailing off.

At first, Kael didn't understand. What lay before him was unlike anything he'd ever seen. It was a sword, to be sure. Like a dark prism, it split the light and cast rainbows in all directions. Its sparkle was like that of a diamond. The thin blade, curved elegantly to the handle, with just a slight arc. And 'handle' wasn't the right word, for the blade and handle were one and the same material, separated only by the shape that was appropriate for their purposes. The handle was cylindrical, decorated will all manner of intricate designs, perfectly sized for the grip of a man. From this, the sword narrowed into a smooth blade with a mirrored surface that reflected the images of things around it. It was the most beautiful thing Kael had ever seen.

"I've never seen its equal," he stated with confidence.

"Indeed," the blacksmith agreed. "...for its equal has never existed, and never will."

For a few moments, the two stood admiring the sword. Then Kael turned to ask the man a question.

The blacksmith held up his hand. "This is not my doing. I am not capable of creating such artistry, neither is any mortal man. I simply removed what was hiding it."

"Hiding it?" Kael questioned. "What do you mean?"

"I began by carefully removing the peeled metal, to see if I could understand how it was applied. I determined that it must have been dipped into molten metal, or had the metal poured over its surface. Once cooled, the metal should be able to be shaped as needed. I decided not to dip it for fear that the glass would shatter from the heat. So I poured the molten metal over the blade, slowly, but it wouldn't stick and rolled off to the ground."

How long have you been working on this?" Kael asked, not taking his eyes off the sword.

"...for the last two evenings. But as I said, it wouldn't stick. Then I realized that I could make a hollow mold, like a scabbard of thin metal, and perhaps a resin to adhere it to the glass. But to do that, I had to remove the peeled metal from the sword. So, I unwrapped the leather cord around the handle, removed the guard, and peeled away the metal."

"And this is what you found," Kael finished the man's statement.

"Yes, but there is more."

The man now had Kael's attention.

"It was dirty and discolored underneath. So I began to wipe it with a cleaning solution and quickly found the cloth and my hand in shreds."

Kael now noticed that two of the fingers on the blacksmith's right hand were wrapped in bandages.

"Then I wrapped a cloth around one of my chisels," he said, reaching down to pick up an object off the floor next to the anvil. He handed it to Kael.

It was a six-inch iron rod, with a flattened spade at one end and blunt on the opposite end, rounded through years of contact with a hammer. The spade end had a deep gouge that nearly clove the spade in two.

"The sword couldn't have done this," Kael replied, handing back the chisel.

The man dismissed Kael's comment. "After I saw that the glass wouldn't be harmed, I put it in the furnace to burn off the grime."

Kael took a deep breath and started to get agitated.

The blacksmith held up his hand. "I knew that it wouldn't be harmed. And it came out gleaming like this, just as I knew it would."

Kael paused, realizing that this man was no amateur. He wouldn't have taken such a risk if he thought there was anything to be concerned about. "And so it's been sitting here, like this?"

"Not exactly," replied the man, a mischievous grin spreading across his face. "Take a look at this," he said, turning around and motioning for Kael to follow.

At the next work station stood an anvil with a cleft running down the approximate center. "What's that used for?" Kael asked.

"That's not used for anything. That's what your sword did to my anvil."

Kael looked back at the sword, shimmering in the light of the furnace, then back to the blacksmith. "You can't be serious."

"I most certainly am. Try it yourself, but watch out for the blade if you value your fingers."

Kael eyed the man suspiciously as he backed away toward the sword. As his fingers encircled the handle, he thought briefly that this could be an elaborate joke. In just a few minutes, Dacien would peer out from the shadows, laughing at Kael as he tried to destroy an iron anvil with a glass sword. But that thought quickly left his mind as he lifted the instrument.

It was light, and weighted perfectly, but wasn't delicate. It felt more solid and dense than anything he had ever felt. As he moved it through the air, the sword seemed to vibrate with a life of its own, and Kael instantly took a liking to it. He walked back to the where the blacksmith stood, and stopped in front of the anvil.

With a quick look around the room to ensure that Dacien wasn't hiding, Kael moved the blade into position over the dark iron mass. He paused, then tapped the blade lightly on the surface of the anvil. Leaning forward, he inspected the surface to find a half-inch gouge in the hard metal.

The blacksmith was smiling now, and backed away from the anvil.

Kael straightened and widened his stance. With his left hand he gripped the butt of the handle, while his right held firm a full handbreadth away to increase the leverage that could be applied. With a two handed grip, he raised the sword over his head and brought it down in one swift movement, putting his full weight behind the force of the attack.

A high pitched hum vibrated from the sword, followed by a piercing shriek as it impacted the anvil. A bright flash of light momentarily blinded Kael. When his eyes adjusted again to the darkness, the anvil lay in two pieces with the sword embedded in the stone floor. Kael pulled the sword free and lifted it to his eyes to inspect for damage.

"There won't be a scratch on it," the man offered.

"Hmm," Kael mumbled after confirming the man's words.

"It is one of the ten," the blacksmith stated, without a hint of hesitation in his tone.

Kael lowered the sword and looked to the man. "What?"

"...one of the ten objects crafted by the gods themselves."

"Oh yes," Kael replied. It was part of an ancient Orud legend to which Kael hadn't ever paid much attention. But now the thought was intriguing. As he moved the sword through the air, getting a feel for how it handled, he continued. "I've traveled to many far away places. And the Orudan are not the only people to have such a legend."

The blacksmith nodded. "I've always thought of it as a fun story, a fairy tale to inspire children, and sometimes men. But until this," he said, pointing at the sword. "...I never actually believed it."

Kael didn't know what to say.

"Look at it. Can the hand of any mortal craft such a thing? It is perfect. It doesn't even bear any marks of its crafting. I didn't know that something could be so smooth or proportioned."

Kael had to agree. It was as if he was holding the idea of a sword, rather than the sword itself. *And not even the idea of a master craftsmen, but the idea of someone capable of imagining more perfect ideas.*

"Surely, the bladesmith who gave this to you was a highly skilled artist. To be able to cover such a thing with metal is nearly an impossible feat."

"He was indeed," Kael replied. Then a question came to his mind, but he stopped short of speaking it aloud. He decided instead to finish up with the blacksmith and leave as quickly as possible. "How much do I owe you?"

The man looked stunned. "...n...nothing," he replied.

"Thank you for your generosity," Kael said, walking back to the furnace to grab the cloth from the floor.

"...b...but" the man stammered. "Might I just keep it one more day...to study it?" he added.

"I'm afraid I must be leaving."

"Of course," the blacksmith replied, sounding dejected.

"I'll give your regards to the General. He was right about you...the best in the Empire," Kael quickly added, trying to distract him with compliments.

"Very well," the man replied.

Kael strode quickly for the door and bade the man a *good evening* as he walked out into the alleyway. He wasn't sure why, but he felt uneasy, like he had secret that needed to be kept. As he approached the end of the alley where it intersected with the main thoroughfare, he glanced back to see the blacksmith standing in the light of his doorway. Kael waved to the man and walked around the corner, out of sight.

After half an hour of waking in the brisk night air, Kael's heart began to beat more slowly and the questions once again rose to his mind.

Why did the old man give this to me?

And why was it disguised? Then, Kael remembered a moment from his time at the fortress city. He had only ever gone into the temple once, after

Matsuri was killed. And he seemed to vaguely remember a glass sword hanging on the wall above the altar.

Is this the sword from the temple?

His mind was now racing as he glanced behind him. After confirming that he wasn't being followed, he patted the object, wrapped in cloth, that he'd unconsciously hidden beneath his cloak.

20

On the morning of the third day of the High Council, Dacien sat in his privileged place among the leaders of the Empire. Plans were proceeding sluggishly as the Emperor tried to concoct a plan from the opinions of the other members present. Dacien kept his mouth closed for most of the discussion, leaving matters to those who were more experienced. The General from the North was trying his best to help put structure to the Emperor's plan, but only occasionally succeeded.

Somewhere in the middle of discussions regarding the impact of the proposed changes on the social life of various major cities, Dacien noted that the court messenger was standing patiently at the back of the Council chamber. A few seconds later, the Emperor noticed, as well, waving the gentleman forward.

His walk was almost a scurry as he moved quickly down the aisle past the council members, and navigated his way to the side of the Emperor. He whispered something into the Emperor's ear, which was received with surprise.

"Gentlemen," the Emperor began, as the messenger walked quickly back through the chambers toward the entrance. "We have an urgent situation to address. We will need to postpone this council until further notice." The Emperor waved his hand and the double doors at the rear of the room opened to reveal six soldiers in waiting.

They were dirty and in full travel armor, a contrast to the men seated around the room in the council. They strode forward with confidence, stopping just behind the council members.

"Your Majesty," their sergeant began. "We have been sent to inform you that a Korgan army marches for Orud. We overtook them three days ago, and we estimate them to now be a day's journey from the outskirts of Orud."

The Generals were already on their feet. "How many?" asked the General from the North.

"...five hundred."

The council chamber immediately broke into a cacophony of sound, as the men began to exchange their opinions. Eventually, one voice rose above the rest and order returned to the council.

"We must evacuate the plantations and dwellings to the north and bring the citizens inside the city walls. Five hundred men will be easily dealt with as soon as they are in range of our ballista." It was the Northern General, commanding the attention of the room.

"We will not allow our citizens to be displaced for such an inconvenience," the Emperor argued. "No, I think you will ride out to meet them."

"Your Majesty, I beg your pardon. It will only risk more lives to meet them on the battlefield without the advantage offered by the city walls."

The Emperor turned to the soldiers. "I assume they are afoot if you overtook them three days ago?"

"Yes your Majesty."

"Very well. Magnus, you will take my army and ride out to meet them before they endanger any of my citizens."

"Your Majesty, your army is supposed to protect this city; you will be vulnerable without their protection."

The Emperor's eyes flashed. "You are bordering on insubordination, General," he yelled. The chambers grew awkwardly silent. "My army will protect this city by riding out in full view of the citizens, with you at the front. You will also take the generals from the East and South. And the city of Orud will see how their Emperor deals with threats, not by hiding and waiting, but by striking out to protect them."

Dacien looked back and forth between the Emperor and the Northern General. "Only us?" he blurted out.

The Emperor's fierce gaze turned on Dacien. "I don't see how the North and South naval forces with be of any use in a land battle. If you have a problem with laying down your life in service of the Emperor, we will have to reassess your new appointment. Do I make myself clear?"

"Yes, your Majesty," Dacien replied. But inside, his mind was screaming in anger. The most powerful man in the Orudan Empire had just played favorites as if he was a child. And matters of war were anything but child's play. Dacien was disgusted by the man's inappropriate use of authority, but there was nothing that could be done except to follow his orders and make the best of the situation. "Generals," he addressed his new companions. "Let's go kill some Korgs."

"Indeed," the Northern General replied, with a nod of respect.

A knock came to Kael's door. He was standing at his balcony, overlooking the city and deep in thought about his strange evening. He had moment of panic, an instinctual response, which disappeared quickly as he realized that the sword was safely hidden. He walked over to the door and opened it cautiously.

"My lord, General Dacien sends you this message" said the soldier, handing Kael a small piece of rolled parchment. "He rides north this morning on an urgent matter. You..."

"What matter?" Kael interrupted.

"To confront an army of Korgs; he rides with the Generals of the North and East and they command the Emperor's army. You are to report to the northern wall as a precaution against a direct attack on the city. Armor and weaponry will be provided. All the information is there," he finished, pointing at the message.

"Thank you," Kael replied to the messenger, who promptly spun on his heels and left.

Kael made it to the northern wall of the city just after noon. The sun was high and blazing, the weather getting warmer with each passing day. He followed the instructions on the message and reported to the Captain of the northern district, who provided him with the standard array of armor and weaponry for an Orud ground soldier—one metal cuirass, greaves to protect both the legs and forearms, a small rectangular shield, and a short sword attached to a belt.

Kael suited up and reported to the wall above the northern gate, a massive arched structure, wide enough for ten wagons side by side. He managed to catch the last of the procession—the Emperor's army—leaving the city. He knew that somewhere, among the bright reflections and red flags, Dacien rode to war, and he wished him well.

Once the cavalry moved beyond the wall, large iron gates were swung into place, securing the northern entrance to the city. The citizens, uninformed about what was happening, lingered about, looking to strike up a conversation to satisfy their curiosity. This marked the end of anything interesting for the remainder of the day and Kael spent his time joking with fellow soldiers throughout the afternoon.

As night fell, everyone's attention was heightened. It was an unspoken rule that enemies attacked at night. And, coupled with the pace that the Korgan were keeping, they could arrive anytime.

Unless Dacien stops them!

Torches flickered at regular intervals along the top of the wall. Kael stood near a ballista, ready to replenish supplies of iron missiles, should the need arise. His eyes were getting heavy, but he shook it off, blinking repeatedly. Every so often, he would scan the darkness beyond the wall and turn to do the same inside the city, to keep his vision fresh. It was nearing midnight when the shift would change.

Kael shifted his stance and breathed in heavily. Out of the silence rose a strange sound. At first, he wasn't sure of its identity. But then it repeated, a loud and clear blast of a horn. It was a distress signal.

Kael cocked his head to the side and waited. The third report allowed him to pinpoint the location; it was coming from the Imperial Palace. The other soldiers shifted uneasily, looking out over the wall.

"It comes from the Palace," Kael shouted.

His fellow soldiers all glanced back to the heart of the city.

"Maintain your posts," commanded the Lieutenant of Kael's small force. "The Palace is sufficiently guarded. Those boys can take care of themselves."

Kael looked around to see concern on the men's faces, and something inside him told him that he needed to leave. He walked over to the Lieutenant and addressed him quietly.

"...permission to be excused, Sir?"

"Didn't you hear me," the man replied. "Stay at your post."

"I am due to be relieved, and something isn't right. I need to go find out what is happening at the Palace."

"You'll stay at your post. The General put you under my command."

"...to lend assistance. I am not under your command. I am going to leave and if I am able, I will report to you what is happening at the Palace. Your men are concerned and they have a right to be. We are here guarding the wall and, meanwhile, something is happening within the city. ...sounds like a distraction to me."

The Lieutenant considered Kael's words, which had been spoken quietly enough not to arouse his subordinates. "...very well."

"Thank you, Sir," Kael replied, turning to leave.

"Report your findings as soon as you are able," the Lieutenant announced for the benefit of his men.

"Yes, Sir," Kael replied, playing along.

After descending a long flight of steps, Kael touched the ground at a run. He quickly discarded his armor, all except for the sword. Fortunately, the streets were clear due to the hour. Kael's leather soles beat steadily across the stone streets, as his heart pumped loudly within his chest. After standing still all day, it felt good to be moving.

It was only a few miles to the heart of the city, where Kael came within sight of the Palace. It was a beautiful and sturdy structure, surrounded by grass and water. Large trees ringed the property in a perfect circle.

Kael could see an orange glow and occasional flicker of flame coming from the western side of the building. Smoke was beginning to rise into the night air. As he ran across the lawn, toward the elaborate columned building, he could see confusion among the guards, some of which were glancing about, unsure whether or not they should remain still or move to the western end of the Palace.

Kael approached quickly and startled one of the men, who lowered his stance and held out his spear. Kael slowed to a stop and held up his hands.

"We were guarding the northern wall and heard the alarm. What's happening?"

The man eyed him suspiciously for a moment, then decided that Kael wasn't a threat. "A small band of men shot flaming arrows into the western wing of the Palace. Something caught fire. We sent out after them, but they disappeared into the night."

"Were they Korgan?" Kael asked.

"We're not sure. They were dressed in dark clothing and their faces were painted."

Kael thought for a moment. "It's a diversion. Who's inside the Palace?"

"The Emperor and Commanders of the north and south naval forces," the man replied quickly. "As well as..."

"You must get me inside quickly," Kael interrupted. "Their lives are in danger."

"We've already sent men to guard the Emperor. It is our first priority."

"It won't matter. He may already be dead. You must help me," he pleaded.

The man paused for a brief moment, then nodded to his left. "...this way."

A maze of hallways passed by in a blur, bringing Kael and the guard to a large wooden door.

"Is the Emperor inside?" Kael asked, breathing heavily.

"Yes. The Royal Guard is with him and the Generals," the man said, then proceeded to bang the butt of his spear against the door in a rhythmic pattern.

When no answer came, he tried again.

"Is there another way in?" Kael asked.

"It's barricaded from the inside, but there is another way." Again they ran, following a circular hallway that surrounded the barricaded room. The soldier stopped abruptly and turned to the wall away from the room. Lifting a heavy tapestry away from the wall, he revealed an opening just big enough for a man to pass through on hands and knees.

"I'll go first," he asserted, disappearing through the dark hole.

Kael followed until he could stand, and found himself in a small stairwell that led downward, back in the direction of the barricaded room. He followed the soldier down the passage that appeared to lead underneath the hallway and below the room where the Emperor was kept. And just as he expected, Kael began to ascend stairs until the soldier stopped at a narrow landing, the ceiling only four feet above the ground.

Crouching underneath a wooden door in the ceiling, the soldier wedged his shoulder against it and flexed his legs. Slowly, the door began to give, but appeared to have something on top of it.

Kael moved next to the man and added his strength to the effort. Immediately, the door gave upward and whatever blocked it and tipped over to land with a crash. Kael helped the man upward through the opening and expected a helping hand to come back down. When nothing happened, Kael grabbed the ledge and jumped, pulling himself up to the floor of the protected room.

Before he even got to his feet, it was clear that they were too late. Bodies could be seen lying lifeless around the room. Kael moved as quickly as he could to his feet and scanned the room for his escort.

The soldier was standing a few feet away, looking down at his Emperor, whose head had been removed from his body. Blood had formed a large pool around him.

Kael took in the rest of the scene at a glance. The naval Commanders were lying together to his left, with puncture wounds to the chest. And scattered around the rest of the room, the ten royal guardsmen lay in various positions of death, slain while defending their Emperor. The quickly spreading pool of blood beneath one man's throat told Kael that all of this had happened only seconds earlier.

"Is there no other way into this room?" Kael asked.

The soldier looked to Kael, startled from his thoughts.

Kael repeated his question.

"No," he answered.

The two doors on opposite ends of the room were still barricaded with large timbers. And the passage that they had just taken showed no signs of tampering. Kael searched the walls for signs of entry. Eventually, his gaze went upward to the rounded ceiling with ten small panels of colored glass set into the dome. In the day, it would have been easy to see, and beautiful to behold. But the dark night sky beyond hid the ceiling in shadow and made the windows nearly impossible to see.

"Is there a way to get up to the roof?" Kael asked with a sense of urgency.

The soldier picked up on his meaning and looked upward. "Yes," he said, with vengeance in his eyes. "...this way."

Kael followed the soldier back through the secret passage. Judging by the size of the timbers in front of the doors, it was a wise choice for the quickest exit. More hallways and turns led them past several fallen soldiers, slain in the same way as the men in the Emperor's safe room.

Spilling out into one of many courtyards within the Palace, the two turned sharply and ran to a darkened corner, which turned into a narrow staircase. Kael pushed past the man and bolted up the stairs skipping many with each stride. His heart pumped strong in his chest as he anticipated a confrontation.

The stairs opened to a sand covered roof surrounded by a low wall around its perimeter. Various large shapes protruded from the sand, structural elements of the Palace construction, each large enough to hide several men. And in the center of the roof was a dome with colored glass windows set five feet apart.

Kael stopped, his eyes scanning the rooftop for signs of movement. His ears told him that the soldier was approaching the top of the stairs behind him. He held out his hand indicating that the man should stop and the footsteps obeyed his instructions.

"You take the left and I'll go right," the soldier offered.

"NO!" Kael said, his voice as hushed as he could make it. "Stay close to me."

Silence followed and Kael took it to mean acceptance. Slowly, he crept forward, trying to listen over the sound of his own heart beat. The faraway sound of voices came from the west as the Palace guards tried to put out the flames, unaware that their efforts were wasted. The goal was already accomplished.

Shadows everywhere. Which one are you hiding in?

Suddenly, movement to the right caught Kael's attention as a shadow darted behind an obstruction.

Kael burst forward, trying to close the distance and get a better look.

It was so fast and silent that it seemed to disappear.

Kael stopped again, letting his instincts tell him where the phantom had gone.

Then it seemed to materialize in the form of a man standing on top of the wall fifty feet away, much farther than Kael would have guessed.

"Ukiru," he called out.

The dark silhouette turned back and cocked its head to the side, with a look of curiosity.

Kael moved forward, brandishing his sword, the Orud guard only a few steps behind him. And then the shadow disappeared. Kael caught only a brief glimpse of a rope, coiled around its leg as it dropped out of sight.

Rushing forward, he confirmed that there was a rope tied to a nearby beam, extending over the edge of the Palace roof. By the time he reached the edge, he could only see the swaying end of the rope, a few feet short of the ground. Looking outward, a shadow melded with the nearby trees and vanished.

Kael sat down on the low wall and looked out over the city. He couldn't quite feel it yet, but he knew that this was going to trouble him deeply.

First Narian...now Ukiru!

Slowly, a deep anger began to burn within him.

21

The mid-afternoon sun filtered down through a blue sky, dotted with patches of cloud. Dacien rode at the front of the column with the other Generals. They were exhausted from their non-stop trip, which carried them north and east to the plains between Orud and Nelhut. There they confronted the Korgs who were moving as quickly as any un-mounted force, taking them by surprise. They were no match for mounted cavalry from the most powerful military force in the civilized world.

Weary and in need of recuperation, Dacien was disappointed to see three riders, bearing the distress flag of Orud, riding north to meet up with the army. A quick conversation with these men told of the Emperor's death, and that of his Commanders.

"The High Council has called an emergency meeting at sunset, and the presence of all the Generals is required."

The General from the north simply nodded in acknowledgement, no signs of exhaustion in his demeanor. "We will be there," he said confidently.

The three riders turned and galloped away to the city, while the army resumed their slower-paced ride back to their home. When they reached the gates of the city, a loud cheer went up from the crowds gathered there. It was nothing unusual, for citizens always showed such support. But on this occasion, the sheer number of people attending was unlike anything they had seen before.

Magnus turned to Dacien and the Eastern General. "We should all take the next few hours to rest, eat and get cleaned up. I'll see you at the High Council chambers at sunset."

Dacien and his counterpart saluted with closed fists to their chests, then entered the northern gate and immediately went their separate ways through hundreds of loyal citizens screaming at the top of their lungs.

Dacien didn't feel much like eating, and went straight to his chambers for rest. Despite his own instincts about the wisdom of striking up a conversation prior to sleep, he asked his guards about Kael. They didn't know were he was, but they relayed the happenings from the previous evening.

"And he left his post?"

"That's the rumor," one man replied.

"I...," Dacien began, but couldn't finish. "I don't want to be disturbed while I rest. If I oversleep, wake me one hour before sunset."

"Yes, my lord," the guard replied.

Dacien collapsed on his bed, exhausted and ready for sleep. But after a few moments, his mind was racing about Kael. *Why would he leave his post? Why did Kael have to get into the Palace?*

Slowly, the feelings that Dacien had kept hidden since their time in Leoran began to come to the surface again. He had a sickening feeling that Kael was the assassin. But he quickly tried to dismiss the idea.

No. He couldn't be. Or could he? He said himself that he had been trained since he was young.

Dacien rose to his feet and paced around the room. Never before had he been so close to such intrigue. The Emperor and his Commanders murdered in the Palace. Emergency sessions of the High Council.

So much for resting!

The mood inside of the Council chambers was quite different than the last time Dacien had been present, and for good reason. Three of the seats in the circle were vacant. An awkward silence lasted for several minutes before the youngest council member spoke.

"It is under grave circumstances that we meet here today. By now, you have all heard of what transpired yesterday evening. I will not recount the story; there will be time for that later. We will have to postpone our mourning to deal with the emergency at hand."

The young man sat back in his seat, and another older gentleman took over. "Our Emperor has been assassinated. The Syvaku have destroyed countless cities in the southern region. And the Korgan have breached the wall in the northeast and taken the city of Orlek. Fortunately, the army that you defeated," he said, pointing to the General from the north, "was the only group to have penetrated this far to the interior of our Empire. While this council is devastated by what has transpired, we must act quickly or all will be lost. This is why we called you together."

The man took a deep breath and continued. "Magnus Calidon, we wish to appoint you as Emperor of the Orudan Empire, effective immediately."

The General from the north stood and looked around the room as murmurs of approval mixed with nods of affirmation. "Does this council understand what is being asked of me?"

"Yes we do," the man replied. "Our Empire is crumbling, and these times call for drastic measures."

"Sir," the General replied.   "With all due respect, this council has opposed many of my initiatives and has consistently chosen to disregard my advice."

"Yes. And look where it has gotten us!" the man said, more to the council than to Magnus. "The economies of the North and East are strong, even amidst the conflict along your borders. And though we haven't given you the support you requested, you have proven your ability to act decisively and defend this Empire."

Magnus looked to the ground while the council chambers were silent. "Very well. I have not asked for this position, but I am first and foremost a servant of the Empire. If this is what is required of me, I will take up this position with the utmost respect and reverence for it. It is my honor to serve you as Emperor!"

Cheers of approval went up from the rest of the council. Dacien stood and clapped as well, a deep satisfaction welling within him. At a time of such turmoil, he was confident that the council had chosen wisely.

Magnus spoke over the applause as it slowly quieted. "We will have to postpone the coronation as well as the funeral due to our urgent situation. However, I think a small celebration is in order. The gods know that we could all use a respite. Tomorrow evening, we will have a banquet, and all of the most influential citizens of the city will be invited. During the feast, I will announce my plans to bring this Empire together and make it strong once again. And I will proclaim the following day as a day of rest and play for the citizens of Orud. No work is to be done within the city until sunrise the next day."

The young man from the council replied. "That's only one day. Will you have enough time?"

"It will be enough," Magnus answered. "Sleep will have to wait. My first order of business will be to appoint our new Naval Commanders."

"Do you have any thoughts on who you will choose?" the older man asked.

"I will start by speaking with the second in command from each navy, although I will not necessarily choose them. I will be looking for strong leaders, regardless of age or seniority. Skilled men are what we need in times like these. I know this has been a point of contention in the past, but I expect your full support."

"You have it. We are ready for change," the man replied.

"Very well. I have a busy night ahead of me, but I will see you all at the banquet tomorrow evening."

"Hail Emperor of Orud," the council members shouted as Magnus walked down the aisle.

Dacien smiled. *Now we're getting somewhere!*

Kael chewed a piece of roasted chicken, while Dacien recounted the events of the past few days. He and the other soldiers from Leoran sat at the table and shared dinner as had become their tradition since arriving in Orud. It was amazing how quickly things could change. One day, Kael was riding back toward his home in Bastul, and now he sat with a General in the Empire's capital city, discussing the appointing of a new Emperor.

He was doing his best to stay engaged in the conversation. And though it was all very interesting, especially the battle with the Korgs, Kael was deeply troubled. He hadn't had a moment alone with Dacien since his return, and it looked like he wouldn't get to speak with him anytime soon. He was burning inside with a vital piece of information, but he'd only shared his history with Dacien, so he couldn't speak openly in front of the others.

The more I think about it, the more it makes sense. Narian leading the Syvaku was strange by itself. But after seeing the assassin... It must have been Ukiru. No else could move like that! And if that's the case, then the logical conclusion is that they are all behind the attacks on the Empire. I need to discuss this with Dacien. I have to get him alone!

"...what do you think?"

"Sorry?" Kael questioned, shaking off his thoughts. "Were you talking to me?"

"Of course I was," Dacien replied. "I said the new Emperor wants to meet you."

"Me?"

"Yes. Well, actually, he wasn't Emperor at the time he asked about you. It was while we were returning from the north. He said he wanted to meet you, so I thought this banquet would be a good opportunity."

"Sure," Kael responded.

"Try not to sound so excited," one of the soldiers said.

"Alright. I would be honored to accompany you to the banquet."

"That's better," Dacien said, raising his glass.

Kael tried to make eye contact with Dacien, who was in good spirits this evening and clearly enjoying his wine. When he finally looked back, Kael tried to get his attention. "...could we..." he began, nodding his head away from the table.

"No," Dacien announced. "No more serious discussion. This is a time for celebration. Eat your food and drink your wine."

Kael shrank back in his chair.

The sound of wheels against the dirt road brought Maeryn out of her seat. She ran to the edge of the porch and saw Magnus' carriage coming down toward the house. She tried to wait patiently, but her wringing hands indicated otherwise. Putting them behind her back, she stared out to the road.

That's strange! What are those soldiers doing with him?

A moment of panic seized her throat as she feared that their secret had been revealed. Trying to calm herself down, she thought of the possible explanations.

He is a general, so he does have soldiers. Perhaps with all that's been happening, he is traveling with increased protection.

The carriage stopped and Magnus stepped out.

Maeryn walked briskly out to meet him. "I've been worried sick. They said that the Emperor was assassinated. Are you alright?"

"Yes, I'm fine," he dismissed.

Maeryn could see that he wasn't fine. His eyes were bloodshot and rimmed with red lids. He looked as though he hadn't slept at all. "Is something wrong?" she asked, looking to the soldiers who had come up beside Magnus.

"Please give us a minute," he asked the guards.

"Yes, your majesty," they replied, bowing low.

"...your majesty?" Maeryn questioned.

"I'll explain. Let's take a walk."

Magnus led Maeryn toward the cliff overlooking the ocean. They were both silent until out of hearing from the soldiers.

"Alright. Tell me what is going on."

"Maeryn. Something incredible has happened. It's tragic, but amazing at the same time."

"What?" Maeryn pleaded.

"You are looking at the newly appointed Emperor of the Orudan Empire."

Maeryn stopped walking and turned to the man whom she had grown strangely attracted to. She put her hand over her mouth and stared at him for moment, taking in his words. Their relationship was strange enough as it was, but now this!

"Isn't it amazing?"

Maeryn removed her hand from her mouth. "They appointed you after..."

"Yes," he replied.

"And now you're..."

"Yes."

"That means..."

"Exactly!" he exclaimed. "Think of what we can do now."

"But how will you explain to the council?"

Magnus smiled. "They don't have to know. But I'm the Emperor now; I can change it all. I can put an end to the slave trade. In fact, that's why I'm here. I'm having a banquet and I want you to come."

"...as what?" Maeryn asked. "I'm flattered, but I won't go back on what I said just because you're an Emperor now."

"I didn't expect that you would," Magnus replied with a gleam in his eye. "You can come as my guest, or anonymously if you wish. But I would like to share this moment with you. I will be presenting the new Naval Commanders and laying out my plan to unite this Empire against our enemies."

Maeryn was silent.

"Will you come?"

"What about Aelia?"

"Of course she can come, as well. So what do you think?"

A slow smile spread across Maeryn's face. "Your majesty," she bowed. "It would be an honor."

22

The feast was being held on a rooftop terrace on the Palace grounds. Kael and Dacien arrived together, but Kael still hadn't been able to inform the General of what he thought was happening. It was frustrating, but he tried to stay in the moment and enjoy the feast.

There will be time tomorrow, after the feast!

The building was surrounded by a double assignment of guards, who pulled their spears apart when they saw Dacien. Kael followed a half-step behind, enjoying the privileges of traveling with his friend.

A short flight of stairs led them to the rooftop, which was lavishly decorated for the occasion. Sconces burned along the short walls surrounding three sides of the building. It was already crowded with honored guests of every powerful family in the region. The members of the High Council were also present. At the far end, a canopy covered a wide table with five chairs facing back toward the rest of the terrace. Behind the center chair, and raised slightly, was an elaborately carved chair with a dark-haired man seated casually. He was leaning forward and speaking into the ear of the man seated in front of him.

"Is that him?" Kael asked.

"Yes," he said, pointing. "In front of the Emperor is the newly appointed General of the Northern Territory. The men to the left are the Northern and Southern Naval Commanders, and to the right is the Eastern General."

"And the empty seat is yours."

"Precisely!"

"So you brought me to this feast so that I could make small talk with strangers?"

Dacien smiled. "But they are the wealthiest citizens in the Empire."

"Well, in that case, I think I can manage."

"You didn't think you would get to sit with the Emperor, did you?"

"No. I don't think that highly of myself." Kael shot back with a grin.

"I must take my seat. Do try to stay out of trouble."

"Certainly," Kael replied.

As Dacien walked to the front of the terrace, Kael glanced around the rooftop.   In the fading light of dusk, the extravagance was impressive. Everywhere he looked, there were servants, both male and female, walking briskly with platters of food and goblets of wine. Kael grabbed a goblet from the nearest tray and moved to the side of the building. Contented to watch the interesting people, he took a seat near the wall.

Dacien took his seat next to the General from the east and immediately struck up a conversation. Kael smiled and looked up to the darkening sky. Dacien was made for this sort of thing. The first time Kael met him in Bastul, he could tell that the man was a good leader.

"Are you hungry, my lord?"

Kael looked up to find an attractive young woman extending a platter of cheeses and olives. "Oh, I'm not a lord; I'm just here to watch all of you beautiful people."

The woman giggled.

Perhaps this won't be such a dull evening after all!

The evening proceeded more quickly than Kael expected it to.   He avoided conversation with the elderly gentlemen who seemed to be professional conversationalists. He wondered if these men ever worked a day in their lives. Instead, he made it a point to talk briefly with the young servant woman each time she passed by. Sadly, she informed Kael that she couldn't stop working and had to keep moving so that her master wouldn't notice. And so the evening went, with spurts of conversation and moments of eye contact from across the room.

Two hours after sunset, the crowded rooftop grew silent, as if coordinated by some signal. Kael, distracted by his new acquaintance, didn't notice what was happening until the very last second. He quickly took his seat as the Emperor rose from his throne. The blonde woman that had been at his side all evening took a seat near Dacien.

"Honored guests," the Emperor began, loud enough for all to hear, without showing any extra effort. "I am pleased that you have joined me in this small celebration. And I hope that the food and drink are to your liking."

This brought a cheer from the crowd. Kael clapped his hands to keep from standing out.

"Until sundown tomorrow, our time of celebration will continue. But amidst our joy, I cannot forget the tragedy that has befallen our Empire. Therefore, we come to the real purpose of this meeting. I have brought you all here so that you may be the first to hear of my plans to restore this Empire to the status that it has fought so hard to attain. There was a time when the name of the Orudan Empire would strike fear into the hearts of our enemies. There was even a time when our enemies had been so defeated, to the point that they were hardly of any consequence to the citizens of this great country. Sadly, those days are over."

Kael caught the eyes of the servant girl and nodded for her to come over. She winked an acknowledgement then began to make her way slowly through the crowd. This time she carried wine and was stopped more often by the other guests.

"...these changes will be difficult for some," the Emperor continued. "...but we have much work to do and it will take our united efforts to regain our former power. And so, over the next few weeks, the laws will be changed thusly—first, the structure of our military forces will be reorganized to eliminate the non-combatants. Soldiers will carry their own provisions and be more self-sufficient, not relying on costly and slow supply trains for food and provision. Secondly, we will create smaller, more efficient groups, able to cover more distance at a time. This will give us flexibility in dealing with the disorganized and often unmanageable way in which our enemies attack. And we will no longer be vulnerable to losing provisions for an entire army by one focused attack."

The servant girl finally made it over to Kael. "Here I am. Would you care for some wine?"

Kael accepted. "I never asked you your name," he whispered in her ear.

"And you still haven't," she wittily replied.

"Alright, what is your name?"

"Julia."

Suddenly, several members of the crowd came to their feet amidst mixed sounds of disapproval and cheering.

Kael wondered what the Emperor had said. Evidently, it was something that had caused the guests to divide into two distinct groups.

"...it is on the backs of these people that our nation has been built. But they are treated as though they have no value." Now the Emperor was shouting. "We, in Orud, are insulated from what is happening in the rest of the Empire. This night, we have an honored guest who has seen first hand the treachery of the enemy."

A feeling of panic shot through Kael's body like a bolt of lightening. He knew the Emperor spoke of him, and knew that he was going to be publicly used to make a point. It was the worst feeling for someone who didn't like attention.

Kael looked to Dacien who was waving at him to come to the front. Kael took a deep breath and began to make his way though the congested rooftop, his heart beating madly within his chest.

"After destroying ten cities along the western shore, the two barbarian armies turned inland and attacked the capital of Leoran. This man to my left," he said, pointing to Dacien, "led the brave Leorans to victory. But the final blow was dealt by this man coming forward now. As the Syvak warlord escaped into the forests, this brave man gave chase, returning with the barbarian's head."

The crowd gasped at the description of war and things that they would rather not know.

"Kneel, servant of Orud. And receive my blessing, for you have shown courage beyond measure and have done what few in this Empire are willing to do, what few have the stomach for."

Kael knelt and bowed his head to the floor as the Emperor neared him, putting a hand on his shoulder. Kael breathed heavily, trying to steady his heart as he did when exerting himself. Slowly, he felt himself calm, helped to a large degree by the sound of the Emperor's voice. It was soothing, yet powerful, with a familiar tone. He was good at speaking and could see why Dacien said he commanded an audience.

Such a familiar sound....

Suddenly, fear gripped Kael's heart and his body felt weak—a fear that went far beyond that of discomfort at being in front of a crowd. It was a primal fear that compelled him to either fight or run.

The High Priest!

The realization hit him like the impact of the ocean after falling from the cliffs of the monastery.

"There was a time when we, as a people, had the stomach to live in a world of barbarians, and carve out a piece of it. A piece that we determined would be our home. A piece of land that we would defend with our very lives. An Empire that could never be destroyed. We have grown weak. We have grown fat. We have grown lazy. We have others do our work so that we may live in luxury. No longer. It will not be tolerated!"

Kael began to sweat and his throat tightened.

I CAN FEEL YOUR FEAR, KAEL...YOU TRAITOR!

The words came into Kael's mind, uninvited.

YOU HAVE EVERY REASON TO FEAR FOR YOUR LIFE.
YOU ARE SURROUNDED BY THOSE YOU BETRAYED!

The words in Kael's mind came from the High Priest, even as he continued to speak audibly to the crowd.

"Rise, brave warrior."

Kael pushed with wobbly knees until he stood in front of the only man he feared. He looked into piercing blue eyes and felt the same horrible presence emanating from the man that he experienced at the Temple so many years ago. He wasn't just a man. There was something else there; something evil and powerful.

LOOK AROUND AND SEE WHAT YOU HAVE FORSAKEN,
FOR YOU WILL NOT LIVE TO SEE THE SUNRISE!

Kael focused his eyes on those that sat at table behind the Emperor. To the far left, he recognized Horace, the Southern Naval Commander. To Horace's left, sat Arden, the Northern Naval Commander. Over the Emperor's other shoulder was Berit, newly appointed to the position of Northern General in the place of the Emperor. Then there was the General of the Eastern Territory. Soren looked intensely into Kael's eyes and another voice entered Kael's mind.

YOU WILL WISH THAT YOU HAD DIED IN THAT OCEAN!

Finally, there was Dacien, beaming proudly at the audible words that the Emperor spoke of his friend.

Kael felt nauseous. He had run from his past for so many years. And now his past sat in front of him, with murder on their minds.

The Emperor released his grip on Kael's shoulder and took a few steps back, motioning to his left. Kael looked over to Dacien who was now on his feet, indicating that Kael should take his seat. The Emperor continued to speak to the crowd and Kael moved slowly in Dacien's direction.

A white-haired man sat against the wall. A servant girl passed by, but not the one Kael knew. These people were oblivious to what was happening. They were entranced by the High Priest and his poisonous tongue.

Instinctively, Kael burst into a run. Using a chair as leverage, he vaulted into the air and over the wall, tucking into a flip as he moved away from the building. Two seconds passed before he felt the fabric of the awning give way beneath him. The sound of tearing and rending of metal supports preceded his awkward landing to the ground.

As soon as his feet were under him, he leapt into a full run, legs pumping as fast as he'd ever run before. The grass passed swiftly underfoot until he met the paved road that circled the Palace grounds. A few more seconds and he passed beneath the great trees that designated the Palace boundary.

Kael ran in a panic, trying to put as much distance between himself and the Palace as was possible. He wasn't sure how long he had run, but when he finally lost his breath, he found himself in a rundown part of the city. Hearing water nearby, he turned to his right and followed a narrow road that hadn't been maintained. The pave stones were lifted out of the ground in many places, making for dangerous footing.

No matter. I can't possibly run anymore!

Kael sat down on a crumbling portion of a bridge that spanned a narrow waterway. It was dirty and probably close to the outskirts of the city. There wasn't much light, but what was available only made the surrounding shacks more detestable.

"Psst."

Kael looked up.

A tall man stood across the water, twenty yards away. It was the white-haired man from the feast.

Kael jumped to his feet.

The man quickly held out his hands, indicating that he didn't mean any harm. "The guards will be scouring the city looking for you. Come with me!"

Kael looked back to the west. "Did you follow me? How did you get here so quickly?"

"Never mind that! Come with me if you want to escape," the man said, his hushed words reflecting off the water.

Kael walked farther down the bank and crossed the waterway via an arched stone bridge. Before he got close to the stranger, the man ducked into an alley. Kael walked quickly to the alley and peered into the darkness, cautious of betrayal.

The man stood at the end of the alley where it opened into another street.

Alright old man. You'd better not get me caught; your life depends on it!

Kael followed the man in a zig-zag pattern through the city. The journey took close to an hour and finally delivered them to the docks of the eastern bay. Kael tried to walk quickly enough to catch up to the man, but it was no use. Short of running, Kael wasn't going to see the man's face. Instead, he followed the stranger out to the end of the dock where he boarded a small sailing vessel.

"...you know how to sail?" the man called quietly.

"Yes."

"Then take the rudder," the man said, moving to the opposite side of the boat.

Kael stepped down on to the deck of the boat, which rocked slightly, keeping time with the surface of the water. He was already standing in the aft section and quickly took command of the vessel, as the stranger cast off the lines, allowing them to drift away from the dock. Releasing another knot, the sails unfurled and caught the breeze.

Kael felt the ship move beneath his feet, and leaned forward to catch his balance. Within minutes, they cleared the docks and headed into the open water.

Kael sat on the bench behind him, with one hand on the rudder, while the other man stayed at the prow of the ship. "Where are we headed?" he asked the owner of the ship.

I hope he's the owner. Or else we just stole this ship!

"Turn a few degrees to the north. We're headed to the shore there," he said, pointing to the northeast.

Kael followed the man's directions and sat in silence for the rest of the journey. An hour later, they approached the shore as the man gave Kael directions. They came to a jolting stop on a sandy shore in front of a small, but secluded dwelling.

"Throw out the aft anchor," he called to Kael.

Kael did as he was told, watching the man do the same with the fore anchor. Then, with the agility of a child, he swung off the deck and landed with a splash in knee-deep water and began to walk toward the house.

Kael followed his example and tried to keep up, but managed only to stay several paces behind. He wondered why the need for such secrecy, but had a feeling that he would find out soon.

There's no way you can hide in a house!

Regardless of the man's unusual behavior, Kael was relieved to be out of the city, and thankful for his help. But he couldn't let his guard down and watched the man carefully, while taking mental notes of his surroundings with nothing more than a glance. The house was a simple wooden structure with one door facing the beach. Kael hung back as the man opened it and entered the darkness. Seconds later, a soft glow shown around the silhouette of the door.

"Please come in," came the voice from inside.

Kael looked for signs of ambush, but didn't sense anything out of the ordinary. Though ordinary was becoming a strange word lately. Pushing the door inward, Kael saw a simple, but clean home, with out any dividing walls. The kitchen and bedroom were off to the left, while a small sitting area occupied the right half of the dwelling. The man had his back turned and was pouring two glasses of wine.

"You have nothing to fear from an old man such as me. Please have a seat."

Kael walked over and sat in a comfortable chair, exhaling as he did so. "You don't move like an old man."

The stranger turned around an offered a glass of wine to Kael. His face came into the light revealing a friend that Kael remembered vividly from his childhood.

"And I've heard that I don't look like one as well!"

"Saba?" Kael said slowly.

"Hello Kael."

The old man's hair had been cropped short and his face was cleanly shaven. Only, he wasn't an old man. Although his hair was white, he looked to be only forty or fifty years of age. Kael sat back quickly, as if he were looking at a ghost.

"Take the wine Kael; we have much to talk about."

23

Dacien sat in the Emperor's war room, with the other Generals and Commanders. Kael's strange behavior prompted the private meeting and it was clear that the Emperor was concerned.

"Frankly, I don't understand it," Dacien admitted.

The Emperor sat forward in his chair. "How long have you known him?"

Dacien thought for a moment before responding. "...since the attack on Bastul. We've been together ever since."

"I see," said the Emperor.

Dacien stopped short of explaining how they met. The more he thought about it, the worse it sounded. *If I tell him that Kael just showed up during the attack, it will sound suspicious. Actually, it might be more than suspicious.*

"I'm told that he was instrumental in fending off the Syvaku. Is this true?"

"Yes," Dacien replied quickly. "I've never seen such a warrior. He was a tremendous help. In fact, it was he who first suspected an invasion. I sent him inland to find proof of his theory, and he returned with that proof." Dacien immediately thought of Caius, fatally wounded during the excursion.

"Yes, of course. And he returned without his escort."

"That's right," Dacien admitted with a frown. His own fears were being echoed by the Emperor. *It's almost as if he's reading my thoughts! How could I have been so gullible?*

"Does this all sound as devious to you as it does to me?" the Emperor asked.

"Well..." Dacien started, then trailed off. The others in the room looked betrayed and Dacien started to realize the gravity of his mistake in trusting Kael. *But how could it be? His story...it all sounded so honest.*

"General Dacien, I suspect that this man is a professional. Such cowards can infiltrate even the very elite of governments. Let me ask you this, how well did you think you knew him?"

"Completely. He told me his entire life story. How he grew up in Bastul as the son of Colonel Adair Lorus and his wife Maeryn."

At this, the Emperor's eyebrows raised slightly.

"His father went missing and the position of Colonel was assigned to another man who was cruel. Colonel Lemus had Kael thrown in jail for coming to the aid of a friend and attacking the Colonel. Before he was executed for his crimes, he was taken away to another prison in the north. Then a mysterious man purchased him from the jailor and took him to a far away monastery where he spent the rest of his childhood studying the arts of war."

"Let me stop you there," the Emperor said, holding up his hand. Looking around the room at the others, he spoke calmly. "This is obviously a made up story. After our initial conversation, I checked the census records and confirmed that such people existed in Bastul. But the jail records show one Kael Lorus being executed and even include details of when and where the body was disposed of. No, I suspect that your friend assumed the identity of an Orudan citizen in order to gain your confidence."

Dacien protested. "But he went to war with us. And the gods will attest that he chased the Syvak warlord into the forest and brought the man back in two pieces!"

The Emperor nodded with a smirk on his face. "Yes, in order to gain access to the inner workings of the most powerful Empire on the face of the earth. Even to kill your own in exchange for the Emperor of the Orudan Empire and two of his Commanders. It seems a fair trade and a brilliant move."

Dacien paused, considering the implications. "You think he was the assassin?"

"You said yourself that he left his post at the northern wall to go to the Palace. And he demanded entrance while the fires at the western wing provided a convenient distraction. Were you ever able to find the guard that supposedly accompanied him through the Palace?"

"No," Dacien replied, his confidence lost. "He apparently disappeared shortly after."

General Soren leaned forward in his chair. "Of course he did; it seems obvious to me."

Dacien slid off his chair and knelt on the ground. "Your Majesty. I see now the error of my judgment and I plead for your forgiveness. I didn't mean to endanger the lives of the Orudan leadership. And now I feel that their blood is on my hands."

"No Dacien. Their blood is on the hands of the assassin who seeks to undermine the strength of this Empire. And we will not let that happen."

Dacien looked to the floor in shame.

The Emperor rose from his chair and pulled Dacien to his feet, looking straight into his eyes. "I'm a good judge of character. And I can see that there was no malice in you intentions or actions. I have also had the privilege of going to war with you and I believe that you are more than worthy of the position of General. That is why I need you. The Empire cannot afford any more turmoil."

Dacien took a deep breath and straightened his stance.

The Emperor put his hand on Dacien's shoulder. "This coward, this assassin still sees you as a tool to be used for his purposes. No doubt he will try to contact you and offer an explanation for his behavior. We can turn this to our advantage and use it to lure him back where we will be waiting."

Dacien nodded, then stopped after some thought. "...that could be extremely dangerous."

"What do you mean?" asked Commander Horace, now on his feet as well.

Dacien turned to the man. "I've never seen his equal in combat. It is as if the gods themselves drive his actions."

Soren, still seated, replied calmly. "You just bring him here, and we'll do the rest."

After escorting Dacien out of the room, Magnus turned back to his pupils.

"...son of Maeryn Lorus?" Soren asked.

"Yes," Magnus replied. "That does complicate things. I never questioned Ukiru about any of your lives prior to your redemption. Well, there is still much that she can do for me with the Resistance. Coen can use her help. She commands a great deal of respect among the slaves and her presence is critical to controlling them."

Commander Arden sat back down in his chair. "Can we trust Dacien?"

Magnus smiled. "I have read his mind and his distrust of Kael goes deep, though his feelings of friendship are genuine. He can be manipulated for our purposes. Besides, with all of you in your positions, we don't have anyone left who is loyal to our cause. Dacien will do just fine."

24

The flicker of candlelight reflected off Saba's face. The bright blue eyes were just as Kael remembered. But it had been twenty years since he last saw his old teacher, and Saba had been an old man then.

"How is it possible that I'm staring into the face of a man who could be my father, when you were once old enough to be my grandfather?"

Saba smiled as he sat back into his chair. "How is it that I'm staring into the face of a child that was executed twenty years ago?" After a quick sip of wine, Saba cleared his throat. "There are many things that I must tell you, but that story will have to wait. There are more pressing matters at hand."

"Oh?" Kael replied.

Saba nodded. "...such as the state of this Empire and the ones who have taken control of it."

"Tell me what you know, and I will do the same," Kael responded.

"Very well," Saba said, downing the last of his wine before leaning forward in his chair. "Many years ago, while we still lived in Bastul, one of your father's friends was found along the western shore, a few miles north of the city. He was badly wounded and it appeared as though his merchant ship had been attacked. He was taken to the temple in Bastul to be cared for where he eventually died. But before his death, his nurse removed an arrowhead from his leg, bearing a symbol upon its broken shaft. Your father gave it to me to research and find some connection between the symbol and his friend's suspicious death."

"Shortly thereafter, your father disappeared. And the local council appointed Lemus to be his replacement. You are, of course, familiar with this part. But after you were sent to jail, Lemus forced me to leave. I stayed in the city for a while and found that your father was able to determine the approximate location of his friend's attack. And I also found out that he and a small crew took a ship from the Bastul navy and went to search the far side of the reef for an explanation. This is when he disappeared."

Kael put his hand over his mouth, starting to put the pieces together.

"After being caught and released, my investigation took me to Orud," Saba explained with outstretched hands, indicating the place they were now in. "In the great libraries, I researched the symbol, but to no avail. Then one evening while walking through these city streets, I was ambushed and captured by many cloaked men. They put a cover over my head and put me into a wagon. I was taken north to a mountainous area where a confinement camp had been constructed. There I was held captive for many years. It wasn't until after my escape that I learned that these men were members of an ancient cult known as the Kaliel."

Kael wanted to interrupt, but he held his tongue and let Saba finish his story.

"The Kaliel worship an ancient and powerful demon god named Rameel, who has been imprisoned for thousands of years. They are seeking to free him. And during my capture I met their High Priest, who acts as a surrogate for this demon. Its spirit can only have contact with this world through the use of this surrogate, who is in and of himself a powerful force. And tonight, I saw this man for the second time in my life. He addressed the crowd as the new Emperor."

Kael took this as his cue. "I know. I used to be a member, though I didn't know them by that name. And they called him the All Powerful."

Saba's eyebrows shot upward as he lifted his head.

"Let me explain," Kael said quickly. "After my imprisonment in Bastul, I was taken by ship to another prison in the north. I spent a few days there with other boys my age until a man by the name of Ukiru paid the jailor to release us. Ukiru took us to an island monastery in the north. We were educated and trained in combat. All the while, they told us that we would be instruments of the All Powerful to reclaim this world that abandoned him. Finally, after we all reached the age of eighteen, Ukiru took us on a long journey to the High Temple to meet the High Priest. It was to be a coming of age ceremony where the High Priest would officially introduce us to the All Powerful. We were supposed to open ourselves up to him so that he could reside in us and speak to us. We were told to yield to his presence in our lives so that he could work through us and make us powerful. But I didn't. I resisted."

Saba smiled with satisfaction.

"It was during this ceremony that I met the All Powerful and I fought against him. I..." Kael struggled for the words. "I cannot describe to you the overwhelming presence of evil that I felt. Not even with Lemus did I feel such a thing. It is indescribable." Kael paused as his voice faltered. When he resumed, his voice was shaky. "As soon as we got back to the monastery, I escaped."

Saba nodded. "The High Temple where you met the All Powerful, it was off the coast of Bastul, wasn't it?"

"I didn't realize it at the time, but yes. And the monastery is north of here on an island near the city of Suppard."

"Kael, these people had something to do with your father's disappearance."

"I know. And what's more, the Emperor's Generals and Commanders were my fellow students."

Saba looked to the ceiling, then rose from his chair to get more wine. Bringing the bottle back to the chair, he poured more for Kael, as well.

"I killed one of them in Leoran."

Saba tilted his head and waited for the explanation.

"After I escaped, I spent many years traveling the world. I eventually made my way back to Bastul just in time to see it sacked by the Syvaku. I traveled north to Leoran with my friend Dacien who was Captain of the Guard at the time. I'm leaving out many of the details, but the point is that the Syvaku attacked Leoran and I was part of the battle. That's when I killed their leader who, as it turns out, was Narian, one of the boys that I grew up with."

Saba shook his head as he began to realize the depth of their treachery.

"It gets worse," he admitted. "The Southern General had been killed in an earlier skirmish, so Dacien was appointed to the position of General."

...strong as an ox!

A memory of a conversation with Dacien came to Kael's mind, interrupting his story. Immediately, he realized another piece of the puzzle.

It was Jorn. Jorn was killed by accident and Dacien took his place!

"What is it?" Saba asked.

"I just realized something that I hadn't noticed before. The Southern General who was killed in an earlier battle was also someone I grew up with." Kael gulped some wine and continued. "Anyway, we were summoned here to Orud to meet with the Emperor. But during the meetings, a messenger warned of an approaching Korgan army. Dacien and the other Generals left to confront the barbarians, while I was stationed at the northern wall. Near midnight the Palace was attacked in secret and the western wing was set on fire. I suspected that this was only a distraction and got into the Palace just in time to find the Emperor and his Commanders murdered. I followed the trail of the assassin and caught up with him on the roof. He escaped and I didn't get to see his face, but I'm positive that it was Ukiru."

Saba shook his head in silence and took a minute to ponder what Kael had said. When he found the words, he spoke. "They used this war to gain control of Orud."

"That's right," Kael replied. "A competent soldier can rise through the ranks quickly in times of conflict. Narian led the Syvaku, and I have no doubt that the Korgan are led by one of them, as well."

Saba stared off to the side as he spoke. "Tell me again the names of the nine."

"Narian I just spoke of. He was tall and strong, but had a good heart." Kael began to remember his childhood friends and relayed more than Saba had asked for. His emotions were clouded, mixed with anger of betrayal and also fond memories of friendship.

"Jorn was a stout child, not just fat. He was built like an ox and incredibly strong. He was the southern General, but was accidentally killed in a battle with the Syvaku. That's how Dacien came to the position of General.

Then there is Berit, the Northern General. He didn't like people and spent all his time in the library. We used to tease him, carrying him out of the library by force, to make him go with us on short excursions."

The Southern Naval Commander is Horace. He was a cocky child who excelled in our combat training, but struggled with our classroom studies.

Arden is the Northern Naval Commander. He was just a bit older than the rest of us and mature for his age. He always had a different perspective and could be stubborn. But he had a good sense of humor.

And then there's Soren. He's the General of the Eastern Territory. He was my closest friend. He had seen many difficult times in his childhood and grew up without parents. He was well acquainted with violence and was the toughest of all the kids. He was the shortest, but we were all afraid to disagree with him out of fear. In spite of this, he loved to laugh and kept us all in good spirits most of the time. He was my competition. In combat as well as the classroom, he was excellent at everything he did. We were always neck and neck except for leadership. This is where he surpassed me. He was a natural leader and I couldn't ever beat him in competitions that required managing others."

Kael trailed off, lost in thought.

"That's six; what of the other three?" Saba asked.

"Rainer was the youngest. He wasn't really good at anything except arguing with Ukiru and knowing how to manipulate people.

Coen was nice... really talkative. He was good with classroom studies, but struggled in combat.

And the last is Donagh. He was just as big as Narian, but a bit thinner. He too excelled in combat due to his size and strength. But he was selfish and got into fights with most of us at one time or another. Except for Soren, that is."

Saba nodded his head, taking mental account of each individual. "So you haven't seen these other three?"

"That's right. I don't know what role they are playing, but you can be assured that they all have some part in this."

Saba leaned to the side and looked out the window. "It is almost dawn."

Kael turned around to see the sky lightening to the east. "Dacien is in danger. He doesn't understand what is going on around him.

"Yes. When the sun comes up, I will go into the city and talk to some people, ask some questions. I want to know the rest of the Emperor's plan and how well it was received. I'll also find out where Dacien is."

Kael nodded, then yawned.

"Why don't you get some rest; it's been a long night."

"Thanks," Kael replied, leaning back in his chair. "Saba?"

"Yes."

"It's good to see you again."

The old man smiled. "...and you, as well."

25

Kael jerked awake, startled by an unknown sound. He lay still, ears probing the silence for an explanation. But all was silent in Saba's house. *Must have been a dream.* The bright sun was beaming in through the windows and Kael judged it to be roughly noon. He rose from his chair and stretched, then walked outside and stood on the sand, staring at the ocean. Seagulls passed by overhead, riding the same soft breeze that caused the long blades of nearby grass to bow to the north.

Kael breathed in the salty air and considered his conversation with Saba. But his mind was still cluttered with a mixture of emotions. Out of habit, he sat down on the sand, crossed his legs, and closed his eyes. During his time at the monastery, there were many times of confusion and anger. And the only thing that helped was to sit above the cliffs and allow the ebb and flow of the ocean and wind drive the confusion from his mind.

With his eyes closed, his mind sought information from the sounds about him. As he had trained himself to do, he quieted his thoughts, forcing his mind to reach out with his other sense, the one he'd never told anyone about. It seemed elusive at first, but gradually, the familiar sensation returned.

He could feel the grass sway, the tiny spiraling currents of wind as they passed by. He focused his sense and pushed it out from him to feel the water at the shore. In this way, he explored his surroundings and, almost immediately, he felt a weight lift off his shoulders. He was at peace again and his emotions began to sort themselves out. He wasn't sure how long it took, but eventually, he began to see things clearly.

The sting of betrayal and the guilt of being associated with these people began to rise to the surface. He felt as though he was responsible for them and their actions. *They are powerful and dangerous! Someone's got to stop them!*

But how could Kael ever hope to stop them. He had always found combat to be easy, until Narian. During that fight, he almost lost. And

Narian wasn't the best in the group. *But I did stop him. He's no longer a factor in this situation.*

Slowly, Kael's fear receded, and in its place was a resolution that something had to be done. He would probably be killed, but there was no one else who could even stand a chance against these people. They had trained their whole lives for this mission, and they would succeed otherwise. *I trained with them. I can't let them succeed.*

The sun was beginning to slip behind the western horizon when Kael caught sight of a small vessel heading straight for the house. Within minutes, he could see that it was Saba's ship with a strange dark object aboard. Kael waited patiently at the water's edge and eventually made sense of what he was seeing. Ajani stood at the bow, holding the reins of Kael's horse. Kael smiled and waved to his friend.

As the sky continued to darken, the small boat came to a stop in the sand. Kael waded out to help lower the cargo ramp and un-board his horse.

"Do you have it?" Kael asked quietly.

Ajani slung two large bags over his shoulders and winked, indicating the presence of the sword.

"Thank you," Kael whispered. He wasn't sure why, but he felt the need to keep it a secret. He didn't yet understand what it was, and so didn't want to talk about it with anyone. Luckily, Ajani rarely spoke.

When Saba neared, they led the horse down the ramp and through the shallow water, draping the reins over the branch of a shade tree near the house.

Saba cooked a simple meal. After they ate, they sat on the porch looking at the firelight from the city reflecting off the rippled ocean.

"He's freed the slaves and given them the same status as the rest of the working class." Saba said, relaying what information he had gathered during his excursion into the city. "You're a free man now," he said, nudging Ajani.

The scarred man smiled indifferently.

"He hasn't been a slave since I found him in Leoran," Kael corrected.

"Of course," Saba offered, apologetically. "It has really caused unrest in the city. But most of the citizens agree with him. Only the ones who stand to lose profits have put up an argument. Normally, this would be a good thing. But I have to wonder why he did it, and how it helps his cause. Clearly, it wasn't out of pure intentions."

"He's building an army," Kael answered. "The Syvaku, the Korgs, the Kaliel, the Orud armies and navy, and now the entire slave population of the Empire are under his control.

They all considered these words for several moments, with nothing but the sounds of lapping water in the background. Finally, Saba broke the silence.

"Kael. There's one thing I haven't mentioned."

"...only one thing?" Kael questioned, knowing that Saba had many secrets.

"...one thing in particular. Your mother was at the feast."

Kael turned to look at Saba, a look of shock on his face. "How is that possible? Dacien said she disappeared from Bastul when the Syvaku attacked. He thought she was kidnapped."

"I don't know, but she was at Magnus' side for portions of the evening. Dacien didn't seem to notice."

"He was Captain of the Guard in Bastul; but it's possible that he never met her," Kael offered, then went silent. After a minute, he spoke again. "So the High Priest, his name is Magnus?"

"Magnus Calidon," Saba clarified. "Does it make you feel different toward him, knowing his name?"

"No," Kael answered flatly.

A seagull screeched as it flew overhead, heading for the water. It offered a momentary distraction as they watched it land a few yards out, ripples of water extending outward from its chosen landing site.

"The Generals and Commanders are staying at the Palace tonight, along with the Emperor. And Maeryn seems to be an honored guest of Magnus', so I would not be surprised if she was staying at the Palace as well. But there is much activity among the ranks of the Orud soldiers. It appears that they are preparing to leave."

"Saba..." Kael said, turning to look at the old man in the eyes. "They have to be stopped."

"I know. I am trying to figure out how to get an audience with the Council, without Magnus attending."

"No," corrected Kael. "There is no time for talking. I have to act, before their plans are finalized. Whatever they're doing, we can't afford for them to get prepared."

"What do you propose we do?" Saba questioned.

"I'm going into the city at midnight. I need to borrow your boat."

"Nonsense. I'll take you myself. What are you going to do?"

"Dacien and my mother can't stay where they are; their lives are in danger."

"Kael," Saba protested. "You said yourself that these men are extremely dangerous. After you escaped, what did they do? While you were traveling the world, they were continuing their training, preparing for what they are doing at this very moment. How can you hope to do anything about it? I say we tell the Council about Magnus' secret dealings. With your testimony, they would surely bring him to trial."

"And then what?" Kael replied. "Magnus is gifted with speech. He could convince them of anything. It wouldn't work."

"And what is your plan?"

Kael rose to his feet and looked down on his friends sitting in the porch. "They planned every last detail, but they didn't account for me. As much as I hate to say it, I'm one of them. And I'm the only one that can stop them."

Saba's boat cut silently through the water, pushed by a stiff breeze. Kael stood at the prow, staring into the distance. He was dressed in a style that Saba had never seen before. The pants were black, loose fitting above the knee for ease of movement, but snug around the calf so as not to get caught on anything. The tunic, if it could be called such, covered his entire upper body, as well as his arms. The same strategy had been applied to this piece of clothing as well, fitting loosely around the shoulders, but tight on the forearms. The back of Kael's hands were also covered by a flap of material and held into place with a loop around the middle finger, such that when he made a fist, his light skin disappeared, leaving only a shadow of dark fabric in the shape of a man. Gone were the sandals of traditional Orud style. In their place, were dark boots of the same black fabric, covering all the skin of his feet. The soles were soft leather which produced hardly any sound when Kael moved across the deck of the ship.

The only thing that could be seen clearly, without straining the eyes, was Kael's head. His hair was gathered at the back and fluttered in the breeze. Kael's hands were free of weapons, holding only a small bundle of fabric that Saba assumed was intended to cover his head.

Ahead and to the port side, a small abandoned dock extended out into the bay. Saba guided the boat toward it. Six miles outside the city limits was a long way, but Kael didn't seem to mind.

Saba concentrated on his approach to the dock while his peripheral vision noted Kael's blonde head disappear into the darkness. A quick glance confirmed that he had pulled a black hood over his head. Saba turned the sails, and they went slack, the boat coasting toward the dock.

"Will you not be armed," Saba spoke into the night air, mindful of the way sound carries over water.

"Men will fall. Weapons will abound," came the reply from the shadow at the prow.

Saba turned his attention back to the approaching dock. He adjusted the position of the rudder, bringing them aside the tip of the dock. When he looked back, Kael was already on the dock, halfway to the shore. Saba hadn't even seen him move.

Kael turned around, only his eyes showing through a horizontal slit in his hood. "Thank you for everything," he said quietly, then disappeared into the darkness.

26

The Palace guard had been doubled due to the strange events over the past few days. Spearmen circled the base of the wall surrounding the Palace, with a detachment moving one direction nearest the wall while a second detachment moved in the opposite direction farther away from the wall. Their pacing was timed such that there was always visual coverage of the entire guarded wall at all times. Archers followed a similar routine along the top of the wall. This was in addition to the guards stationed in hidden places throughout the surrounding fields and trees, keeping watch over the various approaches to the Palace.

Even with the increased security, they failed to notice the shadow that moved silently among them. The darkness of the night couldn't be illuminated properly by the torches scattered throughout the Palace gardens. And through the darkness, Kael moved with stealth and speed.

One particular guard, on his route around the base of the wall, thought he heard something behind him. A quick glance over his shoulder revealed nothing. He looked back to the wall and stopped walking, letting his ears probe the night, but to no avail. After a few seconds, he resumed his march, walking past the base of the guard tower that jutted sharply inward to connect with the wall, resulting in a shadow cast by the torchlight only a few yards back. And only a few yards ahead, another guard approached, boredom showing on his face.

Kael held himself close to the stone, fingers jammed into the crevices, holding his body in the shadow between the guard tower and the wall, ten feet off the ground. He counted to twenty in his head then began to scale the wall as the second guard passed beyond the tower underneath him.

He paused just before the top of the wall, waiting to hear the changing of the guard, which occurred every twenty minutes. His fingers began to shake, struggling to maintain their grip on the stone. After three minutes of holding still, footsteps sounded above, followed by muffled speech. Kael waited another minute, then cocked his head to the side and eased upward to peer over the edge. The new guard was facing his direction, but looking downward as he readjusted his scabbard on his belt.

Kael swung silently over the wall and landed in front of the man. By the time the guard looked up, his vision was already blurry, caused by the pressure against the side of his throat that restricted the blood flow to his brain. Kael held tight as the man lost consciousness. *That'll buy me twenty minutes before they realize I'm here!*

Kael eased the guard to the ground and propped him against the wall, arranging his cloak to appear as if the man had fallen asleep. If he was lucky, he might get another couple minutes out of the charade.

...fifty one, fifty two, fifty three.

Kael eased open the door that separated the guard house from the walkway along the top of the wall. As expected, the archer had just passed. Kael slipped out of the door, across the walkway, and descended the stone staircase that led down to the Palace courtyard.

Once inside the Palace wall, Kael moved more quickly, but still conscious of the occasional archer passing overhead. He swung around the outside of the Palace itself, until he arrived underneath the windows of the guest quarters. Hiding in the shadows, he waited until the passing of another guard, then scaled a vine that ran up the left side of the window. At the third floor, Kael pulled himself over the balcony and dropped to the floor, just inside the room where he hoped Dacien was still staying.

Approaching quietly, he found Dacien asleep on his bed. Kael pulled off his hood and leaned close to hear his friend's steady breathing. Putting his hand over Dacien's mouth, he whispered into his ear.

"Dacien, it's Kael."

Dacien flinched and looked scared for a moment, then recognition came.

"Your life is in great danger and I need to get you out of here. Stay quiet." Slowly, Kael released his hand and Dacien sat up. "I'll explain everything later, but right now I need you to trust me. I only have about ten minutes before the guards discover that I'm here."

Dacien stared blankly, as Kael continued to whisper.

"Where is the Emperor's mistress? Is she staying with Magnus?"

"Uh...I don't think so. Though she's in a room close to his. Why?"

"She's my mother, and I've got to get her out of here as well."

Dacien eyebrows raised. "Let me get dressed and I'll take you to her."

Kael searched the room for weapons while Dacien pulled a tunic over his neck.

"Kael, where have you been? And what's going on?"

"I'll explain later, just hurry," he replied, finding a short spear next to Dacien's armor. Turning back to his friend, he handed him his sword and belt. "We might need this to get out."

Dacien accepted it and quickly fastened the belt around his waist. Within seconds, they were walking briskly through the quiet halls of the Palace, Dacien leading and Kael following. Moving away from the guest quarters, Dacien led them closer to the heart of the Palace. Kael kept his eyes alert, looking for signs of trouble.

"This way," Dacien whispered, ducking down a narrow, unlit hall.

"Isn't the Emperor's room this way?" Kael pointed.

"...only if you want a big reception."

"Alright," he whispered, waving his hands for Dacien to move quickly as he followed.

A few more twists and turns brought them to a thick wooden door, which Dacien hurriedly pulled open. "After you."

Kael rushed inside and found a large room, brightly lit, with maps along the wall. In the center of the room was a raised pedestal with a map of the city upon it. It was the war room of Orud. And leaning over opposites sides of the map, were Arden and Horace.

Kael strafed to the right, covering Dacien with an extended spear. His body immediately tensed up as it had the other evening, upon seeing his old acquaintances. It was an unusual feeling for him.

Horace straightened up and looked over to Kael with a smile on his face.

A grinding clank sounded behind Kael as the door was bolted shut. Kael spun around to see Dacien standing in a defense posture and backing away to the left.

"I'm sorry Kael," was all he said. The look on his face made it clear that he had mixed emotions about what he'd just done.

"Good work Dacien," said Arden, as he moved away from the pedestal, circling to the right.

...EL...AEL...K...KAEL'S HE...HER...HERE...

The sound moved through Kael's head with a reverberating echo; each syllable seemed out of sync, on a separate timing until the sounds collided into each other with vague meaning.

Kael could see the glazed look in Horace's eyes and realized that he was calling out to the others, sending an inaudible message to his brothers. His ability to communicate mentally was not nearly as developed as Magnus' had been during the banquet, but it was still effective.

A hundred yards away lying on his bed, Magnus' eyes popped open, his sleep disturbed by the sound in his head. He rose quickly and dressed, grabbing his cloak and slinging it over his shoulders.

A knock sounded at his door, which promptly opened. Soren stepped through.

"Did you hear that?" he asked his master.

"Yes, I'm going to take care of it." Suddenly, Magnus could feel the frustration emanating from Soren. "You want to kill him," he stated.

It wasn't a question, but Soren replied anyway. "Yes."

"I need you to go get Maeryn and take her away from here. I know your passion and what you shared with Kael as children, but our mission is too critical to take any chances. He's already caused major setbacks."

"Yes, my lord," Soren replied obediently.

"He will try to get to her. Make sure she is safe."

"Yes, my lord."

Kael held his spear in his right hand, the butt tucked underneath his arm.

Arden moved to the right, unsheathing a long sword as Horace moved left to take a spear off the wall.

Kael stood the same height as Horace, while Arden was only a hand shorter. They were both muscular and moved light on their feet. Ukiru had trained them well.

Kael ran for Horace.

Arden moved to close the gap.

Horace's spear jutted out for Kael's midsection.

Kael moved inside the range of the spear tip and deflected the shaft with his forearm. Advancing quickly, he slashed over Horace's spear, using the bladed tip as a sword which cut through the meat of the man's upper left arm. Continuing the motion, he brought the spear around to his back to catch Arden's sword on its way to cleaving Kael in two.

The spear cracked in the collision and Kael dropped it as he moved past Horace and out from the conflict. Pulling two short swords from their crossed position on the wall, Kael spun around in time to meet Arden' forceful attack.

Arden lashed out with a flurry of strikes, ending in loud clangs as Kael fended them off methodically.

Then Kael saw an opening in Arden's attack. Deflecting a jab, Kael countered with a left-handed strike, catching Arden across the chest.

Arden's eyes went wide as he realized the sharp pain in his chest. Kael followed quickly with an over handed cut to the neck, severing Arden's collarbone and burying the blade in his chest.

Blood sprayed like a fountain from the fresh wound, covering Kael's face. For a moment, his vision was impaired. Instinctively, Kael pulled the blade free of the corpse and dropped to the ground, rolling to the left of Arden's body as a spear flew overhead and stuck into the wall.

Rolling to his feet, Kael ran to his left and kicked open the door opposite of where he entered the room. As he ducked through the doorway, he caught a glimpse of Horace pulling an axe and shield from the wall, as Dacien stared in horror at Arden's body.

The exit led Kael into a large atrium with a fountain in the center; a statue of a partially-clothed woman pouring water from a vase into the shallow pool. The wall of the war room was the only solid structure as the ceiling and two other walls were latticed wood with vines filling in the spaces. Opposite the war room, the atrium opened into a courtyard with darkness beyond.

...an escape!

The thought only crossed his mind briefly, but Kael turned to face the doorway he'd just come through, waiting for Horace. He didn't come here to run. He came to face his past and he wasn't about to leave until his own mission was accomplished.

Horace came through the doorway with an odd arrangement of weapons. His shield was rectangular and curved in the fashion of the long spearmen that typically held the front lines of Orud armies. But in his left hand, he held a single-bladed axe, tipped with a sharpened point for jabbing.

Kael slung the blood from his blades and held them outward, stepping forward to meet Horace.

Just as he did when they were children, Horace approached without hesitation. He held his shield tight and swung his axe toward Kael.

Kael strafed right and left, parrying the attacks, following with a few slashes which glanced harmlessly off of Horace's shield.

Horace continued to advance, jabbing sharply at Kael's chest.

With a double slash, Kael blocked the axe with the left sword and chopped the shaft with the right. Horace's axe head fell with a clang to the floor. Dropping his swords, Kael lunged forward and grabbed the top edge of the shield with both hands, jerking it away from Horace. The leather straps broke and sent Kael floundering to the floor.

Horace advanced immediately with a kick to Kael's head.

Deflecting the foot with the inside of the shield, Kael followed with a sweeping kick to Horace's leg. Horace stood his ground, barely affected by Kael's attack.

With one giant step forward, Horace rammed his powerful leg into Kael's ribs, lifting him off the ground and sending him a few feet backward.

The air flew from Kael's lungs as he sprawled on the floor, struggling to regain his footing.

Horace stood still with a crazed smile on his face. He had always been a formidable foe in hand combat. His legs were strong and fast and knew he had Kael outmatched. After watching his enemy beg for breath, he rushed forward to end struggle.

Kael, his head down toward the ground, saw Horace from behind lowered eyelids. As predicted, the man rushed in, confident in the speed and power of his ranged kicks. As Horace neared with a front kick aimed to the head, Kael glided sideways. The kick missed his face by inches. At full extension, Horace's supporting leg was vulnerable. Kael drove his heel into the man's kneecap and felt the crunch of bone as the leg bent the wrong direction.

Horace's arms flailed outward as he sought balance, his momentum now working against him. He folded under his own weight and collapsed to his knees with an anguished shriek.

Kael threw his whole body behind the punch and crushed the man's windpipe, sending him backward to the ground.

Horace's face cringed with panic as he realized that death was imminent.

Kael rose to his feet and glared down at his enemy, watching as Horace's grip on life slipped slowly away. Kael breathed deeply and released a sigh.

After a moment of silence, He turned around and looked to the fountain, his mind not yet ready to process what his next move would be. He was vaguely aware that he still hadn't made contact with his mother yet. But his rigid body was still in combat mode. Then he caught a presence out of the corner of his eye.

Dacien stood in the doorway leading into the war room, a grave look on his face.

Before Kael was even able to identify the emotion that he felt, an overwhelming presence of evil was followed immediately by a suffocating feeling in the air around his body. He looked quickly to his left and saw a dark silhouette coming into the atrium from outside. As soon as Magnus' name came to Kael's mind, he felt an immense pressure on his lungs and the brief sensation of floating before being hurled through the air.

Kael's body crashed into the stone wall of the war room, held four feet from the ground, pinned into place by an unseen force.

Magnus stepped into the light with his hand outstretched in Kael's direction.

The pressure on Kael's lungs increased to the point of strangulation, causing him to panic. But something else was beginning to happen as well. That familiar feeling of awareness, of broadened sensation covered Kael as well. Kael closed his eyes and began to feel the tangible extension of Magnus' power as it stretched through the air and held Kael into place.

Kael focused his own awareness on what was happening inside his body. As his lungs started to collapse, Kael pushed back, expanding the soft tissue until they began to work again. Air quickly returned and Kael felt a moment of peace.

...INTERESTING!
I SEE THAT YOU HAVE POWERS AS WELL.
THEN I SHALL HAVE TO FIND A MORE CREATIVE WAY TO MAKE YOU SUFFER.

The voice of Magnus was strong inside Kael's head, much different than Horace's earlier warning call. Suddenly, Kael's awareness vanished in a flash of sensation, like the loss of vision after looking into the sun. All the texture and detail vanished as if the whole world, air, water, earth, had been melded into one object.

Kael's brain screamed in agony as the pressure moved to his head. With the last shred of strength that remained, Kael focused inside his own head, seeking the location of Magnus' attack. Navigation was difficult without a sense of the surroundings, but by feel, Kael followed Magnus' intrusion.

Focusing all his efforts, Kael resisted, trying to fend off the attack, as helpless as a farmer who attempts to block the hail from destroying his crops. The area was too great, and Kael's powers too limited. And all he could hope to do was delay the inevitable.

Then, Magnus' presence disappeared. Kael's awareness instantly expanded to fill the void. From some distant place, he thought he felt his body fall and hit the ground, but he seemed to be disconnected from his physical self. His consciousness was all that remained.

Ajani rushed across the paved floor of the atrium. He could see Kael pinned against the wall with his hands around his throat, as if he were being choked to death. But Ajani couldn't let that happen. He remembered Lemus' blood-splattered face on that fateful morning, so long ago, and the vision of Kael rushing in with a pitchfork.

Ajani planted his left foot and threw the spear, putting the momentum of his entire body into the shaft of the weapon as it left his hand.

It cut through the air and punctured Magnus' stomach, knocking him backward several steps.

Kael's body dropped to the floor, limp.

Ajani ran toward the injured man who was gripping the spear with both hands and watching the blood from the entry and exit wounds in his abdomen. Just before he reached him, Magnus lifted his hand.

Ajani ran into an invisible wall and came to an abrupt stop. He felt an intense anger come over him just before his bones began to break, crushed from the inside out. In this instant, Ajani felt an all-encompassing feeling of peace. He knew that his life debt to Kael had been paid. And he looked to the sky and prayed that the gods would receive him.

Saba stepped into the atrium and summed up the situation at a glance. He saw Ajani's body fall to the floor and could feel that his spirit had already left the body. Kael was on the floor against the wall to the right, alive but unconscious. General Dacien cowered in the doorway; the fear coming from him was tangible. And at the center of Saba's vision, was Magnus, kneeling in a pool of his own blood, and trying to regain his footing. A dark presence surrounded the man and Saba knew that he was still a threat.

Lifting his hands, Saba contained Magnus' powers and thrust him backwards until he tripped over the low stone wall and fell into the fountain. A visible blue light accompanied the act that made Dacien cower even more.

With one hand extended toward Magnus, Saba knelt down to Ajani.

The scarred slave's body lacked the form that it should have, as if his bones had been shattered from the inside. But his face had a look of peace and Saba smiled, knowing that Ajani didn't go into the afterlife by accident. It was an intentional act on behalf of his childhood friend.

Saba reached down with his right hand and closed Ajani's eyes.

Looking up to Dacien, he made eye contact. "Get Kael out of here," he commanded. "He's still alive."

Dacien looked behind him at the war room, contemplating an escape.

"He came here to rescue you," Saba shouted, bringing the man back to his senses. "...now pick him up and get him out of here. I'll be right behind you."

Dacien snapped into action, lifting Kael's body off the floor and draping it over his shoulders. His legs shook under the weight of Kael's limp body, but within seconds he was moving past Saba and out of the atrium.

Saba released his hold on Magnus and left with Dacien.

The waters of the fountain swirled dark with Magnus' blood. He rose, water and blood dripping from his body. The spear that protruded from both sides of his abdomen broke into two pieces, flying in opposite directions away from him. He stepped out onto the stone floor of the atrium with a look of determined revenge on his face.

My lord is coming, and he will have no mercy on his enemies!

PART III

1

The intrusion came like a stab to the back of the head. Quick. Painful. Uninvited. The man sat upright in his chair, deeply troubled by the penetrating sensation that probed his mind. Troubled because he knew this feeling, though it had been many, many years since he'd experienced it last.

When the sensation passed, the feeling of alarm gave way to acceptance. The man slowly leaned back in his chair and drew in a deep breath. Then, methodically, he raised the lid of the humidor sitting atop his desk and retrieved a cigar. Trimming the end, he placed it into his mouth and struck a wooden match. The thick white smoke curled around his hand and rose lazily to the ceiling as he took steady draws to get it started. At once, his sense of smell was assaulted by the bold and earthen aroma.

...one of life's simple pleasures.

A knock sounded at the door.

"Come in," he replied casually, glancing at the clock on the wall.

The door opened quickly to reveal a young man, in his early forties, dressed in a black suit and tie. His hair was cut short and he had a serious look on his face. Carefully closing the door, he walked briskly across the lavish expanse that separated them, his muscled frame appearing restricted in the expensive clothing.

"Sir, I'm sorry to interrupt you, but something has happened at our facility in Brazil. I have the security footage," the man explained, gesturing to the wall of TV screens seamlessly tiled together.

"Play video," the man behind the desk enunciated. Almost instantaneously, the voice recognition software processed the request and the wall of black glass opposite the desk came to life.

The footage displayed a massive circular room enclosed in safety glass. Around the perimeter were observation rooms filled with laboratory equipment and bustling with personnel. At the center of the room stood a stone dais that seemed to shimmer in the artificial light.

A time display in the lower right corner of the screen read 10:06:24.

A blue light began to emanate from the dais, coalescing into brilliant shafts that stabbed upward, radiating from the center. Then a shadow formed above the surface of the platform, a void that began to take on form and materialize into a dark object that reflected light. Floating above the dais, the object suddenly expanded and shot upward with incredible speed. And like the image burned into one's retina after a lighting strike, the object was gone and only a vague impression of leathery wings was left in the minds of those watching. Suddenly, the glass enclosure shattered and the camera footage turned to snow.

A second later, the perspective changed to that of a camera sitting atop one of the buildings adjacent to the main structure, showing their compound and the surrounding jungle. At 10:06:54, the atrium roof exploded upward as an immense creature unfurled its angular wings and moved quickly out of the range of the camera's vision. At 10:07:22, a column of water erupted from the building and shot skyward, like the trail of smoke left after a shuttle launch. Within seconds, the footage from the second camera was lost in the deluge.

The man behind the desk looked to his subordinate standing at the center of the room. "Check the topographical maps and find the lowest, narrowest section of the surrounding mountains. I want a blasting crew down there immediately to clear out the water. The whole facility needs to be operational as soon as possible; consider it your highest..."

The man behind the desk was interrupted by an audible alarm coming from his assistant's touchscreen computer held at his side.

The younger man lifted the screen and touched the surface, wrinkling his eyebrows. "We have incoming aircraft. The perimeter has been breached and two of our surface-to-air systems have gone down. Wait..." the assistant trailed off as he touched the screen. "This can't be right. It's moving too fast for aircraft. ...a cruise missile?" he mumbled to himself.

The older gentleman rose from his chair. "Turn off our defense systems and tell the men to stand down."

"Sir?"

"It is no threat to us unless attacked. Do it immediately and lock the door on your way out."

"Yes, Sir," the young man replied, leaving obediently.

In the quiet aftermath, the older man walked carefully to the southern side of the room where two large wooden doors opened expectantly, triggered by motion detectors. Moving onto the balcony, he leaned on the stone railing, drew a deep puff from his cigar, and waited patiently.

Across the lush jungle, a dark object appeared on the horizon, somewhat obscured by the mist rising into the humid air from the protective canopy of foliage below. The object appeared to grow exponentially as it neared. And as expected, the penetrating sensation returned to his mind, only duller this time.

Across the treetops, the foliage parted in a wake behind the creature as it moved with blinding speed, coming straight for the man on the balcony. At the last second before impact, its wings shot outward, sending forth a torrent of air as it came to a perfect hover.

The man on the balcony simply shut his eyes as dust pelted his skin. When the air was still, he opened his eyes and lazily brushed the dirt from the lapel of his silk suit. He looked down to the cold cigar in his hand and disappointedly threw it over the railing as the ten-foot creature came to a landing on the balcony thirty feet away.

The man didn't bother to stifle the laughter that came from his throat. "Rameel, you are still just as subtle as you always were. Your...chosen form...is comical, but it suits you."

"And your chosen form is beneath you, Armaros" the creature growled back, not out of anger, but simply because the arrangement of its vocal chords demanded such a sound.

Armaros stepped forward confidently. "I assume you have a good excuse for breaking the oath?" All the humor was gone from his voice now.

Rameel took a step backward and allowed his massive wings to drape around him like a cloak. "It was Sariel. He betrayed me...he betrayed us all."

Armaros narrowed his eyes and inspected his ancient ally, his glistening black skin stretched over a powerfully muscled frame. He looked like a something from a child's nightmare. *Of course, that was the idea.* But far more abnormal than the creature's appearance was the lack of something in particular.

"Where is your key?" Armoros demanded.

Rameel cocked his ghoulish head to one side.

"I see. So your coming here was not intended and you want my help to get back?" Though phrased as a question, it left no room for discussion.

"Yes," Rameel admitted simply.

Armaros nodded, then looked out across the jungle. "And what about your progress? Has this...incident...affected your efforts?"

Rameel growled low in his throat and bared his teeth. "Sariel trapped me inside the portal! Without my key I couldn't complete the journey. He has set me back thousands of years."

Armoros spun around and stalked toward the creature with indignation. "You mean to tell me that you've accomplished nothing in all this time?" he shouted.

"Lower you voice Armaros," Rameel commanded, expanding his wings to emphasize his equality. "I have accomplished much, given my situation. Even now I have hordes of loyal followers waiting to do my bidding. It's in the best of all our interests for you to help me get back. I will kill Sariel and move ahead with preparations. And the next time you see me will be as we all planned."

"Very well," Armaros conceded. "I'll help you, though it may take some time."

2

Maeryn sat in silence as the boat neared the shoreline. A simple dock extended from the rocks and angled to the right. Small waves produced a rhythmic rocking of the ship that Maeryn always found soothing. A slight lurch, as the boat made contact with the dock, was immediately followed by a flurry of activity from the crew. A plank was lowered from the rail of the ship to the deck and Maeryn rose to her feet following the example of her guide. *Actually, guide isn't the proper term.* The dark haired young man would likely be offended if she vocalized her thoughts. He was second in command of the Resistance, just under Magnus. But today, that would change.

Maeryn could hardly contain her excitement and, at the same time, fought back a sense of anxiety about the events to come. Taking a deep breath, she tried her best to clear her mind of emotions and concentrate on the task at hand. After all, she only had one chance to soak up as much instruction as possible.

Maeryn followed Coen off the ship and up the stone steps leading to the sprawling residence above. She had met Coen once before, she recalled. During her first arrival in Orud, he had been the one to show her around the underground passages beneath the temple. He had been a fine host, just the same as this day. Only now, the dynamic of their relationship had changed.

At the top of the steps, the ocean breeze blew freely across the land. It was a bright and clear morning and when Maeryn turned around, she thought the eastern shore of Orud could just be seen low on the horizon across the bay.

"This way," Coen said softly.

She followed him through the arched entrance gate and into the courtyard, which contained a fountain, but lacked vegetation.

Hmm, I'll have to change that.

Across the courtyard were two large wooden doors that came together to form a massive arch. Only now, they were standing open. Coen walked quickly inside and turned to the right, following a long curving hallway with windows to the right and doors to the left. After they had walked roughly half the length of this wing, the hallway opened into a small, interior courtyard, with several tables flanked by comfortable looking chairs. In this room, potted plants adorned either side of the columns that held up the raised timber ceiling.

Interesting. It definitely has a woman's touch.

Coen turned to the left and continued his brisk pace as Maeryn tried to keep up and take in everything that she could. Leaving the sitting area, they entered another short hallway that ended at a closed door. Coen stopped briefly to slide the latch and push open the doors.

At the rear of the house, the land dropped away gradually so that Maeryn could see for miles. The view was breathtaking. Long grasses swayed in the wind like ripples on the ocean, the view broken only by a few clusters of trees and grazing horses. Fifty yards from the main building, sat a guest house, which Maeryn guessed was their destination. It took only a few minutes to walk along the stone path and reach the small building.

"So this is it," Maeryn said aloud.

"You sound as if you're unimpressed," Coen said over his shoulder without stopping.

"Oh no," Maeryn corrected. "I was just thinking out loud. I still can't believe I'm here."

Coen turned back and smiled, then proceeded through the doorway. Inside was a circular room with doors leading to what Maeryn presumed were the kitchen, the bedroom, and the bath. It appeared to be a typical guest house until Coen lifted a tapestry along the south wall revealing a hidden door. He quickly produced a key that Maeryn hadn't noticed him holding earlier, and pushed it into the lock. A sharp twist produced a muffled click and the door swung inward to reveal the top few steps of a spiral staircase. Coen stepped inside and held the tapestry back so that she could follow.

Maeryn stepped over the threshold and, for an awkward moment, stood nose to nose with Coen. He let go the tapestry and the staircase became pitch dark.

"Watch your step," Coen said softly, his receding voice echoing slightly off the stone.

Maeryn picked her steps carefully in the darkness. As she rounded the bend, a flickering light could be seen reflecting off the walls. When she reached the landing at the bottom of the stairs, she breathed in a breath of surprise.

"And now you're impressed," Coen stated, matter-of-factly.

"Yes," Maeryn answered slowly. It took a moment for her to comprehend what she was looking at. The center of the enormous room was raised by a few feet. On this platform was a miniature world, or an Empire, to be exact. The terrain rose and fell to form mountains, valleys, and rivers.

Scattered across the landscape were tiny figurines of various designs, some with flags. At first glance it appeared random, but upon closer inspection Maeryn understood exactly what it meant.

"This is the whole Empire, isn't it?" she asked.

"Indeed," Coen answered confidently.

Maeryn walked around to where Coen was standing. She pointed at the model. "This is the city of Orlek in the northeast. The red figures represent Orud armies, and the flags denote which army."

"That's right," Coen replied, clearly impressed with Maeryn's quick mind. "The major cities such as Orlek, Orud, Bastul, Leoran, and others also have more detailed models. See," he said, pointing across the room. The two walked back around to the south where several other platforms had been constructed, each containing a larger scale model of the major cities within the Empire.

Maeryn gazed back over the enormity of the Empire and suddenly came to a realization. "The size of each figure represents a certain number of soldiers within that army."

"...and navy," Coen corrected, pointing to the ships standing along the flat outer edge of the model.

"And the green figures are..."

"The Resistance," Coen finished her thought.

"I had no idea..." she trailed off. Walking closer to the board, Maeryn noted that there were almost as many green markers as red. She continued, "...that the Resistance was so extensive."

Coen smiled, enjoying the moment. "To be fair, only a small portion of the Resistance are trained soldiers," he replied, fingering a flag with a sword shape embroidered on the fabric. "So in terms of military might, we still don't compete. But we have many supporters among the slave class which makes up a majority of the total population."

"...former slave class," Maeryn countered.

"...of course," Coen agreed. "And as you have experienced first-hand, even one person can make an enormous difference."

Maeryn nodded, looking at the southern-most point of the Empire— Bastul.

"Come," Coen continued. "We have much more to discuss."

Maeryn followed him through an arched tunnel in the north wall to another room, much smaller than the first. This one was cluttered with shelves, stuffed with scrolls and books of all kinds. Along the left wall of the room were maps of the sort that Maeryn was used to seeing during her time in Bastul. And at the center of this display, was a writing desk illuminated by several candles that were nearly spent. At the table, a thin man lifted his head and peered at his guests with sparkling eyes. He was a good deal older than Maeryn. Although he had the look of someone who never made it outside, his skin was tanned and wrinkled nonetheless.

"This is Noster," Coen said, leading her over to the man. "He is our...librarian, I suppose."

"...pleasure," he mumbled, extending his hand to Maeryn.

She grasped it firmly and shook it, looking him in the eyes.

"Noster will prove to be a valuable resource to you in your daily responsibilities. Each morning, the reports will come in by boat from various places throughout the Empire. He will analyze the reports and update the models in the other room based on the new information. He will then document the movements of troops and supplies in writing as a summarization. You will be responsible to approve the summary and deliver it to your...superior, as often as once a day when he is available."

At Coen's stumbling, she realized that Noster didn't know the identity of the Resistance leader. Such a precaution made much sense considering the criminal nature of what they were doing. In fact, she wouldn't be surprised if every member of the Resistance was only trusted with the identity of their immediate superior.

Coen led her out and back to the room of models. "In addition, you will receive orders from your superior and relay them to Noster who will draft them for your approval. These will then be given to the same individuals who bring the reports every morning. On some occasions, you will be issuing these orders yourself. You must remember that the continuous circulation of information is critical to the success of the Resistance. It can be a tiring responsibility, but fulfilling as well."

"Where will you go?" she asked.

"I am needed elsewhere," Coen replied evasively. "Though we have achieved our primary goal of freeing the slaves, there is much, yet, to be done. The beliefs and behavior of citizens cannot be changed overnight. The Empire still needs its share of prodding in order to change the culture of laziness that has plagued our once-great country. And this command center is the key to it all. There was simply no other way to keep track of all the information and movements. And now it is in your hands." As if to make his statement literal, he placed the key to the command center into her hand.

Maeryn could tell that Coen didn't think she was up to the task that Magnus had given her, but she didn't care. "And what of the rest of this place?"

"I must be leaving as soon as possible, but I'll have one of the servants show you around the rest of the property. Ah yes...before I go, I was told you were asking about the guest rooms."

"Yes," Maeryn answered cautiously.

"The north wing of the house should have plenty of room. But you must remember that the servants and stable hands know nothing of what happens here. It would be an unnecessary risk to their lives and your own, should they ever understand what you are doing. I advise strongly that you keep your guests out of these affairs...for everyone's safety."

"Of course," Maeryn replied.

"Well, do you have any questions before I depart?"

Maeryn thought carefully, but felt that she understood exactly what needed to be done. "No," she replied simply.

"Then I bid you farewell...and congratulations," Coen added with a smile.

Kael slowly became aware that there was fluid in his lungs. It was his first conscious thought. The strange part was that he couldn't cough to clear his lungs. He wondered if he had been sleeping. He didn't remember dreaming. He tried to move but it was as if he didn't have a body, only a consciousness. Then, a crack of intense light cut through the darkness. At first it was startling, but he realized that he was controlling it. His eyelids were opening.

So I do have a body.

The intensity of the light faded somewhat and turned into blurred colors. It occurred to him that he should be seeing something, and yet his eyes weren't functioning properly. He couldn't feel his body and could only barely control his eyelids. He wondered if his limbs were missing, but he couldn't lift his head to check.

His vision gradually clarified enough that he could make out a rough timber ceiling. But there was nothing notable within his field of view that gave him any clue where he was. Then, a muffled sound caused him to realize that his ears weren't working correctly either. More muffled sounds echoed through his head at different pitches until a familiar face came into view.

Saba looked down with bright, caring eyes. Kael watched him put a hand against his forehead, but he couldn't feel it. Saba blocked the light with one of his hands, then pulled it away, wrinkling his eyebrow in a look of concern. Kael suddenly felt an ache behind his eyes and closed them, feeling like he needed sleep. He realized there was one consolation about his predicament. If he was severely injured, he felt no pain.

At least I can sleep.

The next time Kael opened his eyes, things were different. His vision was clear, but his head was pounding with each pulse of his heartbeat, bringing a new wave of pain each time. He could also hear clearly enough to know that there were two people in the room. He grunted, and surprised himself.

Saba appeared within seconds, placing his hand on Kael's forehead. The hand felt cold, which Kael guessed meant that his head was hot with fever.

"Can you hear me?" Saba asked carefully.

Kael tried to answer, but it only came out as a weak grunt.

"Do you know who I am?"

Again, Kael grunted.

"Good," Saba replied with relief. "Can you move?"

Kael grunted twice and Saba seemed to understand.

Saba turned his face away and spoke to someone else who Kael couldn't see. "His comprehension is good, but it looks like he's paralyzed." He turned back to Kael. "Are you hungry?"

Kael grunted twice, indicating that he was not. The pounding in his head was all he could feel. Perhaps he was hungry but he just couldn't feel it.

"Kael, do you remember going to the palace?" Saba asked, trying to hone in on the nature of his injury.

Kael grunted once, his throat now feeling raw. At least he could feel his throat, which was progress.

"Do you remember fighting Magnus Calidon?"

Kael thought about the question and didn't remember anything after his confrontation with Horace. He grunted twice.

Saba turned away again. "It appears that he lost consciousness almost immediately during the attack. Kael, I would like to tell you what happened. Can you listen to the story?"

Kael grunted once, suddenly very interested to know how he came to be paralyzed.

"Just let me know when you've had enough and you want to sleep," Saba cautioned, not wanting to push Kael too far.

Kael grunted once.

"Okay. This is one of my homes," he started, sweeping a hand through the air. "We're in the mountains north of Orud. We're far enough away to keep you safe. You've been unconscious for about three months now. When you went to the palace, Ajani and I followed you, though by a different route. When we caught up with you, the Emperor was also there, and you were under attack." Saba spoke carefully, trying to use simple words and explanations.

"Ajani got him with a spear, drawing the attack away from you. He saved your life." Saba's voice fell to just above a whisper. "I'm sorry, but he didn't make it out alive. He gave his life in place of yours." Saba waited for the words to sink in.

Kael breathed in a deep breath. His heart plummeted at the thought of Ajani's sacrifice. His whole life had been pain and suffering, serving cruel masters. And when he finally had his freedom, he gave away his life to save

Kael. *It doesn't seem fair.* And suddenly he felt ashamed and unworthy. His eyes began to well with tears.

Saba waited patiently until Kael was able to listen again. "Magnus was injured in the process, and Dacien and I fled, carrying you out of the palace."

Saba looked away again to the other person in the room, which Kael now realized was Dacien. A strange look washed over Saba's face and when it passed, he continued.

"Unfortunately, Magnus recovered quickly. And during the past few months, he's been very busy making changes throughout the Empire. I travel back to Orud occasionally for supplies and to hear the rumors. Through his own sources, Dacien has been able to confirm much of what I hear. As far as we can tell, he's expanding the Empire's authority as well as his own. And it's causing quite an uproar among the citizens. He freed the entire slave population under the condition that they serve in his army. He's convinced the High Council that it's necessary to bring stability to the Empire through military might. I've also heard that he has promised the slaves ownership of the northeastern wastelands if they can push back the Korgs and conquer their land. The Council likes this idea because it means that the Empire won't lose its labor force. The slaves all have practical skills, such as farming, which they're likely to continue when they own their own land. So, Orud will still reap the rewards of their labor, but the slaves will feel as though they've been given a great blessing."

Kael closed his eyes for a moment, carefully considering Saba's words.

"As we speak, the slaves are being trained as soldiers and shipped to Suppard. Then they travel by land to Orlek where they are assigned to various places along the wall."

Kael wanted to scream. He wanted to get up from his bed and do something about this. As he lay paralyzed, Magnus was making great strides to solidify his grip on the most powerful nation in the known world. But his head began to swim and he had to close his eyes to keep from losing consciousness.

"I'm sorry; I've pushed you too far." Saba rested his hand on Kael's forehead. "Sleep now...there will time to talk more about this later.

But Kael didn't want to wait until later. Later might be too late. When he opened his eyes again, Dacien was standing above him. His eyes were red with tears and he looked much thinner that Kael remembered.

"Kael. I'm sorry for betraying you. I was deceived by the Emperor. He had me convinced that you were the assassin that killed the former Emperor. I shouldn't have listened to him; I should have trusted you. You told me everything and it turned out to be true. I hope you will be able to forgive me someday. I'll never make the same mistake again...I promise."

3

The Palace grounds stretched out before Maeryn, orderly and well kept. Living columns of majestic cedar trees lined the stone walkways which cut across the lush green lawn in wide swaths, like spokes from the hub of a wheel. All paths led inward to the Palace, like a miniature example of the city itself.

The moment the thought came to her mind, Maeryn was reminded of detailed maps and models of the Empire that were now her tools to manage the Resistance. Her heart began to beat faster in her chest as she thought of the double life she now led. The armed guards now escorting her into the Palace would turn on her in an instant if they had any idea who she really was. Fortunately, Magnus found a plausible cover to explain her regular presence.

Once inside, the soldiers led her through a maze of hallways and stairwells, stopping at the door to a meeting room. Maeryn walked inside as the soldiers closed the door behind her. It was a different room than the usual meeting place, but much more desirable. This room had a wide balcony at the back that overlooked the Palace courtyard to the south. The midmorning sun cast long shadows across the courtyard and reminded Maeryn of her balcony in Bastul.

A sudden pang of memory tugged at her heart, but she buried it immediately as Magnus rose from his chair and turned to face her.

"...enjoying the view?" she asked playfully.

"What news do you bring?" he asked, ignoring her question.

Maeryn knew instantly that something was bothering him. Normally, he might have made some comment regarding her beauty as the view he was enjoying. But he passed on the opportunity, clearly distracted by some other thoughts. *Or, perhaps I'm getting old and he doesn't find me beautiful any longer.*

Instead, she pulled a piece of parchment out from under her cloak and handed it to him.

Magnus accepted the report and turned it over in his hands, reading it as he took his seat. He mumbled a few times to himself, but read on as Maeryn waited patiently. By the time he was finished, he was nodding his approval. "This is good," he said aloud, though to whom Maeryn wasn't sure.

"Do you have any instructions?" she asked plainly.

Magnus looked back to the paper, then to Maeryn again. "What do think should be done?" he asked.

"Well, most of our attention is focused on the northeast. Perhaps it would be wise to begin rebuilding in the west while the Empire's infrastructure is weak."

"Yes," Magnus replied with a distant look in his eyes. "That sounds good."

"What's wrong with you?" Maeryn blurted out, louder than she intended.

Magnus turned his head and looked at her, shocked by her tone and volume. "Watch your tongue woman," he snapped back with a commanding voice.

Maeryn shrunk in her chair, feeling like she had stepped over an imaginary line. He had never talked to her that way, but then again, she hadn't ever spoken to him in this way, either. "I'm sorry. It's just that you seem...distracted."

His cold look softened a little. "I have many things on my mind. And the Resistance is in good hands."

"Is that all?" Maeryn probed, wondering if her refusal to marry him was having more of an effect lately. Or maybe it was his injury, though she noted that he was no longer moving slowly.

Magnus turned back to look out on the courtyard. After a few seconds of silence, he spoke again. "I will be going away soon."

"When?" Maeryn asked, after he failed to explain.

"...nine days. The strength of the Syvaku attack surprised many on the Council. They don't understand how deep the grievances run in their blood. And it is now clear that we would be at a great disadvantage in a naval battle. I'm leaving to establish a peace treaty with them. We need their naval skills, both in battle as well as ship construction. And we can't afford another enemy. We must be able to concentrate our efforts on the Korgs in the east."

Maeryn didn't know what to say.

"You may suspend any reports until I return."

Maeryn wasn't concerned about the reports. It would be the longest they've been apart since they met. But Magnus was apparently not thinking about that. *Perhaps you could find a whore along the way,* she thought angrily. *That's what you really want anyway!* "Are we finished?" she said, instead, rising to her feet.

Magnus looked back to her without answering, oblivious to what could have upset her.

Maeryn turned and walked to the door, not waiting for a reply.

The ride back through the city was lonely. Maeryn stared out of the window of the carriage, mindlessly watching the citizens pass by on the street, but not really seeing anything. She was lost in her thoughts. Magnus had been so intent on wooing her initially. And even when she told him that she didn't need another man, he seemed content enough. But lately, he was becoming more and more preoccupied. She knew he had many more responsibilities than ever before, but something had drastically changed in the past few months and it was bothering her, as well.

The carriage came to a stop at the docks. Maeryn rose to her feet and stepped out when her driver opened the door. Before her foot touched the pavestone, she knew something was wrong. One of her guards, dressed in plain clothes so as not to attract attention, stood waiting for her.

"What is it?" she whispered quickly.

"We received a message through the proper channels that someone was trying to contact you. He said he was a friend and that he would be waiting at the meeting place nearby."

Maeryn raised her eyebrows. She didn't have any friends; she only had Aelia and Magnus, and not even him anymore, it seemed. Any other acquaintance of hers would be strictly business and not considered a friend.

"I hope you don't mind, but I took the liberty of checking into the matter. He is, indeed, waiting for you as we speak. ...under very close supervision," the man added.

Maeryn smiled. "Take me at once and keep your eyes alert for any traps."

"As you wish," replied the guard, walking to the door of the carriage.

Maeryn took the man's hand and stepped back inside. After a brief pause, the carriage lurched into motion and Maeryn's mind began to race with thoughts, her disappointment with her previous meeting all but forgotten.

The carriage ride took only a half hour, stopping at a park near the canal that separated the northern half of the city from the southern half. Again, Maeryn stepped out and her guard was waiting to escort her.

"Where is he?" she asked, her curiosity and sense of danger now peaked.

"This way," he replied offering his arm.

She accepted, completing the disguise that these two were simply going for a stroll in the park, a completely common activity. Indeed, on this sunny day, many citizens walked the garden paths or lounged in the shade of the canopy of trees that dotted the rolling landscape.

Fifty yards ahead and to the right, by the water's edge, stood a tall man with short white hair. At this distance, Maeryn couldn't distinguish anything else of him, but didn't see anything familiar, so far. As they neared the low, stone wall at the shore of the canal, the man turned from gazing at the sluggish water, and looked in Maeryn's direction. His skin was tanned from much time in the sun, but his skin was smooth and he appeared very young, despite his white hair. His eyes, she could now see, were bright blue and seemed full of wisdom. Slowly, she began to recognize the face, as if from a dream long forgotten.

As Saba's name came to her mind, a tear rolled down her cheek.

She immediately turned to the guard. "Leave us. I'll call you when I'm ready to go back."

The guard looked concerned, but obeyed promptly. "I'll be at the carriage. Just signal if you need anything," he replied, looking back to the tall stranger.

When the guard was out of earshot, Maeryn walked to Saba and threw her arms around him. She began to weep uncontrollably, though she didn't know why. Saba remained silent and simply held her in his strong arms.

After a long moment, Maeryn regained her composure and pulled away, wiping her eyes and suddenly feeling embarrassed. Saba smiled down at her.

"You look different," were her first words, and as soon as she spoke, she wanted to take them back.

"So do you," he replied with a familiar and comforting voice. "You carry many more concerns that when we last saw each other."

"As always," she admitted, "you seem to know everything. What are you doing here? How did you find me?"

"I have my ways." He nodded his head toward the water. "Let's take a walk."

The two began to stroll along the canal and Maeryn suddenly felt more at peace than she had in a long time. She couldn't believe that Saba was really walking next to her.

"Where do I start?" Saba asked himself aloud.

"I want to know everything," Maeryn replied quickly. "...from the beginning. What happened in Bastul? I assume it had something to do with Lemus?" Just saying the name felt strange to Maeryn.

"Yes. Lemus forced me out of the city under threat of my life. I tried to sneak back in to talk with you one last time to let you know what was happening, but the Captain of the Guard found me. Fortunately, he spared my life and let me go with a warning never to return."

Saba continued talking as they walked, recounting his experiences since Bastul, with a few major omissions. The sun passed its zenith and began its descent as Saba talked about his lengthy travels, careful to leave out anything to do with Kael or the real purpose of his visit. It was too soon for Maeryn.

He needed to reestablish their friendship, at least partially, before discussing any of the pressing matters. Maeryn listened intently, and Saba could tell that it had been some time since she had a friend to talk to.

"...and so I ended up in Orud. But you...you have come a long way."

"I wouldn't say that," Maeryn objected. "Things have been strange for me since Bastul."

"I imagine so. Tell me, how did you ever get free of that man?"

"Well, it's a long story."

"Of course it is. Tell me everything."

Maeryn did just as Saba, recounting her life since they had last talked, only with much more honesty than Saba. Maeryn held nothing back, describing every event and every emotion, as if she hadn't spoken to anyone in all these years. Sadly, Saba came to realize that that was exactly the case.

As the sun approached the western horizon, Maeryn stopped her story just before the recent events at the Palace. They had walked miles along the canal and around the park, and now came to a stop only twenty feet from Maeryn's carriage. Her guard still stood patiently at his post near the horses.

"You should come for supper," she told Saba suddenly. "You don't have any prior engagements do you?"

"None as important as you," he replied. "Supper would be lovely."

"Come on, then," she said happily. "Tonight we will celebrate."

Saba followed Maeryn into the carriage, under the suspicious eyes of her bodyguard. Eager to move on, the driver immediately snapped the reins and the horses jumped into action.

Waves lapped at the side of the boat as it cut through the choppy water of the eastern bay of Orud. Maeryn and Saba sat at the prow while the crew stayed busy on the opposite end of the deck. Having finished her story in the carriage, the two now sat in silence and looked out over the water that reflected the orange glow of dusk.

"I will be delighted to meet Aelia," Saba said, breaking the silence.

Maeryn smiled. "She looks just like her father did. She is strong in her own way, but quiet and sensitive. She has brought much joy into my life."

Again, the two slipped into silence and Saba felt guilty about how he was forced to approach this meeting, which should have occurred under different circumstances. But he had to be careful about what he revealed to Maeryn and when, because one misspoken word would cause his plan to fall apart.

Nothing more was said until they reached their destination at the eastern shore of the bay. Saba was quite impressed at the size of the mansion that was now Maeryn's new home. Sitting atop the rocky shore, it seemed bigger that he imagined it. As they neared the robust looking dock, the crew jumped into action, throwing out lines and securing the vessel.

When the crew was finished, Maeryn took Saba's hand and led him over the plank and onto the docks. They ascended the steep, rocky steps together and entered the house. Maeryn went immediately to the kitchen and had the servant began preparing the meal. She left Saba waiting in a hallway for several minutes. When she returned, a beautiful young woman accompanied her.

"Saba, this is Aelia," Maeryn said with pride.

Saba took her hand and kissed it, bowing low with respect. "It is a pleasure to meet you. Your mother has told me so much about you."

Aelia looked a little worried.

Maeryn spoke up quickly, sensing her daughter's discomfort. "Saba is an old friend of mine and your father's. He used to live with us in Bastul."

"Oh," Aelia breathed in relief. "I thought you'd resorted to arranging a marriage for me."

The three laughed at the misunderstanding and Saba could see the nostalgia in Maeryn's eyes. He realized this was how things used to be many years ago in Bastul.

"Come," Maeryn offered. "I'll show you around the house while dinner is being prepared."

After the evening meal was finished, Aelia excused herself and retired for the night. Saba pushed his chair back from the table and was just about to make himself more comfortable when Maeryn spoke.

"Let's go someplace more comfortable; you look like you have something weighing on your mind."

Saba smiled, and rose to his feet, following Maeryn with a bottle of wine in hand. They made their way to the back patio of the house and took a seat in the garden, which was lit by several torch stands. Saba poured Maeryn another glass of wine and filled his own glass, as well.

"So what's on your mind? I can tell that you haven't been completely forthcoming with me."

"You, on the other hand, have been completely honest with me," Saba admitted.

"I have to keep too many secrets on a daily basis. I find it refreshing to let my guard down because I know I can trust you."

Saba felt ashamed. He took a long swig of wine, wiped his lips, and continued. "What I have to tell you will come as quite a shock. And so I will just start at the beginning."

"Alright," Maeryn said, a worried look creasing her forehead.

"After Lemus forced me to abandon you in Bastul, I went to stay with a friend in the coastal farmlands to the north. As I sorted through my possessions, I came across a note that Adair had written to me just prior to his disappearance. In it, he told me of a friend who had been found injured from an attack and that he was trying to find the attackers. The note was attached to a broken arrow that was the only clue to this mystery. Adair apparently hadn't been able to come to any conclusions based on the clue, so he left it for me to investigate. This was the last communication that I had with him, as he was already missing by the time I read the note."

At the mention of Adair, tears began to roll down Maeryn's face, but she held her composure and listened intently.

"Although it seemed like a meaningless search after Adair was gone, I decided that I owed it to him. Which led me to Orud, where I searched through countless scrolls and volumes of parchment, looking for a link to this clue. Whether researching the materials or style of construction, all of my searching turned up nothing. And then, one night as I was leaving the library, I was attacked and taken captive by a group of cloaked figures. They appeared out of the shadows and surrounded me, leaving me no choice but to comply with them. I was then taken, blindfolded, to an encampment two days journey from Orud. There were other men like me at this camp, and we were all being held against our wills. After weeks, we were paid a visit by their leader. He came cloaked in black, his face obscured and he inspected all of us. Apparently, he found in me what he was looking for, because after this visit, the rest of the men were locked in a building and burned to death. I was the only one spared, and they locked me in a small room with armed guards."

"Who were these people?" Maeryn gasped with surprise.

"Not yet," Saba objected, continuing with his story. "That evening, their leader came into my jail cell and spoke to me directly. During the course of the conversation, he removed his hood and I was able to get a good look at him. I'll never forget that face!"

"But what did he say? Why were you spared?"

Saba shook his head. "Believe me when I say that these details are not what is important about my story. You must let me go on."

Maeryn sat back in frustration and took a sip of wine.

Saba continued. "I was kept locked in that cell for years until I eventually escaped. Then I traveled to distant lands to leave this mystery behind me and escape the danger. But after many years, I returned because I knew that I couldn't just ignore the events that had transpired. I had uncovered something dangerous and the curiosity drove me mad. So I came back, carefully. I purchased several properties in and around the city and began to integrate myself back into the culture and resume my investigation. Again, years passed while I observed. And then things began to happen. A rogue Korgan army broke through the eastern wall and was making its way to attack Orud. The former Emperor responded to this situation by emptying the city of its military in order to meet this threat. Meanwhile, an assassin was rumored to have broken into the Palace and murdered the Emperor and two Generals. Shortly after, the High Council, out of fear of their desperate circumstances, elected the Northern General Magnus Calidon as Emperor."

Maeryn visibly bristled at these words and Saba held up his hand in protest, without stopping.

"I made it a point to attend his feast the day after his new appointment. And that is where two very interesting things occurred."

"I was there," Maeryn interrupted.

"Yes, I know."

Maeryn slumped back in her seat. "You saw me and you didn't bother to even greet me?" she asked, confused.

"I didn't yet understand the dynamics of the events which were unfolding. There would have been no point in risking your life needlessly. As it turned out, my caution was wise."

"What do you mean?"

"I sat to the side of the feast, watching and listening for a clue, for I knew that something was happening, but I just didn't understand it yet. And then, Magnus began to make his speech to the most influential members of society about the changes that would be taking place. And you can imagine my shock when I realized that our new Emperor was the same cloaked figure that came to my jail cell those many years ago." Saba paused and allowed his words to sink in.

Maeryn finished the rest of her wine and looked at the ground.

Saba waited for a reaction, but when nothing came, he continued. "And then, in a grand gesture, Magnus called forth a brave young man responsible for ending the Syvak invasion in the west. And as he was being congratulated in front of everyone, the man leapt over the side of the building and escaped as if he were in danger."

"Yes," Maeryn said, looking up from the ground. "That was...odd."

"Indeed," Saba agreed. "But I didn't stay around to see how Magnus handled the situation. Instead, I left the feast and tracked this young man through the city. When I caught up with him, I invited him to one of my houses to escape the soldiers that were sure to be in pursuit. He welcomed the opportunity and when we arrived at my house, we were finally able to sit down in safety and talk."

"Well..." Maeryn prompted. "Who was he? Why did he leave so abruptly?"

Saba took a breath, set down his wine glass and answered. "It was Kael."

Maeryn, who had been leaning forward with anticipation, sat back and held her breath. "What do you mean it was Kael?" she asked after a moment of silence. She fixed her gaze on Saba's eyes, and repeated the question. "What do you mean it was Kael?" Her voice broke this time.

"I mean exactly what I said. It was Kael. He's alive."

Maeryn put a hand to her mouth and turned away. Her body began to shake as she sobbed.

Saba reached out a hand to comfort her, but Maeryn slid backward and off of her seat, slumping to the ground. Saba went to her and lifted her back to her seat, holding her as she cried. Several minutes passed before Maeryn was able to speak.

"Are you sure? Where is he? I want to see him."

"I will take you to him," Saba promised. "But you must hear the rest of my story."

Maeryn nodded weakly.

"Just as you and I are doing right now, we traded stories and he explained to me what had happened in Bastul. Apparently, Lemus kept him locked in prison, intending to prove a point to Kael before he was executed. But Kael's execution never took place. Instead, he was handed over to someone else who took him by ship out of the city."

Maeryn was smiling now.

"I know this is all very strange, but please listen carefully, because there is more. Kael was taken far away to live at a monastery where he was raised with nine other boys of roughly the same age. These other boys were taken from prison in a similar manner. There, they were educated and trained as soldiers. Kael was grateful for the life he had been given, but as he grew older, he began to suspect that something was very wrong. Then, at the age of eighteen, the boys were taken to the High Temple to meet the High Priest of their order. And this is when Kael's story becomes much like my own. For the group of people that had been raising and training Kael were the very same that captured and imprisoned me in Orud. Kael met the High Priest and it was as terrible an experience for him as it was for me."

"Wait," Maeryn interrupted. "You mean Magnus?"

"That's right," he answered, noticing that this was a new revelation for Maeryn. "I suppose you thought these people were the Resistance?"

Maeryn glanced quickly over her shoulder. "Keep your voice down," she cautioned.

Saba smiled. "No. This group is an ancient cult. They call themselves the Kaliel. They are extremely dangerous, thought to have disbanded centuries ago. They have become a legend in the minds of most people. But I assure you they are not imaginary. Anyway, as soon as Kael returned to the monastery, he escaped and spent his recent years traveling the world aboard a merchant ship."

"This is amazing," Maeryn responded.

"I don't think you understand the point of my story," Saba said bluntly.

"I know," Maeryn objected. "Magnus is their leader. He has always led a double life, and I should be shocked, but I'm not."

"No," Saba clarified. "Listen. Kael returned to Bastul just as the Syvaku were attacking."

"We must have just missed each other," Maeryn mumbled to herself.

Saba pushed ahead. "He helped the Captain of the Guard fight the Syvaku and then traveled with the surviving soldiers to Leoran, where the Syvak made their final attack. But what he discovered was that the Syvak warlord responsible for instigating the attacks was one of the boys from the monastery, one of his childhood friends."

Maeryn wrinkled her eyebrows as Saba continued.

"Then Kael traveled to Orud with the Captain who became General after the previous General was killed fighting the Syvaku. Kael was present when the Korgs were approaching the city. He suspected that the attack was a diversion and went to the Palace where he caught a glimpse of the retreating assassin. And again, it was someone that Kael knew. This time, it was his instructor."

Maeryn had gone completely still as the pieces of the puzzle were beginning to come together.

"Then, after Magnus was appointed Emperor, Kael went to the feast where he recognized Magnus as the High Priest, and the remaining Generals as his childhood companions. And that is why he fled, because he understood what they had done and that he was the only one who knew. Do you understand now?"

Maeryn nodded. "Magnus, the Northern General is also the leader of the Kaliel, and the leader of the Resistance. And while he was leading this triple life, he was also raising and training these boys for a purpose." Maeryn stood up now and began to pace as she worked out the logic. "So he plants them, one by one, like seeds, waiting to be harvested for his own purposes. And in this way, he gains control over the Syvaku and uses them to attack the Empire in order to put pressure on the former Emperor. Then he has the Emperor and other Generals executed, and in an instant, he gains the throne and appoints his new Generals. But, if the Korgan attack was just a diversion, he must control them, as well."

Saba nodded in agreement. "...which means that Magnus controls almost every major group of people in this part of the world, including the Resistance and now the entire slave population, as well. And he's manipulated them to achieve his own goals. "

Maeryn stopped pacing. "What's his motive?"

"I've thought about this quite a bit and what I believe is this. The Syvaku, the Korgs and the Resistance were all means to an end—to gain the throne. But what now? He has already been made Emperor and is working to expand the rule of the Empire even farther. So becoming Emperor wasn't his ultimate goal. No, I believe that his ultimate motive lies with the Kaliel."

Maeryn sat back down, her mind no doubt racing with all the implications of what they were discussing. "But who are they? What is their purpose?"

Saba rubbed his chin. "Legend has it that the god they worship is making preparations to return to this world."

"You're right," Maeryn admitted. "It sounds more like legend than truth."

Saba shrugged his shoulders.

After a moment of silence, Maeryn spoke. "Why did you come here to tell me this?"

"Because you're the only one who can do anything about it."

"Me? Why me? What can I do?"

"You can call together the non-military members of the High Council and tell them what has happened. You have great privileges because of your affiliation with Magnus."

"I..." she stammered. "I can't," she finally said in protest.

"Then I'll go with you," Saba countered. When Maeryn didn't respond, Saba kept pushing. "There's something else you should know. Kael tried to stop them. He went back to the Palace seeking vengeance and killed the two Naval Commanders. He would have finished them all if it hadn't been for Magnus."

"What did Magnus do?" Maeryn asked, her voice shaking with fear.

"He is an evil man, with powers beyond your imagination. He attacked Kael and almost killed him. As we speak, Kael is lying on a bed unable to move or even speak. Fortunately, I was able to rescue him with the help of another young man you know...Ajani."

"Ajani?" Maeryn gasped.

Saba shook his head slowly. "He wounded Magnus and provided a needed diversion, but he didn't survive."

Maeryn buried her face in her hands and stayed like this for a few minutes. "This is all too much. I can't take it," she said, getting up and walking across the garden.

Saba let her go and waited patiently for her to calm down.

Eventually, Maeryn came back to where Saba was sitting and stood in front of him. "What am I supposed to do? I haven't seen you in years and all of a sudden, you show up and tell me this unbelievable story that I'm supposed to tell to the Council. They will have us executed. How can I do this?"

"How can you not?" Saba corrected. "This government has been manipulated and taken over and you are the one with access to these people."

Maeryn pondered these words. "Take me to see Kael."

Saba looked into her eyes to discern her motives and was satisfied that he had accomplished his goal. "Very well," he said. "Come with me."

4

Maeryn left word with the servants that she would be gone until the following evening and to tell Aelia not to worry. But she didn't need to be concerned with Aelia who wasn't prone to worrying anyway. The journey north to Saba's cabin took the remainder of the night. After a long boat ride to the northern side of the bay, the two made their way on horseback through a series of canyons that eventually began to steepen. After hours of ascending into the mountains, they arrived at a small wooden house, nearly invisible against the rocks and covered by trees.

"Welcome to my home."

Maeryn smiled wearily. The sun was just rising in the east and there had been no opportunity to sleep. The only thing that kept her moving was the thought of seeing Kael again, no matter what his condition.

They dismounted and draped the reins over a low branch, leaving the horses to graze. "Are you nervous," Saba asked, looking over to Maeryn.

"Yes."

"Well, don't be. He's grown into a fine young man and you should be proud."

Saba knocked two times, then quickly opened the creaking door. The inside was dark and it took a moment for Maeryn's eyes to adjust. Slowly, she could make out a few chairs and a table, but no decorations.

Saba walked to the back of the room and ducked under a low doorway. Maeryn followed, seeing the kitchen to the left and another small room to the right. Saba led her through the doorway into the small room where a man sat in a chair and another laid upon a bed. A soft morning light was coming in through a window to the right, making this the best lit room in the house. The man in the chair rose to his feet and extended his hand.

"Lady Maeryn. It is good to finally meet you."

Maeryn turned to Saba.

"This is General Dacien Gallus. He served under you in Bastul as Captain of the Guard."

"Former General," Dacien corrected. "I was never fortunate enough to meet you in person while in Bastul, but heard many good things."

Maeryn extended her hand, which Dacien kissed.

"...and this is Kael," Saba said, pointing to the man lying on the bed.

"He's sleeping now," Dacien cautioned. "But he's been doing better. He can move his head now."

Maeryn walked over to Kael and it felt as though everything else in the world ceased to exist. It was only her and her son. He had grown into a handsome man, with features much like Maeryn's. His hair was still blonde, and longer than when he was a child. His skin looked pale and his face bore the stubble of more than a week without shaving. But despite his current condition, he looked strong. His chest rose and fell in a steady rhythm and it was all she could do to keep from waking him. But he obviously needed his rest and so she resisted.

Finally satisfied, Maeryn turned around to Saba with tears running down her cheeks. "Magnus is leaving soon for a goodwill trip to Syvaku territory. He will be gone for months. It will be the best time to gather the Council."

Dacien looked excitedly to Saba.

Saba smiled. "Let us have some breakfast and we can discuss the best way to approach these men."

The river ran sluggishly through the dense forest, its sound consuming all others, providing the perfect meeting place for those who wished to stay hidden. Magnus stretched his legs on the shore as his steed nosed through some wet foliage nearby. The dusk light was quickly fading as night approached.

Out of the mist to his left, a dark figure appeared on foot, holding the reins of a horse following closely behind. The figure was a short in stature, and moved gracefully and silently like a cat.

Magnus turned and walked over to Ukiru and greeted him with a handshake. "How was your trip?" he asked.

"...successful," Ukiru replied with a smile as he reached up to his saddle. Untying a leather strap, he removed a long object bundled in cloths and handed it to Magnus.

With great care, Magnus unwrapped the cloth to reveal an object that made his heart beat fast with an excitement that exceeded any other. He lifted the sword by its handle and turned it so that it caught the fading light. Its crystalline features were a marvel of craftsmanship, with the blade and handle carved from the same material. Though the word *carved* implied crafting this blade with crude instruments, its beauty proved that it couldn't have been made in such a way. And indeed, he knew this to be the case.

"Forged by the gods..." he said aloud. "...and what of your so-called fortress city?"

"...destroyed," Ukiru replied with a blank face.

"This is good," Magnus assured him. "We are on the verge of realizing all that we have worked for these many years."

"And what is next?" asked Ukiru.

"Well, due to your quicker-than-expected success, I've moved up our trip. We leave for the temple in the morning."

"When will you ever find time between your meetings with the Syvaku?" Ukiru asked, sarcastically.

"Ah, yes," Magnus said with a smile. "So you've heard. I have no intention of meeting with them. Though Narian is dead, my influence among them is still strong and without need of intervention. We will have as much uninterrupted time as we need."

Saba met Maeryn outside the Palace grounds. She looked anxious, which only echoed his own feelings. *Anxious to set events into motion that will stop Magnus...nervous at the thought of facing the Council.*

"Thanks for doing this," he said to Maeryn when they were close enough to speak.

"You're welcome," she replied, though she still didn't seem fully behind what they were about to do. "I spoke with one Council member already. He is the leader of the Farming Guild and closer to me than the rest. He seemed deeply concerned about the accusations and called the Council together as soon as he was able."

"Well, that worked out well, didn't it?" Saba replied as they walked through the arched gateway and into the Palace grounds.

"Yes it did," she replied, her eyes on the guards who were watching their every move. "This way, at least he will share some of the blame if this doesn't go as planned."

Saba smiled nervously, feeling sorry that he dragged her into this. But he knew it was the right thing to do. Kael had tried to solve this problem through force, now Saba would use reason and trust that the Council would be receptive to his plea.

Maeryn led them through the elaborate gardens and up the steps into the Palace. She walked with confidence and within minutes, proved that she knew her way around. The guards all nodded in respect as she walked past and Saba knew that he couldn't have accomplished this any other way. After a series of turns and long hallways they arrived at two carved wooden doors that met together to form an arch some twenty feet from the ground.

Soldiers flanked the entrance with their spears crossing one another; a presence meant to intimidate visitors.

"Are they ready?" Maeryn asked.

The soldier on the left nodded, then both snapped to attention, pulling their spears back against their chests in a vertical fashion. Suddenly, the doors began to open silently, revealing the massive interior of the Council room. Saba wondered how the signal was given to open the doors, and how they were controlled, but there wasn't time for such things. Instead, he tried to imagine himself in the place of these Council members and tried to understand how they would react to what he was about to say.

The Council room was large, with high, arched ceilings. A center aisle cut through rows of additional seating for larger meetings. At the end of the aisle, the walkway widened where two semicircle stone tables sat opposite each other. The table on the left was entirely empty, presumably the seating for the military members of the Council. The table on the right was occupied by the six Council members who represented the major trade guilds of the Empire. The High Council was structured in such a way as to balance the competing interest of the major groups of citizens which made up the Empire. And it was highly unusual for such a one-sided meeting to even take place.

Indeed, the Council members all appeared agitated and well aware of the strange circumstances. Saba was disappointed that the meeting would be starting off under this atmosphere, but he fully expected it, nonetheless.

"Lady Maeryn, please come forward with your guest," said one of the Council.

"Thank you all for agreeing to meet with us," Maeryn replied graciously.

The man then turned and addressed his fellow Council members. Saba realized immediately that this man was Maeryn's point of contact, the farming guild leader.

"Gentlemen, yesterday evening Maeryn brought some information to my attention that I consider of grave importance to the future of this Empire. It is under this pretense that I called together this present Council, without our Emperor, Generals, or Commanders. Let me assure you that what you are about to hear will quickly address any concerns you have about meeting under such unusual circumstances."

Saba was impressed by the way that this man quickly spoke to the concerns that were on everyone's minds.

"Lady Maeryn, you have the floor," he finished and sat down.

"Thank you," she replied, stepping forward.

Saba stayed a few steps back, deciding to wait until called upon.

"Council members, this man standing before you today is a close friend of mine. A friend with whom I have just recently become reacquainted after many years apart. And in the course of conversation, he revealed to me..."

"Perhaps he can tell us on his own," interrupted the Council member representing the fishing industries.

Maeryn looked back to Saba and he smiled in return to let her know that it was alright.

Stepping forward, he addressed the Council. "Gentlemen, I can see that you are anxious to hear what I have to say, so I'll not waste your time. To put it bluntly, you are all being manipulated by a devious plan to take control of the Empire. The Emperor you now serve is not the man you think him to be. The Generals and commanders of his army and navy all served under him prior to his appointment as Emperor."

"That's preposterous," one member blurted out.

Saba continued, knowing that convincing them would require a great deal of momentum and he couldn't afford to be side-tracked. "These men were trained for this purpose and intentionally planted by him to give the appearance of an impartial unity among separate military leaders. But this is not the case. And worse yet, the leaders of the Syvaku and Korgan hordes also served under him."

These words produced a collective gasp among the Council.

"These men were also trained and planted so as to induce the attacks that the Empire has recently suffered. The purpose of this was to provide an impetus for change among the leadership...among you. The peak of this treachery was for Magnus to have the former Emperor assassinated by a trained killer. Then, finding yourselves in a desperate situation, you looked for rescue from the one man who had proven himself capable of overcoming such obstacles. And in appointing him to the position of Emperor, you played right into his plan."

"Maeryn," the farming guild leader spoke out. "What do you have to say?"

Maeryn looked to Saba, then to the council. "I know the penalty for such accusations should they prove false. I would not have come here if I didn't believe this to be true."

The Council members were stunned with unbelief and began to whisper among themselves.

Saba continued speaking, now that the situation had turned in his favor. "In addition to this, there is something else you must know. Years ago, when I first came to Orud, I was captured and taken prisoner in the night by a group of men, cloaked in black. They surrounded me and put a bag over my head. I was taken by wagon two days from here and held at a remote compound by armed men. These soldiers are still operating within the boundaries of the Empire and represent a great threat to your security. I managed to escape and have since been able to identify them as the Kaliel."

"Hold your tongue," the youngest council member shouted. "You speak treasonous accusations without proof. And the Kaliel are nothing but a fable."

Another Council member spoke out. "You say that Magnus hired the assassin. But the assassin attacked again and killed the naval Commanders, wounding Magnus in the process. Would you like us to believe that this was only to convince us that there was no connection between them?"

Saba could see that the situation was rapidly deteriorating. "...no, of course not. The second attack didn't come from the assassin; that was simply Magnus' explanation. The second attack came from yet another of Magnus's trained soldiers, one who rebelled against him."

"Where do you get these lies? Where is your proof?" shouted the young man again.

Suddenly, the other Council members began to raise their voices at Saba and he realized that something drastic was needed. He raised his voice to a commanding tone and cut through their cacophony. "I have the so-called assassin."

The room went silent. Maeryn turned quickly to Saba; the agony on her face was unmistakable.

He hadn't meant to risk Kael in this way, but something drastic was needed. Saba repeated the statement. "I have the man who was blamed for the assassination of the former Emperor."

"Where is he?" the young man countered. "Produce him before this Council."

"He is in a safe place and when it is safe to do so, he will testify to what I've said."

The young man smiled and stretched out his arms, his voice much calmer now. "You have no proof, and yet you come before this Council bringing these most serious accusations. Indeed, if what you say is true, our Emperor's actions would be treason of the highest order. But how can we believe such things?"

Saba turned to address the other members. "It was my hope that the seriousness of my allegations would prompt you all to look into the matter for yourselves. In fact, don't take my word for it. See for yourselves if this is true. Surely there would be other signs of proof that you could think of. Perhaps the citizenship papers of the Generals have been forged to appear that these men came from different parts of the Empire."

The young man laughed. "Guards," he called.

In an instant, eight soldiers entered the room and surrounded Saba.

"Take this man into custody."

One soldier grabbed Saba by the arm and the others held their spears ready to impale him at a moment's notice.

"No," Maeryn yelled. "He tells the truth."

The Farming Guild representative stood from his chair. "Lady Maeryn, how can you be sure? Why should this man not be executed this very minute?" he asked, his emotions finally starting to show.

"...because Magnus Calidon is also the Resistance leader. And I know this because he recently appointed me as his second in command."

Saba's heart dropped. He had hoped to keep Maeryn from being condemned, but she had told her secret now. Hopefully it would provide the needed proof.

The soldier lessened his grip on Saba's arm, but still held it firmly.

The Council members looked to each other and began to talk amongst themselves again. When the whispering stopped, another member spoke up.

"You admit that you are the second in command of the Resistance, a group that has infiltrated our Empire and sought to undermine our efforts for many years. They have been our worst enemy in that they live among us. Why would you risk your life to admit such a thing in front of the High Council? Do you think that because of a simple confession, this council will be willing to show you mercy?"

Maeryn shook her head. "There was a time when I was not loyal to the Empire, when I would have liked to see it overrun with barbarians. But I was mistaken and grief influenced my beliefs. I have since realized that it is not the Empire that I hate, but its misuse of power in certain areas. Once Magnus abolished the slave trade and put an end to the Empire's abuse of these people, my perspective changed. And now I see the true reason behind his actions on this matter. I see much potential in the Empire, and I see very clearly that potential being manipulated."

"That hardly counts as loyalty," the young one seethed, eyeing Maeryn with hatred.

Suddenly, something about this young man caught Saba's attention. He noticed the man's sandy colored hair, and the fact that he was fifteen to twenty years younger than any other Council member. His thin and short frame reminded Saba of someone that Kael described from his time at the monastery.

"Rainer," Saba called out.

The young man turned his head out of habit, then quickly turned away.

"You're one of them, aren't you," Saba yelled louder.

The other Council members stopped talking and looked to Saba.

"You're one of Magnus' men. I can't believe I didn't anticipate this."

The remaining Council members looked to the young man, who wrinkled his eyebrows with disgust. "A man condemned to death will say anything."

Saba kept prodding. "Your name is Rainer and I would be willing to stake my life on the fact that your history becomes vague prior to the last ten years. And so Magnus' treachery goes even farther that I imagined. Of course he would have to have someone else on the Council in order to have a majority!"

Maeryn's friend on the Council now looked to the young man. "Durio, Is this true?"

Without warning, the young man grabbed the nearest council member and put a knife to his throat. It was a rash and dangerous move, for the hostage outweighed him by fifty pounds and was a full head taller. The guards immediately released Saba and began to fan outward, surrounding this new threat.

The Blacksmith Guild leader couldn't believe what was happening and it was clear that he wasn't about to be hostage to the small youngster. As Rainer pulled him toward the nearest window, the large man began to struggle. Rainer tightened his grip on the knife, producing a trickle of blood from the man's neck, which spilled down his chest and began to stain his tunic. Instantly, he became compliant.

The room was now dead silent, except for the harsh breathing from Rainer and his hostage. The guards began to close in carefully, now only a few paces from the two men, their spears lowered and ready. Rainer's eyes darted from the guards to the window and back again, calculating his chances.

With his left hand clutching his victim's hair, Rainer's view to his left flank was partially obstructed, or so the guards thought. Simultaneously, the two on either side lunged in. Rainer reacted instantly, jerking the blade across the Guild leader's neck and pushing him into the path of the guard on the left. Then, as if rehearsed, he spun away from the spearhead of the other guard and slashed his knife across the man's face. In the blink of an eye, three men were down while Rainer jumped through the window.

The other guards rushed after him, but stopped at the widow ledge. "He survived the fall," spoke one of the guards, then paused as he watched out the window. "Send out an alert; he's moving south." The other soldiers nodded, then ran out of the room.

Saba looked to the other Council members, who were now pale. He waited for them to respond.

Maeryn's friend was the first to speak. "Maeryn, we will have to reconvene later this evening. I hope you understand, but we can't let you two leave."

"Of course," Maeryn replied, her voice trembling slightly. "May I send word to my daughter so that she knows not to expect me?"

"...certainly. The guards will take you to your quarters. I'll have a messenger sent to you right away."

Though not the expected outcome, Saba felt a sense of relief that at least the rest of the Council now understood. As he watched the pool of blood stretching across the floor from the body of the Blacksmith Guild leader, he shook his head. It was a shame that one of their members had to lose his life in the process. But Saba had seen worse things during his time in captivity under Magnus. Though it sickened him to think it, it was a small price to pay. He took Maeryn's arm and followed the guards as they led them out of the Council chambers.

5

The Council room flickered with yellow torchlight from the sconces mounted to the pillars around the room. The sun had dropped below the horizon less than an hour ago, and no longer gave its light through the stained glass windows. Saba sat beside Maeryn and opposite the remaining members of the High Council, waiting for one additional guest before resuming their discussions.

The large double doors opened inward and two guards entered, standing on either side of the entrance. Everyone turned to watch as Dacien, former General of the Southern Region of Orud, walked confidently down the center aisle to take his seat on the other side of Maeryn and Saba. The Council members watched with a mix of emotions visible on their faces. Some were truly interested in his input, while others were obviously skeptical of this man who was officially an outlaw.

Maeryn whispered to Dacien. "Is he alright?"

"He's still weak, but able to take solid food now. I have the villagers bringing him food several times per day."

Maeryn's friend on the Council stood to address the assembly.

"Friends of the Empire, given the tragic circumstances earlier today, the Council requires no further proof of your accusations at this point. You will, however, testify of these things before a formal trial and provide all the necessary details. That includes persons not present at this meeting," he said, directing his last comment to Saba. "But all that will come later. Right now, we have more immediate issues at hand, such as how to provide the proper motivation for Magnus and his Generals to return to Orud for a trial. And we ask for your input on how to accomplish this."

"Before we get too far down this road of conversation," the Fishing Guild leader interjected, "I just want to clarify something. The accusations are that our Emperor has managed to gain control over the Orudan armies and navy, the Resistance and slave population, the Syvaku and the Korgan, and an ancient cult thought to be nothing more than a myth."

"You sound as though you admire him," Dacien observed.

"Under different circumstances, I might!" he shot back. "My point is that it is absurd to think that this man will do anything we want. He has all the power now and no reason to follow the laws of our Empire."

"...hence the need for this meeting," replied the Farming Guild leader. "Other emperors would have been obligated to return to Orud to stand trial. But these circumstances are much different than anything this Council has seen in the past."

Dacien stood. "May I...?"

"Of course," replied the guild leader, sitting back down.

Dacien took a few steps forward. "It seems simple to me. The basis of this man's power is his military might and his ability to manipulate these different groups of people to achieve his goals. If we look at the events that have transpired, it becomes clear that his intention is not ultimately to harm the Empire, but to gain control of it and make it stronger for his own uses. The attacks of the Syvaku and the Korgs were harmful to the Empire in the short term, but were targeted at cities that had little impact on our infrastructure or our economy. The fact that he commands such military strength is certainly intimidating, but it will also be his downfall. If we directly target his source of power and threaten to remove it, it will be in his best interests to maintain that power. This Council appointed Magnus as the Emperor, and has the authority to place him under arrest on suspicion of treason."

Another guild leader stood up. "What is going to make him comply with our summons? He could simply to choose to ignore it. Or worse yet, what is to keep him from killing us all? Then he wouldn't have any obstacles."

"A revolt..." Maeryn countered. "As Dacien stated, for some unknown reason, Magnus needs the Empire to keep functioning as it does. With all of the recent changes in leadership, and murders under this roof, the citizens would not support an Emperor who kills his opposition. We have hundreds of years of tradition working in our favor; the citizens deeply value the privilege of electing their officials."

"But how would they know if we just disappeared?"

Maeryn smiled. "We start a rumor. We allow word of the allegations against Magnus to reach the citizens. This way Magnus won't be able to do anything rash. And don't forget that I have the means to prepare a revolt should anything happen to us."

The Farming Guild leader spoke up. "How can we forget? I am still uncomfortable about the fact that you deceived me, Maeryn. We have invited three individuals into our Council, who, by all our laws, should have been executed hours ago."

After an awkward silence, Dacien spoke. "So we must send a summons to Magnus, to each of his armies in the east and north, and one to his combined naval command."

"Don't forget," Saba interrupted, "that these men are extremely dangerous as you saw today. It would be a good idea to enlist the help of some soldiers in lower positions of authority within each of these groups...as a precaution against retaliation."

The Council members nodded in agreement. Then Maeryn's friend looked to Dacien. "Dacien, the Council also has a need to reestablish authority over the army at Leoran. Your title of General will be temporarily reinstated until the final outcome of the trial. I think it would be a good idea for you to deliver this message in person."

Dacien smiled. "Thank you; I would like that very much."

The Farming Guild leader continued. "...one last thing. Durio, or Rainer as you called him, has still not been found. I suspect he is either hiding out in this city, or is on his way to Magnus as we speak. The dispatch to Magnus will be alerted of this possibility and will be instructed to take him into custody if their paths cross. Otherwise, the Orud guard will not stop searching the city until he is found. If there is no additional business..." he paused, "then this meeting is concluded."

Magnus sat back from the dinner table and reclined in his chair. The rocking of the ocean and a full belly were just what he needed to finally get a good night's rest. Ukiru sat across the table, silent as always, looking out the small window of the aft cabin at the glitter of the water in light of the setting sun.

Suddenly, Magnus cocked his head to the side, as if listening. He remained in this posture for a moment, then closed his eyes. His lips began to move ever so slightly, as if singing a song to himself.

Ukiru's attention was now intently focused on Magnus, as he had seen this happen many times before. He waited patiently for the event to pass.

Magnus' eyes popped open and he sat upright. He face turning red with anger.

"What is the matter?" Ukiru asked.

"Rainer's identity was uncovered. Maeryn went behind my back and told the Council everything."

Ukiru's usually expressionless eyes widened at these words. "...about the Resistance?

"No," Magnus corrected. "...the Syvaku, the Korgs, the Kaliel...everything."

"How did she find out?" Ukiru asked with an eerie calmness.

"...the old man was with her."

After a moment of silence, Ukiru offered. "At least we know his location now. How do we recover from this?"

Magnus looked out the window as he contemplated the question. Finally, he answered. "We are merely days from achieving our primary goal. Although unfortunate, this matter must not distract us. The Empire is secondary to all else."

Then Magnus stood and opened the door leading to the deck of his ship. "I must alert the others," he said and walked out of the room.

The pounding in Kael's head had eased long enough for him to get a few hours of sleep. If he had been able to move, he would have jumped as the door opened to his room. Instead, the startled feeling was only that, and nothing more. His body, except for head and face, was unresponsive.

This time, it was Saba's face that came into view. He laid a hand on Kael's forehead.

"How are you feeling?"

Kael knew Saba didn't expect an answer, but he wished he could answer anyway. There was so much that he wanted to say. Dacien had told him about his mother and that she had been here only days before to see him. He wanted to ask about her, to see her again. He longed to use his legs, to walk and be able to take care of himself.

Saba's soft words interrupted Kael's thoughts. "I've just returned from the Royal Palace at Orud. Maeryn agreed to help me meet with the High Council and tell them about Magnus and the others."

Kael raised his eyebrows.

"It took some convincing, but in the end, they believed us. Unfortunately, I failed to anticipate that Magnus would also have someone in the Council that he could control. As we were addressing the Council members, I recognized Rainer. I called him out and he took another Council member hostage. And then, before he could be apprehended, he killed his hostage and escaped."

Saba took a seat on a nearby chair. "...tragic," he mused. "But it was more effective than any of our words, and made it completely obvious that we were telling the truth."

Kael's heartbeat quickened in his chest at Saba's words.

"And you'll be happy to know," Saba continued, "that Dacien has been reinstated to the position of General...temporarily, of course. As we speak, he is on his way back to Leoran to communicate the new ruling."

Kael's frustration was mounting. He needed desperately to talk, but his body failed him.

"Meanwhile, the council has sent out dispatches to take Magnus and the others into custody and bring them back for a trial. It is risky, but I believe we have taken the proper precautions to ensure that they won't try to resist."

Saba paused, looking concerned as he noticed Kael's agitation. "I'm sorry. I know it must be difficult for you.   But understand that sometimes a diplomatic approach can be more effective. I think you'll be happy with the results. Anyway, I just wanted you to know that I'm back. Try to get some rest and I'll come check on you in a while." With that, Saba left the room and closed the door behind him.

Kael was furious at his situation. He was helpless. He had never explained to Saba, or anyone, that his enemies could communicate with each other without words. Kael didn't know how close in proximity to each other they had to be. *Is it like talking, where you have to be within earshot?* He didn't know.   But there was a possibility that Dacien, and the other dispatches were riding straight into a trap. *With Rainer's escape, Magnus and the others likely already know what is happening behind their backs in Orud.* And here, on this bed, Kael was a prisoner in his own body.

He screamed in his mind, and willed his legs to move. But it was no use. After several minutes, his temper subsided in the face of his helplessness. His breathing calmed and he felt exhausted. He stared up at the timber ceiling for a long time, his mind blank.

And then a memory drifted into his thoughts. He remembered the sensation, the fear, of falling from the cliffs at the monastery. It seemed to last an eternity. The wind rushed past his face, his clothes threatened to rip apart as he fell faster and faster. It was in that moment that his ability—or whatever it was—came into focus. It was the first time that he pushed the feeling out and away from his body. He could feel the waves of the ocean hundreds of feet beneath him. And he reached out and pushed back at them. It took all his strength, but he slowed his fall just enough to keep himself from being torn to pieces as he hit the water.

If I was able to push my focus away from myself, why couldn't I do the opposite? Why couldn't I focus inwardly?

The thought was intriguing. He hadn't tried to focus his senses since he was injured. It was enough for him to just keep breathing each day. But now he was determined to free himself of this bondage and for the first time in many months, he was hopeful.

He drew in a deep breath and tried to calm his thoughts, and the familiar sensation came easily. Without being able to physically feel his body, his senses compensated somewhat. The effect was similar to falling asleep on your arm and then waking up to find it numb. There was a sensation of the weight of his body and the pressure it exerted upon the bed, but it lacked the life that it should have had. Nevertheless, Kael focused his sense on his legs. He pushed it to inspect his legs, and then his skin. The feeling was odd, as if each hair follicle was a tree, towering above him. The texture of his skin appeared wrinkled, but in a systematic pattern, with groves running in all directions, with hair sprouting from the intersections.

Deeper. There's nothing wrong with my skin. The problem is deeper.

He pushed his sense harder and focused below the skin. He descended layer upon layer through his skin and into the muscles of his thigh. What he saw fascinated him. Hundreds and thousands of tiny fibers ran through his muscles. They pulsed in a unified rhythm. It took a second to realize that it was his heart beat that caused the pulsing. He focused in on one particular fiber and could sense the blood moving through it, like a miniature river driven in time by his heart. He pushed farther and located bone and the connective tissue of his knee where the two met. It was all so intricate and complex.

Time passed quickly as Kael explored the construction of his body. In the back of his mind, he considered that he might be wasting time. But another part of him felt that what he was doing was essential. He had to understand how things were supposed to work before he could recognize where something was broken.

He explored from his toes to his chest before Saba came back into the room.

"Oh my goodness," Saba exclaimed, rushing to Kael.

Kael felt the pressure as Saba wiped a cloth across his face. "Your nose is bleeding," he said, trying to clean the mess.

But Kael just smiled. He didn't care. He felt as though he had regained a small sense of dignity. He might actually be able to do something for himself, something that would allow him his freedom.

"Are you hungry?" Saba asked, his forehead wrinkled with concern.

Kael blinked no.

"...thirsty?"

Kael blinked yes.

Saba quickly brought water and slowly poured some between Kael's parched lips, offering some much needed refreshment. "There," he said when he was finished. "Are you feeling alright?"

Kael blinked yes.

"I'm concerned about the bleeding. I think I'll stay close by for a while."

Kael blinked no, and Saba almost missed it. Instead, he turned back to Kael. "What do you mean? Do you want me to leave?"

Kael blinked yes.

Saba rubbed his chin and exhaled. "I'll be back in half an hour to check on you," he said, then turned and left the room, leaving the door cracked a few inches.

Kael greatly appreciated Saba's care, but right now it felt like a distraction. He had much work to do and wanted to get back to it. As soon as he was able, he calmed himself and resumed his inspection. His chest cavity was fascinating with its heart and lungs. Afterwards, he inspected his arms and found them to be similar to his legs.

Disappointment began to set in as his inspection neared completion and everything seemed to be in working order. *What is wrong with me then?* He let his focus drift out so that he could sense his whole body, then the bed, then the room. It was like stretching a cramped muscle. After a few moments, he started focusing inward again and tried to push farther than before, wondering if he had missed something. He focused past the skin, past the muscles, past the bones, and kept pushing smaller and smaller. Suddenly, a whole new world opened to him. Vast arrays of tiny fibers surrounded him, pulsating with flashes of light like shooting stars.

What is this? These aren't veins carrying blood.

The fibers were bundled in some places like bales of straw, in other places they were connected in erratic patterns like the threads of a spider's web. Kael noticed that the bundles became denser as he moved deeper into his body. He followed them until he arrived at his spine, where the fibers seemed to braid themselves into larger strands and wrap around the spine. It was an amazing sensation to behold, like watching millions of tiny threads weave themselves in and out of a garment, glowing and shimmering with light.

Kael followed these strange threads up his spine toward his head. Then he stopped as a strange notion occurred to him. From his perspective, his sight, his hearing, his taste, and even his voice, when it worked, all emanated from his head. As he thought about it, it seemed that his thoughts and everything that made him who he was, was located in his head. His other sense was no different. And this was why he hadn't yet inspected his head. It seemed illogical to use something as a tool to inspect itself. But it was the only place left.

A smile came to his face as he refocused and followed his spine upwards where it connected to a mass of flesh that he was completely unfamiliar with, folds of what looked like skin lumped together to fill the inside of his skull. He focused tighter, and suddenly activity was bursting all around. Lights flashed and jumped throughout the folds, weaving inside and across from place to place. As he focused smaller and smaller, he saw more and more. It quickly became overwhelming and he had to pull back a little in order to gain some perspective. Then he realized something.

Moving back to where his spine entered this strange place, he realized that there wasn't nearly as much activity. He pushed his focus smaller into the flesh and realized that something was definitely wrong. The folds of flesh seemed to have a different texture than what he had seen before. They seemed dull and damaged. There was only an occasional flash of light.

Kael instantly remembered the feeling when Magnus caught hold of him at the Palace. He felt like a farmer trying to shield his crops from a hail storm. He looked again at the damage before him and realized that this was the crop, ruined, damaged by Magnus' assault. Kael followed the wreckage back to the spine and the bundles of fibers and now noticed that some weren't flashing or glowing. They remained dull. As he followed them back down his spine and into his body, he quickly lost track of them as they spread out to various extremities.

Kael suddenly felt very weak and tired. He had pushed himself farther than ever before, giving no consideration to his condition. He released his hold on his sense and slowly became aware that Saba was in the room again. Before Kael fell asleep, he could feel a cool sensation on his mouth as Saba wiped the blood from under his nose.

6

Borne by the wind, the ship cut through the warm waters off the coast of Bastul. As he was accustomed, Magnus instructed the captain to circle around the reflective circular wall and approach it from the southeast, so as not to damage the hull on the various underwater barricades. The Orud vessel slowed as it approached the gate, which slid sideways to reveal a straight path into the interior of the fortress. The crew had abandoned their Orud uniforms only minutes ago, keeping up with appearances during the majority of the trip. This was the first time that an Orud ship had breached this wall and it made Magnus a little uncomfortable, though the trespass was forgivable under the circumstances.

It took only minutes to dock the ship. Magnus leaped across the gap between the deck and the dock, too impatient to wait for the crew to make the usual preparations. Ukiru was close behind. The two quickly made their way across the docks and onto land, disappearing into the cave entrance into the dark, mountainous island that sat at the center of the secret fortress. Into the bowels of the earth they descended, their senses heightened with anticipation.

Magnus tightened his grip on the cloth-wrapped bundle in his hands and quickened his steps as he made his way down the spiral stairs. In thirty minutes, the two reached the entrance to the high temple and stepped from the glossy stone of the massive arched passage onto the sand floor of the temple. The cavern before them could have fit a small village, but was silent as a tomb, which only seemed fitting under the circumstances.

Striding across the temple floor, Magnus and Ukiru came to a stop at one of the two bridges that rose from the sand to cross the moat of dark water and end at the stone dais in the center of the room. Ukiru stayed on the sand, while Magnus traversed the bridge, stopping cautiously just before the perimeter of the dais.

Unwrapping the bundle, he gripped the hilt of the sword and let the cloths fall to his feet. The sword, a stunning sight, caught what little light was available inside the cavern and reflected it into hundreds of dazzling beams.   Though the form was not familiar to Magnus, he knew Ukiru understood it well. It was an ancient treasure to his people and had been the inspiration for their unique ways. The handle was long, roughly two and a half times the width of one's fist, allowing a two-handed grip with room to spare. There was no guard to separate the hilt from the blade, only a smooth transition where the handle flattened and became the dangerous end of the weapon. Magnus marveled at the beauty, for he knew that in his hands he held a piece of history.

As he had been instructed, he extended the weapon in front of him, over the edge of the dais and waited. Ukiru held his breath, not knowing what to expect. This event had been many years in the making, and now it was here.

Minutes passed and nothing happened. Magnus pulled back his hand and looked at the sword expecting something more to happen. Then he held it out again and waited. The faint whistling of wind could be heard from far away, but it only served to emphasize the silence in the cavern.

Magnus took a few steps backward and raised both his hands, closing his eyes. Then his body shook violently with a jolt, then went still. When he opened his eyes, they were cloudy in appearance and when he moved, his mannerisms were strangely altered, as if he was nothing more than clothing worn by someone else.

Magnus turned the sword over in his hands and inspected it, running his fingers along the flat of the blade. Then, flying into a rage, he squeezed the handle until his knuckles turned white and threw the sword across the moat, where is landed in the sand. Spinning on his heels, he glared back at Ukiru.

"You fool," he shouted. "It is a fake. Are you not able to carry out even the simplest of tasks?" Then Magnus' body shook again and suddenly, he looked fatigued.   He stepped carefully down the bridge with his legs trembling.

Ukiru went to his side and grabbed his arm, lending support.

"I...apologize for..."

Ukiru dismissed it with a wave of his free hand.

Magnus stopped, grateful for not having to explain himself.

"Let's go back to the surface; the fresh air will do you good," Ukiru said.

It was a long walk back, seemingly longer than before when they were anticipating the fulfillment of their goals. Ukiru was right. The fresh sea air seemed to revitalize Magnus. After moments of silence, he gained enough strength to talk.

"It looked exactly as he described it," Magnus explained.

Ukiru nodded in agreement.   "No craftsmen, no matter how skilled, could make such a replica from memory. This rules out the possibility that it was just...art, or some likeness of the real thing. It must have been crafted as a decoy, while the real one was still in his possession. ...clever bastard!"

"...indeed" Magnus agreed. "So the real one was either hidden or taken out of the fortress city. Which means that it could be anywhere."

"So what do we do now?" Ukiru asked.

"I don't know," Magnus replied, realizing that it had been many years since he had ever said those words. "Everything we have worked for has led to this moment."

As the sun began to set, Magnus rose to his feet. "I must tell the others," he said, closing his eyes. His lips began to move slowly as he explained the situation to the remaining members of their group hundreds of miles away.

Ukiru wished he knew what Magnus was saying. He had to fight the temptation to feel envious of the bond that Magnus shared with the other young men. But he was already far too old by the time he had met Magnus. This skill could only be taught to the young, and for this reason, Ukiru was always going to be an outsider. He contented himself with the knowledge that the things he had taught the boys were something that Magnus would not be able to share in. Granted, Magnus was an accomplished warrior, but he would never experience what Ukiru shared with the boys. *They really did receive the best of each of us.*

Magnus drew in a deep breath and opened his eyes, breaking the silence. "...good news," he said, turning to Ukiru. "Berit is on his way here and he says that he brings a gift...one that will solve our problem."

Ukiru raised his eyebrows, waiting for an explanation.

"He'll be here in a few days," Magnus replied. "Then we'll have our answer."

On the morning of the fourth day since their arrival, Magnus and Ukiru were summoned to the observation deck. From this vantage point, they could see a small Orud messenger ship moving in quickly from the north. Magnus gave the authorization to open the gate for this vessel and then descended quickly to the lower levels of the elaborate docking attached to the inside of the wall. Circling the perimeter of the island, they found Berit's ship just as it was being docked.

The crew scrambled to bring in the sails and secure the ship to the dock. As soon as the plank was dropped, Berit came across holding a long wooden box with intricate carvings along its length. His close-cropped blonde hair reflected the morning sunlight coming from the east.

Magnus extended his hand and the two greeted each other. Then Berit looked to Ukiru and bowed slightly. Ukiru returned the gesture.

Magnus gestured for Berit to follow him as he walked toward the mountain. "And what is this gift you spoke of?" he asked.

Berit simply handed the long wooden box to Magnus. "While taking inventory of the Orud treasury, I came across an ancient manuscript documenting items that had been confiscated from our enemies during the early years. Much of it was ordinary family heirlooms, gold and silver goblets and the like. But one item stood out in particular. The author described it as a crude scepter made entirely of glass."

Magnus stopped and turned to Berit with a smile on his face, then looked down to the box he held in his hands. He quickly untied the leather thong and removed the cap, tilting the box so that the contents slid out into his other hand. Then, unwrapping the scarlet cloth, he unveiled an item that matched Berit's description. It was about five feet in length, and looked as though it was the gnarled branch of a crystalline tree. It shimmered in the morning light and the clarity was otherworldly.

Ukiru remembered the replica sword and felt slightly embarrassed that he had ever taken it to be authentic, although he had never looked upon something like this before. Words couldn't describe its beauty.

Magnus clearly felt the same way, holding it up to the light and admiring the fact that it was much lighter than it appeared. "Let us not delay," he said confidently, continuing toward the mountain entrance. For a second time, Magnus and Ukiru descended into the mountain with a prized possession. Berit followed close behind, knowing that he had saved them all.

Ukiru and Berit held their breath as they stood in the sand. Magnus, standing on the bridge before the altar, raised the staff above his head, holding it with both hands. His body shuddered and then was still, standing with an awkward posture. Then, he extended the staff over the edge of the dais.

In an instant, a shimmering streak shot upward like a flash of lightning. But the image didn't disappear; it hovered above them, towering up toward the roof of the cavern, suspended by an unknown force. A faint bluish glow emanated from the dais, bathing the cavern in its luminosity. The light then focused itself into a funnel and began to pull inward until it disappeared.

Magnus' body went limp and dropped to the bridge.

Ukiru and Berit rushed forward, and lifted Magnus to his feet. He was alive, but he had no strength and couldn't stand on his own. "Let's get him to a bed," Ukiru grunted, heaving Magnus' muscular frame away from the dais.

7

The damage was so extensive, that at first Kael didn't know where to start. But after a thorough examination of the surrounding tissue, Kael thought he understood what the damaged area was supposed to look like. And just as he had pushed himself away from the ocean when escaping the monastery, he tried to move things around and repair what had been done.

The first attempts met with failure, but then he stumbled across something by accident. He found that if he focused his sense in a different way, the stimulation caused his body to repair itself. His efforts turned from putting pressure on things, to creating an environment where it happened naturally.

Naturally, he laughed to himself. *There's nothing natural about this.*

It was slow, but effective. After only a week, Kael regained his ability to move his feet. It was an amazing feeling to have gained back some small measure of control. After this first achievement, Kael inspected his body again and learned a great deal about how things were supposed to work. He likened it to clearing debris out of a river. Once it was cleared, the water flowed uninhibited. The strange fibers that were dull and lifeless now pulsed with energy that could be traced all the way down his legs to his toes.

This caused Kael to think carefully about prioritizing his recovery. All he needed was time, but what abilities were most important? He finally decided that being able to communicate would do him more good than anything. So he studied his vocal chords and the fibers that connected them to the damaged part of his head. The complexity was so great that it was impossible to tell for sure if he was working in the right area, but he started with his best guess.

It had been over a week since the incident, and still no word from the All Powerful. It was as if he had disappeared. Usually, Magnus could summon him at will and he would be there as a voice in his mind. Now, there was nothing but silence. At first, it was a relief. For as many years as he could remember, the All Powerful had been there, speaking thoughts into his mind. It had turned out to be profitable for Magnus, but the cost had been equally as great. Every day Magnus struggled to yield to this being who sought complete control over his life. Sometimes, he wondered why he had been chosen. Then, he remembered that he had sought it out. It was he who had gone searching for the darker things of this world. It was he who had been intrigued by the legends of the Kaliel and their practices. *No, I wasn't chosen; I volunteered.*

But after several long days, he began to worry that something had gone terribly wrong. He had forsaken everything in order to make his way to the temple and perform the task that the All Powerful had given him. However, the outcome was not as expected. As time passed slowly, he decided that he must move ahead as though nothing had happened.   His carefully constructed plan to rule the Empire was fraying around the edges and he needed desperately to tie up the loose ends.   He had already given instructions to Coen to move the naval forces. The Orud dispatches would have reached him first, and this move would buy him some time. But there was no plausible excuse to move Soren's forces in the east. The soldiers were committed to fighting the Korgan and it didn't make sense to distract them from their objective.

Magnus drew in a deep breath and looked out over the ocean, forcing his mind to comprehend what had transpired in the past few days. Maeryn and the old man had put him in a difficult position, and it angered him greatly. The first thought that came to mind was that he could kill the dispatches before they reached their destination. But their disappearance would only validate the accusations in the minds of the Council members. They might skip the trial altogether and revoke his position. He needed the Council in his pocket because they were crucial to controlling the citizens. And he couldn't allow the dispatches to reach their destination, because their message would undermine the authority of Soren and Coen with their subordinates. And if they all went back to Orud to stand trial, as the Council wanted, there was no way to explain away the accusations.

As Magnus reviewed his limited options, he realized that the only way out of this mess was to kill the dispatches, then return to Orud and do the same to the remaining Council members. This, of course, would certainly start a riot, for the citizens would not tolerate another change in the structure of their leadership. It would be completely transparent what was happening. But then Magnus would allow the Korgan to break through and invade the eastern half of the Empire. The threat of death had a way of focusing people's concerns on things that really mattered. It would be ugly, but in the end, he would still have control of the Empire and eventually life would return to some semblance of normality.

"Ukiru," he called.

The assassin rose from his meditative position and turned around.

"Prepare my ship. We will leave immediately to intercept the Orud dispatch that will be looking for me in the south."

Ukiru nodded, then walked down the stone stairs leading away from the mouth of the volcano upon which Magnus stood. It was a great vantage point, allowing one to see the entire fortress and surrounding ocean from one place.

Magnus closed his eyes and prepared himself for another communication to his subjects. As he was accustomed, he quieted his thoughts and emotions, and focused solely on the presence of others that could hear and understand him. But something was different this time. Where there was once clarity in feeling the presence of the others, there was now a great deal of confusion. Something was blocking his mind. He focused on the source of this confusion and realized that something was happening below him, in the mountain.

"Ukiru," he called, waving for him to come back, then turned and descended the steps that spiraled from the top of the mountain into the dark hole running down its center. The path, which Magnus rarely traveled, took him along the inside of a fifty foot wide shaft that bored through the middle of the volcano. It was a mystery as to who was capable of constructing such a thing, and without the aid of modern tools. Even if Magnus were to attempt such a feat, he didn't know a single stone mason capable of the mastery evidenced in the High Temple.

After the first hundred feet, the shaft became very dark and the descending steps were almost invisible. Ukiru was only a few steps behind and now the two picked their way carefully down the stairs. After another hundred feet, the stairs ended and the path turned to the left, burrowing into the side of the shaft. It was pitch black inside the cave and Magnus let Ukiru take the lead as he had always proven to be quite agile where others failed. Following Ukiru, Magnus felt the passage begin to veer to the right and descend once more. Eventually, the wall on the right side of the passage opened, and he could see across the cavern of the temple, lit along its perimeter with wall torches. They were still fifty feet above the floor, descending the stairs that were carved into the cavern wall.

Magnus looked over toward the altar and noticed that it seemed different somehow, but he couldn't place it. As soon as their feet touched the sand, they started to run.

Berit had also realized that something was happening. He appeared in the doorway on the other side of the temple, carrying a torch in his hand, and quickly made his way to the center of the room.

It didn't take long to realize why the dais looked different. As soon as he reached the foot bridge, Magnus could see that a section of the shimmering streak of light that remained suspended in the air above the altar was blotted out by a shadow.

...not a shadow...a dark shape

It was about ten feet in length and roughly the width of a man, suspended above the surface of the dais, and rotating slowly. In the faint light of the cavern, it was impossible to make out any features, but it looked somewhat like a cocoon, slightly thicker on the top and narrowing at the bottom.

Magnus and Ukiru stood on one side of the dais, afraid to set foot on it. Berit was on the opposite side, having approached from the other foot bridge.

"What is it?" Berit whispered.

The surface of the shape began to undulate like something rigid moving beneath a skin. Magnus watched in fascination as the cocoon began to open, stretching and expanding outward, unraveling like the blossoming of a flower.

Suddenly, it burst open into a flurry of angled, leathery wings and sharp limbs. A deafening screech exploded in Magnus' ears and he was thrown backward by the force. As his body landed on the footbridge, every torch in the cavern blew out at the same instant. Magnus grasped both sides of his head, trying to cover his ears from the sound, only to find that it resonated inside his head, as well as outside. A rush of images flashed through his mind; memories of recent events that were being extracted. They moved too fast for comprehension. Magnus simply yielded to the overwhelming experience.

At last, when his mind was exhausted, the pain stopped, and was followed by a deafening silence. It took several minutes for Magnus to regain control of himself. And when he could formulate a thought, he realized that the All Powerful had returned. Like the smaller rumblings after an earthquake, he could hear a question echoing in his mind.

WHAT IS THE STATE OF MY KINGDOM?

Magnus realized that he had already answered, or rather, the answer had just been taken from him. He struggled to his feet and could see that Berit and Ukiru were still on the ground, unmoving. He could sense that the All Powerful was still inside the cavern, but couldn't see him. Suddenly, he felt an intense fear of his failings with the Empire and of retribution from his master. He felt completely helpless. Then, just as the emotion threatened to drive him mad, the solution was forced into his mind.

Out of the corner of his eye, he caught a swift movement. Before he could react, a dark creature sped low across the cavern floor toward him. It expanded its wings at the last second, then shot skyward through the opening in the cavern ceiling, drawing a vortex of sand in its wake.

Magnus covered his eyes and crouched to the ground, cowering in fear.

In the silence that followed, Ukiru and Berit regained consciousness and slowly rose to their feet. They both looked to Magnus with questioning eyes.

"We're going back to Orud," he said simply.

Dacien pulled on the reins and his horse slowed to a trot. The other nine men with him followed his lead as the group descended into the valley. Scanning the terrain, he identified a suitable place to make camp for the night—a small stand of pines at the base of a rock outcropping. Dacien pointed to it as the second in command pulled up along side of him.

"Over there," he said to the man. "I'm going to ride on to the next ridge and scout our passage for tomorrow while there is still daylight."

"We'll have something on the fire by the time you get back," the man replied, then led his horse to the right. The other eight men followed him.

Dacien spurred his horse onward and it sped up to a trot. The valley was like everything else the group had seen in the past weeks. The dry terrain was spotted with clusters of brush and groupings of pine trees. Occasionally, they would pass a small stream like the one running through the middle of this valley. Without many obstacles, they had made good time, their progress only slowing when they had to navigate a difficult mountain range.

The sun was just above the horizon and shining directly into his face, but it would drop quickly, so Dacien didn't have much time. Cresting the hill on the southwest side of the valley, he stopped as soon as the brush and rocks afforded him a view of the land. His view was somewhat limited and he had to dismount and climb the rocks. It took more time, but gave him a chance to stretch his legs. When he had found an unobstructed view, Dacien sat down on a large boulder and rested.

Peering out over the land, he could see that tomorrow's ride would be easy, but the last mountain range separating him from Leoran was going to be a challenge. As he studied the valleys, choosing tomorrow's passage, he noted some movement on the horizon.

At first he thought it to be a bird, but as he watched, he realized the proportion was wrong. It was actually much bigger and farther away, but moving quickly. Dacien moved off the rocks and underneath a tangle of brush and continued to watch with curiosity. His horse whinnied and he quickly looked to see that it was shifting uncomfortably, yet staying where he left it.

Looking back to the sky, he shielded his eyes from the afternoon sun that had now just touched the horizon. The intense orange light flooded his vision and made his eyes water as he scanned the sky. Finally, he located the dark shape about a hundreds yards out to the southwest, heading straight for him. The thing, whatever it was, was as large as a man and dark as midnight. Its wings, which were sharply angled like a bat, moved effortlessly and carried it along with such speed that it would have outrun the fastest horse.

Dacien shrank back into the brush and held completely still. In just a few seconds, it had closed the distance. The thing passed swiftly overhead with an eerie howling of the wind. And in an instant it was gone. Dacien crawled out from the brush and stood up, but couldn't see more than twenty feet in the direction it had flown. He quickly made his way down the rocks to his horse and mounted up, turning back toward their camp. Once out from behind the rocks and brush, he caught a glimpse of the dark shape again. It was already over the far end of the valley.

Suddenly, its wings folded back and it dove downward into the valley with increasing speed, like a hawk descending to attack a snake. Dacien realized with a panic that his men were in that part of the valley. He dug his heels in and his horse broke into a run.

Darkness was rapidly choking out the last rays of daylight. The horse's hooves dug into the dry earth as Dacien watched the terrain carefully in the fading light. Then, smoke began to rise from the horizon and Dacien knew that his camp had been attacked. When he was two hundreds yards out he saw the black creature rise into the sky and turn due north. It flapped its wings faster and picked up tremendous speed, disappearing over the valley's ridge to the north.

The creature had been headed east, and with the change in direction, Dacien knew instantly that the attack had been deliberate. He pushed on toward his camp trying to comprehend what had just happened. He had never seen such a thing in all his life. *A winged creature as big as a man?* He couldn't believe it.

When he arrived at the camp in the twilight his worst fears were realized. Though he had seen death all his life as a soldier, he wasn't able to stomach the sight. Arms and legs were strewn about the campsite. The horses had been killed, as well, though not with the same vengeance as his men. Someone had tripped over the fire in the struggle and scattered the wood, sending smoke into the air. A severed head lay by itself, twenty feet from the center of camp.

Dacien had seen a man beheaded when he was a young soldier of sixteen years. It was a surreal experience and never really bothered him, as the man had been tried and convicted of murder. But this sight was very real and very grotesque, and this had been one of his own men. Dacien leaned over the side of his horse as his stomach heaved, but nothing came out.

When he recovered himself, Dacien realized that he was all alone now. The attack had been deliberate, he was sure. But what was the motivation?

He could think of nothing except that they were headed to Leoran under a change in leadership. *Is Magnus associated with this?*

Dacien searched through his saddlebags and found the official communication from the Council, its seal still intact. He put it back where he found it, then pulled on the reins, turning his horse back to the west. Leaning down, he said quietly, "We still have a long way to go." Then he nudged the horse with his heels and resumed his journey to Leoran.

8

Far north of Orud, on a small island off the coast of Suppard, a violent storm was raging. Wind drove the rain hard into the earth, while the ocean swelled and pounded the cliffs on the southeast side with large waves that threatened to break the rocks. Hundreds of feet above the ocean surface sat a stone and wood monastery that had stood the test of time, weathering thousands of storms just like this.

In the pulsing flashes from the lightening strikes, a large winged creature dropped from the sky and touched-down just in front of the main entrance. Folding its wings inward, it wrapped its body as with a cloak. Then it began to walk forward. From a distance, it would have appeared as a very tall man, but nothing could have been farther from the truth.

The creature extended its left hand forward and the thick wooden doors into the main dining hall opened effortlessly. The creature ducked under the doorway and walked into the hall, turning to the right where a fireplace was set inside the wall. Again, it lifted its left hand and a portion of the stone wall next to the fireplace swung inward with a deep, grating sound. The creature entered the passage and descended an unlit stone staircase. The smell of the sea hung thick in the air, as if the door hadn't been opened in decades.

Following the passage, the dark figure descended more than a hundred feet into the earth. Had it followed the passage to its end, it would have seen a cavern at the base of the cliffs, large enough for ships to enter. Instead, it stopped and turned east at a narrow cave that most would have mistaken for a dead end. Twenty feet from the main passage was a small iron door, bolted shut and partially obstructed by rocks and earth that had collapsed.

The creature extended its hand and the debris began to move aside. Had anyone found this door, it would have been useless to try and open it. Aside from the large bolts permanently holding the door against its frame, there were other, more ancient methods of keeping the contents of this room undisturbed.

Placing its hand on the door, the dark figure moved its lips and spoke unintelligible words of a forgotten language. A loud metallic clank rang out, filling the small passage, followed by the escape of air from around the door. Suddenly, the door fell inward to land with a thunderous crash amid a cloud of dust.

When the air settled, the creature walked into the room. The space was a perfect cube, thirty feet across in all directions. At the center of the room sat a very large stone box decorated with intricate carvings, inlaid with all manner of precious stones. It might have looked like a sarcophagus, but for the fact that it was twenty feet in length, taking up most of the space of the room.

The dark figure walked to the stone box, moving with an unearthly gait, as if the force of gravity had no effect on its body. It laid its hand on the box that sat six feet from the floor, and began to walk around it, whispering strange words as it moved. When it had completed one revolution, it stopped at the foot of the box.

"Arise, my son, from your ancient sleep," it spoke aloud. "Arise, great hunter of man, eater of their flesh. Arise to a new world."

After a moment, there was movement from inside the stone box. The lid, which measured a full foot in thickness, unmovable by any man, slid to the side to reveal a small opening. Slowly, an enormous hand of dark flesh came from the opening, its fingers curling around the lip of the sarcophagus. The skin had slight green undertones, more pronounced underneath the fingernails. In form, they closely resembled the hands of a human, but much larger.

Then, the room was filled with emotions of sadness and confusion, wordless communication coming from the coffin.

"...not yet my son," answered the winged creature. "But I have found you a prey worthy of your skills. His name is Kael and he is not far from here."

The great hand lifted and turned, grasping the lid. Then, with unbelievable force, the lid flew from the sarcophagus and smashed against the wall.

9

Ukiru stood at the bow of Magnus' ship looking out over the waters. He was aware of someone's presence behind him, but kept his eyes on the horizon.

"Something troubles you," Magnus stated from behind.

Ukiru waited until Magnus reached the railing beside him. Never one for wasted words, he got right to the point. "I wish to be released from my obligations."

Magnus took a deep breath, but was silent for a few seconds.

Ukiru wondered what was going through Magnus's mind. Almost on a daily basis, he had the opportunity to escape. But Magnus was the only person that he'd ever met who could either stop him, or had the means to hunt him down. For that was the essence of their relationship. Ukiru was indebted to someone who was powerful enough to enforce it. And so Ukiru was forced to appeal to Magnus' desire to keep up the current arrangement.

When Magnus spoke, his voice betrayed the emotions of someone who had few friends. "I have been pleased with your work. And I believe you have more than fulfilled your part of our agreement...but he will never let it happen. No one can ever leave." Magnus' voice was barely above a whisper.

"My agreement was with you, not this...this demon. In all these years, I never believed in the things you did. And I didn't have to; I just had to instruct the boys to do so. But you were wrong about him. He is not the god you worshipped; he is something much worse. And I don't want to have any part of it."

Magnus sighed. "I know. But with him, there is no distinction between what is his and what is yours. Even with Maeryn..." Magnus trailed off, his voice starting to shake.

Ukiru looked over to his master, seeing for the first time the man's own struggles.

Magnus' face visibly hardened. "Everything is his! I'm sorry, my friend, but we both have only one choice in this matter." He turned from the railing and walked away without waiting for a response.

Ukiru looked back to the water, anger boiling in his blood. It seemed that he couldn't escape a life of obligation to someone else, whether it was his childhood elders or his current situation. It seemed impossible to get away from it. But Ukiru wasn't like anyone else...he never was. When something was impossible, he found a way. And that thought was both challenging and comforting.

Ukiru closed his eyes and breathed in the salty air, calming his mind and body as he had instructed his students so many times.

"Saba!" Kael yelled from his bed.

Seconds later, Saba burst into the room, his eyes wide with wonder. "Kael?"

"They're all walking into a trap."

"Kael, you're talking."

"Never mind that," Kael replied. "You have to listen to me. The dispatches that the Council sent out, even Dacien, are all walking into a trap."

"What do you mean?" Saba asked.

"Magnus, and Soren, and all the others... They can talk to each other without using words. They can read each others thoughts. I know it sounds strange, but you have to trust me. Magnus knows everything that Rainer heard you say. Magnus knows what you're trying to do, which means that the messengers are in danger, and so is Dacien."

"Shh," Saba said, calmingly. "You don't have to worry. Coen has already been brought in. Soren's on his way. They didn't resist. We made sure that they knew they'd have a revolt on their hands if they didn't comply. The citizens won't tolerate any more scandalous behavior from their leaders."

"Oh," Kael replied, stunned. "Are you sure?"

"Yes," Saba replied calmly. "Coen is sitting in a jail cell as we speak. Magnus was farther away than anyone, so it has taken more time to reach him. I've never heard of people being able to do what you say, but it doesn't matter. We assumed that Rainer escaped the city and that he would get to Magnus before we could."

Kael breathed a heavy sigh.

"But look at you," Saba exclaimed. "You're talking...that's amazing!"

Kael smiled. "I have a lot of work to do, but it's good to have my voice back. Saba?"

"Yes?" he answered.

"I want to thank you for saving my life, for taking care of me. I know it isn't a pleasant thing to care for a grown man in this way...changing my bedclothes as if I was an infant."

Saba held up his hand in protest. "I've seen worse things. Besides, this is what friends do for each other."

Kael smiled, and blinked as a few tears rolled down the side of his face. He turned his eyes from Saba and looked to the ceiling, which was a sight that had long ago become familiar. "I need a change of scenery," he said. "Can you take me outside?"

"Of course," Saba replied. "Let me fetch some help."

Two days later, Saba loaded Kael into a cart and they rode down the mountain, through the small village, and stopped at the narrow inlet that led to the eastern bay of Orud. There, with the help of some villagers, Saba put Kael aboard his small sailing vessel and the two set out for Orud. Kael had gained some movement in his arms, but not enough to be of any use. The rest of his upper body and all of his lower body remained paralyzed.

Clouds began to move in quickly from the north and, by midday, rain was falling steadily. Saba manned the sails and tried to keep his bearings in the low visibility. Occasionally, he looked to Kael to make sure that he was alright. Usually, Kael just lay still with his eyes closed, whether or not he was sleeping. Saba was greatly relieved that Kael could now speak. It would have been more than awkward to go before the High Council only to have the primary witness unable to testify to the accusations that Saba had made against the Emperor.

By mid-afternoon the rain had stopped and patches of sky were visible between dark gray clouds. The shoreline to the west began to show signs of civilization, with the occasional dock or small living structure close to the water's edge. Saba estimated that they were approaching the main docks in Orud.

Saba turned to check on Kael who was now sitting upright and smiling. "Are you ready to bear witness against these people?" he asked.

Kael's smile disappeared. "I feel completely vulnerable like this. But under the circumstances, I guess I don't really have a choice."

"Don't worry Kael. I'll look out for you. Just tell the Council what you told me and things will work themselves out." Saba knew it was much more complicated than that, but he was trying to be optimistic for Kael's sake.

"Is...my mother going to be there?"

Saba made an adjustment to the sail. "She's going to meet us at the docks."

Kael didn't reply and remained silent until the small boat sailed into the Orud harbor. "When is the trial?"

Saba kept his eyes ahead, navigating the narrow channels through the myriad of floating wooden structures which anchored boats of various sizes. "It's set to begin tomorrow, though the High Council will likely want to meet with us this evening to make sure that we are still prepared to give our testimony."

"Is that her?" Kael asked, looking off to the left at a carriage waiting where the wooden platform connected to the shoreline.

"Yes," Saba replied as he dropped the sails and fastened them to the mast. Then, he carefully rowed the small boat into an empty space at the dock. Kael looked impatient as Saba secured the boat to the dock.

Within minutes they were joined by Maeryn and two of her assistants who helped to lift Kael out of the boat. "Mother," Kael said simply.

Maeryn smiled and stepped forward, touching Kael's face. Then she put her arms gently around him and held him tight.

Kael didn't know what to do, so he just raised his arms and returned the gesture. He knew that it was his mother, though she looked much older than he remembered her. But something felt much different and he was struck at once with the realization that he could never go back to the way things were when he was a child in Bastul.

"You seem to be doing much better," she said as she finally released him.

"I have so much to tell you," he said simply.

Maeryn smiled. "And I have much to tell you. Perhaps after...all this...we will have some time to talk."

"I would like that," Kael replied, as the assistants carried him toward the carriage.

The guards walked slowly as they led Magnus up the steps to the court. The two behind him made a valiant attempt to appear threatening with their spears at his back, but he could feel their fear. He liked it. It gave him strength.

When they had reached the center of the court, the two guards ahead of him diverted to either side of a stone pedestal which stood waist high. One of the men turned around and grabbed the chain that connected his shackled hands and feet, fastening it to another chain that was embedded into the top of the pedestal. Then, they slowly backed away, feeling better that Magnus was now contained.

Magnus simply smiled to himself. Soren and Coen were present, as well, also chained to their own pedestals at the center of the large room.

Councilman Calvus descended the steps which circled the perimeter of the room, and approached. "Magnus Calidon. You, your army Generals, and your naval Commander have been brought to Orud to stand trial for charges of treason of the highest order. In the presence of the Council, what do you have to say for yourself?"

"Where are my accusers and what are their charges?"

The councilman looked to the ground and walked down a few more steps. "Your accusers are expected any moment, but you will not see them until tomorrow. Their charges are that you were behind the Syvaku attacks in the west, as well as the Korgan in the east. You are accused of assassinating the former Emperor and manipulating this council into appointing you as Emperor. Furthermore, the men you appointed to positions of leadership were trained under your command and placed in secret among the various territories, awaiting just such an appointment. You are accused of leading the Resistance, which has long been an enemy of this Empire. You are even accused of leading the Kaliel which, if still in existence, would be a most reprehensible crime."

Magnus stared at the man who seemed to enjoy the fact that he was free to move about the room while Magnus stood chained to a stone.

"Well, what response do you have to these allegations?"

Magnus looked around the room, to Soren and Coen chained in the center, to the remaining council members cowering in fear around the perimeter, to the twenty guards which stood at various strategic positions throughout the room. He looked to the arched ceiling fifty feet overhead supported by massive columns around the perimeter of the room. The sound echoed well in this room and made it easy to hear no matter where you stood.

All the better.

He turned back to stare deep into Calvus' eyes. "If I am guilty of these accusations, I would have to be a very clever and powerful man.   ...a dangerous man!"

Soren and Coen smiled.

Calvus looked nervous.

"And so I have a question for you," Magnus continued. "What type of leverage do you have against such a man?"

There was an awkward silence as Calvus looked back to the other members of the Council. But he didn't receive any help from them. Instead, he stood speechless, unsure of how to proceed.

"Surely you wouldn't bring such a man and his dangerous allies back into your home city unless you were positive that nothing would go wrong?"

"The citizens...," Calvus stammered. "Th...they won't accept..."

"Oh yes, the citizens," Soren interrupted. "We mustn't upset them."

"Oh, Councilman," Magnus said mockingly. "I wouldn't worry too much about the citizens. Adversity has a way of...," Magnus paused for effect. "...of bringing people together."

"What do you mean?" Calvus asked.

A few of the other Council members came down the steps.

Magnus turned to address them. "I think I will make a deal with you. You will all support me and show me the proper respect for someone of my position. You will deliver my accusers to me and then you will make these allegations go away. You will proclaim your allegiance in public and repair the damage caused by these nasty rumors. And in return, I will not remove my armies from the eastern wall. And I will not cause the Korgan hordes to sweep across this land like a plague, to kill every man, woman, and child in this city."

Calvus took a few steps backward, shocked by what he heard.

"It seems a fair bargain to me," Magnus offered. He was feeling powerful now, the strength of the All Powerful coursing through him. Magnus could feel the proximity of his being and knew that he was somewhere in the Palace.

The guards moved in from the perimeter in a show of power.

Magnus laughed, and his voice echoed through the chambers. He lifted his hands and the chains fell to the ground, as did Soren's and Coen's. Then Magnus turned away from Calvus and faced the guards who were now moving inward. He extended both his hands, palms upward.

In an instant, the spears left the hands of the guards and launched themselves toward the center of the room, to land scattered on the ground. The soldiers all backed away as they suddenly found themselves disarmed.

"What manner of sorcery is this?" Calvus whispered.

Magnus turned back to the man and focused on him.

Calvus now felt his neck constricted and grasped with his own hands to fight the invisible force that was chocking the life from him.

"Swear your allegiance to me," Magnus shouted. He walked steadily toward Calvus. "Swear your allegiance," he shouted again.

Slowly, each member of the Council came out from behind the columns, and knelt to the floor. When the last one bowed, Magnus released Calvus, who promptly fell to the floor in exhaustion, fighting to regain his breath.

Magnus turned to the guards. "Bring me my accusers," he ordered.

Maeryn sat opposite from Saba and Kael in the spacious carriage as they made their way to the Palace. It was a wonder for the three of them to be together again. Many times, she had dreamt of just such a gathering during her time in Bastul with Lemus. Eventually, she stopped dreaming because she found that it just drove her into madness. And now she was here with these two men who had ceased to be part of her life long ago. It frustrated her that they weren't meeting under different circumstances. She could sense that this meeting was awkward for Kael and that it would take much effort to reestablish the relationship that should have come naturally, would have come naturally if they hadn't been so violently separated years ago.

Maeryn looked out the window and recognized the tree lined avenue leading to the Palace. She had made this trip dozens of times in the past few months, but never had her heart beat so loudly in her chest.   Just as expected, the trees gave way to a low stone wall topped with an ornate wrought iron fence.   Magnus had told her that trees were deliberately kept well away from the Palace because they made good hiding spots and only aided invaders.   The barren landscape told her that they were approaching the Palace entrance.

Glancing over to Saba, she meant to ask him if he was ready, but something about his tense expression told her otherwise.   Now that she thought about it, he hadn't said a word in the last few minutes.

"Saba?" she asked.   "Is everything all right?"

Saba turned with a distant look in his eyes.   "Something isn't right."

Maeryn smiled.   "...other than the fact that we are going to bear witness before the High Council to prove that the Emperor is guilty of treason?" she said sarcastically.

Saba didn't catch the joke, or else didn't think it was funny.   "Yes...actually," he replied.   "Something is very wrong.   We have to turn around."

"What?" Maeryn questioned, worried that he was backing out of his responsibilities.

"We can't go in there," Saba replied with more confidence.   "Stop the carriage," he told her.

Maeryn couldn't believe what she was hearing.   "How can we stop now? The Council is waiting for us.   And this was your idea to begin with," she said, her voice steadily growing louder.

"Please," Saba pleaded.   "Please trust me.   If we go in there now, we won't come out alive."

Maeryn hesitated, then reached over to the front wall of the cabin and knocked twice with her hand.   The jolting of the wheels over the stone pavers slowed, then eventually stopped.

Kael, who had been resting, suddenly sat upright and opened his eyes.   "I feel it too," he announced.

"Feel what?" Maeryn exclaimed with irritation.

"I'll explain later," Saba offered.   "Just turn this carriage around and get us out of here as fast as possible.

Maeryn wrinkled her eyebrows, then leaned her head out of the window. "Driver, turn around.   We're leaving."   Just before she pulled her head back into the cabin, she caught a glimpse of the guard tower at the gate.   Several guards were pointing.   Two of them started running toward the carriage, while two others ran back toward the palace.

The carriage began to swing left and Maeryn ducked back into the cabin just in time to see the guards again through the window in the opposite side of the cabin.   Now Kael and Saba saw the guards.

"It's happening already," Saba observed.

Maeryn pounded on the wall again. "Hurry up," she shouted. Almost instantly, the carriage lurched forward before it had completed its turn. It momentarily rose up on two wheels, threatening to tip sideways. Then the wheels thudded against the stone road and they began to gain speed as they retreated from the Palace.

Maeryn turned back to Saba and Kael, and carefully sat down, trying not to lose her footing as the carriage vibrated violently. "What do we do now?" she asked, still irritated at the sudden change of plans. "Where are we going?"

Saba turned from looking out the window. "We are no longer safe in this city. Magnus has taken control of the Council, I'm sure of it. We are fugitives from this day forward."

"How do you know this?" Maeryn asked him.

"I just do," he answered without explanation. "I don't know how he did it, but Magnus outsmarted us."

"We could go to Leoran," Kael announced.

Maeryn looked to Saba who appeared skeptical.

Kael continued. "You said yourself that Magnus didn't have the resources to do anything with the forces there."

Saba nodded. "I know you want to see if Dacien is alright, but we don't even know if he made it there alive."

"Actually," Maeryn countered, "it's the only option that affords us some protection. Otherwise we just hide or wander around until Magnus catches us."

Saba and Kael were silent, considering any other possible scenarios.

Maeryn continued. "But we've go to go back to the harbor and get your boat. I have a few loose ends to tie up and I also have a...more sea-worthy vessel and provisions."

Saba and Kael nodded.

Maeryn crawled over to the window and leaned out. "...to the harbor," she shouted to the driver.

They ditched the carriage a short walk from the docks, then went the rest of the way on foot with Maeryn's driver and two assistants carrying Kael. When they found Saba's tiny ship, they stopped.

"Can it carry this many?" Maeryn asked Saba.

"...just," he replied.

They boarded quickly and set a northeasterly course that took them both away from the shore and in the general direction of Maeryn's residence. When they were two hundred yards from shore, Saba spotted a small contingent of the royal cavalry approaching the docks they had just left.

"Everyone, get out of sight," he announced.

Maeryn dropped to the deck and hid behind the railing, while her driver remained at the rudder, the only one standing. They stayed in this posture for half an hour, until they were well out of sight. When her driver altered his course to due east, he announced that it was safe to stand.

Maeryn's heart began to settle back into her chest as they made their way across the bay, but the sense of anticipation mixed with fear persisted. Finally, by mid afternoon, they reached the eastern shore of the bay. Maeryn instructed her driver and assistants to move her guests over to her larger ship, which was designed for fast sailing, and to ready it with all the provisions necessary for a long trip. Then she went ashore and ran up the steps toward her house.

Aelia was in the library, as expected. She turned in surprise as Maeryn entered the room.

"Mother, why have you returned so soon?"

Maeryn walked closer to her daughter, the tears already forming in her eyes. It pained her greatly that they had been living on the run since Bastul. It wasn't fair to Aelia. It should have been the prime of her life. At nearly twenty years of age, she should be wearing fancy clothing and being courted by the wealthy young landowners of Bastul. But that life died a long time ago. Life could just be unfair.

"Remember when we left Bastul?" she asked. "...how I couldn't explain why at the time? And I asked you to trust me?"

"Yes," Aelia replied cautiously, lowering her book, "What's the matter mother? Why are you crying?"

"We have to leave again," Maeryn whispered through lips that wavered.

After a pause, Aelia rose to her feet and drew in a deep breath. Then she smoothed out the wrinkles of her tunic and lifted her chin high. "How much time do we have?" she asked.

Her strength surprised Maeryn, and almost brought forth more tears. But she fought them back. "...not long," she answered. "Gather whatever is absolutely necessary and meet me at the dock in a few minutes."

Aelia tossed her book into the chair. "I'm ready," she stated confidently. "I don't need anything."

Maeryn smiled, then kissed her daughter on the forehead. "I have something I must do."

Leaving Aelia in the library, Maeryn proceeded to the back of the house and made her way to the guest house. As she had done many times since her arrival, she descended the hidden staircase into the basement lit by flickering torches. She passed through the main room which contained the models of the Empire and proceeded through the rear hall and into the communications room.

Noster was not at his usual desk, so Maeryn grabbed a quill and wrote him a note. Just as she finished, Noster walked into the room.

"M'lady...back so soon?"

Maeryn handed him the note. "This must be relayed with the highest urgency."

Noster took the note and moved closer to a candle, squinting his eyes. Suddenly, he looked up with a puzzled look on his face. "Are you sure about this?" he asked.

"...quite," Maeryn replied.

"...into hiding," he mumbled to himself. "It has never been done in our entire history," he said clearly, this time to Maeryn.

"Yes," Maeryn replied. "But it is necessary now! Communicate these instructions or we may all find ourselves in the next life."

"You're leaving," he stated.

"That's correct. And I suggest you make yourself scarce."

"For how long?" he asked.

"...indefinitely," she added. "When it is safe, I will contact you."

Noster walked over to his writing desk and set down her note. "Lady Maeryn," he said. "If we don't see each other again, it has been a pleasure." He nodded his head slightly, without looking her in the eye.

Maeryn repeated the gesture. "Keep safe," she replied, then left the room.

The ship was ready by the time Maeryn got to the dock. Aelia was sitting on a rock at the water's edge with her feet in the water, while the others were aboard the ship. It was obvious that this would be an uncomfortable experience for her. But Maeryn had one more thing she needed to tell Aelia, and it might be received either positively or negatively.

Oh well, I have to do it some time. "Aelia," she called. "It's time to go."

Her daughter shook off her feet, then made her way over to the dock where it attached to the shore. She walked quickly and when she arrived, Maeryn put her hand on Aelia's shoulder and walked with her. "I have someone I want you to meet."

"Who?"

Maeryn wondered if she should surprise her, then decided against it. Aelia had experienced too many surprises lately. "Do you remember when I told you about your real father, and that I had a son with him before you were born?"

"Yes," she answered sadly. "And he died in the prison."

Maeryn smiled. "Well, that's what I thought until just recently. But he's alive and he's here with us."

"What do you mean?" Aelia asked.

"He's aboard that boat," Maeryn explained. "He was taken from the prison and grew up far away from Bastul."

After a silent pause, Aelia began to cry softly.

Maeryn felt awful for having such big secrets from her daughter, but it couldn't be helped. She hadn't even known about Kael until Saba told her. *It must be difficult to grow up as an only child. To be chased from your home and spend your years running in fear. And then your mother tells you that there's another child you've never even met.*

"I'm not jealous, if that's what you're thinking," Aelia said, interrupting Maeryn's thoughts.

"Oh," Maeryn said in surprise. "I thought..."

"I'm happy for you mother. You should have more things in your life that make you happy."

"You make me happy," Maeryn replied. She reached over and embraced her daughter, realizing painfully that this child was no longer a child, but a young woman.

"You know," she said. "I really haven't even spoken to him much since I found out. Everything has been so hectic lately."

Aelia tugged on her mother's arm and started toward the boat. "It sounds like we both have someone to meet."

They boarded the ship and, before they cast off, Maeryn gave her assistants and driver the opportunity to leave. They chose not to and Maeryn decided that they would be a welcome addition to the crew. Since they were not part of the Resistance there was no need to keep up appearances. Maeryn could simply exclude them from any sensitive discussions and it was perfectly normal for servants to be expected to mind their own business.

Maeryn and Aelia made their way to the aft cabin where Saba was looking through the food for something to prepare while Kael rested on a bench.

"Kael?" Maeryn breathed softly.

Kael opened his eyes.

"I would like to introduce you to Aelia...your sister."

Aelia bowed slightly.

Kael smiled. "I apologize, but I'm unable to move. It is a pleasure to meet you."

Maeryn couldn't help but beam with excitement. It was overwhelming to have both of her children together.

Kael looked at Maeryn. "When I returned to Bastul Dacien told me that you had a daughter. But when you disappeared I lost hope that I would ever see you." Kael paused. "...or meet you," he said to Aelia.

Saba pulled a bottle of wine from a crate and tucked it under his arm. "How about a snack?" he asked. "You all look hungry."

Maeryn nodded, then looked back to Kael.

"Aelia, please come sit and tell me everything about yourself. And don't leave anything out."

Aelia looked embarrassed, but excited at the same time.

"Go on," Maeryn whispered. "I've got to go check on something. Make yourself comfortable."

The Councilman droned on about how to explain the new changes to his guild, eager to show the Emperor that he would be successful at keeping the guild members happy.

Magnus grew impatient. "I'm sure you'll think of something," he replied.

At the back of the room, the guards pulled open the doors and Coen walked through.

"That's enough," Magnus barked. "Leave me."

The Councilman looked back over his shoulder, then retreated from Magnus' throne.

Coen brushed shoulders with the man as he made his way forward.

When the Councilman was gone, Magnus looked to Coen. "What news do you bring?"

"...nothing pleasant, my lord. The guest house has been burned down, and the substructure has caved in."

Magnus flexed his eyebrows into a scowl. "And what of the other locations?"

"...the same," Coen replied. "I also tried our other routes of personal communications, but it's as if they've gone into hiding."

Magnus pounded his fist against the arm of his throne. "This is outrageous! What does she think she's doing?" he asked rhetorically. He thought for a moment, then continued. "Did she leave by land or by sea?"

Coen shook his head slowly. "All five of the boats were absent, as well as the carriages and horses. There's no way to tell which method she used to escape."

They are most likely still together, which is good. The All Powerful said he would take care of finding Kael. And when he does, he'll find the others, as well. Now it's only a matter of time. "Thank you, Coen. Return to the fleet and continue with your objectives. I will have need of you before long, so stay in touch."

"Yes, my lord," Coen replied, bowing low.

10

The quickest route to Leoran would have been to cross the canal that ran through the middle of Orud, connecting the east and west bays. From there, the journey around the northwestern part of the Empire was a third shorter than their current heading. But the Orud guard would have been on high alert and they wouldn't have made it through the city.

Sixteen days after setting out from Maeryn's mansion, they rounded the southern-most tip of the Empire. Maeryn pondered the idea of stopping in Bastul, but decided against it. It would only have lengthened their journey and whatever fond memories she had of that beautiful city would have been ruined by seeing its current condition. So they sailed right past the city and turned to the north, and Maeryn did her best to look the other way.

Another ten days traveling north along the western coast brought them to a stretch of shore that flattened out into a beach and stretched inland for a good ten miles. It was the perfect place to go ashore. Unfortunately, there wasn't any cover for her ship. They would have to leave it anchored in shallow water near the shore. And if Dacien hadn't made it back to Leoran and they weren't granted entrance into the city, it was doubtful that the ship would still be there when they returned. It was a risk, but it was the only option they had.

The group loaded their supplies into travel bags and rode to shore in a small dinghy. Though their transportation would have been completely impractical, it would have been nice to have horses for this leg of the trip. It was nearly two hundred miles from this beach to Leoran, and they would have to make the journey on foot. Maeryn recalled her first such journey with the slaves from Bastul. It wouldn't be pleasant, but she had covered many more miles than this before, so she was confident that it was possible.

Once ashore, the group moved inland hoping to reach the shelter of the forest by nightfall. Maeryn's driver and assistants led, while Maeryn and Saba followed. Aelia stayed at the back with Kael, who had somehow regained the ability to move his arms and legs. Walking was still a bit awkward for him, but he demanded to be able to carry himself. He argued that it was the only way for him to get better. So, at the price of sacrificing a little speed, they all agreed.

The sun passed overhead and fell more quickly than expected. Unfortunately, they weren't able to make it to the forest that closed off the northeastern side of the beach. Instead, they found a rock mound which rose twenty feet from the sand. Taking shelter from the wind, they made camp at its base. Everyone was exhausted from walking on the sand, which seemed to make travel twice as difficult.

Saba started a small fire and began to make tea for everyone.

Maeryn leaned over his shoulder. "One of my assistants can do that," she whispered.

Saba turned his head. "I don't mind."

After tea and a simple meal of fish caught during their trip, the group reclined in the sand and stared at the flames. Maeryn was physically exhausted, but doubted she would be able to sleep this night. She looked around at the other faces reflecting the orange flicker, and thought they all looked rather alert. Saba, with his white hair and bright blue eyes, stared into the flames, lost in thought.

"Saba?" Maeryn broke the silence.

"Hmm," he mumbled, lifting his eyes.

"How is it that you look so young?"

"I was going to ask the same thing," Kael chimed in. "When I was a child, you were already an old man."

Saba smiled. "My hair and beard made me look much older that I was. Plus, the sun in Bastul was strong and harsh on the skin. Why, are you jealous?"

"If you know the whereabouts of the fountain of youth, you must tell us," Maeryn's driver replied. This caused the assistants to laugh heartily, which was infectious. Soon everyone was laughing.

When they had gained control of themselves, the conversation turned to other topics, and Maeryn realized that Saba had successfully avoided that question for the second time. But then she felt sleep began to pull at her eyes and she didn't want to miss the opportunity.

"Good night," she announced, then lay back in the sand and wrapped her cloak tight around her.

An hour after the others had fallen asleep, Kael lay still with his eyes closed. He was making great progress at healing himself, but the process was painfully slow and required much concentration. He knew it would be difficult to accomplish much on this leg of the journey, but he didn't realize how physically exhausting it would be. Healing was important, but without a reserve of strength to pull from, he realized that he would have to postpone it until they reached Leoran.   He needed to concentrate on the physical demands that had now presented themselves.

Before allowing himself to fall asleep, he unfocused his sense and pushed it outward from his body.   Immediately, he could feel the wind and the patches of swaying grass that occasionally protruded from the sand. It was a familiar feeling that he hadn't experienced since he began concentrating on healing. This put him into a meditative mood and he quickly drifted off to sleep.

Sometime in the early morning, Kael awoke with a start. He sat upright, his heart pounding in his chest. Something had encroached on his senses and caused him to react with fear. Calming himself, he slowed his heartbeat as he had been taught so many years ago. Then he closed his eyes and allowed his other sense to explore the area around their camp.

Everything seemed to be in order.

Then, at the far reaches of his sense, Kael felt something. He was tempted to push his sense in that direction, but instinct told him to resist. Instead, he just held still, his sense feeling out a radius of fifty feet around their camp.

And then it came again, the feeling. It was like a probing from someone with a similar sense. Kael opened his eyes and relaxed his sense, allowing it to dissipate for fear of being detected. He stood and walked away from camp to the north, gazing into the darkness. Something was out there, and it was searching. So far, it hadn't found them.

Morning came quickly and the group set off again. The air was cool, but the bright sun still warmed them beyond comfort. After reaching the forest, the small trees provided some relief from the sun and travel proceeded more quickly on the solid earth.   Kael scanned the horizons and occasionally searched with his sense, but whatever had awakened him in the early morning was nowhere to be found.

The terrain made for quick travel, with rolling hills and a barren landscape, with the exception of the occasional stand of trees and brush. On the fifth day, they arrived at the south shore of Lake Leoran. It was a welcome sight for the whole group, but Kael felt like he was coming home. He hadn't realized it before, but he dearly missed the city and its people since he left with Dacien.

However, he wouldn't feel at ease until he was safe within its walls, for something had been following them. And with Magnus taking control of the Council, there was no telling what might have happened to Dacien. It was possible that he never made it to Leoran, in which case the armies would not offer them the protection for which they had hoped.

The group turned east and circled around the lake and the mountains that butted up to the southeast side of the lake. This put them into deep forest for the remainder of their travel. On the evening of the eighth day they made camp in a stand of pines. The ground was soft and fragrant with a thick bed of needles all around. The downed wood provided an easy and hot camp fire, around which they gathered for their meal. They would reach Leoran by mid-afternoon the next day. Knowing this, everyone's mood improved and conversation flowed freely.

Out of habit, or because he realized that they were all so relaxed and comfortable, Kael quickly checked the area around their camp, sensing the trees as they swayed in the gentle breeze. Then, he noticed something that seemed out of place. It was tall, and standing against a tree trunk only fifty yards away.

"Kael, are you alright?" Saba asked.

Kael put his finger to his lips, then turned his attention back to the forest. But it was gone. Kael widened his sense, searching. Then he picked it up again, twenty yards away, and to the east. *It's circling in!*

Kael rose to his feet and the conversation ended immediately. "We're in danger," he announced softly. "We need to get away from this fire."

"Kael, what's going on?" Maeryn asked.

Maeryn's assistants were already cleaning up their meal, while her driver went to fetch their packs near the sleeping area.

"Something has been following us since we landed at the beach."

Aelia screamed and Kael turned in her direction just in time to notice something retreating quickly into the forest and away from the light of the fire. He didn't see what it was, and only had time to notice movement. "Where's Trupo?" he asked Maeryn, as he realized that the driver hadn't come back from fetching their travel packs.

"I...I don't..." Maeryn trailed off.

"Everyone come together now," Kael shouted, like a shepherd gathering his sheep.

The group obeyed instantly and formed a circle next to the fire.

Kael sensed the camp and didn't feel any signs of disturbance. He pushed his sense farther out from the camp in the direction that Trupo had gone, but there were no signs of movement in that direction either. Whatever had been following them had taken the man, like a hunter who targets the stragglers on the perimeter of a herd.

Stumbling over to the sleeping area, Kael retrieved the travel packs and brought them back to the group, laying them on the ground. "We have to get moving. We're too vulnerable in the trees."

One of Maeryn's assistants grabbed his pack and started walking.

"Get back here," Kael cautioned. "We have to stick together."

"I can't stay here," the man said with a shaky voice, and turned to walk into the shadows.

In an instant, the man seemed to levitate from the ground as a large shape moved across the darkness behind him.

Something wet splashed against Kael's face.

The man's screams quickly retreated into silence as he was carried away into the darkness.

Kael turned back to the group and wiped his face, noticing the blood on his hands.

Aelia screamed again when she saw her brother.

Instead of fear, Kael felt anger. He wasn't physically ready for any sort of confrontation; meanwhile, the lives of his family were at risk. He was trapped, infuriated that he had allowed himself to get into a position such as this one.

"The women stay on the inside, the men on the outside," he directed, trying to bring some order to the chaos. "Pick up your packs," he said, swinging his own onto his shoulder. "We will move slowly and together. Let's go."

They set off in an easterly direction to get clear of the forest. Kael took the point, leading the group and choosing their path. His ability to walk was still hindered by his injuries, but he couldn't allow anyone else to lead. The scene that had just occurred kept replaying in his mind. *We're being hunted. And the hunter moves like nothing I've ever seen before.* It was quick and silent, and walked upright on two legs like a man, but it was large, perhaps fifteen or twenty feet tall.

It had stayed out of sight for most of their trip. *Why did it attack tonight?* Certainly nighttime would offer it the concealment of darkness, but there had been many other nights before this one. *Has it been studying us, like a hunter studies its prey?* He didn't like the sound of that. That would make this thing a creature of intelligence, and not some brute animal.

Choosing his footing carefully, Kael led the group through the pines, moving at a slow enough pace where he could sense their surroundings at the same time. He realized that from this moment on, he had to be constantly alert. "Stay awake," he said over his shoulder. "It's going to be a long night."

Just after sunrise, they left the forest and entered the open fields to the southeast of Leoran. Kael immediately felt at ease. Here, he could rely more heavily on his sight, and less on his sense. The group had managed to walk the rest of the evening without incident, but Kael was exhausted. Maintaining his sense was like flexing a muscle. After a while, it becomes shaky and difficult to control.

Moving more quickly now, they turned north and began to make significant progress toward Leoran. Perhaps due to the fear of their hunter, they reached the eastern gate by noontime.

Aelia and Maeryn began to cry when they came within sight of the stone guard tower that marked the eastern entrance into the city. Standing at the shores of the lake, it appeared as a formidable blockade protecting the raised road which ran for a mile across the lake to the city walls.

Kael wasted no time and simply walked up to the nearest guard.

"Who are you and what is your business?" the guard demanded.

"...Kael Lorus and my companions. We are friends of Dacien Gallus and seek refuge in your city."

The guard stared back in silence for a moment and Kael wondered if Dacien had ever returned. Then a look of recognition crossed the man's face. "Lord Kael, it is good to have you back. Please come in," the guard replied, pulling back his spear.

"General," the guard spoke softly.

Dacien turned from the window.

"Lord Kael has returned."

"Kael?" Dacien repeated with surprise.

"Yes, my lord. He is at the eastern gate and he travels with four companions. Shall I send them an escort?"

"No," Dacien replied quickly. "Prepare my horse. I will meet them myself."

"A rider is coming," Aelia announced.

Kael looked out the window of the guard tower and could see someone on a large war horse coming along the road from the city. His pace was steady and his manner of dress indicated that he was someone of importance. After a few minutes, Kael recognized him.

"It's Dacien," he said with a smile.

The guards allowed them to exit the tower and wait on the road. And when Dacien pulled his steed to a stop and dismounted, it was as if the group had been holding their breath and only now released it. There was a collective sigh of relief.

Kael could see the look of astonishment on Dacien's face. He walked over to the General, holding both his hands out.

"Look at you...you can walk now?"

"You didn't think I would stay confined to a bed...did you?" Kael retorted.

Dacien embraced Kael, then pulled back to get a better look. "I'm glad to see that you've healed, but you look like you've been through some trials. Is that blood on your face?"

"We have much to talk about," Kael replied.

"Yes we do," Dacien replied with a nod, then looked over Kael's shoulder. "Saba...Maeryn," he greeted, walking over to the group. Saba shook his hand and Maeryn bowed, then proceeded to make introductions.

"This is Grumio, my assistant."

The man bowed in humble and honest respect. "General, thank you for welcoming us into your city."

Dacien shook the man's hand and pulled him up to standing.

"And this is my daughter, Aelia," Maeryn finished.

Aelia bowed.

Dacien took her hand and kissed it. "It is a pleasure to meet you," he said softly.

Aelia looked a little embarrassed, but clearly like the attention.

Dacien turned back to Kael. "Come. Let us get you all settled in. We have beds and food...whatever you need."

Kael and Dacien helped Maeryn up on to Dacien's horse, then they all started along the road to the city gates. Kael looked one last time across the shores and the clearing of land before the forest to the east. Scanning with his sense, he found something large, waiting just out of sight at the edge of the trees. He looked closely with his eyes, but couldn't see anything. Their hunter was adept at his skill and Kael knew that it was a problem that would have to be dealt with. But for now, it appeared that they would be safe inside the city and Kael was grateful for the respite.

11

The chill in the air signaled that fall was coming soon and in response, the city of Leoran was teeming with the activity of the harvest season. Shop keepers were making preparations, while the streets filled with traffic of horses and carts.

Dacien took them to the center of the city and into the walled citadel where he spent most of his time. Guest quarters had been prepared for all of them with fresh clothes and attendants to draw them hot baths. Dacien left them there with instructions to meet him when they were finished.

After everyone was shown to their rooms, Kael went back to his own room and stripped off his clothes, easing into the hot bath. In a matter of seconds, it seemed as if all the weariness of the past weeks evaporated with the rising steam. He slid under the water and everything was silent.

The water bubbled up from the earth and was nearly too hot to touch, but the monks dug a small pool where the water would drain and collect as it cooled. The warm water helped to relax the muscles that had been taxed heavily during the day's physical activities.

Kael lay on his back in the shallow water, his ears just under the surface. He closed his eyes and allowed his body to float, weightless, suspended in water. He quieted his mind and concentrated on his breathing and heartbeat, as Ukiru had instructed them. But instead of trying to hear the voice of the All Powerful, Kael tried to imagine his surroundings. He tried to imagine the water as it swirled behind his hand when he moved. He began to feel a sensation of calm alertness, the restorative benefits of this meditation.

Then, he sensed that someone was coming toward him. He could feel the swirling water, pushed aside as someone tried to sneak up on him. He lay still and exhaled the air from his lungs, causing his body to sink. Then, when his body was no longer visible above the surface, he flipped over and swam toward his assailant. When he arrived, he found his would-be attacker standing still in thigh-deep water, looking for his missing prey.

Kael quickly pulled both the legs out from under his attacker, while pushing off of the sandy bottom. He sprang out of the water to find Donagh, on his back, disoriented, with flailing arms splashing. The others were crowded around the inlet to the small pond, where the water was warmest. They all laughed heartily.

Kael pushed with his feet at the end of the tub until his head came out of the water. Sound came quickly to his ears. No amount of water would wash away his past, he realized. Only actions and time could do that. His past had followed him and was, at the moment, taking control of the world around him. He needed to complete his healing. He needed to undo what they were doing. He needed to speak to Dacien.

Pushing himself out of the water, Kael dried off and dressed in the clean clothes laid out on his bed. After making himself more presentable, he left his room and found Saba and Grumio waiting in the courtyard. The women came out a few minutes later and then they all went in search of Dacien.

They found him in the General's dining hall which overlooked the lake to the south. The sky was a dark sapphire blue with the stars just beginning to shine. The silhouette of the horizon could still be seen against the sky.

A feast had been prepared—roast duck, fish and venison, accompanied by all manner of cheeses and the first-fruits of the vegetable crops. Dacien welcomed them and asked them to be seated. Over the next hour they ate their fill of food and drank wine. When the meal was finished, they excused Aelia and Grumio and retired to Dacien's council chambers to discuss the events that were burning in their minds.

Saba and Maeryn started by telling them of the events at the Palace and that they suspected Magnus had regained control, despite their efforts. This information caused Dacien to visibly cringe as his own leadership and authority rested on backing from the Council that no longer ruled.

Dacien told them of the attack on his riding party. "It was like nothing I've ever seen before. I would judge it to be near ten feet tall, with wings like a bat. Only, it didn't fly in an erratic manner, but more graceful, like a bird of prey. I watched as it flew overhead. But there was also an accompanying sense of fear that came over me unexpectedly, as if it were clothed in dread. It folded its wings and dropped from the sky. By the time I made it back to camp, all of my men had been killed, including their horses. This thing, whatever it was, flew off to the north. And once it was safe, I continued on to Leoran by myself."

Kael shook his head. "We, too, have seen something evil, but not the same. The evening after we came ashore, I was awakened by a feeling that we were being watched. I didn't tell anyone, because there was no way to explain it and it hadn't made any advances. But yesterday evening it attacked us while were eating our meal. We never got a good look at it, but I would estimate it to be fifteen or twenty feet tall."

"I think it was closer to twenty," Saba chimed in.

Kael paused, then continued. "It moved upright on two legs, somewhat like a man. When it attacked, it was always at the perimeter of our camp, just out of sight. It moved quickly and silently. Come to think of it, I never heard so much as a snapping twig. And, in a matter of seconds, it picked off two men from our group before we even had time to react. Then it stayed away for the remainder of our trip."

"Hopefully it's gone now," Maeryn responded.

"Actually," Kael corrected. "It was at the edge of the forest, waiting, when we came into the city. I wouldn't be surprised if it's still out there."

Saba spoke up. "Dacien, you mentioned a sense of fear that came upon you suddenly. I had the same feeling as we approached the Palace in Orud. This was why I asked Maeryn to turn around."

"...asked?" Maeryn countered.

Saba looked at her, then corrected himself. "Alright...demanded. I think these creatures are somehow connected to Magnus."

"So, what do we do now?" Maeryn asked, getting right to the point. "Your forces are the only ones that might be able to oppose Magnus, and he won't allow that to happen."

"Indeed," Dacien answered, "...though I don't think we would be able to contend with the strength of the forces that he has at his command. I will need to think on these matters and I ask that you do the same. For now, recover from your journey. I doubt that Magnus would make any move with winter coming on. In another two months he won't be able to move an army through the mountains. But he has proven to be quite brilliant, so we must continue to think and talk about this."

Satisfied that they had taken the conversation as far as they could in one evening, Dacien dismissed them and each one retired for the evening.

Magnus rose from his chair and left the room, leaving the Council members in mid-discussion. Fortunately, he no longer had to care what they thought of him. They were all cowards, concerned more for their own safety than anything.

Before he got to the door, his head began to pound and he knew what was coming. Finding some privacy in a nearby courtyard, he sat down on a low stone wall and tried to calm himself. Instantly, his mind was filled with thoughts that weren't his own. His head felt as if it was going to burst, like the thoughts were physically shoved in with great force. The sensation lasted only a few minutes, and then it stopped suddenly.

When Magnus regained control of himself, he realized that he had fallen from his seat and was lying on the ground. It would have been embarrassing if anyone had witnessed it, but he had learned how to avoid such things.

The messages from the All Powerful were so much more potent now that he had been freed from his prison. Luckily, he had other important business that kept him away. Otherwise, Magnus didn't know how he would be able to deal with his presence. His recent in-person encounter at the High Temple nearly killed him.

Magnus wasn't sure what the All Powerful was doing with his freedom, but he suspected that it involved traveling into other countries. He was fairly sure that the Orud Empire and the barbaric civilizations of the Syvaku and Korgs were his only resources. But this whole world had once belonged to the All Powerful, and if Magnus was in his situation, he would want to find out the status of the rest of it.

He tried to brush these thoughts aside, knowing that it was a risk to be thinking about such things which the All Powerful could detect in an instant. Instead, he considered this new information. *General Dacien didn't die with the rest of his party and he successfully made the journey to Leoran. The forces at Leoran are now commanded by someone who isn't loyal to me. Maeryn, and the old man are with him. And it is confirmed that Kael is still alive.*

On the one hand, this was bad news. But Magnus had learned to look at the world in a different way since he discovered the All Powerful. The forces at Leoran could easily be dealt with. And the rest of his enemies have now been found all in the same place. Indeed, when considered from the proper perspective, this was good news.

Gathering himself off the ground, Magnus brushed the dust from his tunic and drew in a breath, then headed back to the Council chambers.

The streets of Leoran were relatively clear of obstruction so early in the morning. The sky was lightening in the east, but the sun hadn't yet showed itself above the horizon. Kael was already breathing hard from the pace he had set, but he pushed on, running along the top of the wall that encircled the city. He had completed his healing process in the early evening, and after a terrible night's sleep, decided to rise early and begin his training. Though he no longer suffered the effects of his injuries, his body had grown weak over the past months.

Your body will adapt itself to whatever it is exposed to, Ukiru used to say. And as much as he hated to admit it, some of the things that Kael had been taught while at the monastery were actually true. This only caused him to run faster, pushing himself until his breathing became ragged.

As the water of Lake Leoran passed by on his right side, his thoughts began to drift toward the creature that hunted them. It had been a frightening experience for all of them to see two men taken, then to be hunted like animals for the rest of the night. For Kael though, there were other emotions—regret and anger. Never, since the monastery, had he been as helpless as that night. He had been physically crippled and in grave danger of losing his life. And not because he had decided to do something dangerous, but because something attacked when he was most vulnerable. Since leaving the monastery, he had vowed to never allow himself to be vulnerable. He had violated that vow and he almost paid the highest cost. Never again would he subject himself to another's power. *I will meet this creature again very soon, and this time, it will be on my terms.*

He slowed himself slightly and let his breathing become steadier, then tried to summon his sense. Keeping his eyes open, he could feel it around him, though not as strong as usual. Except for times of intense combat, Kael had always experienced this sensation of awareness separate from any physical activity. It took a great deal of concentration under ideal circumstances, but after their nearly fatal journey to this city, Kael knew that he must learn how to use his sense to accompany his others, and not replace them. After all, his other senses were quite useful and more capable than most. Sight, sound, smell, touch, and hearing all had their purposes. If he could become adept at using it to compliment what he already knew how to do, it might serve him better.

At the moment, it only gave him the limited ability to predict the four descending steps coming upon him in just a few seconds. Kael leapt over them in one long stride and continued running.

It's a start.

Dacien entered the stables and turned down the hall to the right, his boots crunching the fresh straw on the stone floor. He waved away the stable hand, intending to saddle his own horse. He needed to think and nothing worked more effectively for him than to go for a ride.

"Hello," came a beautiful voice from a stall on his left.

Dacien stopped and noticed a young woman inside, brushing one of the horses. "Aelia?" he asked, walking over to the stall.

She smiled and continued to brush the horse who seemed to enjoy the attention.

Dacien just watched for a moment, noticing the care that she took to do it properly. Then it occurred to him that it was a bit strange for her to be here. "Do you always spend your time in stables?"

"No," she replied. "But I miss my horses. You were from Bastul as well," she added.

"Yes, that's right."

"I'll go back some day," she said as she moved around to the left side of the horse.

Now it was Dacien who smiled. "It was a beautiful city, wasn't it?"

Aelia nodded, continuing with her work.

"Do you want to go for a ride with me?" Dacien asked spontaneously.

Aelia stopped brushing the animal and looked up. Her green eyes sparkled as she brushed a strand of dark hair from her face. She was striking to look at and, so far, pleasant to talk to.

"That sounds like fun," she replied.

"I'll get you a saddle," Dacien said, then went in search of the stable-hand.

The morning sun shone through her hair and made her look like an angel. "...you had horses in Bastul?" he asked.

"Three. I used to ride in the forest to the north. But my favorite was to go into the city and watch the people. Mother didn't like it, though; she said it was dangerous."

The moment she said the word *mother*, Dacien felt an awkwardness and a sudden panic.

Aelia must have noticed it. "It makes you uncomfortable that Maeryn's my mother."

It was a statement, not a question, but Dacien answered anyway. "I suppose it does. I served under her in Bastul."

They were silent for a while, until Dacien caught Aelia looking at him. Something about her expression told him that she was just as intrigued as he. He smiled. "You know, I probably shouldn't have asked you to come with me."

"You think I'm too young," she stated. It was as if she could read his thoughts.

"Am I that obvious?" he asked humbly.

She laughed and her face softened into the most beautiful thing he had ever seen. "Don't worry," she said, brushing the hair out of her eyes. "It's not as if we're betrothed...yet," she added, spurring her horse into a gallop.

Dacien pulled his horse to a stop and watched her ride, completely fascinated. Slowly, a smile spread across his face. "Hah," he yelled, kicking his heels into the sides of his steed.

12

Magnus ordered the guards to leave and shut the door, which they obeyed without hesitation. A loud clank signaled that the doors had been locked. Magnus sat down in a chair by the window and closed his eyes. At first, he could only concentrate on the ache in his neck and temples which had become almost regular since the All Powerful's return. Eventually, he was able to ignore this and summon the consciousness of those to which he would speak.

Like seeing campfires on the horizon at night, he could feel the minds of Soren, Donagh, Berit, Coen and Rainer. They were dim at first, but with concentration they became brighter. One at a time, they responded to his summons and, after a few minutes, they were attempting to do the same. It was a meeting of the minds and one of the most effective skills that the All Powerful had taught him.

MY FRIENDS,

OUR ENEMIES ARE GATHERED IN ONE PLACE.

LEORAN MUST BE DESTROYED!

DONAGH, PULL BACK YOUR HORDES FROM THE EASTERN WALL.

SOREN, REMOVE YOUR ARMIES FROM THE EASTERN WALL AND MARCH THEM TO SUPPARD.

COEN, MOVE THE ENTIRE NAVAL FLEET TO SUPPARD AND PROVIDE TRANSPORT FOR SOREN'S ARMIES.

I WILL MEET YOU IN THE NORTHERN OCEAN.

WE WILL NOT WAIT FOR THE THAW OF SPRING TO OPEN A PATH;

WE WILL MARCH ON LEORAN AND STRIKE IMMEDIATELY!

TAKE HEART MY BRETHREN,

WE ARE WITHIN REACH OF ELIMINATING OUR ONLY OPPOSITION.

SOON THE WHOLE WORLD WILL SHAKE AT THE POWER AND MAJESTY OF THE ALL POWERFUL

Magnus opened his eyes and sat back in his chair. The excitement was almost too much to bear. Soon, there would be no obstacles, no loose ends to tie up, nothing to stand in their way. Then, the stage would be set to usher in a new era for Orud. They would once again become the Empire that others feared. Nations would kneel before them in reverence or fall beneath their power. Glorious victory was within their reach.

Kael sat upright in his bed, his heart racing. He quickly pulled back his sense and allowed it to dissipate for fear of being detected.

It had occurred to him the previous day that his sense might be used in another way. He was able to focus it inwardly to heal his own body. He was also able to surround himself with it and feel everything that was happening around him. When he was in Orud, he had heard Soren speaking into his mind and knew that they could also speak to each other. Why then, shouldn't he be able to project his sense farther from himself and detect some of this communication?

When this realization came to him, he tried it immediately. He projected his sense far from himself and allowed it to lose focus. Hearing thoughts was different than feeling objects and required less strength. Within minutes, he heard something. Careful not to reveal himself, he listened. But it wasn't like listening to words with your ears. It was less certain, and more akin to empathizing with someone's emotions.

It took some practice, but he understood the main portions of the communication. The creature was still out in the forest and sending a message to another who was very far away. At first, Kael wondered if it was Magnus in Orud. But eventually, it became apparent that the other being was much farther away, and much more dangerous. Perhaps it was the winged creature that Dacien described, but he couldn't be sure.

The one who had hunted them through the forest had revealed their identities and location to the other being. There was an intense sensation of anger when Dacien was discussed, confirming that Dacien's survival was an accident. Then, there was a deeper and more profound sense of pain and betrayal associated with Saba, which came as a surprise. Kael himself was mentioned as being alive, which was also unknown to the other being. And just before the conversation ended, there were thoughts projected back and forth regarding something that had been lost. This part was hard to follow, like listening to someone speaking a different language and trying to make sense of it by reading the facial expressions of those involved. Then, before Kael could reach an understanding of the topic, the conversation ended.

That had all occurred the previous afternoon, and now he heard another message, this time much more understandable. He rose from bed and paced the floor, trying to put the pieces together in his head. After a few moments, he knew that he had to discuss this with the others at the soonest opportunity. Though the contents of the message were dire, Kael felt a mischievous satisfaction at his new found ability.

The following morning Kael ate breakfast with Maeryn, Aelia, Saba and Dacien. The sunrise over the waters to the east was a beautiful sight and only emphasized the severity of what Kael needed to say.

When they had finished, Kael took the opportunity. "Aelia, would you please excuse us."

Aelia looked back, obviously trying to suppress the confrontational words that were about to escape her mouth.

Kael smiled inwardly, seeing much of his mother in Aelia.

"If you have something important to discuss, you can speak freely. I'm not a child."

Kael looked at Maeryn who just shrugged her shoulders.

"Very well then," Kael conceded. "What I'm about to tell you, I've never shared with anyone before. You are my family and closest friends, so I think you need to understand something about who I am. For many years now I have had an...ability, to do things that others could not. At first, it was something like a heightened sense of my surroundings. Everyone just thought that I had quick reflexes, but the truth is that it was so much more. I could actually feel objects around me as if they were part of my body. Just as I can feel exactly where my hand is and how it is moving..." he said, extending his arm and wiggling his fingers, "...I could feel objects and people near me."

Maeryn and Aelia's faces were wrinkled with concern, while Dacien and Saba wore expressions that suggested they were hearing the solution to a riddle that had been plaguing their thoughts for a long time.

"As you can imagine, this ability has been very useful to me given what I've experienced. And I lived with it for years before anything changed. Then, one day when my life was in danger, I found out that it had another use. Instead of merely reacting to what I could feel around me, I tried to influence it. Which led to the ability to move things."

At these words, Maeryn sat upright and looked around the room. "What do you mean *move things?*"

Kael paused his story. "Like this," he said. Extending his hand toward the table, he focused his sense on a nearby utensil. The knife slide across the table and fell off the edge, landing with a clang on the stone floor.

Maeryn scooted her chair back and stood up, while Aelia sat still, her face white with horror.

"Please don't be alarmed. I don't mean to scare you," Kael pleaded softly. It was extremely difficult to expose himself in such a way, and he had kept this a secret his whole life just for this reason.

Surprisingly, Maeryn sat down, though her chair remained a few feet from the table.

Kael continued. "Then, after Magnus almost killed me, I became a prisoner in my own body. I couldn't move, I couldn't talk, and I only had my thoughts to keep me company. Then it occurred to me that if I could feel objects around me, and move them, that I should be able to figure out what was wrong with me. So I discovered that I could heal myself. It was a tedious process, but successful in the end."

"I wondered how you made such a quick recovery," Maeryn said softly, showing signs of warming up to Kael's words.

"Kael," Dacien interjected. "You have always been special. I've know it since the day I met you. The things I've seen you do on the battlefield are extraordinary."

"Thanks," Kael interrupted. "But I'm not just telling this to you for the sake of confession. "There is another reason that holds dire consequences for all of us, including this city."

Dacien sat forward in his chair.

"Dacien, when we were in Orud together at the Emperor's feast, Magnus and his Generals spoke thoughts directly into my mind. They called me a traitor and threatened me. They are able to speak to each other across distances without using words. This was the reason why I was concerned with the political games you were playing with Magnus."

"What are you getting at?" Saba asked.

"Yesterday afternoon I realized another facet of my ability. If they were able to speak into my mind, I should be able to hear their thoughts as well."

Dacien tilted his head to the side. "What did you hear?"

Kael took a breath. "The creature that hunted us is still out in the forest, waiting for us to leave the protection of the city. It was speaking to your winged terror and revealed our location and identities. Then, last night, I heard Magnus. He instructed Donagh to pull back his hordes from the eastern wall."

"So you were right about him leading the Korgs," Dacien offered.

"Yes," Kael replied. "Then he instructed Soren to remove his armies from the eastern wall and march them to Suppard where Coen will be waiting with the entire naval fleet.

"Did you say Coen?" Maeryn asked.

"Yes," Kael replied.

Maeryn wrinkled her eyebrows. "Does he have black hair and sort of..."

"...feminine features?" Kael finished her sentence. "Yes. Do you know him?"

"He was Magnus' second in command of the Resistance. Magnus appointed me as his replacement because he was needed elsewhere."

Dacien jumped in. "Magnus combined the southern and northern naval fleets under Coen's command after Kael killed the two previous Commanders."

Maeryn inhaled sharply and put her hand to her mouth. "That was you," she said in muffled exclamation. "You came to the Palace that night. And they removed me under armed guard, saying it was for my protection."

"It is likely that they were simply trying to keep the two of you from making contact with each other," Saba clarified.

Maeryn's eyes welled up with tears.

"Magnus is not going to wait until spring to deal with us. He is using the naval fleet to transport the entire northern and eastern armies across the northern ocean. He intends to attack Leoran with all that is at his disposal."

"Then we will fight him," Dacien shot back, defiantly.

"...and he wins either way," Kael countered. "He pits brother against brother, citizen against citizen, to accomplish his plans, whatever they may be. Those soldiers are not our enemies, they are our friends. Magnus and his Generals are the enemy!"

"But how can the two be separated when they are both under his command?" Aelia asked, speaking her first words of the entire conversation.

The room went silent as each person contemplated her question.

13

Kael made his way to the city's northern gate where Dacien was waiting. He pulled his horse to a stop next to Dacien's and sat looking out over the road stretching across the waters to the shore. It was lined with people coming into the city.

"Another villager was taken last night," Dacien said coolly. "...every other week since you arrived."

"Why are they only coming in now?" Kael asked.

Dacien shook his head. "Their whole lives are outside this city. Even though I extended the offer, they haven't accepted until now. But last night's attack was different. One of the villagers caught a glimpse of the creature and word is spreading quickly of the giant monster that stalks the forest. They are scared now."

They sat in silence for a while, watching as the poorer citizens that lived on the shores of Leoran transported all their belongings into the city to find temporary homes. Even the young children who usually ran among the adults, playing with innocent freedom, were now helping to carry their family's possessions with solemn looks on their faces.

Kael could imagine that years from now, when the actual threat was no longer present, disobedient children would be told the story of the giant monster who would come at night and steal them away.

"I'll need twenty men...and supplies," Kael said without turning his gaze from the people.

Dacien looked over to Kael and paused for a moment. "We can be ready in one hour."

Kael turned to look at Dacien. "You shouldn't come. You're a General now; the citizens would be in great danger if you were lost."

"And what of you?" Dacien countered. "...Leoran's champion."

"I suppose..." Kael replied. "We'll meet here, then, in one hour. The men should be armored for battle and we'll also need bows and long-spears."

"...a hunting party," Dacien observed.

"Something like that," Kael replied, steering his horse away.

A cold wind had picked up and the Leoran citizens pulled their cloaks tight around their necks. They had gathered to watch the hunting party that was just now arriving at the northern gate. Kael had only waited a few minutes before he saw Dacien leading a group on horseback. They were ready for battle, as he advised, but there were more than he expected.

Kael spurred his horse into motion and came along side Dacien. "Twenty men?' he asked.

Dacien shrugged his shoulders. "Forty volunteered."

"...even better." Kael replied with a smile.

Riding out of the northern gate, Kael could see that autumn had fully arrived. All along the shore, the forest had turned to shades of red and gold, with only a few patches of evergreens. The lake surface was choppy in the wind and clouds were quickly approaching.

They reached the shore and halted while Kael dismounted and searched the land on foot. He had already been searching with his sense, but the creature was nowhere to be found. Instead, he looked for some sign of passage that he might track.

After searching the open terrain before the shoreline, Kael moved to the forest edge. Dacien's soldiers already looked bored, so Kael decided to make them useful. "How many of these men are experienced hunters?"

Dacien looked back at the group. "Perhaps half."

"Have them spread out and cover this area. Tell them that the creature is big, but moves lightly on its feet. Whatever signs of movement there are will be subtle."

Dacien nodded, then turned his horse around while Kael continued his search. It took nearly an hour before anything turned up. Finally, Kael was called over to one of the soldiers who was looking into the trees. When Kael arrived, the man pointed to a branch about ten feet off the ground.

"See there how that twig is bent back on itself. The base is cracked."

Kael patted him on the shoulder. "Good work," he said. "It looks like the creature was less careful on its way back into the forest. It doesn't like to be seen."

"Thank you, Captain," the man replied.

Surprised at the title, Kael turned to look at Dacien, who just smiled in return. "Lead the way."

Captain? I'll have to talk with Dacien about that later. For now, he looked back to the trees, then walked into the forest on foot.

The day wore on while the soldiers' excitement slowly dissipated, as if the cold wind had sapped it from their bodies. It was an inevitable part of the process, one that most men were not accustomed to unless they were experienced hunters; long periods of silence, looking for the smallest signs of passage that most would overlook. By mid afternoon, Kael knew that they would need to start thinking about a place to make camp. He told Dacien as much and instructed them to stick to areas that had already been searched.

As the sun began to set, Kael came across an imprint in a patch of soft earth. It was only a small indentation, but it gave Kael much useful information. It was the outer portion of the heel and was roughly three times larger than a man's. This confirmed Kael's earlier estimation of the creature's size. Something more revealing, however, was that it appeared to be from a shoe made of soft leather, and not the imprint of an animal's foot. This was bound to have a negative effect on the minds of the men in the hunting party. A shoe implied intelligence beyond a mere animal and there was no way to hide it.

Kael already knew that this creature walked upright on two legs; he had seen that before they reached Leoran. And now he knew that it wore clothing. Could their prey be human?

Impossible! A twenty-foot tall human?

He returned to camp and ate his evening meal in silence. This revelation bothered him and he knew that sleeping would be nearly impossible. He volunteered for the first watch and continued to think on the matter. He was relieved at midnight by his replacement and spent the rest of the night in fits of shallow sleep amid much wakefulness.

The next morning, after the men had eaten their breakfast, Kael called the party together. They came forward and presented themselves in an ordered fashion, lined up single file. "Yesterday, I found a track that has provided great insight into what we are hunting. It was a partial imprint of a heel, nearly three times that of a man's."

Some of the soldiers glanced quickly at each other.

"The imprint showed no signs of animal origin. In fact, it came from a soft leather shoe or boot. This was unexpected, but nevertheless, it is what I found."

Dacien looked shocked, and so did his men.

"I know not what type of creature is twenty feet tall, walks upright on two legs, and wears clothing like a human. But I believe this thing is intelligent, and not some brute beast. Which means that, though our work is tedious, we must be vigilant. Something extremely dangerous is out here and will not hesitate to attack if the moment is right. Keep your eyes open and your weapons ready."

With these words, half of the hunting party mounted up, while the others followed Kael on foot to the sight of the imprint.

Kael looked briefly at it and didn't draw any different conclusions that he had the previous night. As he passed it, he looked back to see the others staring wide-eyed in amazement. None of them offered any different opinions about what it might have been, and Kael was satisfied that his assessment was accurate.

Now the hunter has become the hunted, he thought, as he moved deeper into the trees.

By midmorning, Kael came to a clearing through heavy brush and came upon a secluded meadow, ringed on three sides by low tree-lined hills. A hundred yards away at the far end he could make out a crude shelter, but it was too far away to see anything else. He quickly held up his hand and the hunting party stopped.

His other sense, now a constant presence through practice, didn't alert him to anything. There was no threat in the crude camp. Nevertheless, his heart quickened in his chest, ready for action. Slowly, he moved forward with the soldiers behind him. As he neared the shelter, the smell of ashes came to his nostrils and he was sure that this was where the creature had been living.

Kael looked back to Dacien who nodded, already knowing what Kael was thinking.

Dacien gave the signal for the party to fan out and flank the shelter, setting up a perimeter of control.

Kael continued to move forward, cautiously. He noted that the shelter was nothing more than a creative arrangement of downed timber. Small saplings had been buried in the ground like the pickets of a fence, which comprised the walls of the simple structure. Additional saplings ran across the tops of these, and were tied into place with long strands of grass. A cross-hatched configuration of branches and dense brush comprised the roof. It was a long, narrow shelter. And given the size of the creature, Kael imagined that this was nothing more than a tent to sleep under.

"General," shouted someone from behind the shelter.

The urgency of the man's voice made Kael's heart jump.

"Oh gods," someone else shouted, sounding horrified.

Kael moved around the shelter and made his way quickly to where Dacien and a few others were now gathering. As he approached, the men stepped aside. On the ground, a large skin was stretched and staked to the dirt with sharpened sticks. The pale hide had been scraped clean and was being prepared for other uses. It took only an instant to realize that it was from a human. Next to the clearing was a small pit ringed with stones. Inside were weeks worth of ashes and the unmistakable sight of human skulls and other bones.

Kael turned away in disgust.

Dacien followed, while the others stared in disbelief.

"I've never seen anything like this before," Dacien said as he caught up with Kael, his voice low.

"Nor have I," Kael replied, taking a deep breath. "This thing, whatever it is, is a hunter of men."

"A cannibal from the looks of it," added Dacien.

For a moment, they stood in silence as the wind continued to blow, growing more fierce by the hour.

Kael finally broke the silence. "I think we should set up camp here for tonight and wait for it to return."

"Agreed," Dacien replied. "I'll get the men started. Can you help bury the bones and the..."

Kael waited for Dacien to finish, but it never happened. "...right away," he replied, then walked back toward the camp.

Kael worked with a few other men, well after sundown, burying the various body parts that were found in the creature's camp. By the time they finished, their own camp had been set up a good distance away, and guards were posted on the ridgelines surrounding the valley. No one had the stomach for a meal, so everyone sat in silence around the fire and tried to keep warm. Kael's fingers were numb and he sat close to the flames with his hands extended. There were no jokes this night, or much conversation at all. Everyone bundled themselves in their thick winter cloaks and retired early.

Sometime around midnight, Kael was awakened for the second watch. The wind had died down and snow had begun to fall, dampening the sounds of the night. Kael made his way to the top of the ridge to the north and relieved the soldier from his post. It wasn't very difficult to stay awake. Taking shelter under the branches of a tall pine, Kael pushed his sense out from him to encompass the whole valley. At such a range, he wasn't able to notice details, but felt confident that he could detect any living creature larger than a deer.

He stayed in this posture for several hours, occasionally moving to stretch his legs, before taking shelter under a different tree. The snowfall increased, with large flakes falling straight down and blanketing everything around them. The movement of the snow only made his job more difficult, like trying to pick out a particular voice amid a cacophony of sounds in a crowded market. *If I was going to attack the camp, this would be the moment.*

As the thought ran across his mind, his heart began to race. Suddenly alert, he probed the areas around the camp, outside of the tree-lined hills. Instead of searching the whole area at once, he focused his sense to a ten foot area and then began to sweep back and forth, moving it from the center of camp outward.

After half an hour, he spotted some movement to the southeast, from the direction that his own party had entered the camp. He quickly left his post and descended the hill toward camp, which was situated between himself and whatever was out there. As he neared camp, he could feel the thing move backward. Kael stopped walking and focused his sense only on the thing that moved.

It suddenly went still, making it more difficult for Kael to read at this distance. Somehow, the creature knew of his awareness. So far, it was working to Kael's advantage. He didn't want to confront the thing in the night, when the men would be without sight to guide them. He wanted to catch it in the daytime. If his awareness was keeping the creature at bay, then so be it. After several minutes without any movement, Kael lost his perception of where the creature was. Like staring at an object in the dark, after a while you begin to lose your sense of perspective and wonder if you're looking at anything at all.

Kael allowed his sense to spread out, losing focus, in an effort to regain his bearings. Immediately, the creature bolted away from the camp. Kael tried to focus his sense on it and get a better feel for what it was, but it moved twice as fast as a horse at a full run, and Kael couldn't keep up. After only a few seconds, it had moved beyond the range of Kael's sense.

His heart beat loudly in his chest as he tried to calm himself. Then he realized that the creature had moved in undetected between the two guards posted at the mouth of the valley. He sent out his sense once more and located the guards at their posts. There was no movement or sign of alarm on their part. Even during its full speed retreat, they were within twenty yards of it and hadn't noticed it.

Kael looked down at his feet that were buried in the calf-high snow, then looked back at his tracks leading up the side of the valley into the trees, quickly disappearing in the falling snow.

We can track it!

"Get up. Get up," he yelled, rousing the camp. He ran to where Dacien was sleeping. The General was already on his feet with his sword drawn.

"It was here."

"Where," Dacien asked, scanning the valley around him.

"There," Kael pointed. "...to the southeast. It fled. We can track it if we move quickly. We don't have much time."

Kael and Dacien ran to their horses and swung themselves up into the saddles.

"Soldiers," Dacien shouted. "We ride."

Kael's horse was already at a full sprint, with snow flying from its hooves. Kael leaned forward and grasped the reins tightly, scanning the snow for tracks. He found what he was looking for at the entrance to the valley and followed the tracks as they veered due east after clearing the dense brush. He didn't bother looking back, knowing that the rest would catch up eventually.

The snow stung his eyes as he raced across the blanketed earth. The tracks were steady, each footprint showing a stride of fifteen feet. Kael knew that it was only a matter of time before the distance between him and his prey would grow so great that the falling snow would obliterate the tracks. His horse was breathing hard, with plumes of steam gushing from its nostrils in the cold night air.

After twenty minutes, the snow stopped falling and the night sky began to appear. Kael smiled.

Nowhere to hide now!

He pulled his spear from its saddle sheath and held it against his hip, ready for the kill. As the clouds dissipated, the moon cast its light across the new fallen snow and illuminated the landscape. It was nearly as good as daylight.

After a few more minutes, the tracks veered sharply to the right. Kael slowed his horse and followed them around a cluster of scrub oak. When he came into another clearing, the tracks turned back in the direction that he had just come from.

Oh no, he thought, instantly alerted to the danger. *It's doubling back!*

The tracks wove through more patches of brush and ran straight into a stand of pines. The sound of many horses told Kael that Dacien's approaching party was very near. Kael steered his horse to the right, and tried to make his way back to his own tracks, hoping to cover more distance in the open land. He knew that the other men were in danger, but he just couldn't cover the distance fast enough.

As soon as the forest opened into a clearing, he spotted his tracks and followed them back toward Dacien. Within seconds he caught sight of the group, their silhouettes stark against the bright snow.

Suddenly, a large shape exploded from the trees to the left and plowed into the group of forty. As Kael's horse ran at full speed, still fifty yards away, he could see several horses and riders go down amidst a tangle of legs and hooves. Then, the creature darted into the trees on the right and disappeared.

Chaos ensued as the panicked horses reared up and ran in circles. Men were shouting.

Kael grunted with frustration as he tried to close the distance as quickly as he could. Just as he reached the fray, he sensed movement in the trees to the right. Before he had a chance to react, an enormous shape launched itself from the shadows at a full run. Kael dove off his horse and landed hard on the snow. A low thud, followed quickly by several cracks and slashing sounds assaulted his ears. Kael came to his feet with his spear ready, but there was no foe. Only the wreckage left in its wake.

Kael looked around at the bodies of horses and men lying on the ground. The snow was splattered with blood. Six men lay still, while three others writhed in agony with unknown injuries. Four horses were down, including his own, which had apparently taken the brunt of the last attack. It was lying on its left side with its ribcage collapsed. Blood flowed from its nose, and the wake of snow piled up around the animal showed that it had been broadsided by something incredibly strong.

Kael turned in anger and walked toward the forest where the creature had disappeared. He cast his sense into the trees and only caught a fleeting glimpse of movement, already more than a hundred yards away.

COWARD!

His mind screamed at the retreating form, sending out the message with his sense.

COME BACK AND FIGHT!

COWARD!

14

General Soren sat atop his horse, overlooking the port city of Suppard from a cliff above the shoreline. Below, the Orud navy filled every available space along the docks, with even more ships anchored a short distance from shore, awaiting their turn. The local fishing and trade vessels had been cleared to make way for this occasion. As far as the eye could see, row upon row of soldiers marched in formation and lined up at the docks, waiting their turn to board the ships.

Suddenly, he cocked his head to the side, as if listening. From somewhere far away, a message came to his mind. But it wasn't a message from Magnus, nor was it the fear-inducing presence of the All Powerful. No, this was something more distant...faint, but familiar.

Kael! The message was confrontational and offered a challenge. Soren knew it was directed at someone else, but smiled to himself as his reply came to mind.

"There are no cowards here," he said aloud. "We're coming for you!"

The sun rose to a clear sky. All around, the trees were covered in white. The temperature had risen slightly from the previous day, and already the snow was beginning to melt from the ground. Dacien, Kael, and the remainder of the hunting party buried their dead along with the horses, finishing around noon.

Exhausted, Kael collapsed on a rock next to where Dacien was sitting. No one had spoken since the attack the previous night, and for several minutes, the two stared out at the beautiful scenery, unable to appreciate it for the pain in their souls.

"I'm sorry I got you into this," Kael said, finally breaking the silence.

"You've nothing to be sorry for. I volunteered, and so did these men."

"Still, I have a suspicion that this thing is here because of me. I think I've put everyone in danger."

Dacien had no response.

They sat in silence again, each one staring at the landscape as though the peaceful beauty would cleanse how they felt inside.

Kael turned to Dacien. "It just occurred to me that if this monster is a hunter of men, and it is really only looking for me, then we've been going about this all wrong."

"What do you mean?" Dacien asked, wiping the sweat from his forehead.

"We should be letting him hunt us, or me, to be specific."

Dacien smiled and wrinkled his eyebrows at the same time. "And how do you propose we do that?"

As the sun began its descent toward the western horizon, Kael moved cautiously through the grass, looking for signs of the creature's passage in the patches of snow and wet earth. Behind him, in a V-shaped formation was the rest of the hunting party. Each man was within a few yards of each other to reduce the opportunity for someone to be picked off. The only exception was Kael, who was purposefully a good distance on point.

Once they found a trail, they moved quickly, covering much ground in a short amount of time. Kael scanned the ground, while the rest of the party scanned the surrounding trees, keeping watch for signs of movement. What the others didn't know, however, was that Kael was announcing their presence with all his might.

COWARD!

COME OUT AND FIGHT.

He sent out the message with his sense, knowing that the creature was watching and listening.

YOU MUST FEEL AFRAID.

IS THAT WHY YOU HIDE IN THE TREES?

I AM A WARRIOR.

DO YOU EVEN KNOW WHAT THAT IS?

A WARRIOR WALKS IN THE OPEN.

BUT YOU ARE A COWARD!

IF IT'S ME YOU WANT, I'M HERE WAITING.

The hours moved on as they continued to track the beast as it apparently moved northeast. As the sun touched the horizon, the sky began to slowly darken. Kael wondered if the creature would take the bait. If it didn't, they would find themselves in danger once again during the night. Kael didn't want this to happen and could almost feel that something was about to happen.

DON'T LET THE SUN GO DOWN.

I WANT TO SEE THE FACE OF THE CREATURE THAT STRIKES FEAR INTO THE HEARTS OF MEN.

IF YOU WAIT TILL NIGHTFALL, I'LL KNOW THAT I'VE WON.

I WAS HOPING FOR A CHALLENGE, FOR SOMEONE TO MATCH MY SKILLS.

IF YOU WAIT, I'LL LOSE INTEREST AND RETURN HOME.

I HAVE NO DESIRE TO WANDER IN THE FOREST, CHASING A FRIGHTENED ANIMAL.

COME TO ME!

TAKE MY SKIN IF YOU CAN!

COWARD!

"Kael," Dacien said softly. "...on your left."

Kael lifted his head and looked to the treeline about fifty yards away. The setting sun was casting long shadows across the clearing, but when he shielded his eyes, he could see something standing just inside the trees, cloaked in shadow. It was half as tall as the trees around it, massive and frightening to behold.

As they had prepared, the formation of soldiers stopped all forward movement and began to spread out. Kael altered his course to due north and moved at a casual pace toward it, with one hand on the hilt of his sword, the other loosely gripping the spear at his side. Though his heart pounded into his throat with fear, he choked it down, ready to have a conclusion to this hunt.

The silhouette in the trees remained still, so still that Kael began to doubt his eyes. He stopped in the middle of the field and squinted his eyes.

All the trees were swaying slightly in the soft breeze, while the man-shaped blot of darkness remained fastened in place like a statue.

Suddenly, it was out of the trees and moving with blinding speed across the clearing, heading straight for Kael. Like seeing a bolt of lightning and not realizing its image until the instant afterward, Kael finally realized what was happening. In the split second that it took to comprehend the situation, the creature had already covered half the distance between them.

Though sluggish by comparison, Kael began to run forward as well.

Dacien's heart pounded in his chest as he watched the beast charge for Kael. He had never seen something so fast and so intimidating in all his life and he knew immediately that Kael wouldn't survive. For an instant, it looked like Kael didn't see it. Dacien began to move forward in Kael's defense, just as Kael came to his senses and began to run at the monster.

In a matter of seconds, the creature had crossed the meadow and was upon Kael. Just before impact, Kael dropped to the ground and a brilliant flash of white light exploded from the confrontation. The creature fell to the ground and tumbled, unable to control itself due to its momentum. Something flew through the air and landed next to the beast as it finally came to a stop.

Kael rose to his feet with the dark crystal sword in his hand. He looked down at its brilliance, reflecting the orange of the setting sun. Across the field, the soldiers stood motionless, their image blurred momentarily by the steam coming from his own breath on the cold air. Forty feet away, the giant rose to its feet, realizing that its right arm was missing, severed clean above the elbow. Blood began to gush from the wound.

Only now did Kael get a good look at his adversary. From this distance, it looked proportionally human, despite its massive size. It was a male. His skin was dark with green undertones, like a corpse. It had long black hair that fell to its shoulders. It wore human hide as clothing, darkened by fire such that it didn't reflect light. This was why the creature was so difficult to see at night. What he could see of the beast's frame appeared to be lean and muscled.

It looked to the ground and noticed its arm lying near. Raising its head, it screamed in rage, blanketing the meadow in a frightful wail. When it looked back at Kael, its face had a look of intelligence, and all the signs of its animal-like expressions were gone.

"What are you?" Kael asked.

Then it spoke a quick, guttural sentence in a foreign language—not the screeching of an animal, but a complex arrangement of sounds that was unmistakably intelligent, but foreign.   It took a step forward, then wavered and fell to one knee.

Kael moved forward in the snow, ready to finish it off.

All of a sudden, the giant sprung from its crouching position and collided with Kael, knocking him backward.

Kael instantly found himself on his back with the giant on top of him, staring him in the face. The weight of the giant's body threatened to crush Kael's bones, while the enormous hand squeezed his neck. He could feel the fibers of his neck muscles burst as the creature began to slowly crush him to death.

Just as the darkness of unconsciousness threatened to engulf Kael, the grip around his neck lessened. Kael could see the creature's facial features begin to lose their intensity. With his last ounce of strength, Kael twisted the handle of the sword that had penetrated the giant's rib cage. Its heart must not have been in the same place as a human, or it would have died instantly.

In that moment, as Kael stared deep into the dark eyes of the monster only inches from his own face, he sensed a deep sadness emanating from it. It was a longing for something, or perhaps a person. Was it regret? He couldn't tell.

Slowly, the giant fell to one side. Kael didn't have the strength to hang on to the sword and it was ripped forcefully from his hand as the beast fell dead on the ground.   For a moment, Kael lay still, looking up at the darkening sky, the light of the sunset now turning to a deep violet.

He heard the sound of many approaching footsteps, but couldn't move. He heard a few gasps of surprise from the soldiers. Then he saw Dacien's face come into view.

"Kael, are you hurt? Are you alright?"

"I'm alright," Kael mumbled.

Dacien and another man grabbed hold of Kael's shoulders and pulled him out from under the giant's legs. When he was clear, they pulled him to his feet.

Kael took a deep breath and walked over to the giant. It was grotesque to look at. Its features were entirely human, only three times larger. Kael wondered where this thing had come from, what it was, and why it came after him. He knew his mind wouldn't be able to comprehend the matter for some time, as was the case with most intense situations that he'd endured. Instead, days from now, he would realize what had taken place. And only then, would he try to make sense of it.

Reaching down, he grabbed the hilt of the crystal sword, now slick with the giant's blood. In one swift movement, he wrenched it free of its victim.

"Friends," he said to the soldiers standing around him. "It's time to go home."

15

The morning air was clear and cold as they approached Leoran. The citizens were gathered on the ramparts, eagerly awaiting the return of their General and their champion. Dacien had come to love this city, more than he ever felt for Bastul. He knew Kael felt the same way. There was a sense of peace inside the city walls, and the citizens were fiercely loyal. Despite the cold air, he felt his heart warm at the sight of the citizens along the walls of the city, cheering them on.

The procession of hunters moved at a comfortable trot with plumes of steam coming from both the horses and their riders. As the sun climbed above the mountains to the east, its light reflected off the men's armor in flashes as they moved.

Dacien and Kael steered out of the forest and headed for the northern road. The contingent of soldiers at the guard tower cheered as they passed underneath the stone arch. The wind picked up as they moved along the road with water on either side. Dacien pulled his cloak tighter about his neck and continued to lead the procession.

As they entered the city, citizens began to gather around them, even before they could dismount. But Dacien only saw Aelia, his gaze fixated on her. She made her way through the cluster of people, clamoring to see if the monster had been killed.

Dacien swung his leg over the saddle and stepped to the ground. When he turned around, Aelia waiting close by, threw her arms around him. He held her tight and felt instantly at ease.

"I'm glad you're alright," she whispered into his ear.

When they released each other, Dacien noticed Maeryn in the crowd over Aelia's left shoulder. His childish smile quickly left his face as he saw the look of concern on hers. "Didn't you talk to your mother yet?"

Aelia turned around and locked eyes with Maeryn, who now looked confused. "I didn't know how to tell her," she said as she turned back to Dacien.

"We'll do it together then, tonight, when everyone is in a festive mood."

"So you were successful?"

Dacien smiled with mixed emotions. "We lost some good men, but we accomplished our goal."

Aelia looked relieved.

Dacien looked to the crowd. He raised his voice above the drone of conversations. "There will be a feast today, for we have reason to celebrate," he announced.

Cheering went up from the crowds and several people left immediately to make preparations.

Shortly after mid day, the feast began. The roasted meats were now coming off of the spits and making their way to people's plates, along with a variety of accompanying dishes. The wine flowed freely and people's spirits began to lift as they realized that the monster who stalked the forest was dead. There would be time to mourn their fallen, but this day would be dedicated to their success. In a few moments, Dacien would tell the story to the guests at his table, but before that happened, he and Aelia pulled Maeryn aside for a private conversation.

When they were alone, Dacien spoke calmly. "We wanted to tell you first, of our love for each other," he said. Aelia leaned close to him and took his hand.

"I gathered that much already," Maeryn replied. "It's just so sudden. Don't mistake infatuation for love; they are very different."

Dacien felt awkward, like a child who had done something wrong. But he hadn't. And he wasn't a child. He was the General of Leoran and didn't need anyone's permission. Even though the situation was ridiculous, he did his best to be respectful of Maeryn's feelings, considering all the events that she and her daughter had been through together.

"Haven't you loved in the past?"

Maeryn's eyes welled up with tears instantly. "Yes...my first husband...Aelia's real father."

"I was not yet part of the Bastul Guard when he ruled, but I have heard that he was a good man."

"...the best," Maeryn answered softly.

"How old were you when you met?" Aelia asked.

Maeryn paused, counting in her head. "Younger than you are now," she replied hesitantly to her daughter.

Aelia smiled as if she had won a small victory.

"But that doesn't matter to me. What matters is that you understand your own feelings. Your heart can be deceitful and make you believe something that isn't true."

Dacien looked carefully at Maeryn, knowing that statement had nothing to do with him. Maeryn wasn't concerned with Dacien, but with her daughter.

"Who's daughter do you think I am?" Aelia replied. "Have I ever been one to make decisions hastily? Have I ever been careless with my emotions? You were always trying to get me to be more like other girls."

Maeryn put her arms out and stepped forward, embracing her daughter and only friend for so many years. Aelia began to cry now as well and Dacien felt even more awkward.

"You're right," Maeryn admitted. "I'm sorry, I just want the best for you."

Dacien smiled. "...careful now. I may take offense to that."

Maeryn smiled in return, her eyes red. "So when are you planning to be married?"

"Soon," Dacien answered quickly.

"We have your blessing then?" Aelia asked.

"Yes," Maeryn answered after a pause of consideration. "Yes, you do!"

That evening, Kael sat near a fire in Dacien's palace. Saba and Maeryn sat to the right, while Dacien and Aelia sat on the opposite side of the fire ring. They all stared into the flames as the heat warmed their bodies. Dacien took a sip of wine, while Aelia whispered something into his ear. He smiled, then whispered something back.

It was good for them to be in love. Though it was forbidden, Kael had felt love of that kind at one point in his life. It seemed so long ago, and so unfortunate that the object of his affection was given to another man in an arranged marriage. But he felt no jealousy. He was happy for Dacien. And the fact that he would marry Kael's own sister, didn't feel as strange as it sounded.

Kael sat forward and put his glass of wine on the table next to him. "I don't mean to ruin the mood, but I continue to hear voices and they're getting stronger."

Dacien looked up and Maeryn leaned forward.

"Can you tell how far away they might be?" Dacien asked.

"Not exactly," Kael answered. "I can tell direction, but that's all. If I had to guess, I'd say they were in the sea north of Orud."

"What are we going to do?" Aelia asked.

"I've been thinking about this," Kael continued. "Magnus believes that all his enemies are gathered in one place. But it doesn't make sense for Leoran soldiers to fight against the armies of the north and east. They are all citizens of the same Empire."

"What do you propose we do?" Saba asked.

"I see this as an opportunity," Kael replied. "In an effort to finally remove the remnants of his opposition, Magnus has made a mistake of his own. All of my enemies will be gathered in one place, as well, and I will go out to confront them."

Dacien looked shocked.

Saba spoke up quickly. "Kael, he almost killed you last time you encountered him. Magnus is extremely dangerous and powerful. It would be suicide."

"It doesn't matter," Kael countered. "I can't let the men of this city and all the other citizens be slaughtered because of the manipulations of one man. I have to stop him."

"Kael's right," Dacien agreed. "They believe this is the final battle and have combined all their resources. It is an opportunity, but you're not going alone. I won't allow it." Dacien directed his last comment at Kael. "You must let us help you."

Kael rose to his feet. "...very well. Let's discuss strategy in the morning."

Saba stood up also. "...a good idea. I must get some rest too."

16

Winter had fully descended on the land by the time Magnus' ship ran aground in the bay to the north of Leoran. The waters were sluggish and the trees along the shore covered in white. The crew dropped a plank down to the pebble beach, which made a wet crunch as Magnus stepped off his boat.

Behind him, hundreds of ships were making their way to the shore, carrying thousands of soldiers. To his right, Magnus noticed Soren coming across the beach. On his left, Coen, Berit and Rainer were just stepping off their ships. Magnus felt the power that was at his disposal, and he would use it to crush his opposition. Most likely, the army at Leoran would surrender under such a show of force, offering up Maeryn and the others at the first opportunity. It would be quick, but disappointing. He wanted a fight.

It took hours for the soldiers and horses to come ashore and assemble into formation. It might have been much quicker except that there were also siege weapons to unload, which were difficult to transport across such rough terrain. A dock would have made the situation much easier, but such things were merely details given their ultimate goal. Magnus knew it would be difficult passage. The snow would present a challenge and might slow them considerably. He estimated five days until they reached Leoran.

Once all the cargo was unloaded, Magnus gave the order to set up camp. Tomorrow would be a long day and the extra sleep would be needed.

The following morning, Magnus' armies set off from the shore in five groups, led by his most trusted men. Each army had the full allotment of cavalry, spearmen, archers, foot soldiers and heavy equipment handlers. Magnus and his army led the procession to the south. The progress was slow as expected, with a great deal of effort expended to clear a passage for the siege towers and battering rams that traveled at the rear of the column. Magnus rotated the path-clearers every hour to ensure that this task was given the most important priority as it set the pace for the entire mission.

By midday, his men were exhausted. He allowed Soren's army to take the lead, not out of pity for his men, but in an effort to keep the procession moving as quickly as possible. By dusk, Soren's men were useless, as well, and they stopped on the east side of a canyon where the ground was dry as a result of its position relative to the sun's passage. Scouts were sent out immediately and, by the time they returned, the evening meal was prepared. A light contingent of guards was posted on either side of the canyon to the south, on high ground where their vantage point would allow easy sight of an approaching force.

This was, of course, only a formality as Magnus didn't expect much opposition. The sudden change in activity was making itself evident in the ranks. After several weeks at sea, a full day of travel across land was an abrupt transition. Even Magnus succumbed quickly to the pull of sleep and retired early in the evening.

Sometime in the middle of the night, Magnus woke as if startled. It wasn't a dream, but something he heard. He paused for a moment, listening. But his ears didn't detect any sound. Instead, he heard thoughts in someone's mind.

...THOUSANDS OF THEM!

This time, he understood immediately what was happening. It was Kael!

...FIVE GROUPS. SO IT'S TO BE A SIEGE!

Magnus rose quickly and grabbed his sword, fastening the belt around his waist. Having slept in his clothes, he was able to leave his tent in a matter of seconds. He made his way to Soren's tent only to find the General already coming his way.

"I heard it too," he said quietly. "Rainer is awake, but the others didn't hear it."

"Go wake them," Magnus ordered. "And make sure that no one communicates in the usual way; I don't want to alert Kael."

Soren nodded, then moved away into the darkness, disappearing almost instantly.

Magnus looked across the canyon to the crest of the hill on the opposite side. He knew Kael was up there with someone else and he knew their general direction. The problem was that if Magnus advanced, Kael would spot him. They had to wait until Kael had completed his reconnaissance. Then they would follow him and eliminate the nuisance that had plagued Magnus since the death of Narian.

It took another hour until Magnus could feel Kael's departure. He had been thorough, just as Ukiru had taught him. By this time, Soren and the others were anxious to make a kill. As soon as Magnus gave the signal, they moved quickly and quietly across the canyon and up the opposite side.

After cresting the hill, they moved south and were able to gain on Kael as he seemed to be moving at a casual pace, unaware that he was being followed. Finally, after another hour, they came within sight of Kael who was accompanied by another man, the two of them riding their horses at little more than a walk. As they chose their path carefully, Magnus and his men moved quickly on foot, fanning out to cover the flanks, positioning themselves to attack.

They followed Kael and his companion into a tangle of scrub oak and were able to gain even more ground as the horses weren't as nimble at finding a path through the brush. By the time the two men exited the brush and rounded a hill, Magnus and his generals were within twenty yards of the pair. The moment had come.

Magnus moved into the lead and sprinted across the short distance of open land, stopping at the base of the hill, and waited for the others to catch up. This time, there would be no mistakes. He would destroy Kael's mind quickly, turning him into an invalid within seconds. He wouldn't stop to savor the moment like last time. Then, they would move in and finish the task with hard steel.

Magnus looked the others in the eyes and they all nodded, indicating that they were ready. Magnus nodded in return, then ran around the hill.

The men on horseback turned at the sound, but Magnus knew it was too late for them. He extended his hand toward Kael and focused his energy.

Suddenly, something struck Magnus in the chest, pushing him back a few steps. Looking down, he saw a feathered shaft protruding from his tunic. His breathing quickly felt restricted and the delayed pain reaction finally caught up to him, exploding from his chest in searing waves that ran down to his legs. Magnus felt the strength suddenly leave his body and he was unable to keep himself upright. As he fell, he caught the sight of dozens of men on horseback coming out of the trees to surround him and his Generals.

Kael heard the approaching footsteps and turned just in time to see the arrow strike Magnus in the chest. For a second, Kael feared that the Emperor might be wearing a cuirass, but the look on his face said otherwise.

The timing couldn't have been more perfect. Dacien's cavalry came out of hiding, just as the other Generals came around the bend. Magnus dropped to the ground, rendered ineffective by the arrow, though Kael didn't completely dismiss the man.

Turning their horses around, Kael and Dacien drew their swords and charged at the same time as the cavalry moved in.

Rainer turned to retreat, then noticed that there were men on horseback behind him as well.

Kael drove his horse toward Soren, his next priority. But Soren bolted to the left, dodging behind the nearest approaching rider. Coen ran in the opposite direction, but there was nothing to hide behind.

Quickly changing plans, Kael redirected his steed toward Coen. There was a second of nothing but the sound of horse's hooves, then it disappeared in a wave of shouting and the ringing of metal on metal. Kael's horse collided with Coen, knocking him to the ground and trampling him. The crunch of his bones was somehow audible over the other sounds. A sudden flicker of reflected light caused Kael to flinch to the left as a blade tore through his tunic. He slid off the saddle and, as his feet made contact with the ground, he felt the warm rush of blood at his right side just under his ribs. He dismissed it instantly, knowing it was a superficial wound.

The horse continued forward, and when it was out of the way, Berit moved in for the attack, stabbing with his sword for Kael's mid section. Kael already had his Orud short-sword drawn and parried the blade to the left, followed by a sharp kick to Berit's knee. A loud snap could be heard and Berit immediately went to his knees in agony. Kael quickly followed with a forehand slash, but Berit brought his sword up and blocked the attack, the clash of steel ringing loudly in the air.

For a moment, the two stayed in this posture with their blades crossed, each pressing with all their might. Then, Berit's features became an exaggerated look of surprise as one of Dacien's men pushed a spear through his midsection from behind. Kael pulled his sword back and Berit fell forward to the dirt.

Then, the sound of combat ceased, replaced only by the sound of heavy breathing. Kael quickly scanned the area and took note of his enemies.

Magnus is down. Coen...trampled. Berit is taken care of. Rainer is... he paused, looking around. Another body lay by the base of a tree. The thin frame told him it was Rainer. "Where is Soren?" he called out.

Dacien pointed to the east where three of his men lay on the ground. Kael was about to speak when Dacien said, "They're already in pursuit."

Kael let out a breath he'd been holding, then walked over to where Magnus lay on his back. As he approached, he could see his chest rising and falling, with the arrow embedded in it, like a flag atop a hill. His breathing was shallow and rapid, and his eyes looked at the sky, though Kael was quite sure that Magnus wasn't seeing anything.

"Can you hear me?" Kael asked.

There was no response.

Kael knelt down and put his left hand on the man's arm, while his right gripped the hilt of his sword, ready to use it at a moment's notice. Closing his eyes, Kael summoned his sense and entered Magnus' thoughts. Immediately, the man's emotions flooded over Kael. There was a great deal of fear and anger, but an undercurrent of sadness.

MAGNUS, CAN YOU HEAR ME?

Kael felt his recognition, but there was no reply.

I KNOW YOU'RE LISTENING

YOUR PLANS HAVE COME TO AN END, MY HIGH PRIEST!

LOOK AT THE MESS YOU'VE CREATED.

YOU HAD NO RIGHT TO DO WHAT YOU DID TO US.

WE WERE JUST CHILDREN!

YOU'VE PUT ME IN AN AWKWARD POSITION.

MOST OF THE OTHERS ARE DEAD NOW...AND THE REST WILL SOON BE!

For a moment, Kael could sense the man's regret. There was even a fleeting thought about Maeryn and a sense of loss. But this quickly gave way to a powerful feeling of hatred that felt very familiar to Kael. The he realized that it wasn't coming from Magnus, but from somewhere else. Kael focused his sense, seeking out the source of the hatred. When he located it, he instantly recognized it.

AH YES—THE SO-CALLED ALL POWERFUL.

IS THIS HOW SUCH A BEING ACCOMPLISHES HIS WORK; BY USING SOMEONE ELSE'S BODY?

Kael could feel the hatred swell like a wave, preceding the response.

YOU INSOLENT INSECT—I AM COMING FOR YOU!

AND WHEN I FIND YOU, I WILL MAKE YOU SUFFER LIKE NO ONE ELSE!

Kael smiled inwardly as he thought of a response.

WE MET ONCE, JUST LIKE THIS—YEARS AGO.

YOU TRIED TO INVADE MY MIND AND BODY, AND YOU FAILED!
DO YOU REMEMBER ME?

The tendrils of the All Powerful's consciousness snaked out toward Kael.

YOU HAVE SOMETHING OF MINE AND I AM COMING TO RETRIEVE IT!

Kael gritted his teeth.

YOU WILL GET IT BACK WHEN I PUT IT THROUGH YOUR HEART—THE SAME WAY I KILLED YOUR SON!

This last comment produced a momentary pause, followed by a desperate anger that engulfed him, like vines that grew up around a tree and chocked the life from it. Kael could feel the All Powerful reach out to grab hold of his mind. But Kael was ready. He had felt this before and had prepared himself for this moment many years ago. Focusing his sense, he pulled with all his might and broke free of the grasp on his consciousness.

When he opened his eyes, he could see Magnus' body begin to twitch. Without hesitation, he pushed on his sword and drove the sharpened point into the chest, piercing Magnus' heart. Instantly, the body relaxed and was at peace. Even through his own feelings of hatred, Kael felt pity on the man that lay before him. Somehow, long ago, this man had given himself over to an evil being and had never gotten himself back.

Dacien's voice cut through Kael's thoughts.

"Men, let's mount up. If Soren manages to evade pursuit, he will head back to his army. Let's go."

The return trip to the ridge overlooking the valley was much quicker the second time. But after they arrived, they waited for another hour without any sign of Soren. Finally, two of Dacien's riders came back.

They stopped in front of their General. "He just kept riding east and eventually we lost his trail."

Dacien looked to Kael. "What do you think?"

"It's possible that he won't return to his army. Magnus' control over the Council was only under the threat of force. It wasn't legitimate. Perhaps Soren knows that he is powerless without Magnus' backing."

"Then we should leave," Dacien concluded. "We still have much work to do."

Kael hesitated, but decided that Dacien was right. "Lead the way," he said to his friend.

Colonel Aulus Sentiun woke early in the morning to find that his General was missing. It was highly unusual for Soren to be absent for any reason. After some questioning of the upper ranks, it quickly became apparent that the Emperor and other Generals were missing as well. Being the next ranking officer, Aulus ordered the scouts to search the surrounding areas.

By midmorning, a scout returned to the camp and informed Aulus that the bodies of the Emperor and three of the four Generals were found a few miles to the east in a clearing. There was no sign of Soren. Aulus wondered briefly whether Soren was responsible, but the scout continued his report and noted that there were horse tracks everywhere around the bodies and that it looked like they had been ambushed. Aulus dismissed the scout and ordered a search party to recover the bodies.

"Colonel," said the captain standing behind him. "We're ready to move. What do you want to do?"

Aulus looked up at the sun now standing high in the sky. The air was warming and clumps of wet snow fell from the branches of trees all around. "It is our duty to carry out our orders."

There was a moment of silence and Aulus knew what the captain was thinking. Aulus was thinking the same thing. *Why should we continue with this ludicrous mission?* But Aulus was a soldier and a man that lived by rules. As long as he was able to continue with their standing order, he was obligated to do so.

Aulus turned around and locked eyes with the captain, which was all that was needed. The other man looked at the ground. "...right away, Sir," he replied.

Another four days of grueling travel over terrain that alternated between wet or frozen—depending on the movement of air—brought the armies to the northern border of Leoran. As soon as they exited the forest and set eyes on the beautiful stone city on the lake, Aulus knew that something was wrong.

It was uncommonly quiet. He sent a patrol of scouts to search the shacks and common buildings at the shoreline. They returned to report that all were vacant.

"Come with me," he said to his captain. Riding down to the shore, the two men along with the scouts, made their way to the guard tower protecting the raised road that crossed the lake and entered the north gate of the city. Just as the scouts had said, it was vacant.

They passed underneath the tower through a wide stone arch and continued along the northern road. Surprisingly, when they reached the gate to the city, it was ajar. They rode in cautiously, expecting an ambush, but after an hour of searching found the city to be empty as well.

Slowly, a smile crept over Aulus' face as he came to understand what was happening.

"We could track them," the captain offered.

Aulus pulled his horse to a stop. "No. Our orders were to march on Leoran, and we've done just that. Set up camp for the evening. We leave for the boats in the morning."

The captain couldn't help but smile. "What about the city? It would be easier to use..."

Aulus cut the man off in mid-sentence. "No. We'll make camp in the forest tonight. This is someone else's home."

"Yes, Sir," the captain replied, riding off to carry out his new orders.

Aulus dismounted and walked up the stairs to the ramparts overlooking the lake. As the wind picked up, blowing tiny flakes of snow through the air, Aulus breathed a sigh of relief. "Clever...very clever," he mumbled to himself.

Dacien sat atop his horse, with Kael at his side, watching the citizens of Leoran file back into the city after the Orud armies had departed. The past year had been a difficult one for these people, with the Syvaku attacks, the nightmares of a monster stalking their forests, and now, being displaced from their home. Still, Dacien had to admit that this was the best possible outcome and had turned out much more successful than he had originally hoped.

He looked over to Kael, whose neck was a variety of dark colors, bruised by the hand of the giant. Kael was smiling as well.

"Thank you, Kael. This was a brilliant idea."

Kael turned. "I just hope this is the last of their suffering. They deserve to live in peace."

"Indeed!" Dacien agreed.

"And thank you for helping me with Magnus..." Kael's words trailed off as he wasn't sure how to say it.

"You're welcome."

For a moment, they sat in silence and watched the procession of citizens leading back into the city. Then Dacien spoke. "Come on; let's go home."

17

The winter at Leoran was always long, the citizens eager to see the first signs of spring. But this particular year was different. After surviving such hardships, everyone enjoyed a time of peace. Even though it should have been a difficult time of year, it wasn't. The time passed quickly. Spirits were high. And it seemed that all were enjoying their new-found freedom and security. Life returned to normal and everyone seemed to like it that way.

In late winter, Dacien and Aelia were married. They originally intended to wait until spring, but as the winter months passed, they found that they couldn't keep apart from each other. The occasion was celebrated for three days with feasting, dancing, plays and musical performances in the royal palace. Aelia quickly adapted to her new position of authority, helping Dacien where she could. He found her to be a great asset on matters of city governance.

Eventually, spring returned. The air warmed and the snowfall turned to rain. The farmlands to the southwest of the lake became busy with horses, plows, and workers all rushing to get their crops planted. The lake was again populated with fishing boats and the city seemed to come to life.

After just a few weeks, when the mountain passes began to clear, Dacien invited Maeryn, Kael, and Saba to dinner. They all came to the dining hall overlooking the lake and took their seats.

"So what is the occasion?" Maeryn asked.

Dacien looked to Aelia sitting next to him, then back to Maeryn. "We've decided that I will go back to Orud."

Although Kael was ready to be rid of political affairs, he knew this was coming. "You wish to be Emperor?"

Dacien didn't answer immediately, choosing his words wisely. "Though I love this city and its people, I am the only rightful successor to the throne. And the Empire is in a fragile state. The damage that Magnus caused will take time and effort to recover from."

"And you think you can fix it?" Maeryn asked.

"Yes I do," Dacien shot back.

"I'm sorry," Maeryn apologized. "I didn't mean it like that. I'm just concerned. Aren't you ready to live in peace? Magnus is gone."

"There are still a few left," Kael warned.

Dacien continued. "And the Korgan are still a threat. Meanwhile, the High Council is left to make all the decisions. They will look to matters in the only way they can, monetarily...which is exactly their function. But they need a counter-balance, the other half of the Council that sees events from a military perspective. This is the structure that has kept the Empire safe and prosperous for generations. I want to live in peace," he admitted, turning to smile at Aelia, who smiled in return. "I believe that peace is within our grasp, but it is not yet obtained."

"Are there others who would vie for the position of Emperor?" Saba asked.

"Perhaps," Dacien replied casually. "The Colonel from Orlek used to outrank me, but he served directly under Soren and his loyalty is in question. All I need to do is go back to Orud and present myself to the Council. If they are reasonable, they will have to conclude that I am the next Emperor."

"When will you leave?" asked Maeryn.

Dacien paused for a moment. "That's why we asked you to dinner tonight. Of course, you are all welcome to stay here in Leoran. But Aelia has decided to accompany me. We will leave by the end of the week. And Kael, I could really use you by my side."

Kael nodded his approval.

"Well I'm not letting my daughter go halfway across the Empire without me," Maeryn stated.

"I will go, as well," Saba chimed in.

"It's settled then," Dacien concluded with a smile.

Soren stood at the docks of the High Temple and stared out across the shoreline where thousands of loyal followers were gathered. Still more were standing on the decks of their ships in the harbor. The docks were filled, every available slot taken by a ship whose passengers were now standing, listening to his address. Hundreds of ships and thousands of followers had made their pilgrimage in response to his announcement. And now they waited to hear his words.

"Brothers," Soren shouted to the crowds. "Our years of obedience to the words of our High Priest have reached their fulfillment. Many of you know that he has fallen. But he was only a servant. His duty was to point you toward the All Powerful and to show you what is possible when you yield to his will. For thousands of years, our god has been absent from this world, driven away in sorrow, for there was no one left who honored him. But we honor him now. And our ranks have grown."

The crowds cheered at these words so that Soren couldn't have heard himself speak.   He waited patiently for the noise to subside before continuing. "Because of our honor and our loyalty, he has returned."

Again, the crowd cheered, even louder than before.   It was several minutes until they calmed themselves to the point of listening.

"Men of the Kaliel..." Soren shouted, his voice threatening to go hoarse. "...bow in reverence to your god, to the one who is All Powerful!"

Almost in unison, the crowds dropped to their knees and looked upward.

The thick rain clouds that blanketed the sky overhead began to swirl inward. The eye of the vortex began to protrude, dropping like a funnel. The clouds flashed, followed by peals of thunder. As the funnel lowered and grew wider, lightening arced between the top of the mountain and the bottom of the vortex. The humid air suddenly grew warm. Then, the vortex opened like a mouth.

Out of the opening, a black creature slowly descended. Its wings were outstretched, spanning thirty feet, as it glided on the wind in a controlled fall. It came to land on the top of the volcanic mountain and retracted its wings, enfolding itself in a cloak of leathery darkness.

The lightening stopped and the clouds stopped swirling, as if they, too, obeyed the All Powerful. The crowds were no longer cheering, but deadly silent, watching in fascination.

Suddenly, Soren felt its presence in his mind and the look on the faces around him told him that they could hear the thoughts also.   The All Powerful was speaking to them, without the nuisance of words. Instead, thoughts came into their minds and they suddenly received a revelation.

The Empire had chosen to deny the leadership of the High Priest. They had made their decision and it would prove to be a costly mistake. Now, the All Powerful had returned to his world, to lay hold of it by force. There would be no mercy shown to the citizens, whether man, woman, or child. The time for mercy had passed. Everyone understood what had to be done, and it made perfect sense. Then the thoughts disappeared and everyone became aware of themselves and their surroundings.

As Soren regained control of his own senses, he looked to the top of the mountain. The dark figure seemed to shrink down, then burst into the air, finally unfolding its wings as its ascent began to slow. The giant wings pumped the air, causing it to hover a hundred feet above the mountain. It extended its hands to the people below, then turned them palms upward. In response, a massive roar was quickly followed by a wall of water, shooting upward from the ocean immediately surrounding the outer wall. It came back down in a torrent, drenching those standing along the wall, creating a wave in the harbor that rocked the ships.

The crowd gasped in awe at the sheer power their god possessed.

The All Powerful began to rise higher into the sky and turn toward the northeast. Then, with a quick burst of speed, it shot forward and quickly disappeared over the wall.

18

The pastures were already green with new grass. The buds on the trees were just beginning to open, but the trees still looked bare. Kael leaned down and whispered to his horse, patting it on the neck before urging it to continue.

Up ahead, Dacien and Aelia rode together. Things hadn't been the same between he and Dacien since the marriage. But it was understandable. The bond between a man and wife was special and something to be celebrated. Still, the thought didn't keep Kael from feeling lonely.

"We couldn't ask for more pleasant weather," Saba said, riding up alongside Kael.

Kael looked around and drew in a deep breath. "It is beautiful, isn't it?"

Maeryn looked back over her shoulder. "It would be even better if we were aboard my ship."

Saba laughed.

"It was too nice to last for very long," Kael called ahead. They had left the ship anchored southwest of Leoran in their haste to get to the city. Unfortunately, the scouts that Dacien sent out reported that it wasn't where they had left it.

"Someone out there is enjoying a most fortunate discovery," Saba said with a smile. "Maeryn still hasn't gotten over it."

Kael shrugged his shoulders. "It was a great ship," he said in his mother's defense.

A small boat made its way through the harbor of the High Temple and toward the exit. The guards, seeing Ukiru aboard the ship, promptly opened the gate, letting the massive armored panel slide sideways, revealing the open sea beyond. The crew below deck began to row and the ship lurched toward the opening in surges.

As the vessel left the confines of the High Temple walls, a soft thud sounded behind Ukiru and he spun around. At the stern crouched Soren, rising to his feet after jumping to the deck.

"Where are you going, old friend?" he asked with a calm intensity.

"My service to Magnus was concluded at his death. I am leaving."

The boat continued to push forward on the strength of the rowers, seeking open water before raising the sails. The two men stood twenty feet apart, eyes locked on one another, adjusting their stance with each movement of the ship in order to maintain balance.

"Your service is to the All Powerful and it is a lifelong decision; there is no leaving!"

Ukiru knew that this moment would be awkward, which was why he wanted to leave in private. "My service was never to the All Powerful. All these years, I could never hear his voice. My charge was to train you and teach you to hear his voice. I was already too old by the time I met Magnus."

Soren's eyes narrowed into a scowl. "You're an unbeliever, then. And the worst kind, an impostor. Why didn't Magnus discover this?"

"He knew," Ukiru admitted. "I didn't hide it from him."

"And what now, now that you have seen the All Powerful with your own eyes?"

"It is a demon, and not something to be worshipped!"

Soren's scowl turned into a mask of rage. "...traitor!" he hissed through his teeth.

"Don't you realize that I could have left anytime? I was indebted to Magnus for what he did to help me. In exchange, I served him with honor. That debt has been repaid and now I'm leaving."

"You can't leave!"

Ukiru put his hand on the hilt of his sword. "I can and I will."

This infuriated Soren, who drew his sword and charged at Ukiru, swinging his blade for the older man's face.

Ukiru crouched and spun away from the attack, striking Soren's leg as he moved out of the way.

Soren came to a stop and looked down at his thigh. His tunic was cleanly separated into a three inch cut, while the warm blood began to flow down his leg.

"Have you forgotten, already, what I taught you?" Ukiru asked, calmly. "Heightened emotions will cloud your ability to think clearly and act wisely." He knew Soren would chafe at the instruction and only stir up more emotion, which was exactly what he wanted for his opponent.

Soren spun to his right and locked eyes with his former teacher. In an instant, the expression left his face and he appeared calm, even disconnected. "Here's something you never learned, old man." Soren's eyes turned white and he began to twitch slightly.

Ukiru had seen this many times with Magnus, and realized that the All Powerful was inhabiting Soren's body. He lunged forward, attempting to take advantage of Soren's temporary distraction. He raised his sword and brought it down toward Soren's head.

The sharp clang of steel sounded across the deck as Soren swiftly brought his blade into a defensive posture. Shoving Ukiru's sword backward with his own, Soren attacked rapidly, slashing from different angles.

Ukiru stepped backward, fending each blow, the muscles in his wrist struggling to maintain control of the sword. Soren's strength and speed were beyond anything Ukiru had experienced.

Soren paused his attack and changed his position so that he could drive Ukiru into the starboard railing.

Ukiru took the opportunity and drove forward, striking laterally with a two-handed grip.

Soren lunged to the side, dodging the blade and brought his own sword down on top of Ukiru's extended weapon, trapping it against upward movement.

Ukiru pulled his weapon back and spun around, but Soren's blade was already in place, blocking the next attack as well. His defenses were too quick and each time their weapons met, Ukiru could feel his own strength being sapped from his arms and hands. He had to keep on the offense if he was going to survive.

He retracted his sword and then quickly lunged forward with a stabbing thrust. The attack went farther through Soren's defenses than expected. Soren flinched backward and brought his blade in a circular motion up to his neck, knocking Ukiru's sword to the side, leaving a shallow cut across his collar bone and shoulder as he cleared the threat away from his neck.

The sideways force on the sword was too much for Ukiru and he felt the handle slip from his grip. He was now off-balance and his opponent had his sword in a ready position. He knew instantly that this was the moment it would happen. In a last desperate attempt, Ukiru jumped and twisted around to bring his left heel toward Soren's face. It was a risk because he couldn't see his opponent until the last minute.

As his body came around, building momentum, Ukiru's face spun just ahead of his foot and he saw, at the last moment, that Soren wasn't there. His foot followed its path, committed to the attack and kicked the air. Ukiru landed awkwardly on the deck, off-balance and vulnerable.

From the left corner of his vision, he could seed Soren moving in. In an instant, Ukiru felt his chest expand with an intense pressure and then the air left his lungs. He looked down to see the tip of Soren's sword coming through the front of his rib cage. It lingered there for a second, then disappeared with a violent backward motion.

Then, the pain set in like being burned from the inside out. Ukiru turned, his knees losing strength, and saw Soren standing over him, his sword dripping with blood. Ukiru collapsed from weakness and lay on the deck. As he looked up at the blue sky, with soft clouds passing overhead, he felt regret that he had lived his whole life doing someone else's bidding. Then the pain disappeared and darkness enclosed on his vision.

19

The mist clung to the foothills in the south, revealing only the tops of the mountain range. Dacien's horse walked along a gravel road that cut through fields of long grass, setting an easy pace for the others to follow. Late in the morning, the gravel road suddenly became a paved road, signaling that they were nearing Orud.

Aelia rode up alongside and slowed to match Dacien's pace. "What will we do once we get to Orud?"

"We'll go straight to the Council and explain what Magnus and his Generals were attempting."

"Emperor Dacien Gallus..." Aelia mumbled to herself.

Dacien turned to his wife with raised eyebrows. "It may not be as easy as that," he cautioned.

Aelia smiled. "Still, it's fun to think about."

"Empress Aelia Gallus," Dacien said.

"That's fun to think about too," Aelia replied.

The southern wall of Orud slowly emerged from the fog, its massive height foreboding as it stretched from east to west as far as the eye could see. Dacien continued along the road, maintaining the lead position as the group made its way to the nearest gate. The portcullis was flanked by a pair of square towers with arched windows that overlooked the plains to the south, as well as the area in front of the gate. All of the window covers were propped open, which was an unusual sign that the city was on alert. Though the mist made it difficult to see, Dacien knew that archers stood at each of the windows ready to unleash their missiles upon anyone suspicious.

Just before they were within range of the archers, Dacien pulled his horse to a stop and allowed the others to catch up. "The city is on alert for some reason. Stay here; I will go and speak with the guards alone."

Aelia looked concerned.

Dacien winked at her, then bumped his heels against the flanks of his horse. Another hundred yards brought him right up to the iron portcullis.

"Halt," commanded a voice from the ground level of the left tower.

Dacien stopped his horse and waited, keeping his eyes on the arrowheads that were now visible just inside the windows of the upper levels.

A guard came out from the protection of his tower and approached Dacien.

If Dacien hadn't dressed in his uniform, they might have stayed in their tower and shot him for looking suspicious. It was a good sign that he was being greeted face to face.

"State your name and purpose," the guard ordered.

"General Dacien Gallus of Leoran. I am traveling with my wife and friends and wish to enter the city."

The man's suspicious countenance changed instantly. "My lord, I apologize for the nature of our welcome."

Dacien nodded. "What's going on here, soldier? Why is the city on alert?"

"It's the Korgs, General. They're coming to lay siege to the city."

"...siege? Where did this information come from?"

"General Aulus of Orlek."

Dacien looked back to the others, hardly visible now as the fog began to thicken. He looked back to the guard. "I must speak with the Council immediately."

"Yes, my lord," the man replied obediently. He ran back to the tower and disappeared through a doorway. Seconds later, the portcullis began to lift from the ground. Squeals of iron pierced through the dampening affect of the mist as the sharpened ends of the gate became visible, like the teeth of some giant monster.

Dacien turned around and waved for the others to come forward. When they arrived, he led them through the gate and into the city with a wave to the guards as they passed through. Once inside the city, it became apparent that the guard's story wasn't exaggerated. Citizens and soldiers were rushing everywhere. The city seemed on the verge of panic.

"Follow me. We need to ride quickly," Dacien said over his shoulder. Kicking his horse into action, the group sped to a gallop and wound their way through the city streets. Even at their pace, it took half an hour to reach the center of the city where the Palace was located.

After entering the Palace gates, they came to a stop at the southeastern wing where the Council chambers were located. Dacien dismounted and gave the reins to Aelia. "I'm sorry, but they will be expecting to see everyone but you."

"That's alright," Aelia answered. "Where are the stables?"

Dacien smiled. It was one of the things that he loved most about her. She was uncomplicated and hardly ever got her feeling hurt over such things. "...at the back of that building there," Dacien replied, pointing to the north.

Saba, Maeryn, and Kael dismounted, as well, and each handed Aelia the reins. "Thank you," Saba offered.

The halls outside the Council chambers felt cold. Torches lined the stone walls, illuminating the arched ceilings, but doing nothing to warm the interior. Dacien walked confidently, heading for the main meeting hall where the Council members would be. As they approached the large wooden doors, a man rose to his feet from a nearby bench and stepped toward Dacien.

"General," the man called.

Dacien hadn't ever met the man, but suspected that he was the former Colonel from Orlek.

"General Aulus Sentiun of Orlek," the man confirmed, extending his hand in greeting as soon as Dacien was near.

Dacien wasn't sure that this man could be trusted, but shook his hand anyway, just to be polite. Saba, Maeryn, and Kael stood behind a few paces, watching in silence.

"We missed you at Leoran," the man said forwardly.

Dacien wasn't sure how to take the comment, but decided to meet it head on. "We learned that you weren't just coming to visit."

Aulus squinted. "Indeed we were not. And I must apologize on behalf of my army. Our leadership was acting without our support, or that of the Council. Unfortunately, I was obligated to follow orders, as were my men."

"Of course," Dacien replied, warming up to the man.

"But I suppose that doesn't matter now, does it?"

Dacien smiled but didn't say anything, not wishing to incriminate himself.

Aulus continued. "The Council was quite relieved to learn of their deaths."

"And what about you?" Dacien asked, getting right to the point. "Are you relieved?"

"Very much so!"

"Tell me," Dacien continued. "What is this that I hear about the Korgan?"

"Well..." the man paused. "...after finding Leoran mysteriously deserted, we were pleased to march back to our ships and set sail for Orud. When we arrived in late winter, I informed the Council of our Emperor's death, and that of his Generals. This is when I learned that the Council hadn't approved or even been informed of the mission."

Maeryn, Saba, and Kael stepped forward to hear his words more closely.

"I also warned them that Magnus had ordered nearly all of the northern and eastern forces to leave the wall near Orlek. This left us endangered by the Korgan hordes in the wastelands. They immediately ordered us to return to Orlek. We arrived at Suppard in early spring and I sent scouts at once to assess the situation in Orlek. They returned before we were even finished unloading the ships. They told me that Orlek had been completely overrun by the barbarians, the whole city burned to the ground. One of the survivors told them that the hordes moved west after the attack and that there were hundreds of thousands of them."

"...hundreds of thousands?" Dacien repeated, not sure if he heard correctly.

"Yes, that's right. Of course, he was a commoner and was likely exaggerating. But even if there were half that number, it's still an incredible threat. We've battled the Korgs for nearly a decade in the east. And they've always been disorganized, fighting like wild animals. And we've never seen that many."

Dacien shook his head in wonder.

"So I ordered the fastest ship to be relieved of all its cargo and I returned to Orud as quick as possible. I've only been here a few days and I've been meeting with the Council every day to discuss the matter."

"Discuss the matter? Is that all that the Council has managed to accomplish in this time?"

"Well," he replied, taken aback by Dacien's accusing tone. "Preparations are underway as we speak."

Just then, the doors opened and a guard walked out. "General, the Council will see you now."

Dacien turned and walked toward the doors.

The guard immediately lowered his spear into Dacien's path.

Dacien didn't even slow his stride. "At ease soldier," he said, pushing the man's spear aside and walking through the doorway. As he entered the Council hall, he heard Aulus speaking to the guard, presumably making allowances for what just happened.

But Dacien was too upset to give regard to formality. His blood was pumping hard through his veins, driven by an intense frustration at what he had just heard.

"General Dacien. What brings you back to Orud?" one of the Council members called out.

Dacien strode down the center aisle and approached the meeting arena where all the seats were filled in one half of the circle. Apparently, the two guilds that had lost their representatives last year had appointed new ones.

"I've come to discuss my qualifications for serving as Emperor, but I see that there are more pressing matters."

"Now wait just a minute," Aulus called from the back of the room. He walked quickly down the aisle toward the Council as Maeryn, Saba and Kael came slowly into the room. "I've served as Colonel for many years in a capital city, faced with defending the northern wall against the Korgs on a nearly constant basis. Your experience has been as a Captain in some far away city to the south."

Dacien smiled inwardly, though he remained stern on the outside. He expected this and didn't fault the man for trying. "Yes. And I quickly rose to the position of General during times of war, where I've served for a year and a half. And now we are the same rank. But, as I was saying before you interrupted," he said, turning back to the Council members. "I've just learned that a large Korgan force is marching toward Orud from the east. What is the Council doing about this threat?"

"We are considering several strategies. The first is..."

"Unacceptable," Dacien interrupted, raising his voice. "You've met for days now and you are still *considering* strategies."

"I beg your pardon, General," one member countered. "But it is a complicated matter."

"For you perhaps," Dacien shot back. "You all aren't experienced military leaders. And I don't fault you for that. However, if these reports are true, then this Council needs to reach a decision today. There is no time for indecision. We must be moving troops into positions this very hour if we have any hope of stopping this siege."

Though several Council members looked on the cusp of saying something, no words were spoken and the chambers were silent for a few seconds.

Dacien took the reins. "Colonel, how many do you have at your command in Suppard?"

"Twenty legions," Aulus answered quickly. "Two of cavalry, two of archers, five of spearmen, and the remainder are foot soldiers and siege equipment operators."

Dacien turned back to the guild leaders. "And last I knew the Orud guard was comprised of ten legions."

One council member spoke up. "The slaves make up another ten legions, but they are still in training. I don't think they even have all their weapons ready, yet. Their progress ground to a halt when Magnus set his sights on Leoran."

"Alright," Dacien replied. "And my forces at Leoran are too far away to be of any use. So that gives us forty thousand men."

"...against hundreds of thousands?" Maeryn spoke up.

The room went silent again.

"But don't forget," Dacien finally said. "If we don't go out to meet them and we allow them to come up against the walls of this city, they are the ones at a great disadvantage. Their hundreds of thousands might prove useless against our catapults. If we utilize our resources correctly, this could be an easy victory."

"I appreciate your optimism General," Aulus replied. "But I would advise you not to underestimate the Korgan. They are clever bastards and their tactics have improved immensely over the past ten years."

Dacien looked over to Kael whose brow wrinkled at the comment. He knew that one of Kael's childhood companions was now leading them and had likely brought a great deal of organization to the barbarian hordes.

"There are more soldiers at our disposal," Maeryn offered.

Dacien understood instantly, looking to the Council just in time to see a few of the members cringe.

"As you know," Maeryn continued, "I have held a position of authority within the Resistance."

Dacien had never spoken to Maeryn about her involvement with the Resistance and hadn't even considered the possibility. "Would they help?" he asked.

"Yes," Maeryn answered. "In this instance, I believe they would."

"Maeryn, how many men could you muster?"

Maeryn looked to the ground as if counting in her head. "...in the surrounding area...ten thousand."

A collective gasp came from the Council. The farming guild representative stood from his chair. "That many?" he asked quietly.

It was clear to Dacien that the Council had grossly underestimated the strength and numbers of the Resistance. And to be fair, he had, as well. If there were ten thousand in the immediate vicinity, how many members did they have throughout the Empire?

"We would greatly appreciate any help they could offer," he said to Maeryn, who simply nodded.

Saba put his hand up. "Uh... might I suggest that there are others, still? You men all represent guilds of hundreds, even thousands. Your skills could prove quite useful in times like these...especially the blacksmiths."

The new blacksmith guild representative stood up. "My guild has already pledged to work day and night to provide weapons and armor."

"Good," Saba replied. "And what about the breeders? Your horses could turn foot soldiers into cavalry. And the farmers. The city will need food if the siege lasts for an extended period of time. The carpenters can make arrows and defense equipment. The citizens can fletch arrows. We need to think broadly. It isn't just the soldier's responsibility to help defend the city."

Mischievous smiles began to appear on faces around the room.

"Do we have an agreement then," Dacien asked. "We will put all discussions of the Emperor's title on hold until this threat is dealt with. For now, we will each contribute in the way that we can. We will bring our disparate resources together to meet our common enemy."

"Agreed," one Council member stated, rising from his seat.

One by one, they all followed suit.

20

The morning sun rose, but failed to pierce skies darkened with thick clouds. Rain fell in sporadic patches around the city. Aulus knew that it would make traveling more difficult, but he was glad, nonetheless, to have his orders. He watched as the crew untied the ropes that fastened his ship to the dock. The anchor had already been pulled up. And within minutes, oars came out from the flanks of the ship and began to cut into the water, moving his ship out into the bay where his sails could be used.

He looked down at the folded and sealed piece of parchment that detailed his orders. It gave him a steady sense of purpose that had been missing from his life for many years. He had served under Soren for a long time, to his dissatisfaction. And the culmination of that was an attempted attack on men of his own country. Now all that was past. It happened so rapidly that he hardly had the time to consider it.

But daunting as it may be to have the Korgs marching for Orud, and the battles that were only days ahead, Aulus felt truly happy for the first time in many years. He looked out across the bay and watched the westerly wind drive the rain at an angle into the ocean surface. It would be a quick trip back to Suppard.

He smiled. *The Korgan will never expect what is about to happen.*

Maeryn stepped out of the carriage and shielded her face from the rain. Moving quickly, she walked toward the building and stopped in front of a door, third from the left. The arched overhang offered a dry area just in front of the door. She hoped her information was accurate.

Reaching up, she lifted the iron knocker and rapped it against the thick, wooden door. It took a few minutes before she began to hear rumblings of movement behind the door. Maeryn glanced over her shoulder and saw that the two soldiers stood guard on opposite ends of the carriage. The driver looked slightly nervous. Maeryn wished the soldiers weren't so obvious.

Quietly, the door swung inward a few inches.

Maeryn turned around to see a familiar face that was now bearded. But the pale skin and squinting eyes were unmistakable. "Noster?"

The door opened a bit more and he peeked his head out, looking over Maeryn's shoulder at the Orud guards behind her.

"It's alright; they're with me," she explained. "May I come in?"

He thought for a moment, then opened the door.

Maeryn walked through the doorway and into the foyer. Instantly, the smell of parchment and ink came to her senses.

Noster shut and locked the door behind her, then walked through another doorway at the back of the foyer.

Maeryn followed. The house was arranged in the typical fashion, with the bedrooms, kitchen, and washroom extending from a common central courtyard area. Noster walked to the back of the house and into a workroom, farthest from the entry. Scrolls were arranged on shelves around the room, with a familiar writing desk in the center.

"I didn't expect to hear from you so soon. And you came in person...with Orud soldiers."

Maeryn smiled. "I'm sure you know what's happening?"

"Though the Resistance is in hiding, my ears still hear many things."

"And what do they hear recently?" Maeryn asked.

"...rumors of a siege."

Maeryn walked over to the desk. "They're not rumors."

Noster turned from his casual inspection of scrolls and looked at Maeryn. "So the Empire will finally get its due for how it has dealt with the Korgan over the years."

Maeryn breathed a sigh, then sat in the chair that faced the desk. "Noster, how much do you know about our leadership?"

"Nothing. And they like it that way."

Maeryn nodded. "Well, I know plenty. Let me be completely honest with you. The Resistance leader didn't really care about the causes that you and I worked for. He was using our military might to keep pressure on the Empire's forces, so that there was always a constant threat that needed to be managed. You see, the leader was actually part of the Orud military. And when his own personal progress through the political hierarchy slowed, he would order the Resistance to attack something. Over the years, this worked to undermine everyone's confidence in the Emperor due to his inadequacy at dealing with the Resistance."

Noster sat down on a low shelf. "You keep referring to him in the past tense."

"Our leader was Magnus Calidon, the General of the Northern army, who then became our most recent Emperor."

Noster raised his eyebrows, then looked to the ceiling, considering the weight of this new information. "So we've been fighting ourselves?"

Maeryn continued. "Magnus had many ways of manipulating things. He also had control over the Syvaku in the west, and the Korgs in the east. He used them in a similar manner."

"But the Emperor is dead now," Noster observed. "Why are you telling me this?"

Maeryn could see his disappointment. "Because you have given your life for a cause and have lived in secrecy. I believe that you deserve to know what has happened. Your efforts have not been in vain. Before he died, our leader freed the slave population in order to bolster the quantity of his armies. But he died before he could make use of them, before he could manipulate them. You and I have stayed true to the original meaning of the Resistance, even though our leadership abandoned those principals long ago. We now have a great opportunity and I need your help."

"...opportunity?" he asked.

"Before he died, Magnus stirred up the Korgs and readied them for attack. Now he is gone and has left a mess in his wake. They are marching toward Orud as we speak, and have devastated everything in their path. Their numbers are in the hundreds of thousands. The Orud Council is strategizing on how to meet this threat. As you can imagine, the Korgs outnumber us by a significant margin."

"...us?" Noster asked with suspicion. "We are not the Empire."

"The people of this Empire have never been our enemies, rather, the Empire's policies and practices. And our main objective has been achieved, no matter the motivation. Now we have an entire slave population indebted to us, as well as to our military forces. Now is the time for the Resistance to take its rightful place among this Empire. No more hiding. No more secrecy. The Empire needs our numbers and we can offer them on our terms. We have the opportunity to position ourselves in such a way as to have a much greater influence on the government than ever before."

"That sounds risky," Noster cautioned. "We'll be completely exposed...and for what, the hope that we'll be accepted?"

"I've already been to see the Council. The Empire is changing by the day. Our armies are operating under individual leadership, independently from one another. The Trade Guilds are supporting this effort in every way they can. It's very different than the Empire we used to struggle against."

Noster considered her words, scanning the floor with his darting eyes. Finally, he lifted his head. "You've told the Council about your involvement with the Resistance and they let you walk out alive?"

Maeryn smiled and lifted her hands, as if to offer proof that the plan would succeed.

"I suppose you want me send the wake-up call to the Resistance? What should I tell them?"

Maeryn fished in her cloak for a folded piece of parchment, then handed it to Noster. "This is the plan," she said.

He held it for a moment without looking at it. Then a smile came over his face. "I must say, it has been a tremendously boring winter. It is good to see you again."

Maeryn smiled, then stood up to leave. "These are exciting times, and it's my hope that this is only a new beginning for us."

Dacien walked along the northern ramparts of the city with the Orud Captain of the Guard, inspecting the fortifications. He was impressed by the defenses, which were a more elaborate version of what he experienced in Bastul and Leoran. What he hadn't seen before was that the buildings and other structures outside the city walls were pushed back to a pre-determined distance so that they couldn't be used as shields. The forces along the walls also knew the exact distance of certain features of the terrain in front of their station, which would prove useful for estimating the distance of enemy forces.

Large catapults were positioned at regular intervals along the walls, with smaller trebuchets, stone throwers and ballista between them. The ammunition for these pieces of equipment was being stocked by masses of laborers as Dacien traversed the fortification.

"General Aulus tells us that the Korgan have traditionally fought as savages, with little organization."

"That's true," Dacien replied. "But their tactics have been steadily evolving over the past ten years. Their latest Commander is highly experienced in the ways of modern warfare. We shouldn't be surprised by the sight of siege towers, catapults, and the like."

The captain nodded.

Dacien looked out across the bare fields between the walls and the beginning of the outlying buildings, hundreds of yards away. Deep trenches traversed the landscape which were sloped on the side toward the city. The earthen slopes were spiked with iron spears embedded in the dirt and rock underlayment. As Dacien made a mental note of this in his mind, an idea began to form in his mind. "In a city this size, you must have access to pitch and oil."

"Yes," the captain replied cautiously.

"How much?" Dacien asked.

The captain looked out over the battle fields, then back to Dacien. "Let's go find out."

The line of citizens coming through the northern gate was long and slow moving. Saba and Aelia were attempting to help the guards who were overwhelmed by the masses.

Saba waved another farmer forward.

The man walked next to a pair of oxen pulling a large cart, periodically smacking the nearest beast's rump to get it moving. Behind him was a woman leading another cart, with a third being led by a boy of fifteen years or so. The farmer stopped in front of Saba, eyeing the old man suspiciously.

Saba had already experienced this several times throughout the day. The citizens didn't take well to being directed by others who were not in uniform. "What is your crop?" Saba asked.

"...wheat," the man grumbled. "It's all we had stored up."

Saba nodded, then walked to the back of the cart to inspect the goods. The woman also looked sour and tired of waiting. It was understandable. At a time when they should be out in their fields planting, they had been told to abandon their homes and bring everything from their storehouses into the city. Saba smiled at the woman, then walked back to the man at the front of the cart.

After estimating the weight of the cargo and getting the man's name, Saba made some notes on a piece of parchment. "Grains are being stored in the warehouse district, fourth street up and to the right."

Without a word, the man smacked one of his animals and the cart lurched forward into a slow roll.

Saba breathed a sigh, then looked over to Aelia two rows away. She looked just as exhausted.

"Ten legions," Kael said.

The instructor looked at the group of former slaves gathered in the massive training arena. "...nine hundred and forty," the man clarified.

Kael scanned the group, trying to assess their alertness. "Have any been trained on horseback?"

"...no cavalry here, my lord. Not yet anyway. We started with wrestling and hand combat. Most of them excelled. Then we trained with the short sword, shield and spear. And for the last two months...long spears."

Kael knew that these men needed at least another year to be fully battle ready. Unfortunately, they didn't have that much time. "...any archery training?"

"No, my lord."

"I assume you haven't started them on group training at specific tasks. But I need you to make a judgment today. What is your assessment of their skills?"

"Well," the man said, pausing to consider his answer. "Six hundred would function well as spearmen...the rest as foot soldiers."

"Very well, Lieutenant. You have my permission to take what you need from the armory. Get these men prepared to take part in the third phase of the defenses. I'll contact you when you're needed."

"Yes, my lord."

As the sun declined in the east, Dacien sat at a long table with Aelia at his side. Saba, Maeryn and Kael sat across from them, enjoying the feast of roast duck, fish, a variety of fruits and cheeses, accompanied by a strong wine from the Royal vineyards. It had been silent for most of the meal, with each one lost in his own thoughts.

"The scouts came in today," Dacien stated.

"Oh?" Kael responded. "What did they report?"

"The original estimate was wrong. There are approximately six hundred thousand."

"Six hundred..." Maeryn started, then went silent.

Dacien continued. "They're moving in three formations and their progress is slowed by the equipment they bring."

Kael lifted his head. "Equipment?"

"Unfortunately, yes. They have siege towers, battering rams, catapults and ladders."

Kael nodded and his eyes gleamed with a look that Dacien hadn't seen before.

"Donagh has been hard at work."

"What was he like?" Saba asked.

Kael lifted his wine goblet and took a long swallow, then carefully set it down. "He was tall and muscled, even more so than Narian. And he knew how to use his size to get what he wanted. He was always a bit immature, but that disappeared as soon as he got into the training arena. He was a gifted athlete and among the best in hand-to-hand combat. His downfall was that he was extremely self-centered, which made him weak when it came to leading others. People would only listen to him out of fear that he'd react violently. But they didn't respect him. I would expect him to be much the same now."

"That's good to know," Dacien said. "If these hordes are driven by fear, they can easily be disheartened. Our fight would be much more difficult if there was a great deal of loyalty among our enemies."

"Don't be so sure," Saba cautioned. "The Korgan have a long history of defending themselves against more advanced peoples. They are primitive, but their culture is based on very different motives than anything you or I know. They have a distinct hierarchy, much like a pack of wolves. The one who is most fierce in battle earns the right to lead and all the others either fall into line or challenge the leader. They kill each other as a means of establishing their order."

Maeryn chimed in. "That sounds like any other group of men. What's so different?"

Kael immediately thought of his time at the monastery and was inclined to agree with his mother.

"I heard," Aelia added, "that they mark their skin with designs after they kill."

"That's right," Saba replied. "It's a way of showing the other people in the tribe, as well as their enemies, how dangerous they are. You can also see this in other parts of nature. In the far south regions, where the trees and bushes grow so thick that they block out the light of day, there are animals that are brightly colored, such as frogs and snakes. These are usually the poisonous ones. Their colors are a warning to predators."

"How do you know all these things?" Aelia asked.

Maeryn leaned forward. "Saba is a very wise man. That's why your father and I chose him to be Kael's mentor."

Saba looked at Aelia and shrugged his shoulders.

"Nevertheless," Dacien stated. "If their motivation is anything other than loyalty for their country and their own people, their spirits will be easier to break."

Saba held up his hands. "I only caution that it would be unwise to underestimate them."

Kael spoke up to move the conversation past this point of contention. "How far away are they?"

"The first wave will arrive tomorrow, but if they're smart," Dacien said, looking over at Saba. "...they won't attack until their siege equipment has caught up." Then, he raised his goblet. "We've made all the preparations that we can. Now we must leave it to the gods to sort things out."

Kael raised his goblet, even though he didn't agree with Dacien's toast. Whatever gods there were, they would have nothing to do with this war.

21

Dacien surveyed the plains from his position atop a guard tower along the northern wall of Orud. The main road ran in a direct line toward the city and underneath his tower. It was the only way into the city along the thirty mile stretch of land that separated the west and east bays. He knew it would be the focus of any attack. Spanning the road at intervals of two hundred feet were three smaller guard towers restricting passage to anything larger than the standard ox cart. If the enemy's siege equipment was going to be moved into range and be effectively used, it would have to come along this road. Across the fields, small, dark shapes began to move among the buildings that were just out of range for the longest catapults. The enemy had arrived.

Since the horizon was populated with structures of various kinds, there was no way to see the masses that were likely gathering just out of sight. But the noise of their arrival was like a dull drone in the background, low and constant. The first wave of Korgs had arrived hours ago, but now their siege equipment had caught up and it seemed that they were readying themselves for attack.

At the limits of his vision, Dacien could see something moving along the road. As it neared, its long and low shape identified it as a battering ram enclosed in an armored housing. The housing usually protected the ropes and pulleys that powered the thrust of the head, which meant that the Korgs had, indeed, become more sophisticated in their tactics.

The battering ram was pushed and pulled by dozens of men, who only appeared as dark, earthen colored shapes from this distance. The ram moved quickly on the well constructed road, its great wheels turning rapidly. Though it was now within range, Dacien withheld any attack.

It came to a stop in front of the first guard tower, six hundred feet out from the walls of Orud. The guard tower was comprised of two square columns on either side of the road with a wall between them. A giant iron portcullis sat in the center of the wall, with its bottom teeth embedded into the receiving ports in the ground. The gate was securely locked and the tower abandoned by the soldiers who usually manned this position.

The men who had moved the battering ram into position were now scrambling around the rear and sides of the wood and iron machine, readying it to do its work of destroying the iron gate.

Dacien looked to his left and then to his right. The catapults atop the guard towers on either side of his were ready.

Dacien lifted his hand, then let it drop.

A soldier behind him, copied this motion with a bright red flag.

A loud clank split the air and the sound of rushing wind was followed by two burning streaks arching through the air toward the battering ram. The oil-filled projectiles both hit their marks. The one on the left exploded at the base of the battering ram. Flaming oil burst from the projectile and covered the men, the ground, and the base of the left side of the battering ram. A second later, the one on the right hit the armored side of the ram and engulfed it in flames.

Half of the barbarians ran back along the road to safety, while the others scattered in different directions, trying to put out the flames that had attached to their skin and clothes. In seconds, the battering ram became a ball of flames, sending a dark streak of black into the midmorning air. And, after a few minutes, it became another obstacle for the attacking enemy to overcome.

The writhing mass of men gathered between the buildings, parted quickly at the sight of their Commander. He approached from the rear, head and shoulders taller than the rest. His waist and thighs were loosely draped with furry animal skins. Across his shoulders hung a cloak, gathered at one side with a torc made of bone. The rest of his muscled frame was bare, except for the black tattoos that covered every inch of his skin. The intricate swirls and shapes wove together and spread over his body, like vines that engulf a tree, covering even his chiseled face and shaven head.

Though the crowds were thick, they parted immediately so that Donagh never had to break his stride. He entered a building and ascended stairs that led to the roof terrace. From this new vantage point, he could look out over the fields which separated him from his objective—the city of Orud. To his left, a burning pile of wood and iron sat in front of the first gate, blocking passage along the road.

His eyes lifted to the sky and took note of the dark gray clouds that hung overhead, ready to release their burden on the earth. A determined look spread across his face while he smiled inwardly. He barked a quick command in a guttural language, and one of the men standing nearby, ran away to relay the orders.

The Captain of the Orud guard came up the steps of the guard tower and walked toward Dacien who was looking out over the north fields. "General, why are they waiting?"

"The rain," Dacien replied. The Korgs hadn't made a move in hours and the Orud soldiers were getting restless. "As soon as this storm begins, they will attack. Tell your men to be patient; we have no reason yet to deviate from the plan."

The afternoon passed agonizingly slow. The anticipation of the siege had created a city-wide panic that required a great deal of planning and labor to manage. Likewise, the soldiers had stocked all the necessary ammunition for each catapult and projectile weapon along the walls, ready to use them at a moment's notice. The arrival of the Korgs and the first confrontation created a destructive glee among the guards. But all that had faded in the hours spent looking at the enemy from a distance.

The clouds were thick overhead, and smears of darkness could be seen descending from the sky in the east. It was raining elsewhere, just not on the battlefield. The ambient light that made its way through the storm above began to darken as night descended.

Dacien felt a raindrop hit his face. He stood and walked to the front of the tower, looking out over the wall. The other soldiers watched him carefully, excited at the prospect of action.

A mile away to the northwest, sheets of rain were falling on the land and moving steadily closer. "Alert the guard," he said to the man who followed his every move.

The man raised his small red flag and twirled it, receiving an identical signal from the towers on either side seconds later.

Then it finally happened. First, the ground began to darken, one tiny spot at a time. Then, the sound of raindrops could be heard as they fell on different surfaces, creating a steady but random sound that drowned out all else. Within seconds, Dacien's hair and clothes were soaked. In the distance, he could see movement among the enemy ranks.

In perfect unison, the enemy line exploded into motion. As far as the eye could see in either direction, the Korgs began to advance upon the fields. They came out from between the buildings and set foot upon the grassy fields, one after the other without end. As one man came to the battlefield, another came behind him, and so on. The sight of their numbers was enough to drive fear into anyone's heart.

But Dacien had been anticipating this very moment and had planned accordingly. He waited until the first wave of the enemy reached the first trench running across the field. As anticipated, the ranks became very dense behind the frontline, due to the ten foot drop.

Dacien's eyes narrowed as he raised his right hand, then let it drop. With only a few second's delay, the long range catapults released a volley of melon sized rocks through the air. The time between release and impact seemed endless as the dark round shapes arched through the rain and became visually smaller by the second.

The only indication of the volley doing its work was the appearance of tiny pockets of movement among the ranks of the enemy, appearing one after the other just as long grasses move in response to the wind. Though he couldn't see it clearly, Dacien could imagine the impact six hundred feet away. "Catapults...fire at will," he shouted.

As the north battlements became engulfed in the noise of battle, Dacien shifted his gaze to the north road at the front of the enemy line. Already, he could see the vague outline of more machines being lined up. A mischievous smile spread across his lips. So far, the enemy was acting in a predictable manner. They would use the benefit of their numbers to draw the catapult fire away from their machines, which would be moved into position by way of the road. It would be physically impossible to get machinery in range of the Orud walls any other way.

The masses of Korgs kept coming forward, now reaching the second trench, and still more were pouring out from between the buildings at the edge of their range. It was like lifting a rotten log to find hundreds of termites wriggling inside. Only in this case, it was hundreds and thousands of full grown men bent on destroying the city.

Dacien again waited until the enemy ranks swelled up behind the second trench, then gave the signal for the rock throwers to engage. They were smaller catapults using fist-sized rocks and their range was much shorter.

In between the clanking metal and low, loud sound of the long-range catapults, a facet of brighter and sharper sounds was added. Now Dacien could see the enemy falling in response to their defenses. Because of the sheer density of the invading forces, every shot found its mark. Korgs were falling by the hundreds, but more kept coming. Rain pummeled the field. Catapults and rock throwers release their ammunition. The shouts of the enemy came across the field in waves. And the machines began to move.

Dacien turned his attention to the road. Lined up in a procession were numerous battering rams being both driven and pulled by scores of men. Dacien turned to his signal officer and nodded. The man raised his flag and waved it in a different pattern this time. The catapult atop Dacien's tower groaned and creaked, as it was turned to target the battering rams. The Orud defenders were adept at quick changes, and the process took less than a minute. Looking back to the field, Dacien saw projectiles begin to crash into the rams and the surrounding men. The impact was devastating. Their aim was perfect.

The unfortunate men charged with moving these massive constructions received the brunt of the attack, mowed down by the inertia of the boulders. One projectile from the right side catapult destroyed the first two wheels of the second ram in the procession, causing it to tilt to one side and run into the ground. The first battering ram carried forward, but the rest were held up behind the newly created obstacle. The others would try to go around it and would only make them more vulnerable as they slowed to accomplish the task.

The hordes of foot soldiers reached the third trench and Dacien signaled for the bolt throwers to engage. The four foot long wooden bolts were normally fitted with long iron tips to penetrate enemy armor. But in preparation for the masses of Korgs who fought in nothing more than animal skins, they had been fitted with broad bladed tips to increase their effectiveness. The wisdom of this decision was proven within seconds of their use. Each bolt took down two or three men, as opposed to only one.

The rain continued to fall, and the afternoon light was now completely gone. The sound of thunder echoed across the fields, accompanied by flashes of light among the clouds above. Each flash illuminated the battlefield for only a moment, revealing thousands upon thousands of glistening bodies, surging toward the city walls.

Dacien squinted through the rain and tried to see if anything had changed at the border of the battlefield and the outlying buildings, but it was too far and the visibility was poor. Provided that nothing had gone wrong, General Aulus should be making his move any minute.

After stalking the tracks of the Korgan hordes for days, General Aulus Sentiun and the combined northern and eastern armies of the Orud Empire had finally arrived at the outskirts of the city. With the walls of Orud spanning the thirty miles of land between the western and eastern bays, it appeared that the enemy had spanned out to take up roughly ten miles of that space, centered on the northern gate. Within these ten miles, their forces were spread thin and long, congregating mostly between the buildings that had sprung up over the years along the edges of the battlefields.

Aulus liked the scenario that had presented itself to him. The darkness of night and the buildings would provide the needed cover. The rain would muffle the sound. It was likely that the front lines of the Korgs would never know what was happening at their rear until it was too late.

Aulus ordered the enemy flanks to be covered by spearmen. The traditional Orud formation was ten rows of soldiers, with those in the rear carrying the longest spears and those in the front carrying the shortest. In this fashion, each of the first five rows of men were protected by an impenetrable wall of spearheads. Behind the spearmen, foot soldiers with short swords and shields were arranged in another tightly packed formation to quickly dispatch any who managed to get by the spearmen. Behind the foot soldiers, archers would send volleys of arrows overhead to thin the enemy ranks before the pikemen ever made contact.

These forces would move in from the right and left while Aulus led the cavalry straight on, followed by another formation of foot soldiers. The goal, as General Dacien had explained it, was to push all the Korgan forces onto the field and trap them there. Aulus liked the strategy. Though he didn't know what Dacien planned beyond this, he was eager to find out.

The General glanced to his right and left, seeing that his men were ready. Their faces were illuminated by periodic flashes of light from the clouds above. With a gentle nudge, he started his horse into a trot. He pulled his sword free of its scabbard and it rang with a sharp metallic tone. Though he had faithfully served for decades defending the city of Orlek from these barbarians, this type of battle suited him better. For once, he would attack and the Korgan would defend.

Moving slowly down a paved street, Aulus rounded a bend and the backs of hundreds of Korgs could be seen. Though they were still more than a mile away from the battlefield, these barbarians were packed into the streets, awaiting their turn to enter the battle.

Aulus kicked the flanks of his horse and its trot increased to a gallop. The men beside him followed his lead, their own horses picking up speed to match his. The sound of the hooves on the stone pavers alerted the first of the Korgs, causing them to turn and face the attack. But in the confines of the packed streets, there was nowhere for them to go.

Aulus' war horse collided with the rear ranks, trampling men as it plowed through. He swung his sword in broad strokes, cutting and hacking through flesh and bone. The barbarians swung their crude iron swords in panicked overhead strokes, but they were no match for the cavalry. Every enemy that fell gave Aulus just a bit more satisfaction as he thought of all the horrendous acts that these people had perpetrated upon the citizens of Orlek.

He left a swath of fallen bodies in his wake. He was already breathing hard and the night had just begun. He had heard stories from old veterans that in prolonged battles, a bloodlust would overtake you and you would forget all feelings of pain or exhaustion. He knew this night he would join the ranks of those veterans.

22

"General Dacien," shouted a voice from across the guard tower.

Dacien turned as the Orud Captain of the Guard strode across the smooth stone. He wore a look of concern on his face.

"Captain?"

"Black ships have entered the eastern bay under the cover of darkness," the man shouted above the din of battle. "A small force of men has taken control of the eastern gate from the inside. It appears that they are trying to open the gate for the invading forces aboard the ships."

"Who on the inside would do this?"

"I don't know," the man yelled, covering his ear as the long range catapult released its load.

"And what of the Orud navy?" Dacien asked.

"They are trying to mobilize, but they won't be able to keep the black ships from reaching land. They came too quickly. I need to take half of our ground forces to secure the gate and prevent them from breaching the city walls."

Dacien glanced over his shoulder at the battlefield below him. "I'll secure the gate," he replied.

"Very well. And don't worry about us," the man offered. "Everything is going as planned on the northern front. We will have victory before daybreak tomorrow."

Dacien nodded. "May the gods smile upon you," he said, clasping the man's forearm.

Kael had just finished saddling his horse when Dacien rode into the stables. Kael knew instantly that something had changed. "What is it?"

Dacien pulled the reins to the left to turn his horse around. "...change of plans. A fleet of black ships has invaded the eastern bay."

"The Kaliel," Kael breathed.

"They are working with a small force on the inside that has taken control of the eastern gate. The captain has given us half the ground forces to secure the gate and keep the invaders out. Are you ready to ride?"

"...just," Kael replied quickly. In one swift movement, he swung up on to his horse and slid his feet into the stirrups. "I'll round them up."

Within minutes, half of Kael's cavalry was riding a full speed with Dacien in the lead. Running behind them were spearmen and foot soldiers, with the understanding that the cavalry wouldn't wait. They would engage the enemy as soon as possible.

The streets of Orud were barren at this hour. All of the citizens were holed up in secure areas in anticipation of a breach. This made maneuvering through the city much easier than normal, despite the fact that the streets were completely dark and wet.

They reached the eastern gate in fifteen minutes. Kael and Dacien slowed their horses as they assessed the situation. The portcullis stood open. Through the arched gateway, ships could be seen only a few yards out from the docks. Atop the guard tower, a few dozen armored men in black clothing held the high ground. Archers rained arrows down on the Orud guard, while infantry held the stairs on either side. The few remaining Orud guardsmen took cover behind nearby buildings. The bodies of their fellow soldiers littered the streets and stairs leading up to the tower.

"I'll take the right," Kael shouted, kicking his steed into a sprint.

In unison, the cavalry separated with half following Kael toward the broad stairs to the right of the tower, while Dacien veered left.

At once, arrows glanced off the stone underfoot. Two riders behind Kael were hit and fell from their horses. Kael rode hard and reached the stairs, his horse ascending the steps in long strides. The infantry closed their ranks and descended the steps to meet him. Just before he reached them, Kael slid his leg over the saddle and dropped to the stairs, ducking behind a column that shielded him from the archers to his left. Kael could see that these soldiers were also of the Kaliel. How they got inside the city, he didn't know.

Springing from his position behind the column, Kael surged forward, drawing the curved crystal sword free of its scabbard. White light scattered in a million directions as the sword seemed to reflect and amplify the moonlight.

The Kaliel infantry slowed their advance at this strange sight.

Kael kept moving.

When he was within range, the first Kaliel soldier swung a double-edged sword in a forehand cut.

Kael did likewise.

A brilliant flash of light burst as the swords met. Kael expected resistance, but felt almost nothing. His sword continued on its path, cutting cleanly through the other man's sword as well as the upper portion of the man's chest and shoulder. The pointed half of the man's blade spun through the air and Kael flinched as it nearly hit him in the face.

The man slumped to the steps.

Kael had developed a deep respect for this weapon, but also realized that it would take some getting used to, and could be dangerous if not used properly.

Another two approached. The one on the right stabbed for Kael's midsection.

Kael parried the sword with the side of his own blade and stepped forward, inside the man's defenses. With a two-handed stroke, he cut through the man's belly and raised his sword to block the attack of the next.

In a matter of seconds, he would be surrounded. He could feel the enemy soldiers moving around his right flank, trying to pin him against the wall on his left. The other cavalry had dismounted and were moving up the steps.

Kael's sense detected a solution and he immediately obeyed. Lunging to the right, between two men, he broke free of the immediate tangle and struck out with a rapid flurry of attacks. Limbs were severed and swords dropped to the steps.

All of a sudden, Kael found that he had plowed through the small group and had thinned their numbers by half. He now stood a few steps from the top and had the high ground. His other men were engaged at the bottom of the stairs. Only six Kaliel remained facing him.

Behind them in the courtyard, the Orud infantry were still pinned down by the archers.

Kael surged forward, drawing attacks from two men who came forward to meet him. They both slashed for him, but he pulled back and let their attacks hit nothing but air. Then he moved in and took them down with one backhand slash.

The other four tightened their stance and moved in as a group, swords stabbing outward.

Kael moved back and ran into the wall.

They surged toward him again, thrusting with double-edged swords.

With a quick two-handed slash, Kael sliced through their swords. The blade tips fell to the steps, ringing loudly on the stone. Stepping back in the opposite direction, he cut through the three men on the left before he lost momentum.

The last man jumped back as his fellow soldiers slumped to the ground, dead before they touched the steps.

Kael quickly moved forward and plunged his blade into the man's chest. His aim was perfect; the man's heart stopped before he even realized what happened.

Kael pulled his sword free and ascended the steps, reaching down to pull a body off the stairs. Heaving the fleshly shield in front of him, he stepped out from behind the wall at the top of the stairs. Suddenly, the body was riddled with arrows. With one hand holding the body and the other his sword, Kael moved across the wall toward the gate, trying to make as much progress as possible before they got off another round.

He made it within a few feet of the first archer when they released their second volley. His shield took the brunt of the attack, but one of the arrows pierced his exposed left forearm as he lifted the body in front of him. He dropped the dead soldier and advanced, knowing that he only had a few seconds before the next round.

Bolting forward, Kael cut through the first man at a full run.

He dropped the second and third easily while they fumbled for the next arrow from their quivers.

The forth managed to let loose his next bolt, but it went wide and glanced off the stone wall to Kael's right. Kael cut through the man's bow and chest in one motion.

The last archer had retreated ten yards away to the arched doorway leading to the gate mechanism room. He stood with his bow fully drawn, aiming for Kael's chest.

Kael switched his sword to his left hand and moved a few cautious steps forward.

He could feel the man's intentions, like he was looking through his eyes.

The man made the decision to let go of the bow string.

Kael felt it.

The fingers loosened their grip.

Kael felt it.

The string went taught and projected the arrow forward.

Kael was already moving into a spin, raising his right arm and bringing it in front of his body.

The arrow passed by as Kael's back was turned from the archer.

The timing was perfect. The shaft of the arrow slid through Kael's fingers and held at its balance point. Continuing to spin, he used the velocity of the arrow to bring him around to face the enemy once again, releasing it back on its owner.

The arrow stuck in the man's neck and he dropped his bow. A look of complete shock came over him. Blood spurted from the wound and he grabbed for it, trying to hold it in. He dropped to his knees and looked back at Kael in unbelief. Then his face lost its color and he fell to the stone.

Kael looked down to the arrow protruding from his left forearm. The arrow head had gone clean through. He grabbed the shaft and pulled it the rest of the way through his arm, then cast is aside. His hand was tingling, but still had some sensation. He transferred the sword back to his right hand.

Through the arched doorway, he passed by large iron gears, ropes and pulleys that comprised the control mechanisms for the portcullis below. Toward the back of the room, a four-inch thick rusted iron rod was mounted on the stone wall with a swivel, allowing it to be moved into place to lock one of the main gears. One look told him that it was damaged and wouldn't operate as designed.

Kael gripped his sword with both hands and raised it overhead. As he brought the sword down, he pulled inward with his left hand, bringing the hilt closer to his body, causing the blade tip to accelerate with tremendous force. He felt the impact as the blade dug into the iron. A sharp clang deafened his ears as a flash of light blinded his eyes. A second later, the upper half of the iron rod fell to the floor, the severed end shiny and clean.

The freed gear spun rapidly and the squealing sound of the portcullis could be heard under his feet. Seconds later, a loud thud rumbled the earth as the portcullis slammed into the street beneath the arched gate.

Kael quickly moved to the opposite doorway and waited to the side.

A Kaliel infantryman came into the room with his sword drawn.

Kael slipped behind him and grabbed him by the neck, pushing his sword through the man's back and into his belly.

The soldier cried out in pain and surprise. His injury wasn't fatal, but he instantly became compliant.

Kael turned him around and pushed him through the door.

The nearest archer swung around and loosed his arrow right into the man's chest.

Kael pulled his sword free and pushed the man aside, dispatching the archer with one swift cut.

The remaining archer turned at the sound of the commotion.

Dacien, who had been pinned behind the wall on the opposite side, used the distraction to his advantage, lunging forward from his hiding spot.

The archer turned back and released his arrow.

Dacien was already too close and knocked the man's bow to the side with his sword. Blood from the man's hand splattered the wall as the arrow flew wide. Dacien dropped his shoulder and rammed into the soldier, pushing him backward and over the edge of the wall.

The Kaliel archer fell backward, thirty feet to land hard in the courtyard below.

Breathing heavily, Dacien rose to his feet.

Kael met his eyes for a moment, but neither said a word.

They both exhaled a sigh of relief.

Then Dacien walked over to the nearest arched window and pushed open the wooden shutter, looking for the ships in the bay. "It looks like half of the ships have docked," he said, almost breathless.

Kael was already waving for the Orud guard to come out of hiding. In the distance, the infantry from the northern wall had just arrived.

"We need to get these catapults armed and firing," Dacien said.

"Reinforcements are here," Kael announced. They had seen his signal and were now moving up the stairs on either side of the guard tower. As he turned back to Dacien, a thought occurred to him. "Dacien," he shouted over the rising sound of marching footsteps.

The General turned.

"What about the western bay?"

Dacien thought for a second. "The captain didn't say anything, but..."

"Exactly!"

Dacien paused, thinking through the possibility. "Take the cavalry and go as fast as you can. We can hold them now that the gate is shut."

Without a word, Kael turned and ran back through the doorway to the other side of the guard tower.

23

The sun peaked above the eastern horizon, sending bright rays across the wet landscape. The clouds were beginning to break up and reveal blue skies. All across the northern battlefield, the bodies of the Korgs covered the ground.

The captain smiled at the sight of the sun. They had made it through the evening without the walls being breached. It was quite an achievement. But now, the Korgan equipment was in place and they were beginning to launch their catapults. And still the masses continued to pour onto the fields in seemingly inexhaustible numbers.

To his right, a projectile landed on top of the wall between two towers. It missed the catapult, but took out a five foot section of the wall and three soldiers, raining debris down into the courtyard. The real battle had begun.

The captain looked out over the fields and waited for the signal.

General Aulus was completely exhausted. His arms felt so weak that he had trouble holding onto his sword. He was covered in Korgan blood from head to foot. Sometime during the night, one of the barbarians had cut his horse out from underneath him. He had fallen hard from the back of his horse and he was sure that bones in his left shoulder were shattered.

He gritted through the pain and struggled to hold his shield up. Only a half hour earlier, they had given up trying to slaughter the barbarians. They were only a few more yards away from the battlefield and he and his fellow soldiers were now resigned to literally pushing the Korgs out of their hiding places.

With a loud shout, he surged forward and his companions followed his lead. With shields locked into an impenetrable wall, they dug their feet into the ground and pushed with all their might. At first, it seemed impossible, but slowly, the crowds began to move.

As the enemy gave way to the power of the Orud infantry, it became easier and easier. The enemy started trampling one another in an attempt to get away.

Suddenly, Aulus' feet met with wet earth.   They had reached the battlefield. *Only a little farther now.*

The Korgs began to turn and run.

Aulus and his men ran in pursuit. All along the battlefront, he could see the spearmen and infantry surging forward. Their plan had succeeded.

The Korgs fell over the side of the first trench and were impaled on the long iron spikes embedded in the earth. Eventually, the bodies covered the ground and the rest of the barbarians landed safely on a cushion of their fellow soldiers.

Aulus stopped running. Turning back to the buildings behind him, he waved. Seconds later, bright red flags were being waved from the rooftops. Aulus turned back toward the city, wondering what was supposed to happen.

The catapults stopped firing.

Then in unison, as far as the eye could see, all the long range catapults atop the city walls sent up a volley of flaming projectiles. They hung in the air a moment before descending rapidly to land in the first trench and explode into flames.

Aulus walked forward a bit.

The flames began to spread quickly. It seemed odd that the oil inside the projectiles would spread so evenly. Within seconds, the entire trench was on fire. That's when Aulus realized that the trenches had been oiled.

The wall of flames shooting up from the trench burned hot and smelled of charred human flesh. Aulus looked down the length of the trench and saw nothing but flames in both directions. As soon as he gathered his wits, he began to move for the road that ran straight through the trenches and into the city gate. It was the only area that wasn't on fire.

"Follow me," he yelled. "If they try to escape, they'll use the road to do it."

Walking as quickly as his legs would carry him, he made his way to the mouth of the road twenty yards away. His men followed him, as did the remaining Orud soldiers that were now in disarray, scattered across the field between the buildings and the first trench. Before they could assemble, Korgs began to pour out of the opening in the flames. Aulus began to run. He wasn't sure where the strength came from, but he felt an urgency that bordered on panic. They had to keep the Korgs from escaping.

Already, some of his infantry who were nearer to the road were engaging the enemy. They were attacking at random without the usual disciplined formations, caught off guard by the moment.

Aulus arrived at the road and moved into the fray. He could now see down the road which was covered with the enemy. It was like looking through a gate of fire. Each successive trench was blazing and the Korgs that had managed to stay out of the ten foot deep gouges in the landscape were now trapped between walls of fire.

Suddenly, Aulus' eyes focused on one of the enemy. He stood a full head and shoulders above the rest of his counterparts. His tattooed skin and shaved head glistened with sweat and blood. He was surrounded by Orud infantry and was swinging a long, double-edged sword in wide arcs around himself. Everywhere he turned, soldiers dropped dead at his feet.

Aulus made his way toward the man that he knew to be the Korgan warlord. He had a score to settle. When he was only ten feet away, a dull thud sounded as a catapult boulder bounced off the road and slammed into the warlord. It violently shoved his body aside, crushing bone upon impact.

Aulus swung his sword wildly at the fleeing Korgs, cutting them down like wheat as he tried desperately to reach the enemy leader. When he arrived, he could see that the errant catapult fire had done the job that he wished for. The massive barbarian lay on the ground. The lower half of his body was twisted from the upper half as if they each had a mind of their own and decided to go their separate ways. His spine was clearly shattered, as well as his legs, which were splayed at odd angles.

Aulus looked down on the man with mixed emotions. He felt satisfaction that this beast of a man was dead. He felt a sense of relief that perhaps the struggles of the past decades were over. He felt cheated out of the glory that he wished for himself. But above all, he felt exhausted.

From atop the central guard tower along the north wall, the Captain of the Orud Guard watched as the enemy, trapped between the blazing ditches, fell beneath a shower of catapult fire. General Aulus' forces had succeeded in pushing the remnants of the enemy out of the buildings and onto the field, and now it was a slaughter. As predicted, the Korgs who couldn't move forward or backward began to press toward the road running to and from the captain's guard tower. All the catapult fire was concentrated in this densely populated area and they were ordered to keep firing until their ammunition was exhausted.

Most of the Korgs tried to escape, but some actually moved in toward the city walls. This was a mistake. When they cleared the last trench, they were within range of the archers. A thick rain of arrows fell on the closest of the invading forces and quickly stopped them from mounting an attack.

As the bolt throwers and other defensive machines began to run out of ammunition, the captain signaled for the ground forces to move in. The delay was longer than expected, but after several minutes he could see groups of cavalry, spearmen, and infantry moving across the fields between the trenches. Ahead of them, waves of the enemy scattered in retreat. But without anywhere to escape, they fell by the hundreds. The captain surveyed the fields and after hours of battle, concluded that the hundreds of thousands of barbarians had been nearly wiped out. The battle was won.

"Fire," Dacien yelled.

The rear line of archers released a volley of arrows over the top of the eastern wall, while the front aimed through the arched windows. The combined attack fell heavy on the forces of the Kaliel that were now assembled on the shore between the harbor and the city. The enemy soldiers, who had been expecting to breach the city through an open gate, were now trapped.

The gate was closed, and in the harbor, the Orud navy had finally assembled. An array of ships spread out to form a blockade preventing any escape. They were steadily moving inward, closing the gaps between them.

Some of the rearmost Kaliel ships turned to meet the navy. Dacien watched as two ships collided. Grappling ropes were thrown across the deck of the Kaliel ship, securing its retreat. Instantly, soldiers jumped from one deck to the other as hand-to-hand combat ensued.

"General," one of the frontline archers shouted.

Dacien ran toward the man and saw the uppermost supports of a siege ladder peering above the wall. Instinctively, the archers concentrated their fire at the ladder, but they only managed to hit half of the Kaliel that were quickly scaling the apparatus. Dacien was prepared. He waved for the infantry that were assembled in the courtyard to prevent a breach.

The first of the attackers came over the top of the wall and dropped six feet to the walkway. He was instantly met by Orud infantry hungry for some action. One by one, men came over the wall only to find that the city was well defended.

When the infantry had beaten back the attack, they pushed the ladder away from the walls with long poles. It finally fell backward on the crowds assembled below.

This appeared to be the last straw as the Kaliel began to retreat to their ships.

"General," a messenger announced from behind.

Dacien turned.

"They're ready."

"Perfect," Dacien replied. "Bring them up and get the catapults loaded."

"General, shall we give chase?" asked a lieutenant.

"Not yet," Dacien corrected. "Let them board their ships."

"Yes, Sir," the man replied, then ran away to convey the orders.

The retreat happened rapidly, and while the Kaliel boarded their ships and prepared to try their chances with the Orud navy, Dacien gave instructions to the soldiers manning the catapults. "Each one choose a ship. Aim carefully. Stay well away from our own ships. The navy can deal with any that slip by."

By the time Dacien got back to his vantage point, the catapults were ready and the Kaliel were moving away from the docks and entering the harbor. Raising his hand high into the air, Dacien brought it down and yelled, "fire!"

Of the first wave, only about a quarter found their mark. But the damage inflicted by the flaming projectiles was severe. Upon impact, the enemy ships were covered in flame. A few shots were slightly short and hit the hull of the ships at the waterline. The breached hulls quickly took on water and the ships began to sink.

"Reload," Dacien ordered.

Within seconds, he received the ready signal.

"Fire," he commanded a second time. This volley was more successful, with nearly three quarters of the shots finding their mark. As the ships burst into flames or sank into the calm water of the bay, Dacien signaled for the gates to be opened. The infantry moved out of the city and headed for the harbor, ready to intercept the hundreds of enemy soldiers flailing in the water, trying to reach the shore.

Dacien grinned with satisfaction. He and his men had succeeded in turning back the invading forces. He only hoped that Kael was faring as well.

24

The sound of hooves on stone rang out through the city streets. Kael drove his horse hard and the rest of the cavalry kept pace. The midmorning sun was obstructed by thick, low-hanging clouds which turned the light into a hazy gray. The streets were still wet from last night's rain.

As he had now become accustomed to doing, Kael felt out the passage ahead with his sense. The more he made use of his ability, the easier it became. Then something passed overhead that grabbed his attention.

Turning in the saddle, he looked to the clouds behind him and saw just the faint outline of something large and dark moving within the mists. Though a signal of fear went through his heart, he couldn't help but smile. The All Powerful was heading east and would only find that his forces had been defeated.

Turning around to face front, Kael concentrated on the immediate task of making his way to the western gate. No doubt, the All Powerful had just come from there. And if that was the case, the situation wouldn't be favorable to him and his men. Of that he was sure.

After a few minutes, the terrain began to slope downward toward the bay. The elevation wasn't steep enough to view the bay from his vantage point. The surrounding buildings obstructed the view of everything but the sky, but he knew that they were nearing the western gate.

Sending out his sense in a broad effort, Kael surveyed the streets leading toward the gate and the docks beyond. Everywhere he searched there were pockets of men fighting in the streets and the buildings. The Kaliel had breached the city walls. Everywhere they spread, the Resistance soldiers were struggling to hold them back, defending the Empire that had once been their enemy.

Kael veered to the left and down an alley heading for the densest part of the confrontation. As soon as he came out of the alley he had to dodge men on foot. Orud archers were retreating quickly, stopping occasionally to shoot some arrows at the few Kaliel infantry that were in pursuit.

Kael pulled his sword from the scabbard on his waist and turned to the right. Heading straight for the Kaliel infantry, he was surprised to see that they didn't even try to evade his cavalry. They had clearly grown brave and were focused on chasing down the archers.

The men on horse trampled over the Kaliel. Kael held tight to the reins with his left hand as his trained horse plowed through the insignificant obstacles. Those who didn't fall beneath the hooves of the beasts were cut down with swords.

Continuing west, Kael's cavalry entered another narrow street, this one packed with Resistance soldiers. Looking down the street, Kael could see that it opened into a wide courtyard where hundreds of Kaliel were gathered. It looked as though the men of the Resistance were trying to use the benefit of the narrow streets to their advantage. The Kaliel were held in the courtyard and any attempts to make further advances would lead them into the narrow corridors where their numbers couldn't help them.

"Make way," Kael shouted as they approached the rear of the Resistance line.

As soon as they saw the cavalry, the men gladly parted.

Kael was the first to burst free of the crowd and enter the courtyard. The Kaliel scattered before him and his cavalry, which gave them time to assemble into formation. A second later, they veered to the left and began to circle the courtyard.

The enemy began to cluster in groups to meet them.

Kael spurred his horse faster. Slashing in forehand, then backhand strokes, his crystal sword cut through flesh as if through water. There was almost no resistance as heads and arms were separated from bodies. First the right side, then he attacked on his left. Kaliel blood began to darken the stones underfoot.

Behind him, he felt one of his men go down. The enemy was packed so tightly that the horses were beginning to slow down. Kael pulled the reins slightly to the right and his horse broke into a pocket of open area. The others followed him and they immediately picked up their speed.

Kael looked ahead and sensed the path that they should take through the sparse areas where their speed and height could be used to its full advantage. They were now on the western side of the circular courtyard and starting back to the east. Kael made sure to steer for the outskirts of the crowds, taking down rows of the enemy with each pass.

To his dismay, the Resistance soldiers were emboldened by the presence of the cavalry and began to push out of the narrow streets. This increased the density of people in the courtyard and by the time they had returned to the eastern end, it was unsafe to continue.

Kael steered out of the courtyard and down the nearest street, moving slowly and awkwardly through the ranks of the Resistance who now wore smiles on their faces. Once free of the crowds, Kael pulled to a stop and counted his men. As he suspected, only one fell in the skirmish.

"Captain, where do we go now?"

Kael held up his hand while he searched with his sense. About twenty yards to the northwest was one of the main thoroughfares that had been vacant only moments ago. Now, Kael could feel hundreds of Kaliel soldiers marching in formation down the wide street and making considerable progress into the city.

"This way," he hissed, kicking the sides of his horse. Heading down an alley, he crossed two narrow streets before coming out onto the main road.

On both sides of the street, Orud archers had just assembled on the rooftops and were firing down upon the Kaliel infantry. Without shields, the Kaliel began moving more quickly to break free of the attack overhead. Unfortunately, there weren't any opposing infantry on the ground to stop their advance. They came straight for Kael and his cavalry.

Kael turned his horse to face the enemy and pulled back on the reins, causing his horse to stand on its hind legs and strike the air with its front hooves. When he came back to the ground, his men were lined up beside him and the archers above were cheering.

"Strike and move, men. Don't let them bring you to a stop or you won't last long."

A shout went up from the rest of the cavalry. They burst into motion and headed straight for the oncoming enemy.

The collision was audible as sword struck sword and horses trampled men. With the sudden change in motion from a run to a stop, one of Kael's men went down, then another. Hacking his way free of the tangle, Kael circled back to the open space. With only a second's pause, he headed back, taking a diagonal strike at the front lines. The rest of his men followed suit, attacking at random. It was effective and already the bodies were becoming obstacles for the other soldiers to get over. But every couple minutes, another of Kael's men fell. In all, he had lost five, already.

Then, Kael circled back away from the advancing enemy and stopped. "Fall back," he shouted.

His men looked confused, but obeyed, quickly circling back to Kael.

"What are we doing?" one of them asked.

The Kaliel army shouted in triumph and surged ahead.

Kael looked back to his men. "Just wait."

As the Kaliel neared, the horses began to fidget, anticipating the confrontation. The men gripped their swords tighter, growing nervous with each step of the advancing soldiers.

But Kael remained still, staring defiantly at the crowds.

Suddenly, Resistance infantry began to pour out from the alleyways on either side of the street. They were armed with swords and quickly filled in the space between the cavalry and the enemy. There were only about eighty men in all, but the sight of such a group made the Kaliel slow in their tracks.

Kael turned to his men, who now numbered only nineteen. "Follow me. We can be more useful approaching from a different angle."

Ducking down an alley to the right, Kael came out into a narrow street. He turned left and rode up several streets before turning left down another alley, heading back for the main street and the enemy. He had judged the distance correctly and they were now barreling down a narrow passage that would open into the enemy ranks about ten yards behind the front lines.

In single file, the cavalry broke out of the alley and into the ranks of the Kaliel. Kael struck swiftly and tried to clear a path for those behind him. His sword slashed in broad strokes, felling men on all sides. Behind him, the other cavalry stabbed and slashed their way through, keeping up with Kael's pace. In less than a minute, they broke free of the battle and entered an alley on the opposite side. When they came out into another narrow street, Kael paused and waited for the last man to catch up. All nineteen survived.

They looked exhausted and most were covered in blood.

Kael lifted his sword and used it to point at an alley a few more streets up. "Shall we?" he asked. The men smiled in return, but their expressions quickly changed. Kael looked back and saw the previously deserted street filling up with dark clothed soldiers, coming out of the alley they were going to use for their next attack.

The fifty foot soldiers quickly lined up in formation before a rider came into sight. It was Soren, atop his warhorse, and this meeting was no accident. His eyes were locked on Kael.

For a moment, the two stared defiantly at each other. Then Kael sensed Soren's thoughts as he prepared to call his master. "Are you such a slave to him that you can no longer fight on your own?" Kael yelled, his voice ringing off the stone walls and street.

Suddenly, he felt Soren's distress call evaporate before it even began.

"I see you carry the sword that has killed hundreds of my brethren. It appears we all have our crutches." The seething words were filled with hatred.

Kael dismounted from his horse and began to walk down the alley toward Soren. The cavalry followed, but at a distance, knowing instinctively that this was a private fight. "The difference," Kael shouted, "is that I don't need this to kill you."

Soren smiled and Kael was instantly reminded of how easily this man could be made to laugh when he was only a boy. He had a contagious sense of humor and enjoyed telling jokes even more than he enjoyed their combat training.

Soren's soldiers parted, understanding the situation without orders.

"...very well then. Man to man. No tricks," Soren replied, dismounting his horse.

"Indeed," Kael replied, lowering his sword to the ground.

As Soren moved forward between his guards, he pulled two swords from scabbards on either side of his belt. He held one by the base of the blade, ready to toss it to Kael, but hesitated.

Kael left the crystal sword on the cold stone and walked several steps away from it with his hands held outward, showing that he could be trusted.

Soren waited, then tossed the sword to Kael.

Now, they were evenly matched.

"Finally, after all these years...a worthy opponent," Soren said, walking a few steps forward. "I hope you don't disappoint me like Ukiru. He died so easily that I couldn't even enjoy it."

Kael gripped the sword with two hands and raised it to a ready position. Questions ran through his mind. *Soren is deceived just as I was. Can he be reasoned with? What did they do to him while I was away? If they would only stop attacking, then none of this would be necessary!* There was so much to say, so much that had occurred since they last saw each other. But in this moment, it didn't matter. Nothing would be resolved with words. Words were useless; he could see it in his enemy's eyes.

Soren mimicked Kael's actions with precision, keeping his sword at just the right position so that neither man would be at a disadvantage. They slowly circled each other and moved inward, making slight adjustments to the position of their grip, the angle of their swords, or their stance. It was a face-off that wouldn't have made sense to other less-informed warriors. But both men understood that all it took was a split second to gain the upper hand.

The smell of rain on stone.

The sound of distant battle.

The cool breeze flowing down the street.

Kael's senses drank in the moment, heightened in self-preservation. He shifted his weight, feigning a mistake and Soren attacked instantly with a downward cut. Kael was ready and blocked the attack, countering with a flurry of strikes to the head, which Soren blocked one after the other. The clang of steel on steel rang down the street.

Both men returned to their defensive postures and studied each other, weighing what they had just learned from their first encounter. Kael was impressed with Soren's speed and strength. It was clear that he had kept current with his training.

Soren attacked again, rushing in with a stab to the midsection.

Kael dodged to the side and parried the thrust.

Soren continued to advance steadily, attacking at random to see how Kael would react. He was studying his enemy, probing to see what lurked beneath the calm exterior.

Kael knew what he was doing and decided to play into it. He blocked all of the attacks effortlessly, but deliberately left himself vulnerable on his right side.

After the third such mistake, Soren went for the kill, slashing at Kael's abdomen.

Kael was ready and stepped into the attack, blocking the sword with his own in a one-handed grip, while he grabbed Soren's wrist with the other. He pivoted on his right foot while violently wrenching Soren's arm and flipping his body over an outstretched leg.

Soren lost his balance and fell to the ground, his sword slipping from his paralyzed hand.

Kael quickly followed with a knee to Soren's face, snapping his head backward as a spurt of blood shot from his mouth.

Soren rolled to his back to get free from the situation, now at a great advantage.

Kael pursued him, slashing as Soren began to rise to his feet.

But Soren was quick, dropping back into a roll and spinning, knocking Kael's feet out from under him. Then he pounced on Kael, pinning him to the ground where Kael's sword was useless.

Now on his back, with Soren on top of him, Kael dropped his sword and pulled his arms inward to block his face as Soren began to beat on him with his fists. Most of the blows glanced off Kael's arms, but a few connected with his face and stung.

Soren, not satisfied at the result, reached down and grabbed two handfuls of Kael's hair. He tugged sharply, lifting Kael's head off the ground, then slammed the back of Kael's head into the stone.

An explosion of pain shot through Kael's skull and threatened to take his consciousness. He knew he wouldn't survive another such attack. He quickly pulled his right leg in and delivered a powerful kick to Soren's midsection that lifted him in the air.

It knocked the wind out of Soren's lungs and caught him by surprise.

Kael took the opportunity and rolled to the side, getting to his feet as swiftly as possible. When he gained his footing, Soren had also recovered.

Now the two faced each other. Soren's mouth was covered in blood coming from his nose. Even though he wore a blank expression, Kael knew that he was enjoying himself. Kael could feel his own face bleeding from a gash above his eye. Both men were now breathing hard.

Kael lunged forward.

Soren met him with a spinning kick.

But Kael was already inside and blocked the kick with his shoulder, delivering a sharp kick to Soren's supporting leg. As Soren fell to his knees, Kael rammed his fist into his face and the man spun to the ground.

For a moment, Kael though it was over.

But Soren raised his head and smiled, his face a bloody mess.

Kael looked past his face and saw that one hand had closed around the hilt of the crystalline sword on the ground.

Kael backed away with caution.

Soren rose to his feet with a triumphant look in his eyes.

Kael knew the time for fighting man to man was over. If Soren was too much of a coward to finish this the way they started, then he would only die that much quicker. Kael drew in a deep breath and closed his eyes, calming his soul to engage his sense.

The change must have been visible because Soren went on guard immediately.

When Kael opened his eyes, he could feel Soren's fear and anger. As Soren advanced, Kael could feel and anticipate the movement of every muscle in the man's body.

Soren raised the powerful weapon and charged.

Kael stood his ground and stretched his arms out to either side of his body, feeling the volume of space contained between the walls on either side of the street. Every soldier, horse, and weapon, was an extension of his body. And just as if they were other appendages, the two swords lying in the street only a few yards away began to obey him. They shot into motion and slid across the pavestones until they made their way into Kael's hands.

In the instant before Soren attacked, Kael dropped into a crouch with one sword shielding his left shoulder and the other extended in a low swinging arc.

Soren slashed at the air where Kael had been.

Kael's crude blade tore through Soren's abdomen with a deep gash, while the crystalline blade just missed his own head, slicing through his other sword and cutting into the flesh of his left shoulder.

Soren crumpled to the ground next to Kael, his face suddenly pale. The crystalline sword dropped from his hand and he fell forward, propped up on one hand.

Kael remained on his knees, looking into Soren's eyes.

The narrow street had suddenly grown quiet.

It was a fatal wound and Soren knew it. He turned to look at Kael.

The two men stared at each other, neither saying a word, but communicating nonetheless. They had been friends at one time. They had shared joy and pain, experienced trials and triumphs together. But it all seemed so long ago, another life.

Kael watched the life slowly drain from Soren's face, as he lowered himself to the ground. With his face pressed against the cold street, Soren's breathing became shallow. His eyes continued to stare into Kael's and it seemed that long moments passed.

Eventually, Kael realized that there was no more life in the eyes. He wasn't sure of the exact moment it happened, but he knew now that he was only looking at a corpse. Kael reached over and closed Soren's eyes. He wanted to say something, but words seemed grossly inadequate. Instead, he lingered for a moment, then grabbed his own sword and rose to his feet. Behind him, the cavalry waited for a signal. In front of him, the Kaliel soldiers stood ready, trying to comprehend their loss.

Kael knew that the war wasn't over. The enemy wouldn't stop just because they lost Soren. But then a familiar sound rose. From all around them, the sound of marching echoed off the walls and rang through the streets. The footsteps grew louder and louder. With each stomp, he could now hear the clank of metal and the grunts of men's voices, chanting as they marched.

Kael backed away from the Kaliel, who now looked worried. Turning back to the east, Kael ran down the street and ducked into an alley. When he emerged onto the main thoroughfare, he saw that the crowds of Kaliel had stopped their forward march.

To the east, the wide road disappeared around a bend and the first ranks of the Orud spearmen could be seen. Just in front of them, Dacien and the Captain of the Orud Guard rode on horseback. Row upon row of men followed them. Now infantry could be seen. At the left and right flanks, archers marched as well. There were thousands. The reinforcements had arrived.

Kael looked across the street and down the alley, seeing more red cloaks, the color of Orud. He turned back to the alley from which he had come and could see men moving west along that street, as well. The fact that Dacien and the captain were both present meant that the other battles had been won. Now all the Orud forces had gathered to meet the Kaliel in this part of the city. And they were surrounding the enemy on all sides.

The formations marched forward until they were fifty yards away. Then they stopped in perfect unison. Again there was silence.

Dacien's voice rang out. "You will never prevail against the armies of Orud."

Defiant shouts burst forth from the Orud and Resistance soldiers, filling the streets with such a mighty sound that nothing else could be heard.

Slowly, the Kaliel began to move backward, clearly outnumbered.

Dacien's voice rose above the noise. "Charge," he shouted. Instantly, the ranks of spearmen burst into motion, advancing at a run while maintaining their formation.

Kael stepped aside into a nearby alley and let them pass. Row after row of soldiers marched toward the Kaliel, who were now in retreat. After the last row of spearmen, the archers followed, firing their arrows overhead as they moved. After the archers passed, Kael stepped out to meet Dacien and the captain.

Dacien looked down from his horse. "We couldn't let you have all the fun."

Kael smiled.

"Where's your horse?"

Kael looked back through the alley. "...on the next street. You go ahead; I'll catch up." He patted Dacien's horse on the rump and turned back down the alley.

Suddenly, a loud shriek echoed through the streets, deafening the ears. The sound of marching stopped almost instantly, followed by an eerie silence. Kael was tempted to search with his sense, but he already knew it was the All Powerful. Turning back, he walked slowly and when he reached the end of the alley, he stopped and peered around the corner. He saw the backs of the Orud infantry as they slowly stepped backward, as if scared to make a sound.

Over their heads was a ghastly sight. Between the Orudan army and the Kaliel, an area had opened up free of soldiers from either army. In the void stood a black-skinned creature, ten feet tall. It had veined skin wings like a bat, translucent except for the bones that ran through them, supporting their thirty foot span. Its body rippled with thin muscle as it extended its arms as an open invitation for someone to challenge it. In one hand it held what looked to be a dark crystalline walking stick.

Kael looked down to his own sword, knowing that he was witnessing something significant that would require consideration when this was all over.

The creature took a step forward, and the Orud soldiers took several steps backward in repulsion and fear. The creature's face reminded Kael of the giant beast-man he encountered in the forests of Leoran and he knew without a doubt that the beast was the offspring of this winged monster.

Slowly, the wings pulled inward and wrapped around the creature, draping its frame like a cloak. Then it lunged forward and swung the crystal stick into the ranks of infantry. Several men went down, while others flew through the air and landed against the walls of the nearby buildings, before dropping dead to the stone street.

The crowds backed up, not wanting to break formation, but not able to overcome the fear that now gripped their hearts. With a look of amusement, the creature held up his hand and the first twenty rows of Orud spearmen burst into flames. They immediately scattered in all directions, screaming hysterically and beating themselves to put out the fire that consumed their flesh. This unbelievable sight drove fear into the hearts of all who witnessed it, a tangible overwhelming fear.

Kael looked down and closed his eyes. *This is it. This is the moment.* His breath seemed loud in his ears, interrupted only by the sound of his beating heart. *You've always known that your death would come violently,* he told himself. *Let it be glorious!*

Kael choked down his fear, then stepped out of the alley and into the street, to join the ranks of the Orud armies who were standing motionless. As he looked into the eyes of the soldiers, he saw a fierce determination; he saw men who had just come to terms with their own mortality and were seconds away from the end of this life; he saw courage mixed with sadness, and he realized that he was not alone.

Slowly, the armies of Orud began to move forward, first at a walk, then at a jog, then at a sprint.

Kael ran with them, his knuckles white as he gripped the crystalline sword, hungry to spill demon blood.

The winged beast appeared to shriek in rage, but he was drowned out by the triumphant shouts of the soldiers.

At a full run, the frontlines of the pikemen moved into formation, forming a wall of shields with foot-long spear heads protruding at different lengths. This formed the center of the force, while the infantry followed suit. Their shields were larger and created an impenetrable barricade, separated only by steel blades of their short swords. The archers dropped back so that the spearmen and infantry filled the entire width of the street.

At this sight, the Resistance soldiers turned around to face the winged beast and his armies. They raised their swords in the air and charged as well.

Kael ran as fast as his legs would carry him, focused on the All Powerful. As he and other soldiers came within feet of the creature, it leapt into the air and unfurled its wings. The powerful downward thrust sent the creature fifty feet into the air and sent shockwaves through the ranks below.

Kael was pinned to the ground by the wind as it rushed past his face. His ears felt like they would explode. When the sensation passed, Kael got to his feet and looked up.

The All Powerful hovered for a moment, looking down on the masses below, then flew off to the west. The Kaliel army followed their god, retreating at a full run, and by the time the sun was touching the western horizon, the western gate had been shut and the Kaliel were sailing away from the docks toward the northern ocean.

Kael stood on the western ramparts next to Dacien, watching the retreating silhouettes of the black ships. "This will be a day that people will remember," Kael said quietly.

Without taking his gaze from the ships in the bay, Dacien replied. "Indeed...men of the Empire as well as the Resistance, standing side by side against a common enemy. The Empire has been united. We're stronger now than we have been in many years."

The shouts of the surrounding soldiers were deafening. Kael raised his voice over the crowd. "I assume there will be a celebration tonight."

Dacien turned. "I imagine so!"

After a few minutes, the ships faded into the horizon and the cheering died down.

Dacien turned around and watched as the soldiers clasped each other's arms and embraced, enjoying the victory.

Kael continued to watch the horizon as the sun shrank by the second. "You know..." he mused. "I know where they're going."

Dacien turned around. "What did you say?"

Kael turned to look at him. "...the High Temple. It can hold hundreds of ships within its walls."

Dacien paused for a moment, studying Kael. "You're not done fighting, are you?"

"No," Kael replied honestly. "That demon is still out there. As long as he's alive and people are willing to fight for him, the Kaliel remain a threat."

"What do think you can do against such power?" Dacien countered.

Kael smiled. "Yes...power. But why did it hold back? Why didn't it just annihilate our forces in an instant? Surely not for lack of ability! It's because it fears for its own life. And something that fears can be killed!"

Dacien pondered these words for a moment. Then, he answered carefully. "I would much rather celebrate with these good men, but I have to agree with you. I can have the navy ready in two hours."

"Good," Kael replied.

"Tell me about this temple. Where is it and what will be our plan of attack?"

Kael smiled and put his hand on Dacien's shoulder. "I'll tell you on the way."

25

The journey from the eastern bay of Orud to the eastern coast of Bastul took five days by boat. The Council was ready to forget about their troubles as quickly as possible, but Dacien managed to convince them of his need for thirty of their warships and the full complement of soldiers. They agreed, reluctantly. But that was good enough.

While they traveled, everyone caught up on sleep from the exhausting battle. Kael and Dacien planned their strategy as Kael divulged everything that he could remember about the High Temple. The soldiers worked at mounting bolt throwers to the decks of the ships in preparation for a battle at sea. And then they waited.

As they neared the southern tip of the Empire, they slowed their progress, intending to attack under the cover of darkness. Bastul was still miles away, but the end of the coastline could be seen on the horizon as the sun sank into the west. Dacien ordered his ship to a stop and set anchor in the shallows of a nearby sandy bay. He decided it would be a good opportunity for everyone to stretch their legs and rest before the battle. The other ships fell behind and lined up along the beach.

When they were all ashore, Dacien had a small meal prepared so that everyone had sufficient energy. As they ate boiled fish and bread, Dacien found Kael sitting alone on a rock, just near enough to the rest of the soldiers to hear the conversation. He sat down next to his friend. "Are you ready to do this?" he asked.

Kael looked up from his meal. "I've wanted this for many years, but I haven't been ready until now."

"How are you going to do it?" Dacien asked, suddenly concerned for his friend's life. "I've seen you do amazing things, but..." he trailed off.

Kael waited for him to finish his thought.

"...this winged creature is unlike anything I've seen. It's like the gods of old have been resurrected."

"Hmm," Kael mumbled, nodding in confirmation.

"This is suicide," Dacien said, finally reaching his point.

"I thought you were behind this. Why are you telling me this now?"

Dacien was worried for his friend's life, but somehow it didn't seem like a good enough reason to call off the attack. Instead, he looked out over the ocean. "Here we are on the verge of another battle and it occurred to me that we've already won. There aren't enough of them to be a threat to the Empire. You and I have a safe place once again to call home. And the more I consider it, the more I think this is unnecessary."

Kael turned to look at Dacien with a distant gaze in his eyes. "I have no home," he said quietly.

Dacien was taken aback. "Look around you," he countered, not bothering to hide his anger. "These men have come here for you. They are risking their lives for you."

"And I have risked my life for them, as well. I had a home once...many years ago. And it was stolen from me and I from it. I haven't been the same ever since. Do you remember when we first met in Bastul?"

"Of course. You saved my life," Dacien replied, his tone softening.

"I was lost, Dacien. I was lost and searching. I only came back to Bastul because it was the only place where I ever felt safe. And what I realized that day was that I couldn't get back what was stolen from me. I was without purpose. And then you befriended me and it was some small measure of consolation to kill the Syvaku who had destroyed my home. I have enjoyed our time together, and living in Leoran is the closest I've come to happiness. But it's not my home. And I suspect it won't be yours soon enough."

Dacien looked down, not knowing what to say.

"But you know something? When I think back on all the events of my past, I now see a purpose. I probably won't survive this night, but this demon won't either. And that is my purpose. I was meant to put an end to all of this. They trained me and made me what I am. And if I die tonight, then so be it. Because this ability that I have, these skills that you find so intriguing, are really only a curse under any other circumstances."

Dacien opened his mouth to speak, but he didn't have the words. It troubled him deeply to hear his friend talking this way, but he couldn't think of an argument. After a long pause, he finally spoke. "You may be right, Kael. If anyone could put an end to these people, it's you." Dacien rose to his feet. "We'd better push off if we want to arrive at midnight."

Kael looked up with a determined look in his eyes. "Thank you."

Dacien smiled. "If we don't see each other after this night, it's been an honor to fight along side you. Now get up and let's go before I change my mind."

"This is the spot," Kael said, barely above a whisper.

"Okay men, this is the spot," Dacien echoed.

The crew untied the ropes holding a small boat to the hull of the larger ship. Slowly, they lowered it into the water.

Kael let the other two men go over the side first, then followed them until he was seated at the stern of the small rowboat. Each of the men grabbed an oar and immediately began to dig into the water. As they moved out away from the larger sailing vessel, Dacien came to the railing and put up his hand. It was a silent goodbye.

Kael waved back, wondering if this was the last time he would see his friend. Minutes later, Dacien's ship began to glide to the south with the wind filling its sails. Turning around, Kael gazed west over the smooth waters of the ocean. In that direction was the reef that followed the coastline all the way to Bastul. With the western shore of Bastul to the rear, the small rowboat sat directly east of the High Temple with only the shallow waters of the reef separating them. The plan was to approach unseen over the reef, while Dacien and the Orud navy would approach the Temple from the south where a passage in the reef had been cleared for deep hulled ships. Hopefully, the distraction would allow Kael to get into the Temple without much conflict. And that was as far as his plan went.

Kael waited, and waited, while the two men rowed silently. The night sky was black, but for the multitude of stars shining. The moon hung low on the northern horizon. Even with the faint light, Kael felt confident that they could make it all the way to the walls of the temple without being seen. That was, if Dacien did his job.

Kael studied the pattern of the stars and determined that it was nearly midnight. And though he couldn't see it, he could feel the temple due west about a half mile. "We're getting close."

The two men glanced back over their shoulders between strokes. "I don't see anything," one of them replied.

"And you won't until were almost upon it," Kael responded.

The minutes passed tensely, as Kael contemplated what he was about to do. It didn't help to think about it too far in advance. But now that the moment was here, he ran through the consequences in his mind. He remembered his encounter with Narian in the forests of Leoran. It was the first time since leaving the monastery that he fought someone who presented a challenge. And it had taken him by surprise. Since then, from Arden and Horace in the temple, to Soren in the streets of Orud, Kael had been better prepared.

But the All Powerful? How do I prepare for a fight with a being so formidable? What he did to those soldiers...I don't stand a chance! This had to be something more that a suicide mission. Kael had to succeed, even if he had to sacrifice his own life in the process. *Otherwise, all of this—these men*

*risking their lives to get me into the temple–is for nothing! I can't let them
down. And I can't allow a demon to walk this earth.*

Kael took in a deep breath of the sea air and tried to clear his mind.

Straight ahead, the temple came into view. Now only a hundred yards
out, it was still difficult to see, even when you knew what to look for. The
polished metal sheets that covered the exterior of the circular wall served to
reflect the image of the surrounding sea, camouflaging it from all but the
most determined eyes.

Kael held up his hand and the rowers stopped. It quickly grew quiet.
Kael looked up at the stars. It was now past midnight. He listened intently.
Finally, he heard the clank of a bolt thrower.

"They are engaging the enemy. Let's move."

The rowers hauled back on the oars and the boat lurched forward.

As they neared the temple wall, Kael sent out his sense with caution,
trying to determine if anyone was on the western wall. He had to be careful
not to reveal himself to the All Powerful, so he concentrated his efforts only
on the top of the wall. After a few minutes, he sensed the passing of two
guards, running in the direction of the southern gate, but no one else.

Inwardly, he smiled with satisfaction. There was no need to guard the
western side of the temple because it butted up against the reef which
protected it from any sizeable threat. And with Dacien's forces moving in
from the south, all attention was drawn there.

After a few minutes, they reached the wall. Kael scanned the seams of
the metal sheets for a crevice large enough to get his fingers into. After
moving around slightly to the north, he found one that ran up to a lookout
portal.

He pointed to it and the rowers nodded silently, carefully dipping their
oars into the water. As the boat glided over to the wall, Kael stood and
reached out, sliding his fingers into the gap between the metal sheets. Then
he turned his hand so that it was wedged into place. He followed suit with
his other hand, then stepped out of the boat and hung from his hands, with
his feet flat against the temple wall.

He turned back to the Orud soldiers and nodded.

Quickly and quietly, they turned the boat and headed back toward the
west.

Compared to the walls of the Royal Palace in Orud, it was a relatively
easy climb of thirty feet. Kael stopped where the seam ran into another panel
of metal that was hinged at the top and unfastened on the other three sides.
It was a lookout window that opened from the inside. Sending out his sense,
he found no one on the other side. Quietly, he pried his fingers under the
metal and lifted. The window opened slowly on its own weight. Kael pulled
himself up into the opening and slid over the threshold, dropping to the

walkway. He rolled on his back and then to his feet, pausing for a second to take in the sight with his eyes.

The walkway on which he stood ran all the way around the temple. Beneath him were stalls where boats had once been moored, but were now empty. To his left near the southern gate, there was much activity as boats were lined up in the harbor, waiting to exit the gate and meet Dacien's attack. In the sky, an object blotted out the stars as it flew to the south. Its shape couldn't be discerned from this distance, but Kael knew who it was.

After waiting until it was safe, Kael stood and straightened his Kaliel uniform, confiscated from one of the unfortunate invaders of Orud. Then he began to move north along the walkway, away from the activity.

Dacien had hoped to reach the temple quickly enough to prevent the Kaliel's ships from getting clear of the channel that had been dug at the southern side. But the enemy responded more quickly than he expected. When it became apparent that his primary plan would have to be abandoned, he had his signal man light a torch and send the message to the other ships to fan out.

Implementing the secondary plan, his lighter and smaller ships took up the center point of the attack with the larger and heavily-armored ships behind them. The midsized ships moved to the left and right flanks and held their position. Then, they lowered their sails and masts, and put out the oars. It was an unusual formation, and one that Dacien hoped would confuse the enemy.

The Kaliel fleet was still large, even after their defeat at Orud. Already, forty ships of various sizes had exited the outer wall and still more were waiting inside. They moved in single file along the cleared route until they reached deeper water where they spread out into a wider formation.

Dacien gave the signal and his midsized ships advanced along the flanks. As soon as they were within range, they utilized the bolt throwers and focused on the single file ships trapped inside the passage that had been cleared through the reef.

Within seconds, two of the enemy ships began to sink as their hulls were penetrated by the iron spears. Almost immediately, the Kaliel returned fire.

Dacien was surprised to see several of his own ships go down. The projectiles from the enemy ships skipped across the water until they lost momentum or slammed into the hull at the water line. Their weapons were much more effective.

Feeling that he was loosing the upper hand, Dacien gave the signal for the rest of the ships to begin the charge. There were roughly an equal number of Kaliel ships in open water which meant that his attack would have maximum effectiveness. He moved to the prow of his large, armored war ship and readied himself for the attack. Just off the starboard bow, one of his smaller and faster ships took the lead and began to distance itself from his own. Dacien's heartbeat quickened at the impending confrontation.

The Kaliel projectiles skated across the water on either side of his ship, missing by only a few feet. Fifty yards ahead, the smaller ship neared the first of the enemy ships. It was on a path for a head-on collision. Dacien held his breath in anticipation. Just before impact, the smaller ship veered sharply to one side and pulled its oars in. The midsized Kaliel ship didn't have time to react. The smaller Orud vessel just dodged the prow of the enemy vessel and raked its port side along with all the oars. As the two ships narrowly missed each other, broken oars littered the water. The soldiers in the enemy ship, not understanding what had just happened, continued to row for a few strokes on one side, causing it to turn and expose its flank.

Dacien crouched and grabbed hold of a railing as his larger vessel with its armored prow rammed the starboard flank of the Kaliel ship. The timing was perfect and the strategy was devastatingly effective. Dacien almost lost his footing as the ram shattered the hull and deck of the enemy vessel. After the initial impact, he jumped to his feet and raced forward with a spear in his hand. The rest of his crew did the same. Just as he reached the bow of the ship, a Kaliel soldier came over the railing and landed awkwardly on the deck.

Dacien rushed forward and speared the man in the chest before he could get his bearings. The man pitched backward over the railing and fell into the water. The other Kaliel soldiers that had gone overboard at the collision were quickly dispatched by the Orud archers.

Dacien looked ahead to the smaller Orud ship now advancing on another enemy and smiled. To his left and right all his other ships had been successful, as well. Roughly fifteen Kaliel ships had gone down in the first charge.

"Alright Kael," he said to himself. "We're doing our part, now do yours."

The gigantic cavern that stretched out before him was just as he remembered it. The perfectly flat ground was covered with sand. The torches that lined the perimeter were never allowed to go out, and cast a menacing glow throughout. At the center of the cavern was a moat with a stone dais at its center.

This is it, the place where I first met and defied the All Powerful. How fitting then, that it should also be where all this trouble comes to an end.

Kael walked out into the cavern and surveyed his surroundings. Though he knew that Dacien was out there, right now, fighting on his behalf, he couldn't bring himself to face the All Powerful, yet.

Am I crazy? Can I really defeat him?

Suddenly, something bright at the corner of his vision interrupted his thoughts. Kael turned his head. Something shiny lay against the wall to his right. He walked to it and knelt down.

To his surprise, it was another sword like the one in his hand. He reached down and picked it up. It was slightly heavier. He compared the two side by side. The similarity was remarkable. Then he looked at it with the aide of his sense and could see that it was only ordinary glass.

A confused smile crossed his lips as he realized what he was holding. The master blade smith at the fortress city had given him the crystal sword, encased in more ordinary trappings. Surely such a treasured possession would have a place of honor among his people, but he had disguised it and given it to Kael as he left the city. Perhaps he hadn't wanted it to fall into the wrong hands. *...which would explain the need for this impostor to take its place. What a clever old man!*

But Kael wondered how this fake had made its way here. After a moment, he gave up on the thought. He was grateful for the momentary distraction, but now it was time to face the reason for this journey. He dropped the sword into the sand and stood up, walking back to the middle of the arena. When he was near the moat at the center, he sent out his sense, pushing it through the hole in the ceiling and into the open sea air, searching for his enemy.

26

The initial attack had gone perfectly and Dacien was encouraged by its success. Though the Kaliel's weaponry was superior, the skill of the Orudan naval tactics had placed them all in close quarters where projectiles didn't matter. And the Kaliel had lost almost half of their ships in the process.

Dacien waited with the other soldiers on the deck of a large and heavily armored ship. In unison, the men heaved on thick ropes and pulled the smaller Kaliel vessel toward them; the grappling hooks held fast to the enemy ship and secured it from escaping.

As soon as the flanks of the two ships touched, a loud cry went up from his men as they charged over to the enemy ship and boarded it by force. Dacien prepared to run, but stopped when a bright flash to his left caught his attention.

He turned and saw that one of his midsized ships sitting a hundred yards to the west had burst into flames. His first thought was that the temple had catapults using flaming projectiles. But there were no signs of anything coming from the temple.

As he pondered the strange sight, something moved across the night sky, blocking the light of the stars above. It was quick as lightening and before he understood what was happening, he felt a rush of wind on his face. Something flew low across the deck of his ship and collided with the ranks of his soldiers, knocking twenty men overboard. A familiar sickening fear came over him like a wave of nausea and he realized instantly what caused it—the winged creature.

He lost sight of it momentarily, then reacquired it as the main mast of the ship next to him exploded into a shower of splinters. The top of the mast came crashing down on the crew below.

Dacien gritted his teeth as he watched it glide over the waters to the east, then circle back. With a newfound sense of urgency, he ran to the nearest of three bolt throwers mounted to the foredeck of the ship. "Turn this around," he yelled above the commotion.

The soldier manning the catapult looked confused, but obeyed, pivoting the machine.

Dacien looked at the men standing behind the two other throwers. "Target that thing when it returns."

Their blank expressions told him that they hadn't seen it.

Dacien pushed the man away from the machine and took up the position. "Follow my lead," he told the other two as he grabbed the handles and braced his body against the weapon. He scanned the horizon and it only took a second to locate it, now that he knew what to look for.

"There," he pointed. "It flies low above the water."

"Aye, General! I see it!"

"Wait until it's in range," he cautioned.

Just then, the mast of another ship caught fire. In the face of such raw power, Dacien felt fear begin to take a hold of him. But more intense than his fear was the bloodlust that came over him during times of battle. He wished to put a bolt through the center of this monster and watch it fall into the ocean. He wanted it so badly that he could taste it.

"Here it comes," he breathed. "Hold fast and don't waste your opportunity," he said, more to himself than the others.

The dark object moving silently through air was getting closer. *A hundred yards...fifty...twenty five.*

A sharp twang sounded as the first bolt was fired.

The creature banked slightly and the bolt went over its left shoulder, missing by four feet.

The second soldier fired next.

Dacien watched intently, waiting for just the right moment.

The creature veered sharply, extending its wings to catch more air. The second bolt was low by only a few inches.

Dacien aimed ahead of it and fired. The sharpened iron rod flew toward the creature and disappeared in the darkness. For a moment, he wondered if he missed.

Then the monster banked and came straight for them.

"Reload," Dacien yelled. But there was no time.

In a matter of seconds, it was upon them, flaring its wings and coming to a sudden stop in the air. Then it dropped to the deck with the grace of a bird of prey.

Dacien was stricken with fear. Somehow, he knew that this thing need only to wave its hand and he would drop dead. He had never felt so utterly inferior to anything in his whole life.

Then it looked directly at him, locking eyes.

Dacien knew that his time had come, but he suddenly didn't feel ready to die.

The creature took a step forward, then its head snapped to the side.

Dacien was startled, ready for something terrible to happen, but instead he watched in fascination. It almost seemed like it was listening to something.

Then it turned again and looked Dacien in the eyes, just before leaping into the air and thrusting its wings downward. It moved quickly away from the ship and headed toward the temple.

Dacien smiled with mixed emotions of relief at knowing that Kael had made it to his destination, and a sad fear that Kael wouldn't survive the confrontation.

Kael could feel the All Powerful getting closer. When it was inside the temple walls, he retracted his sense and waited. A few seconds later, he watched as it slowly descended through the hole in the ceiling of the cavern. Dropping softly to the sand, it retracted its massive wings and began walking in Kael's direction.

Kael stood motionless in the sand. He gripped the hilt of his crystal sword and held it in a ready position, anticipating a sudden attack.

SO, YOU ARE THE ONE THAT IS TRYING TO RUIN MY PLANS!

The words came into Kael's head like an intruder, louder and clearer than he'd ever experienced before. He decided to respond likewise, sending out a message as he walked toward the winged monster.

I'LL DO BETTER THAN TRY!

The two stopped walking when they were only a few feet from each other. Finally, Kael could see the object of his childhood fears. The All Powerful towered over him at ten feet tall, with hairless skin darker than the night. His body was thin, but powerfully muscled at the joints like an animal built for speed. His wings, now retracted, hung from behind his shoulders like a long skin cloak. Beneath the loose skin, Kael could see the outline of an array of bones which provided structure to translucent wings. He briefly remembered seeing a bat for the first time as a child, and the mixture of revulsion and fascination.

"The old man taught you how to cast your thoughts," the All Powerful stated audibly. His voice sounded like several different people speaking at once. The sound was complex, with high and low pitches that seemed threaded together to produce the words.

Is he talking about Saba?

A smile crossed the All Powerful's dark face, which was so perfectly structured that it might have been beautiful under different circumstances. "Saba? Oh...I see. He's lied to you as well."

Kael kept silent, gripping his sword tightly.

The All Powerful looked down to Kael's hand. "You brought my sword; I hope you haven't grown attached to it."

"I brought it here so that I could put it through your heart," he replied calmly, while his heart pounded wildly in his chest.

A deep laugh came from its mouth that pierced the silence of the cavern.

Kael backed away, ready for something to happen.

The laugh slowly died and the once calm face became distorted with rage.

"You insignificant slave! Do you think that even one of your kind can do anything that is not ordered by the gods?" The deafening barrage of sound reverberated off the cavern walls.

Kael stumbled backward, trying to cover his ears, but one hand was occupied by the sword. His eardrums threatened to burst.

The All Powerful reached out and the crystal sword tore away from Kael's grip, flying through the air to rest in the demon's hand.

"Now that you have served your purpose," he bellowed, "you will learn obedience."

Suddenly, Kael felt an immense pressure upon his body that forced him to the ground. He locked his legs and tightened his muscles, trying to resist. But the pressure increased. His legs began to shake. Then something in his knee snapped and he crumpled to the ground. His leg throbbed with pain and the air was squeezed from his lungs. He began to panic at the thought of drowning in the open air. Darkness showed at the corner of his vision and he knew that he was losing consciousness.

Out of desperation, Kael reached for his sense. It was still there, like a trusted friend. As his normal state of conscious became paralyzed, Kael slipped into the other. Even though he could feel his body being crushed into the ground, he felt some measure of freedom.

Focusing on the face of the All Powerful, he could feel the skin twisted into a grimace of pleasure, the eyes darkened with hatred. Kael focused smaller until he felt nothing but the iris of its right eye. Veins ran across its surface, disappearing into the pupil. Suddenly, Kael lashed out with all his might and invaded the eye with one swift strike.

The All Powerful stumbled backward and the pressure on Kael's body immediately released. Now able to control his body once more, Kael opened his eyes and lifted his head from the sand.

The All Powerful pulled his hand away from his right eye and stared at it. Blood covered his hand and streamed down his face. Where his eye used to be was now a mass of ruptured, indistinguishable flesh.

The All Powerful raised his head and leveled his one good eye at Kael.

Kael struggled to his feet, his left leg useless. With his sense, he focused it to a sharp point again and thrust it from himself. It gained speed as it moved across the cavern floor, aimed at the heart of the beast.

But then it stopped, hitting some sort of barrier.

The All Powerful flexed his muscled body and Kael's sense was pushed backward with violent force, lifting his body from the ground. For a moment, he felt nothing under his feet. Then his body slammed into the cavern wall and slumped to the floor. He knew instantly that several bones had been smashed, including a few ribs. He could feel the blood pouring from each nostril from the trauma to the back of his head.

Standing between him and the dais at the center of the cavern, the All Powerful opened his wings to their fullest extent and let out an earth shaking scream of rage. Waves of noise propelled concentric rings of sand radiating from the demon, engulfing Kael and overwhelming his senses.

As his skin began to bleed from the coarse grains attacking his body, Kael clawed at the ground, trying to crawl away from the attack. Then the stinging sensation began to change into something else. It took a moment to figure it out what was happening, but when the smell of burned flesh assaulted his nostrils, Kael realized that he was on fire. Quickly taking refuge in his other sense, he could feel the tremendous power emanating from the creature as it forced the air around Kael to constrict and become excited. He could feel the sand beneath him start to fuse together as the heat turned the sand into glass.

Glass!

Kael realized in a split second what to do. Focusing his sense on the ground beneath him, he raised a wall of sand between himself and the All Powerful. Almost instantly, Kael felt relief as the sand melted and formed a barrier from the scorched air. Kael kept pushing his sense, building layer upon of sand that quickly fused into a molten shield.

Then the attack stopped.

Kael retracted his sense and waited, crouching behind his glistening defense structure, listening. In the eerie silence, Kael felt something underneath him. Reaching into the sand, his hand closed around the hilt of a glass sword. A smile spread across his face. He knew the end was near and he wanted to die like a warrior. Even if it was utterly useless against his enemy, he wrenched if free of the sand and struggled to his feet. Stumbling out from behind his shield, Kael looked across the cavern at the All Powerful.

The demon stood perfectly still, with his one good eye watching Kael in unbelief, the other ruptured eye socket weeping blood.

Kael hobbled forward on one good leg, fighting to stay conscious as stabs of pain shot through his midsection. He looked down at his body and saw that his clothes had disintegrated. His skin was bright red in sections, while other areas were charred and smoking. Looking back to the god of his childhood, all of the bitterness and feelings of betrayal from his time at the monastery came flooding back into his mind. As tears ran down his face, Kael feebly raised his sword in a gesture of challenge.

The All Powerful slowly raised his own sword, mimicking the gesture. Then he pulled in his wings tight around his body and broke into a run, coming straight for Kael.

This is it, Kael thought.

The All Powerful closed the distance quickly, his clawed feet digging into the sand as he built speed.

Kael raised his sword, his frail arms shaking from the exertion.

The All Powerful reached back and swung his sword to take Kael's head off.

Kael swung his sword upward to meet the attack.

A bright flash of white light erupted from the contact.

Shards of glass stung Kael's face as his sword cut cleanly through the other and hacked deeply into the All Powerful's neck.

Their two bodies collided.

Kael was thrown aside like rubbish.

The momentum of the demon's body carried it forward until it tumbled through the sand and slid to a stop.

A moment of silence followed as Kael lay in the sand. Then he used his last ounce of strength to pull himself to his knees and crawl over to the creature. The All Powerful was lying in a spreading pool of blood. The cut had gone through half of his neck.

Kael could still sense some life in the body, but it was quickly diminishing. He looked down to the sword in his hand that he had switched with the fake, then back to the All Powerful. "Arrogance and presumption...those were your weaknesses."

Unexpectedly, the one good eye rolled in its socket and stared at Kael.

THE AWAKENED HAS COME!

The words passed through Kael like a fierce wind through a forest. It was different than before. This message wasn't directed at him, but at someone far away.

"What is the awakened?" Kael grunted with pain.

But it was too late. The creature that Kael had once worshipped was now dead.

Kael collapsed in the sand and rolled over, wincing at the pain stabbing through his chest and abdomen. When he found a position on his back where the pain was lessened, he lay still against the cold sand and closed his eyes.

"He's here."

The words startled Kael from his sleep.

A few seconds later he felt someone touch his neck.

"He's alive."

The voice didn't sound familiar.

"Kael. Can you hear me?" The second voice he recognized instantly.

Kael opened his eyes and saw Dacien looking down at him. He appeared shocked, then concerned, and then gradually a smile came to his face.

"You're safe now. We're going to get you out of here."

Kael glanced over Dacien's shoulder and noticed that the cavern was bright with daylight coming through the hole in the ceiling.

"You were supposed to...create a dis...distraction..." Kael's words came out slurred.

Dacien smiled again. "Well, that was the plan. I hope you don't mind, but we went ahead and destroyed their whole navy and invaded the temple. They're all gone now."

Now it was Kael's turn to smile.

"Come on," Dacien said. "Let's get you out of here."

27

The days passed quickly in Orud as Kael split his time between healing himself and talking to friends and family who came to visit. Though he was bedridden at the Royal Palace, he felt truly happy for the first time in many years, as though an enormous weight had been lifted from his shoulders. The bitterness and anger that always lurked beneath the surface of his thoughts had dissipated.

Maeryn came to visit and told him about the debates taking place among the council members. Dacien was still asserting that he should be appointed as the next Emperor. Unexpectedly, some council members felt that Maeryn should be appointed Empress, due to the unwavering support among the former slaves and resistance soldiers, who now constituted a majority of the Empire's population. Either way, the council seemed reluctant to make any appointments, given the turmoil of the last year.

Dacien visited more often than anyone. Sometimes, Aelia would come with him. But it was becoming more and more difficult for her as her pregnancy progressed. Dacien beamed with pride when they were together. He was excited to become a father.

As the time passed and Kael healed, questions began to form in his mind. Initially just nagging thoughts, they eventually grew into an obsession that had to be dealt with. As people came to visit him, he found himself distracted. He knew it wasn't polite and that he should pay attention when others had gone out of their way to visit him, but he couldn't help it.

After a few days, he sent for Saba, who always seemed to have answers for everything. Saba finally came in early one evening, just after sunset.

"How are you feeling," he said as soon as he entered the room.

"Better every day," Kael replied, looking down at the dark scabs that covered his arms. "But something is bothering me."

"Oh?" Saba questioned.

"That's why I asked for you."

Saba paused. "Shall I sit down? This sounds like it may be a long conversation."

"Yes," Kael replied. "Please do."

When Saba was comfortable in a chair next to the bed, Kael continued. "Why did the All Powerful mention you?"

Saba's eyebrows raised up. "Did he?"

"Yes...in the temple. He called you the *old man*. How did he know about you?"

Saba took in a deep breath and got to his feet, walking over to the window that overlooked the palace grounds.

"And why do you only look old enough to be my father, when you should look like my great grandfather? And when Magnus attacked me in the Palace, how did you and Dacien get me out of there without getting killed?"

Saba smiled at the quick series of questions. "For a long time now," he began, "I've wanted to tell you a story. But I didn't want to interfere with how events were supposed to unfold."

"...supposed to?" Kael questioned. "What do you mean? Why are you always talking in riddles?"

Saba turned around. "This story that I'm about to tell will likely raise more questions than answers." He paused. "No human has ever killed one of my kind. So I think it is safe to assume that you are the one."

...one of my kind? Kael sat up in the bed, anxious and suspicious all at once. His feeling of satisfaction at how events had turned out was quickly being replaced by a suspicion that he was about to hear some horrible truth.

"I will tell you a grand story. One of magical beings, colossal beasts, and a great evil perpetrated against mankind and the earth. But more importantly, I will tell you of the prophecy spoken about the one who will set all this right. The one destined to carry out vengeance against mankind's enemies—The Awakened."

Kael's body went rigid as he remembered the words.

THE AWAKENED HAS COME!

"That's right," Saba said. "I heard the proclamation just as you did."

Kael looked at the man standing by the window as if he were a stranger. In fact, there was much he didn't know about his childhood mentor.

Saba looked back. "Thousands of years ago, when the earth was still young, mystical beings guarded the earth and watched over mankind. But they began to lust after the daughters of men, and so they came to earth to take wives from among the human women. Though it was our duty to protect you, we betrayed the Most Holy and our original purpose. In all, there were two hundred of us who descended upon the earth and left our home among the heavenly realms."

"...us?" Kael questioned, his voice barely above a whisper.

"Semjaza, our leader, Arakiba, Rameel, Kokabiel, Tamiel, Ramiel, Danel, Ezeqeel, Baraqujal, Asael, Armaros, Batarel, Ananel, Zaquel, Samsapeel, Satarel, Turel, Jomajael, and myself. We were each chiefs of ten. You know me as Saba, but I was originally known to your kind as Sariel."

28

Kael stood in front of the dais. Its surface was polished like marble, and seemed to emit silver light. Just beneath the surface, as if encased in ice, was a strange pattern of concentric circles like the rings of a tree that had been frozen, then shattered. Overhead, sunlight streamed down in a brilliant column through the hole in the ceiling of the temple, illuminating the cavern where he first met the so-called All Powerful. Behind him, Saba stood in the sand, holding the crystal scepter that had been crafted for him thousands of years ago. In his own hand, Kael gripped the crystal sword that had been used to slay its owner.

"They'll wonder where you went. And they will be hurt that you didn't say goodbye. What should I tell them?"

Kael turned to look at his friend. "Tell them the story that you told me, then they'll understand."

Saba hung his head.

He initiated this, but he knows there's no other way. "Who's to say this is goodbye?" Kael offered.

Saba smiled at his optimism.

"I'll see you again," Kael stated simply. Then he stepped onto the dais and walked to its center. Almost immediately, he began to feel an immense weight upon his body, like it was being pushed from all sides. Saba stood at the edge of the moat surrounding the dais, tears running down his cheeks. Then his image began to distort sideways, like Kael was watching through the heat of a campfire. The image of Saba and the cavern began to spiral inward toward Kael. Suddenly, a blue light flashed in his eyes, sending a jolt of pain through his head.

THE AWAKENED HAS COME!

The words still echoed in Armaros' mind. He would have been tempted to dismiss them if not for the fact that he felt Rameel's life slip away from the physical realm shortly after. And this fact, combined with the proclamation, was deeply troubling.

Of course, it could have been Sariel who killed Rameel. But then why would Rameel mention The Awakened? Sariel was the only one who believed the prophecy anyway. Why would Rameel validate Sariel in that way? Unless he didn't. Unless it was a human that killed him. Could it be that Sariel was right after all these years? Could it be that the prophecy is real?

Even as Armaros stood at the water-damaged ruins of his Brazilian fortress, watching masses of soldiers descend into the abyss that housed the portal, he had a sick feeling in his stomach. He looked to the man standing next to him, the Commander of his ground forces in this region.

"Miguel, sooner or later a man is going to come through there."

"Another man, Sir?"

"Yes. The first was not important. But the next one who comes through...he is to be killed by any means necessary. I want no less than two-thousand armed men on guard at all times, on a rotation so they don't get lazy."

"Yes, Sir," the Commander replied, having heard this order several times now. "And at your request, we had the whole compound rigged with explosives, just in case..."

"Very good Miguel," Armaros replied with confidence, but inwardly, he still had his doubts.

ABOUT THE AUTHOR

Jason Tesar lives with his wife and two children in Colorado. He works in the microelectronics industry improving and developing processes, and writing technical documentation for integrated circuits manufacturing. In his personal time, he enjoys graphic design, playing guitar, reading books, watching movies, and doing anything outdoors with his family. THE AWAKENED is his first fictional writing. To learn more about Jason, THE AWAKENED, and future writing projects, check out his blog at www.jasontesar.com

Lightning Source UK Ltd.
Milton Keynes UK
UKOW050955020512

191857UK00001B/137/P